THE EPIC CLIMAX OF THE FIRST ROBOTECH WAR

# ROBOTECH

## THE MACROSS SAGA

# DOOMSDAY

Robotech novelizations based upon the animated science fiction series produced by Harmony Gold and available from Titan Books.

## THE MACROSS SAGA: Battlecry

Genesis
Battle Cry
Homecoming

## THE MACROSS SAGA: Doomsday

Battlehymn
Force of Arms
Doomsday

## THE MASTERS SAGA: The Southern Cross

Southern Cross
Metal Fire
The Final Nightmare

THE EPIC CLIMAX OF THE FIRST ROBOTECH WAR

# ROBOTECH

## THE MACROSS SAGA

# DOOMSDAY

# JACK McKINNEY

**TITAN** BOOKS

Robotech – The Macross Saga: Doomsday, Vols. 4–6
Print edition ISBN: 9781803365695
E-book edition ISBN: 9781803365725

Published by Titan Books
A division of Titan Publishing Group Ltd
144 Southwark Street, London SE1 0UP

First Titan edition: February 2024
10 9 8 7 6 5 4 3 2 1

A CIP catalogue record for this title is available from the British Library.

Printed and bound by CPI Group (UK) Ltd, Croydon, CR0 4YY.

# KAMIKAZE RUN

"**B**RACE FOR RAMMING!" GLOVAL BELLOWED. THE ENGINES SHOOK the great ship and drove it into a death-dive.

The two huge booms that reared above the ship's bridge were aligned directly at the space mountain that was the nerve center of the Zentraedi fleet. The booms were separate components of the Main Gun, reinforced structures. Around their tips glow the green-white fields of a limited barrier-defense, making them all but indestructible.

The Zentraedi, prepared for close broadsides, only realized in a list, horrified moment what the SDF-1's intention was. By then, it was too late. The SDF-1 had become an enormous stake being driven straight into the heart of the enemy.

# CONTENTS

BATTLEHYMN

09

FORCE OF ARMS

149

DOOMSDAY

351

VOLUME 01

# BATTLEHYMN

FOR GABRIELA "GABBY" ARANDA

# 01

As far as I'm concerned [Gloval] has already disobeyed his orders; I'd urge the council to proceed with a court-martial if I could only come up with someone to replace him. What do you think, [name withheld], perhaps I could talk [Admiral] Hayes into accepting the position and kill two birds with one stone?... This issue of the civilians aboard the SDF-1 has turned into a real mess. Personally, I consider them expendable—along with Gloval, along with the whole ship, if you want to know the truth. Let's face facts: The thing has already outlived its purpose. You and I are where we wanted to be. Why not give the aliens their damn ship and send them back where they belong?

Senator Russo, personal correspondence
(source withheld)

THERE WAS SOMETHING NEW IN THE COOL SUMMER NIGHT SKIES of 2012... You remember sitting on the backyard swing, hands tightly gripping the galvanized chains, slender arms extended and head tossed all the way back, gazing up into the immeasurable depths of that black magic, teasing your young mind with half-understood riddles of space and time. All of a sudden, your gaze found movement there where none should have existed, as if an entire constellation had uprooted and launched itself on an impromptu journey across the cosmos. Your heart was beating fast, but your eyes continued to track that mystery's swift passage toward the distant horizon, even though you were watching it upside down now and in danger of toppling backward off the swing. A screen door slammed, its report a signal that your cries had been heard, your father and his friends beside you trying to follow the rapid flow of your words, your shaking forefinger, pointing to unmoving starfields. "Past your bedtime," your father said, and off you went. But you crept down the wide carpeted staircase later on, silently, invisibly, and heard them in the library talking in low tones, using words you couldn't fully comprehend but in a way that proved you weren't imagining things. You'd glimpsed the fortress, a heavenly city returned from the past, massive enough to occultate the stars... savior or harbinger of dark prophecies, your father's friends couldn't decide which, but "a sign of the times" in either case. Like blue moons, unexplained disappearances, rumors of giants that were on their way to get you... And on the front page of the following day's newspaper you saw what the night had kept from you: a mile-high roboid figure, propelled by unknown devices twice its own height above a stunned city, erect, legs straight, arms bent at the elbow, held out like those of a holy man or magician in a calming gesture of peace or surrender. It reminded you of something at the edge of memory, an image you wouldn't summon forth until much later, when fire rained from the sky, your night world annihilated by light...

In direct violation of United Earth Defense Council dictates, Captain Gloval had ordered the SDF-1 airborne. It was not the first time he had challenged the wisdom of the Council, nor would it be the last.

The dimensional fortress had remained at its landing site in the Pacific for two long months like an infant in a wading pool, the supercarriers *Daedalus* and *Prometheus* that were her arms positioned out front like toys in the ocean waves. And indeed, Gloval often felt as though his superiors on the Council had been treating him like a child since the fortress's return to Earth. Two years of being chased through the solar system by a race of alien giants, only to be made to feel like unwanted relatives who had simply dropped in for a visit. Gloval had a full understanding of the Council's decisions from a military point of view, but those men who sat in judgment were overlooking one important element—or, as Gloval had put it to

them, 56,000 important elements: the one-time residents of Macross
Island who were onboard his ship. Circumstance had forced them to
actively participate in this running space battle with the Zentraedi,
but there was no reason now for their continued presence; they had
become unwilling players in a game of global politics that was likely
to have a tragic end.

There had already been more than 20,000 deaths; how many
more were required to convince the Council to accede to his
demands that the civilians be allowed to disembark?

The Council's reasoning was far from specious, it was crazed,
rooted in events that had transpired years before, but worse still,
rooted in a mentality Gloval had hoped he had seen the last of.
Even now the commander found that he could still embrace some
of the arguments put forth in those earlier times—the belief that it
was prudent to keep secret from the masses any knowledge of an
impending alien attack. Secrecy had surrounded reconstruction
of the dimensional fortress and the development of Robotech
weaponry, the transfigurable Veritech fighters and the Spartans
and Gladiators. This was the "logic of disinformation": There was
a guiding purpose behind it. But the Council's current stance
betrayed an inhumanity Gloval hadn't believed possible. To
explain away the disappearance of the 75,000 people of Macross,
the military had announced that shortly after the initial lift-off
of the SDF-1, a volcanic eruption on the order of Krakatoa had
completely destroyed the island. To further complicate matters,
GIN, the Global Intelligence Network, spread rumors to the
effect that in reality a guerrilla force had invaded the island and
detonated a thermonuclear device. *Global Times Magazine* was then
coerced into publishing equally bogus investigative coverage of a
supposed cover-up by GIN, according to which the actual cause of
the deaths on Macross was disease.

Just how any of these stories could have functioned to *alleviate*
worldwide panic was beyond Gloval; the Council might just as easily
have released the truth: that an experiment in hyperspace relocation
had inadvertently ended with the dematerialization of the island. As
it stood, however, the Council was locked into its own lies: 75,000

killed by a volcanic explosion/guerilla invasion/virus. Therefore, these thousands could not be allowed to "reappear"—return from the dead was an issue the Council was not ready to deal with.

The 56,000 survivors had to remain virtual prisoners aboard the SDF-1.

And if the Robotech Defense Force should win this war against the Zentraedi? Gloval had asked the Council. What then? How was the Council going to deal with the victorious return of the SDF-1 *and* the return of the dead? Couldn't they see how misguided they were?

Of course, it was a rhetorical question.

Gloval's real concern was that the Council didn't consider victory an acceptable scenario.

Which is why he had taken it upon himself to launch the SDF-1. He was going to focus attention on the civilians one way or another...

There was panic on the ground and panic in the voice of the Aeronautics Command controller.

"NAC. ground control to SDF-1 bridge: Come in immediately... NAC. ground control to SDF-1 bridge: Come in immediately, over!"

On the bridge of the dimensional fortress there were suppressed grins of satisfaction. Captain Gloval put a match to his pipe, disregarding Sammie's reminders. He let a minute pass, then signaled Claudia from the command chair to respond to the incoming transmission.

"SDF-1 bridge to NAC. ground control, I have Captain Gloval. Go ahead, over."

Gloval drew at his pipe and blew a cloud toward the overhead monitors. He could just imagine the scene below: the eyes of Los Angeles riveted on his sky spectacle. He had ordered Lang and astrogation to utilize the newly revamped antigrav generators to secure and maintain a low-level fly-by, and so the enormous triple ports of the foot thrusters were scarcely a mile above the streets. There would be no mistaking this for some Hollywood stunt. And not only were people getting their first look at the airborne SDF-1, but also of the formerly top-secret mecha that flew along with her—fighters, Guardians, and Battloids hovering and circling a mile-high bipedal Robotechnological marvel. Forget the majestic colors of those sunset clouds, Gloval wanted to tell them. Here was something really worth photographing!

"Captain Gloval, low flights over population centers have been strictly prohibited except in extreme emergencies."

Gloval reached forward and picked up the handset. "This *is* an emergency. We must maintain a low attitude holding pattern. Our gravity control system is not perfected, and the lives of our 56,000 civilian detainees are in jeopardy."

Lisa Hayes turned from her station to throw him a conspiratorial wink.

"But sir, you're causing a panic down here. Increase your altitude and fly out over the ocean immediately. It's imperative."

*I have them where I want them!* Gloval said to himself.

"I will comply with your order if you can give me permission to disembark these civilians."

The speakers went silent; when the controller returned, there was incredulity and urgency in his voice.

"Sir, that's impossible. Orders from UEDC headquarters state that *no one* is to leave your ship. We have no authority to countermand those orders. You must leave this area at once."

It was time to let some of the anger show. Gloval shouted, "I will not rest until those orders are changed!"

He slammed the handset back into its cradle and leaned back into the chair. Vanessa had swiveled from her screen to study him; he knew what was on her mind and granted her the liberty to speak freely.

"Sir, isn't it dangerous to be making threats while we're on the aircom net?"

Claudia exchanged looks with Gloval and spoke for him. "This fortress is a symbol of the Council's strength," she told Vanessa. "If it gets out that the captain is resisting orders, the Council would lose face—"

"And there's a chance," Lisa added, "that our communication *was* being monitored." She turned to Gloval. "Isn't that true, Captain?"

Gloval left the chair and walked forward to the curved bay.

The cityscape was spread out beneath the ship; Veritechs flew in formation, and great swirls and billows of lavender and orange sunset clouds filled the sky.

"I'm prepared to keep the SDF-1 here until we *are* monitored, Lisa." He turned to face Claudia and the others. "I don't think there's much chance that the Council will reverse its decision. But politicians can sometimes be helpful, and it's possible that someone in the government will get wind of this, see an opportunity, and step in."

"But the Council isn't going to like your tactics, sir," said Vanessa.

Gloval turned back to the bay.

"Even if I face prosecution, this is something I must do. Civilians have no place onboard this ship. No place in this war."

But for the time being the SDF-1 was stuck with its civilians. However, it had been outfitted with a reworked shield system. Dr. Lang had dismantled the pin-point barrier and liberated the lambent energy which animated it—the same energy which had materialized with the disappearance of the spacefold generators some time ago. His team of Robotechnicians had then reanalyzed that alien fire, careful to avoid past mistakes, tamed and cajoled it, and fashioned a newly designed harness for it. Where the former system relied on manually operated maneuverable photon discs that were capable of covering only specific portions of the fortress (hence the name "pin-point" system), the reworked design was omnidirectional, allowing for full coverage. It did share some of the weaknesses of its prototype, though, in that activation of the system drained energy from the weapons systems, and full coverage was severely time-limited.

If only the personnel of the fortress could have been similarly outfitted... but who has yet designed a shield system for the heart, a protective barrier, pin-point or otherwise, for the human soul?

Roy Fokker was dead.

The VT pilots of Skull Team had their own way of dealing with combat deaths: The slain pilot simply never was. Men from Vermilion or Indigo might approach them in Barracks C or belowdecks in the *Prometheus* and say: "Sorry to hear about Roy," or "Heard that Roy tuned out." And they would look them square in the eye or turn to

one of their Skull teammates and ask flatly, "Roy who?" Some might
think the Skull were kidding with them and press the question, but
the response remained the same: "Roy, who?" Nobody broke the
pact, nobody spoke of Roy, then or now. Roy simply never was.

Except in the privacy of their quarters or the no-man's-land of
their tortured memories and dreams. Then a man could let loose
and wail or rage or throw out the same questions humankind has
been asking since that first murder, the first death at the hands of
another, the one that set the pattern for all that followed.

Perhaps that shell game the Skull Team played with death had
found its way to the bridge, or maybe it was just that Fokker's death
was too painful to discuss—the first one that hit home—but in any
case no one brought it up. Claudia and Rick were each separately
cocooned in sorrow no one saw fit to disturb. Kim and Sammie talked
about how sorry they felt for Claudia, knowing how much she missed
Fokker, knowing that underneath that brave front she was torn up.
But neither woman ever approached her with those feelings. Even
Lisa seemed at a loss. That afternoon she had followed Claudia to the
mess hall, hesitant at the door, as if afraid to intrude on her friend's
grief… Did it occur to her that Claudia and Rick—the lieutenant at
the observation deck rail and Claudia seated not fifteen feet away—
might have been able to help each other through it, or was Lisa also
one of the speechless walking wounded, wounds in her own heart
reopened, wounds that had been on the mend until Fokker's death?

It was Rick she approached that afternoon, the City of Angels
spread out below the observation deck like some Robotech circuit
board. Rick looked drawn and pale, recuperating but still weak
from his own brush with death from wounds he had suffered
indirectly *at her own hand*. There was no mention of Roy, although
it was plain enough to read in his dark eyes the devastation he felt.
And the more she listened to him, the deeper she looked into those
eyes, the more fearful she became; it was as if all light had left him,
as if his words rose from a hollow center, somber and distanced.
She wanted to reach out and rescue him from the edge. There was
music coming through the PA, a song that had once welcomed
both of them back from a shared trip to that edge.

"That's Minmei, isn't it, Rick? Have you two been seeing each other?"

"Sure," he answered flatly. "I watch her on the wall screen, and she sees me in her dreams."

No help in this direction; Lisa apologized.

Rick turned from her and leaned out over the rail.

"She's been spending a lot of time with her cousin Kyle. You know, family comes first."

"Well I'm glad you're all right, Rick. I was worried about you."

That at least brought him around, but there was no change in tone.

"Yeah, I'm feeling great, Lisa. Just great."

She wanted to start from scratch: *Listen, Rick, I'm sorry about Roy, if I can be any help to you—*

"So I hear we've got a new barrier system," he was saying. "And I guess we need it more than ever, right? I mean, since the Council is refusing to allow the civilians to leave—"

"Rick—"

"—and it isn't likely that the Zentraedi are going to call off their attacks."

She let him get it all out and let silence act as a buffer. "The Council will rescind their order, Rick. The captain says he'll keep the ship right there until they do."

Rick smirked. "Good. And the sooner it happens, the better. I know we're all anxious to get back into battle."

Rick's eyes burned into hers until she could no longer stand it and looked away. Was he blaming her somehow for Roy's death? Had she suddenly been reduced to some malevolent symbol in his eyes? First Lynn-Kyle and his remarks about the military, and now this… Below she watched the traffic move along the grid of city streets; she looked long and hard at the Sierra foothills, as if to remind herself that she was indeed back on Earth, back among the living. But even if the Council had a change of heart, even if her father came to his senses and allowed the civilian detainees to disembark, what would become of the SDF-1 and her crew?

Where and when would they find safe haven?

# 02

LAPSTEIN: In light of the, well, "psychological" problems which beset the Zentraedi after the SDF-1's successful return to Earth, isn't there some justification for suggesting that Khyron should have taken over command of the Imperial Fleet?

EXEDORE: (Laughs shortly) We would not be having this interview, of this I can assure you.

LAPSTEIN: Of course… But in terms of strategic impact?

EXEDORE: (After a moment) It could be said that Khyron was more aware of the dangers of cultural contagion than many of us, but he was no longer thinking as a strategist. The SDF-1 was not his main concern; that the ship contained a Protoculture matrix was of little importance. He had by now come to believe that by destroying it he would put an end to what he regarded as a psychic threat to his race. I will leave it to your "psychologists" to examine his underlying motives. But I will add this: He was responding in pure Zentraedi fashion—he recognized potential danger and moved to eliminate it. My hope is that this will rescue his image from what many of your writers have termed "humanness."

Lapstein, *Interviews*

Khyron was possessed by the Invid Flower of Life; without being aware of it, he was by now working against the Zentraedi imperative.

Rawlins, *Zentraedi Triumvirate: Dolza, Breetai, Khyron*

WELL WITHIN STRIKING DISTANCE OF EARTH, TWO ZENTRAEDI cruisers moved through space, silently, side by side,

Gargantuas from an unholy realm. A day would come when the commanders of these ships would stand together at the gates of an even blacker void, released from an artificial past and feverish with exhilaration for a present in the making, hands and hearts linked, an evil pact made good, laughing into the face of death… But today there were harsh words and recriminations, a taste of what was to come for the rest.

Khyron slammed his fist down on the command post console, his right hand pointed accusingly at the projecbeam image of Azonia, her arms folded across her chest, as much in defiance as in defense.

"It can't be!" the so-called Backstabber shouted. "Why are they ordering us to fall back?"

His lowered head and narrowed eyes peering from beneath bangs of sky blue gave him a demonic look.

Azonia addressed the projecbeam image on the bridge of her cruiser.

"I'm not at liberty to explain, but our orders are clear, Khyron: Until this new operation is terminated, you will do nothing but stand fast and wait. Is that clear?"

She tried to sound calm but knew that he would see through it. Khyron glared at her.

"Don't play games with me, Azonia. That ship grows stronger day by day, while we sit and do nothing."

"Khyron—"

"Your meddling in my plans allowed the Micronians to reach their homeworld. But it is not too late to undo the damage you've done: Destroy them now!"

"Enough!" she screamed at the screen. But he paid her little heed. An angry sweep of dismissal with his arm, bared teeth, and he was gone. The projecbeam compressed to a single horizontal line and vanished, but Azonia tried to raise him nevertheless.

"Khyron, come in, Khyron! Come in at once!"

Too late. She leaned forward to steady herself on stiffened arms, palms still flattened against the com buttons. She knew him well enough to fear him, but it wasn't fear that was threatening to overcome her. These were darker feelings, utterly devoid of light, far worse than fear. And suddenly she recognized what it must be: Commander in Chief Dolza had relieved Breetai of his command, had entrusted her with the mission to retrieve Zor's ship, and she had *failed* him.

*Failed him!*

Just then Miriya was admitted to the bridge, and Azonia felt a glimmer of hope. If anyone could help her deal with Khyron, it would be Miriya, the Zentraedi's most skilled pilot. But Azonia was soon to learn that Khyron had already undermined these plans also.

"I'm glad that you're here," Azonia welcomed the female ace. "Commander Khyron is jeopardizing our mission. I'm going to need your help to keep him in line."

Miriya lowered her gaze. "Commander, I..."

Azonia approached her with concern. "Miriya, what's wrong? Out with it."

"I have come to request your permission to enter the dimensional fortress... as a spy."

Azonia was shocked. "Micronized?!"

"Yes. I have been studying the enemy's language, and I am confident that my presence will profit our cause."

"But why? Why would our finest pilot want to become a Micronian? You're not making sense!"

"Please, Commander, I have no choice."

"Nonsense! Tell me. I order you."

Miriya's deep green eyes flashed; she tossed back her mane of thick hair and locked gazes with Azonia.

"I have been defeated in battle... bested by a Micronian, an insignificant *bug!* I must find and destroy that pilot. Until then I'm of use to no one. You must permit me, Commander, for the glory of the Zentraedi."

*Defeat!* thought Azonia. *Failure! What was to become of their once glorious race?*

Khyron wasted no time putting his attack plan into effect. Moments after breaking contact with Azonia he was on his way to the cruiser's Battlepod hangar, where his lieutenants and squadron leaders would receive their briefing. Every minute lost brought the Zentraedi that much closer to defeat; of this he was certain. The Micronians were making repairs, taking on stores, readying themselves for another round...

*Defeat*... There was a time not long ago when the very *word* found no place in his thinking, let alone the idea. But recent events had reshaped his world view; dangerous possibilities were now entertained where none had existed before. This operation directed against the Micronians of "Earth" was beginning to assume portentous dimensions. Left in the dark to puzzle out the intricacies of this war that was not a war, Khyron had been forced to rely on instinct and rumor; he had implicit faith in the former but little use for the latter unless, as in the present case, he found corroborating evidence of his own. And at the center of the complexities was Zor's ship, the Super Dimensional Fortress. That the fortress, with its Protoculture matrix, was a trophy worthy enough to justify the expenditures of the operation was beyond dispute. And that it had to be kept from the Invid, equally so. But surely the Robotech Masters would concede that at this point the fortress was expendable; the Micronians, having already unlocked some of its secrets, posed a threat greater than loss of the ship itself. And threats were best dealt with directly. But what should have been a straightforward eradication and mop-up exercise, no different from scores of similar operations effected throughout the quadrant, had become a hazardous hunt—an attempt to recapture the fortress intact *at any cost*. Had the Commander in Chief forgotten the Imperative?

*The Zentraedi were a race of warriors, not gamesters.*

Just what were Dolza and Breetai up to? Over and over again Khyron had put the question to himself. Were they serving the Robotech Masters or some rebellious design of their own? His suspicions had been temporarily laid to rest when Breetai had been relieved of his command, but now he was beginning to consider that this, too, was part of their plan. That Azonia had been chosen to head up the operation was disturbing—maybe a sign that the Old One was in fact losing his grip—but beside the point in any case. Azonia's time had run out; once under way, the present attack plan would accomplish a secondary purpose in seeing to that. But Dolza's next move remained to be seen; should Breetai be returned to command, Khyron would have no choice but to accept his rebellion theory as truth. But he also understood that a schism now would only add to an already perilous course. That was why the present situation had to be defused.

In the cavernous lower chambers of the Zentraedi cruiser, the assault group was assembled. In addition to the usual complement of Botoru tri-thruster assault ships, carapace fighters, and scout recons, there were scores of specialized mecha outfitted with ECM and radar jamming devices. Khyron laid out his simple plan: The dimensional fortress was to be destroyed.

As Khyron prepared to strap into his Officer's Pod assault ship, he exchanged some final words with Grel, who would man the helm in Khyron's absence. The square-jawed face of the First Officer was on the overhead screen in the central hold.

"Wait until I approach the fortress and activate ECM before you follow and land your fleet, Grel."

"Although Earth's atmosphere makes it difficult to maneuver, we will obey."

"See that you do. Intelligence reports indicate that the Micronians care a great deal about their miserable world, so if we bring the fight there, the fortress and the planet will be ours for the taking." Khyron noticed Grel's eyes shift back and forth. "Questions, Grel?"

"No, sir... But we are going against Azonia's orders again, aren't we?"

Khyron laughed maliciously. "Just carry out your orders. I'll take care of her after we return."

Khyron lowered the canopy of the Battlepod. He ingested two dried leaves from the Flower of Life and brought his mecha to the edge of the cruiser port.

*The first controlled firing of the main gun, the* Daedalus Maneuver, *the return to Earth: three "whoopees" in two long years of warfare...*

But now there was cause for genuine celebration on the bridge of the dimensional fortress: Gloval's ploy had worked. The North American Ontario Quadrant, one of a growing number of separatist states seeking autonomy from the Council's stranglehold, had agreed to accept the civilians. Ontario had its own reasons for doing so, but the captain wasn't about to ask questions. Gloval felt as though an enormous weight was about to be lifted from his shoulders—he could practically feel the worry lines on his face beginning to fade. Now, if Dr. Lang could only figure some way to transfer Macross City as well, lock, stock, and barrel.

News of the recently received crypto-communication spread like wildfire through the ship. Spontaneous parties were already under way in the streets of the city, and Gloval would have been given a ticker-tape parade if there had been any ticker tape available. Residents were hastily packing and making preparations to leave, embracing one another, sobbing good-byes, taking last looks around. As expected, there were more than a few who wished to remain onboard, but there were to be no exceptions to the captain's orders: All civilians had to go. Perhaps when the war was over, like some "city in flight" the SDF-1 would be taking Earth's children to their destiny...

But most of that was for starry-eyed dreamers and science-fantasy buffs; most of Macross wanted out. The tour was finished; it was time to get back into the real world, reconnect with family left behind, tear up the premature obituaries, and start living again. No more alert sirens waking you up in the middle of a false night, no more military scrip or play money, no asteroid showers, no more—*thank heavens!*—modular transformations. Many of the residents forgot that these same hopes had been dashed only short weeks before.

The Defense Force was never polled as to its feelings, though the results no doubt would have proved interesting. To some, Macross was the ship's heart, and they had fought hard on Earth and in deep space to protect that transplanted center. To be appointed guardian of their homeworld would have been a fair enough trade-off, but that was not to be the case. The Council had already made this clear: Their orders were to lead the aliens away from Earth, to bring the war back into deep space where it belonged, to act as a decoy until such time as the Earth was suitably prepared to deal with invasion. In other words, they had been singled out for sacrifice. If there was supposed to be some sort of grandiose nobility attached to this, it was not readily apparent. But fortunately for the Council, the Earth, and the dimensional fortress commanders themselves, there were few members of the Defense Force in possession of all the facts.

Rick was belowdecks in the *Prometheus* when Max and Ben brought him the news from the bridge. He was in uniform, number-two torx driver in hand, standing alongside. Skull One— Roy Fokker's Veritech. An opened access panel in the nacelle below the cockpit broke the unity of the fighting kite insignia, but Rick missed the symbolism. Nevertheless, he stared into the exposed circuitry, even tinkered a bit, as if searching for memories of his lost friend. The fighter had been fully repaired and serviced; there were no signs of damage, no evidence of the fatal rounds sustained, but that didn't mean the exorcism had been complete. Roy's presence lingered palpably.

Rick closed the panel as the two corporals approached. "Just doing some maintenance," Rick said by way of explanation. *Yeah, self-maintenance.*

"I'm not surprised," said Max. "Lisa Hayes told us you were down here."

Ben eyed the fuselage numerals. "Hey, this is Commander Fokker's Skull One, isn't it? I didn't know you were going to be flying it."

"Uh, yeah," Rick answered distantly. "Guess I was lucky to get it as my aircraft assignment."

He turned away from them and put his right hand against the mecha almost reverently. "Nice touch of irony, don't you think? Commander Fokker was always so proud of the fact that he'd never gone down. Now he's... gone, and I get his plane. Me... the guy who's always being shot down—even by our own ordnance. Just kind of ironic, that's all."

Rick's friends exchanged concerned looks, but Max broke out of it and into a smile. He told Rick about the civilians, and the lieutenant said, "Terrific." Undaunted, Max continued.

"Apparently the North American Ontario Quadrant will be accepting them, and the official announcement will be given tomorrow by Captain Gloval."

"So how's about we get a jump on the celebration?" Ben said, full of good humor. "We could hit Macross for some food, drink, whatever else comes along."

"You could use the recreation, Lieutenant," Max hastened to add.

Rick's slow smile was a signal that he'd already made up his mind. He had to climb out of his funk somehow, and he didn't see how low spirits could stand a chance in Macross just now.

"It sounds good, guys. In fact, it'll be my treat."

Ben beamed. "Well how about that, Max?" He moved between his friends, a head taller than both, draping his arms over their shoulders and leading them away from the Veritech. "Doesn't that sound like something the new pilot of the Skull One would do? C'mon, let's get going before he changes his mind."

Rick glanced over his shoulder at the silent mecha; then he surrendered himself to Ben's lead.

Khyron's assault unit launched from the cruiser and plunged into Earth's atmosphere, triple-thrusters brilliant orange against a peaceful field of cloud-studded blue.

The dimensional fortress, still configured like an upright winged techno-knight, was over the city of Toronto when radar alerted the bridge of the impending attack.

Vanessa leaned over her console and entered a series of commands. She leaned back in her chair as "paint" and directional symbols began to fill the large screen.

"Multiple radar contacts in five, six, and seven. A squadron of alien spacecraft." Her words came in a rush. "Pods, recons. Small ships, mostly. Coming in from an altitude of twenty miles, north-northwest."

Gloval didn't want to believe it. "Are you sure?"

"Yes, sir," she answered emphatically.

Sammie moaned, "Oh, no!" as both Lisa and Claudia turned from their forward stations to regard the threat board.

"Just as we were entering the Ontario Quadrant."

"Exactly," said Claudia in a way that meant: *typical!*

Gloval had not moved from the command chair; his hands were

tightened on the arms, as much to prevent himself from rising as to get a grip on the situation.

"We cannot afford to come under attack here," he announced. "Commander Hayes, order all pilots to red alert immediately!"

"Here you are, mister, one giant top sirloin, medium rare," the chef said as he placed cutting board and cut in front of Ben.

He, Max, and Rick were in the Kindest Cut, one of Macross City's finest steak houses. They had elected to sit along the circular counter which ringed the central grills—"close to the action," as Ben put it. Exhaust fans and an enormous copper hood overhead took care of most of the smoke, but you had to be a real red-meat lover to deal with the odors, the sizzle and pop that were inescapable up front.

"Thanks a lot, pal," Ben said, pulling the platter-shaped cutting board toward him.

His friends were staring at the steak in disbelief.

"Does this smell great or what?" He had knife and fork poised, ready to dig in.

"Looks like a lot to eat," Max said tentatively.

A massive hunk of meat was impaled on Ben's fork. "I'm so hungry, I might order another one!" He laughed loudly, then opened his mouth widely, the forkful a scant inch from his mouth when an announcement blared over the citywide PA.

"Attention, all fighter pilots: red alert, red alert. This is not a drill…"

Max and Rick were already on their feet and heading for the door by the time the message was repeated. Ben, however, was still anchored to his seat, wondering if he had time for just one more bite.

"Hey, Ben, move out!" he heard the lieutenant say.

Ben stood up and contemplated the top sirloin, the small, round potatoes, the heavenly garnish of mushrooms and onions…

"Don't move," he told the meal. "I'll be back."

# 03

And, lo, I saw a winged giant walking among the clouds in the western sky, haloed within a globe of radiant glory, and his body set to gleaming silver in the sun. And tho his hands might be raised in supplication, his heart burned with all the fury of holy fires. And I say unto you that this is the Temple of Mankind, risen and returned to do battle with the forces of evil!

Apocrypha, *The Book of James*

VERITECHS WERE ALREADY BEING MOVED TO THE FLIGHT elevators by the time Rick, Ben, and Max reached the hangar of the *Prometheus*. They had their "thinking caps" and harness packs on, likewise their respective red, gold, and blue flight suits. Cat crews and controllers were keeping things orderly; after two years of almost constant fighting, they had the routine down to a T. Lisa's voice was loud and clear through the speakers:

"All fighter squadrons: red alert, red alert. This is not a drill, this is not a drill…"

They wished each other luck, separated, and ran for their individual fighters. Skull One was waiting patiently for Rick, wings back and Jolly Roger—emblazoned tailerons folded down. He clambered up into the cockpit and strapped in as he ran a quick status check. He thought of Roy as the canopy descended.

*Well, Big Brother, looks like I've been elected to fill your shoes. I'm not looking forward to it. Now, don't get me wrong… But piloting your fighter in combat is going to take some getting used to.*

Rick was waved forward to the elevator. Once on the flight

deck, he spread the mecha's wings and raised the emblemed tailerons while coveralled hookup crews readied the ship for launch. Finally the go signal was given. Rick flashed thumbs up and dropped back against the seat. A fleeting image of Roy Fokker appeared on one of the commo screens.

"Well, ole buddy, this one's for you," Rick said aloud. Then, flipping toggles, he contacted the bridge and added, "This is Skull Leader. We're movin' out."

The engines were activated, power and sound building. The cat officer dropped, the shooter ducked, and seconds later Skull One was accelerated off the flatdeck's hurricane bow and airborne.

On the bridge of the SDF-1, Claudia turned to Lisa. "Did he say, 'Skull Leader'?"

"That's right, Claudia." There was almost a note of *pride* in her voice. "Lieutenant Hunter's taking over Commander Fokker's Skull One as of today."

It took Claudia by surprise, but she smiled and turned to the bay, hoping to catch a glimpse of the takeoff.

"Roy would have liked that."

"Skull Leader to Skull wing: I've got bogies on my screen. Estimate fifteen seconds until first contact."

Rick and his men were in a delta formation; below them, also in triplicate, were Indigo and Vermilion, along with several other VT teams. Max and Ben were on the lateral commo screens in Skull One's cockpit.

"Are both of you ready to get the job done?"

"You bet we are, Lieutenant," Ben said.

Max added, "Ready for combat."

Rick felt a reawakened sense of purpose that bordered on sheer exhilaration. It was not the usual prebattle adrenaline rush or any other endorphin high but a settling of the storm that had raged inside him since the ship's return to Earth and had peaked with Roy's death—a storm that had whipped him into a frenzy and left him depleted of spirit, faith, the very will to go on. But now, out in this wild blue yonder, those storm clouds were breaking up, and with them that ominous sense of doom and impenetrable darkness. Skull One was airborne again; Rick Hunter was airborne again. Where before he had seen irony, he now felt a curious but calming harmony. He would prevail!

In the lead ship of the alien assault group, Khyron was thinking the same thing. But where Rick's thoughts were tuned to life, Khyron's were attuned to death—as clear an example as any of the differences that separated human from Zentraedi. "They're dead ahead," Khyron told his pilots. "Keep your shields up and fire when ready. Let's get them now!"

So saying, he engaged the ship's boosters, signaling his wingmen to follow suit, and threw his forces against Hunter's.

The two groups met head-on, filling the skies with thunder. Explosions bloomed and erupted like some hellish aeroponic garden. Brilliant blue and yellow tracers crisscrossed with contrails and the smoke and fire falls of destroyed ships. Wingmen broke away from their leaders to engage the enemy mecha one on one in an aerial free-for-all. VT pilots sometimes used the analogy of boxing versus street fighting: There were no rules; your opponent was unskilled but mean-spirited and more than likely unstoppable.

Zentraedi snub-nosed tri-thrusters, triple-finned and resembling stylized faucet controls, tore through the Veritech formations, plastron cannons blazing, blue fire holing craft and pilots alike. Twin top-mounted rockets were elevated to firing positions, launched, and more often than not found their mark, throwing fiery debris into the arena. Balls of flame that were once Veritechs plunged from the sky.

But the Robotech forces hit back.

Skull One banked sharply to avoid the debris of an exploded craft, angry blue fire deep within its aft thrusters, red-tipped pyloned heat-seekers eager for release. Rick trimmed his ship only to find that he had four more bandits on his tail. He led them on a merry chase, up into a booster climb to the edge of night, then down in a power dive they hadn't anticipated.

Rick threw down the G lever and thought the mecha through to Guardian configuration. He flew into the face of his pursuers like a bird of prey, taloned legs engaged and rear undercarriage guns erupting when he'd cleared their formation. Orange fire blazed from beneath the wings.

A Zentraedi ship exploded, then a second, as it kamikazeed in on Skull One, an expanding cloud of orange death. *Divine wind, indeed,* thought Rick.

The Guardian was ho vering now, utilizing the downward-pointing foot thrusters for loft and stability and pouring out fire against the two remaining ships. And once again, Rick's thoughts and shots found their mark.

He heard Ben's voice above the racket on the tac net.

"Hey, Skull Leader, that was mighty fine flying, but you've got to be more careful!"

But it was Ben who wasn't being careful: An enemy mecha had him locked on target and was about to open up. Fortunately, Max Sterling had been monitoring the approach; he had the craft lined up in his reticle, and he loosed two rockets to take it out.

Rick heard Ben's cry of surprise, then delight, as Max brought his blue-trimmed ship alongside Dixon's port wingtip.

"You okay, Ben?" Max asked, a lilt to his voice. "Yeah, sure, now I am, thanks."

"Well, stay alert, big guy."

"Better believe it. Nobody tunes out Ben Dixon!"

Rick was too involved in the battle to notice that several alien ships had peeled away from the attack group and established a holding pattern not far from the SDF-1. This did not go unnoticed on the bridge of the fortress itself, however, or onboard the cruiser commanded by Khyron's second.

Grel, arms folded across his chest, studied the blue projecbeam field. Deep within a schematic representation of the planetary rim, a bright red light bar flashed once, then twice more. And over the com came the voice of one of the fleet commanders.

"Sir, the radar-jamming tactic appears to be working. Shall we now proceed?"

Grel leaned forward over the console. "Yes, proceed as planned."

As he gave the word, five enormous warships began a slow descent toward Earth.

Gloval stood at the forward bay of the bridge, white cap pulled low on his head, eyes heavy with concern. In the western sky flashes of devilish fire marked the battle zone, discs and crescents in the dusk. South, a cluster of enemy craft in a curious holding pattern, and below the fortress, a city in chaos—a city in peril. What were the residents to make of these unannounced fireworks? Gloval wondered. The SDF-1 was headed north at a good clip, but would it clear these population centers before the battle escalated? He knew it would. He closed his eyes to shut out the scene. He had brought the fortress here to disembark the civilians, and in so doing he had endangered yet another group. Was there no winning this thing—on any front?

"Sir, radar is destabilizing."

Gloval didn't bother to turn and face Vanessa; wearily, he said, "The Zentraedi are jamming our signal... One thing after another... Alert Skull Team to begin a recon sweep of the area." Then he swung around. "Put the new barrier system on standby and be prepared for new enemy activity."

Claudia exercised her prerogative by pointing out that activating the shields would draw power from the weaponry systems, but the captain was way ahead of her; he had little patience left for ground already covered. "I understand the problem, but I must consider the safety of *all* personnel aboard. Now, put the new system on standby immediately!"

"Yes, sir," Claudia deferred. "Stand by to engage..."

Meanwhile, a solitary ship of bizarre design was on a low, silent approach to the dimensional fortress, taking advantage of a ridge of low hills to conceal itself from detection and involvement in the raging battle. The mecha was insectlike in appearance, with a globular twin-hemisphered body, pincer arms, two cloven legs, and a pointed proboscis cockpit module. It was not a Botoru ship—one of Khyron's Seventh Mechanical Division—but a Quadrono. And held in the grip of the armored right hand, contained in a transparent chamber similar to that which had delivered three micronized spies into the SDF-1, was the female ace of that fleet, Miriya Parino. She wore a sleeveless blue-gray sackcloth of a dress, belted with rough cord, and carried no weapons.

It was this last that worried the female pilot of the mecha. Seloy Deparra had visual contact with Miriya via the curved screen in the cockpit, audio through the helmet communicator.

"Miriya, this is dangerous!" Deparra said, "Are you certain you want to board the Micronian ship with no weapons?"

"I won't need weapons."

"But Commander Azonia is already upset about the failure of this operation…"

"Upset, but not with me. It's Khyron who has made a mess of things." *And some of us are aware of the* special *rivalries that exist between Azonia and Khyron,* she wanted to add. But Miriya had no quarrel with the Backstabber. He was now doubly responsible for her mission and her present micronized size: first by alerting her to the Micronian ace who had bested her in battle, and second by launching yet another unauthorized attack against the SDF-1. The battle had simplified the infiltration considerably. But these facts were of no use to the pilot. "Just deliver me to the Micronian ship," Miriya said sternly.

Khyron had removed himself from the aerial arena; his command mecha was positioned at the southern perimeter of the skirmish, and he had managed to raise Grel on the com. The lieutenant's face appeared on a secondary commo screen in the cockpit while explosive flashes of battle light strobed against the outer hull of the ship.

"We're hovering above the surface, awaiting your further orders, my lord."

Khyron was pleased enough to compliment his second. "Excellent, Grel, you've done a superb job. Now, prepare your attack, but don't open fire until I join you."

"My lord!" Grel saluted.

Following Gloval's orders, Skull Team had also temporarily absented themselves from the battle to recon south of the fortress.

Rick had patched the infrared scanners, wide and long-range, into the commo system; center and lateral screens now afforded him an image-enhanced sweep of the horizon. In a moment he had radar contact and upped the magnification on the screens. Gloval was right: Zentraedi cruisers!

Rick activated the scrambler and went on the tac net.

"Lisa, are you monitoring?"

She answered, "Affirmative," from the bridge and notified the captain: "Skull has visuals on five alien cruisers; range, seventy miles, south-southeast, vector headings coming in now…"

"All right," said Gloval, hands behind his back at the forward bay. "Claudia, activate the omnidirectional barrier at once!"

In the new shield system control room, more than a dozen techs and specialists readied themselves. Situated aft and well below the bridge in a huge hold, the room itself was little more than a flyout platform equipped with a central readout table and numerous manned consoles and viewscreens. But the device responsible for the energy barrier was something else again. Blue rings of pulsed energy filled the hold as Gloval gave word to engage the system. Power began to build in the field generator—an enormous gearlike dish with eight hydraulic closure teeth—while its mate telescoped down on a thick shaft from the hold overhead. Short of meshing, the generators exchanged phrases of fire, forming and containing a sphere of effulgent energy.

On the bridge the energy sphere registered schematically on Claudia's console monitor as a globe-shaped grid fully encompassing the upright SDF-1.

Externalized, the sphere was a yellow-green cloud that grew and expanded from the ship's center, gaseous and slightly luminescent, haloing the fortress in the night sky.

Grel was viewing its formation on the command center screen as Khyron entered, his harness pack and hip blasters still in place.

"What's going on?" he demanded.

Grel didn't bother to salute. "There's a large energy shield surrounding the Micronian ship."

Khyron snorted. "I don't care. Open fire, now!"

· · ·

It was as if someone had scribbled across the sky with a light crayon… that many rockets were launched from the Zentraedi warships. Ninety-eight percent of them found their mark, enveloping and obscuring the dimensional fortress in a minute-long symphony of explosions. But to the amazement of human and Zentraedi alike the shield absorbed the deadly storm, and the fortress was left unscathed.

"It's unlike anything we've encountered," said Grel, commenting on a profile schematic of the Micronian shield. "And it seems to be fully protecting the ship from our attack. So what now?"

"Yes…" Khyron answered slowly. "Advance the group and continue firing until I order you to cease."

And continue they did, employing pulsed lasers and cannon fire. Streaks of horizonal lightning converged on the SDF-1, but to no avail. What the shield didn't absorb, it simply deflected.

Captain Gloval was cautiously optimistic; the barrier system was holding, but Vanessa's threat board showed that the enemy had advanced well into the yellow zone.

"The enemy is continuing their attack," she warned him.

His hopes dashed, the captain gave voice to his fears. "This time they won't stop coming until they've destroyed us."

Sammie turned her frightened eyes to him. "Sir, couldn't we radio headquarters and ask for some support or something?"

"That won't work," Lisa chided her. "The captain knows a request like that would just be ignored."

"Because we've been making so many demands about the civilians?" Kim asked.

It was the wrong time for foolish questions, but Gloval fielded them patiently. "It has more to do with our proximity to the ground," he told her. He'd placed his own head on the chopping block; it was unlikely that anyone in the Council would come to his rescue.

"Message, sir."

Gloval turned his attention to Claudia's overhead monitor. It was one of Lang's Robotechnicians.

"We've got a serious problem, Captain. The barrier system is beginning to overload!"

. . .

Rick and the members of Skull Team had been watching the bombardment in awe, but Lisa was now ordering them to counterattack the warships.

"You've got to draw their fire, Lieutenant Hunter. The shields can't take any more. If you fail…

"There isn't going to be any ship to return to."

Her eyes shifted on the screen, as if trying to find his across miles of sky. "It looks bad, Rick. Captain Gloval wants you to know that as of this moment, the safety of every single person on this ship rests in your hands."

*The safety of every single person on this ship rests in your hands…* Bottom of the ninth: bases loaded, two outs, Hunter on deck…

Skull Team descended on the cruisers like vengeful eagles. They had reconfigured to Guardian mode for the drop and to Battloid now as they touched down on the first warship, skimming over its armored green hull, blue foot thrusters blazing like power skaters. Gatlings resounding, they moved toward the stem, taking out turret guns and sealing weapons ports. But that still left four ships emitting unbroken lines of blue death.

The once clearly defined schematic sphere was now a vaguely circular blotch bleeding sickly colors across the Zentraedi projecbeam field.

"You see," Grel said knowingly, "their energy readings are dropping quickly. The shield is at its limit."

Khyron laughed through his teeth. "Now these Micronians will be mine. *Mine!*"

Inside the SDF-1 the barrier system generators lost their grip on that shared and maintained globe of energy; the ball flattened, grew savagely oblate, then lost its circumference entirely and began to arc untamed throughout the hold.

The bridge was in chaos.

"Barrier generators four and seven are losing power due to intense core overheating," Claudia reported to Gloval. Her monitor schematic revealed weakened coordinates along the shield grid.

The captain quickly ordered her to switch to subsystem power.

Meanwhile three of the nine screens at Kim's station and two at Sammie's had blacked out; two others were flashing a field of orange static.

"We have an overload situation in the outer field circuits…"

"Number seven converter has exceeded its limit…"

"Emergency backup crew, report to your service areas."

Lisa brought her hands to her ears and went on the aircom net. "Skull Leader, keep your comline open for emergency orders."

The threat board showed the Zentraedi warships continuing their advance. "They've just entered the red zone, Captain!" Vanessa shouted.

Then, suddenly, there was a blood-curdling scream through the patch lines from the shield control room and primary lighting failed. The bridge crew looked like the living dead under the eerie glow of console lights. Klaxons and warning sirens were blaring from remote areas of the fortress. Sammie's station screen had gone fully to orange.

"It's reaching critical mass," she yelled. "It's going to explode!"

Rick heard the panic in Lisa's voice. "Skull Leader, evacuate your team at once—the barrier system is about to chain-react. Evacuate—"

Rick, Max, and Ben thought their Battloids through an about-face. Beyond the rim of the Zentraedi warship they could see the barrier transubstantiate: What appeared as the selfsame shield was in fact shot through and through with submolecular death.

Rick watched as radiation detector gauges came to life in the cockpit. He raised his teammates on the tac net and told them to clear out on the double.

Behind them the shield expanded, its internal colors shifting from green through yellow and orange to deadly red; then, after a blinding flash of silent white light, the shield was gone. In its place a hot pink hemisphere began to form, an umbrella of horror fifty miles wide.

The three pilots ran their Battloids along the armored hull, past turrets and singed bristle sensors already slagging in the infernal heat; they reconfigured to Guardian mode and launched themselves, the spreading shock wave threatening to overtake them.

Rick glimpsed one of the warships rise from the pack and accelerate to safety. But the rest were annihilated, atomized along with every standing structure and living thing on the ground.

Skull One was tearing through fuchsia skies, fire nipping at the fighter's tail. Inside, Rick searched desperately right and left for a sign of his wingmen. Max's ship came into view to port, but Ben was nowhere in sight.

"Ben, Ben!" Rick cried.

"Behind you, Lieutenant!"

Rick found Dixon's radar blip on the screen; Ben was converting to Guardian for added thrust.

"Hit your afterburner—now! Do you copy?"

Ben's voice was terror-filled: "It's too late, Rick! I can't make... Aaarrrggghhh!..."

Rick shook his head wildly, as much to deny the truth as to keep the sound of death from his ears.

He crossed himself as Ben's radar image began to fade. A second friend lost... color gone out of the world...

# 04

All of a sudden it seemed everything was out of control. Here we were back on Earth, feeling more displaced than we'd felt in deep space. The Council refused to hear us out. The Zentraedi attacks continued unabated, we'd lost Roy Fokker and Ben Dixon, and thousands of innocents had been killed. I wasn't alone in feeling this sense of hopelessness. But it was something we weren't supposed to discuss, as though we had all agreed to some unspoken rule: By not talking about it we could make it go away... Day by day it was becoming more difficult for us to find any sense of comfort or acceptance in Macross, and here was Lynn-Kyle adding fuel to the fire, spearheading a peace movement which could only farther undermine our attempts to defeat the aliens. Not that there wasn't ample justification for civil unrest. But we were one ship, one cause—no thanks to Russo's Counoil  an independent nation at war with the Zentraedi! I had personal reasons for disliking [Kyle], but I now found reasons to distrust him as well. That he had turned Minmei against me, I accepted as given. But I couldn't stand still and allow him to threaten the ship, that military/civilian integrity essential for our survival.

The Collected Journals of Admiral Rick Hunter

THE ENEMY ENERGY POURED INTO AND ABSORBED BY THE barrier cloud had chain-reacted; at the center of the ensuing explosion the SDF-1 was left relatively untouched, but on the ground countless thousands were dead. Within a twenty-five-mile radius from the fortress the Earth's surface was scorched and flayed beyond recognition.

As a consequence, the Ontario Quadrant subcommand had refused to allow the SDF-1 civilians to disembark; those onboard who had heard the rumors early on ceased their premature celebrations and faced the heartbreak.

Eight of the twenty-one techs who manned the barrier system controls had been killed, and the rest were listed in critical condition. The air corps had suffered heavy casualties.

Ben Dixon had tuned out…

But the really big news in Macross City focused on Lynn-Minmei: She had been hospitalized for exhaustion.

Reporters caught up with Lynn-Kyle on the steps of Macross General. The long-haired star was angry enough to create a scene, but he thought better of it and decided to use the news coverage to his advantage. He left their rapid questions unanswered until they got the hint and backed off to let him speak.

"What does Minmei's doctor say?"

"What is the prognosis?"

"Kyle, how long will she be hospitalized?"

"Come on, give us *something*—you're her closest friend."

"How is this going to affect the shooting schedule for the movie the two of you are doing?"

"All right, listen up," Kyle said at last. "I want to make a statement concerning the war. In the midst of all that's going on, all this continual destruction and loss of life, you people want to ask me about Minmei's health. Are you all blind to the realities of this situation or what?"

One of the reporters smirked. "I get it, we should be focusing on *your* needs, huh?"

Kyle shot him a baleful look. "Have you ever stopped to consider the priorities? You're prisoners aboard this ship, we're still under attack, the Council has written you all off, you're being lied to left and right, and you spend your time chasing after a celebrity who's fainted from overwork! Forget this nonsense. We've got to find a way to put an end to this war."

"What would you have everyone do, Kyle?"

"Are you planning to head up a new peace movement?"

"Open rebellion, passive resistance, letters to Command—what are you advocating?"

Kyle held up his hands, then pointed toward one of the group as he responded. "It's *your* responsibility to expose these cover-ups. Point out the lies and contradictions. Show the people of this city the military leaders *as they really are.* We've got to begin pressuring them. We're fifty thousand strong, and we *can* put a stop to this.

"Right now all we've got is devastation and destruction—no winners, only losers. This is an inhumane, no-win situation. The only *conquest* that should concern us is the conquest of our warring nature."

Kyle V-ed the fingers of his right hand and held it aloft.

"*Peace* must conquer all!"

While Lynn-Kyle was urging the press to smoke out enemies of peace from Senator Russo's Council and the SDF-1's leadership command, Earth's fate was under discussion several billion miles away. Khyron's cruiser, the lone survivor of the barrier shield chain-reaction explosion, had refolded to Dolza's command fortress with trans-vids of the catastrophic event. The Zentraedi Commander in Chief was viewing these now, shock and deep concern on his ancient stone face. Breetai, on the other hand, wore a self-satisfied, knowing grin.

Wide-eyed, Dolza ordered a replay of the video—a second look at that enormous canopy of destruction, that hemispheric rain of death, a hapless Micronian city atomized, a verdant land utterly denuded.

"These Micronians are more ruthless than I first believed," the Old One was willing to admit. "They were prepared to sacrifice an entire population center simply to defeat four small divisions of attacking mecha!" Without turning to Breetai, he added, "I suppose their determination comes as no surprise to you, Commander."

Breetai swung around to face Dolza, his grin of self-vindication still in place. He placed one arm on the table and said simply, "No, sir."

"Commander Azonia's inexperience with these beings has proved to be an obvious liability. I am therefore sending you back to take charge of our forces."

Breetai narrowed his good eye at the pronouncement; he'd anticipated this moment for some time. "On one condition," he told Dolza, taking delight in the Old One's disgruntled reaction. "I must request that the Imperial Fleet be redeployed and placed under my command."

"Why such a large force?" Dolza demanded.

Breetai gestured to the wall screen. "You have seen what the Micronians are capable of. They are unpredictable and dangerous. I'm going to need the extra resources."

"Very well, then. You have them," Dolza said stiffly.

Breetai rose and brought his right fist to his left breast in salute. "Your lordship."

Dismissed, he started for the door, but Dolza called out to him, "One more thing, *Commander*."

Neither one of them turned around: Dolza sat stone-faced in his chair; Breetai stood straight and unmoving, right hand clenched at his side. He glanced over his shoulder.

"I expect you to give me better results this time." The words dripped with menace, the implication clear.

"You'll not be disappointed with my performance, m'lord."

When Breetai reached the sliding door, Dolza added, "For your sake, I hope not."

Exedore was waiting for him in the corridor, eager to learn the results of the brief meeting. Breetai brought his adviser up to date as they returned to the flagship. The first stage of the journey—one that suitably suggested the enormous size of the command center—was on foot. The two Zentraedi walked for several minutes until they reached an egress port, where a curved platform jutted out into the command center's central chamber. This was a vast low-g space of water-vapor clouds and what might have appeared to human eyes as blue skies. An open-aired-hover-dish met them at the edge of the railed flyout and transferred them to a waiting shuttle, one of several "anchored" in antigrav stasis. In true Zentraedi fashion, these shuttlecraft resembled nothing more than oddly shaped fish, with two small circular "mouths," one above the other at the ship's snout, and ventral forehead slits and bilateral gill membranes aft, which were actually the exterior drive housings. The shuttlecraft conveyed them through the heart of the chamber—over a veritable city given over to the Robotechnological devices which maintained the command center—to the main docking area where ships-of-the-line, cruisers, destroyers, and battlewagons were anchored. Ultimately they were delivered into the flagship itself. Breetai insisted that they go directly to the bridge.

The observation bubble and the command post's circular viewscreen were in ruins, unchanged since Max Sterling had piloted a VT through them over two months before. But at least the debris had been carted away and the commander's chair and twin microphonelike communicators were intact.

"I'll be most eager to hear what our spies have to report when they return from their mission," Breetai was saying.

"Yes, our emergence from hyperspace will be the signal they've been waiting for." Exedore continued, "Their observations should prove most enlightening, my lord. Surely we'll learn to what extent the Micronians have applied their knowledge of Protoculture. From there it should prove a simple step to redesign our offensive campaign."

"Let us hope so, Exedore," Breetai said noncommittally. "Now, give the order to all vessels of the Imperial Fleet to prepare for an immediate fold operation."

Exedore turned to his task. Klaxons were soon sounding, and announcements issued over the command network.

"All vessels move to fold position… Axis pattern adjust to flagship's attitude… countdown has begun… Hyperspacefold to commence in exactly one minute…"

Exedore surveyed the vessels of the Imperial Fleet as the countdown sounded. He was pleased with Breetai's reawakened confidence. But there was something… some nagging doubt remained at the edge of his thoughts. Words of warning from the ancient texts continued to erode his strength. A secret weapon, *a secret weapon*…

One million warships readied themselves for the fold.

And Exedore wondered: *Will they be enough?*

...

On the way to his quarters in Barracks C, Rick heard himself being paged and walked over to one of the yellow courtesy phones.

*Minmei.*

"Rick, I'm so glad I got you. I guess you've heard the news that I passed out. Well, it's true. I'm in the hospital now, but I don't want you to worry about me. It was just overwork, and now I'm catching up on some much-needed rest… Oh, Rick, why don't you come over and visit me. It would be great; I could really use the company. You don't have to bring me anything—"

He replaced the handset in its cradle, stood there staring at it for a moment, uncertain, then walked off. Again he heard his name on the PA, but this time he ignored it.

He went straight to the computer keyboard in his quarters, sat down, and began to hammer away at the keys methodically and without pause. He commanded the printer on-line and tore free the single sheet he'd completed.

"Dear Mr. and Mrs. Dixon," he read aloud. "As your son's commanding officer, it is my sad duty to inform you that—"

*Ben, hit your afterburners—now!*

Rick crumpled the paper in his hands and threw it aside in anger. "I just can't do it!" he shouted to the monitor.

Beside him on the desk was a photo of Ben and his parents taken years ago, along with a letter from them that had arrived too late. Rick took hold of them and stood up.

*They were both so proud of him! There's nothing I can say to make this any easier. It seems like such a waste!*

There was a knock at the door; he replaced the items and went to answer it, a weary stranger in his own room.

At the door it all caught up with him. Palms pressed against the cool metal for support, he stood there and sobbed, letting his pain wash out uncontrolled. Then suddenly he spun round at the sound of a familiar voice, a ghostly hallucination his mind wanted desperately to embrace.

Ben was leaning over the computer, as though reading what Rick had written, one foot crossed in front of the other, his characteristic grin in place.

*Lieutenant, old buddy—hi!… Hey, I know you're feelin' bad, but it couldn't be helped. It was just my time to go.*

Rick turned away from the apparition, complimenting one part of himself for a nice try. But he wasn't about to let himself off the hook that easily.

He hid his face and tears from Max as the door slid open. Sterling spied the photo and letter but said nothing. He reminded Rick that the two of them were due on deck shortly, and they left the room together a minute later.

Why wasn't Max equally broken up about Ben's death? Rick asked himself. He considered what his mind had materialized only moments before. *It couldn't be helped, it was just my time to go…* Was there something to that?

In the elevator Max seemed to read his thoughts.

"I guess it's tough being in command," he told Rick. "I mean, after a while you start feeling responsible for everybody who's serving under you, right?"

Rick turned to him. "You don't know how helpless I feel each time we go into battle. Each time we… *lose* someone. It's like letting someone slip from your grasp and fall. You're always wondering if there wasn't something more you could have done, something you overlooked."

"I wonder if I'll feel that way when I get *my* first command."

Max's response surprised him; he wasn't going to get the sympathy he'd expected.

"It's probably coming soon," Max continued. "Command just promoted me to second lieutenant, and it's barely a month since I was promoted to third lieutenant."

They were ascending the wide staircase that led to the starboard observation deck overlooking the *Daedalus*. Rick stopped to look at Max.

"I'm sure you'll make a good commander."

Rick's tone was flat, but he meant it; Max not only had the required skills, he had the faith and will to carry on—he knew how to stow away the horrors. Rick thought he'd achieved that after Roy's death. Before the battle he had felt renewed, but with

Ben's death that feeling had faded. In its place was a hopelessness he could barely bring himself to confront.

A female tower controller's voice rang out over the ob deck speakers: "Unloading will commence in exactly one minute. Please be sure all cargo bay doors are open to receive supply consignments from helicopter shuttle groups. Under flight decks should now be clear and convoy vehicles in place to continue transfer to warehouse distribution centers…"

The SDF-1 was back at its original landing site in the Pacific, floating now in Cruiser mode like some techno-island. For days, huge cargo carriers and choppers had been flying in all make and manner of supplies and provisions. Trucks and transports lumbered through the streets of Macross city day and night, confirming the worst fears of the civilians aboard: The battle fortress was no longer welcome on Earth.

Max pointed out a fancy-looking double-bubbled jet chopper coming out of pink and lavender sunset clouds to set down on the carrier deck. In addition to the Robotech insignia, it bore black and gold Earth Council markings.

"Gotta be somebody important," Max guessed.

"It's from Alaska HQ. I'll bet they brought lift-off orders. We're the only thing standing between Earth and the Zentraedi, but they're ready to toss us to the sharks, anyway."

Following Rick's lead, Max put his elbows on the rail and leaned over for a better look at the chopper. "You think it's true about us being banished from Earth?"

Rick nodded and straightened up. "They've pulled in the welcome mat. This ship is going to be our home for a long time to come."

"Then this might be the last time we get to see the Earth from the surface," Max mused. "Guess we'd better enjoy the view."

The sun was setting. Rick stared into the orange glow; there was a finality to the moment too frightening to contemplate.

She was an attractive woman with pleasant features and a crop of long brown hair, but she carried herself stiffly and kept her officer's cap pulled too low on her forehead. Besides, she had brought bad news.

She turned around in the doorway to Gloval's quarters and saluted.

"I'll let headquarters know the orders were received." Two white-jacketed, blue-capped aides, brass buckles of their belts gleaming, registered looks of distaste and followed her down the corridor.

The captain remained seated at the desk in his spacious quarters. A Defense Forces flag stood to one side of the desk in an area partitioned off by a tall bookcase and dominated by a large wall screen. Insignia carpets, bright throw rugs, and potted plants warmed the room; the leatherbound volumes and computer consoles lent just the right air of officiality.

Gloval had the orders in hand. He lighted his pipe and leaned in to read through them. *Yes*, he said to himself, thinking about the female officer, *the orders have been received.* And she could tell those idiot generals back at headquarters that they were received in silence, *completely under protest.*

It was unthinkable—expected but unbelievable nonetheless. The Council members didn't have an ounce of pity in their hearts.

Gloval got up and paced, then returned to the desk.

What was he supposed to say to the people of the ship?

Silently, he read: *The United Earth Council hereby orders that you remove the dimensional fortress from any close proximity to the Earth. You are also ordered to detain until such time as this governing Council sees fit all civilian refugees onboard. Should you fail to carry out these orders to the letter, this Council will recommend to the Joint Chiefs of Staff—*

Gloval threw the papers aside in disgust. He responded to a knock on the door and bade Lisa enter. She picked up the note of anger and frustration in his voice and asked if there was anything wrong.

Gloval had his back to her, smoke rising from his pipe like steam from an ancient locomotive. "Yes, there's something wrong—as wrong as can be." He gave her a sidelong glance. "But it's just as we feared: We've been ordered to leave Earth immediately."

Gloval heard her sharp intake of breath, but she rallied quickly and offered to fix him a drink. She was a trooper all right.

"After the explosion I expected the ship to be exiled. But to force fifty thousand innocent civilians to become refugees from their own planet—"

Lisa handed him a Scotch on the rocks; she had fixed herself one as well.

"I guess we should drink a toast to our last moments on Earth, Lisa."

"Perhaps we should drink a toast to the civilians instead."

It seemed an appropriate gesture; they raised their glasses and took long pulls of the expensive stuff.

"These orders go into effect as soon as we've finished taking on supplies. That means we'll be forced to break the news of our banishment to everyone just moments before we take off."

"Do you want me to announce it?" Lisa volunteered.

"No, I'd better make the broadcast myself."

Lisa left to make the necessary arrangements. Gloval dropped down into his chair, took a deep breath, and punched for the bridge on his phone. Claudia informed him that loading was almost complete.

"Now, listen to me carefully, Claudia," he began. Sweat was even now beading up on his forehead; how would it be when he went out in front of the entire ship? "I want you to quietly begin preparations to move out."

"To where, Captain?"

"I'll have astrogation furnish you with the coordinates immediately. You see, we're leaving Earth."

# 05

It is no secret (nor should it come as any surprise) that humankind's most noble impulses often surface during the most trying of times, that human spirit rises to the challenge when faced with adversity, that human strength is born from human failings... Is it any wonder, then, that the SDF-1 crew became a tighter family after the fortress had been exiled than it had been before?

From the log of Captain (later Admiral) Henry Gloval

IN THEIR DARK AND DANK HIDEOUT DEEP WITHIN THE BOWELS OF the dimensional fortress, the three Zentraedi spies sat down to their last Micronian meal; soon they would attempt an escape that would end either in their deaths or in a successful rendezvous with the ships of the main fleet. The three—Rico, Konda, and Bron— agreed that their mission would have been judged superlative had they only been able to leave the fortress to reconnoiter the Micronian homeworld; but oddly enough, few of the Micronians had been allowed to disembark. Nevertheless they were pleased with what they had managed to amass over the course of the past three months by Micronian reckoning. The operational Battlepod which they had been lucky enough to obtain was ready for flight, crowded now with the results of their many forays into Macross City in search of espionage booty, Micronian artifacts, and, well, *souvenirs*—two video monitors, a few tables, a refrigerator, a grand piano they had smuggled home in pieces, disc players and discs, candy and foodstuffs, and, of course, a wide assortment of Minmei dolls and paraphernalia.

Bron, as always, had prepared the meal.

"Something called beef stew," he explained.

"Smells terrific," said Konda, purple hair now below his shoulders.

Metal plates and bent silverware in hand, the three agents, looking unwashed and shaggy, their clothing soiled and threadbare, were seated on short lengths of cowling and empty cans around a blazing liquid-fueled camping stove, currently crowned by a large, lidded stew pot. Rico had switched on the portable CD player; Minmei's "Stagefright" was filling the little-used storage room with pleasing sounds.

Rico put aside the device that would alert them to the rearrival of the Zentraedi fleet and said, "Listening to Minmei helps my food go down better."

"She makes *everything* better," Konda seconded.

Their spirits were high, ebullient; even Bron, who managed to burn his hands while removing the stew pot from the flame. As always. He placed a coffeepot on the STOVE and sampled a bit of the day's fare.

"What about my cooking, boys—do you think it's improved some?"

"Yeah," said Konda, straight-faced, "it takes me over an hour to get indigestion now."

Bron's response was equally low-key. "That *is* better. It used to take you fifteen minutes."

"When he first started cooking, *I* used to get sick just *thinking* about it!"

Rico broke up, and his comrades joined in. The coffee, meanwhile, was boiling away, running down the sides of the pot and adding sizzle to the fire.

But Bron grew serious all of a sudden. "To be honest, I'm going to miss this Micronian food."

The subject broached, other disclosures followed.

"Well, I hate to admit it, but you're right—me, too."

"And that's not all. I've been thinking, I'm gonna miss a whole lotta things—like happy people, music—"

"Yeah, the music. The thing I'll miss most is hearing Minmei sing every day."

The corners of Bron's mouth turned down. "I don't even want to *think* about that."

"And you remember those females we met that one time?" Konda poured himself a cup of coffee. "Dancing was fun."

"Yeah, that Kim was really something else," said Bron, the enthusiasm returned. "She had me laughing almost all day!"

"And that girl Sammie," Rico was quick to add, hand to his face demonstrating a Micronian gesture he'd observed. "When she spotted us with the Minmei doll... 'My heavens!'" He mimicked Sammie's voice.

They shared a good laugh, but again the mood deteriorated. "Yeah... And you remember what we heard that Micronian talking about—about trying to put an end to the war?"

"That frightened me," said Rico. "Without war we'd have no reason to live!"

"Maybe," Konda answered him. "But I kinda feel like I understand what the Micronian was talkin' about."

Rico reached out and touched the gravity-wave indicator beside him on the floor. "It's hard to believe that by tomorrow morning we'll all probably be back in uniform."

"Yeah..."

"I can hardly wait..."

Claudia Grant also found herself breaking out in a cold sweat as she relayed the captain's orders to the bridge crew.

"Takeoff?" said Vanessa. "You mean to say all those rumors about leaving are true?"

"Let's be realistic. We caused an entire city to be wiped out." Kim's hand was at her mouth, as though trying to stifle the truth.

Sammie looked over her station innocently. "We weren't responsible—it was the barrier overload. Blame it on the Zentraedi."

"But we shouldn't have been there," Kim argued.

"The captain was thinking of the civilians, Kim—"

"What's going to happen to them?" Vanessa broke in.

Claudia was on tiptoes, throwing switches to activate the overhead monitors at her and Lisa's stations. She turned around, a hint of impatience in her voice. "Since they've already been declared dead and nobody on Earth wants to accept them, I guess they'll stay with us. Now, hurry up with those final checks; we're running out of time."

Sammie struck a daydreamer's pose at her console. "Lisa's father is a bigshot in the United Earth Council. Maybe if she sent him a message, he'd hold up our orders until we figured out—Oh—"

Claudia, hands on hips, was standing over her.

"Don't you *think* about suggesting that to Lisa, do you understand? As an officer aboard this ship, she knows her duties. Now, see to it that you carry out yours!"

Lovers watching the skies that night thought they were viewing an unannounced solar eclipse. The full moon wore a diamond ring of brilliant light. But wait… *an unannounced solar eclipse?* The sun had set over four hours ago!

Amateur astronomers were similarly puzzled, as were seismologists and sailors; graphs and gauges were going wild, and Earth's oceans were rising to dangerous heights… But there were a few scientists scattered across the planet who recognized the phenomenon; they'd witnessed these gravity-wave disturbances once before, a little over two years earlier. But where that initial event had brought awe, the present event brought terror.

To three beings on the planet, however, the event was little more than a signal.

"That's it!" said Bron, deactivating the transceiver. "Let's move out!"

The agents were already inside the Battlepod, strapped in and alert. They ran the pod ostrichlike across the hold, metal hooves loud against the floorplates, echoes granting them an illusory sense of company, stopping a few feet short of the exterior hull. Bursts from the mecha's twin lasers concentrated blue-white energy on the hull. The steel glowed red, then white, slagged, and began to fall away; flames leapt forth, and the small hole enlarged. Within minutes there was an enormous breach, large enough to accommodate the pod's passage into the cool Pacific night.

Foot-retros eased the pod into a controlled descent; it plunged several hundred feet into the ocean, the thrusters carrying it scarcely half a mile from the fortress to a coral outcropping.

Rico raised the mecha to its feet and initiated a series of booster commands. Thruster flame shot forth from the cockpit sphere as it disengaged from its bipedally designed undercarriage. The three micronized agents were airborne and on their way home.

Had there been a little less preflight commotion aboard the dimensional fortress, perhaps some tech or sentry would have noticed the hole that the agents burned in the hull; but as it was, ship personnel had just enough time to complete their own assigned duties let alone check up on someone else's station. And the bridge was by no means exempt from this frantic pace, especially when radar informed them of interspatial disturbances emanating from beyond the moon.

Lisa was already on the bridge and the captain was just making his crouched entry when the reports began to pour in.

"…We're not sure, but it appears to be the fallout from a massive number of hyperspace-fold operations," Gloval heard someone from radar report.

"Gravity-wave disturbance from the moon," said Vanessa, slender fingers flying over the keyboard to bring schematics to the threat board.

Gloval was standing over her, anxious. "Are they certain it is a fold?"

"It's more severe than that, sir," she told him. "It appears to be multiple folds!"

"Can you estimate the number?"

"Trying…"

"Wait!" said Sammie, and all eyes turned to her. "Maybe they've come in peace this time." Blank stares of disbelief grounded her hopes. "Right," she said, swinging around to her console, "probably not."

That same male voice from radar announced an unidentified object flying directly over the ship.

Gloval turned to Lisa. "Do we have any fighters on patrol?"

"Negative, sir."

"Radar again, Captain. Our monitors show a large alien vessel moving toward Earth from lunar space. It appears to be on a collision or rendezvous course with the object we've been tracking."

Gloval studied the schematic and ordered Lisa to move all

Veritech groups to condition yellow at once.

"Picking up a second wave of gravity disturbance," said Vanessa. She gasped as new readouts filled the screen. "I calculate the number of enemy ships to be in excess of … *one million!*"

Gloval narrowed his eyes and looked over at Lisa, as if to say: *Yes, your reports to the Council are now verified.* Gloval wanted to see those generals live to eat their words.

"I don't think it matters how many ships the enemy brings in," said Claudia confidently.

"But a *million* of them…" said Sammie.

"We'll never be able to outmaneuver them," added Kim. But Claudia remained undaunted. "We beat them before, and we'll beat them again."

Gloval's thoughts were still focused on the Council. He was certain they were monitoring this latest move by the Zentraedi, and yet there was no word from them.

"Then we're completely isolated," he told the crew.

"Why?" Sammie wanted to know.

The time had come to let them know the truth. Gloval realized that his life for the next twenty-four hours would be filled with many such moments. And yet he couldn't help but ask himself what would happen if he did nothing to counteract the present threat. Had the Zentraedi been pushed beyond their limit? Were they ready to hold the Earth hostage? What did they want, and what would the fools who governed the Council do if Gloval refused to acquiesce to either group's demands?

But Henry Gloval was simply not built that way.

"I guess you might as well know," he began. "The Council has decided that the best way to protect the planet is to use the dimensional fortress as a decoy. We have been ordered to draw the aliens away." He let that much sink in while he moved to the command chair and sat down; then he added:

"This ship and its passengers are considered expendable."

Although Mayor Tommy Luan had at one time expressed concern that Macross had little in the way of newsworthy stories, there was now enough daily news to run morning and evening editions. There wasn't a man, woman, or child in the city who hadn't heard rumors to the effect that the Ontario Quadrant subcommand had withdrawn its offer. Then there were the further exploits of Minmei—whew! had that idea ever exploded far beyond his plans!—and, lately, those of her cousin and costar, Lynn-Kyle—one to keep a close eye on for several reasons. And of course the disagreements, quarrels, and fights two months of imposed confinement and stress had unleashed. And tonight Captain Gloval himself was planning to address the entire ship, as rare an event as had occurred thus far.

Gloval and Lisa had left the remaining preflight preparations to Claudia and the crew, exiting the bridge only minutes after the Zentraedi had made their reappearance. Gloval could simply have raised the ship and delayed the address until they were in deep space, but he wanted it behind him. He had no idea what the enemy's next move was going to be, and he planned to ask the residents of Macross for their cooperation and support no matter what course of action he might be forced to take.

They had arrived at the Macross Broadcasting System studios only moments ago, interrupting a live special starring Minmei and Lynn Kyle. The two cousins, along with Lisa Hayes, stood off to one side of the center-stage podium just now. There were three cameras trained on Gloval; the lights were too bright and way too hot. He was already perspiring under his blue jacket and white cap. He had opted against using the prompter or cue cards, for effect as well as because of failing eyesight. One of the engineers leading the quietly mouthed countdown threw him a ready sign, and he began:

"This is Captain Gloval speaking, with a very important announcement that will affect the lives of everyone aboard this ship. Since our return to Earth, as some of you may already know, I have made numerous appeals to both the United Earth Defense Council and the governing bodies of several separatist states for permission to allow you to disembark and resettle wherever you might choose. I'm certain that you are all aware by now of my feelings regarding your continued presence aboard the fortress. Be that as it may, time and again my appeals have been turned down, for reasons that must remain undisclosed for the present. However, I always felt that progress was being made on those requests, until in light of recent events I have been forced to entertain second thoughts about the Council's position."

Gloval was silent a moment; his throat felt parched, and he began to wonder whether the in-close cameras were picking up the slight tremor of his hands. But he dared not risk looking at himself in the monitors. Rather, he cleared the quaver in his voice and continued.

"My friends and fellow shipmates, I have some very bad news to report to you. I received word just a while ago that this ship and all its passengers have been ordered to leave the Earth immediately."

Gloval heard the cameramen and grips gasp; he imagined a collective gasp rising up from the entire city, strong enough to register on the air supply systems in engineering.

Now for the most difficult stretch…

"If we do not evacuate Earth, we've been warned that we risk attack by elements of our own Defense Forces. I know that you must find this unthinkable, but it is most unfortunately true. You cannot have failed to notice that for the past few days we have been taking on a wide assortment of supplies and provisions. I know it is of minor consolation, but I anticipate that we have enough in stores to undertake the journey ahead. And just where is that? You must be asking yourselves. Well, I will tell you: That journey will be to *victory!*"

Without an audience, Gloval had no idea how it went over, so he risked a quick look at Lisa, who flashed a smile and thumbs up. But were the civilians buying it? Did they still have confidence in his ability to lead them to victory?

Those lights seemed even hotter now; he felt dizzy from strain but pressed on.

"I desperately need all of your cooperation in this moment of terrible responsibility. We must all work for the day when Earth will reaccept us. Until then, we will survive as best we can… I give you my most humble apologies…"

*No, this can't be happening!* he shouted to himself.

But it was: He was sobbing, still on camera and sobbing.

And suddenly Minmei was beside him, her hand on his shoulder. She picked up the mike from the podium and began to speak, the cameras tracking mercifully away from Gloval to close on her.

"Listen, everyone, the captain really needs our support right now. Look, I don't understand politics—after what Captain Gloval has told us, I'm not sure I want to—but I do know that the only way we'll survive this is to pull together.

"We've been on this ship for a long time, and I don't know about you, but I think of the SDF-1 as my home now. Don't forget, we have almost everything here that we could ever have on Earth—our own city and all the things that go along with it. We've all been through quite a bit, but look at how strong we've become because of it. I have more friends *here* than I *ever* did on Earth. You've been like a big family to me.

"Someday we'll return to our real home—we'll never give up hope. But for now, I'm *proud* to be a citizen of Macross City and this *ship!*

"No matter where we go in space or how long it takes, our hearts will always be tied to the Earth. So to help all of us express our feelings at this moment, I'd like to perform a song for you and dedicate it to the Earth we love so dearly…"

And Minmei actually broke into song; white dress swirling, blue eyes flashing, she broke into song. And more than half of Macross joined her. She had touched something. Her words had given voice to some unarticulated feeling the residents of Macross shared. Throughout the city, people shook hands and began to view themselves as a new nation, a new experiment in human social evolution. It was true that many of them had family out there on Earth, but hadn't most of them come to Macross Island in the first place to escape most of what passed for world events? Did anyone really want to be governed by such a heartless group of puppet masters as the United Earth Defense Council?

So they celebrated a bittersweet victory. They shelved their dreams for the last time, and they took a long look around their city, as if for the first time. And many of them crowded to the ports and lights in the hull as the fortress lifted off, Earth already a memory, the unknown ahead.

# 06

They [the Zentraedi troops] reacted like adolescents released from the behavioral constraints of their guardians. Suddenly there were worlds of pleasure and pure potential awaiting them—worlds that they'd been denied access to but that were now theirs for the asking, if not the taking... One doesn't have to look far into the history of our own race to find examples of the same impulses at work. The so-called counterculture of late-1960s America comes immediately to mind, especially with regard to the central place given music and pleasure, and arising as it did from a decidedly antiwar movement.

Zeitgeist, *Alien Psychology*

"Talk about your 'charms to soothe the savage beast' [sic]... She had enough talent—enough magic—to bowl over an entire empire! So why not call it as it was?—a Minmei cult!"

Remarks attributed to Vance Hasslewood,
Lynn-Minmei's agent

T HE MILLION VESSELS OF THE IMPERIAL FLEET FORMED UP ON Commander Breetai's flagship, positioning themselves by rank in the staging area—a multirowed column of Zentraedi firepower that stretched for thousands of miles into Luna's dark-side space.

In what was left of the command post bowl, Breetai stood tall and proud, his dwarfish adviser by his side, equally confident for the first time in months. The three returned agents were being regenerated in the sizing chamber, and here was Commander Azonia's troubled face in the projecbeam field. Breetai had already informed her of his reinstatement. Exedore moved to the communicator to check on regeneration status while Azonia offered her reply.

"So I hear," she began. "You've assembled quite a fleet to deal with one small Robotech ship."

Breetai laughed at her sarcasm, gleaming faceplate riding the wrinkles of his grin. "You noticed… that 'small Robotech ship,' as you call it, has caused quite a bit of trouble. Even you, *Commander*, were beaten and humiliated."

"My defeat was humiliating only in that Khyron was responsible for it."

"A good commander keeps his troops in line," Breetai started to say. But Exedore interrupted him deferentially.

"Uh, sir, the sizing chamber… Our agents are ready to deliver their report."

Breetai regarded him briefly, then turned back to Azonia's projecbeam image. "I'll give you your assignment later," he said dismissively.

"But wait, I haven't given you *my* report yet! Miriya Parino has—"

"That will be all," he told her, arms folded across his chest. "More pressing matters require my attention."

"Breetai  " she yelled as the image faded.

"Ah, well done, my lord!" Exedore congratulated him. He then motioned to the corridor. "I believe they're waiting for us."

"This report may turn the tide in our favor," Breetai said as they left the command post.

Breetai had no reason to doubt that this would be the case. He had no inkling then of the bizarre reversals that awaited him not only from his own agents but from another whose micronized presence onboard the SDF-1 was to come as a complete surprise.

Rico, Konda, and Bron, clothed once more in the red uniforms of their rank, were brought to Breetai's personal conference chamber, a sparsely furnished circular room dominated by an enormous exterior bay, currently filled with a view of the Earth and its cratered moon. Central to it was a round table surrounded with comfortable high-backed lounging chairs. The piled artifacts the agents had brought back with them made for a most curious centerpiece.

Breetai reached out and pulled an item loose from the jumble. He regarded it quizzically, its three-legged form misleadingly heavy in his open hand.

"The Micronians call that a 'piano,' m'lord," Rico explained.

"'Piano,'" Breetai repeated. "What function does it serve?"

Rico instructed him to press down on the keyboard of small white teeth. Breetai did so, displeased and strangely disturbed with the noise it emitted. He placed the thing out of reach on the table. Exedore studied it while Breetai hastily examined several other objects.

"Is it alive? Some sort of Protoculture-animated Robotech device?" Exedore wondered aloud.

"No," Rico continued. "It makes music. Music is when different sounds are put together for entertainment. It's really quite interesting when you get used to it. We came to enjoy it very—"

"Explain 'entertainment,'" Breetai demanded.

Rico thought for a moment. "Uhh... diversion, m'lord. This, for example." He selected a small, monitorlike device from the pile and held it up for Breetai's scrutiny. "These seem to provide electronic images in much the same fashion as our own vid-scanners. But several of these can be found in each Micronian quarters for the purpose of observing and listening to 'entertainment.'"

Exedore made a thoughtful sound. "Undoubtedly the means by which they familiarize themselves with battle plans and such. Continue," he told Rico.

But all three agents started to talk at once, excitedly, eager to report their findings. A little *too* eager; Exedore began to worry.

"One at a time!" Breetai said, silencing them. "Don't force me to repeat the threats of our last debriefing."

Rico stood up. "What we brought back represents only a small part of the Micronian society and its customs," he calmly began. "You see, they live a much different life than we do—"

"They're proficient at making repairs within their ship," Konda interrupted, on his feet now and gesturing nonstop. "Indeed, they rebuilt an entire population center onboard using only salvaged materials. They adapt quickly to unfamiliar environments—"

"And," Bron blurted out, unable to contain his enthusiasm, "there are many Micronians besides soldiers onboard the ship. In fact, they join together many times during the day and move about freely—"

"Males and females are together!" Rico shouted.

Breetai and Exedore, who had been trying to follow these rapid deliveries like spectators at a high-speed tennis match, suddenly turned to each other in near panic.

"Males and females together," Rico was repeating to utterances of affirmation from the others.

"As a matter of fact, it doesn't seem to be as bad as we thought," Konda started.

"We forced ourselves to adapt to the presence of females all around us and were unable to discover any negative side effects," Bron finished.

Already Breetai had heard more than enough, but it went on like this for several more hours before he silenced them again, as confused as he was nauseated by their reports. If the results of the penetration operation had demonstrated anything, it was that further contact with the Micronians could not be permitted. It was obvious that his three agents had been brainwashed by some Micronian secret weapon, and to make matters worse, Exedore was now suggesting that he be allowed to investigate Micronian society firsthand!

Dismissed, the three agents later regrouped in secret at Konda's insistence.

"I kept some Micronian artifacts in my pocket," Konda was confessing to his comrades now. "Did you show them everything you had?"

"No, I held out," Bron admitted. Ditto for Rico.

"Let's see what we've got," Konda said, pulling things from the deep pockets of his red jacket.

Six hands began piling souvenirs on the table, a veritable dollhouse garage-sale assortment of miniatures: a doubleburner stove, a small refrigerator, a circular end table, several video monitors, a chest of drawers, a space heater, a commode, a/v discs,

CD players, a teddy bear, a set of golf clubs, a guitar. Konda said, "I'd rather have these than the cruiser commands we were promised."

"I brought along two of Minmei's voice reproductions," said Rico, Minmei's first CD edged between his thumb and forefinger.

Bron leaned in to take a look. "How about trading me one of those for something, eh?"

"What piece do you plan to trade?" said Rico, a profiteer's glint in his one good eye.

"I've got a Minmei doll…"

"Deal!" Rico answered.

Bron squinted at the CD photo of a veiled Minmei.

"You know, the other guys would sure be impressed if they could see this stuff."

Konda was nodding his head. "Yeah, we could get away with showing just a select few, don't you think?"

Within an hour there were eleven soldiers gathered around the table in what had become the agents' clubhouse. Word had spread quickly through the flagship. There wasn't a soldier aboard who hadn't expressed some interest in hearing about the peculiarities of Micronian life, and now that there were, well, *artifacts*—actual objects to handle, look at, and listen to—Rico, Bron, and Konda couldn't have kept them away if they tried. Of the eleven uniformed troops, three were already in dereliction of duty.

The agents passed the artifacts around, pleased to be at center stage to be sure but sincere in their desire to share their experience and adventures aboard the Robotech ship with their comrades. Candies were sampled, objects examined, nuances of Micronian culture explained. But it was soon obvious which artifact among the lot was the hottest property.

"'To be in love,'" sang the doll as it took tiny steps along the tabletop, electronically synthesized voice full of pleasant vibrato, arms in motion, black hair buns like mouse ears.

The soldiers were disturbed, then astounded, but ultimately captivated.

"It looks like a Micronian, but what are those noises?"

One of them, a massive, mop-topped, sanguine-faced brute

betraying an uncharacteristic concern, squatted down, crossed eyes level with the tabletop, when the doll tipped over and ceased its song.

"Uh, did I hurt it?"

Konda set the doll back on its feet. "No, dummy. You can't hurt it. It's called a Minmei doll, and that 'noise' is called singing."

"You call that a 'Minmei'?" someone said. "It's incredible—I've never heard anything like it."

"Amazing," said another.

"We should let some of the others hear this."

"Quiet! I can't hear the Minmei when you're talking."

For the remainder of the Zentraedi day, the doll repeated its two-song repertoire over and over again. More and more soldiers stopped by the clubhouse; rap codes and secret handshakes were exchanged, and Minmei's name was being whispered like some password throughout the ships of the Imperial Fleet.

While the "Minmei" continued to gather a secret following among the troops of Breetai's armada, the inspiration for that doll was attending a party at the plush Hotel Centinel, Macross City's best, only a stone's throw from the new skyway overpass. The dimensional fortress had left Earth, and while most of the city's residents were making the painfully difficult readjustment to life in space, Macross's who's-who were drowning their sorrows in tabletop fountains of recently acquired sparkling spring water and vintage champagne. But this was no sour-grapes affair; it was an all-out bash held in celebration of the premiere of SDF Pictures' first release, *Little White Dragon*, starring Lynn-Minmei and Lynn-Kyle.

The film's financial backers were there, some of the crew, engineers from EVE, the mayor and his crowd, selected extras, and assorted hangers-on. Kyle, too, a little surly tonight but looking dashing in a lavender suit, crimson shirt, and bow tie. But the female lead was conspicuously absent from the indoor merriment, the tables laden with gourmet foodstuffs, the wine and spirits. She had absented herself to the balcony for a breather; show biz was getting to her.

There was a downside to it, she decided. The real thrill was in the performing, the real reward in the applause. But these parties weren't fun at all; they were business, a place for the sycophants and profiteers to gather. This was where they performed, and money was their applause.

Minmei wasn't feeling jaded; it was too soon for that. But she couldn't help but question some of the new directions she was taking, the new directions Macross seemed to be taking. She thought back to the early days, the communal spirit that had rebuilt the city, the family ties that had developed, the sense of equality that had reigned. But things were changing all of a sudden, not only physically—what with skyway ramps, exclusive hotels, and gourmet foods—but *spiritually*. It seemed as though more than a few people had merely given lip service to the idea of SDF-1 "citizenry"; now that existence aboard the fortress was an open-ended reality, those same hypocrites were seeking to claim for themselves the best this place had to offer. A new class system was beginning to form itself, and the last place Minmei wanted to find herself was among a reborn aristocracy. It was so important to stay in touch with one's past, to remember the people who helped you find your place—

"Hey, doll, what's going on?"

Minmei turned from the view to face the sender of that slurred intrusion. It was Vance Hasslewood, her business manager, at least two drinks past his limit.

"You're the star of this party," he said, toasting her with the drink he carried. "You should be inside having fun. What's the problem?"

"Looks to me like you've been celebrating enough for both of us." She didn't bother to conceal her disapproval, but Vance was too caught up in party momentum to catch it. He loosened his tie coyly, eyes closed behind the aviator specs.

"Well, I'll admit that I'm enjoying myself a bit... but I've got one heck of a reason. After the movie premieres you'll be a star. We're talking major talent, big, *big* bucks. You'll need two more hands just to haul the money home."

He couldn't have been happier.

"I'm already a star, Vance," Minmei reminded him. "What else can you offer me?"

Vance laughed and put his arm around her. "Hey, it's payday, kid. You want something, I'll get it for you."

"I need a front-row seat for the premiere; it's for someone I want to invite."

Vance made a troubled gesture. "Front-row seat? Now? Those seats were filled weeks ago… I don't know Minmei."

She looked directly at him. "Vance. Just do it, okay?"

"All right," he said at last. "I'll see what I can do." Minmei thanked him, and he wandered off, glass in hand.

Smiling suddenly, she leaned her elbows on the balcony rail.

"I wish I could be there to see the expression on Rick's face when I tell him."

Jan Morris was no stranger to people who talked to themselves— she'd talked to herself for years now—but given her present condition it was unlikely that she even heard Minmei's solitary remark. Cocktail glass precariously pinched between her fingers, the former star (and someday mystic) was winding her way toward the railing. Two years in space, self-pity, and drink had taken their toll; she was aged beyond her years, a bleached-blond caricature in long white gloves and strapless gown.

"Minmei, I've been looking all over for you. How are you, dahling? Wonderful party! Having a good—oops!"

Minmei deftly avoided the launched cordial; thick liqueur red as Jan's gown splashed against the retaining wall beside her.

"Excuse me. How *clumsy*, I could just die!" Jan was all false apologies. "Lucky I didn't get any on your dress, dahling. And it's such a *quaint* little dress, isn't it? So full of *charm*; it's really lovely, dear. Did you make it yourself?"

*I'll have you know that this lime-green silk cape alone costs more than—* Minmei wanted to say. Fortunately, though, she didn't have to say anything, because Jan was already slaloming her way back inside. An older man had appeared and expressed an interest in meeting "the young star of the film," and Jan was now tugging him away from the balcony doors.

"She's not so terribly interesting," Minmei heard her tell him. "Just a child, really. Now, why don't we go sit down somewhere and I'll read your palm."

Minmei was thinking about hiring a bodyguard when Kyle called to her.

"Your manager told me to tell you it's seat A-5. They'll hold the ticket at the box office."

Minmei clasped her hands together under her chin. "Great, Kyle! Thanks."

"Thank Vance," he told her, and led her inside. He had that protective look on his face she'd come to recognize. He placed his hands on her shoulders.

"You've got a big day tomorrow. Why don't you call it a night and I'll walk you back to your room."

"Deal," she answered. "I need to make a call, anyway."

Big day or no big day, there was to be no sleep for her that night. She left a message for Rick at the officers' barracks, but he never called back. The large suite SDF Pictures had supplied only served to return her to that evening's earlier train of thought. At Vance's insistence she joined him in the rooftop lounge for a nightcap, but even that didn't help. She yearned for her blue and yellow room above the White Dragon, her few possessions, her treasured memories.

# 07

Eventually, *Little White Dragon* would find a larger audience, a less involved one to be sure, and critical reaction was mixed, to say the least. More than one reviewer dismissed it as "home movies for the space set"; another called it "low-art therapy... propagandist fantasy... a misdirected death-wish fable." But several praised it unconditionally as "a prescient warning from the collective unconscious."

*History of the First Robotech War,* vol. LXXXII

MIRIYA PARINO, LATE OF THE QUADRONO BATTALION AND NOW an unauthorized micronized operative inside the dimensional fortress, marched briskly down Macross Boulevard. The somewhat Teutonic outfit she had pilfered to replace the sackcloth garment she'd arrived in was well suited to her traffic-stopping martial stride, although she didn't understand what all the stares were about. Perhaps, she wondered, the uniform was inappropriate. If she could have seen herself as passersby saw her—radiant green hair, tight-fitting lavender vest, knickers, white stockings, and high-heeled "Mary Janes"—she would have understood at once.

It had not been an easy week. She had been forced to steal food and moments of rest when opportunities presented themselves. Once or twice she was tempted to accept assistance offered at least a dozen times daily by Micronian males—but thought better of it. Early on she had spotted Breetai's three agents among a crowd gathered in front of a vid-scanner listening to some long-haired male talk of *peace* and *ending the war!* But she saw no reason to make contact with the three and hadn't seen them since.

*Peace...* Micronian ways were baffling, unthinkable. But she was enjoying the challenge. Unfortunately, though, she had yet to find the pilot who had bested her in battle, despite the many soldiers she passed in the streets.

Ahead of her now was yet another gathering of Micronians, the largest she'd encountered thus far, and certainly the loudest. Cheering groups of males and females were standing twenty deep in front of a strange-looking building, a backlit message display of some sort jutting out above the entry.

"Little... White... Dragon," Miriya read aloud, trying out the feel of the words. She knew that the first meant "small" and that the second referred to the absence of color, but she was unfamiliar with the final word.

There was a line of long vehicles with tinted observation ports discharging strangely uniformed males and females in front of the building. The people in the crowd were craning their necks and rising on their toes to catch a brief glimpse of these heroes as they ascended the entry steps, waving and smiling. Adulation was heaped on two in particular: a small dark-haired female someone in the crowd called "Min-mei" and an equally dark-haired male—*the same who had been spouting peace from the vid-scanner!* They were ceremoniously ushered into the building without having to show the passes required by the ordinary citizenry of the population center.

Miriya had little doubt that her quarry was inside, about to be honored for defeating her in battle. It might have even been that long-haired male. Why else would so many attend? She had no pass, but she did have a trick up the sleeve of that white blouse with the ruffled collar. She had noticed that certain facial contortions from a Micronian female could open many a locked door. So giving her thong-laced vest a downward tug, she approached the guard at the gate who was accepting the passes and flashed him her most brilliant smile...

Spotlighted center stage inside the Fortress Theater, where an SRO crowd filled the lobby and upper gallery tiers, stood the president of SDF Pictures, Alberto Salazar (chairman of the board of Macross

Insurance Company in his spare time), tall and well built, with a thick walrus mustache and blue-tinted triangular shades.

"…Once again I want to thank you all for your support in the making of this film—the first but certainly not the last filmed entirely onboard the ship. And now, without further ado, I'd like to introduce the stars of the film, Minmei and Lynn-Kyle!"

Salazar made an expansive gesture to the wings, where a second spotlight found the leading couple. They walked arm in arm, acknowledging the applause with a wave or two. Salazar led Minmei to the microphone stand.

"Tell us what it was like to star in your first movie."

"It was thrilling, Mr. Salazar. I just hope the audience enjoys my performance."

The crowd went wild, and Salazar grinned.

"I'd say you already have your answer. Sounds to me like the people of Macross love *everything* you do. And how about you, Kyle? Have you got something to say to all your fans?"

"I just want to thank everyone involved in the production," he began rather shyly. "Especially Minmei, for all the support she's given me. I'm a newcomer to this ship, but I'm pleased to discover how easy it is to make friends here. I'm hoping we can continue to turn out movies to entertain you during our time together. This was a great experience, and I thank you for it."

While Kyle was speaking, Minmei stole a glance at the front row, searching for Rick. She found the mayor, Aunt Lena, and Uncle Max, but A-5 was vacant. *He didn't even call for his ticket,* she said to herself.

But Rick was there all right, pressed shoulder to shoulder with the rest of the standing-room—only crowd in the rear of the theater. He had received the message that Minmei had called but not the part about the ticket reserved for him. There had been no response when he phoned her at the Centinel; she was in fact with Vance Hasslewood at the time, sipping at a kahlua and cream on the hotel roof, thinking about Rick. He was in good spirits nevertheless, happy to be there even when he heard someone nearby say, "I hear that Lynn and Minmei are dating. It wouldn't surprise me if they get married!"

Minmei was singing now, the crowd swaying to her song, and Rick began to move with them, caught up in the moment. *What is this power she has?* he asked himself.

Standing stiffly and in obvious discomfort a few feet away, Miriya Parino asked herself the same thing.

In a review written by two science fiction writers who had been covering the SDF-1 launch for *Rolling Stone* on the day of the spacefold, *Little White Dragon* was billed as "a *kung-fu* fable"; it was to previous martial arts flicks what *Apocalypse Now* was to war pictures. No one would deny that it was an ambitious undertaking from the start, especially for a fledgling company in a three-cinema, fifty-thousand-plus market with little hope for a general release. But it more than fulfilled the expectations of its creators, in much the same way that the Miss Macross pageant had. Financial rewards aside, the film was conceived of as an effort to keep morale high onboard the ship; shot entirely inside the SDF-1 (thanks to the EVE engineers), it created jobs and indirectly helped to perfect some of the "normalizing" techniques used in Macross City.

Set in some undisclosed era of Asian prehistory, the film opens on the barren, evil-looking island of Natoma, where a wizard named Kirc is briefly introduced. The young magician is in possession of a strangely configured seagoing vessel, the bow of which has been fashioned to resemble a dragon's head and neck, the stern a barbed tail. Folded wings form the ship's bulwark and gunwales. It is soon apparent that Kirc is not the rightful owner, and while an army of blood-crazed giants—massive sanguine-fleshed hairless mutants dressed in harem pants, cummerbunds, and vests—move in to repossess the ship, he utters a spell which results in its dematerialization.

Cut to a second island in more familiar waters, tropical and peaceful. Some of the inhabitants become familiar, including the island's resident Zen master and a beautiful girl named Zu-li (played by Minmei, her long hair lightened and braided). Zu-li is a visitor to the island, but after scarcely a month there she is known by one and all. Her quiet songs fill the night air, lulling the inhabitants to sleep and bringing a sense of peace and harmony to everything they touch. Her eventual leavetaking, however, is delayed when a mysterious mist blows in and envelopes the island. Out of this enters the dragon ship.

Most of the islanders are frightened by its appearance, but a band of adventurous men and women led by the Zen master board the ship and bring it in. Zu-li and a handsome *kung-fu* student named Taiki—Lynn-Kyle—(a peaceful young man forced by circumstance to fight to save the people he loves) are among the master's following. On closer inspection the vessel is even more marvelous than its stylized exterior suggests, almost uncannily lifelike and filled with curious devices the islanders strive to comprehend.

Time goes by, and on the trail of the ship come the evil giants seen earlier. Seemingly recognizing the enemy at hand, the ship defends itself with an outpouring of fiery dragon's breath that destroys most of the attackers. Terrified by these developments, the chief orders the Zen master and his followers from the island. They set sail aboard the ship and are chased around the world by the giants in a series of perilous and exciting episodes, culminating in their attempt to return to their homeland. Zu-li, meanwhile, has discovered the true power of her voice: She learns to produce a tone that weakens the giants while at the same time strengthening Taiki's martial arts skills. He vanquishes enemies the dragon ship encounters during its long journey home—blue-uniformed, scimitar-wielding assailants and armored warriors with bows and arrows—and lays waste to the giants with *kung-fu* energy bolts and soaring leaps.

In the thrilling climax Zu-li is captured by the enemy and rescued by Taiki, and the island, which has refused to allow the journeyers home, is devastated by the giants.

Well before the credits ran, Lisa Hayes left her seat and exited the theater. The final color-enhanced kiss had been too much for her to take. When she looked at Lynn-Kyle, she saw Karl Riber; it was Karl's voice she heard when Kyle spoke, Karl's sentiments about war and death… Since that first day in the White Dragon she had been drawn to him, moth to flame. He was antiestablishment, antimilitary, antieverything her life had become, and yet she couldn't put him from her mind. She could close her eyes and remember every detail of his face, every word she had heard him tell the reporters about his hopes for peace when all they were interested in was Minmei's health; she could vividly recall standing next to him at the MBS studio the night Captain Gloval addressed the ship; and now there he was, ten times larger than life on the silver screen. *Another giant in her life.* And seemingly in love with Minmei. Minmei again. What magic did she possess? First Rick, now Kyle. It sometimes felt as if the entire ship was haunted by her presence, much as it was haunted by her songs.

Lisa could hear applause coming from inside the theater. Soon the lobby was going to be jammed, and she didn't want to hear everyone talking about how *wonderful* Minmei was, how *beautiful.* She stopped for a moment to glance at the film's colorful glass-encased poster and was about to move off, when all at once someone grabbed her behind! Not a grab, actually, more like a shove! She'd had enough of that waiting in line to get in and was certainly in no mood for it now. Enraged, she spun around, white trench coat flying, high red boots and fists ready, *just like in the movies…*

And found Rick Hunter groveling on the lobby floor in front of her, apologizing for his clumsiness.

"Commander!" he said, full of surprise. "I *am* sorry. I must have tripped or something…"

Lisa folded her arms across her chest. "And I just *happened* to be within reach, is that it?"

Rick's eyes widened. "Well, what do you think? I can't imagine another reason why anyone would want to, er, grab you."

"That's tellin' her, pal," said someone in the crowd that was gathering around them.

"I don't know, Hunter, first I find you prowling around in a lingerie shop and now you're molesting women on the street…"

"Let him have it, sister," someone else added. "Shove her again, pal!"

Lisa turned an angry face to their audience and grabbed Rick by the arm. "Come on, Lieutenant, we'd better continue this discussion elsewhere."

That brought out even more comments and a few catcalls, but Lisa ignored them. She practically dragged Rick down the wide staircase, complaining all the while. "Of all the nerve, intruding on a private conversation like that, how embarrassing, those imbeciles." Appropriately enough, Lisa didn't come to a halt until she had both of them positioned inside one of the black and yellow diagonally striped danger zones. Then she turned on him again. "Now, what in the world were you up to back there?"

"I was just coming out of the movie," Rick said innocently.

"Why didn't you stay to see the ending?"

The blare of warning sirens silenced Rick's reply; he and Lisa looked around. People were already running for shelter, and Sammie's voice was on the PA:

"Attention: Prepare for modular transformation. Please move to the nearest shelter immediately. Avoid the marked danger zones and move to the nearest shelter immediately!"

"A modular transformation?!" Rick said in disbelief.

"Something's wrong. We're supposed to be having a drill. That's why Sammie's on the com."

"A sneak attack?"

Lisa shook her head. "Impossible. Even so, we'd have more advance warning than this."

"We better get to a shelter, anyway." Rick took her arm, but she shook him off.

"Shelter? What's the matter with you? We've got to get back to the base as soon as—"

The street had begun to vibrate and shake. Lisa and Rick exchanged worried glances and hesitantly looked down. Their colorfully striped section of sidewalk was elevating rapidly. They held on to each other as they were carried high above the city streets. Down below people raced for cover. Cars pulled over, drivers and passengers leapt out. The scene in front of the Fortress Theater bordered on pandemonium. Sirens continued to blare and shriek.

The telescoping shaft came to an abrupt stop; then it lurched into upward motion again, but not before Rick and Lisa had managed to leap off. They were far above the third tier of Macross now, beyond EVE's blue sky illusion in the uppermost regions of the dimensional fortress—an area of massive cooling ducts, recycling conduits, transformational servogenerators, and miles of thick cabling. But Rick thought he knew a way out. He led a skeptical Lisa through a maze of human-size corridors; "portholes" every few feet afforded glimpses of junction boxes and circuit boards inside the walls.

"I think we're near the end," Rick said confidently. "All we do is bear right here."

"You don't say."

"Just follow me. I'll get you out of here. Nothing to it."

A minute later, they were in a cul-de-sac and Rick was scratching his head.

"Nothing to it," Lisa mocked him.

"Must've taken a wrong turn back there."

From somewhere close by came the *click! click!* and hum of activating machinery. There was something about that wall in front of them ... that seemed to be moving *forward!* They turned and started to run, only to find their exit blocked by a descending hatch. They stood rooted to the floor while one section of wall continued to advance; then, blessedly, it shuddered to a stop.

Lisa breathed a sigh of relief and regarded the thirty-foot-high metal walls of their prison. She dropped her shoulder bag and turned to Rick, exasperated.

"Hunter, aren't you the one who was lost somewhere in this ship for two weeks?"

"Look, how was I supposed to know? We had no choice! Anyway, none of this would have happened if you had gone with me to a shelter like I told you in the first place!"

"That's no way to be talking to a superior officer!"

"What, now you're going to pull *rank* on me?"

Rick made a dismissive gesture and slumped down sullenly against the bulkhead, knees up, hands behind his head. Lisa followed suit in the opposite corner of the box, too frustrated to hold on to her anger. Distant rumblings filtered in.

"Maybe we were attacked," Lisa posited. "Of course, it could be target practice, Phalanx fire or the Spartans ... I wonder how Sammie is doing. She's new at this. But someone has to act as my backup. Claudia has her hands full, and of course Vanessa and Kim..." She looked over at Rick. "You're not listening to a word I'm saying, are you?" No response; Lisa smirked. "Are you planning to sulk for the rest of our time together? You know, you're acting pretty childish, Rick. Come on, damn you, I'm going to go mad in here if you don't talk to me!"

"Well now, there's a surprise," Rick said suddenly. "Lisa Hayes actually needs somebody."

"Just what's that supposed to mean?"

"I figured you were too tough to need anybody."

She glared at him, then softened. "All right, Rick, I'm sorry I exploded back there."

Rick smiled. "Me, too." After a minute he added, "Reminds me of when we were stuck in that holding cell on Breetai's ship."

"Don't remind me. This place looks too much like it."

Rick looked around. "True enough. But even if this ship was designed by aliens, it's our ship now—our home. We'll just have to wait until she reconfigures."

"If it is a drill, that won't be much longer."

They both grew quiet and introspective; but when another twenty minutes had passed, Rick broke the silence.

"I still can't figure out the Zentraedi's tactics. We haven't scored a decisive victory once. They're always saving us from their own attacks."

"The captain thinks their command is divided. One side is convinced that we're derived from Protoculture; the other disagrees."

"The magic word... if we only had some idea what it was."

All at once there was a third voice in the room; Rick and Lisa glanced up and saw a Petite Cola robo-vendor coursing around the upper landing of their enclosure.

"What soft drink would you like?" the machine was saying.

"Hey!" yelled Rick, on his feet in a flash.

Lisa got up and moved to his side. The machine peered over the edge. "We're out of that brand. Please choose again."

Rick shook his fist in the air. "You empty-headed tin can, bring some help! Help!"

"We have ginger ale, Petite Cola, and root beer. Make your selection and deposit appropriate amount." The vendor was circling around making whirring sounds.

"You piece of junk, you no-good—"

"Stop it," Lisa said, tugging at his jacket. "It's not doing any good to yell at it. It's just a machine."

Resignedly, Rick said, "Yeah, I know." He joined Lisa on the floor. "*That* is what Protoculture is all about. Whatever it is that makes those machines behave like idiots."

Lisa laughed. "I don't think so, but we'd have to consult Dr. Lang to be sure."

"No *thanks.*"

Again they both retreated to inner thoughts and fantasies, punctuated by muffled explosions from overhead.

"I think Protoculture is more like the *kung-fu* force in the movie," Lisa said at last.

Rick's eyebrows went up. "Oh, so you *were* in the theater."

"Yes, I was there. I know the manager. I had a seat in the back. Why are you so surprised?"

Rick shrugged. "Just hard for me to imagine you at a movie."

"I *do* get out, you know." She felt her anger building again.

"Guess I always pictured you as a shut-in."

"And I picture you as a jerk, Hunter!"

Rick made a show of acting miffed. "But sometimes I can read minds…" He put his forefinger to his lower lip in mock concentration. "Let's see, you wanted to see this movie—even *though* it was a chop flick—because you've got a crush on one of the stars."

"Forget it, Hunter," she said, turning away from him.

"Right. You went to the trouble of reserving a ticket and dealing with those crowds just to see a film starring Minmei. No way. It has to be Kyle. Am I right?"

"Back off, Rick. Besides, how do you feel about Minmei now—Minmei and *Kyle*, I mean? You're still in love with her, aren't you? Aren't you?" Rick had lowered his head and grown silent. Lisa apologized. "I was just trying to get you to stop making fun of me. I didn't mean to bring up any bad memories. Believe me, I know what that can be like."

"Then tell me the truth," he said without facing her. "You left the theater for the same reason I did. You couldn't stand to see the person you're in love with kissing someone else?"

Lisa nodded, tight-lipped.

"What a joke," Rick continued. "Both of us running out of the theater at the same time. But how could you fall in love with that guy? He's against everything you stand for."

"He looks exactly like a man I was in love with. *He* had to go away, and then he died before we had a chance…" She began to cry in spite of all her efforts to be strong. "Sometimes when I see Kyle, Karl's face comes back to haunt me and I just can't bear it…"

Rick passed her his kerchief.

"But where would we be without love?" Rick mused. "Minmei's the only meaning I have in my life."

"You're right, Rick," she sobbed. "But I just don't want to feel this way. I just don't want it."

They held on to each other for several minutes, neither of them speaking.

"I'm glad I'm here with you," Rick told her.

"You're not so bad yourself, Hunter."

"Yeah?"

"Yeah. In fact, I think I could even get to like you—if you could stop being such a chauvinist sometimes."

Rick smiled at her, discovering her eyes as if for the first time. "That's funny, 'cause I was thinking the same about you."

Perhaps they would have kissed each other then—no *alien* pressure this time, no hastily hatched escape plan in mind—but all-clear sirens and Sammie's muffled voice on the city PA broke the spell.

"Attention, please: The drill has ended. The ship will now be returning to its normal mode of operation."

"Time to return to reality," Rick said as bulkheads retracted and hatchways lifted.

Lisa stood up and brushed herself off. "Guess I should get back to the bridge."

Rick got to his feet. "I suppose so. But let's not rush, okay?"

Lisa grinned. "With you leading us, I don't see that we have any choice."

Rick reached out and took her hand. They began to retrace their steps.

There were numerous wrong turns, reversals, and dead ends, even a few hairy moments and tricky descents; but mostly there was a feeling of togetherness and a fresh spirit of adventure. Ill prepared for the modular transformation and coming as it did with so many people in the streets for *Little White Dragon*'s premiere, Macross City suffered more than its usual share of damage. Rick and Lisa passed overturned vehicles, debris from traffic accidents, and fallen girders and piers in new construction zones. Ambulances and fire crews tore through streets all but deserted now and unnaturally quiet. They would learn later that a mistake had, in fact, been made; what was supposed to have been a simple drill had escalated into a small catastrophe. Sammie still had a lot to learn. Max Sterling, whom the bridge bunnies had spent so much time talking and worrying about, had never even left Macross, let along the fortress. According to the latest reports, Max was off in hot pursuit of some green-haired beauty in knickers who had caught his eye at the premiere. Minmei and Kyle had left the theater together and hadn't been heard from since.

No sooner did Rick and Lisa arrive on level one near the skyway, when a Petite Cola machine sidled up to them, begging a handout.

"My drinks are undamaged. May I serve you, may I serve you?"

Rick was ready to deliver a few well-deserved *kung-fu* kicks, but Lisa stopped him. She also insisted on paying for the drinks.

"All right," Rick allowed. "But only because I'd like to take you out to dinner next week."

Rick was just removing the cans of soda when he saw Kyle and Minmei walking toward the Hotel Centinel. He pulled himself and Lisa into hiding behind the machine.

"You better stay here," he told her without explanation.

Later on he'd feel foolish, but right now he was feeling protective.

"What's going on?" she wanted to know.

Rick was peering toward the hotel. "I didn't want you to get upset."

Lisa gave a look: Arms linked, the leading man and leading lady were entering the lobby.

"Like I said before, welcome back to reality. Guess we'll just have to live with it."

"Look, Rick, let's not worry about them. It's not unusual for cousins to show affection and be close to each other."

Rick snorted.

"Let's get out of here," said Lisa.

"Barracks time, huh?"

She shook her head.

"Let's walk. I don't have to report in until oh-eight-hundred."

"Just you and me?" he gestured.

"Yeah," she said, taking his arm. "Just you and me."

# 08

Say what you will about the retrospective critiques of *Little White Dragon*, it was Breetai's review that mattered most!

Rawlins, *Zentraedi Triumvirate: Dolza, Breetai, Khyron*

A world of things we've never seen before
Where silver suns have golden moons,
Each year has thirteen Junes...

Lynn-Minmei, "To Be In Love"
(the rallying cry of Rico's Minmei cult)

"IT APPEARS TO BE SOME SORT OF BATTLE RECORD," EXEDORE was saying.

Breetai agreed. "A primitive fighting style at best. I don't understand their interest in viewing such a record."

The Zentraedi commander and his adviser were side by side in the flagship command post. In the astrogational section of the bridge the rectangular field of the projecbeam glowed, outlined by the jagged, fanglike remains of the observation bubble. Lynn-Kyle, *Little White Dragon*'s male lead, was up a tree dodging arrows loosed by a small army of bowmen led by a crazed bearded commander with a black eyepatch and a plumed helmet.

"Possibly an instructional requirement for their soldiers," Breetai continued as Kyle's leap carried him out of frame.

Still anchored in space on the far side of the moon, the mother ship of the Imperial Fleet had locked into low-band transmissions emanating from the dimensional fortress. The two Zentraedi had been viewing these for some time, first with puzzled interest and now with growing concern. This longhaired Micronian in the black slippers and belted robe had executed some truly amazing maneuvers, albeit primitive, and now here he was soaring through space unleashing bolts of brilliant orange lightning from his fingertips. The recipient of these, a curiously uniformed hairless mutant wearing some sort of power-collar, was paralyzed and felled a moment later by the Micronian's follow-up leap and kick.

"Did you see what he just did? What was that?!" Breetai was aghast; reflexively he had unfolded his arms and adopted a defensive stance.

Exedore's pinpoint-pupilled eyes were wide.

"Perhaps it is that legendary force the Micronians are said to possess."

"It's a death ray! Our soldiers cannot win against such an incredible force!"

"It seems beyond the power of Protoculture or Robotechnology."

Breetai straightened up decisively. "We must report this information immediately to Commander in Chief Dolza."

Elsewhere in the flagship *Little White Dragon* had a second audience, the dozen or so members of the growing Minmei cult. They were gathered around a monitor screen, jaws slack in amazement. Rico, Bron, and Konda had recognized Minmei in spite of the Zu-li over-the-shoulder braid.

"She doesn't look the way I thought she would," said one of the group.

"Yeah, what happened to your beautiful female?"

"Bubbleheads," Bron said calmly. "This is just a monitor. She's much better-looking in person."

"That's right," Rico added knowingly. "You have to see her in real life. We were hanging out with the girl all the time."

This drew astonished looks from the cultists; they turned now to Konda, who added nonchalantly, "In fact, the three of us all became her close personal friends for a while."

On the screen, Kyle was going through his F/X routines, dispatching giants left and right and hurling lightning bolts.

Rico recognized him. "These recordings must have been made before the Micronian began to think about putting an end to warfare."

"An end to warfare?" said one of the confused cultists.

"'Peace' is the Micronian word for it," Bron explained.

But what grabbed the attention of this captive audience was the kiss Lynn-Kyle planted on Minmei's lips after effecting her rescue. Cooing sounds surfaced through the speakers.

"How strange," said someone in the audience. "I've never seen anything like that before."

"It's weird… Why do they do that?"

"They seem to be enjoying it."

"Yeah," Bron explained. "Something makes them do that all the time. It's required."

"They *make* their people press their lips together?"

"Yeah, it happened every day," Rico answered, ringleader and gifted liar. He had his chair tipped way back, hands behind his head.

One of the heavy-banged clones took his nose from the screen. "That's fantastic! I wouldn't have thought you could stand it. Did they force you to do such a thing with this girl?"

"Yep, they sure did," said Rico.

"Often," from Konda.

Shocked faces, some gray, some yellow, some pure white, swung to catch each spoken word, each nuance.

Then Bron picked up and carried for a while: "My lips got sore from always being pressed."

It has been said that there comes a point in the growth of every powerful cult or movement when something is needed to carry it over the top, to open it up to those who are aware and prepared but who have been afraid to act alone. *Little White Dragon* served this purpose for the Minmei cult. But it had less to do with the "death ray" Breetai saw than with the need to protect the film's leading lady. Singing had reawakened long-lost emotions and impulses; music had reopened a long-locked pathway to the heart.

There was scarcely a soldier in the Imperial Fleet who hadn't heard of the singing doll by now. The film had instilled the rumors with a new momentum; sensational tales of the wonders onboard the SDF-1 were talked about in every corridor and discussed at every watch. The password spread. Micronian words were spoken and memorized. Posts were abandoned, duties left undone. Fights broke out over whose turn it was to carry around the life-size color poster of Minmei. Shock troopers and sentries began to rap on the clubhouse door and beg admittance, their armed and armored presence lending a new element to the gathering of green-uniformed cultists—an element that would soon spell peril for the Zentraedi high command…

The little two-song dot-eyed doll continued to work its tabletop magic, melting hearts hardened by conditioning and countless military campaigns and conquests. Rico's roomful of former galactic warriors came to sound more like a maternity ward visited by a host of proud fathers.

"So this is what they call 'singing,' huh?" said one soldier as he watched the doll go through its motions. "I think I like it."

"Singing is a way the Micronians make each other feel good," Konda explained.

"Makes me feel kinda funny."

"Makes me feel great!"

"Is it true," asked another, "that we could hear the real singer if we became spies and lived among the Micronians?"

"It's the truth," said Bron.

Rico folded his arms across his chest. "You'd like the real thing a lot more than you like this doll."

"Yes, but it's unlikely that we'll ever get the chance to see for ourselves, Rico. You three are surveillance operatives; we are soldiers."

A grin spread across Rico's face, and he leaned forward conspiratorially, arms on the table. "This is something we should discuss…" he told them.

It is also said that "loose lips sink ships."

Khyron's second in command, Grel, reported to his commander that there was trouble afoot. Khyron had been brooding about his defeat and near death at the hands of the Micronians during the shield explosion and as a consequence ingesting powerful amounts of the dried Flower of Life leaves, so Grel braced himself for the worst.

"You say there's chaos aboard Breetai's flagship?" said the Backstabber disinterestedly.

"That's right, m'lord. Exedore's spies—Konda, Rico, and Bron—returned from their infiltration mission aboard the Robotech ship with a singing doll that is wreaking havoc."

"A 'singing doll'? What are you talking about, Grel?"

"A... *device*, Lord Khyron. It emits sounds that have affected the thoughts of the crew. Discipline has become a problem."

Khyron wore a look of distaste. "And you have seen this... *device*?"

"No, m'lord, but—"

Khyron turned his back to Grel. "I don't think we need to concern ourselves with rumors."

But Grel persisted. "It's a lot worse than that, sir. There is talk among many of our own soldiers about defecting to the Robotech ship to lead the Micronian way of life!"

Khyron spun around, fists clenched. *"Defecting?!"*

"M'Iord!" snapped Grel. "That's what I heard. And not just a few—"

"Enough!" shouted Khyron. "Is anyone in the higher command aware of this?"

"No, m'Iord."

"As I thought." Khyron sneered. "Everyone is losing their minds over what's happening on the battle fortress..." He raised his fist. "Well, let them! Let them perish through their own stupidity! Khyron will survive and prevail! Khyron will live to see that ship destroyed! Khyron *alone* will rule the Fourth Quadrant of the universe! And woe to anyone who stands in his way!"

It was true that neither Breetai nor Dolza had received word of the incipient desertions, but the commander in chief had reasons of his own for wanting the Micronians annihilated. Breetai had dispatched a ship to the command center with trans-vids of the "death-ray" sequences he and Exedore had viewed. There, Dolza had come as close to fear as his Zentraedi conditioning allowed.

A trans-vid of his response was quickly returned to Breetai. The fleet commander and his adviser screened this on a rectangular monitor that had been installed behind the remains of the spherical one Max Sterling's VT had finished off some months ago. The brief message did not take either of them by surprise.

"I am now convinced that the Micronians have discovered the secrets of Protoculture," Dolza stated flatly. "And as a result they are extremely dangerous to us. Any prolonged contact with them can only have a disastrous effect on our troops. I am therefore ordering you, Commander, to begin preparations for a final assault on the Robotech ship. You are to infiltrate the fortress and secure the Protoculture matrix. Failing that, you are to destroy the ship. And understand me, Breetai: This time I expect results. Succeed or find yourself facing the fury of my fleet."

Word of the impending assault threw the Minmei followers into a state of dismay.

"What do we do now?" asked one of the cultists, Minmei poster in hand. "When we attack the fortress, we'll probably kill this girl. We'll *never* get to hear her sing!"

"We want to hear her sing!" yelled another.

There were at least twenty of them in concealment behind a row of Battlepods in one of the flagship docking bays. All eyes were on Rico now.

"It's not just singing. In the fortress population center they have loads of things we don't have. *All* that will be lost if we attack them!" He struck a determined stance. "Why don't we save them, and save ourselves as well?"

"How?" several voices said.

"We can't do anything by just *thinking* about our future. I say we look for a way to remain aboard the enemy ship when the attack begins."

There was a moment of stunned silence. Even in their weakened state, enough residual conditioning remained to leave them fearful in the face of Rico's suggestion, and more than one forehead was beaded in sweat. But Rico had given voice to their wishes, and soon Bron and Konda were slapping him on the back, full of encouragement and congratulations.

"If they catch us, we'll be executed," said one of the few holdouts.

But Rico was on a roll. "That's the chance we'll have to take," he said, scanning each face.

"Then count me in. I want all those things I've never had before."

"Me, too," said another, and another. Shock trooper and duty officer alike continued to cast yea votes until it was unanimous.

"Okay. We're in it together," Bron said finally. "But before we can enter the enemy ship we've got to become Micronians."

Again there was a moment's hesitation as the irreversibility of their decision set in. Then someone asked, "Do you know how to work the sizing chamber well enough, Bron?"

"No," he confessed. "It takes a specialist to operate it, right, Karita?"

All eyes focused on a meek, docile-looking blond soldier at the outer perimeter of the group. Nervously, Karita clasped his hands together as Bron put the question to him. It was true. He knew the secrets of control levers eight and nine.

"Without *permission*?" he seemed to whimper.

"Of course, you fool. If the plan is discovered, we're all dead!"

"You want to hear *real* singing, don't you?" said Rico, trying a gentler approach.

Karita turned his back to them and stammered, "Sure I do, but, well, uh…"

Bron took the Minmei poster from someone's hand. "If you help us, this picture *and* the singing doll are yours. What do you say to that deal, Karita?"

"Well… I don't know…"

"We've got to work like a team," said Konda. "If we stick together now, we'll all be able to enjoy a new life with the Micronians."

Karita turned to face them. "All right. I'll do it. But you'll have to promise to take me with you."

Bron went over to Karita with a big grin and put an arm around him. "You just operate the converter. We'll see to it that you get into the ship."

. . .

Meanwhile, aboard the dimensional fortress life was busy imitating art. *Little White Dragon*, finally shown in its entirety, had received ecstatic praise from one and all, and more than ever Lynn-Minmei's voice seemed to weave a magic spell over the ship. During a follow-up concert carried live by MBS, there wasn't a man or woman who didn't feel somehow *transported* by the star's songs and gentle lyrics. On the bridge Captain Gloval grew introspective, remembering better if not quieter days. Vanessa, Sammie, and Kim, ever-present cups of coffee in their hands, slipped into a sort of collective daydream fantasy where those "silver suns" and "golden moons" were almost tangible and love was something no longer sought but found and embraced. Claudia Grant walked through London snow she hadn't thought about in years, arm in arm with Roy Fokker, her lover still in that interior realm unlocked by Minmei's magic. Even Lisa, who only the day before had walked out on the film, succumbed; but it wasn't Karl Riber she thought of but Kyle, who brought into question all that she had lived and worked for, all that she was.

And from the stage wings of the Star Bowl Kyle watched his cousin perform as though for the first time, feeling at once threatened and comforted, concerned about how much attention was lavished on her and how little was focused on ending the war but at the same time recognizing how all-important Minmei had become to morale and the personal strivings of all those onboard the fortress.

Not for a moment, though, did the singer herself question her gifts or her purpose. Tearfully she accepted the applause, the flowers and love, but in a strangely distanced state of being, as though outside herself, her songs on the side of love in the eternal struggle of good against evil.

And was there anyone more aware of Minmei's cause than Rick Hunter, standing now outside the Star Bowl as she finished one of her tunes, his ear pressed up against one of the posters that adorned the amphitheater wall? *She* was his cause from the beginning, and it seemed certain now that she would be his cause at the end.

# 09

Although films like *King Kong*, *Attack of the Fifty-Foot Woman*, and *Devil Doll* had understandably enough become popular onboard the SDF-1, perhaps we should have been paying more attention to a little-known classic called *One Touch of Venus*, wherein a statue of the goddess comes to life and sings a song that weaves a spell of love over everyone.

Lisa Hayes, *Recollections*

THE RIGHT ARM OF ZOR'S SHIP DREW BACK AND HURLED ITSELF forward as if it were part of a living being, its steel-hulled supercarrier fist punching through the armor plating of the Zentraedi cruiser and crippling it; only then, with the ship so impaled, was the forward ramp of the carrier lowered and the full firepower of the Micronian Destroids unleashed.

"The '*Daedalus* Maneuver,' as it is called," said Exedore. "Apparently named after the oceangoing vessel itself."

Breetai ordered a replay of those trans-vids which had captured the Micronian battle maneuvers for study: the deep-space destruction of Zeril's cruiser and the fiery death of a destroyer under Khyron's command when the SDF-1 had been temporarily redocked on Earth. Exedore was arguing that it might be possible to *force* the Micronians into employing the maneuver once again, but in such a way as to prove advantageous to the Zentraedi. Breetai was trying to keep an open mind, despite the fact that there was precious little in the way of reinforcing evidence to warrant optimism at this point. If two years of fighting (by Micronian reckoning) had established anything, it was that one could only expect the unpredictable from these Micronians. Still, there was too much at stake to completely rule out Exedore's plan. He had been as shocked by Dolza's threats as Exedore had been. That the Micronians presented an unprecedented danger was not to be argued; but to destroy Zor's dimensional fortress in lieu of capturing it was madness. Without the knowledge contained aboard that ship the Zentraedi would never be able to break free from the yoke of the Robotech Masters. Dolza knew that better than anyone.

Breetai stroked his chin as the trans-vids ran to completion. "We would be taking a great risk," he said to his adviser.

"True, m'lord. But even so, we stand to gain everything if we succeed. If we can force them into executing a *Daedalus* attack, we might be able to insert a Regault squadron into the fortress without detection. Then we would be in a position to capture the ship intact."

Breetai uttered a sound of approval. "That has been my design all along. But how can we make certain the Micronians fulfill their part in this?"

"First, we must rely on the fact that they judge our actions to be as predictable as we judge theirs to be unpredictable. Then we must take care to so maneuver the flagship that they launch their attack at the bow of our ship. We are strongest there, and with our troops suitably forewarned, it would prove a simple matter to get our infiltrators aboard."

"Hmm… you've thought this out carefully, Exedore."

The misshapen Zentraedi bowed slightly. "May I be permitted to speak freely, m'lord?"

Breetai gestured his assent.

"With the one million ships of the Imperial Fleet at our disposal and Zor's Protoculture matrix in our possession, we would be a force to be reckoned with. Both Dolza *and* the Robotech Masters would have to deal with us."

Breetai grinned. "And what of the Invid? Have you given this thought, too?"

Exedore's pinpoint-pupiled eyes widened at the mention of the name, but he regained his confidence soon enough.

"Those enemies of life as we know it will surely search us out," he told Breetai coldly. "But they will be made to suffer the same fate as the Micronians, and anyone else who presumes to tamper with Protoculture!"

The flagship sizing-chamber had been the scene of frantic activity since Breetai's sounding of general quarters. True to his word, Karita had operated the reduction converters, secretly "micronizing" some twenty Zentraedi soldiers; and Rico, as promised, saw to it that Karita along with three other Minmei cultists found a place in one of the Battlepods. Sometime later the Zentraedi commanders would learn that fewer Battlepods went out than pilots, but it was not something they needed to concern themselves with at the moment; the Zentraedi were not as fussy about this sort of thing as the Micronians were.

Several conversion kits for the pods had been secured, but not enough to go around. Bron and Konda therefore offered last-minute advice and instructions to the micronized pilots who would be manning the standard pods. Then, in sleeveless sackcloths once again, the three infamous operatives regrouped and climbed aboard the mecha that would deliver them back to the SDF-1 and its world of delights.

Hundreds of Battlepods pressed plastron to plastron filled the launch bay of the flagship. Pilots ran their craft through systems checks and prepared themselves for battle. Rico, Konda, and Bron were at their stations inside the pod when a change in the attack plan was announced from the bridge: All Regault squadrons were being ordered to move to the bow of the ship and await further instructions.

"Now what?" asked Konda in a sudden panic.

"Just calm down," Bron told him, already beginning to move their Battlepod forward with the rest. "The plan is still to attack the battle fortress, isn't it? We'll get our chance, so stop worrying about it."

Aboard Khyron's cruiser, meanwhile, the attack mecha of the Botoru Battalion were readying themselves. The Backstabber's Officer's Pod headed up four shipshape columns of the Seventh's finest fighters. Khyron was addressing them over the net:

"The Micronian ship is almost within range. As soon as their fighters are launched, we will take to space and engage them. Do not concern yourselves with losses; think only of *victory!*"

Khyron lowered the visor of his helmet. *The stage is set,* he said to himself. *Nothing can save the Micronians now!*

From inside the flagship command bubble Breetai ordered his attack force into motion—a relatively insignificant number of ships but appropriate for the occasion. He wanted the Micronian commander to feel confident, not unduly threatened.

"Follow my lead toward the enemy fortress," he spoke into the communicator. And he thought to himself: *Let the games begin!*

Sammie's scream broke them out of the trance Minmei's songs had sired.

Lisa and Claudia furiously began to tap commands into their console keyboards, while Kim let out a call that brought Captain Gloval running. Vanessa sat hunched over the threat board controls like some maniacal organist.

"Thirty ships," Lisa said, as Gloval tried to make sense of the overhead monitor readout. A schematic showing the fortress's position relative to Earth revealed that a triangular formation of enemy paint had emerged from behind Luna and was presently on an intercept heading with the SDF-1.

"Thirty," Gloval said, puzzled. "Why, when they have so many at their command? What can they be planning?"

"Estimate of TOA and DOA coming in, sir," said Vanessa.

Gloval turned to the threat board and back to Lisa.

"Sound general quarters. Scramble the Veritechs." Gloval took to the command chair and exhaled wearily as alert Klaxons blared throughout the fortress.

*Thirty ships,* he kept repeating to himself. Not an arbitrary number, but somehow calculated. The enemy was actually communicating with him, offering up just this number of ships as a tease. Not enough to overwhelm the fortress, though just enough to ensure a tight fight. So why was he experiencing such an unusual sense of dread? He couldn't put his finger on the cause, but he likened the feeling to those small warnings your mind transmits just as you're stepping into an accident. Something says "oops!" to you even before you've committed yourself to an action, but your body refuses to listen: It moves forward into catastrophe in some irrevocable fashion, obeying laws of causality as yet unknown.

Gloval stared at the monitor screen, watching the radar blips move closer and closer to the fortress. Well, here was all the advance warning anyone needed, and still he could not bring himself to turn tail. *How that would surprise those Zentraedi bastards!* he said to himself. If he just refused to engage them, if he just set the ship on a course of retreat… What response *did* they expect from him this time? he wondered. Once again he would be forced to choose between shield and main gun. Or he could simply wait it out until the enemy began to turn on itself, as had so often been the case. But no, that would go against his training.

Gloval made up his mind that he would simply meet the ships head-on, no second thoughts about it. Brute force against brute force, one on one. He'd bring the *Daedalus* into play if he had to. Just punch those ships from space, one after another. Starting with that lead monster up in lights on the radar screen. Yes, the SDF-1 would start with her: an all-out *strike* to the front of the formation!

Rick was still leaning against the curved wall of the Star Bowl when the sirens went off. He joined a group of VT pilots who had raced from the amphitheater and flagged down a taxi. Together they piled inside and ordered the driver to put the pedal to the metal and get them to the *Prometheus.*

The hangar area was a study in controlled chaos. Pilots ran to their ships, pulling on helmets and cinching harness straps. Flight controllers directed prepped Veritechs toward runways and launch bays, while groups of techs unloaded heat-seekers from antigrav pallets and locked them into undercarriage pylons. Supply trucks and personnel carriers screeched across the floor ferrying ammo canisters and cat officers through the madness, often narrowly missing one another. Shouts and elevator and engine noise erased the gentler sounds of radio communiques, canopy descent, and rapid heartbeat.

Rick threw himself into Skull One, throwing levers and toggles as he fastened straps and adjusted the seat. The alphanumeric displays of the HUDs and HDDs came to life, glowing brightly as systems ran themselves to self-check status. Rick ran through a self-check himself, then worked the foot pedals and interfaced with the HOL microprocessor, ordering the Veritech forward to the elevator. He had his hands on the Hotas—the so-called hands on throttle and stick—when Lisa appeared on the central commo screen.

"Thirty alien craft approaching from section twenty-four, Skull Leader, do you copy?"

"Affirmative, Commander."

"These aren't ostriches, Rick. Radar shows cruisers and battlewagons. No mecha as yet. Your threat evaluation displays should be registering their signatures now, do you copy?"

Rick turned to a side screen: Thirty bandits in a flying wedge formation were revealed.

"I copy, Commander," he told Lisa. "Locked and loaded; I'm outta here."

"Rick, this looks like a big one, so be careful, okay?" He pulled his visor down. "You don't have to tell me."

Rick goosed the VT forward at the urgings of a flight controller and positioned it on one of the elevators. He completed his checks as the fighter was raised to the flight deck and stabilized for hookup. As the cat officer and his shooter went through their well-oiled routine, he ran through one of his own. He summoned up an image of Roy Fokker in his mind's eye, then Ben Dixon. He held on to those for a moment and allowed them to fade in the presence of another. Minmei filled up his thoughts as the VT was catapulted off the hurricane bow of the supercarrier and launched into space.

"Six bandits within range," Rick shouted into the tac net. "Switch over to your targeting computers and fire on my command."

Local space was reduced to a grid on his forward screen, with clusters of Veritechs assigned to each section. Skull One led a formation of five VTs into one of these.

Death, parcelled out.

The enemy pods opened up, disgorging pulses of blue fire into the night. An Officer's Pod was out front—its flashing signature plain as day on Rick's threat evaluation screen—"hand-guns" and top-mounted cannon spewing flame. The Veritechs danced between the deadly lines, thrusters carrying them out of harm's way as nose gatlings blazed a reply.

"Send 'em home, boys!" Rick shouted.

He engaged the VT's afterburners, propelling it farther out in front of the pack. Behind him, one of the newcomers sustained a direct hit and disintegrated in a silent sphere of blinding fire. Two other fighters broke across each other's courses and accelerated into flanking maneuvers on either side of the enemy contingent. Pod gun turrets swiveled to find them without effect, bolts of uncreased lightning telescoping into the void. They broke their formation and scattered in pairs, dangling bipedal legs behind themselves now, boosters blazing pink and white, cyan fire erupting from their plastron cannons.

Skull One loosed six red-tipped missiles into their midst, orange crescents and small suns filling the skies as they found their mark. Pods exploded, human and Zentraedi pilots died, and Death clapped joyfully from the sidelines.

It was a free-for-all, rockets and pulsed beams crosshatching space haphazardly. No one was safe, no one immune.

Inside the flagship Breetai watched the battle from his command chair, Exedore stone-faced beside him. The fleet commander was pleased.

"So far they are following their usual attack pattern."

Off to the right of the observation bubble, two indicator lights flashed on. Breetai and Exedore turned to these.

"This is operations," said someone from the launch bays. "All our Battlepods and mecha have been deployed."

"Good," Breetai responded, directing his words to the communicator. "Inform all the cruiser commanders that I want them to continue on course. But make certain they allow the flagship to maintain the lead."

"At once, my lord," came the reply.

Breetai rose from the chair. "Prepare to fire main batteries."

Pinpoints of blue light flashed into life across the front of the cruisers; bursts of pulsed energy rained from the front of each of these, regular as clockwork.

Meanwhile, pods and VTs continued to slug it out. Rick found himself up against that Officer's Pod again; the enemy mecha was in ascent, thruster glowing between its legs while it exchanged fire with Skull One and its wingships. Aft and slightly port, a VT exploded—one of the less-armored tan and white ships piloted by yet another newcomer. Engaging the undercarriage and lateral thrusters, Rick piloted the VT up and over the enemy fusillade; one of his wingmen followed but was tagged and blown to debris. As enemy fire mysteriously ceased, he cut away from the silent Officer's Pod and went after one of the regulars, executing a Fokker Feint, then rolling over and taking it out with gatling blasts while it floated stationary in space. The Officer's Pod tracked Rick as he completed the move, encasing Skull One in streaks of fire from which it emerged miraculously unscathed.

The SDF-1, however, was not faring as well. While the VT teams were successfully shielding it from the stings of enemy mecha, the fortress was sustaining salvo after salvo from the rapidly approaching whalelike ships of the attack group. Bristling guns discharging unbroken lines of lethal energy, the warships closed on the SDF-1 like deep-sea monsters in a feeding frenzy.

The massive ship was shaking violently. On the bridge Captain Gloval gripped the arms of the command chair for all it was worth. The women worked feverishly at their stations, tireless and unfailing in their duties, the occasional scream notwithstanding.

"Damage reports coming in, Captain," said Kim.

"Later!" he answered.

Claudia reported that the Veritech teams were taking heavy losses.

"Keep them deployed as long as we can!" Gloval shouted to her as an explosion rocked the bridge. "Lisa, we're going to have to use the *Daedalus* to take out those cruisers one by one!"

Lisa turned from her console to signal her understanding, then reached up for the remote mike cradled alongside the overhead monitor.

"Stand by to launch *Daedalus* when you receive my command," she said.

Full of sinister intent, streaks of light radiating from what looked like eye pods and the suggestion of a mouth turned up in a crooked smile, the Zentraedi flagship continued to bear down on the fortress. Concealed behind bulkheads and hastily erected reinforcing partitions in her bow waited scores of Battlepods, erect on their hooved feet, turret guns aimed and ready.

Inside one of the pods the three operatives received word of the imminent Micronian counterattack. Rico and Bron were standing on the seat, each positioned at one of the projecting levers that controlled the mecha. Konda was down below near the foot pedals. Bron held a communicator in his hand; through this he was in touch with the rest of Rico's band of micronized would-be deserters.

"Are you ready?" he said into the mike. "Our moment has arrived."

"To our deaths, or our rebirth!" said Rico in a rallying cry.

The three raised their hands in salute to one another.

Rico grew serious. "Once inside the fortress, we'll have to take care."

"The wrong place at the wrong time and we could be killed—by Micronians or Zentraedi," cautioned Konda. "We'll have to stay out of sight until the proper time. Then we'll abandon the pod and lose ourselves among the people of the population center."

"He's right," said Bron getting back on the mike. "I'll pass the word."

The Macross Amphitheater was shaking and quaking—not to thunderous applause or the rhythm of the band but to the frenzied beat of war. Half of the Star Bowl's 30,000 had fled for shelter at the first warning sirens, and many more began to filter out as the sounds of battle invaded the ship, but a surprisingly large number remained—mainly those who were guided by the past, the unfortunate ones who continued to believe that Macross would always be immune to attack.

Minmei was introducing a song when the first major jolt was felt. She cried out as she almost lost her balance, and this started a wave of panic in the audience. Suddenly the diehards and risktakers were having second thoughts. People were screaming and rising halfway out of their seats in dismay, as if to get a general fear-level reading before making up their minds to exit or stick it out.

Kyle could almost smell the panic brewing. He took to the stage in a leap and ran to Minmei's side.

"Minmei, you've got to keep singing," Kyle told her.

Only moments before he had been watching Minmei's performance from the wings, fascinated by how her mere presence could overshadow the war. And now he glimpsed a way that her power might be put to good use in lulling the audience back into a state of calm.

She turned to him, panic in her eyes, smudges of run mascara beneath them. "What?" she said, not comprehending.

"Gimme that," he said, taking the mike from her hands. "Hey, everybody, we're going to continue the concert, so please take your seats. There's no reason for panic. We've all been through this before. So please calm down and return to your seats. Minmei's going to go on with the show."

Another jolt rocked the ship, and the screaming escalated. Minmei had her hands over her ears, but Kyle was shaking her by the shoulders and telling her to sing.

"In your strongest voice!" he told her.

She looked up at him, wide-eyed and childlike, but nodded her head.

"Be courageous and sing," Kyle said calmly. "You can do it."

Reluctantly she took the mike and stepped forward on trembling legs. She walked out of the stage's inlaid five-pointed star and perched herself on the edge. The band, taking this as a cue, gave her an intro. She motioned them to pick up the tempo and began to belt out "Stagefright." People returned to their seats. Minmei turned and winked at Kyle. He smiled at her and mouthed: "You're great!"

On the bridge, Lisa Hayes gave the word. With a little luck the destruction of the lead ship would result in an explosion that would take out the others as well.

In space the right arm of the SDF-1 drew back and hurled itself forward, as if it were alive...

# 10

"What you fail to grasp is that Commander Breetai's decision to allow the SDF-1 to retreat was entirely in keeping with the Zentraedi tradition of open warfare, that is, move and countermove. It was most certainly not a tactical blunder... Moreover, it is for precisely this same reason that it never even occurred to Commander in Chief Dolza to hold the planet Earth hostage for the return of Zor's ship. Through no fault of your own you imagine this to be unthinkable. Which, then, is the more barbaric of the two races—yours or mine?"

Exedore, as quoted in Lapstein's *Interviews*

THE STEEL-PLATED BOW OF THE SUPERCARRIER *DAEDALUS* punched through the nose of the Zentraedi flagship.

It was an encounter of mythic proportion, worthy of inclusion in that short list of eternal struggles—angel and demon, eagle and snake, snake and dragon: *a giant techno-knight in gleaming armor, its fist locked in the jaws of a deep-space armored leviathan...*

The two-foot-thick bow plate of the *Daedalus* swung up and away from the body of the ship, its massive top-mounted hinges groaning in protest. Unseen servodevices locked while others disengaged, motors whined, and hydraulic couplers hissed in a symphony of mechanization. A triple-hinged forward rampart unfolded itself into the hold of the Zentraedi ship while a fan of brilliant energy was loosed from Destroids in the carrier belly. Structural piers and pylons were blown away; girders and tie beams slagged in the infernal heat. Supply crates and storage tanks exploded, filling the air lock with concussive sound and deadly fumes. A bulkhead just inside the breach was holed by concentrated firepower.

Golden alloy-armored Destroids now began to descend the ramp, their lasers at rest. They were early products of Robotechnology, bipedal and nearly as tall as Battloids but somewhat cumbersome-looking, with large square feet and skeletal laser-gun arms. Following their programmed directives, the three-man units moved into the hold and took up positions for a second and more lethal assault. But they were not quick enough.

Battlepods suddenly leaped from places of concealment and opened fire. Pulsed beams tore through the thin skins of the mecha, dropping them in their tracks. There were attempts to return fire, but the situation was instantly beyond hopeless. The Destroids were vastly outnumbered and easily overrun; minutes after the skirmish erupted, their silent forms were heaped at the base of the ramp.

Then the Battlepods reversed the order, taking to the ramp and making for the *Daedalus*. By this time, however, word of the defeat had reached the carrier command center, and the arm of the SDF-1 was already retreating, ripping out the steel tendrils the flagship defense systems had attached to it in an attempt to seal the breach. There was barely time enough to insert a quarter of the battle-ready pods. As the final few hopped gracelessly into the carrier hold, the ramp folded, retracted, and slammed shut.

The Zentraedi had been given no clear-cut orders, save to enter the Micronian ship and inflict as much damage as they could without destroying it. Breetai's hope was that at least some of the pods would make it to the bridge of the fortress and effect a capture of the commanders. Short of that, the pods could attempt to incapacitate the ship's reflex drives.

Some of the Zentraedi soldiers, however, had their own ideas.

Once inside the *Daedalus*, in an orgy of indiscriminate destruction, they began to fire at everything in sight. Provisions, mecha, vehicles, and Gladiator teams were wiped out. Techs left their stations and picked up weapons to combat the intruders, but not one lived to give details of the battle. The Zentraedi hurled fire against the control towers and communications stations, incinerating systems and personnel with equal abandon. The hangar areas of the carrier were fully aflame by the time the pods took to the main corridors of the SDF-1.

They still had no idea where they were going, but it was easy enough for anyone to tell where they had been. A path of utter destruction led from the supercarrier, up through the right arm of the fortress and into its heart—Macross City itself. The pods moved wantonly through service corridors, extending their reign of death. Coveralled techs were fried by bolts of unleashed fury; shaking hands reached out weakly for comlink phones and panic buttons but seldom found them. Meanwhile the pods continued their sweep. The Zentraedi were finally repaying the Micronians for two years of frustrating defeats. The mecha soldiers were so caught up in vengeance that not one of them noticed the disappearance of several of their number—a group of awkwardly piloted pods that seemed curiously loath to engage in battle.

Captain Gloval's leg shook uncontrollably while he awaited Lisa's reply. "Come on, Lisa, come on," he said, hoping to hurry along the flow of data.

She was bent over her console, fingers flying over the keyboard. "I have no contact at all with the *Daedalus*, sir. It's as if it doesn't exist!"

Something was very wrong. The oblate bow of the Zentraedi warship filled the bay of the bridge, dark green in color, menacing, enormous. It looked to Gloval as if a whale had mistaken the arm of his ship for a giant fishhook. But the calculated collision had not worked out as planned. Whatever the firepower unleashed by the Destroids, it had not been sufficient to affect the cruiser. In fact, the ship was still hurtling forward, now pushing the fortress along in front of it. And the bridge had lost contact not only with the Destroid squad but with the entire supercarrier garrison as well.

"Pull the fortress back!" Gloval shouted suddenly. "All power astern and redeploy the shield energy!"

As Kim and Sammie relayed continued commands to engineering and astrogation, the fortress began to vibrate to a steady bass drone. The engines were powered up and engaged; then the contained explosive fire of the reflex core erupted from the ports of the pectoral thrusters, carrying the ship away from its aggressor, pulling the *Daedalus* arm free of the flagship's hold.

Gloval breathed a sigh of relief.

The fortress responded with an unprecedented sounding of Klaxons and alert sirens.

Claudia was on the comlink; she lowered the handset and turned to face the command chair, a look of unmitigated terror contorting her face.

"Enemy Battlepods have entered the ship through the ramming arm!"

Gloval's eyes opened wide. "The enemy's on board?"

This had happened *only* once before, when an overeager Zentraedi pilot had given chase to Max Sterling's Veritech and battled it briefly in the streets near Macross General Hospital.

"The *Daedalus* is on fire," Claudia continued. "The pods are attacking Macross!"

"Quickly! Patch us into the civil defense network!"

The captain and his crew turned their attention to the speaker system, hoping against hope.

"Ten enemy pods on Lilac Street," said a horror-stricken voice. "We're trying to hold… *Aargh!*"

"This is area B control—we can't seem to hold them back, we need help—"

"…retreating from the Tenth Avenue gate. We're getting our—"

"Switch it off!" Gloval shouted from the chair. He dropped his head and said weakly, "God help us all."

Destroids, Spartans, and Gladiators were waiting for the Battlepods when they reached the outskirts of Macross City. For those battle-weary residents who had yet to reach shelter, the attack would recall a similar one two years earlier. But this time they knew their enemy. This time they knew how much they had to fear.

Bent on nothing less than complete destruction, the pods advanced through the street, blue fire spewing from their upper and lower guns, panicked pedestrians scattering beneath their hooved feet. Explosions launched fragments of glass and steel into the artificial air and tore gaping holes in the streets, exposing raw power lines and rupturing water conduits. Raining showers of electrical sparks, store signs dangled dangerously from fractured rooftops. The facades of buildings fell and burned, sending up clouds of dust and thick smoke.

A pod, its twin guns blazing, stepped out from behind the remains of a clothing store to face off against a Gladiator positioned at the end of the block. Bursts of blinding fire were exchanged again and again until both pod and mecha exploded, while elsewhere rockets fell and flames spread. A massive multibarreled autocannon swept along Macross Boulevard, sending ground-to-air heat-seekers against airborne mecha. EVE's star-studded sky veneer was stripped away, revealing in stark detail the naked terrors of war.

Not all the pods were blasting away, however. Some were actually looting the shops for souvenirs, raking in whatever appeared intact with the mecha's grappling hooks and waldo gloves. Two of the pilots got a fix on an external sound source that was similar to Minmei's "singing"; and the pair moved off together, homing in on the Macross Star Bowl.

Inside, Minmei was still on stage, wedded to her audience in some sort of unrehearsed litany of song.

Without accompaniment, she sang, "To be in love…"

And they chanted: "Stagefright, go'way, this is my big day."

She was grasping the mike tightly in both hands, though she was certain that the power had gone off. But her face betrayed no fear. Kyle was standing stiffly by her side, his fists clenched, urging her to go on. From what she could tell, the city beyond the amphitheater rim was engulfed in apocalyptical flames; thick black smoke was billowing toward the ceiling of the hold, and a light rain seemed to be falling from the overhead water-retrieval system. Electrical power had shorted out in most areas of the stadium. The spots were off. The band had fled. And those in the audience who weren't singing were crying. It felt like the end of the world.

Then, all at once, two Battlepods appeared on the upper tier of the amphitheater, their cannons aimed ultimately at the stage, and she dropped the mike.

Kyle stepped forward and raised it again to her mouth. "You've got to continue singing, Minmei. Give it all you've got!"

He put his arm around her, and she found the courage to pick up where she'd left off. The audience followed her; she believed they would have followed her anywhere.

"Now, don't be afraid," Kyle was saying into her ear. "They're not going to hurt us."

And it truly seemed that way for an instant—as if the pods were just part of the audience—until a bolt of blue energy flashed overhead and struck the upper reaches of the stage canopy. It had not been launched by either of the pods and was in fact a stray shot from outside the amphitheater. But that made little difference. The crowd panicked. And worse still, the blast had loosened one of the large overhead spotlights. For a second it looked like it wouldn't fall. Then something snapped and gave way, and down it came.

Kyle spied it in the nick of time and moved in to cover Minmei. He succeeded perfectly, taking the full force of the impact on his back, the spotlight driving both of them violently to the floor.

Outside the fortress, things were not much better. The SDF-1 had managed to put some distance between herself and the Zentraedi warships, but furious space dogfights were continuing. Rick was locked into the vacuum equivalent of a scissors finesse with the Officer's Pod that had been hounding him since the word go. Each time he tried to break or jink, the pod stuck to his tail, loosing cannon fire, and now here was Lisa on the right commo screen vying for his attention. Fortunately, Max had been monitoring the aircom net and was coming in to give Rick some relief. Sterling came in low under the Officer's Pod and chased it off with Stilettos; Rick angled himself out of the immediate battle arena and went on the net to the fortress bridge.

"*In* the ship?" Rick repeated in disbelief.

Lisa reaffirmed it. "They're destroying everything, Rick. Return to base immediately!"

*Minmei!* Rick screamed internally. "Lisa, have they hit the amphitheater? You've got to tell me!"

"I don't have a status report, Rick. Just get back here on the double." As she signed off, Max appeared on the left screen.

"I'm with you, Commander," said Sterling. "I'll follow you home."

Which was easier said than done.

First the two Veritechs had to navigate a web of pulsed fire laid out by the Officer's Pod and its three cohort ships, then direct themselves through the continuous bombardment the fortress was receiving from the enemy warships. Rick raised the bridge and asked Lisa to see to it that one of the SDF-1's ventral docking ports was opened for their entry; it would have been not only a longer route to Macross via the *Daedalus* or *Prometheus* but a more dangerous one as well. No one in fact had ever *piloted* a VT through the arms of the fortress.

Rick rehearsed his moves as he closed on the air lock; he visualized a map of the city streets and began to plot a course, almost as if allowing the mecha to familiarize itself with the plan.

Skull One and Skull Two zoomed into the fortress, unaware that four Battlepods had followed them in, Khyron's Officer's Pod in the lead.

Miriya was as surprised as anyone to see Zentraedi mecha in the streets of Macross City, and just now she was possibly the only person alive in those streets. Most of the Micronians had taken to the shelters long ago, but many had remained in the amphitheater to witness the workings of some sort of psychological weapons system. For some unknown reason the Battlepods had also chosen to concentrate their might there, and as a result the Micronians had sustained heavy personnel losses. In addition the pods had laid waste to much of the surrounding city. Fires continued to burn, explosions could be heard and felt from all quarters, and a steady rain of embers, soot, and debris fell from the ceiling of the enormous hold.

Miriya had been one of those who remained unsheltered in the amphitheater. She had been trailing the long-haired Micronian warrior ever since the populace had turned out in such force to honor him at the trans-vid screening of his battle records. It seemed likely that the female warrior shown in those trans-vids was the same one who had drawn such a fanatical following to the amphitheater. The vocal noises she emitted had been discomfiting; they had left Miriya feeling debilitated and ill at ease, much as she had felt upon recognizing that the female warrior was in some way the *consort* of the long-haired male!

Until moments ago Miriya had been convinced that the male warrior was the one who had defeated her in battle, but something had happened to alter her thinking. She had seen him crushed by the falling illumination device and, while working her way down the aisles toward the stage, had spied a blue-trimmed Micronian fighter streak overhead. Certain that she recognized the mecha, she had taken to the devastated streets to watch the pilot of that ship in action against her allies.

The fighter was reconfiguring to bipedal mode now as she watched, fascinated, from her place of concealment. The pilot was about to bring the gatling into play. Surrounded by pods, he twisted and trap-shot one from the air, then spun around and took out a second that had landed behind him. Agilely sidestepping the blast of the exploding pod's foot thruster, he utilized the earned momentum to position himself for a bead on a well-situated third. Yet another pod mistakenly thought that height would be advantageous and lifted off, foot thrusters blaring and top guns blazing away. But the Micronian merely sent his mecha into a beautifully executed tuck and roll and came up shooting as the pod came down beside him. Again the foolish Zentraedi pilot tried to leap and fire, but the blue ace had already decreed his fate: Bolts of lightning striking around him, he raised the muzzle of the cannon, fired, and holed the pod with a shot right through the front viewscreen. While the mecha blew to pieces in midair, the Micronian set off in search of greater challenges.

Miriya was depressed by the Zentraedi pilots' poor showing—it was no wonder Breetai's troops were losing!—but elated at having at last discovered the object of her long search. Now she simply had to hunt him down and confront him.

...

Elsewhere in Macross Rick had also set Skull One down in Guardian mode and reconfigured to Battloid, shooting his way to the Star Bowl area of Macross, where the fighting was thickest, charging down city streets he knew so well and closing on the amphitheater. He had literally just bowled over two stationary Battlepods when Max raised him on the tac net.

"How bad is it where you are?" Sterling wanted to know.

Rick panned his external cameras across the burning cityscape to take stock of the scene: There wasn't a storefront left undamaged—it looked as if some of them had been *looted!* The streets were torn up from explosions and the hooflike feet of who knew how many enemy mecha. EVE's "sky" had taken a beating—most of it had in fact fallen—and few of the deadly fires had been brought under control.

Rick went on the net: "It's worse than I even thought, Max."

"Any civilians about?"

"None that I can see," Rick answered, calling for zoom on the scanners. "Looks like most of them made it into the shelters."

Static crackled through Skull One's speakers.

"Same out here. What's your next move?"

"I'm going to check the Star Bowl. See that everybody got out of there all right."

"Minmei…"

"Right, Max."

"All right, Skull Leader, I'm signing off. Rendezvous with you at the Star Bowl. Over and out."

Rick took a deep breath and relaxed back into alpha. He hit the foot pedals hard and began to think the mecha back into a jog. Enormous explosions erupted behind him as he started out, the gatling in the Battloid's right hand, metalshod left clamped on the cannon for added stability.

Rounding a corner at a good clip, he ran smack into heavy fire. Several pods had taken to the rooftops here and were throwing blue bolts at anything that moved. Up ahead a grounded pod sustained a hit in the back and keeled over as Rick approached.

Rooftop rounds were impacting all around him, and he was forced to dive Skull One sideways to the street, left arm straight out for counterbalance as he went into a double roll. The muzzle of the galling was up before he completed the move, just in time to sear off the right leg of a pod that had leapt from an upper-story support. The enemy mecha rolled over on its back, flame blazing from what was left of its leg, and exploded.

Meanwhile Rick was back on his feet again and already resuming his pace. But not fifty meters down the street a pod stepped from the shadows of a department store doorway and almost succeeded in nailing him. At the last minute, Rick saw it and launched the Battloid like a high jumper over blinding flashes of cannon fire. As he rolled into a front flip, he opened up with the cannon and caught the pod between the legs, transuranic slugs lifting it off the street before it burst to pieces in a ball of orange and purple flame.

Skull One landed hard on its back, smoking gun still clutched tightly in its right hand.

Inside the cockpit Rick shook his head clear and found himself staring straight up at a gaping hole in the hold overhead and two more rooftop pods that were now pouring rounds at him. He thought his mecha into a roll and twist to the right, which ultimately brought it to a kneeling position, the muzzle elevated and armed. Trigger finger on the Hotas, he squeezed, bringing the mecha's left hand up and around to fasten on the forward section of the galling. The street quaked as explosive-tipped projectiles spiked into the area around him.

Rick sprayed the pods right to left seemingly without effect, the gun sputtering and overheating in the Battloid's grip. Then it gave out completely. But after a moment of dramatic stillness, the pods fell headfirst from their ballet poses on the building ledge. Trailing fire, they crashed on either side of Skull One, fulminating.

Thinking the Battloid erect, Rick shouted, *"Minmei!"* and continued his charge on the amphitheater.

# 11

I can't imagine what he was thinking when he grabbed me like that, pinning my arms and forcing himself on me. Why do they all have to fall in love with me? Why do they all need to possess and control me? ...All I could think about was what happened on Thursday, when Kyle saved me from falling into one of the modular transformation troughs and I looked up and saw Rick's face in place of his.

From the diary of Lynn-Minmei

KHYRON AND SIX OF HIS FINEST SWAGGERED THEIR PODS DOWN Main Street, mopping up what was left of the civil defense patrol Battloids and Gladiators. The Backstabber couldn't have been happier. The fortress's population center was in flames, Zentraedi mecha were overrunning the last few remaining pockets of resistance, and soon the heart of the ship would be secured. It would only be a matter of time before they moved against the ship's command centers.

"Victory will be mine!" he shouted from within his Officer's Pod.

But something was about to occur that would rob Khyron of this false apotheosis, something that would give new meaning to his nickname...

"Destroy everything in sight!" he commanded his troops. "We can do anything we want this time!"

Two Battloids suddenly appeared in the distance; they had taken up positions on either side of the street a few blocks ahead and were now leaning out from behind buildings, directing pulsed cannon fire against Khyron's methodical advance. But the

Zentraedi commander never even broke stride; he casually took out both of them with hand-gun hip shots.

He was beginning to increase the pace somewhat when three Battlepods darted out across his path from a perpendicular side street with an obvious purpose in mind. Khyron signaled his own troops to halt and opened his comlink to the preoccupied pods.

"Just a moment," he said, stepping forward, his voice full of suspicion. "Where in the name of Dolza are you three going? Answer me at once!"

The three pods stopped and turned to him. Vocal salutes and sounds of surprise came across the net.

"Respond!" Khyron repeated.

After a moment one of them said, "We are hoping to find Minmei, Commander."

"Minmei?" Khyron said uncertainly. "I've never heard of a Minmei. What are its ballistic capabilities?"

"She's not a missile, sir," said another. "She's a Micronian female!"

All at once the three of them were laughing with delight. Several other pods had skulked out of the side street to watch the exchange.

"The most incredible creature in the universe!"

"We've got to meet her in person. Hear her sing—"

"Silence!" Khyron cut them off.

The pods snapped to, but muffled laughter continued. Khyron narrowed his eyes. So the rumors Grel had reported were true, he said to himself. Defection: It was unheard of.

Khyron's voice dripped menace when he spoke again.

"I presume you plan to tell me what you're laughing about."

"I'm sorry, m'lord," one responded, attempting to stifle his laughter, seemingly unaware that Khyron was bringing one of his hand-guns to bear on him. "It's just that I'm so overcome with joy at the possibility of finding Minmei—"

Khyron fired once, his round entering the pilot chamber through the central viewscreen and exploding.

"He's out of his mind!" Khyron heard over the comlink as the pods ran for cover. "Run, run!"

"Stop!" he commanded them, looking around and realizing that even members of his own crack unit were abandoning him. "All of you, come back!"

Khyron threw his pod into pursuit mode, hooved feet pounding along the city streets. Not one of them would live to see the end of this day, he promised himself. Already he had one of the deserters centered in his top-cannon reticle.

"Come back here, soldier, and face me like a Zentraedi! You can't run from me forever!"

"I'm sorry, my lord," came the meek reply over the net, "but I—I can't explain what *joy* it is to be among the Micronians."

*"What?"* Khyron shouted. "I've never heard anything so crazy in my life! You're completely *mad*, do you hear me? You're telling me that you'd prefer to be with *them*?!"

Khyron heard an exclamation of fear but no explanation. He shook his head knowingly and pronounced sentence as the chase continued: "Well now, my little friend, I'm afraid I must deal with you in the same way I dealt with your companion."

The Officer's Pod right hand-gun fired once. The pod took the hit in the rear end, was lifted up as though goosed by fire, and was blown clear from the street.

Khyron fired again and again, pursuing the Battlepods through the ruined streets into the city's night.

Minmei summoned her strength, heaved once, and managed to drag herself out from under Kyle's dead weight. She felt bruised and mangled, and her red gown was in a sorry state. The large canister spotlight that had beaned her cousin was several feet away, tipped over on its side amid plaster chips, shards of plastic, and other bits of fallen debris. The amphitheater appeared to be deserted, but there were flames and thick smoke in the distance and the sounds of sirens and explosions.

Wondering just how long she'd been out, she began to tuck stray hairs back into their bunlike arrangement. Kyle made a groaning sound, and she went over to him, helping him to his feet and walking him to the wings, where they both sat down.

He was breathing hard, and his forehead was cut. Minmei took a handkerchief from his pocket and dabbed at the blood. As he came around, she said, "I'll make it better," and started to make funny faces for his benefit. She crossed her eyes, stuck out her tongue, puffed out her cheeks, uttered some strange sounds, and in a minute had him laughing.

"There. All better," she announced in a motherly tone, stroking his face with the kerchief.

Had she been less concerned about what was to prove to be a very minor injury, perhaps she would have noticed the look that began to surface in his dark eyes and would have been able to avoid the awkward scene that followed.

Kyle was so used to taking care of himself that Minmei's attentiveness overwhelmed him. In his still weakened state he found his feelings for her confused but undeniably powerful. She was so much stronger than he had ever thought possible, so talented, such an amazing *presence* in the lopsided world they inhabited together…

So he expressed these thoughts and feelings the only way he knew how: He reached out for her and kissed her full on the mouth.

They were kneeling face to face on the stage; it was dark, and maybe he didn't see her eyes go wide with bewilderment and fear—or maybe he just didn't care. Perhaps he somehow misread her attempts to push him away. But it is more likely that he pinned her arms in the hope that his love for her could silence her fears, much as his mouth was stifling her protests. He needed to make her understand how he felt. Once she was made to understand his needs, she would surely give herself freely to him…

But ultimately Minmei pushed him away and told him in no uncertain terms that he was never to do that again.

Kyle did not understand.

And neither did Rick, who had arrived at the amphitheater in time to witness the kiss but who turned his Battloid around too soon to see the rebuff.

...

The computer-generated graphics from civil defense command

had been patched through to the fortress bridge. A schematic bird's-eye view of the city streets showing the deployment of CD and enemy troops filled the screen of the threat board. Gloval and his crew had been spared actual video footage of the devastating attack, but it didn't take much imagination to visualize the horrors that were befalling the place. These were the streets and landmarks of their world, just as surely as the bridge and base were. Each and every injury inflicted there affected the entire fortress. What happened to one happened to them all.

Gloval was not really a religious man, despite what his verbal expressions may have suggested. But more than once during the past two years of warfare he'd come close to finding some sort of divine, intervening, benevolent intelligence at work in the cosmos. And most often it had been the Zentraedi's sudden and inexplicable strategic reversals which had given rise to those theological revelations. The captain was in the middle of one of these at the moment, standing stock-still behind Vanessa's chair and staring uncomprehendingly at the novel troop movements on the screen.

"The enemy's actions have become totally chaotic," Vanessa said, stating the obvious.

Gloval nodded his head slowly. "I see it… I see it… I don't *believe* it, but I see it."

Initially it had appeared that the Zentraedi command was merely relaxing its methodical march and allowing its forces to scatter—to loot or pillage or engage in whatever it was that giants did in Micronian cities. But on closer examination the board revealed that certain pods were chasing, *routing* others. One pod in particular—an Officer's Pod according to its schematic signature—was actually *destroying* them. Gloval let his mind rake quickly over the possibilities: There was Lisa's two-faction theory, a schism in the Zentraedi high command; the chance that some of the VT pilots had for some reason commandeered several pods; and then there was… *God*. And perhaps any or all of them spelled God in the end, Gloval decided, as he turned forward to face Lisa and Claudia.

"Alert all auxiliary groups to assemble and lock in on sectors seven, nine, ten, and eleven. We should be able to box the pods in near the Macross amphitheater." Gloval regarded the board briefly and added, "See if you can raise the Skull team and ascertain their position."

Lisa went to work carrying out the captain's orders. Brown, Indigo, and Green squads were taking up positions near the amphitheater when she finally succeeded in contacting Skull Leader. It had been a long while since Rick had radioed in, and she found herself as relieved as she was angry when he came on-line.

"Uhh, sorry, Commander." He sounded distracted and distant.

"You haven't been reporting in, Rick. Where are you? What's going on?"

"They're here," he answered sadly, turning his head from the cockpit camera. "Kyle and Minmei. Send a rescue group to the amphitheater."

"The amphitheater?" she said in alarm. "Rick, you've got to get them out of there!"

Rick said nothing.

"Have they been hurt, Rick? Answer me. Has something happened to Kyle?"

Lisa saw him reach out for the kill switch, and a second later the monitor screen signals on the bridge went diagonal in static.

Skull One turned its back on the lovers' kiss; dejectedly, the Battloid walked from the amphitheater's tier, head down, arms hanging loosely at its side, interfacing with and mirroring the emotions of its pilot.

Rick felt as devastated as the city itself, at once angry at himself for spying and heartbroken by the result. It had been far worse than that tender cinematic kiss that had riled him so.

*How could she have done it? How could she have been so blatantly unfaithful to him?*

There wasn't a trace of irony in his inner voice. He desperately *wanted* to feel betrayed, and he meant to put the anger that welled up from the wound to good use.

Max Sterling was waiting for him at the exit gate.

"Did you find her?" Max asked over the net.

"Find who?" Rick spat back.

"Minmei, buddy. Is she in the shelter already?"

Rick almost raised the muzzle of the cannon on his friend. "She's only one person aboard this ship, Max, you got that?

My job is to defend the SDF-1, nothing else."

"Sure," Max said, backing his Battloid away a bit. "Then you'll be happy to learn that you've got your job cut out for you. CD has herded the enemy right into our lap."

Inside the cockpit module Rick stomped on the foot pedals and primed the gatling cannon.

"Then let's go get 'em," he said to Max.

There were eight Battlepods waiting for him on the shattered street and burning rooftops. He acknowledged them with a nod, raised the cannon, screamed a throat-tearing war cry, and launched himself into their midst, skull and crossbones prominently displayed.

The pods poured fire into the street and descended on him like rabid birds of prey. Running headlong into a horizontal rain of blue death, Rick kept the gatling at waist level, discharging searing fusillades against his ship's enemies. He sustained hits his mind refused to feel and blew away one after another of the galloping pods. Explosions relit the artificial night.

He jagged to the right as one pod took to the air and trapshot it, two hands on the cannon now and screaming his war cry all the while. He twisted left and blew the legs out from under a second, screen-shot a third. Even when the gatling had expended itself, his blood lust was far from diminished. He went close in, using the cannon as a club; when he lost that, he continued to fight, metalshod hand to hand.

On the other side of town six pods played dead.

The double-pulled hinged hatch of one these opened, and three small faces peered out. Explosions could still be heard off in the distance, but from the sound of it the fighting was sporadic and winding down. Thanks to Khyron, the Micronians had been able to snatch victory from the very jaws of defeat; their troops were mopping up what the Backstabber's timely escape from the fortress had left unfinished. But the micronized Zentraedi soldiers inside the undamaged spheres had no bones to pick with him. Quite the contrary: *Thanks to Khyron!* indeed.

Rico, Bron, and Konda rappelled to the street on ropes thrown from the cockpit; had they been aware of the Micronian custom, they would surely have kneeled down and offered a kiss. Other Zentraedi began to follow their lead, and soon the entire cult was reunited.

These six pods had managed to keep together since the assault; they had peeled away from the main strike force just before the destruction of the population center had begun. Consequently they had come through the battle relatively unscathed, but most of their fellow deserters had not been as fortunate. Several pods, only a few of them containing micronized Zentraedi, had been unlucky enough to cross paths with Commander Khyron. The diabolical lord of the Botoru Battalion had meted out punishment on the spot. There was no way of guessing just how many soldiers he had put to death; but as word had spread through the ranks, many had given up their hopes for resettlement among the Micronians and fled into space.

As the lucky ones now began to take a look around their dreamland there were mutterings of disappointment and regret. One of their number had found a foot-high Minmei doll on the sidewalk, its embroidered red robe stained and tattered. He was holding it in both hands cheerlessly.

"What's wrong with it?" one of his companions asked. "Why isn't it singing?"

"It seems we've damaged it."

"That doll's not the only thing we've damaged," said Karita, gesturing in general to their surroundings.

"You mean it's not supposed to look like this?"

Bron stepped in and took the doll. "Karita's right. This population center was once beautiful and peaceful."

"The Micronians know how to repair things," Konda added. " Then they'll rebuild all this?" Karita asked hopefully.

Rico nodded. "They know the secrets of *Protoculture*."

This brought surprised gasps all around, even from those micronized Zentraedi who had no understanding of the word but knew enough to recognize it as the shibboleth of the command elite.

"But what do we do now, Rico? If we're discovered by the Micronians, we'll be executed for our actions against the fortress."

"Yeah, now what?" others chimed in.

Rico thought for a moment. "There's a Micronian who was trying to convince everyone that the war had to be stopped the one I pointed out to you during the battle record trans-vids we watched. He was talking about peace all the time."

"What's 'peace'?" asked one of the clones, but the others shushed him.

"Go on, Rico."

"Well, I think we should turn ourselves over to the Micronian high command. We'll tell them that we've come in the name of *peace*."

# 12

I remember my parents telling me about a popular amusement center
that existed before the [Global] War. The place was called EPCOT,
and it was located in the southeastern Panam, in what was then
called the state of Florida. There you could walk or ride through
any number of pavilions, each representative, architecturally and
culturally, of its nation of origin. Pop was fascinated by the Mexican
exhibit. Apparently, once inside the building, it was easy to surrender
yourself to the imagineers' illusions. A marketplace, an ancient
pyramid, even a smoldering volcano—all under a twilight dome full
of redolent aromas. Pop was so taken with the pavilion that he went
back to it over and over again, and one day he was allowed in before
those illusions were in full swing. Much to his later disappointment.
Because without that starry sky and that cool and gentle breeze, he
was well aware of where he was: *inside a human-made environment*.
The pavilion would never be the same for him again. And this is how
the dimensional fortress civilians felt when they left the shelters after
the Zentraedi attack. It was all too plain that they were inside an
alien spaceship; Macross was changed forever.

The Collected Journals of Admiral Rick Hunter

MAYOR TOMMY LUAN WAS ONE OF THE FIRST TO LEAVE THE
shelters. He had set out immediately on an inspection tour of
Macross that by day's end had left no proverbial stone unturned. But
every step along the way proved to be an ordeal. The fires had been
extinguished and the thick smoke exhausted through the enormous
exterior ports, but the air still reeked of molten metals and plastics.

The hold windows and bays, the so-called starlights, were encrusted with the same resinous grime that seemed to have settled on every horizontal surface in the city. The streets were potholed, cratered, and torn up, running with water loosed from subsurface and overhead conduits. Recyclable sewage from the devastated oubliette system had been heaped up here and there or blown into the air to adhere to street signs and buildings. There didn't appear to be an intact piece of glass anywhere; shards littered the sidewalks, the lobbies, the interiors of offices and homes. In the most unlikely places one was able to stumble upon pieces of mechanical debris, a car part here, the leg of a Destroid over there, a Battloid finger buried in a wall. Perhaps worst of all, there were those holes in the sky.

Residents were sorting through the mess like zombies, trying to locate fragments of their past lives, staring shell-shocked at standing walls that no longer embraced a home, walking eerily to and fro calling out names of the displaced, the lost, and the dead— of which there were miraculously few.

For the most part casualties had been confined to the area around the amphitheater, which had seen the worst fighting by far. The Star Bowl itself would not house a concert for a long while, and the surrounding buildings were damaged beyond repair. Here there was hard evidence of the battle: the silent husks of pods and Gladiators still locked together in war-memorial poses, undetonated missiles projecting from storefronts, craters that were in effect immeasurable.

The Macross amphitheater, however, wasn't the only landmark to have been hit. The Hotel Centinel had collapsed like a layer cake, and the neighboring skyway was in shambles. Numerous monorail line pylons had been felled; street and store signs were down. Much of Macross Central Park had burned—the only "living fire" the SDF-1 would ever witness. Electrical power was out in many sections.

Macross was a disaster area.

But Tommy Luan was already rolling up his shirt sleeves and putting things back in order. On the one hand there were several things to be thankful for, he told the populace from a makeshift podium set up on the boulevard not far from the Fortress Theater.

The aliens had been beaten back. True, they had leveled quite a bit of the city, but they had not penetrated any of the command areas of the ship—astrogation, engineering, or even the Robotech Defense Forces base. There was certainly an enormous amount of work ahead of them, but they had already rebuilt once before and they would be able to do it again. Luau called on them to think back to a time even earlier than the spacefold accident and recall their experiences during the Global Civil War, when scarcely a city on the planet had escaped devastation in one form or another. Robotechnicians would come to their aid and provide the know-how once again, Luan promised, and Macross would meet those technicians halfway supplying the strength and spirit required to implement their designs. "Rome wasn't built in a day," he reminded them. "Macross City was!"

It was a rousing address, and the city applauded its mayor and spokesperson as much for his determination as for his optimism. There were few among the resident population who doubted that renewal was possible, but an alternative to rebuilding had presented itself to some: Just open the air locks, they publicly maintained. Let space suck out the debris and the memories, and then simply start again from scratch.

For a small and select group of victims the disaster actually facilitated the procurement of much-needed supplies—a different sort of uniform for starters.

"Clothes!" Bron reiterated. "How many times do I have to tell you: Some of the Micronians are soldiers, and some are civilians. The soldiers wear uniforms; the civilians wear clothes. Now repeat it—*clothes*."

"Clothes," said the club members, hangdog expressions on their faces.

"I don't know…" Rico said uncertainly. He turned to Konda and Bron for reinforcement. "Can we get away with this?"

The Minmei cultists had abandoned their Battlepods and hiked crosstown—a troop of curious-looking scouts in sackcloth dresses. It had been decided that Rico, Bron, and Konda would surrender themselves to the SDF-1 high command and explain the reasons for their desertion from the Zentraedi forces. Since the others had little command of the Micronian language, Rico thought it best that they go into hiding for a while. He was actually more concerned about their overeagerness to partake in the Micronian way of life, although he didn't tell them this. All along he'd been proclaiming to have sampled widely of the population center's offerings, and now his followers were beginning to press him for answers he simply didn't have. "When do we get to meet Minmei?" "Can we begin to kiss her immediately?" "How long are we supposed to keep our lips pressed together?" Rico felt like he needed to run off somewhere and hide, but it would probably work out better for everyone if he hid *them* instead.

A hideout would be easy enough to come by, but at some point the micronized soldiers were going to need food. Which meant that one of them was going to have to go out unescorted into the streets. Which meant that clothes were essential. Rico shuddered when he recalled how the Micronians had laughed at Bron when he stepped out in female clothing. Rico shuddered again at the thought of Karita or one of the others stepping out into Micronian society. But *something* had to be done—and *fast!*

Konda, who had the best sense of direction among them, led them through a maze of ruined streets and ultimately into a relatively undamaged department store he remembered from the surveillance visit. The Micronians were just beginning to emerge from their battle shelters as they entered the well-stocked store. Rico turned the group loose and regretted it almost immediately. Karita and the rest scattered and started stuffing all sorts of objects into their sackcloth gowns— toys, small appliances, hairbrushes, entertainment discs, time devices, earlobe ornaments ... whatever they could lay their hands on. It took well over an hour for Rico, Konda, and Bron to round them up; Karita and a second cultist had to be forcibly restrained from lip-pressing every fabricated female form they passed.

"Clothes!" Bron shouted angrily when they were all regrouped. "We're here for clothes and nothing else. Is that understood?"

Sheepishly they promised to behave and followed Konda up a stairway (which under normal circumstances would have been mechanized) and into an area of the store set apart exclusively for apparel.

"Now, pick what you want and be quick about it!" Rico yelled as they ran off, their eyes lit up by the display.

Konda was the first to see them return from their foray: Rico and Bron caught his slack-jawed look and followed his gaze. Down to the last, they had picked out female attire—long thin-strapped gowns cut low in front and back; A-lines and pleated skirts; high-waisted sleeveless frocks; sweater and skirt ensembles; ruffled blouses; lingerie, hosiery, and high-heeled shoes.

It took another hour to get everyone properly outfitted, but by the time they left the store there was no reason to doubt they could pass for Micronians. Except, that is, for the three leaders. *Their* next move was to get themselves identified as Zentraedi, and they reasoned that the original sackcloth uniforms might help that along.

The sidewalks and streets were filled with Micronians now, most of whom were busy clearing rubble or sorting through debris. Food and drink booths had been opened for the needy. Armed soldiers and battle mecha patrolled while huge Robotech vehicles hauled away the remains of pods and multigunned civil defense units. The population center was already mobilizing, breaking up into teams and relief groups to deal with the damage. Not fifty paces out of the department store, Rico and the others were assigned to one of the work crews.

At first it looked as though involvement in the detail was going to spell disaster, but Rico's concerns were shortly laid to rest. To the Zentraedi, "repair" was not only a foreign notion but a magical process. Karita and the others had been handed digging devices called shovels and pickaxes and after a few moments of familiarization were completely absorbed in their tasks. They were joyfully swinging and shoveling, shoulder to shoulder with Micronians, even *joining them in song!* It was too perfect, Rico told himself: They would be fed and cared for and looked after. Now, as long as none of them had to speak...

With Konda and Bron in tow, Rico managed to weasel out of the area. The three former operatives had far more important things to concern themselves with than clearing debris from the walkways.

It was time to turn themselves in.

Expecting nothing less than complete acceptance and full cooperation, Rico and his cohorts brazenly approached one of the nearby patrol posts and confessed to being Zentraedi agents. But something was wrong; Rico wasn't being taken at his word. The soldier was actually *laughing* at them. So he grew more insistent.

"I'm telling you, we're Zentraedi. We came into the fortress inside one of our battle mecha—"

"You're a little short to be a Zentraedi, aren't you, buddy?" the soldier interrupted.

"We've been through the resizing process," Bron attempted to explain. "We're micronized."

The soldier exchanged winks with one of his companions. "'Micronized,' huh? Well, why didn't you say so in the first place?" He put his hand on Rico's shoulder and spun him gently left. "You want that place, right over there. You see, where it says, 'medical assistance.'"

"'Medical assistance,'" Rico repeated. "All right, thanks." He turned to Bron and Konda and said, "Come on."

"Shell shock," the lieutenant said to his corporal as the three sackclothed men walked away. "Some kind of martyr thing by the look of it."

At the first-aid station they went through an almost word-for-word repeat performance. But eventually a female wearing a white uniform with a red-cross emblem escorted them into the office of a man who introduced himself as Dr. Zeitgeist.

The room was large and spacious and lined floor to ceiling with archaic document displays. The "doctor" himself was a portly Micronian with an abundance of facial hair but very little on his cranium. He spoke with an accent that made his curious utterances and phrases even more difficult to comprehend. But undaunted, Rico proceeded to recount the details of their desertion from the Zentraedi.

Zeitgeist gave a long "I seeeee…" when Rico finished, and leaned back in his swivel chair. He regarded the three couched men in sackcloths for a moment, then began to review what they'd told him.

"So you three think you're Zentraedi soldiers," said Zeitgeist. (What he actually said was closer to: "Zo you zree zink you're

Zentraedi zoldiers.") "You were first sent here as spies, but you grew to so love our…" he consulted his notes, "'Micronian' society that you decided to desert your armed forces and live with us."

"Yes, that's it," the three said in unison.

"I zeeeee…" said Zeitgeist.

It was the most richly detailed case of guilt-induced Type-Seven behavior that it had been his pleasure to diagnose in many a day. Certainly a step up from the space phobias, null-g sickness, and separation anxieties he'd been nursing along for the past two years. And so *thorough* and laden with symbolism—from the flagellants' robes to the talk of espionage and "micronization"— that wonderful word which really captured the human sense of displacement one felt inside the alien dimensional fortress. Why he could almost see the journal paper writing itself: "Micronization: The Phobia of Containment."

"And you would ez-timate your actual height," the doctor continued, "to be approx-zimately fifty 'Micronian' feet?"

Rico turned a sober face to Bron and Konda.

"He doesn't believe us."

Bron got to his feet: "We can prove it," he told Zeitgeist. "Bring us to one of your commanders. We'll tell him things about our battle mecha that will convince him."

Over the course of the next few hours the good doctor saw his hopes for a journal paper dashed, but he did begin to think about opening up a counseling clinic for disaffected extraterrestrials. Meanwhile the three Zentraedi were prodded, poked, searched, examined, analyzed, interviewed, tested, scoped, scanned, evaluated, appraised, and assessed. They were moved from office to office, city to cell, and barracks to base. They saw more different types of uniforms than they would have believed existed in the Fourth Quadrant of the known universe. And finally, they were brought before the fortress's commander in chief, Captain Henry Gloval.

Gloval had done little more than browse through the foot-high stack of reports on the debriefing room desk—psychiatric evaluations, intelligence test reports, military and medical examinations, interview transcripts—but he had seen enough to convince him that the aliens' claims were true. What they knew about the workings of the Battlepods alone would have been sufficient evidence. And their very existence in "micronized" size had fully substantiated Lisa's aftermission reports regarding some sort of reduction device aboard the enemy flagship. The clone issue would have to await the results of the medical tests. That these three had actually been in the fortress previously was as amazing as it was discomforting; it was no wonder that Dr. Lang was dying to get his hands on them. First, however, it was up to Gloval and the high command to decide exactly what to do with them. What, in fact, did they want? And how many others like them might be aboard the SDF-1 at that very moment?

These were questions he hoped to have answered before the special session with colonels Maistroff and Caruthers convened.

Lisa Hayes and Max Sterling were now admitted to the room, and shortly thereafter the three aliens were escorted in.

Lisa's first impression erased all doubts that she might have had; in fact, there was almost something *familiar* about these three. Rico put a quick end to her puzzlement.

"We were present at your interrogation," he explained. "Remember when you kissed one of the male members of your group?"

Even though that tidbit had been included in her report, she blushed at hearing about it—from a *Zentraedi*, no less. Rico went on to give details of that meeting with Dolza that were more complete than Rick, Lisa, and Ben's collective recollection. Then he went on to talk about Breetai and Exedore and someone named Khyron, who had been responsible for turning the tide during the attack on Macross City. The alien also mentioned Protoculture and Zentraedi fears concerning a Micronian secret weapon. They wanted to stay aboard the fortress—this much was clear—and more than anything they wanted to see *Minmei!*

By this time Gloval looked like someone on the verge of sensory overload. His eyes were wide, and his mustache was twitching. "That's enough for now," he said, holding up his hands. "We'll carry on with this session in the presence of colonels Maistroff and Caruthers. And Lisa," he added as an aside, "I want you to request that Lieutenant Hunter join us immediately."

# 13

When one sits down to a serious side-by-side study of the log entries
of the two commanders [Gloval and Breetai], a curious pattern
begins to emerge which I believe has been overlooked by many of
[the Robotech War's] commentators and historians... And by the
time we've reached those entries written just prior to Dolza's direct
involvement in the war, this parallel pattern has become self-evident,
especially with regard to Lynn-Minmei's importance, the growing
disaffection among the ranks, and the defiant stance adopted by
both Gloval and Breetai toward their respective high commands (the
UEDC and Dolza). It is almost as if two years of space warfare had
created what two centuries ago was called a *folie à deux*.

Rawlins, *Zentraedi Triumvirate:*
*Dolza, Breetai, Khyron*

"LIEUTENANT HUNTER'S PRESENCE IS REQUESTED IN HQ SPECIAL
Sessions chamber immediately." No explanation, no afterword,
Rick told himself. What, he wondered, had he done now?

There had been no sleep following the battle; the fortress
was still on red alert, and all available men and women in the
Defense Force were on duty. Most of the tech, engineering, and
construction crews had been assigned to Macross, where the
civilians had organized work details and clean-up was already
under way. Indigo and Brown VT teams patrolled the city streets in
Battloid mode, wary that some Zentraedi might have survived. The
SDF-1 was swept stem to stem for infiltration units, but save for
the *Daedalus* arm and the city itself, there were no signs of enemy

penetration. Although casualty counts were not yet complete, there was little doubt that the losses sustained would number well into the hundreds, and this didn't take into account a civilian body count. It would take days to sort through the rubble surrounding the amphitheater alone—a good deal of which Rick and Max had been responsible for after the CD squads had successfully stampeded a horde of Battlepods right into their laps.

His blood lust quenched, Rick felt like some sort of overstimulated incandescent bulb; sleep, even if it was granted by his superiors, would probably elude him for weeks. And when that burnout point was finally reached, it was going to be one heck of a downhill run to hell... He had been ordered to the *Prometheus*, where he was supervising mecha triage when the request from Lisa Hayes reached him.

Standing outside the Special Sessions chamber now, he returned a sentry's salute, tugged at the hem of his jacket, tried in vain to dewire himself somewhat, and rapped decisively on the door.

The large room was familiar to him from two other occasions— when he had been awarded the titanium Medal of Valor and during his debriefing after imprisonment aboard the Zentraedi flagship. Command would be seated behind a somewhat U-shaped desk above which was the kitelike Robotech emblem centered in an embossed Defense Forces silver shield. There were bound to be one or two armed sentries positioned on either side of the door, a session transcriber, and of course some hot seat in front of the desk, which Rick hoped had not been reserved for him.

"Lieutenant Hunter reporting as ordered." Rick saluted.

"At ease, Mister Hunter. That was a request, not an order." Rick wasn't about to relax; he quickly scanned the room. Gloval was seated casually below the shield, elbows on the desk; to his right were Max Sterling and Lisa. On the captain's left, as stiff as ever, were colonels Maistroff and Caruthers, burly veteran commanders both, thick-jowled, tight lipped clones in different color uniforms.

Three men were in the hot seat.

As Rick moved closer, he could see that they were similarly dressed in coarsely woven dark-colored robes. Their strangely unnatural skin tones and hair color varied greatly. And yet there was something familiar about them, something that caught Rick in the pit of his stomach when the three turned around to regard him, something his thoughts and voice refused to make clear but his face betrayed.

"Yes," Captain Gloval said. "These... *men* are aliens."

Rick shook his head. Had Gloval taken leave of his senses?

The Zentraedi were giant warriors, *killers*! Their huge body parts and remains were scattered all over Macross City for one and all to see. Rick had seen to that! But even as his mind was shouting all this to his inner ear, an irrefutable realization was fighting its way to the surface.

"B-but *how*?" Rick stammered.

"Apparently those *were* reduction chambers that we saw, Lieutenant Hunter," said Lisa, picking up on his confusion and distress.

"It's pleasant to see you again, Lieutenant," said the grayfaced Zentraedi.

"Yes, not long ago you were in a similar position," added the heavy one.

A *similar position?* Rick asked himself. Then recognition joined realization: These three had been present during the interrogation!

"But what are they doing here, Commander?" Rick held his hands out in a gesture of uncertainty. "Were they captured, or, uh..."

"They have come in peace, Hunter."

"Voluntarily and at great personal risk," said Lisa. "They're asking for our protection."

Rick was stunned. "Protection? Are we supposed to say, 'All is forgiven, be my guest,' or what?" He turned to Gloval. "Have you seen Macross, Captain?"

"Relax, Lieutenant."

"Then what do you want from me—my tacit approval?"

"You're here for the same reason that I asked Commander Hayes and Lieutenant Sterling to join us: because you've had prior contact with the aliens."

Rick turned to the aliens. They were pressed together on the hot seat couch, expectant, almost jubilant looks on their faces.

"Why? What are your reasons for deserting, for wanting to join us? You don't know anything about us."

"We want to live the Micronian life," said Bron.

"There is happiness aboard this ship," said Kanda.

"Minmei is here," said Rico.

Rick was speechless. Did the alien really say "Minmei" or had he just imagined it? All of a sudden he felt nauseated. His voice sounded thin and strained as he asked them how they knew about Micronian ways and... *Minmei*. And their answer was even more surprising than he had feared.

"We have already lived among you as spies."

For Rick's benefit the captain recapped what had been learned in previous debriefing sessions with the aliens. How they had been inserted into the SDF-1 at the same time Lisa and Rick's Vermilion Team had made their great escape; how the three agents had walked unnoticed for weeks through Macross City; how they had made their own great escape from Bird Island; how tales of their exploits and disaffection with war had spread through the Zentraedi fleet; how there were more than a dozen others like them aboard the fortress even now; and how Minmei was at the center of it all.

"...And the most beautiful things of all were Minmei's singing and the fact that males and females, er, stayed together."

"Some people even spoke out against fighting," Rico added.

*Kyle!* Rick said to himself.

"Once we became used to it," Konda was saying, "we started to like living here."

"We can't go back," Bron reminded them.

"And what would be the sense, since it is known that you control the Protoculture."

All heads turned to purple-haired Konda.

"Exactly what is this 'Protoculture'?" asked Caruthers, speaking for the first time since Rick's entrance.

"You know exactly what it is," Bron said flatly.

"It's not nice to make fun of us."

Rico seemed to be sincere about it, but Gloval wanted to avoid the issue of Protoculture during this first session. He cleared his throat and asked Rich how he would feel about granting the aliens political asylum.

Rick had sensed it coming for a while and had been slowly formulating his thoughts. "I would be in favor of it," he told the panel. "If only as a first step toward a possible truce or peace." There was no need to mention the obvious military advantages to be gained once the aliens had been fully debriefed.

"I can't believe what I'm hearing," said Caruthers. "Just a moment ago you were reminding us of the atrocities that these... *creatures* had perpetrated on Macross, and now you're willing to grant them asylum."

"Really, Captain Gloval," Maistroff added, picking up the ball. "Don't you think we should be consulting with someone who has a clearer understanding of this entire matter? I, for one, am not convinced of their claims. This is a ruse."

"Hmmm," Gloval mused. "Anything you want to add, Hunter?"

Rick faced the colonels. "The aliens are bred for war and conquest. It's the only life they've known. But contact with our ways has erased who knows how many generations of aggressive conditioning almost overnight. Singing, marriage, love. Even a kiss can set them off—Commander Hayes and I indicated that much in our report."

"There has to be some attempt made at peace."

"Good lord, man!" said Caruthers, his fist striking the desktop. "You're talking about living with *aliens!*"

Maistroff mirrored the gesture. "They may *look* like us, Lieutenant Hunter, but don't be fooled: I'm certain that this is some sort of Zentraedi trap."

"You weren't aboard that Zentraedi cruiser, Colonel. I'm telling you, these three had their first taste of freedom aboard the SDF-1, and the word has already started to spread. By granting them asylum we're demonstrating that ours is the better life. We can create a mutiny in that fleet."

"If three are willing to desert," said Lisa, "three hundred will, then three thousand."

Caruthers laughed shortly. "Now, there's some nice emotional logic."

"We must make them understand that there are alternatives to war," Lisa continued. "If we can get them to understand another way of life, one that's not a matter of win or die, maybe we can change the focus of their lives and live with them in peace."

"Very eloquent," said Maistroff, applauding, his voice dripping sarcasm. "A truly excellent speech, Commander Hayes. But these are *aliens* we're dealing with. You can't possibly expect them to adapt to our way of life."

The three still-couched Zentraedi were turning their heads from speaker to speaker, trying to follow the conversation. Frowns of concern had replaced their initially confident expressions. Rico was about to say something, but just then someone knocked at the doorway and entered the Special Sessions room unannounced. It was one of Lang's white-frocked, glassy-eyed Robotechnicians.

"What is the meaning of this?" demanded Caruthers. "How dare you barge in like this?"

The man was carrying a file which he presented straightaway to Gloval, undaunted by Caruthers's reprimand. The captain returned a salute and aimed a dismissive gesture toward the colonel. "I asked Lang to have this sent to me as quickly as possible."

Gloval began to run through the file, uttering sounds of interest and surprise.

Max, Lisa, and Rick exchanged glances.

"What's he got there?" Sterling whispered.

"Lang's medical profiles on the aliens," Lisa returned.

The colonels were halfway out of their chairs peering at the file. "Well, what is it, Captain?" Maistroff asked at last.

Gloval passed him the file. "I had the laboratory analyze the aliens' cell structure. You may find this intriguing. As a matter of fact, I'm certain you will."

Save for the sound of pages being turned, the room was silent while Maistroff and Caruthers read. Ultimately the file began to shake in the colonel's hands.

"It's incredible! Why, their blood types and genetic structures are virtually identical to ours! We're effectively the same beings!"

This seemed to shock the three Zentraedi as much as anyone else in the room.

"I expected something like this," Lisa remarked.

"You could be right, Commander," said Max. "We might have a common ancestor race, after all."

"Well now, it seems to me that we can no longer treat these, ah, *people* as aliens. I believe we're safe in proceeding with this case as we would with any other request for political asylum."

"Hold on a minute, Gloval," Maistroff protested. "First of all, I don't think that the results of one lab test should influence the decisions of this council. As far as I'm concerned, Lang's evidence is inconclusive. Lord knows the man has reason enough to want to keep these three aboard. But that's beside the point. And so what if we *are* of similar genetic background? These men—and I use the term advisedly—are the enemies of this ship and all aboard her. I move for imprisonment until such time as their true purpose for being here can be ascertained."

Gloval listened closely, nodding his head, then said, "And as captain of this vessel, I say we grant these gentlemen political asylum."

The three Zentraedi were on their feet hugging each other even before the last word left the captain's mouth. Rick, Lisa, and Max risked guarded smiles. But Maistroff was enraged, standing at his chair and pounding the desk with his fist.

"We can't make a decision as important as this without first consulting the United Earth Defense Council!"

"You better hear him, *Captain*," Caruthers was saying.

"I accept the responsibility," Gloval answered them firmly.

Red-faced, Maistroff swallowed whatever it was he was going to say. He motioned to Caruthers that they should leave, but at the door he turned and promised: "You haven't heard the end of this, Gloval."

"Captain," Lisa said after a moment.

Gloval acknowledged her.

"We're going to have trouble with them. They won't let it go at this. They'll make contact with Earth HQ and try to get your decision overturned."

Gloval turned a weary face to all of them. "We are forced to take extraordinary measures. If the Earth Council wishes to continue denying the facts, then so be it. But aboard this ship I will decide. Let them doom themselves if they wish, but they will no longer sit in judgment of our fate."

# 14

"Rick, I'm going out of my head," [Max Sterling] would say to me.
"I've been searching the city since I saw her at the premiere, and no
one seems to know her or know where she lives. I mean, how can
that be? I thought everybody knew everybody in Macross! I swear
I'm in love with her; I'm going to ask her to marry me if I ever see her
again!" ...And I remember saying to him, "Sterling, you're going to
marry a girl with green hair?" It was a foolish enough remark given
the fact that Max had worn a blue tint in his hair ever since I'd known
him, but an absolute *riot* considering who Miriya turned out to be!

The Collected Journals of Admiral Rick Hunter

QUADRONO ACE MIRIYA PARINO DID A DOUBLE TAKE AS THE
Micronian work crew passed her on Macross Boulevard. It wasn't
the big smile on the foreman's face that caught her attention—
she was used to those appraising looks by now—but the equally
silly faces of a group of stragglers who seemed to have attached
themselves to this particular crew. This whistling happy-go-lucky
subgroup of males—there must have been ten of them—carried
their shovels and crude digging implements as if they were sacred
relics, and the ear-to-ear grins they wore (not directed toward Miriya,
in any case) appeared to radiate from some newfound inner sense of
wonder and exuberance. This in itself was not uncommon among
the Micronians, even in the midst of all the present devastation, but
there was something about the posturing and enthusiasm that led
Miriya to believe things were not entirely as they seemed.

She began to follow them along a course that wound its way

through the devastated city streets, across planks that spanned battle-created craters, through the burned-out hulks of houses and buildings, around carefully organized and sorted piles of debris and the slag-heap remains of mined mecha, and finally into the heavily damaged amphitheater, where the workers began an assault on the rubble. Assisted by massive Robotech droids and processors, the men and women threw themselves into the task with an unmatched display of discipline and commitment. The stragglers were no exception to this. But as Miriya moved in for a closer look, she recognized one of them: It was *Karita*—the Zentraedi officer assigned to the sizing chambers aboard Commander Breetai's flagship! Even those finely tailored Micronian trousers and that cardigan sweater could not disguise him.

As Miriya began to look around, she recognized several others from Breetai's ship and instantly realized what was going on. She had to congratulate the Commander on a brilliant plan. Obviously the Zentraedi attack against the population center was more in the way of a diversionary action. The actual purpose of the raid was to see to it that a sizable contingent of micronized agents was inserted into the dimensional fortress. Their mission was to infiltrate the work crews and attain firsthand knowledge of the Protocultural process that enabled the Micronians to effect repairs to their damaged Robotechnological devices—information long withheld from the Zentraedi by their Robotech Masters but something Zor would have wanted them to possess.

Miriya was content, she would be able to return to her own mission without having to concern herself with the progress of the war. Breetai was doing his part, Miriya, hers.

She left the amphitheater, pushing her way through throngs of busy Micronians, deliberately stepping between male-female couples whenever she had the opportunity.

Miriya was on her way to one of the fighter pilots' training centers— at least that was what she reasoned it to be. VIDEO ARCADE, she read above the doorway. Whatever that meant. Inside were two floors of electronic fighter-training devices for young Micronians. It was no wonder the so-called VT pilots were so adept at handling their mecha;

they were trained from infancy to fly and fight. Several of the training devices were even designed to perpetuate archaic hand-to-hand combat techniques. Miriya had become fascinated by one of these in particular, a device called "Knife-Fight." It was possible that when the time came for Miriya to face off with her Micronian archenemy, there would be no battle mecha available. She therefore planned to prepare herself for any and all eventualities.

"What are you looking at, Rick?"

"That girl," he started to say.

"She was pretty rude if you ask me, pushing between us like that when she could just as easily have stepped to the side."

"Yeah, but that green hair…"

"You find that attractive?"

"No… no, of course not, Lisa. It's just that Max has been looking all over for some green-haired girl, and that might be her."

"Tell Max she's rude."

"Yeah, sure, but did you see where she went?"

"I really wasn't looking, Rick."

"Must've turned off into one of those stores, maybe the arcade."

"Do you want to stop and look for her or what?"

"Huh? No, no way. I'll just let Max know that I saw her."

"You do that."

They were on a walking tour of the damage; no particular place to go. People were scrambling around getting things done, taking care of business, fixing this and that. "Public works," one of Rick's more cynical VT friends had said, "keeps their minds off the war."

"Is it like this all over?" Lisa asked, wanting to change the subject.

Rick nodded. "Nearly every part of the city was damaged in the attack."

"I wonder what the casualty figures will be like."

"I don't know," said Rick. And he didn't want to know.

Eventually their wanderings brought them around to the White Dragon. (*Let Rick have the lead and you always seem to end up here,* Lisa told herself.) The building itself looked untouched, but an overturned delivery van was still smoldering in the street. There were enormous breaches in the overhead tier in this section-jagged holes and lightning fissures. Uncle Max and his wife Lena, Macross City's oddest couple, were just exiting from the hexagonally shaped doorway. Rick called out to them and broke into a run.

"Rick!" said Max. "What in the world are you doing here? Are you all right?"

"I'm fine, but what about you? Where are you two off to?"

"We've been worried sick about Kyle and Minmei," said Aunt Lena. "We heard that the Star Bowl was practically destroyed, and I just can't stand waiting around here any longer, praying they'll show up."

Max took his wife's hand and gave it a reassuring squeeze.

"They're at the hospital," Rick told them. "But there's no need to worry; they're both fine."

"Oh, thank God!" said Lena.

"Kyle is bruised up, but Minmei just went along to hold, ah, look after him, see that he was all right."

"Do you think we'd be allowed to see them, Rick?"

"It's a bit of a mess over there right now," said Lisa. "But they'll let you through, I'm certain of it."

Rick suggested that they give it a try and spontaneously volunteered to keep an eye on the restaurant during their absence. Lisa agreed to help, and Rick's surrogate family hurried off.

Inside, they had their work cut out for them. Large portions of water-damaged gypsum board had collapsed from the ceiling; water dripped from a broken overhead pipe. Tables and chairs were overturned; pictures had fallen from the walls; the remains of dishes and glassware shaken from cabinets littered the floor. On every horizontal surface from the smallest ledge to the only still-standing table was a gritty black coating of resinous ash. Ultimately the entire place was going to need a couple of coats of paint, but until then they could at least take care of the custodial chores—cleaning, sweeping, scrubbing.

Rick opted for the shovel and broom detail while Lisa attacked the tables and chairs with a detergent fluid. Rick noticed that she hummed to herself while she worked. It brought a smile to his face each time she stepped from behind that commander's mask.

Here she was being *domestic*… Here *he* was being domestic! And he actually felt good, just losing himself in the mindlessness of it and seeing immediate results for a change. There was a beginning and an end to this task.

Two hours later the mess had been cleared, the tables and chairs uprighted.

"You know what would be good right now, Rick? A cup of fresh tea. I'll do the honors."

Rick said, "Be my guest," and walked over to straighten one last picture. It was a framed photo of Minmei taken over a year earlier, sometime after the Miss Macross pageant. He reached out a gloved hand and tipped it back to vertical, the harsh memory of that stage kiss replaying itself as he did so, a continuous loop that time and endless viewing had yet to erase. *It's over now,* he was saying to himself when Lisa entered from the kitchen with two cups.

*I've lost her to stage, screen, Kyle, and now to the enemy!*

"Don't burn yourself," she warned him.

They sat at one of the tables overlooking the street. Work crews had moved into the area to cart off debris and undertake floor-by-floor searches of each building. Lisa watched a group of strange-looking men busy themselves clearing rubble as she sipped her tea. They seemed downright *enthusiastic,* and it got her to thinking.

"You know, Rick, these simple activities don't mean much to us, but to the Zentraedi our everyday, humdrum world must seem wonderful by comparison. It doesn't surprise me at all that Rico and those other two decided to defect. Sometimes I think *I'd* like to desert. Just forget about the military and get myself back to basics." She laughed to herself. "Get myself *back.* Listen to me. I've never even *been* there."

"Are you thinking about the Zentraedi or Kyle?" Rick asked smugly.

She grinned wryly. "It's a pipe dream, and I know it. I'm Ms. Military, and he hates the military. Great way to begin a relationship, right? But it's true that I've been nursing some doubts since I met him. He's a ghost who's come back to haunt me. Everything about him: his looks, all his antiwar speeches. I keep seeing Karl. And it doesn't help any when we've got to hear Maistroff and Caruthers expressing the same old… you know what I'm talking about."

"So much for playing it by the book, huh?"

"Who knows? And as for Lynn-Kyle, he doesn't know I exist. I've got two strikes against me: this uniform and Minmei." She saw Rick's face grow long and apologized.

"If you don't want to talk about it..."

"There's nothing to talk *about*." Rick turned his face away. "I'm angrier at myself than I am with her. I mean, how could I have been so *sure* that we shared something when as far as she was concerned we were just friends? Someday you'll have to get me drunk and I'll tell you all about our wonderful two weeks together in the basement of this ship."

"I'm a good listener, Rick. I'm not going to judge you or anything."

He shook his head. "Maybe some other time. I'm just sick of getting all twisted up by the whole thing. Let her stay with her cousin. Let her marry him for all I care. I just wanna have all this behind me for a change. It's really *bizarre*, and that's the long and short of it. Back on Earth I could at least move to another town or another country. But we're all stuck on the ship for the duration, the whole nine yards. Just one big happy family of space wanderers."

He had tears in his eyes when he looked at Lisa again, but his voice was self-mocking. "This was probably how it was at the beginning, a few thousand hominids running around the Serengeti and every one of them in love with the wrong person."

Lisa laughed and covered her mouth with her hand.

"I think you're writing yourself off too soon, Rick. Maybe it'll just take time. Have you ever actually told her how you feel?"

Rick shrugged. "My actions speak for me."

"Not enough. Sometimes it's just not enough. You have to tell her. Otherwise, she's in the dark and Kyle *will* take her away. Of course, you'll get to hold on to your regrets and your self-pity..."

Lisa recalled Claudia telling her as much.

"Is that what I'm doing? Is that how you really see it?" His watery eyes were locked on hers, searching.

She exhaled slowly.

And a warning siren went off outside.

"Another attack!" said Lisa, jumping up from the table. "You better get back to the base! I'll lock up in here and meet you at the rail line!"

"Don't take too long," he told her from the doorway. "Sammie can't handle your station!"

"Be careful!" she called after him, but he was already gone.

"Enemy battle mecha," said Claudia Grant. "Course heading zero-zero-niner, Third Quadrant. Looks like the same group to me, Captain."

Gloval agreed with her assessment after studying the readout. The same two dozen Zentraedi pods and fighters had appeared on the threat board after the attack on Macross, moving erratically from quadrant to quadrant, half the time in pursuit of the fortress and at other times speeding from it. There was reason to believe that these were the very ships that had escaped from the fortress after the CD forces had gained the upper hand. Perhaps, Gloval now speculated, under the command of this apparently crazed Zentraedi officer named Khyron, whom the three defectors had mentioned over and over, sometimes referring to him as "the Backstabber." Rico had actually credited him with more Battlepod kills than the combined total of the Defense Forces.

"Skull Team is up and away, Captain," Gloval heard Sammie report from Lisa's station. He noticed that her foot was tapping nervously. "Kirkland," she continued, "prepare to supply cover. They'll be coming about on your right flank."

"*Left* flank," Claudia corrected her. "Their cat's away from *Prometheus.*"

"Uh, scratch that, Kirkland. Look for Delta on your left flank. Indigo, your signal is 'buster.' Return to base immediately. Uh, uh… *Damn it!* Where is Commander Hayes? I'm going crazy—"

"Right behind you, Sammie," Lisa said breathlessly. She turned a quick salute to the captain: "Sorry I was delayed, sir."

"It's all yours," Sammie said, stepping aside.

"Estimate five minutes to contact," said Vanessa.

Gloval glanced over at the board. The Zentraedi warships were still holding at their postattack coordinates. What could this small contingent of pods have in mind?

"Looks like a kamikaze run," said Claudia. "They should know better than that by now."

Lisa turned to her. "Judging from what the defectors had to say, I wouldn't put it past them to try anything from now on." She raised Skull Leader on the net. "Bandits will be in your face in three minutes, Lieutenant."

"Roger," Rick answered her. "I show them on wide beam."

"Try telling them to go home, Lieutenant Hunter."

Rick's laugh came through the speaker, followed by a loud and seemingly sincere, "Go home!"

Still unwilling to rule out miracles, Lisa checked the displays.

"Uh, sorry, Skull Leader. Nice try, but it didn't work."

"I copy that, Commander. Guess we've gotta speak to them in the only language they understand."

Lisa's screen began to light up; the enemy mecha had opened fire. Skull and the other teams were engaging them. Radar blips began to disappear from the board, VTs and enemy paint.

"Never say die, Rick," she said softly into her mike.

# 15

...But if such a contest existed, I would cast my vote without
hesitation for Khyron—history's principal man in the middle.
Distrusted by Dolza, dismissed by Breetai, feared by his own troops,
and now fixed upon by the "Micronians," Khyron had moved into
what might be called transparanoia (or better still, metanoia). He
simply was all those things normal paranoid personality types delude
themselves into believing: persecuted, grandiose, and essentially
pivotal in the great scheme of things.

Rawlins, *Zentraedi Triumvirate: Dolza, Breetai, Khyron*

THE ZENTRAEDI FLAGSHIP HAD SELF-SEALED ITSELF; AN
undetectable patch of green armor covered the damage done
to its blunt nose by the ramming arm of the fortress—a design
feature the Robotech Masters had engineered into the ships of
the fleet. Would that breaches in command were so easily sealed,
thought Breetai, and breaches in discipline.

Just now he was pacing the floor of the observation booth, as
always, under the analytical gaze of his misshapen adviser.

Though limited in emotional range, the Zentraedi commander
had run the gamut of available responses since the inception
of Exedore's plan to assault the SDF-1 right through to Khyron's
news of mass desertion among the ranks. Things had looked
good early on: He had forced the Micronians to launch their so-
called *Daedalus* Maneuver, their Destroids had been destroyed, and
Regault squads had been successfully inserted into the fortress.
There were indications of a massive battle having taken place in the

population center inside the Robotech ship; the Micronians had recalled most of their fighters to deal with the threat, and follow-up transmissions on the tac net suggested that the Zentraedi had scored a decisive victory. Much to Breetai's and Exedore's surprise, Khyron's Botoru teams had also infiltrated the enemy's defense. Breetai had grown confident of a sure Micronian surrender. Zor's Protoculture matrix would soon be his, and with it would come greater glory than any had hitherto known.

But then word had been received from Khyron about the desertions.

Breetai refused to believe it.

"This must be the tremendous force the Robotech Masters have been speaking of," Exedore said. "The legends have been most specific: Continued contact with Micronians is to be avoided at all costs. They are said to be in possession of a secret weapon which could ultimately destroy us, leaving this quadrant wide open for an attack by the Invid. I have long dreaded this day, m'lord."

Breetai expected no less; his advisor had been quoting the legends to him since that first day when the fleet defolded from hyperspace near the Micronians' homeworld.

"So you think I should have paid attention to those ancient warnings, do you?"

"Perhaps, m'lord."

"And what of Commander in Chief Dolza, Exedore? What would we do about him?"

"The question remains not what we *would* have done, Commander," Exedore countered, "but what we *will* do about him."

Desertion had turned the battle around. Although Breetai had yet to formulate a clear picture of the events, Commander Khyron reported that he had been forced to take punitive measures against some of the Zentraedi troops. Soldiers had been abandoning their mecha and expressing a wish to live among the Micronians. Some sort of psychological assault had been launched against them— Khyron said that the deserters had referred to it as a "Minmei." Obviously the perfected form of the weapon the Micronians had been experimenting with for at least a year by their own reckoning.

Breetai recalled those early days: the low-frequency transmissions from the fortress which had so confused Exedore's three Cyclops operatives, and later, the disturbing effects produced by the male and female captives. Subsequently there was the strange behavior of the returned spies and the trans-vids of that Micronian battle record and death ray demonstration.

*The secrets of Protoculture were theirs!*

Driven from the dimensional fortress, Khyron had since been pursuing a group of potential deserters, dispatching them one by one. He now had them regrouped and headed again toward the SDF-1 on a suicide run. Breetai, however, was having second thoughts: It was too late to undo any of his past mistakes, but he might yet be able to profit from this latest upset. Commander Azonia had informed him that Quadrono leader Miriya was still aboard the fortress. Surely she'd see to it that the deserters wouldn't live long enough to do the Zentraedi any harm. And as for these few stragglers...

"Tell Khyron to call off his attack," Breetai now told his advisor. "We will remove all our troops from Micronian influence immediately."

Exedore bowed slightly. "And then, m'lord?"

"Interrogate the deserters. You must see if you can determine the nature of this power the Micronians have exerted. We may yet find a way to resist their control."

"It shall be done."

Khyron had centered one of the Battlepods in his targeting screen. It would require only a glancing blow to the upper right of the sphere to bring the thing back into line. Mustn't let them stray too far from the fold, he said to himself. *All Micronian sympathizers have to stick together.* He was just elevating one of the mecha's handguns and bringing it to bear on the pod when Exedore raised him on the comlink.

Breetai's orders were relayed.

"Isolate the deserters and lock them up?!" Khyron shouted into his communicator. "Exedore, are you mad? What next, if we let them get away with this?"

"You have your orders, Commander."

Khyron slammed his fist down on the control console of the Officer's Pod. "We might just as well surrender to the Micronians!"

"Order your troops about, Commander. Commander Breetai has ordered me to employ the nebulizer if you fail to comply."

"And what about the deserters aboard that ship?" Khyron demanded. "Do you realize what damage they can do?"

"Miriya will see to them, Commander."

Khyron was stunned. "Miriya? Miriya Parino is aboard— *micronized?!* Why wasn't I informed of this?"

"That is Commander Breetai's prerogative," Exedore said plainly. "Bah!"

Khyron shut down the comlink. So this was how it was going to be, he said to himself. New lines were being drawn. And sooner or later he and Breetai were going to find themselves on opposite sides. A sinister smile began to surface. Let Breetai have his deserters, the infected ones. The illness would spread through his fleet like an epidemic, and Dolza would hear about it. With both Azonia and Breetai out of the way, Khyron would be put in command. Then the real purge would commence; and not just against the Micronians but against *all* those who defied the Zentraedi imperative!

Human and Zentraedi mecha met head-on, crisscrossing silently in space at skirmish speed. The Veritechs held back their fire until the last possible moment, then unleashed a storm of missiles and gatling rounds at the Battlepods and triple-fins. Spherical explosions threw short-lived light against the night. Below them was the dark face of the Earth, undisturbed and unconcerned.

Skull One's retros flared briefly to bleed the fighter of velocity as ventral thrusters provided its lift, tipping the ship over so that Earth was now above Rick for a moment. Most of the pods had also doubled back but had yet to return fire. VTs from Vermillion and Blue teams were blowing them out of space like sitting ducks. And where Lisa had been expecting a kamikazelike attack, there was only a full-scale retreat. Rick moved to within striking distance of two ostriches, his front fuselage guns blazing, but the enemy refused to engage him; they simply rolled and showed him the red glow of their foot thrusters.

"Certain reluctance out here or am I imagining things?" said Vermilion Leader over the tac net.

"I copy that, V Leader," someone added.

"Skull One, do we pursue?"

"Uh, affirmative, V Leader," said Rick. "Let's go see what they're up to."

The Veritechs regrouped and boostered off after the retreating Battlepods. Rick was the first to spot the Officer's Pod; it seemed to be taking aim at one of its own, herding the mecha back into formation with the rest. Rick hit his afterburners and homed in on it.

He couldn't hold the enemy officer in the reticle but had a good view of the ship on his forward scopes. It had to be the same one! Rick convinced himself. There were no telltale markings of any kind—it was easily as worn, scorched, and scratched as the rest of them—but that pilot seemed to have his own signature. And from what the defectors had divulged, the name attached to that craft would be "Khyron"—someone they seemed to fear above all else.

Rick noticed two VTs from Blue making their approach against the Officer's Pod. But Khyron was alert to their scheme and went after them in a frenzy, handguns blasting away, top-mounted cannon erupting in salvos of death. Both Veritechs sustained hits and disintegrated in the ensuing explosions.

Meanwhile Rick was certain he had the drop on the pod. Distracted by the two fighters, his quarry had turned his back to him, all guns forward. But as Skull One sped in for the shot, the pod swiveled and caught sight of him. Rick launched three missiles regardless, but pulsed bombardment detonated the first, and the second and third fell to fratricide.

The tables were turned all of a sudden. The pod had a good opportunity to tail Rick and slide easily into position for that lethal cone release, but in the interim, Khyron's charges had escaped his control. So instead of jumping on Rick, the pod turned around to reshepherd its widespread flock.

"They seem to be breaking off for good, Lieutenant," said the Vermilion Leader.

Rick breathed a sigh of relief before he went on the net. "Have your teams pull back to the fortress." He then raised Max on the commo screen.

"Scanners show warships along our heading, Skull One."

"All right, Max. Looks like they decided to go home, after all. Let's do the same."

One by one the Veritechs retroed and began to reverse their headings. The SDF-1, reconfigured to Cruiser mode now, was waiting for them in the space above Earth's sunny side.

Later, Lisa met with Captain Gloval in his quarters. Ever since colonels Maistroff and Caruthers had walked out on the asylum session, she had been searching for some way to counteract their influence with the United Earth Defense Council. Should the UEDC leaders overturn Gloval's ruling, there was no telling what might become of the defectors. For all anyone aboard the SDF-1 knew, Rico and his companions could possess some means of spreading the word, good or bad, back to the Zentraedi fleet. They had stated that there were ten other micronized soldiers in hiding. And perhaps those ten were prepared to engage in acts of sabotage if asylum was refused. Things hadn't gone very well with her father the last time they met, but surely he would have to be open-minded now, in light of these recent developments and the new physical evidence of a possible link between humans and Zentraedi. She told Gloval as much.

"You know I'm right, sir. When we granted asylum to those defectors, we changed this whole conflict. We're defending their desire to adopt our values. If I don't go to Earth and line up some support, we might very well be ordered to send them back."

Gloval had his back to her while he listened. But now he swung away from the starfield view out the portside bay and faced her. He was skeptical.

"Our dealings with the Council have proved less than satisfying so far. What makes you think you'll be able to convince them now?"

"I'm not *promising* anything, Captain. But we do have new evidence on our side. If I can just get my father behind us."

"That's a very large *if*, Lisa."

"The results of Dr. Lang's lab tests should be enough to reopen a dialogue with the Council if nothing else. The Zentraedi race and the human race are essentially the same. They could be our long-lost brothers and sisters. If that isn't compelling enough, I don't know what is."

"You're determined to make this work."

"Yes, sir. I'm aware of what you said after the session—that you're no longer going to let the Council dictate to this ship—but I would hate to see things go in that direction. No matter how disaffected the civilians are, Macross will never be the same after that attack. They have to be disembarked and resettled on Earth. What can we do otherwise? Search the galaxy for some hospitable world? If we still had our fold generators that might be possible, but given the speeds we can attain... I don't have to tell you this, Captain."

Gloval waved his hand dismissively. "You're right to say it. I need to hear it sometimes."

Lisa perched herself on the corner of his desk. "We've been lucky. But how much longer can this go on? Even if the Zentraedi never achieve a decisive victory, they're going to succeed in whittling us down to nothing. Our stores are not inexhaustible. And God knows, our Defense Force isn't inexhaustible. And no matter what the Council proclaims—no matter what they threaten us with—this ship is *not* expendable. We are the only thing that stands between the Zentraedi armada and the Earth itself." Lisa motioned out the bay to the stars. "They have over one *million* warships out there! We're losing sight of that because we've been lucky and they've been foolish. But even in the best of winning streaks luck has an uncanny way of reversing itself. We have to come to terms with the Council and the Zentraedi. I think the appearance of the defectors is the first step in that process, and *they* took it. Maybe we've already done our part by offering asylum, but I'm convinced we have to go further. I've got to get to my father before Maistroff and Caruthers get to him."

Gloval tugged at his mustache. "It could be risky, Lisa."

"How, sir?"

"Because your father wants you off this ship. And if we lose you now..."

She smiled at him. "You have Sammie, Captain. She'll get the hang of it."

Gloval snorted. "Sammie will someday make a proper First Officer, but she lacks your overall knowledge of this fortress. You are needed here, Lisa."

"Thank you, sir," she said, lowering her gaze. "But this war *must* be stopped. Let me try this approach, Captain. I promise you I won't let my father prevent my return."

Gloval nodded and exhaled loudly. "All right, you have my permission. But think carefully before you decide to disobey any orders from the Council. Remember who and what you are, Lisa."

She stood up sharply and saluted him. "I'll begin working on a joint report tonight and have a draft for you in the morning."

Gloval stood up and extended his hand to her. "You'll leave as soon as possible."

Lisa was already formulating her report when she left the captain's quarters, experimenting with wording and editing, choosing the phrases and approach that would work best with her father. She was so wrapped up in this process that she got halfway to the bridge before realizing that she was supposed to be headed to her barracks. Turning around, she became preoccupied with a different train of thought: It was possible that she might never set foot on the bridge again. Captain Gloval was right; her father wanted her off the SDF-1, and he would try to make good his demands this time—especially after hearing the news she was bringing. She could hear him now: *What?! Aliens aboard the fortress?! A-and Gloval's granted them political asylum? A-and you expect me to allow you to return to that ship of fools?!*

This started her thinking along the line of "last thoughts": This might be the last time she walked this corridor, the last time she slept in her quarters, the last time she saw her crewmates— Claudia, Sammie, Kim, Vanessa… and Rick. What would Rick say if he knew she was leaving?

Had Lisa walked directly to the elevator, she would have had an opportunity to ask him in person, because the lieutenant had stepped off a moment before she arrived. And it would have been doubly interesting considering that he had been wondering how she might react to his asking her out to dinner.

But fate operated along the same lines then as it does today, and her autopilot wrong turn along the corridor had erased all chance of a meeting. Dinner would have to wait—for quite a while if the truth be permitted at this stage of the narrative. And not onboard the SDF-1, either. Events were about to take a twist everyone had feared but no one had dared anticipate. The war was about to escalate. Death was about to gain the upper hand. Rick and Lisa *would* meet again, but against a landscape that would overshadow any joy such a reunion might ordinarily bring.

# VOLUME 02
# FORCE OF ARMS

FOR BONNIE BADER,
AND HER WORK ON THIS PROJECT

# PART 1:
# SHOWDOWN

# PROLOGUE

IN THE 1990S, A GLOBAL CIVIL WAR SWEPT ACROSS THE PLANET Earth; few wanted this war, but no one seemed to be able to avert it. It absorbed all the smaller disparate wars, rebellions, and terrorist struggles in the same way a huge storm vacuums up all the lesser weather systems around it.

The War was fought with conventional weapons for the most part, but by 1999 it was clear that its escalation pointed directly to an all-out nuclear exchange—planetary obliteration. There seemed to be nothing any sane person could do about it. By then, the War had a life of its own.

As the human race prepared to die—for everyone knew that the final phase of the War would surely exterminate all life on Earth, the fragile lunar and Martian research colonies, and the various orbital constructs—something like a malign miracle happened.

A damaged starship—a super dimensional fortress created by

the dying alien mastermind, Zor—appeared in Earth's skies. It crashed on a tiny Pacific island called Macross. Its descent wreaked more havoc than any war: there was tremendous damage and loss of life and numerous natural disasters. The human race was compelled to pause and take stock of itself.

Zor had served the evil Robotech Masters, but he had resolved to serve them no more and had hidden his ultimate secrets concerning Protoculture—the most powerful force in the universe—in the fortress. The Robotech Masters needed those secrets not only to conquer the universe but to protect themselves from the vengeful attacks of the savage Invid, a race of creatures sworn to destroy them.

Thus, the focus of an intergalactic conflict came to bear on the formerly insignificant Earth.

The super dimensional fortress was Earth's first inkling of the greater events taking place outside the bounds of human knowledge. Earth's leaders saw at once that the wrecked SDF-1 could be rebuilt and become a rallying point that would unite a divided human race.

A ten-year project began, incorporating the brains and energies of the entire planet. But on the day the SDF-1 was to be relaunched to guard humanity from alien attack, disaster struck again. The Zentraedi—the Robotech Masters' giant race of ferocious warrior clones—struck, bringing devastation to the Earth in an effort to recapture the SDF-1.

The desperate crew of the SDF-1 attempted a spacefold jump to get clear of the attack. Yet a miscalculation resulted in the ship's reappearance far from its intended destination: The SDF-1 and most of the civilian population of Macross Island were suddenly transported out to the orbit of the planet Pluto.

And so the long, perilous voyage back to Earth began. The SDF-1 battled for its life, hounded by the Zentraedi armada at every turn. Returning after more than a year, the crew found that it was no longer welcome on the homeworld—in the view of the ruling powers, they constituted too much of a danger to Earth's safety as well as the rulers' own authority.

A renewed Zentraedi offensive resulted in horrendous casualties on Earth and reinforced the Earth leaders' determination to refuse haven to the SDF-1—even though it had waged the only meaningful resistance to alien invasion.

So the great star battleship was forced to ride an orbit to nowhere, its crew and civilian refugees struggling desperately to stay alive. The Zentraedi continued to plot new war plans, determined to have the ship and the secrets of Protoculture.

Alien agents were planted within the ship, reduced from their fifty- and sixty-foot heights to human size. These spies found themselves strangely affected by the experience of human life as their long-dormant emotions were awakened by the sight of humans mingling and showing affection and in particular by the singing of Minmei— the ship's superstar and media idol and the mainstay of its morale.

Upon their return to the invasion fleet, the spies' stories and souvenirs of their experiences among the humans led to the defection of a dozen and more of the Zentraedi and disobedience in the ranks of those who remained behind.

Aboard the SDF-1, human life fell into patterns of conflict and emotion. Lieutenant Rick Hunter, fighter pilot in the Robotech Defense Forces, experienced constant confusion and turmoil over his love for Minmei and simultaneous attraction to Commander Lisa Hayes, the SDF-1's First Officer.

This triangle formed the core of a larger web of loves and hates, the sort of human emotional blaze that the colossal Zentraedi found so baffling and *debilitating*.

Nevertheless, the Zentraedi imperative was battle, and battle it would be. The aliens deployed a million-plus ships in their armada, restrained from all-out attack only by their need to capture the SDF-1's Protoculture secrets intact.

Breetai, commander of the invasion force, moved in his own intrigues against two of his rebellious subordinates: Azonia, the female warlord, and Khyron the Backstabber, psychotic demon of battle.

But the Robotech War proved to be far more complex than any of them—Zentraedi or human—could have ever imagined.

Dr. Lazlo Zand,
*On Earth As It Is in Hell:*
*Recollections of the Robotech War*

# 01

I guess Max was the most conspicuous example of the growing war weariness and hunger for peace. As the top VT pilot, he was revered by all the aspiring hot-daggers and would-be aces.

When he came back from a mission, his aircraft maintenance people would always stencil the symbols for his latest kills on the side of his ship; that was their right. But like a lot of us who had been in the eye of the storm for too long, he began avoiding the jokes and high-fives and swaggering in the ready rooms, barracks, and officers' club. He was still top man on the roster, but it was plain that his attitude was changing.

The Collected Journals of Admiral Rick Hunter

"YA AIN'T SO BIG NOW, ARE YA, YA FREAKIN' ALIEN?" THE BIG BRUISER said, shaking a scarred first the size of a roast in his face.

Well, no, he wasn't. Karita *had* been a Zentraedi soldier some forty feet tall. But now, having been reduced to the size of a human and defecting to their side in the Robotech War, he was only a medium-build, slightly-less-than-average-height fellow facing three hulking brawlers eager to split his head wide open in a Macross alley.

Even as a Zentraedi, Karita hadn't excelled at combat; his main duty had been tending the Protoculture sizing chambers, the very same ones in which he had been micronized. The situation looked hopeless; the three ringed him in, fists cocked, light from the distant streetlamps illuminating the hatred in their faces.

He tried to dodge past them, but they were too fast. The biggest grabbed him and hurled him against the wall. Karita dropped, half-stunned, the back of his scalp bleeding.

He cursed himself for his carelessness; a slip of the tongue in the restaurant had given him away. Otherwise, no one could have told him apart from any other occupant of the SDF-1.

But he could scarcely be blamed. The wonders of life aboard the super dimensional fortress were enough to make any Zentraedi careless. The humans had rebuilt their city; they mingled, both sexes, all ages. They lived lives in which emotions were given free expression, and there was an astonishing force called "love."

It was enough to make any Zentraedi, born into a Spartan, merciless warrior culture with strict segregation of the sexes, forget himself. And so Karita had made his error; he had gone into the White Dragon in the hopes of getting a glimpse of Minmei. He didn't realize what he was saying when he let slip the fact that he had adored her since he had first seen her image on a Zentraedi battlecruiser. Then he saw the hard looks the trio gave him. He left quickly, but they followed.

During the course of the war, everybody aboard had lost at least one friend or loved one. The Zentraedi, too, had suffered losses—many more than the SDF-1, in fact. That didn't stop Karita and the other defectors from hoping for a new life among their former enemies. Most humans were at least tolerant of the Zentraedi who'd deserted from their invading armada. Some humans even *liked* the aliens; three of them, former spies, had human girlfriends. But he should have known there would be humans who wouldn't see things that way.

The three closed in on him.

One of the men launched a kick Karita was too dazed to avoid. It was not so much a sharp pain he felt as a tremendous, panic-making numbness. He wondered woozily if his ribs were broken. Not that it mattered; it didn't look like his attackers were going to stop short of killing him. They didn't realize that they had picked on one of the most unmilitary of Zentraedi; given a different one, they would have had more of a fight on their hands.

One of them drew back his heavy work boot to kick Karita

again; Karita closed his eyes, waiting for the blow. But the sudden sound of shoe leather sliding on pavement and the thud of a falling body made him reopen them.

He looked up to see one of the assailants down and the other two turning to face an interloper.

Max Sterling didn't look like the conventional image of a Veritech ace. The brilliant Robotech Defense Force flier was slender, wore blue-tinted aviator glasses—with *corrective* lenses—and dyed his hair blue in keeping with the current fad for wild colors.

This young RDF legend looked mild, even vulnerable. In a time of crisis, Max Sterling had risen from obscurity to dazzle humanity and the Zentraedi with his matchless combat flying. But that hadn't changed his basic humility and self-effacing good-naturedness.

"No more," Max told the assailants quietly. The bully on the ground shook his head angrily. Max stepped between the other two, went to Karita's side, and knelt, offering his hand.

Minmei's Aunt Lena had watched the ominous trio follow Karita when he left the White Dragon; it took her a few minutes to find Sterling, so Max said, "Sorry I'm a little late."

This bookish-looking young man who held the highest kill score of any combat pilot in the ship offered the Zentraedi his hand. "D' you think you can stand?"

The attacker Max had floored was back on his feet, eyeing Max's RDF uniform. "You have two seconds to butt out of this, kid."

Max rose and turned, leaving Karita sitting against the wall. He took off his glasses and dropped them into Karita's limp hand.

"I guess there's gonna be a fight here, so let's get one thing straight: In case you missed the news, this man isn't our enemy. Now, are you going to let us by or what?"

Of course not. They had looked at Karita and automatically thought, *We can take him!* And that had decided the matter. Now here was the pale, unimposing Max, and their assessment was the same: *We can take him, too. No sweat.*

So the one Max had knocked down came at him first, while the others fanned out on either side.

Max didn't wait. He ducked under a powerful, slow haymaker and struck with the heel of his hand, breaking the first one's nose. A second attacker, a thick-bodied man in coveralls, hooked his fist around with all his might, but Max simply wasn't there. Dodging like a ghost, he landed a solid jab to the man's nose, bloodying it, and stepped out of the way as he staggered.

There wasn't much fighting room, and Max's usual style involved plenty of movement. But it didn't matter very much this time; he didn't want to leave Karita unprotected.

The third vigilante, younger, leaner, and faster than the other two, swung doubled fists at him from behind. Max avoided the blow, adding momentum with a quick, hard tug so that the man went toppling to his knees. Then Max spun precisely so that he had his back nearly up against the first attacker and rammed his elbow back.

The man's breath rushed out of him as he clutched his midsection. Max snapped a fist back into his face, then turned to plant a sidelong kick to the gut of the one in the coveralls. The incredible reflexes and speed that served him so well in dogfights were plain; he was difficult to see much less hit or avoid.

Karita had struggled to his feet. "Stop!"

The three attackers were battered up a bit, but the fight had barely started. Max Sterling wasn't even breathing hard.

"No more fighting," Karita labored, clutching his side. "Hasn't there been enough?"

The first man wiped blood from a swelling lip, studying Max. Indicating Karita with a toss of his head, he said, "Him and his kind killed my son. I don't care what you—"

"Look at this," Max said quietly. He displayed the RDF patch on his uniform, a diamond with curved sides, like a fighting kite. "You think *I* don't understand? But listen t' me: *He's* out of the war. Just like *I* want to be and *you* want to be.

"But we're never going to have peace unless we put the damn war behind us! So drop it, all right? Or else, c'mon: Let's finish this thing."

The first man was going to come at him again, but the other two grabbed his shoulders from either side. The young one said, "All right—for now."

Max supported Karita with his shoulder, and the three stepped aside to let them pass. There was a tense moment as the pilot and the injured alien walked between the attackers; one of them shifted his weight, as if reconsidering his decision.

But he thought better of it and held his place, saying, "What about you, flyboy? You're goin' out there again to fight 'em, aren't ya? To kill 'em if ya can?"

Max knew that Karita was staring at him, but he answered. "Yeah. Maybe I'll wind up killing somebody a lot like your son tonight. Or he'll wind up killing me. Who knows?"

Max put Karita into a cab and sent him to the temporary quarters where the defectors were housed. He didn't have time to go along; he was late for duty as it was.

Waiting for another cab, Max gazed around at the rebuilt city of Macross. Overhead, the Enhanced Video Emulation system had created the illusion of a Terran night sky, blocking out the view of a distant alloy ceiling.

It had been a long time since Max or any of the SDF-1's other inhabitants had seen the real thing. He was already defying the odds, having survived so many combats. The EVE illusion was nice, but he hoped he'd get to see the true sky and hills and oceans of Earth again before his number came up.

Elsewhere on the SDF-1, two women rode in an uncomfortable silence on an elevator descending to a hangar deck, watching the level indicators flash.

Commander Lisa Hayes, the ship's First Officer, wasn't at ease with many people. But Lieutenant Claudia Grant, standing now with arms folded and avoiding Lisa's gaze as Lisa avoided hers, had been a close friend—perhaps Lisa's only true friend—for years.

Lisa tried to lighten the gloom. "Well, here I go again. Off for another skirmish with the brass."

That was certainly putting the best face on it. No previous effort had convinced the United Earth Defense Council to either begin peace negotiations with the Zentraedi invaders or allow the SDF-1 and its civilian refugees to return home. Lisa had volunteered to try again, to present shocking new evidence that had just emerged and exert all the pressure she could on her father, Admiral Hayes, to get him to see reason and then persuade the rest of the UEDC.

Claudia looked up. They were an odd pair: Claudia, tall and exotic-looking, several years older than Lisa, with skin the color of dark honey; and Lisa, pallid and slender, rather plain-looking until one looked a little closer.

Claudia tried to smile, running a hand through her tight brown curls. "I don't know whether it'll help or not to say this, but stop looking so grim. Girl, you remind me of the captain of a sinking ship when he finds out they substituted deck chairs for the lifeboats. It's gonna be hard to change people's minds like that. Besides, all they can do is say no again."

There was a lot more to it than that, of course. Admiral Hayes was not likely to let his only child leave Earth—to return to the SDF-1 and the endless Zentraedi attacks—once she was in the vast UEDC headquarters. Neither Claudia nor Lisa had mentioned that they would probably never see each other again.

"Yeah, I guess," Lisa said, as the doors opened and the noise and heat of the hangar deck flooded in.

The two women stepped out into a world of harsh worklights. Combat and other craft were parked everywhere, crammed in tightly with wings and ailerons folded for more efficient storage.

Maintenance crews were swarming over Veritechs damaged in the most recent fighting, while ordnance people readied ships slated for the next round of patrols and surveillance flights. The SDF-1's survival depended in large part on the Veritechs; but they would have been useless if not for the unflagging, often round-the-clock work of the men and women who repaired and serviced and rearmed them and the others who risked their lives as part of the flight deck catapult crews.

Welding sparks flew; ordnance loader servos whined, lifting missiles and ammunition into place. Claudia had to raise her voice to be heard. "Have you told Rick about the trip, or have you been too busy to see him?"

Busy had nothing to do with it, and they both knew that. Lisa had concluded that her love for Rick Hunter, leader of the Veritech Skull Team, was one-sided. By leaving the SDF-1 on a vital mission, she was also almost certainly giving up any chance of ever changing that.

"I thought I'd call him from the shuttle," she said.

Claudia exercised admirable restraint and did not blurt out, *Lisa, stop being such a coward!* Because Lisa wasn't—she had the combat decorations to prove it, medals and fruit cocktail that any line officer would respect. But where emotions were concerned, the SDF-1's competent and capable First always seemed to prefer hiding under a rock someplace.

The shuttle was near the aircraft elevator-air lock that would lift it to the flight deck. Lisa's gear and the evidence she hoped would sway Admiral Hayes and the others at the UEDC were already aboard. The crew chief was running a final prelaunch check.

"The shuttle is nearly ready for launch, Captain," a female enlisted-rating tech reported. "Launch in ten minutes."

Captain Henry Gloval crossed the bridge to glance at several other displays, stroking his thick mustache. "Any signs of Zentraedi activity in our area?" His voice still carried the burred r's and other giveaways of his Russian mother tongue.

Vanessa answered promptly, "There's been absolutely no contact, no activity at all."

The stupendous Zentraedi armada still shadowed and prowled around the wandering battle fortress. Time and again the aliens had attacked, but in comparatively insignificant numbers. The defectors' information was only now beginning to shed light on the reasons behind that.

"There's been nothing at all?" Gloval asked again, eyes flicking across the readouts and displays. "Mm. I hope this doesn't mean they're planning an attack." He turned and paced back toward the command chair, a tall, erect figure in the high-rolled collar of his uniform jacket, hat pulled low over his eyes. He clenched his cold, empty briar in his teeth. "I don't like it, not a bit..."

Lisa was his highly valued First Officer; but she was also much like a daughter to him. It had taken every bit of his reason and sense of duty to convince himself she was the logical one for this mission.

The first enlisted tech turned to Kim Young, who was manning a position nearby. She knew Kim and the two other enlisted regulars on the bridge watch, Sammie and Vanessa, were known as the Terrible Trio, part of what amounted to a family with Gloval, Lisa Hayes, and Claudia Grant.

"Kim, does the skipper always get this... concerned?"

Elfin-faced Kim, a young woman who wore her black hair in a short cut, showed a secret grin. She whispered, "Most of the time he's a rock. But he's worried about Lisa, and, well, there's Sammie."

Sammie Porter, youngest of the Terrible Trio, was a high-energy twenty-year-old with a thick mane of dark blond hair. She usually didn't know the meaning of fear... but she usually didn't know the meaning of tact, either. She was conscientious and bright but sometimes excitable.

Lisa's departure had meant a reshuffling of jobs on her watch, and Sammie had ended up with a lot of coordinating duties Claudia and Lisa would have ordinarily handled.

"Yellow squad, please go to preassigned coordinates before requesting computer readout," she ordered a unit of attack mecha over the comcircuit. The mammoth Robotech war machines were part of the ship's defensive force. Excaliburs and Spartans and Raidar Xs, they were like some hybrid of armored knight and walking battleship. They were among the units that guarded the ship itself, while the Veritechs sortied out into space.

Gloval bent close to check on what she was doing. "Everything all right? No trouble, I hope."

Sammie whirled and snapped, "Captain, please! I have to concentrate on these transmissions before they pile up!" Then she went back to ordering the lumbering mecha around, making sure that the gun turrets and missile batteries were alert and that all intel data and situation reports were up to date.

Gloval straightened, clamping his pipe in his teeth again. "Sorry. I didn't mean to interrupt." Kim and Vanessa gave him subtle looks, barely perceptible nods, to let him know that Sammie was on top of things.

Gloval had come to accept Sammie's occasional lack of diplomacy as a component of her fierce dedication to duty. Sometimes she reminded him of a small, not-to-be-trifled-with sheep dog.

Gloval considered the Terrible Trio for a moment. Through some joke of the gods, it had been these three whom the original Zentraedi spies—Bron, Konda, and Rico—had met and, not to put too fine a point on it, begun dating and formed attachments to.

The normally clear lines between personal life and matters of concern to the service were becoming quite muddied. The Zentraedi seemed decent enough, but there were already reports of ugly incidents between the defectors and some of the SDF-1's inhabitants. Gloval worried about the Terrible Trio, worried about the Zentraedi—was apprehensive that, after all, the two races could never coexist.

On top of that, he couldn't shake the feeling that he ought to be setting curfews, or providing chaperones, or doing *something* paternal. These things troubled him in the brief moments when he wasn't doing his best to see that his entire command wasn't obliterated.

"Shuttle escort flight, prepare for launch, five minutes," Sammie said, bent over her console. She turned to Gloval.

"Shuttle's ready, sir. Lisa will be leaving in four minutes, fifty seconds."

# 02

Of course, idle hands are not the devil's workshop; that is
a base canard.

Rather, it is the sort of hand that is always driven to be busy,
turning itself to new machinations, keeping the brew boiling, that
causes the most trouble. Those who wish to dispute this might do
well to consider what happened whenever Khyron grew restive.

Rawlins, *Zentraedi Triumvirate: Dolza, Breetai, Khyron*

MAX STERLING, FLIGHT HELMET CRADLED IN HIS LEFT ARM,
strode through the frenetic activity of the hangar deck and
heard Sammie's voice echo over the PA. "Sammie's substituting for
the commander," he said.

At his side was a Skull Team replacement, Corporal Elkins, who
had been transferred in from Wolf Team to help fill the gaps in
Skull's ranks after the last pitched battle with the Zentraedi. Elkins
remarked, "I hope she stays calm. Last time she had me flying
figure eights around a radar mast."

Max chuckled, then forgot the joke, distracted. "Hey." Elkins
saw what Max meant. The techs had rolled out a prototype ship,
something everybody in the Veritech squadrons had heard about.
It was like the conventional VT, a sleek ultra-fighter, but two
augmentation pods were mounted above its wing pivots.

The conventional VTs were a kind of miracle in themselves,
the most advanced use of the Robotechnology that humans had
learned from the wreckage of the SDF-1 when the alien-built battle
fortress had originally crashed on Earth twelve years before. The

SDF-1 had murderous teeth in the form of its mecha, its primary and secondary batteries, and its astoundingly powerful main gun, but the VTs were the ship's claws. And this new, retrofitted model was the first of a more powerful generation, a major advance in firepower and performance.

"Wouldn't that be something to fly?" Max murmured. He hoped it checked out all right in test flights; the humans needed every edge they could get.

"Whenever they're ready to give me one, I'll take it," Elkins said. "Anyway, watch yourself up there, Max."

At the top of the shuttle boarding steps, Lisa said, "I've made notes on everything that might be a problem."

"Don't worry about a thing," Claudia told her. Then she put her hands on Lisa's shoulders. "I'll see you back here in a few days, okay?"

Lisa tried to smile. What do you say to someone dearer than a sister? "I hope so. You look after things." One of the ground crew whistled, and Lisa stepped back into the shuttle's entry hatch.

The mobile steps moved away from the tubby shuttle. Claudia threw Lisa a salute for the first time in so long that neither of them could remember the last. Lisa returned it smartly. The round hatch swung to, emblazoned with the Robotech Defense Force insignia.

There were no other passengers, of course; contact with Earth had been all but nonexistent since the UEDC rulers decided that the dimensional fortress was to be a decoy, luring the enemy away from the planet. Other than a few canisters of classified dispatches and so forth, she had the passenger compartment to herself.

Lisa found a seat at the front of the compartment, near a com console, and asked a passing crewman, "Is this a secure line?"

"Aye aye, ma'am. It's best to make any calls now; never can tell what glitches we'll run into outside."

"I will."

He was wandering a quiet side street of Macross when the paging voice said, "Repeating: Lieutenant Rick Hunter, you have a call."

For a moment he wasn't even sure where he was, shuffling along in civvies that felt rather strange—the first time he'd worn anything but a uniform or a flightsuit in weeks. He'd been brooding a lot longer, trying to sort things out, to understand his own feelings and face up to certain truths.

He went to one of the ubiquitous yellow com phones and identified himself. The incoming call carried a secure-line encryption signal, keying the public phone with it. While the machines went through their coding, Rick looked around to make sure no one was close enough to eavesdrop.

People were just passing by, not even sparing a glance for the compact black-haired young man at the phone. He didn't mind that; he needed a few hours respite from being the Skull Team's leader—some time away from the burden of command.

He had been a cocky civilian when he first came aboard the dimensional fortress two years before. He had been drawn into military service only grudgingly by Roy Fokker, his unofficial Big Brother—Claudia Grant's lover. Rick Hunter had survived more dogfights than he could remember, had written so many condolence letters to the families of dead VT pilots that he forced himself not to think of them, had stood by at the funeral of Roy Fokker and others beyond counting. He only wanted to shut them out of his mind.

He was not yet twenty-one years old.

The comcircuit was established. "Rick? It's Lisa."

He felt as though he had been under observation as he walked the streets aimlessly. Lisa and Minmei; Minmei and Lisa. His brain failed him in that emotional cyclone where his feelings for the two women swirled and defied all analysis, all decision.

"What can I do for you?" Ouch. Wrong. He knew that as soon as he said it, but it was too late.

"I wanted to let you know, Rick. I'm leaving the SDF-1. I'm on my way to Earth to try to get them to stop the fighting."

He looked around again quickly to make sure no civilians had any chance of hearing. There was enough unrest in the dimensional fortress without spreading new rumors and raising expectations that would in all probability be dashed. At the same time, he felt an emptiness. *She's leaving!*

"Why wasn't I told ab—"

"It's all top secret. Rick, I might not be allowed to come back." Lisa cupped the handset to her, staring at it sadly, as the shuttle was moved onto the aircraft elevator for the trip to the flight deck. Max Sterling's VT was next to it.

"So… I want to tell you something," she struggled. *Oh, say it!* Claudia's voice seemed to holler at her. But she couldn't.

"I appreciate all you've done, and it's been an honor serving with you," Lisa said instead. "Your observations about our captivity in the alien headquarters will be an important part of my report when—"

"What are you talking about, Lisa?" Something that had been murky to him moments ago was crystal clear now. "I don't care about reports or anything else if you can't come back here!"

*Tell him! Say it!* But she ignored the voice, couldn't face the rejection. He loved the luminous superstar, Minmei, and Minmei cared for him. Who could compete with that?

She found herself saying, "Please watch over the Zentraedi defectors, Rick. A lot of our people haven't had time to reason things out yet, and the aliens are in danger."

The stubby shuttle was on the flight deck, boxed up for launch by the cat crew, the hookup people clear, the blast deflector raised up from the deck behind the spacecraft. Off to one side, Max's VT swept its wings out and raised its vertical stabilizers.

Lisa held the handset tenderly. "We're launching. Good-bye. And thanks again."

"What? Wait!" But the circuit was dead.

He got up to an observation deck just in time to watch a tiny cluster of distant lights, the drives of the formed-up flight, dwindle into the darkness.

"Shuttle craft and escorts proceeding according to flight plan," Vanessa told Gloval quietly. Nobody had actually *said* that Lisa's flight was to be monitored so closely; but no one had objected to the idea, either, and the Terrible Trio were keeping close tabs.

Back at her duty station, Claudia was alert to every nuance of voice, like everyone else there. When Vanessa said, "Captain!" in a clipped, alarmed tone, Claudia's heart skipped a beat.

"Elements of the Zentraedi fleet are redeploying. They're on intercept course, closing in on the shuttle."

Gloval looked over his situation displays, threat boards, computer projections. Claudia kept one eye on the board, one on Gloval.

He sounded very calm. Now that battle had come, he was a well of tranquility. "Order them to take evasive action as necessary or return to the SDF-1 if possible."

Claudia almost blurted out a plea to send reinforcements, but she could read the displays as well as anyone. More Zentraedi forces were moving into place, apparently to cut the shuttle off from the dimensional fortress. Pummeled and undermanned, the SDF-1 could ill afford to risk an entire VT team to save one shuttle and its escorts.

No matter who might die.

Alarms and emergency flashers brought Lisa out of a dim gray despair. The shuttle pilot was announcing, "Enemy craft approaching. All hands, general quarters. Secure for general quarters."

There was a heavy grinding sound as sections of padded armor shielding slid up into place around Lisa's seat. She calmly pulled her briefcase into the questionable safety of the metal cocoon with her, securing her acceleration harness, and the ship's drive pressed her back into the seat's cushioning.

Max Sterling accepted the news almost amicably. The heritage that was the fighter pilot's proud tradition remained strong. Dying was sometimes unavoidable, but losing one's cool was inexcusable.

"Enemy approaching on our six," he said, with less emotion than most people used talking about the weather. "Form up in gamma deployment and stick with your wingmen."

The other VTs rogered and moved to comply. Max was going to give Lisa an encouraging wave, but the armored cocoon had already swallowed her up.

He peeled off to take up his own position. The aerodynamic maneuvers of the VTs looked strange in the airlessness and zero g of space, but the pilots came from a naval aviation tradition. They thought a certain way about flying, and thinking was half the key to Robotechnology. The aerodynamic maneuvers wasted power, but Robotechnology had plenty of that.

Max hoped this was another feint. Like Gloval and many others, he had noticed that there seemed to be two distinct factions— almost a schizophrenia—among the enemy. One side was playing a waiting game, determined to capture the SDF-1 intact for reasons that the humans still couldn't guess and that the low-ranking defectors, not privy to strategic information, couldn't clarify.

The other element—rash, unpredictable, almost irrational— mounted sudden, vicious attacks on the dimensional fortress, apparently intent on destroying it with no thought to the consequences. It was becoming clear that the enemy commander responsible for this had a name known to, and even feared by, all Zentraedi.

Khyron the Backstabber.

"Commander, the target has changed course," a Zentraedi pod pilot said, the facebowl of his combat armor lit by his instruments. "And the Micronian fighters are redeploying for intercept."

The alien mecha, two dozen and more, were in attack formation—huge ovoid bodies quilled with cannon muzzles, mounted on long reverse-articulated legs so that they resembled headless ostriches. Most would have been considered "armless," but the Officers' Pods mounted heavy guns that suggested gargantuan derringers.

In the lead pod was Khyron the Backstabber.

He didn't fit most stereotypes of the brutal warlord. Quite contrary to the Zentraedi conventionalities—their Spartan simplicity, their distaste for mannerisms—Khyron would have been called a fop if such a word or concept had existed among his race.

Youthful-looking and sinisterly handsome, he gazed into

the screens of his pod's cockpit, contemplating the kill. He had been forbidden to attack the SDF-1 again on pain of immediate execution, but no one had issued any orders with regard to a juicy little convoy.

Four times now, the Micronian vermin had humiliated him. With each defeat, his hatred had grown geometrically. It went incandescent when he saw the sorts of perversions the humans practiced: males mingling with females, the sexes somehow coming into contact and expressing weak-willed affection for each other. They behaved seductively, something unknown to the Zentraedi. The Micronians paired off, sometimes forming lifelong bonds, driven by impulses and stimuli Khyron was only beginning to perceive.

It repelled and fascinated him; it obsessed and possessed him. So he knew he had no other choice but to destroy the Micronians utterly or go completely insane.

"Nothing can save them," he gloated. "All units: Attack immediately!"

The pods closed in, riding the bright flames of their drives, guns angling, answering their targeting servos. The VTs swept out to meet them.

"Captain, the shuttle has reached coordinates Lambda thirty-four," Sammie called out. "Should we send reinforcements?"

The bridge crew watched Gloval, hoping he would say yes as much as he himself wanted to. But that would have left the SDF-1 underprotected; the Zentraedi had already tried similar diversionary maneuvers to set up a major attack.

With the number of spaceworthy VTs critically low until the Robotech fabrication machinery could produce replacements, he simply couldn't risk sending out another team of fighters or risk the pilots who were so crucial to the ship's survival.

"Not unless we absolutely have to," he said stonily. The women turned back to their jobs in silence. Gloval did not elaborate on the question of reinforcements, but he had already decided: He couldn't risk a flight of VTs, but there *was* one desperate gamble he could take if the shuttle's situation got worse.

...

In the volume of empty space designated Lambda thirty-four, Max Sterling's Veritech went through a lightning change. It was what Dr. Lang, the eerie Robotech genius, termed "mechamorphosis," the alteration of the fighter's very structure.

Max had pulled the lever that sent the ship into Battloid mode, thinking the mecha through its change. The VT shifted to Battloid, looking like a futuristic gladiator in bulky, ultratech armor, bristling with weapons. Two pods drove in at him, cannon blazing.

# 03

That undisciplined showoff? That wet-nosed civilian joystick pilot?
What a waste of time and effort!

Remark attributed to Lisa Hayes upon being informed that
trainee Rick Hunter had qualified as a YT pilot 2009 A.D.

THE PODS FIRED AWAY WITH THE PRIMARY AND SECONDARY GUNS
that protruded from their armored plastrons, but the blue bolts
converged on utter vacuum. Max's Battloid wasn't where it had
been a split second before.

The Battloid had its autocannon in its metal fists, riding its
backpack thrusters with the agility of a gymnast, darting like a
dragonfly. It whirled on one pod, opening up.

The chain-gun was loaded with depleted transuranic rounds, big
as candlepins and much heavier—high-powered, extremely dense
projectiles that delivered terrific amounts of kinetic energy. The
pod's armor flew like shredded paper; it exploded in an outlashing
of energy and debris.

Max was still dodging with blinding speed, turning his sights on
the second pod. He riddled it before the enemy pilot could draw a
bead on him, putting a tight shot group of holes in the center of the
egglike alien mecha. The pod became a brief fireball.

No system of manual *or* computer controls could have come
up with such astounding maneuverability, such instantaneous
responses and deadly shooting. Only the "thinking cap," the
interface of mind and mecha, could work the seeming magic of
the RDF.

Other VTs had already paired off against the foe. The mecha swirled and pounced; their missiles corkscrewed and sizzled while energy bolts and powered gatling rounds lit the darkness. But the pods had the advantage of numbers by more than two to one, enough to occupy every Veritech and leave more pods to go after the shuttle.

The shuttle pilot was taking evasive action and running for safety at full emergency power. But there was no safety; the shuttle was no match for the pods' speed, and the Zentraedi closed in, firing. The shuttle's light armaments and lack of maneuvering ability made it easy prey, but the shuttle skipper did his best, trying to evade. He was hoping he could eventually make a dash for the tantalizingly nearby Earth, knowing that the UEDC would never allow any of its forces to intervene or otherwise risk turning the Zentraedi wrath on Earth itself. He could hope for no help from that quarter.

A Zentraedi cannon burst stitched holes in the shuttle's port wing in a line of three, ringed by molten metal. Lisa felt the ship rock in her armored cocoon, and gripped the padded armrests, waiting to see what the outcome of the battle would be.

The attacking pod was a modified standard type, carrying augmentative particle-beam cannon for added firepower. It turned to come back for the kill, but just then Max arrived, his Battloid diving headlong into the fight. The Battloid knocked the pod aside like a football player, driving a huge, armored shoulder into it.

Then the Battloid that was Max Sterling flipped neatly on foot thrusters and fired. The rain of armor-piercing slugs punched a dozen holes in the enemy, and it was driven back like some wounded living thing. There was no secondary explosion—very unusual, since the enemy mecha's power systems usually turned them into firecrackers once their armor had been pierced.

Two more pods came in at him, one with extra missile racks and another with the strange rabbit ears of a Zentraedi signal-warfare ship. Max went at them, juking and evading to stay out of their cross hairs, his Battloid firing short bursts from the autocannon.

One of the escort VTs had been lost, another damaged by the first onslaught. Several more were still engaged in combat, but the rest, like Max, had come through their first duel and were taking on new opponents. Some help arrived, and Max began to feel confident that he could keep the pods away from the damaged shuttle.

But just then, Elkins yelled over the tac net, "More pods! We've got more pods coming at us—half a dozen!"

Max's mouth became a thin line as he drove in to deal with his current opponents as quickly as he could. He thought back with a certain pilot's superstition on what he had said to the men in the alley. Perhaps the taboos were right and it was lethal bad luck to talk about not coming back.

"The escorts are outnumbered," Kim called over her shoulder without taking her eyes from her instruments.

"More pods closing in on them!" Vanessa added. "Cutting off the shuttle's escape."

Gloval sat slumped in his command chair with his cap visor pulled down low over his eyes. A Veritech flight couldn't possibly get there in time, and he didn't have them to spare. But...

"How long would it take the armored Veritech prototype to make it there?"

Sammie already had the figures. "Approximately four minutes from launch at max boost."

Claudia bit her lower lip, watching Gloval. The captain's head came up. "Prepare it for launch!"

Claudia relayed the order, sending up a silent prayer, while Sammie asked, "Who'll be flying it, sir?"

"Get Lieutenant Hunter to the hangar deck at once. Tell him we don't know how much longer Sterling can hold out."

The ship's PA and a few seconds on a comcircuit had Rick on his way, anxious and very intense, in a commandeered jeep he flagged down in the middle of a Macross boulevard. The enlisted driver was a capable man who liked having an excuse to break all traffic laws.

Rick suited up virtually on the run, and minutes later the aircraft elevator was lifting the humpbacked-looking armored VT to the flight deck.

"Lieutenant, your destination is Lambda thirty-four," Sammie told him over the command net.

"Lambda thirty-four? What're you talking about?"

On the bridge, Claudia turned to Sammie. "Didn't you see to it that all pilots had the new map-reference codes?"

Sammie looked devastated. "I was so swamped—I didn't think he'd need one until he went on duty later."

Aircraft status was relayed; the armored VT was boxed and ready for launch. Sammie gritted her teeth, ignoring the silent stares of the rest of the bridge watch, especially the ominous quiet from Gloval. She couldn't let her mistake spell Lisa's death!

Sammie opened the mike gain, concentrating, eyes shut, matching coordinates and codes by memory. "Coordinates in superseded code are at Weasel twenty-one!"

Rick launched without taking time to acknowledge. The armored VT poured on speed like nothing any other human-produced mecha had ever demonstrated. A single man in an untested ship, flying out against terrible odds—and if he lost, the woman who was humanity's best hope for peace would die too.

From the first, Max had known that the chances of help arriving from the SDF-1 were slim. Now he was resigned to the fact that there would be no help, though he didn't let on to the dwindling survivors of the escort flight.

The other VT pilots had flown well and bravely; their kill ratio was high, but still they went down to oblivion, one by one, in the silent globular explosions of a space rat race—a mass dogfight. Max Sterling flew like no pilot before him, a grim reaper, a deadly wraith, an undefeatable mecha demon in the form of a Battloid.

The Battloid changed vectors and zoomed out of a pod's salvo, jamming some of its missiles with ECM equipment and dodging the rest, a masterful performance. Max turned the gatling on it and hosed it with a tracer-bright stream of heavyweight rounds, blowing it away.

But still the enemy came, and more were arriving. It looked like a day for dying.

He turned to get back with Elkins, to stick together and protect the shuttle to the last. But Elkin's ship vanished in an ugly blossom of fire and shrapnel. The escort had been whittled down to five. Four times that number came in at them now.

Hanging back from the action in his Officer's Pod, Khyron watched gleefully. He suspected that the enemy leader, the amazingly fast and deadly blue-trimmed Veritech, was the same one who had sent so many Zentraedi to defeat and death—had even humbled the vaunted Miriya, female ace of aces of the Quadronos.

Khyron was in no hurry to lead the attack and tangle with the Micronian devil in person; it would be enough to dispose of the rest of his command by attrition and pull the Veritech wizard to bits by sheer weight of numbers. Then, Khyron would have a boast to fling in Miriya's face and the faces of all the others who secretly laughed at him!

More pods converged. But at that moment a newcomer arrived.

"Only one," a pod pilot reported, and Khyron dismissed the matter coldly. One more Veritech wouldn't matter now.

His opinion changed a moment later. The fighter accelerated to unprecedented speeds, maneuvering more nimbly than any Micronian mecha ever had. Its humpbacked profile didn't match any computer ID.

Then the strange new machine let forth a storm of fire: murderously fast and accurate missiles of some new type; autocannon rounds with even greater velocity, delivering far more kinetic energy on impact; phased-array laser blasts as powerful, at close range, as any plasma bolt.

The new arrival, faster than the escort leader, was in and out among the pods, striking and vanishing, blowing two Zentraedi mecha to smithereens and going on to take out another while the first two explosions were still ballooning.

Suddenly, the pods were like so many fat pigeons before the attack of a rocket-driven hawk.

Rick's initial success was so overwhelming, so pronounced and irresistible, that he got careless.

After seeing a dozen and more of the ambushers go up in flames, he began to switch to Guardian mode. But he'd forgotten what a hot ride he had, and the ship's sudden retro thrust almost put his head through the instrument panel and split his thinking cap down the middle.

He barely recovered, shaking his head, the breath knocked from him by the strain of the safety harness across his torso. Trembling, he got control of himself and his ship and pressed the fight again.

And once more the Zentraedi pods were fat targets at his mercy. He went swooping in at them, the VT laying out a staggering volume of fire, skeeting pods as if they were clay targets.

Khyron had seen enough; he had no desire to go up against this bewilderingly fast, fearsomely armed intruder. He made sure his own withdrawal was well under way before he ordered his troops back.

It didn't mean his thirst for revenge was slaked, of course; if anything, it was worse. It was a constant torment now; it would be until he destroyed the enemy insects once and for all.

Max's report came over the bridge speakers. "The enemy has broken contact and withdrawn. The shuttle has sustained minimal damage and is continuing on.

"With your permission, I am returning to the SDF-1 with the remaining escort ships, due to damage suffered during the attack. Lieutenant Hunter will escort the shuttle to Earth."

Gloval granted permission. To Claudia's doubtful look, he responded, "That armored Veritech has so much speed and firepower, it's the equal of ten regular fighters."

*And a thousand more like it wouldn't put us on an equal footing with our foe,* he thought to himself. *Still, we must have as many as we can, as fast as we can!*

Sammie stretched and yawned. "I'm exhausted! I wish Commander Hayes was back."

Claudia glared at her. "We almost lost her permanently with that code snafu of yours!"

Sammie looked dismayed, young and tearful; she was even more upset by the danger to Lisa than by Claudia's temper, which could lead to *very* serious problems for anyone who angered the bridge officer.

But Claudia softened after a moment. After all, Sammie *had* pulled things out of the fire.

"That's okay, kiddo," Claudia said, turning back to her console. "Everybody learns from mistakes."

Gloval thought about that, silently gazing through the forward viewport. Did that apply to the Zentraedi, too? And the UEDC rulers?

Could they all be convinced the war was a catastrophic mistake?

The protective shielding swung back to show Lisa a passenger compartment that seemed unaffected by the battle. She was still a little winded and bruised from the tossing around she had taken in the padded, armored cocoon.

The shuttle pilot had kept her abreast of the battle and she felt a bit limp with relief. It was so vital that she get to Earth, that she speak for peace—long ago she had resigned herself to the likelihood that she would die in war, but to have died at that moment was a tragedy too vast to contemplate.

"Commander Hayes," the pilot's voice came over the intercom. "We have a commo call for you from Lieutenant Hunter, who's now flying escort for us. I've patched it through."

So Rick was the one who had ridden to the rescue in the armored VT; she had hoped it was and yet had feared for his life all through the fight. She picked up the handset.

Armored panels were sliding back from all the viewports. She was looking out at the humpbacked new-generation Veritech. "Lisa, are you all right?" she heard him say.

"Yes. Because you came to help." She saw him through the VT's canopy, looking at her worriedly.

*I was never cut out for emotional drama*, she thought. *I should have known I couldn't get away with a rehearsed exit speech.*

"No problem," he was saying. "Now, what's all this about you not coming back?"

"There are reasons, Rick."

"Even though your father's on the UEDC?"

"*Especially* because of that. Besides, they aren't going to like what I'm going to tell them."

There was a choppy sensation as the shuttle entered the Earth's atmosphere. He fumbled for something appropriate to say, knowing he had to turn back in seconds. "I hope you'll be safe" was all he could come up with.

"Thanks. I'm sure I'll be fine."

"Um." He knew the call was patched through the shuttle's com system, accessible to the pilots—presuming they weren't busy with their atmospheric entry maneuver. "There's something else—sorta private. Here; look."

He had fallen back, out of the pilots' line of vision, up close to the shuttle. She could see him clearly, watching her. She was confused. "What is it?"

"Prosigns." He began flashing his VT's running lights in prosigns—brief dot-dash combinations that represented whole words, for quick manual Morse code communications. Lisa was a little rusty but found that she could read it.

LIKE YOU MUCH. COMPLAIN SOMETIMES BUT
BELIEVE IN YOU. MISS YOU MUCH IF YOU DON'T
RETURN. PLEASE RETURN SOONEST.

He could read her lips, so close were VT and shuttle. *I'll try. So long, Rick.*

He threw her a salute—a joke between them, given his lack of military discipline when they had first met and clashed.

The armored VT peeled off and vectored for the SDF-1, the blue vortices of its thrusters shrinking to match flames, then disappearing. The shuttle jostled more as it hit the denser atmosphere.

# 04

I have familiarized myself with the enemy's culture, to better carry out my espionage mission. What a repulsive, contemptible thing it is!

All seems to revolve around their gruesome, sadistic method of reproduction, and it obsesses them constantly. The humans—Micronians—even make up false legends about it! They immerse themselves in stories where males and females poison one another or stab themselves or simply expire from some unexplained thing called "pining away." Or else the imaginary couples go off together and spend all their time in revolting, pointless intimacies.

Our enemies languish in these falsehoods the way we might enjoy a hot soak at the end of a long campaign.

What perversion! Truly, this is a species that must be exterminated!

Miriya Parino, from her interim notes
for an intel report to the Zentraedi High Command

SHE WAS STRIKING ENOUGH TO DRAW STARES EVEN IN THE crowded Macross plaza, where people were usually in a hurry and some of the more attractive women in the dimensional fortress were to be seen.

Boots clicking on the swirling mosaics of the plaza, the green-dyed hair flowing with the speed of her walk and the light air currents of the ship's circulation blowers, she looked neither right nor left. People made way for her; she was barely aware of their existence, even that of the men who looked at her so admiringly.

Miriya, greatest combat pilot of her race, exulted a bit. *I've finally discovered one of the reasons these Micronians have developed such amazing skill in handling their mecha!* It wasn't the reason she had come to the SDF-1 as a spy, but it was a step in understanding her quarry, and that was elating. The intelligence data would also be of interest to the Zentraedi High Command, another coup to her credit.

Not that Miriya needed one. As a demigoddess of battle, she was without equal, her kills and victories far outnumbering her nearest rival's. She had lost only once in her life and had submitted to micronization and come to the SDF-1 to make amends for that.

Miriya left the street and its EVE noonday, entering the dark and blinking world she had only recently discovered. All through the media-game arcade, people stood or sat hunched toward the glowing screens, playing against the machines.

The screen-lit faces of the players were so intent, their movements so deft and quick—what could account for it other than military indoctrination and the hunger for combat? What other motive could there be for the Micronians' relentless practice? They were so highly motivated that they even subsidized their own training, feeding money into the machines.

The young ones were the best and most diligent, of course. *By the time they reach maturity, they will be superb warriors!* she thought. This, even though the very concept of human reproduction, the parents-child-adult cycle, made her feel queasy and dizzy. The discovery of that vileness, as she thought of it, had rendered her inert and dazed when she first stumbled on the truth of it. But in time, bravely, she had shaken off the horror of human reproduction and resumed her search.

Miriya came to the most significant machine, though they were all cunning and instructive. She vaulted into the little cockpit, inserting a coin in the slot. One hand went to the stick, the other to the throttle, as she watched the screen. Her feet settled on the foot pedals.

Her finger hovered near the weapons trigger as she waited for the game to begin. Miriya looked around quickly to see if her nemesis was there.

She couldn't spy anyone who might be that greatest of Micronian pilots and therefore assumed he wasn't present. Surely a pilot who was good enough to have defeated Miriya Parino, the indisputable champion of the Zentraedi, would draw great attention and recognition. She would know him when he came or when someone mentioned him. She would find him eventually.

And then she would kill him.

The face in the family portrait was pale, thin—but open and kind, the mother's features very much like the daughter's. Admiral Hayes glanced down at the framed photo, not realizing that many minutes had gone by while he sat, thinking and remembering.

He was looking at himself, years ago, only a lieutenant commander then. Next to him in the photo was his wife, and in front of them a shy-looking little girl wearing a sun hat and sun dress with a Band-Aid on one knee.

*Whenever I look at this picture, I wish Andrea were still here to see how her little girl turned out—to see what an extraordinary soldier Lisa's made of herself.*

A comtone from his desk terminal broke his contemplation. "Pardon me for interrupting, sir," an aide said. "But you left word that you be informed when the shuttle made final approach."

Hayes shook himself; there had been that last, terrible fear when the shuttle was attacked and not even he could countermand UEDC orders and send help. More to the point, there was no help that Earth could send that would be of any use; the SDF-1 and its Veritechs were the only effective weapons against Zentraedi pods. Hayes could only wait and hope.

When the shuttle survived its gauntlet, he had nearly collapsed into his chair, staring at the photograph of the past. There was so much to heal between himself and his daughter, so much to put behind them.

Now, he looked to the aide's image on his display screen. "Thank you."

"The craft should be landing very shortly. Shall I meet you at the elevators, sir?"

Hayes pressed against his big, solid oak desk with both hands, pushing himself to his feet. "Yes, that would be fine."

The headquarters of the United Earth Defense Council was a vast base beneath the Alaskan wilderness. Very little of it was aboveground—surveillance and communications equipment, aircraft control tower—but the surface was guarded by the few remaining Battloids on Earth.

Years before, when the SDF-1 made its miscalculated spacefold jump out to the rim of the solar system, it took with it most of its Robotech secrets and all the fabricating equipment humanity had discovered in the huge vessel when it originally crash-landed on Earth. Earth had turned back to largely conventional weapons for its defense with the exception of one gargantuan project that was already under way: the Grand Cannon.

The Grand Cannon took up most of the sprawling, miles-deep base, a doomsday weapon that let the UEDC live the fantasy that it could defend itself against an all-out Zentraedi onslaught. Admiral Hayes had been largely responsible for the Grand Cannon's construction; Gloval's simple disdain for such a massive, immobile weapon system was one of the major stresses that had ended their friendship.

Waiting by the landing strip, the brutally cold arctic wind whipping at his greatcoat, Hayes recalled those days, recalled the bitter words. His once-warm bond with Gloval, solidified during their service together in the Global Civil War, had shattered as Hayes accused the Russian of timid thinking and Gloval sneered at the "hidebound, Maginot-Line mindset" of the Cannon's proponents.

Hayes's thoughts were interrupted by the aide. "Admiral, we've just received word that the shuttle's ETA has been moved back by twenty minutes. Nothing serious; they're just coming around for a better approach window. If you like, I' II drive you back to the control tower; it's warmer there."

The admiral said distractedly, "No, I'll wait here. It's not that cold, anyway." Then he turned back to watch the sky, barely aware of the biting wind.

The aide sat back down in the open jeep, shivering and buttoning up his collar all the way, burrowing his chin down and tucking gloved hands under armpits. He always thought of his commander as rather a comfort-loving man; certainly, Hayes's living quarters and offices gave that impression.

But here was the Old Man, indifferent to an arctic blast that would send an unprotected man into hypothermia in seconds. None of the base personnel knew much about this daughter; her last visit to the base had been rushed and very hush-hush. Hayes rarely mentioned her, but he had been remote most of the time since he had received word she was coming. The aide shrugged to himself, swearing at the shuttle, wishing it would hurry up.

In an officers' mess onboard the SDF-1, Max sat toying with his coffee cup, glancing over at the table a few yards away where Rick Hunter sat immersed in thought, an almost palpable cloud of gloom surrounding him.

*He's been sitting there by himself for half an hour twiddling his spoon, and it's like his food isn't even there,* Max reflected. He made a quick decision, rose, and went to approach his team leader.

"Lieutenant, it's too early to be depressed about this," Max jumped right in. "I'm sure Commander Hayes will get back here somehow."

Rick turned away from him, chin still resting on his hand. "First of all, I'm *not* thinking about her, and secondly, what makes you think I'm depressed?"

Rich decided it was all far too complicated to explain to Max Sterling, the bright-eyed boy wonder of the VTs, the cheerful, unassuming ace of aces. A man who never seemed unhappy, at a loss, or in doubt of what he was doing. *Eager beaver!* Rick thought huffily.

"Maybe you need a little excitement—some distraction," Max persisted. "How about a game? I know just the place! Let's go!"

Before Rick could object or even consider pulling rank, Max had him by the arm and yanked him to his feet, tugging him toward the door. It seemed easier to give in than to start a tug-of-war in the middle of the officers' mess; Rick went along compliantly.

It didn't take long to get there; Max even paid for the cab. The Close Encounters game arcade was alive with noise and lights, like some Robotech fun house.

Max's eyes were shining. "Great place, huh? You're gonna love it!"

*More war games?* Rick groaned to himself. "I don't know. Maybe I'll just head home—"

But Max had him by the elbow again. "A coupla games'll make you feel like a new man, boss."

"Max, I don't think—"

"Look, I've been here before; I know what I'm talking about!" He dragged Rick through the entrance.

As they moved deeper into the arcade, Rick recognized a face. Jason, Lynn-Minmei's little cousin, had stopped to watch a young woman playing a game. Rick went past without saying anything to attract the child's attention; talking to Jason would only remind him of his feelings for Minmei and compound his doubts and gloom.

In passing, he did notice the young woman: a very intense player with green-dyed hair and an expression like some beautiful lioness ready for the kill.

The shuttle had barely rolled to a stop when Hayes reached it, running. His aide watched him in astonishment.

By the time the ground crew got the mobile stairs in position, Lisa was waiting in the open hatch. The wind tugged at her long, heavy locks of brown-blond hair and her too-light trench coat. She was wearing fur-trimmed boots she had borrowed, but the cold sent ice picks through her and numbed her skin instantly.

She halted, shocked to see her father waiting for her. Their previous meeting and parting had been anything but cordial, with the admiral doggedly taking the UEDC line against Gloval's common sense and compassion. Coldly formal to her in the meetings, her father had later sought to get her reassigned to headquarters base, to get her out of the danger of her SDF-1 assignment. Lisa had torn up the conciliatory note he had sent her and returned to the dimensional fortress with Gloval. She was unaware of how that tormented her father.

Now, looking up at her, he said, "Lisa! Thank goodness you're here at last!" She came down the stairs carefully, holding the railing with one hand as the wind buffeted her, clutching a dispatch case.

"You're finally off that cursed alien Flying Dutchman." He was smiling, tears forming. "We've got a lot of talking to do!"

But when she reached the bottom of the stairs, she came to

attention and snapped him an exacting salute. "Admiral, Commander Lisa Hayes reporting, sir. I'm carrying a special dispatch from the captain of the SDF-1 to the United Earth Defense Council."

He was taken aback, the smile wiped from his face. It was her turn to be formal and distant now, her right, as it had been his the last time.

If she was giving him back his own, he was willing to accept it. Nothing was as important to him as the fact that his daughter, his only family, was with him again. He returned her salute crisply, straight-faced.

"Welcome home."

Dante's Inferno was one of the more popular games there, but Rick just didn't feel like following old Virgil down through the nine circles to the demanding Ultimate Player level. Dragonbane, with its swirling nightmare reptile attackers and Nordic swordsman, seemed a little too much like his own duel with inner demons.

Nor was he inclined toward Psycho Highway Chainsaw Bloodbath. Eventually, though, Max convinced him to take on a pair of side-by-side Aesop's Gauntlet machines, mostly because the easy chairs before them were thickly upholstered and comfortable.

Down below, on the main level, Miriya sharpened her skills at the Veritechs! game. She found grim amusement in being a simulated Micronian pilot, blowing Zentraedi Battlepods to whirling fragments. She was disappointed that there were no Quadrono powered-armor opponents in the game; her own unit was by far the elite of the alien armada.

She also approved of the training machine—as she thought of it—for not introducing trainees to the realities of warfare at this early phase of their instruction. It was clear that the gamesters would need a little hardening and proper military discipline before they could deal with the horror and bloodshed of real warfare. This clean, neat gaming gave them appropriate affection for combat without any confusing exposure to certain unpleasant aspects of a real warrior's life. Clever.

She sent another pod to computer-modeled oblivion, pretending it was that of Khyron, whom she had come to despise.

The score credit flashed, and little Jason, still watching, piped up, "Wow! Look at that!"

She tried to ignore him as tokens stamped with a big M poured into the payoff tray. The little Micronians were intriguing to her, but disquieting. And the small ones were always so boisterous or emotional—certainly impulsive and rather simpleminded. At first she thought that they were a slave underclass, but that didn't square with the indulgent treatment they got from the bigger Micronians. She forcefully shut from her mind the truth about human childbearing; compared to it, the war and slaughter were simple, comprehensible, painless things.

And such thoughts were not in keeping with her true mission aboard the SDF-1. She looked around, wondering when she would find her quarry. The memory still burned in her: of how the Micronian ace had outflown her and then, in the very streets of Macross itself, she in her Quadrono superarmor and he in his Battloid, faced her down, made her flee.

Her face burned again at the thought of it. She had difficulty eating or resting and would until she regained her honor.

The dimensional fortress was big, but not big enough that her enemy could hide forever.

# 05

Considering the staggering expense involved in any Robotech operation, the match that took place in the arcade that day certainly ranks as the most cost-effective VT mission of the war—and perhaps the most fateful.

Zachary Fox Jr., VT: *The Men and the Mecha*

EVERY ANIMAL IN AESOP'S BESTIARY SEEMED TO HAVE IT IN FOR Rick, while Max progressed through the ascending levels with ease.

"The points're piling up, Lieutenant," Max said, referring to his score. Rick, teeth gritted, was trying to wax the fox that was leaping for the grapes. Damn thing moved faster than a Zentraedi tri thruster.

After a lot of bleeping, ringing, and flashing from Max's machine, a flood of tokens, glittering like gold, slid into the payoff tray. The tokens could be used for more games, of course, or redeemed for prizes, vouchers of various kinds, or—if one really pressed the issue—cash.

"That's great! I always make more than I can cart off."

"Well, you left *me* behind," Rick admitted. *Wasn't this supposed to make me feel better?*

Actually, it did. "Max, look at that!" More and more tokens slid down into the tray until they were spilling all over the place.

Close Encounters's assistant manager, Frankie Zotz, a nervous young man in white pancake makeup and black, owl-like hairdo, rushed into the manager's booth. "Hey, boss! We're gettin' wiped out at some of our most difficult machines!"

Blinko Imperiale, the manager—he of the goggle shades and two-tone Mohawk and vaguely intimidating lab coat—sat with chin on fist.

"Dincha hear me?" Frankie Zotz yelped. "That pilot's upstairs again, and the green-haired dame's inside turnin' a VT game every which way but profitable!"

Blinko didn't even move, sadly staring off at nothing. "Oh, boy. I knew I never shoulda opened this place near where those RDF maniacs hang out!"

The split-screen comparisons were obvious even to nontechnical personnel. The DNA strands and analysis workups spoke for themselves.

The presentation flashed along as Admiral Hayes muttered, "Interesting... hmmm..."

It was much more than that; it was astounding. It shook the very foundations of human knowledge.

It had long been thought that wherever the basic chemical building blocks of life coexisted in the universe, they would preferentially link to form the same subunits that defined the essential biogenetic structures found on Earth. In other words, the ordering of the DNA code wasn't a quirk of nature. Tentative evidence dated back to long before the SDF-1's crash landing on Earth, both from meteoric remains and from spark-discharge experiments.

The new data pointed up to a universal chemistry—that the formation and linking of amino acids and nucleotides was all but inevitable. The messenger RNA codon-anticodon linkages that blueprinted the production of amino acids seemed to operate on *a coding intrinsic to the molecules themselves*. This meant that life throughout the universe would be very similar and that *some force dictated that it be so*.

Admiral Hayes skimmed over all that; it had little to do with the war. He skimmed some of Dr. Lang's hypotheses and preliminary findings, too: that somehow the very energies that drove Robotechnology were identical to the shadowy forces governing molecular behavior. There was also mention of this irritatingly mystical Protoculture, something none of the alien defectors had had sufficiently high clearance to have learned much about.

Lang, it appeared, was monumentally frustrated that the hints and suspicions couldn't be verified. But he was vocal about his suspicion that this Protoculture the Zentraedi were so obsessed with was the key to it all-molecular behavior, the war, the origins of life, ultimate power.

The point of the presentation was obvious even to an aging flag-rank officer whose Academy biochemistry classes were far behind him. "Let me see if I'm completely clear about what you're telling me.

"You believe our genetic backgrounds, the Zentraedi's and that of the human race, are similar. And because of the possibility that we might all be part of the same species, you hope to promote peace talks."

Lisa was nodding, wide-eyed as the little girl he remembered. "But will all this convince the UEDC to open negotiations, sir?"

He sighed, the heavy brows lowering, staring down at the briefing file before him on the coffee table. Lisa held her breath.

"I'm not sure," her father said at last. He looked up at her again. "But I'll present it to them and make sure they listen, then we'll see what they say."

For the first time since she left the SDF-1, Lisa smiled.

Miriya bent over the VT machine, refining her game. Next to her, on the floor, were two plastic pans filled with playing tokens. Frankie Zotz had had to refill the game's reservoir twice to pay off all her winnings. She ignored his sweaty invitations to go play some other game—or, better yet, take a rain check and just go—with a slit-eyed amusement and a dangerous air that kept him from pressing her too hard about it.

Max came downstairs with Rick, holding his own tray of tokens. Suddenly, he stopped yammering his overcheerful encouragements about how Rick would eventually get the hang of the computer games. That was fine with Rick; he had had just about enough light banter.

Max paused on the stairs. "Oh! *That girl!* Sitting at that game!"

Rick looked at the green hair. She wore a tight brown body suit that showed off a lithe figure, and a flamboyant yellow scarf knotted at her throat. "So? What about her?"

"Isn't she incredible?" Max said, more excitedly than Rick had ever heard Max talk about anything. "I've been seeing her everywhere."

"Well, she *is* sort of attractive," Rick had to admit, his mind too full of Lisa Hayes and Minmei for him to go on at any greater length.

Max, the renowned VT wizard, wasn't much when it came to the pursuit of females; his few fumbling attempts with one or another of the Terrible Trio had failed, and he retreated completely when Sammie, Vanessa, and Kim became involved with the three Zentraedi ex-spies, Konda, Bron, and Rico.

Max's modest, self-effacing shipside persona made him a sort of uninteresting doormat for women. Perhaps he wasn't suave or seductively menacing enough. So when he wasn't out in a Veritech, he kept to himself for the most part.

But this was different; the Close Encounters arcade was his turf. "Maybe I can get her in a game with me!" Max said, as he went racing down the stairs.

There was quite a crowd around Miriya; she had rolled up one of the largest scores ever on the Veritechs game. She felt a little irritated, even a bit strange, with all these Micronians gathered around. Yet she endured their gaze, proud and pleased to show off her prowess.

She briefly considered the idea that her strange sensations had something to do with the damned Micronian food. It was nothing like the cold, processed, sanitized rations of the Zentraedi; human food had strange textures and flavors, odd biological constituents. It was all animal tissue and plant substances, and she suspected it was affecting her system.

She shook off the feeling and kept playing, rolling her score higher and higher, until she went over the top, beating the game, and more tokens poured into her tray. Getting enough money to survive in Macross had been no problem for Miriya since she had discovered the arcades.

Now someone pressed through the crowd: an unremarkable-looking VT pilot with a tray of token winnings in his hands. She was inclined to dismiss him; dozens of men had made overtures to her since she first came to the SDF-1.

But there was something different about this one, she thought.

Max worked up the nerve to say, "'Scuse me; would you be interested in playing a game with me? From what I've seen, I think we'd be equally matched. Don't you?"

He looked so young and eager that she almost laughed in his face and ignored him. Then she considered the tray of tokens in his hands. Miriya knew enough about the arcades to appreciate how good he must have been to have accumulated so many of the glittering pieces.

Of course it was beyond the realm of possibility that this slim youngster could be the premier enemy killer, but if he provided some competition, it might make for useful practice.

She looked at him languidly beneath long black lashes. Max felt his heart pounding. "Are you willing to bet all that?" Miriya asked.

He gasped happily. "Yes, I am!" He set his tray down next to hers, then scooted around into the seat opposite her. He babbled, "This is absolutely terrific! I know we're gonna have a great game!"

Watching from the sidelines, Rick wondered if there wasn't something else Max could do to screw up his chances of impressing her. Trip over her, maybe, or throw up.

But once in his seat, Max took on the air of confidence and aplomb that was his in matters regarding the VTs. "How about starting with level B? All right with you?"

She shrugged, somehow making it seem alluring and yet indifferent. "Fine."

"All right. Here we go."

He deposited the tokens, and the screen lit. Miriya had picked red for the color of her VT; Max selected blue, for the trim on his own ship. He didn't notice that Miriya's eyes suddenly narrowed at that choice.

Little animated Minmei figures walked out from either side

of the screen to strike a gong in the center, and the action began. They guided their VTs through the twisting, changing computer-modeled landscape, using control sticks and foot pedals, maneuvering at each other and firing.

It didn't take long for Miriya to lose her nonchalance. Try as she might, she couldn't gain the advantage on him, couldn't shake him once he'd gained on her. A frown crossed her face, then a sudden flare of rage, when his fighter destroyed hers. She hid the expression in an instant, looking at him more closely.

The video warriors gathered around them were aghast. It had been a master-level fight. Max grinned at her. "Whoops! Looks like I won, huh? Wanna go on to level A?" He winked at her.

Rick groaned to himself. Somewhere along the line, Max had learned *exactly* how to antagonize beautiful young women.

She regarded him coldly. "Yes. Let's go on to level A. That should prove quite interesting." This time she would give the fight serious attention.

Max fed in more tokens; this time a blue hemisphere sprang from the game, a holoprojection. The muttering of the growing crowd became louder, until the real purists silenced everybody.

The miniature Veritechs flew over the flat surface of the gaming table now, going to Battloid mode and taking their autocannon in hand at high port. There was a moment in which Miriya gazed through Max's blue-trimmed, ghostly mecha, through his blue aviator glasses, into his eyes.

Somehow, she knew in that moment; all the rest of the game would only be proof of what her instincts were telling her.

The little Battloid computer images looped and fired, maneuvering on each other, going to Guardian or Veritech as their players decreed. There were outbursts and yells from the onlookers as the game moved. It was the fastest, most canny maneuvering anyone had ever seen; even though side bets were strictly illegal, everybody was making them.

Frankie Zotz projected it onto the arcade's main screen. Veteran players looked on in awe at the amazing dogfight. Tiny missiles and tracers spat; the computers could barely keep up with the instructions coming from the control sticks. The minuscule mecha circled and attacked.

Miriya used the same tactics she had used that day in her Quadrono armor; his responses were the same. For a moment, it seemed to her that her simulacrum Battloid had *become* a miniature Quadrono. Any doubts she had were swept away.

Max was thinking, *Boy is she beautiful!* as he played his best at the machine. Another VT pilot, a lady's man, might have lost to Miriya on purpose. But then, another VT pilot probably couldn't have won.

People were whooping and cheering on the sidelines. In her mind's eye, Miriya saw the apocalyptic combat in the streets of Macross, as her own powered armor smashed through buildings and wreaked havoc, backpack thrusters blaring. She also saw that one-on-one final confrontation, when she had bolted rather than die in a point-blank shootout.

And just as his autocannon rounds had defeated her that day, Max's VT image destroyed hers. The red VT fragmented and flew into modeled, spinning bits, then de-rezzed to nothingness.

The blue hemisphere faded away, leaving her open-mouthed and blinking. *I lost! This cannot be! I will not be humiliated again!*

The victorious Battloid image's head turret swung back, and a little figure that looked suspiciously like Rick Hunter appeared, crying the word "STRONG!!" as a tiny Minmei raced up to throw her arms around his neck, kissing him and kicking her feet. The real Rick Hunter, still standing on the staircase, edged back in order to be more inconspicuous and thought dark thoughts about the sense of humor of video game designers.

An onlooker was saying to Max, "I dunno how you pulled that off, buddy."

"Aw, there were a couple of tight spots in the middle and near the end, but all in all, it wasn't too tough."

"*Oh!*" Miriya breathed. The insult of it. So she'd presented him with little challenge, eh? She rose, turning on one booted heel.

Max forgot his warm victory feelings and plunged after her. He caught her wrist, not knowing how close he was to getting a fist in the throat. "Wait, I've been wanting to speak to you for a long time.

I think you're wonderful, and I want to get to know you better. This is my only chance to get your name and phone number."

His grip was very strong, but not painful, his palm very warm. For a moment Miriya felt as though her wrist were burning.

"My name is Miriya," she said coldly. "And I don't currently have a phone number." She turned to go, tugging at his grip. The feel of his skin against hers made her feel a typical Zentraedi loathing of contact between the sexes but stirred something else, something she couldn't put a name to.

Now that she had met her archenemy, Miriya was confused. Killing him on the spot was out of the question; she suddenly didn't know *how* to cope with her mission. What he said about her brought back the strange, blurry feelings that the Micronian food gave her.

Max kept hold of her wrist. "Then, would you meet me in the park this evening? By the Peace Fountain, at nine o'clock?"

*Fool! You've sealed your fate!* she thought. Somehow the thought of slaying him made her angry rather than exultant. "Oh, whatever you want! Just let me go!"

His fingers loosened, and she snatched her wrist away, saying an icy, "Thank you." Then she whirled and ran, fleet as a deer, driven by a storm of conflicting emotions.

Max watched admiringly, breathing, "Isn't she something? Whew!"

Looking down from the staircase, Rick silently wished Max better luck than *he* was having.

# 06

When you're caught up in a war and thinking mostly about the enemy, it's easy to forget that there are other fronts on which you should at least attempt to strike a truce.

Lisa Hayes, *Recollections*

IN A CORRIDOR DEEP IN UEDC HEADQUARTERS, LISA HAYES SAT fretfully, shifting and fidgeting. She heard footsteps approaching and looked up to see her father. "Well, I talked to them," he said.

Tension twisted her middle. "Did they make any decisions?"

"You can never be certain about these things, but I think they're ready to accept the idea of peace talks."

She drew an excited breath, then smiled at him fondly. "I'm so proud of you for having the courage to take on this fight!" She stood on tiptoe to kiss his cheek.

Later, as they sat on an upholstered bench in a lift car, she asked him, "Is anything wrong, Father?" He had been staring at her strangely for minutes.

"I've been thinking of how you remind me of your mother. And how proud she'd be."

She blushed, very pleased. "Thank you, Father."

He shocked her by saying, "So, tell me how your love life's going these days. Are you going out with anyone special? Anybody I should know about?"

It took her so off guard that she found herself admitting, "Well, there *is* a young man…"

"He's military, of course?" her father said.

"Yes, he is. In fact, he's the one who rescued me from the alien ship."

Admiral Hayes nodded slowly. "Ah yes. Sounds like a good man."

They walked and chatted as they hadn't done in more than three years. The admiral led Lisa through the enormous base, coming at last to a vertical shaft nearly a mile across. It was lined with operations ports, energy systems, and power routing. High above, at ground level, a faceted dome like a cyclopean lens covered the shaft.

"Was there something in particular you wanted to show me out here?" After the relative confinement of the base passageways, it *did* feel like being outside.

Her father led her out to the end of a gantry overlooking the cavernous shaft. They could see down for miles, see up almost as far.

He waved a hand at it. "I wanted you to see the Grand Cannon, Lisa. Before we enter into any peace negotiations with the aliens, we're going to fire it at them."

She couldn't believe her ears. "What?" The cry seemed lost in the abyss that was the cannon's barrel.

Admiral Hayes wore a grim look, his strong jaw set. "Even though the satellite reflector system isn't in place yet, we expect to wipe out a large segment of the enemy fleet by pulling off a surprise attack spearheaded by a volley from the Grand Cannon. Once they've seen its power, we think they'll enter the negotiations in good faith."

The original plan had been to put huge orbiting mirrors in place to direct the cannon's bolts as needed; otherwise, its field of fire was very narrow indeed. But with the alien warships so numerous and so close to Earth, it was really only a matter of time before part of their fleet drifted into range.

Lisa spat, "This Grand Cannon probably couldn't wipe out a small division of Battlepods, much less one of their nine-mile-long mother ships! Don't you understand? We *have* to approach them without trying to escalate the war!"

"Some of them have defected to us already! I'm sure the Zentraedi will listen to our peace proposals *without* the use of weapons."

The admiral looked out at the barrel of the gun. "Lisa, how can you be so naive?" He turned to her. "The only thing a warlike power understands is a demonstration of *greater* power! We can't let the

Zentraedi mistake our peace overtures for a sign of weakness. We must deal from strength!"

He paced to the observation platform at the very end of the gantry, hands clasped behind him. "How can you expect peaceful intentions from a race bred and trained for nothing but war? Even if their genetic structure is identical to ours, we have no real knowledge of what factors in their background motivate them, or how strongly."

"But Father," she began hopelessly.

He forged on. "No, Lisa! If history tells us anything, it's that caution and strength are needed when dealing with an unpredictable foe. We've already set a date for the firing of the cannon; we'll see about the peace talks after that."

She stood mutely, hair stirred by air currents in the yawning shaft. "I'm sorry, dear," he told her. "But there's nothing more to discuss."

"Yes. So I see."

Even with strange rumblings of unseen events on the war front, the public demanded that its hunger for other news be fed. The interest in celebrities and media idols was never satisfied for long.

A press conference had been called in the lobby of Macross General Hospital. It was crowded with print and broadcast journalists, shoving and elbowing, aiming lights and lenses and microphones. In the middle of it all was Lynn-Minmei, the reigning queen of Macross and the SDF-1.

Not even nineteen yet, she was used to the lights and attention, a gamine, black-haired lovely. Her tremendous charm and vivacity had bolstered the ship's morale through its darkest moments and won the heart of almost everyone on board.

Next to her sat her costar and third cousin, Lynn-Kyle, a saturnine, sullen young man with flowing black hair that reached down past his shoulder blades. Kyle, the pacifist who was nonetheless an unbeatable martial-arts expert, wore a bandage around his head. He was completing his convalescence after having saved Minmei from a falling spotlight during a Zentraedi attack on the battle fortress.

Lynn-Kyle glared at the reporters and the camera and sound

people. He always held the public in some contempt, scorning them for their willingness to let the military prosecute the war. "Minmei," one man was saying, waving a mike at her, "is it true you've been helping Kyle recover, remaining *right beside his bed for the whole week*?"

Minmei frowned at him, and Kyle glowered, but they were used to that kind of innuendo by now. "I don't think I'd put it quite that way," she replied.

A woman persisted. "Rumor has it both of you are about to get married. Got anything to say about that?"

"Absolutely untrue!" she fired back.

That didn't keep another guy from asking, "Can you tell us how your ex-boyfriend reacted when you told him about these marriage plans?"

She felt like blowing her stack, then saw that this might be a chance to divert the focus of the interview. "Oh, you must mean Rick Hunter." She gave a silvery laugh. "He was just a friend."

Sitting up on his bunk, knees clasped to himself, watching the live coverage, Rick made a sour face, shaking his head. "Yeah. I guess that's all I was."

He felt like an idiot, a complete sucker. Time and again he had convinced himself that Minmei cared for him.

There was something about her, something flirtatious and impulsive. It was something that didn't want to release anyone who had fallen under her spell because, he supposed, that would be too much like rejection. So every time he had come close to getting over her, she had shown up to raise his hopes all over again.

Well, it looked like that wouldn't be a problem anymore. A little trip down the aisle for the two darlings of stage and screen would at least cut Rick free once and for all.

But the reporters weren't having any of Minmei's evasion. "Oh, come on, now! That's not what *we* heard!" "You used to be pretty close to him, right?" "You mean to tell us you and Hunter never discussed marriage at all?"

Minmei looked vexed but didn't answer. Rick thought back once again to those long days they had spent together, stranded and lost in a remote part of the SDF-1, when they first met. When it looked like they weren't going to make it, she had admitted to Rick her lifelong desire to be a bride.

They held a mock ceremony, marked by a very real kiss, only to be interrupted by rescuers before they could say their vows. Rick wondered if any of that was passing through Minmei's beautiful head or if she had dismissed it from her mind as she seemed to dismiss anything that didn't fit with her desires and attitudes of the moment.

He told himself that he would probably never get a clearer sign. It was finally time to put her out of his thoughts and try to get back to living his life.

In other quarters, the micronized Zentraedi defectors were gathered around a screen, utterly enthralled as they gazed at Minmei.

They were dressed in ordinary work clothes and came in the assortment of sizes and shapes that any random group of human males might include. Except for a few skin tones that seemed a little odd—mauve, albino-white, a pale, pale green—there was nothing to mark them as alien. Since the incident with Karita and the muggers, they all took great pains to avoid trouble. The military's decision to keep them all confined to their quarters chafed but was accepted.

The SDF 1 authorities had provided them with quarters and rations and so forth and were spending long hours debriefing them, though as low-ranking warriors there was little of strategic value the defectors could tell. No one had yet begun a systematic orientation program to familiarize them with human life; since the military believed there was always the chance they might return to the Zentraedi fold, the less they knew, for now at least, the better.

But they could watch Minmei and listen to her voice—the voice that had enticed them away from war making.

Now, one of them said, "Rico, what do they mean by 'marriage'? Why do they keep talking about it?"

There was some grumbling, as others were troubled by the enigma, too. Rico considered his answer. He understood only a little more about human existence than the others, but they looked to him for answers, and he didn't want to seem at a loss.

"Um, because marriage is something important. When two people get married, they go off someplace private and spend their time pressing their lips together."

This business of pressing lips had been mentioned before among the Zentraedi, had been one of the prime matters of fascination that had led to the defections. But still, the thought of such unbridled contact between the sexes sent the erstwhile warriors into a tizzy.

"Maybe they won't make us do it?" "My lips aren't ready for that sort of thing!" "I dunno; something tells me it might feel good." "Lemme at 'er!"

Some babbled and exclaimed to one another; others started shaking visibly or gnawing their fingernails. A few tried rubbing their top and bottom lips together and concluded that they were doing it wrong somehow. At least one swooned.

At the interview, Kyle found another microphone shoved into his face. "Tell the truth: *have* you proposed marriage to Minmei?"

He was calm, unflappable, on the outside. "No, I haven't."

He and Minmei were not close by blood, although their families had kept close bonds due to friendships and shared business investments in the White Dragon and Golden Dragon restaurants. He had grown up with Minmei very much like an adoring little sister to him.

But that had changed over time, as much as he'd fought it. It was the tremendous battle inside him compared to which mere physical fights were children's antics. Everyone thought the self-discipline he brought to the marital arts was a reflection of his inner calm; in fact, it was a reflection of the iron will that barely kept him from yielding to temptation. He'd spent all his young adulthood locked in fierce battle against his own impulses.

And most difficult of all were the movies they made together, the shared work and intensity of their scenes, especially the love scenes. It was so easy for acting to slide over into the real thing. The impulses were very patient and unrelenting. He drove them off each day, only to have them return fresher and stronger than ever the next.

But no more. Being with Minmei aboard the SDF-1, seeing the

others who coveted her, had decided Kyle. No one else could have her.

"Sounds like a pretty weak denial." The interviewer grinned at him. "Maybe you just haven't had the chance, right?"

Kyle said in his calm, measured tones, "No, I've been thinking about, um..."

The newsman was watching him like a ferret. "Yes?"

"Thinking about how I'd actually say it to her. Because I don't mind telling you, it's something I've considered."

He heard Minmei's gasp next to him, and the mass intake of breath by the reporters. Flashbulbs began popping, and everyone began talking at once.

"Minmei, what d' you have to say?" "Have you set the date?" "Tell our viewers: Would you accept if he proposes?" "Give us a shot of you two holding hands!" "Kiss 'er, Kyle!" "Where d' you two plan to honeymoon?"

But they paid the reporters no attention. "Kyle, are you serious?" Her eyes looked enormous. They sat there, gazing at each other, while the furor boiled around them.

His screen switched off, Rick lay with head pillowed on elbows, feeling utterly wretched. *I can't believe it. All this time she's been waiting for Kyle to propose to her.*

There was a knock at the door, and Max showed up, dressed in civvies: sports jacket, slacks, sweater, and tie. He wore a cheerful, eager look that made him seem sixteen or so.

"Sorry to bother you, boss. But I'm thinking of wearing this tie to meet Miriya. And I wondered if it made me look too sophisticated, you know? Or maybe I should go the other way, wear a gold chain..."

After Rick got rid of Max, he decided to get some fresh air. He wandered up to a parklike area on one of the observation decks and stared out a viewport as high as a billboard and longer than two.

Earth swung by above him, a crescent of swirling blue and white in the darkness. He sat and tried to spot Alaska.

After a while a familiar voice, holding a trace of mischief, said, "Well, if it isn't Lieutenant Hunter, as I live and breathe!" He looked up to see Claudia standing nearby. "Oh. Hi, how're you?"

They hadn't seen each other a great deal lately, partly because they had been so busy and partly because they both still ached with the grief of Roy Fokker's death, and seeing each other brought it up all over again.

But now she came over to sit next to him. "Not bad. But what're you doing up here at this hour?"

"Couldn't stand my quarters anymore."

"Ah. You saw the press conference."

"Mm-hm."

She sat down, crossing her knees, resting her chin on her hand, helping him watch Earth. "You *could* get along without her. She isn't that terrific."

"She is to me!" Rick wouldn't have taken that from anyone else now that Roy was gone. But Claudia had an honesty that was hard not to respect and give its due. And she was quite capable of getting mad right back at you if she felt it was warranted. Claudia was not someone you wanted to be mad at you if you could avoid it.

"You're bright; you should be with somebody else," she said after a bit.

"I don't know that I want to be. I'm stuck on her."

"Why, Rick?"

"I don't *know* why! Maybe she's just my type."

Claudia put one finger to her chin, eyeing him sidelong. "I don't know. I sorta picture you being with somebody more mature. You know: someone more experienced? Who's been through a big romance and a broken heart?"

*Oh, great, just what I need!* Rick thought. *Some other walking wounded to hang around with!* But he couldn't help listening very closely.

"It'd be good for you to be with someone who can appreciate a relationship. Those people're around, y' know. Sometimes they turn out to be your next door neighbor. Or even... your superior officer."

"Huh?"

She rose. "Gotta go."

"Claudia, you mean Lisa, don't you?"

She glanced back over her shoulder at him. "Did you hear me mention anybody by name? I only said people like that are around. Sometimes they've been known to pass by so close, you can't even see them."

She started off once more, throwing back over her shoulder, "Now, don't stay up too late. Things will look a lot better in the morning."

He watched her go and said very softly to himself, "Wow."

Rick sat, watching Earth again. The way he had it figured, the SDF-1's orbit would bring Alaska into view in a little while. He went over the message he had flashed to Lisa by prosign dots and dashes.

He wished he had said more.

# 07

The myths of selfless humility and humble allegiance to ideals aside, there is no warrior culture, not that of Japanese samurai, medieval knight, or any other, that does not, upon close scrutiny, have a ruthless, entirely practical side to it. Also universal are egotism and a hypocritical willingness to dispense with all the high-flown language and poetic vows when the grim business of life and death is at hand.

How much more so, then, among the cloned, bred-for-battle Zentraedi? In the case of Miriya Parino, female warlord of the Quadronos and arguably the greatest fighter of her race, the matter is certain: Her soaring pride and utter self-confidence had been her hallmark until she was bested both in the air and on the ground by Max Sterling. Her emotional ferment was such that the law of her kind, the vendetta, was the only road open to her—vengeance, by any means possible.

Is it any wonder, then, that what happened next has provided fuel for songs, arguments, dissertations, and grand opera for generations since?

Altaira Heimel, *Butterflies in Winter: Human Relations and the Robotech War*

THE SUPER DIMENSIONAL FORTRESS PROWLED CAUTIOUSLY through the void, vigilant against attack and yet resigned to battle as only a seasoned veteran can be.

The Zentraedi had come pressing battle upon the ship many times before, would come again. Life in between clashes was, therefore, to be lived that much more fully. Death was all around—

the war had gone on for years; nobody aboard thought, any longer, that it couldn't as easily be *their* number that would come up the next time around.

In the center of Macross was a park, lovingly and carefully put together by the inhabitants almost blade of grass by blade of grass. Overhead was an Earthly summertime evening, courtesy of the EVE system. There was even the sound of crickets—descendants of good-luck pets who had somehow survived the war.

Max Sterling paced fitfully under a streetlamp near the Peace Fountain that trickled and gurgled a few yards away. He checked his watch for the seventh time in two minutes.

"Jeez; it's almost nine. I hope she's all right."

He was worried that Miriya wouldn't show up—worried even more, really, that she would. Just an average-looking young man straightening his necktie and hoping his only sports jacket didn't look too shabby, and recalling with a sudden sinking feeling that he had forgotten to pick up the flowers he had ordered.

He didn't know that death hunted afoot and that the pounce was near; he wouldn't know for several seconds yet that cruel eyes were watching him from the shadows.

"I can't believe I asked her to meet me in the park—a girl, at night!" he muttered. "She could get mugged or something."

In fact, street crime in Macross was all but nonexistent. And punishments were such that recidivism was just about nil; but that sort of reasoning meant nothing to a young man waiting for a woman who had him mesmerized, entranced, enraptured. A woman he had met only a few hours before.

A woman who stood in the dark poised, to kill him.

Then he heard running footsteps behind him, and her voice. "Maximillian, prepare for your doom!" It was a literal translation of a Quadrono war cry.

Miriya had gotten to the spot well in advance, seen him arrive, watched him. She had been set to kill him precisely at their appointed meeting time, a quarter hour before. But she had only watched him, hating him all the more but feeling strange—feeling drawn to him in some mysterious way she couldn't fathom.

She told herself she was merely studying her enemy's movements and possible vulnerabilities and fought down the *liking* she had for seeing him in motion. She told herself that she was merely waiting for the most opportune moment; yet though that part of the park was absolutely deserted, she let the minutes slide by.

Miriya observed his eyes, his lips, the way he moved. She felt a trembling in herself that no military mind/body discipline known to her could quiet. But at last, by a tremendous application of will, she hurled herself into battle.

Max was unaware of all of that, of course. At first he thought it was some kind of joke.

He saw her charging at him with the quick grace of a panther, a gleaming knife held high. Miriya's heavy waves of green-dyed hair snapped and flew behind her like a flag. She still wore the brown body suit, the knee-high boots of blue-dyed leather, and the yellow scarf at her throat.

Her eyes started madly. She was Quadrono, a Zentraedi warrior, and yet this miserable human had somehow made her vacillate—made her feel weakness where once there had been only strength! But that would end; Sterling would die, to expiate his sin of defeating her, and she would once more be Miriya the unconquerable.

Max was fumbling through a little greeting he had been rehearsing, his habitual whimsical half smile appearing on his face. "Miriya, it's nice to see you… glad you could… uh…"

This, while she bore down on him, the blade gleaming. The knife was a kind of hybrid cross between a Japanese-style *tanto* and one of the midlength Randall hunting models, with a circular guard. She saw that she had a lot of ground yet to cover and, afraid that he might elude her, hurled it at him, clawing in the meantime for her second blade.

The knives weren't quite like the Zentraedi weapons she was used to, but the balance and heft weren't too different. Although a firearm would have been faster, her incandescent need for revenge had made Miriya choose a more traditional weapon. It had to be reflexes, muscle, eye-to-eye confrontation, and cold steel that settled her score with the hated human.

And in that moment Max Sterling proved that all those dogfight kills weren't some kind of fluke. His psychomotor responses were the fastest the SDF-1 meds had ever measured—his coordination and reflexes were unprecedented.

Max was still trying to figure out what she was talking about when his body saw the flash of steel, understood, and ducked; he was doing his best to recall the awkward, rather romantic little speech he had meant to make to her when those supreme and somehow *strangely given* combat reflexes cut in.

His evasion was barely a flicker of movement; the knife flashed past him to land solidly in a tree trunk.

This was the first time she had ever missed. But she kept corning at him.

Stunned, Max watched her charge headlong toward him. She threw the sheath of the first knife far from her; it made no sound, landing in the grass.

"Hey, are you crazy?" Everything had suddenly slid into place within him; he already loved her so, but the physical Sterling, the part that made him unbeatable, was broadcasting warnings and threat updates, putting his body in motion.

She drew a second, sheathed blade from the open front seam of her body suit. "I am Quadrono Leader Miriya Parino: Zentraedi warrior!"

Max gulped. "There goes our first date."

But something in him had already changed; his balance was forward, on the balls of his feet—he felt nearly weightless—and his hands were curled into the fastest fists on the SDF-1.

However, he was still infatuated with her; he held himself in check when all his impulses were to counterattack. A little thing like attempted murder couldn't alter the fact that he was hopelessly in love with her.

She had seen him pacing, heard his concern for her. The weakling human fears—for the safety of an imagined loved one, of all things!—were so contemptible and misplaced, and yet...

Somewhere deep inside of her she knew, with a clear and pure knowledge, that Max's worry was a reflection of his regard for her.

Who else, in the course of her matchless military career, had ever shown such simple, loving concern for Miriya Parino's well-being?

No one. Not ever. The very thought galvanized her, launched her forward to murder.

The sheath hissed briefly with a metallic rasp as the blade glimmered wickedly under the soft park streetlights. "You're such a fool! Fight for your life!"

There was something nauseatingly vulnerable and adoring in his eyes; the expression with which he regarded her was unworthy of any true warrior—but it sapped her determination so.

Yet inside her, a furnace as hot and powerful as any Protoculture engine burned. *Kill him! Kill him now, at once! Before… before he can…*

"My life? But why attack me?" Max asked bewildered; but his body was already set—they were both so locked into the physical language of hand-to-hand that a fight was inevitable.

She brought the glitter of the blade up into their line of sight like a fencer so that they could both consider its cold blaze. "*I will have my revenge!*"

His hand went to the hilt of the knife embedded in the tree trunk, and she made new calculations based on his being armed. Sterling's having a knife was so much the better as far as Miriya was concerned; she wanted to kill him in a fight on equal terms, wanted to humble him as he had humbled her—before… before he could…

His hand came away from the haft of the knife—very reluctantly, very slowly, very deliberately. He turned back to her. "I'm afraid I don't know what this is all about."

He left the weapon aside when he might have taken it. His life was in danger, but in another way his life was there, staring at him, a knife in her hand—the person, he was sure, he couldn't live without.

*I wonder what the court-martial punishment is for falling in love with the enemy?*

"What d' you mean, revenge? If you're a Zentraedi, I understand why we have to—to fight." He barely got the word out. "But why d' you want *revenge?*"

She held the short, *tanto-style* knife high, a miniature samurai blade, burnished and keen, that threw the light back like a mirror. "I… have… *reasons!*"

With that she sprang at him, fast as any jungle cat.

But Max Sterling's emotions and misgivings were subject to a sudden override; body and reflexes took over.

An edge so fine that it would have cut a hair floating in the air sliced through the spot where he had been standing, with a curt, sinister sibilance. Max was already aloft.

She spat a Zentraedi oath in frustration, watching him dive and flip to momentary safety. He whirled on her when he might as easily—and more sanely—have run for it. "Miriya, what'd I ever do to you?"

She wasn't blind to his decision to stand when it would be more advisable to run. Like a Valkyrie, she lifted the knife blade again, so that it threw back shards of light.

"You defeated me. And you don't even know who I am, do you?"

She swirled the blade around, *en garde,* so that there was a contoured trail of light between them. "I am the Zentraedi's greatest pilot! And I will not be humiliated by a human *insect!*"

She plunged at him, the razor-sharp edge slitting the air. In less than a second she executed two masterful infighting moves that would have disemboweled a lesser opponent.

But Max Sterling simply wasn't there. He made no countermoves, but he avoided the cuts and thrusts like a shadow. Miriya was even more enraged to see that he wasn't terrified, but rather mystified. That he still felt weakling human emotions for her.

She fought down the chaotic impulses that flared up within her. She slashed again, but the knife hissed through empty space once more.

And she began to know a certain fear. *By the Protoculture! He's so fast!* Her fear had nothing to do with dying; she was Zentraedi. In this strangest battle of her life, she wasn't quite sure *what* that ultimate and most dire of terrors was, the dread that was somehow bound up in Max Sterling. She had had many mental images, wondering about what this utter demon of war would be like; none of them were anything like the truth.

"The first time you were lucky! The second time was your final victory!"

She cut at him, barely missing, Max dodging with that same uncanny speed. "Nothing can save you now!" Miriya hissed. *"I will defeat you!"*

She hurled herself at him, the blood thirsty edge coming around in an eviscerating arc.

# 08

There are old soreheads and young soreheads in our ranks who still denounce the events that occurred near the Peace Fountain that night. Chances are, they won't get the point of this book, either.

To paraphrase Robert Heilbroner, "These people bring lots of *rigor* to our cause, but alas, also *mortis*."

Betty Greer, *Post-Feminism and the Robotech War*

MIRIYA WAS QUICK, TOO, NEARLY AS QUICK AS MAX, AND A clever knife fighter. She maneuvered the next sequence of cuts so that his route of evasion would be past the tree's great roots, and sure enough, he stumbled and went down.

She dove at him gleefully, the white throat open for her death cut. By all rights the duel was hers; it needed only the flick of a wrist to end Sterling's life and expunge her shame. Nothing could explain her slight hesitation, she who had never hesitated before and had lost to no other foe. Nothing could explain it except the sudden vivid image of what he would look like when she killed him.

Flat on his back, Max looked up at her. *This* was the powered-armor pilot he had fought to a standstill days before, first in a furious dogfight over the SDF-1, then in a toe-to-toe confrontation in the streets of Macross itself.

He should have been afraid for his life. But all he could think of was the fact that, squaring off with Miriya's mecha, he'd kept hearing Tex Ritter's old song from *High Noon*, "Do Not Forsake Me, O My Darlin'," echoing through his head. And now he just couldn't help hearing that haunting line—*on this, our weddin' day-ayy…*

Miriya sprang at him; the blade cleaved the air, aimed at his heart. His body responded before he had time for coherent thought; he held up a flat disk of rock, and the knife point skidded from it, striking sparks, nearly taking two of his fingers off but missing by a hair's breadth.

The miss put her off balance; he worked a leg trip. As she rolled to get free and try for his life again, he catapulted toward the first knife, which was still buried in the tree.

She was after him at once. To kill him before... before he could...

"It's no use!" she cried triumphantly, slashing at him. They maneuvered and feinted, the other knife's haft only inches beyond Max's reach. "You're no match for me! Oh, you may be a great man, but what's a man compared to a Zentraedi?"

He faked her away from the tree, turned, and had the knife in his hand like magic, her belated cut only chipping bark.

"Now, we'll see." He held the knife in a fencing grip, almost hesitantly. She went at him.

Impossibly, they set aside any sane knife-fighting style to fence as if they held sabers. The knives struck scintillas of light from each other. Max had learned to fence in school and had sharpened his combat skills in the Robotech Defense Force; Miriya was a Zentraedi—she lived and breathed warfare.

Amazingly, Max engaged her blade in a bind, whirling it around and around, whisking it from her grip. It flew high, landing yards away. The point buried itself in the ground, tantalizingly close and yet so far, too far.

Max held the point of his knife close to her throat. She raised her chin proudly. "I guess I win again," he said, yet there was something in his tone that made him sound unsure.

It was the moment Miriya Parino, warlord of the Quadrono, had never thought she would face. And yet there was such a thing as dignity in defeat, such a thing as her warrior code.

"I've lost to you."

*This is a shame I cannot endure.* She sank to her knees, pulling the scarf down and baring her throat. She waited for the cold kiss of the blade, hoping it would come soon to end her suffering. She couldn't help it, but tears welled up in her eyes—not from fear or even anger but from impulses to which she could put no name.

He was hesitating for some reason; she thought that perhaps he was going to show the cruelty a Zentraedi might in his position. She didn't blame him and was bravely determined to endure whatever he might mete out, but she thought that perhaps he simply needed a word from her to acknowledge her defeat.

"End my life." She lowered her head; the long green tresses hung about her face. "Please. Do it now."

But what she felt wasn't the final cold fire of the knife's edge. His fingers were under her chin, lifting her face. "But I couldn't! You're so beautiful…"

Suddenly everything was so unreal, so difficult for her to understand, that it came as only a minor shock to see that he had let the knife fall.

Miriya looked up blissfully into a face that held confusion, wonder, and a certain something else she was only beginning to comprehend.

She never felt herself come to her feet; perhaps she didn't, and the zero-g, flying feeling was real. One final spasm of Zentraedi warrior training made itself felt, telling her to stop him, to stop him before … before he could…

But he already had, and they were kissing, embracing, Miriya in Max's arms. For a while, in the little meadow in Macross's darkened park, there was a place apart from all other worlds. No word was said for a long time, until Max got up his nerve.

"Miriya, this is gonna sound crazy, but—will you marry me?"

"Yes, if you wish. Maximillian, what's 'marry'?"

The three former Zentraedi spies, Rico, Bron, and Kanda, were sitting in the RDF crew lounge not far from the bridge, doing their best to show the Terrible Trio a good time.

Sammie, Vanessa, and Kim were feeling down hearted. It seemed that the SDF-1's voyage would never end, that there was no refuge for the starship anywhere.

No one wanted to guess how much longer the dimensional fortress could last against the Zentraedi armada that hounded them, but the unspoken consensus was that it had pushed its luck to the limit and that they were all living on borrowed time.

"D' you think the Canadians will offer sanctuary to the SDF-1, Kanda?" asked the burly Bron.

If the Canadians could be persuaded to defy the United Earth Defense Council and let the ship land, offer her crew and refugees asylum, there might be hope. It would be the most strenuous test yet of the UEDC's authority as opposed to the autonomous rights of its member states, could perhaps lead to a new civil war, but it was the SDF-1's only hope.

Bron's friend and fellow warrior chewed a bit of food. "I'll tell you one thing: If our request is denied, it means we'll be stranded out here in space *forever*."

The three young women exchanged agonized looks. Little Sammie shook her head, intense and frightened. "Konda, please don't say anything like that!"

Kim, her coffee cup forgotten in her hands, suddenly looked lost and vulnerable. "Surely… *someone* will help us!"

Konda didn't contradict her, but neither did he agree. The six usually had fun when they were together, but now they just stared gloomily into their coffee.

"We must have faith," Rico said—an odd thing coming from one whose only belief had, until some months ago, been the Zentraedi warrior code.

None of them noticed Max Sterling pass by, looking every which way for his commanding officer. "Ah! Just the man I want to see," he muttered, spying Rick Hunter.

Rick sat alone at a table on an upper level of the place, lost in thought, staring out the deck-to-overhead viewports that had space on three sides of him. He was exhausted from the constant flight duty and the added burdens of being a team leader. He was worried about the ship, about his men, and about what he could possibly do to set his love life straight.

Rick looked surprised when Max broke in on his reverie, but he invited him to sit. "It's about last night," Max began. "I think I'm gonna get married."

Rick spat out his coffee and choked a bit until Max patted his back. "That's the most ridiculous thing I ever heard!" he sputtered at last. "You only went on one date! Man, you know she won't be leaving town, so why don't you take some time?"

Max looked stubborn, struggling a bit before he said, "We're in love."

Rick plunged into a lecture that he never would have imagined giving before he became Skull leader. But before he could get too far into why no one should rush into matrimony and how that went triple for VT fighter pilots, Max cut him off.

"Lieutenant, that's not the part that's bothering me." He mopped his brow with his handkerchief. "Y' see, it's ah, I'm not sure how to say this. She's the enemy. Miriya confessed to me that she's a Zentraedi."

Rick stared at him blankly for a long moment. If it had been practically anyone else, he would have doubted his sanity; but he was Max's friend, and besides, he had seen his latest psych evaluation. "How could you let this happen?"

"I love her," Max said, a bit more forcefully than he usually said anything.

"You're talking nonsense! What could you possibly have in common with her?" This, even though the three former spies and the bridge bunnies were keeping company on the other side of the lounge. Rick had been trying to unsnarl his *own* stormy emotional life and couldn't see why other people would want to complicate theirs.

"I'm telling you, I love her," Max insisted. He suddenly hit the table with his fist, making cup and saucer dance. "And there's no problem love won't solve!"

*Oh yeah?* Rick thought ironically; he wished that for just a moment he could do something about his hopeless yearning for Minmei, could understand his complex feeling toward Lisa Hayes. *Max, you've got a lot to learn!*

"There's one problem it won't solve, pal, and that's your silly idealism. Love isn't gonna make you happy, take it from me."

Max was furious. "It doesn't matter what you say, Rick. I'm going to marry this woman with or without your approval."

"Okay, look, so you're attracted to her. How many times does *that* happen to a guy?"

"*She's special!*"

"Take it easy; I'm sorry. I can tell you like her very much."

Max calmed a bit. "I want you to meet her."

"This should be interesting," Rick said, realizing someone had come up to the table.

Miriya Parino of the elite Quadrono battalion of the Zentraedi hordes looked like the cover of a fashion magazine. Rick didn't know what he had expected; he had never met a female Zentraedi and had seen few males who didn't look ugly enough to stop a clock.

What he *hadn't* expected was a gorgeous young woman in a simple, graceful pink summer frock set off by a blue sash about her slim waist. She wore her dark green hair in a single lush tail drawn forward over one white shoulder.

"We were just talking about you," Max told her with a sublime, starry-eyed smile.

Rick blinked, flabbergasted, then got out haltingly, "You were right, Max. She *is* beautiful. I—I think I understand now."

Miriya smiled serenely. "I'm so pleased to meet you. You look just the way Maximillian described you."

She was terribly happy that she and Max were to marry, though this odd, strangely thrilling human custom was more a mystery than anything else. She suddenly looked and felt nothing at all like a Zentraedi commander and warrior, but she didn't mind. Everything was so clear and bright and wonderful…

Max's decision to buy her new clothes had plainly been a good one; the looks she'd drawn from people, and from Rick in particular, were not the kind one directed at an enemy.

It was difficult to believe that only hours before, she had been trying to kill Max. He had spent much of the intervening time trying to clarify what "love" meant. She decided she wanted more clarification—a lifetime's worth.

"You're a lucky man, Max," Rick told him, without taking his eyes off Miriya. Then he grinned. "And forget all that nonsense I told you."

Max was all smiles again. Rick added, "And to guarantee you two have a great wedding day, I plan to be there to kiss the bride!"

Max shrugged and nodded cheerfully, a little irony creeping into his tone. "I knew I could count on you, boss. Only—"

He reached out to take Miriya's hand. "You'd better hold off on that until I explain it all to the future Mrs. Sterling. The RDF forces are shorthanded as it is, and I'd hate to see Skull Leader wind up in intensive care."

The preparations for the wedding began that same day. Gloval was strangely silent, except to give his permission and authorize the sort of major bash the ship's media moguls hungered and cried out for. Rick knew Gloval well enough to know that the captain had good reasons for a move like this, and he wondered what those might be.

News of the coming nuptials had the entire dimensional fortress abuzz. It galvanized crewpeople and refugees alike, a reason at last to celebrate and forget the war for a while. Mayor Tommy Luan and the director of the in-ship broadcasting system and a hundred others threw themselves into the arrangements.

Somewhat to their surprise, they found that Gloval had ordered that no effort be spared in making the occasion a major event. Miriya could have had ten thousand bridesmaids if she wanted; the RDF people and the Veritech pilots in particular kicked out the chocks to mount a pageant worthy of a royal wedding.

The preparations went quickly; the marriage became the center of existence for quite a few people. They were sewing, cooking, decorating; the RDF personnel rehearsed their drills, and the engineers rigged the most special of special effects.

All the activity didn't go unnoticed. In the alien armada, cold and merciless eyes watched the peculiar goings-on. Fateful, dire decisions were near.

# 09

These letters pile up, Vince dear, perhaps to be read by you someday or perhaps not, but today especially I have to set down how full my heart is—more so than at any time since Roy was killed.

I heard Gloval murmuring something astounding while he was sitting in his command chair: "Capulets and Montagues." I thought he was going soft; heaven knows the rest of us have. But when I looked at the clipboard he had been studying, it was an intel rundown on books Miriya had screened from the Central Data Bank while she was here—when she was hunting Max. Shakespeare was there, of course.

I don't know what to think, except—damn it! We've got to change the ending this time!

Lt. Claudia Grant, in a letter to her brother Vincent

THE SPECTACULAR FIREWORKS LIT UP THE SPACE ALL AROUND THE SDF-1. It was only the beginning, but *what* a beginning. The whole area was illuminated in bright colors; civilians and RDF people alike crowded every available viewport, oohing and ahing.

Then the fighting mecha appeared, to execute their part in things. From the flight decks of the fortress and the two immense supercarriers that had been joined to it like stupendous metal forearms, Veritechs swarmed out to take up their places.

A broad, flat roadway of light, radiant in all the colors of the spectrum, sprang from the bow of the flattop *Daedalus*, like a shining runway. The Veritechs zoomed out, retros flaring.

Excitement hit fever pitch all through the ship. It was more than just the occasion of a wedding—even the first wedding that anyone could think of that had taken place in outer space. There was something about the joining of a human and a Zentraedi that spoke directly to the humans' longing for peace and a return home. It was a ray of hope that the terrible Robotech War might yet be ended short of catastrophe.

For Max and Miriya, it was simply the happiest day of their lives. They came swooping out of the void in Max's VT fighter right on schedule, Max wearing his tux and sitting in the forward seat, piloting. Miriya sat in the rear, making constant corrections to the fall of her wedding veil, the arrangement of her bridal bouquet. She had won so many decorations for bravery and courage under fire, yet she found herself unable to stop trembling.

The VTs had gone into Battloid mode, looking like giant ultratech knights. They positioned themselves in pairs, facing one another across the rainbow runway of light. They lifted weapons, the long gray autocannon that had been used on other occasions to wage savage war on the Zentraedi.

Now, though, the weapons had been fitted to throw forth brilliant beams of light into reflective aerosols that had been misted around SDF-1 for just that purpose. They shone like scores of crossed swords over the gleaming approach path. Max flew his ship under the military salute at low speed as Miriya looked around at it open-mouthed, delighted beyond words.

The fighter set down on *Daedalus*'s deck, and there were more mecha—the attack machines of the tactical corps ground units. Monstrous Destroid cannon, Excaliburs, Raidar Xs, and the rest sent harmless beams to form a canopy overhead as Max taxied for the elevator that would lower his ship to the hangar deck.

Cameras were already tracking the VT, and close, total coverage was planned for every portion of the ceremonies. Max and Miriya didn't mind; they wanted everybody to share in their total joy.

But not everyone did.

Breetai, the mountainous commander of the Zentraedi armada, gazed into the projecbeam image from intercepted SDF-1 signals. "This is the oddest Micronian custom we've observed yet, is it not,

Exedore? Can you explain to me what Miriya Parino is doing?"

*What* she was doing was evident: She was walking slowly next to a blue-haired human, dressed in a rather elaborate and inconvenient-looking outfit, clutching what appeared to be a handful of plants.

She was also clinging to the Micronian's arm, causing Exedore to speculate that perhaps she had been wounded in the leg or fallen ill. Although she didn't *look* ill; she looked—Exedore didn't know *what* that expression on her face could mean.

Breetai gazed at the image. He was a creature who would have had no trouble passing for a Micronian himself, except that he was some sixty feet tall. Terrible wounds received in battle against the Invid species, implacable enemies of the Zentraedi, had left him with a glittering metal half cowl covering the right side of his skull, the eye replaced by a shining crystal.

Next to him was Exedore, a hunched and fragile-looking Zentraedi, far smaller than Breetai—almost a dwarf by the standards of his race. But within Exedore's big, misshapen skull was most of the accumulated lore and knowledge of his kind and a mind that Breetai relied upon heavily.

Exedore's bulging, lidless, pinpoint-pupilled eyes were fixed on the projecbeam image of the wedding, too. "Your Excellency, if I am not mistaken, she is getting 'married.'"

They were standing in Breetai's command station, overlooking the vast bridge of his colossal flagship. The flagship, nine solid miles of weapons, shields, and armor, was in a state of disrepair after its furious engagements with the SDF-1 and the RDF mecha. The transparent bubble surrounding the command station had been shattered; only jagged pieces of it remained around the frame.

Zentraedi were warriors, not slaves or drudges; they had little taste for anything that smacked of common toil, and even less talent for it. Those prejudices were approved of and reinforced by their Robotech Masters; without the Masters, the Zentraedi would sooner or later find themselves without functioning tools of war.

Exedore explained, "According to my research, it is a condition in which male and female Micronians live together."

Breetai was stunned. His harsh, guttural bass voice filled the command station. "Live together? Miriya Parino and this puny Micronian male?"

"Correct, m'lord."

But for what reason? The towering Zentraedi warlord, master of a cloned race that didn't know love, family, or sex, tried to imagine what the purpose could be, why male and female might conceivably desire such *intimacy*. But when he tried, he was assailed by waves of distaste and confusion, by nameless half-seen visions that made him physically ill. He shunted the images aside.

Breetai lowered himself into his enormous command chair, still considering the import of the wedding. "It seems she's taking this spying mission of hers very seriously. Perhaps more seriously than she should."

His first conclusion was that Miriya the dedicated fighter was simply undergoing the tremendous torment of such behavior to infiltrate the enemy and learn the perverse secrets of their obscene social practices. But Breetai saw something in Miriya's face, something that made the towering commander doubt this analysis.

It was like the three spies, Konda, Rico, and Bron, all over again. Breetai felt a certain dread. "Unless my senses deceive me, it would seem she's enjoying herself in some peculiar fashion. Could it be that she too has found the Micronian way of life too enjoyable to resist?"

Exedore answered, "It would appear, sir, that she cannot resist the charm of that Micronian pilot."

Breetai had seen kissing demonstrated when he captured Rick Hunter and Lisa Hayes. He shuddered, recalling the disgusting display, and wondered how any intelligent creature could bring itself to indulge in such baseness.

But the lure of the humans was undeniable; scores of Zentraedi soldiers had secretly conspired to undergo micronization and had gone to live among their former foes. It was the first such mutiny ever to have taken place in the history of the warrior race. Part of the madness had to do with the young human female Minmei and the oddly hypnotic power called "singing" that she exercised.

"Our forces may be in more jeopardy than we believed," Exedore said. "What if the traitors who went over to the human side were not merely mental defectives, as we thought, but rather the first wave in a sea of such deserters?"

Breetai rubbed his huge jaw, the one giant black eyebrow lowering. "It appears this 'love' business is a very powerful thing."

Exedore replied, "I'm afraid I agree with you, sir. It's an emotional factor against which we Zentraedi have no defense. This 'love' could be used as a powerful weapon against us."

Breetai scowled at the image of laughing, joyous humans, of the radiantly happy Miriya and proud, smiling Max. "Weapon, eh?"

"Yes. We must beware."

The intercepted coverage of the wedding showed them flashbulbs popping and people applauding as Max and Miriya cut their cake. The wedding cake was a ten-foot-high model of the SDF-1 in its knightlike Attack mode.

Breetai, growling in his rumbling bass, watched the proceedings angrily. What was there about the blissful looks of Miriya and the Micronian that exerted such a fascination, such a deep pull, on him? He told himself that it was only a commander's need to study a dangerous enemy, refusing to believe that he could feel such a thing as envy for the puny foe.

At the reception, the master of ceremonies was calling for quiet.

"Ladies and gentlemen, today is a very special day. It's more than just a wedding celebration; it's the bonding of two souls dedicated to the protection of our Robotech colony. I'd like to introduce the man who's done so much to make this a unique occasion, the commander of the SDF-1, Captain Henry Gloval!"

There was plenty of applause even though people were still passing around cake and freshening up their champagne after the several toasts that had been drunk.

Gloval stood up, decked out in his dress uniform, laden with medals, braid, and campaign ribbons galore. Rick, who knew the captain a little better than most people there, got the impression that they were going to find out why he had spared nothing to turn the wedding into a major occasion.

Gloval spoke. "Well, to begin with, I extend heartfelt

congratulations to Max and Miriya. This wedding carries with it a great historical significance.

"As you all know, Miriya was a Zentraedi warrior who destroyed many of our ships. She comes from a culture that we have grown to fear and hate."

*Oh, no!* Rick thought. What could Gloval be thinking of? Miriya sat rigid as a statue, staring down at her plate. Max was white. The gathered guests were listening in stunned silence.

"It is the Zentraedi who have caused our present situation," Gloval pressed on. "They alone prevent our return to Earth—our homes and our beloved families." One hand was balled into a fist now. "It is they who have caused injury, destruction,

and endless suffering!"

"Captain, *please!*" Max burst out, just at the same moment that Rick yelled, "Captain!"

Gloval forged ahead. "Now, I know what you're thinking: 'Why is he choosing this time to remind us of these terrible things?' I remind you of them, ladies and gentlemen, because we *must learn to forgive our enemies.*"

His image and his voice went out over screens throughout the fortress—in the barracks, the lounges, the giant monitors in the public squares of Macross City. "Not blindly, not out of ignorance, but because we are a strong and willing nation. We cannot blame the Zentraedi for their inexplicable lust for war. They have never known another way of life, and it has been their only means of survival."

All through the battle fortress, people gazed up at the screens in amazement—some with burgeoning hope, others with growing antagonism.

"Nor can we condemn individuals of that society for the mass insanity of their leaders. Instead, we must look to their good nature. As you may know, dozens of Zentraedi defectors are now aboard the SDF-1, having been reduced to human size. They have made a request to stop the fighting, and I believe it is a genuine request."

He turned to indicate the newlyweds. "The blood of these young people was tested before the ceremony. Zentraedi blood was found to be the same as human blood."

That started murmurs and whispers in the reception hall; in the ship and the city at large, it ignited a thousand arguments and marked a turning point in human thinking.

In the White Dragon, the Chinese restaurant belonging to Minmei's uncle Max and aunt Lena, Mayor Tommy Luan and some others had come over to watch the ceremonies on television. They heard Gloval say, "There is no reason why we cannot coexist in peace. Let this occasion represent a future where all people live in harmony."

Cheers and applause were rising, evidence of the general hunger for an end to war. Gloval held his hands up to silence it. "Please, let me speak a moment longer."

Voices in the background were heard, saluting Gloval for his leadership, courage, and convictions. In the restaurant, Mayor Tommy Luan nodded his head and wiped at a tear. "Captain Gloval is truly a man of peace. A great man."

There were others in the ship who didn't feel the same way, others who smashed bottles in the street or shook a fist at Gloval's image. There had been so many losses, so many deaths, and so much suffering since the aliens' first attack that the hunger for revenge would not die easily.

Gloval had anticipated that, of course. "All of us have lost loved ones, and it will be difficult not to harbor ill feelings toward the Zentraedi. But somehow we must overcome these feelings! We must stop this senseless destruction."

Far beneath the surface of the bleak Alaskan tundra, in the lowest levels of the United Earth Defense Council's headquarters base, Admiral Hayes pointed a remote unit at the TV, and it went dark.

He turned to his daughter and spat, "He's crazy! I don't understand Gloval talking about peace at a time like this!"

Lisa was quick to spring to Gloval's defense, both because he was her former commanding officer and because he was inarguably right. "Father, it's the only way to avoid our own destruction! If we don't start talking peace, it will mean the end of this planet, and not even you would want that!"

He suddenly looked pained. "Lisa!"

"I'm sorry," she told him, "but you *must* stop the Grand Cannon operation immediately!"

Admiral Hayes stubbed out a cigarette and avoided his daughter's gaze. "Plans for use of the Grand Cannon are already set. There's nothing to be done about that now."

# 10

I heard someone next to me saying something about a marriage literally made in the heavens. I held my tongue and was glad no one took the obvious bait, to mention a honeymoon in hell. I silently said my chants for the newlyweds and for us all.

Jan Morris, *Solar Seeds, Galactic Guardians*

GLOVAL STILL HELD HIS AUDIENCE TRANSFIXED. "EACH AND EVERY citizen must develop a responsible attitude toward the efforts for peace. We must learn greater tolerance and meet this challenge. I'm not proposing we lay down our arms but rather that we *extend* the hand of friendship.

"There is a chance for a peaceful solution, and we must make it come to pass. As Max and Miriya, here, have done.

"The Zentraedi are a strong and intelligent people. Let this ceremony stand as a symbol of our desire for peace. We must emulate Max and Miriya: They are the heroes of today and our hope for tomorrow."

It took a moment to realize he was finished, as Gloval turned to let the newlyweds retake the spotlight. Then all at once the cheers and applause were deafening. Streamers and confetti showered around the SDF-1 cake, and everybody was hailing Max and Miriya and blessing their union.

The crowd hailed Gloval as well, and friendship between human and Zentraedi. The Terrible Trio threw themselves into the arms of the three onetime Zentraedi spies—Vanessa to the husky Bron, little Sammie with Rico, and Kim embraced by purple-haired

Konda. The joyous crowd called out toasts and salutes to peace.

Gloval hoped that it had been enough—hoped that the commitment and the determination would still be there when the cheering had stopped.

The headquarters of the Zentraedi supreme commander, Dolza, hung like some titanic hive in the blackness of space. It was the size of a planetoid, an armored moonlet so immense that Breetai's flagship and hundreds of thousands more like it could fit within. Around it, the Zentraedi Grand Fleet was assembling, a force so incredibly vast as to dwarf even Breetai's armada.

Dolza, the Old One, largest of his race, paced within his headquarters. Standing at attention before him were his assembled subordinates. Dolza stopped pacing and looked down at them.

"We can no longer permit this condition to exist. It's becoming a significant threat to Zentraedi power. It seems that we have underestimated the powers of these Micronian vermin."

In the end, it seemed Breetai's trusted adviser Exedore was right: The ancient Zentraedi warnings against any contact with Micronians had been handed down for good reasons, though the reasons had been unknown until now.

A race that could subvert the Zentraedi, make them violate their warrior code—a race that could weaken them so with talk of love and peace! Dolza had seen that it was a threat infinitely more dangerous than the ravaging Invid, that it was something that could end Zentraedi greatness forever, at a single stroke, unless something was done immediately.

"The battle fortress has become too dangerous to continue to exist. Even though it means destroying so many of Zor's secrets and losing valuable knowledge, you are ordered to totally annihilate the SDF-1. The Grand Fleet will soon be mustered and prepared to set forth."

The subordinates smote their chests with their right fists, roaring in unison. "*Ho!*"

Then, Dolza thought grimly, *we shall incinerate the planet Earth and end this threat once and for all.*

...

At the reception, there was the roll of a snare drum, and the master of ceremonies brought out Lynn-Minmei. Rick Hunter sat with his arms folded across his chest and didn't know what to feel.

She was even more beautiful than the first time he had met her—a black-haired, blue-eyed stunner with a naturally winning stage presence. She wore a gold lame gown cut high on her left hip.

She took the microphone; the crowd was eating out of her hand before she even opened her mouth. Minmei paid lavish compliments to the newlyweds, then broke into one of her biggest hits, "To Be in Love."

Rick recalled the first time he had heard it, marooned with Minmei in a deserted portion of the SDF-1, lost and seemingly doomed. He had fallen in love with her there and had thought she felt the same.

Her wonderful voice took the notes with a sure, sheer beauty, caressing the words, taking the crowd under her spell.

Rick saw Miriya take Max's hand shyly. The three alien ex-spies were hugging the bridge bunnies. Konda and Bron and Rico had initially been won over to the human side by that same voice, that same face.

Claudia was trying not to cry; she had done a good job controlling it since Roy was killed, but Minmei's voice had something mystical about it. Rick saw moisture on Claudia's cheek.

Rick looked out the viewport to the emptiness of space. Roy, his best friend, was gone—and Ben Dixon and how many hundreds, how many thousands upon thousands of others? The losses had been terrible.

Deep under the frozen Alaskan ground, Lisa had turned the ceremonies back on. She watched Minmei work her magic and despaired of ever being able to compete, of ever being able to win Rick's love. *How can I? She's so beautiful; her singing—it's like a kind of miracle.*

The broadcast was also intercepted by the armada as it swam like a school of a million bloodthirsty deep-sea creatures in the depths of space. The great warships, bristling with weapons, spiny with their detection and communication gear, prowled hungrily.

In his command station, Breetai looked up at the image and heard the music. "This woman has a voice that… can make a man feel sorrow," he said slowly, heavily. Exedore looked at him worriedly.

Just as Minmei was about to start another song, a priority signal replaced Minmei's image. One of Dolza's staff officers looked down at him.

"Commander Breetai, forgive this interruption, but I bring you top-secret orders from Commander in Chief Dolza."

Breetai shot to his feet, hand outflung. "Hail, Dolza!" He shook off the effects of Minmei's siren song.

"You are ordered to begin a full-scale assault on the SDF-1," the officer informed him. "There are to be no survivors whatsoever, no matter what the cost. That is all."

He disappeared, and Minmei was singing once more. "Well, Your Excellency?" Exedore asked softly.

Breetai stared up sadly at Minmei's image. "It grieves me that the time has finally come. I do not look forward to this task at all, Exedore. That may sound strange, but it's true."

And the haunting beauty of Minmei's voice put that same heavy sorrow in him once more, until he willed himself to reach out and shut it off.

Loyal, insightful Exedore looked at his lord with concern. Half a dozen times he almost spoke of the fear and apprehension that those words, coming from Breetai, put into him. But in the end the small, slight giant held his peace.

But Breetai did not have the only receiving equipment in the fleet. Everywhere in the teeming warships it was the same: Clusters of huge, hulking warriors had gathered around to watch and listen to Minmei—and had heard Gloval as well. The first sounding of the alert signals, the call to arms and to glorious Zentraedi warfare, had touched off more dissent than they had ever experienced before.

"I don't *want* to fight," growled a much—decorated pod commander. He was staring at something tiny that lay in the palm of his hand as though examining his own heart line. Another PC, standing near, tried to get a look at whatever it was; but the first closed his fist.

He did it carefully; he didn't want to damage the tiny Minmei doll that lay there. Bron had given it to him before he and the others defected, seeking shelter and an uncertain future among the humans. The PC had listened to the doll sing until the batteries were all but exhausted. He couldn't explain its appeal… or the power of Minmei's music over him… or why he was unwilling to go out and destroy the SDF-1 when his former comrades in arms were aboard.

The harsh Zentraedi language had few or no words for these concepts, but that didn't change the PC's feelings.

All around them, colossal warriors raced to don combat armor, seize weapons from the racks, grab gear, and get ready for the great assault. The decks thrummed under their massive iron-shod feet.

The second PC opened his palm to the first for an instant. They had been thinking the same thing, for he held another of the tiny souvenir Minmei dolls. He closed his fist again. Opposing the war felt much different, sparked a higher flame of hope, when each realized that the man facing him felt the same.

"It's as though I'm going to be fighting against my own people," the second PC said, struggling to put his thoughts into the limited Zentraedi battle tongue.

NCOs and officers were yelling at various scurrying units to move it, move it, move it. Go! Go! The deck-plates thundered.

But one body-armored NCO, having caught a bit of the exchange, skidded to a halt, his disrupter rifle gripped in one hand.

"D' you realize what the penalty is for disobeying orders in combat?"

Others had been listening to the two pod commanders, half swayed by what they were saying, recalling Gloval's words and Minmei's song. But all of them knew the dreadful punishment the NCO was talking about. Death would be preferable.

One of the bystanders declared, "He's right! We will *have* to fight!"

"Let's move!" someone else cried, and with that they were in motion, scrambling to prepare and race to their battle stations. Everyone, that is, but the first PC. He watched the others go as he reclined back on his bunk, hands behind his head, brooding. At last he brought his hand forth and spent a long time looking at the tiny Minmei doll.

The vast armada began shifting formation, spreading and realigning for the attack.

At the wedding reception, alert sirens began sounding at just about the same time Gloval took the call on a mobile com handset and got the crowd's attention. With the banshee song of the sirens behind him, he announced, "Ladies and gentlemen! It grieves me to say this, but we are now on red alert."

He had to raise his voice to speak over the confusion and outcries of the crowd. "All military personnel report to battle stations at once. Civilians proceed to emergency duties or to designated shelters. The SDF-1 is about to come under full-scale attack."

He swallowed once, with effort It was the first time the enemy had thrown its massed strength at the fortress, and there was little question as to what the final outcome would be.

"God be with you all. Now, move quickly!"

Only a few actually lost their heads and bolted; everyone aboard had been through the fire of battle, and most moved swiftly but with a deliberate calm.

The Terrible Trio finished what they were eating and swapped hugs with the Zentraedi spies before dashing off to the bridge. Striding for the door, Rick Hunter exchanged a brief glance with Minmei but had no time to stop and talk to her, though he wanted to do that more than anything in the world.

A VT duty officer halted amid the flow of people and looked back to the wedding party's table as Max came to his feet, unable to believe what was happening.

"Max, you're excused from duty. Captain's orders! You sit this one out!" Then he was on his way.

Max slowly tugged his bow tie, opening his collar. He sighed deeply, feeling Miriya's eyes on him, and turned to her. "I can't let them down when they need me the most, love."

She drew off her wedding veil. "Of course not, Max. I'll go with you."

He stared at her. "*Huh?*"

Miriya came to her feet. "I've seen your Veritechs, even flew yours for a bit, remember? I can handle one as well as any of your pilots."

"No—"

"I promised in our vows that I would stay by your side, and I will. From now on, we fight together."

And a brief fight it might be, he knew. The RDF needed every hand it could get, and Miriya's battle skill might be a critical plus. He took her hand, and they managed an even more loving look than they had exchanged during their vows.

"Then I guess I have no choice," he said. "Even though we may die together."

"Oh, but Maximillian! I would accept no other death!"

"Me, either." He kissed her quickly, then they raced off hand in hand. "There goes the honeymoon," he said as they ran.

"I don't think you understand true Zentraedi determination." She smiled.

Alone in the ballroom, the master of ceremonies had no more strength to seek shelter or follow the war over the screens. The wedding had been the best thing that had happened to him in two years aboard the SDF-1, the thing he was suited to, that he did best.

Now he sank to his knees, head lowered to the forearm he rested on the shambles of the wedding party's abandoned table. The fortress model, symbol of Max and Miriya's wedding, looked down at him. He sobbed what everyone in the ship was thinking, as the Zentraedi dreadnoughts moved in in their hundreds of thousands.

"Please, save us all."

# 11

Dolza, my old friend, old watchdog; the naive straightforwardness of the Zentraedi could be your downfall someday.

All things are so simple to you: The eye sees the target, the hands aim the weapon, a finger pulls the trigger, an energy bolt slays the enemy. You therefore conclude that if the eye sees clearly, the hand is steady, and the weapon functions properly, all will be well.

You never see the subtlety of the myriad little events in that train of action. What of the brain that directs the eye and the aim? What of the nerves that steady the hand? Of the very decision to shoot? What of the motives that make the Zentraedi obey their military Imperative?

Ah, you call all of this sophistry! But I tell you: There are vulnerabilities to which you are blind.

Remark made by Zor to Dolza shortly before
Zor's death   known only to Dolza, Exedore, and Breetai

AGAIN THE BAYS OPENED, THE ELEVATORS LIFTED THE FIGHTERS to the flight decks. The SDF-1 and the *Daedalus* and *Prometheus* catapult crews labored frantically to launch the all-important fighters as fast as possible. On the flatdecks, waist and bow cats were in constant operation, and the crews' lives were in constant danger; it was very easy for something as small and frail as a human being to meet death during launch ops, especially in the airlessness of space.

The Veritechs rose to the flight decks, deploying ailerons and wings that had been folded or swept back to save space on the hangar decks. Their engines screamed like demons, and they hurtled into space in a meticulously timed ballet, avoiding collisions with one another and forming up for combat with the sureness of long experience.

Gloval watched from a tall viewport as Rick Hunter went out, leading Skull Team. And the rest, scores of them, fell in behind to do battle against the aliens' total attack.

"May every one of you make it home safely," Gloval murmured, the old briar pipe gripped in his teeth. But he knew it was too much to hope for.

Rick was running the fighter wing now; even though there were those who outranked him, there was no one with more expertise.

"Remain in Fighter mode until I give the word," he told them. "We are now approaching intercept zone."

Flying at his wing was Max, with Miriya in the seat behind wearing an RDF flight suit and "thinking cap."

The pods were coming in droves to soften up the target and eliminate and suppress as much counterfire as they could before the Zentraedi heavyweights came in for the kill.

Rick's autocannon sounded like a buzz saw multiplied a thousand times; high-density slugs went out in a stream lit by tracers to pierce an oval armored body through and through. The enemy disappeared in an expanding sphere of red-hot gas and flying shrapnel an instant later.

The Veritechs peeled off, wingmen trying their best to stick together, and threw themselves into swirling, pouncing dogfights against the enemy. The pods advanced in an unstoppable cloud, as the desperate VTs twisted and swooped.

Gloval agonized over the fact that ongoing repairs and retrofitting made it impossible to fire the ship's main gun. But the ship's primary and secondary batteries opened up, turrets swinging, barrels traversing, hammering away.

A pod was hit dead center by an armor-piercing discarding—sabot round and blew to incandescent bits. Another was riddled by kinetic-energy rounds from an electromagnetic rail-gun, projectiles accelerated to hundreds of thousands of g's, hitting at such high speed that explosives would have been redundant. A VT in Guardian mode spun and tumbled, chopped to fragments by the energy blasts of a pod's plastron cannon.

But more and more pods came at the humans in vast waves, pushing them back. The SDF-1 was surrounded by the globular explosions of space battle, hundreds of them every second.

Max had a pod square in his gunsight reticle, thumb on his stick's trigger, when Miriya cried, "No! Wait! Don't shoot!"

"Huh? But they were right in my sights."

She took over, maneuvering until the computer-aided sights were centered on a structure behind the articulation apparatus that joined the pod's legs. Whatever it was, it wasn't on the VT pilots' menu of sure-kill shots.

But Miriya told her husband, "*Now!*" Max zoomed in on a close pass, letting a short burst fly. The target structure disappeared in a burst of flame.

The Zentraedi wobbled and careened out of control, its main thrusters sputtering and coughing every which way, guns going silent after a moment. Trailing fire, it drifted away, limping toward safety with feeble gusts from its attitude thrusters.

VT pilots were taught to go for the sure-kill shots at areas of the enemy mecha most likely to expose themselves to fire, He felt like he had just been taught a secret *Shao-lin* pressure point.

"But we could've lost him while we were trying for that shot," he pointed out, craning around to look over his seat at his bride of less than an hour.

"I don't want anybody else to be hurt in this war," she told him.

"But Miriya, we don't want to jeopardize our own lives, right? Or the ship?"

She looked him in the eye. "Remember what the captain said? Max, it's time to do more than just talk. We must act. And now I've given you the key."

"Oh, boy. You're right. We'll just have to give this a try."

"Thank you, Maximillian."

Max took out two more to make sure it really worked.

"What in heaven's name is going on in that plane?" Rick yelled over the tac net.

He saw Max's face on one of his display screens. "Boss, I'm sorry those last few weren't kills."

"Don't bull *me*, Max." Rick could see what was going on. "I think I understand."

He dove at a pod, his forward lasers vaporizing the vulnerable component that Miriya had revealed. "We'll stop this war *without* bloodshed!"

Captain Gloval was right. "The time has come for peace," Rick muttered.

The secret of popping the enemy pods without killing anyone within was made easier to share because the small, vulnerable component was located behind and slightly below the leg juncture. This made it easy and even fun for the VT fighter jocks to tell each other where to shoot and to vie with each other at making perfect shots.

The structures were also located in a spot difficult for the pods to defend. The VTs had never concentrated on that place before because most of that area was heavily armored and the target in question was so small.

But once they knew what they were after, the VT pilots began enthusiastic, almost crazed disabling runs. Pods got their fundaments blown out from under them by VTs on long passes, predatory banks, high deflection shots. One guy on Ghost Team got three in one pass.

But the pods had closed in tightly around the SDF-1 as the alien battlewagons came up behind. The dimensional fortress shook to a ferocious blast of concentrated fire.

"Captain, our number two thruster's been damaged," Vanessa said.

Gloval gritted his teeth, saying nothing; he knew it was going to get worse.

. . .

The Zentraedi officer dashed angrily into the ready-room hatchway, furious when he saw the crew there had not even so much as donned their armor.

"Lord Breetai commands that you prepare to attack!" he roared.

One crewmember was standing by a viewport, looking out at the starlit darkness, holding a tiny Minmei doll in his palm, small as a pea in his giant hand.

"So beautiful yet so small," he whispered to himself in his rumbling voice as the others looked over his shoulder. He thought of her songs again, and the memory filled him with longings no Zentraedi career could ever answer. He closed his enormous fingers gently around the doll.

The officer bawled, "You're all in direct violation of Lord Dolza's orders! Report to battle stations at once, or I'll have you all court-martialed!"

They were Zentraedi beguiled by the songs and peace talk of humans; but they were still Zentraedi, with the pent-up fury of their race. One whirled on the officer, bringing up an assault rifle, checking off its safety.

"*What* did you say?"

Others turned, weapons clacking, and the officer found himself staring into a half dozen rifle muzzles and then a dozen. "Don't be insane!" he screamed. "Think of what you're doing!"

"It doesn't matter what you say," one of them told him icily. "We aren't fighting anymore. We have friends on that ship. We have vows we've sworn with those friends, sacred warrior oaths. We won't attack them; that's where we draw the line. Now, *leave!*"

He threw the rifle to his shoulder, bracketing the officer in his sights, finger tightening on the trigger. The officer gave a yowl and disappeared from the compartment hatchway, boots echoing on the deck.

The warriors stood listening, lowering their weapons. "Look at him run, like a trog with his tail between his ears," one said, laughing.

Breetai spun on Exedore. "What? It's mutiny!"

"Your Excellency, a large number of our best pilots will not leave the mother craft. *They refuse to acknowledge that the order was given!* Mutiny in time of battle is a thing that has never happened before in Zentraedi history."

*Although,* he added to himself, *those warnings from the ancients must have had a basis. If they're right, we face disaster!*

"But—with all respect—they have some justification," Exedore went on.

Breetai glowered down at him. "There is no rationale for mutiny!"

"But you know there are Zentraedi on the battle fortress. And now they know, too. To attack their own is a direct violation of the laws that bind us together as comrades in arms—"

"Enough!"

"And then there is this baffling new tactic of the enemy, disabling our pods rather than destroying them, sparing our warriors when they could more easily have killed them. Some pod commanders in the attack force are preparing to turn on their fellows if the attack isn't broken off—"

Breetai turned and strode away. "Exedore—"

Exedore hurried his shorter strides to catch up. "And the transmissions from the wedding—"

Breetai stopped and pivoted instantly. "*I said enough!*" His boulderlike fist hung near Exedore's face, clenched so tight that the huge knuckles and tendons creaked loudly, trembling with Breetai's anger. Exedore fell silent.

After several long seconds, Breetai retracted the fist almost unwillingly but regained control of himself. He started walking again, the overhead lights gleaming off his polished skullplate and crystal eye; Exedore followed meekly.

"Stop your blathering," Breetai rumbled. "I'm aware of the situation. Issue the order to withdraw immediately! Recall all Zentraedi mecha."

Exedore halted, mouth agape. "Yes, sir, but that is in direct disobedience of the Zentraedi High Command—of Dolza's own orders!"

Breetai stormed on his way, neither looking back nor answering.

. . .

On the SDF-1's bridge, no one quite knew how to take it.

"It's a miracle," was all Sammie could say.

"Yes, we're very lucky," Gloval said softly, sitting in his command chair. *Could it have to do with the wedding? Did it work?*

Claudia began calling the Veritechs home.

The newlyweds had received generous offers of living quarters in crowded Macross City, even from some who could ill afford the space. But there was no question of staying so far from the fighter bays while the current emergency remained.

Ship's engineers had hurriedly taken out the partition between two adjoining compartments to give the Sterlings a small connubial bower: a living room-kitchenette and a tiny bedroom. There hadn't, however, been time to soundproof it; that would have to wait until the next work shift.

So Rick Hunter lay in his bunk, head pillowed on hands, listening to the muffled turmoil in the kitchenette on the other side of the bulkhead.

"Max, why is it on fire?" came Miriya's voice. "Is this another weird human recipe?"

"Uh, honey, get out of the way; I'll put it out," Max yelped, and there was the gush of a small fire extinguisher. Rick didn't hear the ship's main fire-fighting systems cut in and concluded that Max had gotten it.

"Strange, strange day," Rick sighed.

He caught snatches of their conversation without meaning to. What had she done? Just used a dash of that liquid, the cooking oil. Nothing on the bottle *said* it shouldn't be used in the coffeepot.

Max would be perfectly willing to do all the cooking for a while; Miriya insisted that she wanted to do her share. That was what comrades in arms and lifelong mates *did*, she insisted.

After a bit longer, they were both giggling and the hatch to the bedroom closed. Rick slugged his pillow like he was in a title fight, then threw his head against the mattress and pulled the pillow over it.

*I hope they'll be happy,* he forced himself to think. Then he found himself thinking about Minmei, and of Lisa, and then of Claudia, grieving for Roy Fokker—so brave; stronger than Rick would be in her place.

Roy had tried to tell him something once, something the original Skull Leader had discovered during the course of his tempestuous love affair with Claudia Grant.

Before you can love someone, you have to like them.

The thought came into Rick's mind unbidden, along with the image of long, light brown hair and a slender form—a quick, disciplined mind and a commitment to a set of beliefs that Rick found more worthy every day. And—there was the remembrance of a kiss before alien captors, a kiss that had been so much more than he had expected and had haunted him since.

*I like Lisa; maybe I even—*

He tossed on his bunk, head on top of his pillow now, staring out at space through his cabin's viewport. Next door there was still silence.

In a few moments he was blinking tiredly before he could sort out just what it was he felt.

*I'm so beat. I feel like just—*

He fell asleep with Lisa's face before him.

# 12

Khyron was always different from the rest of us, and the ways of the Micronians held some dark fascination for him, however much he fought it.

But the Micronians are mad! Is it any wonder this drove him over the brink, so that as he perceived it his only relief was to liquidate them all?

Grel

"ALIEN VESSEL, BATTLESHIP CLASS, SIR," VANESSA SAID TIGHTLY from her monitoring station on the bridge.

This time Gloval was ready. "Prepare to fire main cannon! Lock all tracking systems to target!"

In the respite that had followed the last attack, engineers had completed retrofitting and new installation. At long last, the SDF-1 had been brought into Attack mode without major damage to Macross City and accompanying loss of life.

The ship could use its fearsome main gun in this configuration, standing like a monumental armored gladiator in space with the two tremendous supercarriers held out like menacing forearms.

"All systems go; booms now moving into position," Claudia said in clipped tones. The booms had stood like horns above the fortress; now, brute servomotors swung them down so that they pointed out straight from both of the ship's huge, bulky shoulder structures.

"Main gun standing by to fire on your command, Captain," the message was patched in from engineering. Claudia couldn't help but wish Lisa were back on the bridge. The Terrible Trio and the other techs were good and were doing the best they could, but nobody except perhaps Dr. Lang knew as much about the ship as Lisa.

Sammie watched the preparations, wide-eyed. "I bet this is a trick or something," she declared in her young, breathless voice. "A Trojan horse!"

Kim spared a moment from her own problems to gaze at Sammie dubiously. "Trojan horse? They know we'd never fall for that! Where on Earth would you get an idea like that from?"

"The Trojan War! Besides, that's the way it always happens in the movies."

*For two years now, they've been trying to wipe us out, and she still thinks about movies!* Kim groaned to herself and went back to her job, resolving to slug Sammie later.

Sammie said with high acrimony, "Okay, if you've got a better theory, let's hear it!"

Vanessa cut through the squabble.

"Captain," Vanessa said, "I have a message coming in in cleartext from the alien ship."

Gloval came halfway out of the command chair. "*What?*" He tried not to let himself hope too much.

"They're asking permission to approach the SDF-1. Shall I put it up on the monitor, Captain?"

Gloval grunted approval, and Vanessa complied. Suddenly, Sammie's flight of fantasy didn't sound so zany.

"I say again: We are sending an unarmed ship to dock with your battle fortress. We request a cessation of hostilities. Please hold your fire."

The enemy flagship drew near at dead-slow speed, straight into the line of fire of the main gun. The battleship might be nine solid miles of supertech mayhem, but surely by now the Zentraedi knew that it would be as defenseless as a helium blimp before the holocaust blast those massive booms could generate.

"Let them come," Gloval told Claudia. "But stand ready to fire."

Claudia flipped up the red safety cover with her thumb, exposing the trigger of the main gun. Sweating, she watched the battlewagon close in, ready to fire the instant Gloval gave the order but forcing herself to be calm. She was unaware that everyone else there, captain and enlisted ratings alike, was glad that Claudia—whom they saw as a tower of strength—was trigger man that day.

Gloval let the flagship come at him, come at him. Sammie's Trojan horse remark was much in his mind. He wondered about this Breetai, whom Lisa and Rick had described to him. The three Zentraedi spies and the deserters who had come after them had contributed more, as had Miriya. Gloval wondered and hoped the vagaries of war would let him meet Breetai face-to-face; he suspected that the alien commander felt the same.

The flagship slowed to a stop, a sitting duck of a target, reassuring him. But abruptly there were dozens of streamers of light swirling from behind it, bearing in on the fortress at high speed. Gloval didn't have to look at the computer displays; he had seen these performance profiles before.

Vanessa yelled, "Picking up large strike force of tri-thruster pursuit ships, closing rapidly!"

The tri-thrusters were right in the line of fire; Claudia's forefinger hovered by the trigger.

*What are they up to now?* Gloval thought with dismay. Peace had seemed so suddenly, tantalizingly close. But what could this be except betrayal?

The tri's were out in front of the flagship, closing in on the SDF-1, their drives leaving bright swirling ribbons of light behind them. The command to fire was on Gloval's lips.

But all at once a hundred batteries in the enemy flagship's forward section opened up, and the tri-thrusters were blown into fragments, dozens per second disappearing in ballooning clouds of total annihilation. The blue-white lines of energy from the enemy dreadnought, thread-fine against its enormous bulk, redirected immediately upon destruction of a target, to the next. In moments, the massive sortie fell apart and space was full of briefly flaming junk.

. . .

Gloval swallowed. "Secure the trigger but stand by," he said.

Claudia closed her eyes for a moment, breathing a prayer, thumbing the safety cover over the trigger. But as he had ordered, her thumb rested on it still.

Breetai stood at his command station, hands clasped at the small of his back. As he expected, Khyron the Backstabber didn't take long to appear by projecbeam image.

*"Breetai, have you gone mad?"*

Breetai studied him coldly. "Your ships were interfering with a diplomatic mission, as you well know. And so I disposed of them. Henceforth you will address me by my proper rank."

Khyron fought a fierce internal battle, then managed, *"Commander, what happens now? I refuse to spare the Micronians! We all know Dolza's orders!"*

"You know nothing, Khyron! And I will hear no further word from you on the subject. Just consider yourself lucky you didn't choose to lead your troops this day!"

*"Ridiculous!"*

Breetai swung his command chair away from the screen, cutting the communications circuit, muttering, "Hardly."

Like some immense killer whale, the flagship came to a stop directly in front of the SDF-1's most powerful weapon.

"They're just sitting out there, Captain; I guess they're waiting for us to make a move." Claudia's thumbnail stood under the edge of the trigger's cover.

*If they don't want peace, why would they destroy their own fighters? Why would they not overwhelm us, as they so easily could?*

"They wish to send an emissary. Very well," he decided. "So be it."

The Veritechs flew forth accompanied by other mecha, like the cat's-eye intel ships, detector-loaded and studying everything about the emissary pod.

The pod was standard except that it mounted only auxiliary comma gear: no weapons. The cat's-eyes and other emissions-intelligence detectors said that it wasn't the Trojan horse of Sammie's nightmares.

Rick Hunter quieted his Skull Team, telling them he *knew* it was weird and getting weirder all the time but reminding them the team hadn't suffered any casualties in a while.

That strangest of all convoys came to rest in an SDF-1 bay, the VTs now in Battloid mode with their chain-guns leveled at the pod.

Things moved quickly to the hangar deck, while PA voices went on about the normal checklist procedures and the extraordinary precautions surrounding the emissary's arrival. No one wanted to take any chances on a double-cross or, perhaps worse, on a vengeful human's violent act robbing the SDF-1 of this chance for peace. Security was—in some ways literally—airtight.

The enemy mecha knelt, its prow touching the deck as the rear-articulated legs folded back. A rear hatch swung open; a Brobdingnagian enemy trooper stomped forth to glare around.

"Aren't you forgetting something?" called a reedy, highly miffed voice from within the pod.

The mountainous trooper was immediately contrite, almost afraid, "Oh, please forgive me, your Eminence! My humblest apologies!"

The trooper reached carefully into the pod and came out with a small figure, which he set down with exaggerated, painstaking care. It had been explained exactly what would happen to him if he allowed his micronized passenger to come to any harm.

Exedore, dressed in the blue sackcloth robe that was all the Zentraedi had to give their micronized warriors, stepped off the warrior's armored palm.

His toes clenched, and his arches arched a bit higher against the cold deck. "*Hmph!* How *do* these Micronians survive with such frail little bodies?"

He turned to regard the huge flight deck, but it made little impression because its size would have been imposing for human *or* Zentraedi.

Exedore's pilot was another matter, staring eye to eye with a chain-gun-wielding Battloid. "Rather an imposing sight, aren't we, hah?" he said, rubbing his jaw.

Still, he was one among the Zentraedi to know that size didn't count for everything—counted for nothing, in some cases.

"Ten-HUT!" the PA said as a line of military vehicles came screeching up. The Battloids snapped to present-arms, and to Exedore's great pride, the Zentraedi pilot stood at perfect attention. Exedore abruptly noticed that there were Micronian personnel, ground crew and what-not, scattered around the compartment as they, too, came to attention.

Men leapt from the cars to form ranks smartly, and a man in a uniform not so different from Zentraedi's own came toward Exedore, hand extended.

"Colonel Maistroff, Robotech Defense Forces, sir. I bring you greetings from the super dimensional fortress commander, Captain Gloval."

Exedore sighed a bit to see that Maistroff was taller than he, to see that all of them were. Perhaps there was something in the micronization process that dictated that, or perhaps it was just something about destiny.

Anyway, Maistroff's open hand was out to him. Exedore blinked at it in bewilderment. "This is how we greet friends," the human said.

Ah, yes! The barbarian custom of showing that there was no weapon! Exedore put his dark mauve hand into the other's pale pink one, trading the grip of friendship.

"I am Exedore, Minister of Affairs."

Maistroff, a former martinet and xenophobe who had been salted and wisened up a bit in the course of the Robotech War, looked him over. "That sounds rather important, sir."

Exedore shrugged blithely. "Not really." He smiled, and Maistroff found himself smiling back.

The colonel indicated his staff car. "If you're ready, we'll get you some more comfortable clothes and then take you to the captain. Have you eaten?"

Exedore sorted that out, recalling the wedding transmissions and dreading a lot of ceremonies stalling the beginning of the peace talks. "Ah, yes; yes."

As they walked, ground-shaking impacts began on the deck behind them, jostling them as they moved. They turned to see that the Zentraedi pilot had naturally fallen in to follow his lord. The Battloids hadn't *quite* brought their chain-gun muzzles back up.

Exedore was quick to see the problem and also to understand some of the humans' apprehension.

Maistroff kept his composure. "Excuse me, Minister Exedore, but—could you ask him to wait here on the hangar deck?"

"Oh!" It didn't take a genius of Exedore's caliber to see that those little hatches wouldn't allow for much full-size Zentraedi wandering. Clever!

He turned to look up at his pilot. "Stay here and guard the pod." It did irritate him how much higher and less forceful the transformation had made his voice.

The pilot pulled a brace, biting out, "Yes, sir!"

Maistroff turned and jerked a thumb at two aides. "You men find him something to eat."

They saluted as one, "Yes, sir!" under the eyes of the Zentraedi warrior, just as precise as he. Then they watched as Maistroff cordially aided Exedore in boarding the staff car, just about as unlikely a sight as anything yet in the war. Motorcycle outriders led the way, and the motorcade moved off.

The two staff officers relaxed, looked up at the Zentraedi, then looked back at each other. "Something to eat?" the first one exclaimed. "He's got to be kidding!"

"Maistroff *never* kids," his companion answered. They both had comrigs in their jeeps, and the second staff officer reached over now to get a handset, telling his friend, "You call ration distribution and break the bad news."

Then he turned to his own mission. "Hello, transportation control? Listen, I'm gonna need a coupla flatbeds…"

The thoroughfares of Macross City were as confusing to Exedore as they had been to the spies. So much undisciplined, disorganized activity! So much aimless milling about! There seemed to be no point to a lot of it—all this gaping through display windows and strolling haphazardly. He wondered if it was some deceptive show that had been mounted for his visit.

And, of course, he averted his eyes from the males and females wandering the city holding hands or with arms around each other's waists. Of the tiny-model Micronians, the noisy, poorly regimented smallscales that the humans called "children," Exedore could make neither head nor tail. Just seeing them gave him a shuddery feeling.

But he had to admit the ship was in a good state of repair, especially after two years of running battles with the warrior race. There would have been no hiding the damage in a Zentraedi ship, no fixing it. Intelligence reports had already indicated what Exedore saw evidence of all around him: The Micronians knew how to rebuild—perhaps how to *create*. It was an awesome advantage, a critical part of the war's equation.

Very few Micronians were in uniform; none of them appeared to be under close supervision.

"Why, this is our shopping district," Maistroff explained when Exedore asked.

"Ah, yes! I believe this is where you use something called money to requisition goods."

Maistroff scratched his neck a bit. "Um. That's not too far off, Minister."

They cruised along a broad boulevard, and Exedore suddenly broke out into a cold sweat and began to shudder. Maistroff sat up straight, wondering if something about the ship's life support was incompatible, but that was impossible.

Then he saw that Exedore, teeth clenched, was staring up at a billboard. The billboard advertised the Velvet Suntan Clinics, with a photo of the languorous Miss Velvet, a voluptuous, browned, barely clad, supremely athletic looking young woman whose poster popularity in Macross City was second only to Minmei's.

"Ee, er, oh, th-that picture on the building over there," Exedore got out at last, looking like he was having a malaria attack. "Would you mind explaining it?" He forced his gaze to the floor of the staff car.

Maistroff reached up to the back of his cap and tilted the visor down over his eyes to keep good form with the minister, coughing into his other hand. "Well, actually, it's a little hard to explain."

Exedore crossed his skinny arms on his narrow chest and nodded wisely. "*Aha!* A military secret, no doubt! Very clever! Indeed!"

Maistroff didn't even want to think about what damage he might have done to interspecies relations—didn't want to complicate things.

He tilted his visor farther down. "Right, that's it. Classified."

The motorcade raced for the conference room.

# 13

RUSSO: What are they doing up there, Alexei? Don't those RDF pantywaists of yours even know how to fight?
ZUKAV: I believe that what we should worry about, Senator, is that they and the aliens are teaching each other how not to.

Exchange believed to have taken place between
Senator Russo and Marshal Zukav of the UEDC

T HE SDF-1 AND THE FLAGSHIP FACED EACH OTHER, UNMOVING across a narrow gap of space, almost eyeball to eyeball.

Gloval left instructions with Claudia that she open fire with the main gun if there was any hostile action at all. A few minutes later he sat at a judicial bench in the ship's biggest hearing chamber with Colonel Maistroff on his right, an intelligence major to the left, gazing down at Exedore. Except for a few functionaries, the place was empty.

The misshapen little fellow fell far short of Gloval's mental image of a ravaging alien warmonger, the captain had to admit to himself. If anything, he seemed rather… prissy.

"At last we meet face to face, Captain," the alien said in a not-uncordial voice, glancing at him from the distant witness stand.

"Yes," Gloval allowed.

An attractive young female ensign brought a tray and put a glass of orange juice where Exedore could reach it. Gloval and the others watched Exedore's reaction to the woman closely, but apparently he had gotten his responses under control as he merely nodded his head in gratitude.

Exedore raised the glass and took a cautious sip. The flavor was delightful, but the beverage had a certain savor, something he couldn't define. It was something dizzying, almost electric.

"Mmm. This is very refreshing." He looked up at her. "What is it?"

She checked with Gloval by eye to make sure that it was all right to answer. Gloval gave the barest nod, which Exedore in turn caught. "It's orange juice, sir. From our own hydroponics orchards."

Exedore didn't quite understand for a moment. When he spoke, he tried to keep the tremor from his voice. "You mean, you *grow* it?"

She looked a little confused. "We grow the fruit the juice comes from."

"Ah, yes; just so. That is what I meant." He downed the rest of the orange juice to hide his amazement.

These creatures consumed food that had been alive! Who knew; perhaps they consumed things that still *were* alive! He shuddered and reminded himself that this was only the juice of a plant, but his self-control was tested thoroughly.

Here was something those three imbecile spies hadn't mentioned, or had perhaps omitted from their reports on purpose, or had even failed to realize. Zentraedi food, of course, was synthesized from its chemical constituents; that was as it had always been, by the decree of the Robotech Masters. To eat living or once living food was to risk the consumption of rudimentary energies somewhat related to Protoculture.

Exedore finished the glass so as to give no hint of what he was thinking—fearing. It crossed his mind that perhaps these men were testing him. If so, he would reveal nothing.

"That was very refreshing," he enthused.

The ensign gave him a bright smile. "Here, have another." She picked up the empty and gave him a full one from her tray.

"If you insist," he said lightly.

Gloval was rubbing his dark mustache. To Maistroff, he said, "I think we're missing some people, aren't we?"

"Some." The colonel nodded. "But they should be arriving any minute now. In fact, this may be them."

He was indicating the door signal. Max and Miriya entered,

both in RDF uniform. Max snapped off a sharp salute. "Sir. Reporting as ordered."

Exedore was on his feet, the drink put aside. "Ah! Hello, Quadrono Leader!"

She gasped as she turned to him and saluted by reflex. "I'm sorry, sir; I didn't realize *you* were the emissary."

He shrugged to say it was unimportant. "I found your pairing ritual—marriage?—quite... provocative."

She didn't know what to say. "You are probably wondering why we did it."

"Yes, just as you're no doubt wondering what *I* am doing here. And this must be the male half of your pair."

Suddenly Miriya looked young and a little forlorn, standing before the great genius of her race, the Eldest, the repository of all Zentraedi lore. "Ah, that's right, sir."

"Gee, y' don't sound too thrilled about it," Max murmured. He almost gave in to his impulse to take her in his arms and kiss her, top brass or no, and remind her emphatically of what their pairing *really* meant.

But just then Rick Hunter reported as ordered, saluting. Then he spied Max, who was in a bit of a snit. "Hey, you don't look so good," Rick confided.

Exedore was still on his feet. Now, he pointed at Rick and Max, yelling, "That's it!" He clucked to himself. "The micronization process must have affected my memory! *You're two of the hostages from Dolza's flagship, aren't you?*"

"Does somebody want to tell me what's going on here?" Rick asked slowly.

"This time the circumstances are a bit different," Exedore rattled on excitedly. "But tell me: How did you and the others manage to escape? Was it some hidden Micronian power?"

What had really happened was that Max had come aboard in a Battloid disguised in a Zentraedi uniform, but Rick wasn't sure he should let that particular cat out of the bag. He didn't see Gloval or the others giving him any help, so he improvised, "Uh, I guess you could say that."

The frail little emissary sat, fingering his jaw. "Hm, another one of your military secrets." It was all so confusing and illogical, even to him. Who knew what eons of eating live food had done to these creatures?

The door signaled again, and Gloval said, "Here are the others now." Rico, Bron, and Konda filed into the hearing chamber. They caught sight of him and cringed as he gave them a death's-head smile.

"It's Minister Exedore!" they all yelped at once, looking like mice facing a hungry lynx.

"I did not expect to see the instigators of our mass defection show up here today," he remarked.

Trembling, Rico drew himself up. "Your Excellency, it *wasn't our fault!*"

"That's right! It was just something that we couldn't help!" Konda put in. And the stout Bron maintained, "We had no control, sir!"

Exedore brushed that aside with a prim flick of his fingers. "You may relax. I have no intention of harming you."

The breath they let out was audible as they wilted with relief. When everyone was seated, Colonel Maistroff said, "Captain Gloval, the ship's computer will record the proceedings."

Gloval squared his cap away. "Very good; let us begin." To Exedore he said, "Minister, we are unclear as to the exact purpose of your mission here. You've told us very little so far. Won't you please enlighten us?"

Exedore's eyes swept across them. "Your curiosity is understandable, but—not everyone is present yet, Captain."

"What?" Maistroff growled under his breath.

"We would like to know more about two of your kind, gentlemen. The first possesses powers and fighting skills that are truly extraordinary, and there is a female who is the core of your psychological assault."

"Incredible," mumbled Gloval, watching Exedore.

Colonel Maistroff had read some of the defector debriefing reports. In an aside to Gloval he said, "I think he means that movie, *Little White Dragon*. They must've seen it too, and think Lynn-Kyle's movie stunts were for real."

*Little White Dragon* was the first feature film produced on the SDF-1. It featured Lynn-Kyle in some spectacular stunts and fights, downing ferocious giants with his fighting arts and using a death beam that he could shoot from his hand thanks to an enchanted medallion.

"There is clearly a misunderstanding here," Gloval told Maistroff. To Exedore he declared, "I can't think of anyone who would be at the core of a psychological assault. It would be helpful if you could be more specific about this female."

Exedore blinked at him with bulging, pinpoint-pupilled eyes. "She appears to be performing some kind of ritual. A strange little chant."

Bron leaned over to his fellow ex-spies. "Do you think he means—"

"No! He *couldn't*!" Konda whispered.

"Sure he could!" snarled Rico.

"*You* know," Exedore said impatiently. And he rose to stand next to the witness chair, strike a coquettish pose, and sing:

Stage fright, go 'way,
This is my big day!

Rick groaned, not wanting to be the first to say anything. If he wasn't seeing what he thought he was seeing, Colonel Maistroff would probably report him to the flight surgeon and get him grounded on a mental.

But the three spies burst out, "He *is* talking about Minmei!"

Exedore went on singing "Stage Fright" with a terrible, cracking falsetto that was seriously off key. He struck poses and postures that looked like he was auditioning for Yum-Yum in an amateur production of *The Mikado*.

Gloval drew his head down into his high, rolled jacket collar like a turtle, making a low sound. "I do not believe this."

"They must think Minmei's singing is a weapon of some kind," Maistroff observed.

"Have the girl brought here," Gloval ordered. "And her cousin as well." Then he tried to figure out what the most direct and yet diplomatic method would be for asking the emissary to please stop singing.

. . .

As soon as Minmei appeared in the doorway, Exedore cried, "That's her! Yes!"

She stood looking around like a startled deer. A moment later, Kyle slouched into the room, sulking and hostile, saying, "I'm getting tired of being pushed around by the military."

"Now," Minmei said in a tired voice, "would someone mind explaining why it was so important for us to come here?"

She was as beautiful as ever, delicate and haunting as a princess from a fairy tale; try as he would, Rick couldn't keep the familiar longing from welling up in him.

Kyle stepped before her as if to shield her from harm, glaring all around. "Don't expect any answers from them. They only care about their fascist war schemes; they don't care about people, and they—"

"Enough of this nonsense!" Gloval thundered, and even the truculent Lynn-Kyle was a bit intimidated. Exedore thought how like the great Breetai this Micronian commander was.

"You will answer our questions," Gloval said to the two of them. "These proceedings are strictly classified, and if you mention them to anyone, I will personally see that you rue this day. You will give us your total cooperation. Do you both understand?"

"Yes." Minmei nodded. When Kyle stood unspeaking, unresponsive, she put a hand to his shoulder. "They need our cooperation. Hostility won't do us any good, don't you see?"

Gloval had turned to Exedore; he let his irritation show in his voice. "Now, Mr. Minister, if you would *kindly* tell us what your mission here is all about?" He began stoking up a favorite meerschaum.

"All in its proper sequence," Exedore said earnestly. "But I assure you: My reason for being here is of crucial importance for you as well as for the Zentraedi."

Gloval puffed out a blue cloud that his officers tried to ignore. *Reading this alien's mind is impossible,* he reflected. The song and dance had convinced him of that. *I'll just have to wait and hear him out.*

In the UEDC's subterranean complex, Lisa Hayes sat at the end of long rows of techs who were manning monitor screens. All attention was focused on the SDF-1; Lisa had gotten the impression, in subtle ways, that the world rulers were chewing their nails, waiting to see what would happen.

She had stopped wishing that she was back onboard to help in what was going on; it hurt too much. The emergency, the shortage of good officers, the dangers of space travel during the current hostilities, the fact that she had had access to classified UEDC information, her value as an intelligence source—her father had a dozen justifications for keeping her right where she was, and there was little she could do about it.

Now, she stared up at her own master console. The more she learned about the Grand Cannon, the more convinced she was that it would serve little purpose except to get the Zentraedi angrier.

She started, realizing that her father had come in to bend down near her. The other technical officers and enlisted ratings kept diligently at their work; it was unwise to be seen letting one's attention stray when Admiral Hayes was around.

She was beginning to understand that her father wasn't a popular officer. She had never found it easy to make friends, and now that she was known as the admiral's daughter, she was effectively frozen out.

She removed her headset in time to hear him say, "How do you like your new job? Everything okay?"

"Fine, fine," she lied, and attempted to smile. "I understand that the SDF-1 and the Zentraedi fleet have reached a ceasefire agreement."

"That's what I hear," her father said noncommittally.

She tried to sound as upbeat as she could. "Well, if things keep going this way, maybe we won't have to use the Grand Cannon, after all."

"It's possible, but I doubt it."

She turned away, dropping her eyes in discouragement. They were all so blind down here in their little rabbit warren! Then she felt his hand on her shoulder.

"Listen, Lisa. We can't trust the Zentraedi; we have to *prove* what we can do."

It would do no good to tell him again that the SDF-1's main gun was easily a match for the Grand Cannon, and it hadn't kept the Zentraedi from waging their war. The UEDC planners, engineers, and rulers had too much at stake and only scoffed when she tried to make the point.

He saw she wasn't going to yield the point; she simply gave up arguing it for the time being. He turned to go, saying, "I have work to do. If anything comes up, I'll be in the central core."

"Yes, sir," Lisa said wearily.

# 14

I was close enough to Lang in those days to be certain that he had no confidential knowledge of the hidden Protoculture source to which Exedore was referring. Had he but known the secret of those great, sealed reflex furnaces, he might have formulated an immortal update to Einstein's remark: Protoculture doesn't play dice with the universe, but It certainly knows how to palm an ace at the crucial moment!

Excerpted from the personal log of Dr. Lazlo Zand, 2030 A.D.

"OFFICER LYNN-KYLE, WHAT IS YOUR MILITARY RANK?" EXEDORE asked in the vaulted hearing chamber.

Kyle gave him a surly look. "I'm a civilian."

Exedore made a brief, mocking chuckle. "With your superpowers? I doubt it."

Kyle bared his teeth at the alien. "I have no idea what you're talking about!"

Exedore looked around, confused. He was satisfied that these Micronians were doing their best to, to "level with" him, as Colonel Maistroff had put it on the way over.

Gloval intervened. "Mr. Minister, he's telling the truth. This man possesses no superpowers. For that matter, none of us in this room possess the powers you're referring to."

Gloval was taking a gamble. The bluff of human superpowers hadn't made the enemy go away and couldn't be sustained for very long. But there was something murky about the whole war, something that made him suspect that a basic breakdown in communication was responsible for the whole thing. It was time for someone to try to get to the bottom of it.

"But—we saw him on our monitors," Exedore protested. "Oh, that was a *movie*, merely a form of entertainment," Gloval replied, scratching his head to try to think how to explain better. "It's not true, it's… simply for enjoyment."

Exedore decided to table that for now; he knew the enjoyment he found in the ancient lore and history of the Zentraedi, but those were *factual*. "Then what about your energy barrier and destruction waves?"

"These are merely defensive and offensive weapons based on technology discovered in this ship when it originally crashed on Earth."

"Ah, but you've forgotten the Protoculture!" Exedore said slyly. "The great genius of the Robotech Masters' race, Zor, hid the secrets of Protoculture and its last great manufacturing source in this vessel before he dispatched it here."

Now, at last, Gloval was seeing some of the aliens' cards, and he was sure the talks were worth it. All the questions of who the Robotech Masters were, who Zor was and why he had picked Earth, had to be set aside, intriguing as they were. The life of the human race might be measurable in hours, even minutes.

Gloval opened a comline. "I think we're ready for Dr. Lang now."

Lang entered, the greatest mind of his time, an intellect worthy to sit with Newton and Einstein and yet a man frustrated by the many mysteries of Robotechnology. He had been monitoring the exchanges in a waiting room and was eager to talk to Exedore.

The Zentraedi, Minmei and Kyle, and the others there who had never seen Lang before got a bit of a shock and understood why he shunned the limelight. Normal-looking in every other way, the man had eyes that seemed to be all dark, liquid iris—no pupil or white.

Gloval remembered that day well, hours after the SDF-1's crash in 1999, when he, Lang, and a few others had first boarded the smoking wreck. They had discovered an astounding technology, fearsome mecha guardians, and bewildering time paradoxes.

They had also discovered a recorded warning that they couldn't fathom. And Lang, yielding to an unquenchable thirst for more knowledge, more interface, had somehow subjected himself to direct contact with whatever it was that animated the ship. That was when his eyes changed, when he himself became *different*, as if he were hearing celestial music. Nevertheless, it was his genius that had allowed the rebuilding of the SDF-1 and the construction of the Robotech Defense Force.

Now, Lang said to Exedore, "We've heard Protoculture mentioned many times, Emissary. Will you tell me now what it is?"

Exedore's brows shot up. "You mean you still insist that you Micronians don't know? Protoculture is the most powerful energy source in the universe."

Lang's deep, dark eyes bored into him. "I have been able to find nothing of that nature in this vessel, and I've been searching since your fleet first arrived in the solar system. But I believe I know what has happened. Will you come with me, please?"

Gloval rose but told the others, "You will all kindly remain here, please."

The jeep was waiting, and the trip through the huge passages and byways of the battle fortress took only a few minutes. Very shortly they were in the engineering section, just forward of the huge reflex engines that were the ship's power plant.

They were in a large compartment that had once held the ship's spacefold apparatus. Now there was some leftover machinery from the pin-point barrier system that had been the ship's main defensive weapon on its precarious trip across the solar system. As there had been for years, there were also the lights.

"When the Zentraedi first attacked Earth, we made our spacefold jump to get to safety," Lang was explaining. "We had no time to experiment, no time to test. A jump that was meant to take us beyond our moon's orbit took us instead to the orbit of Pluto."

"I remember well," Exedore said, scratching his cheek, staring at the giant, almost-empty compartment. "You made the jump too close to the planetary surface; we were convinced that you were suicidal."

"You gave us no choice," Gloval said in a low voice, thinking back to the appalling devastation and loss of life that day. He did his best to put it from his mind.

"But in the wake of the jump," Lang went on, "the spacefold apparatus just... disappeared. Utterly! Simply faded from view and was never seen again. And in its place were *those*."

Lang meant the lights: darting, glowing sparks, fireflies and tiny comets that swanned and drifted through the space where the spacefold apparatus had once been. Exedore turned to him. "May I borrow some of those instruments you've brought, Doctor?"

It took only a little time to prove his suspicions. "Ah, yes: definite residual Protoculture signature here, but the Matrix is gone. And I detect no other great manufacturing mass, only the lesser animating charges of your weapons and the reflex furnaces."

Exedore lowered the detector numbly. "The secrets of Zor, gone! This long war fought for nothing!"

Lang patted Exedore's shoulder commiseratingly. "Perhaps someday we will find it again; who can say?"

Gloval was shocked to see how quickly the two had become easy in each other's company. "I think we'd better get back to the hearing room," the captain said. "We still have a great deal to talk about."

*Deep within the sealed fastness of the mighty reflex engines, something stirred and then was quiet again. It could not be detected by Lang's relatively primitive instruments, was capable of hiding itself even from the Zentraedi's scanners at this range.*

*As Zor had provided, the last Protoculture Matrix was safe, biding its time, waiting until his great Vision should come to pass.*

"It does appear we've made a great mistake," Exedore confessed when they were all back in their places. "But! You cannot possibly deny the power of the female's singing!"

"I wouldn't dream of it," Gloval responded simply, drawing a doubtful look from Colonel Maistroff.

But Bron was on his feet. "He won't deny it because it's true!"

"Minmei's song has incredible power!" Rico added, jumping up too.

Minmei, for her part, gave a shy smile that seemed to have some secret wisdom behind it.

"This is not the first time the Zentraedi have encountered something like this," Exedore told them all. "A very long time ago we were exposed to a culture like yours, and it nearly destroyed us."

"How do you mean that?" Gloval was quick to ask.

Exedore's protruding, pinpoint eyes roamed the room. "To a Zentraedi, fighting is a way of life. Our entire history is made up of nothing but battle after glorious battle. However, exposure to an emotionally open society like yours made our soldiers refuse to fight.

"This, of course, could not be tolerated, and the infection had to be cleansed. Loyal soldiers and the Robotech Masters themselves came in to exterminate all those who had been exposed to the source of the contagion."

The three spies in particular were pale and silent. The rest looked at one another. Exedore went on. "Dolza, our supreme commander, will do everything in his power to avoid making the mistake our ancestors did. When and if he reads my report, he will certainly launch an all-out attack on Earth, especially in light of the fact that the Protoculture Matrix is no longer on the SDF-1."

Gloval's eyes shifted to Rick. "That's the same one mentioned in your report?"

Rick licked his lips. "Yes, sir." *Almost five million warships!*

Exedore nodded. "I know what you're thinking. But you see, these new developments—the defections, the Minmei cult, the mating of our greatest warrior with one of your pilots—change the entire picture."

He looked around at them, the center of their riveted attention. "For, you see," Exedore said, "unless some solution can be found, we—Breetai's forces—are in as great a danger from Dolza and the Grand Fleet as you."

Breetai sat in his chair in the command station overlooking his flagship's bridge.

A projecbeam drew a two-dimensional image of Azonia in the air, the woman who had replaced him in the war against the humans, failed to bring it to a successful conclusion, and been replaced in turn by Breetai.

"Commander!" she began. "How long do you intend to allow this situation to continue?" She was a medium-size, intense Zentraedi female with a quick mind and high aspirations. Her short, frizzy hairstyle puffed within the confinement of her high, rolled collar.

Breetai, arms folded on his great chest, answered in his rumbling, echoing bass, "Any continuation of hostilities would be unwise in light of recent events."

She sneered at him. "Well, I expect a different solution when the Grand Fleet arrives!"

He leapt to his feet. "Grand Fleet? *What have you done?*"

She gave him a smug smile. "I've reported my findings to the supreme commander. And his Excellency Dolza has decided to set the fleet into motion."

"So Dolza has decided the Micronians are a threat, has he?"

"He has," she said triumphantly.

Breetai's anger welled up like a volcano, but suddenly he found himself laughing like a grim god at the end of all worlds. It was the last thing Azonia expected; she watched him, his head thrown back, roaring, light flashing off his metallic skullpiece and the crystal eye, and she felt a sudden sinking sensation in the pit of her stomach.

"You imbecile!" he managed when he could talk again. "You know nothing of history, do you? No, no self-respecting Zentraedi cares! Well, know *this,* my scheming friend: We're doomed along with the humans! We have been infected, and all of us—all—are now considered plague carriers."

"You're certain of this?" Exedore asked quietly, holding the handset tightly in a trembling fist.

The communications patch had been set up hastily, with no chance for the aliens to encrypt their exchange. Exedore would certainly know that human techs had monitored whatever Breetai had said. Therefore, the captain bent forward, certain that he would hear whatever it was at once.

"You know what this means, then," Exedore said. "I understand." He returned the handset to its cradle and looked at Gloval.

"Captain, you must prepare yourselves to escape this star system. We will help you."

Gloval's face hardened. "And leave the Earth defenseless?"

"Yes."

Gloval squared his shoulders. "Out of the question! We are sworn to defend our planet."

Exedore was nodding wearily. "Yes, I understand. We Zentraedi would not act any differently. What's more, without your help, escape for us would be all but hopeless. The Protoculture Matrix was our great hope for success; the armada's supplies are all but exhausted."

He sighed. "It seems we shall soon be fighting a common enemy."

Maistroff exploded. *"What did you say?"*

Exedore looked to him. "My Lord Breetai has just informed me that the Grand Fleet is headed for this star system. That means four million eight hundred thousand ships with the destructive force of a supernova."

"All right, then," Gloval said matter-of-factly. "A fight it shall be."

"You're crazy!" Lynn-Kyle was on his feet. "There's no way you can beat a fleet like that! We're finished!"

Max had taken Miriya's hand in his. He told her gently, "I'm so afraid that this might be the end of us. Just when we've found each other."

She squeezed his hand. "I don't care, my love, as long as I'm at your side in battle."

Rick, on the opposite side of the U-shaped table, looked across at them with envy. "Together," he said under his breath.

Exedore had been watching the various reactions carefully and was satisfied. He could tell mighty Breetai that among the military, at least, there were worthy allies.

Now he raised his voice to say, "It's not over yet! There might still be a way!"

"Explain," Gloval bade him, stone-faced.

"Thus far, this vessel has proved itself unbeatable. I will need more information before I can be sure, but I believe there is a way that we can win."

# 15

I have therefore concluded that Breetai and his subordinates and all those under their command now entertain such primitive behavioral quirks and abstruse thought processes as to set them completely outside the Zentraedi species and make them a threat to us all.

Every available unit will therefore be mustered in the Grand Fleet to take the action dictated by our ancient lore.

From Dolza's personal log

"**R**EPEATING THIS ANNOUNCEMENT, ALL MILITARY PERSONNEL ARE to report for duty at once. All leaves are canceled. All reservists are to contact their units for immediate mobilization. Civilians are directed to stand by for further directives, we will be making announcements as soon as further information is available."

Lisa wheeled her jeep into the headquarters' cavernous parking lot on two wheels, snapping off the radio. She hadn't been able to get anything on the military freqs, and the civvie bands just kept repeating the same thing.

She dashed into the HQ, flashing her security badge, and, in the situation room, heard the classified announcements.

"Sensors are still picking up extremely high energy levels from lunar and near-Earth regions. This activity is characteristic of enemy spacefold operations. However, they are of a magnitude never before encountered."

She spotted her father and ran toward him. In her mind's eye was the Grand Fleet as she had last seen it, or at least part of it, in and around the moonlet-size hive that was Dolza's headquarters base.

"It doesn't look good," Admiral Hayes was saying to a G3 staff commodore.

"Admiral!"

Her father looked at her, traded salutes with the staffer, and came over to her. He took her by the arm, leading her to a conference room. He sounded brusque as the door slid shut. "Well? What is it?"

She drew a deep breath. "Father, what's going to happen to the SDF-1?"

He didn't reprimand her for the lapse in formality, as he once would have. But there was no sympathy in his voice. "It will be destroyed. We're committing it to drawing the enemy fire away from Earth and the rest of our forces."

"You can't!"

"I'm sorry, Lisa." He didn't sound sorry at all. "There's no other choice."

She accepted that; she'd been around headquarters long enough now to realize that her father was no longer a leader. He was an apologist, an errand boy, for the real rulers of the planet.

She gathered her self-control. "Father, I want to ask you a personal favor. I want you to send me back to the battle fortress."

"No! That's completely out of the question!"

Now it was her turn to flare. "My place is with my crew, my captain!" She waved her hand around to indicate the scurrying futility of the UEDC base. "It's not here, in a hole in the ground, when the people I fought beside need me."

He knew then that he'd lost her. For a moment, he saw the place through her eyes and wondered how he could ever have been so deluded. The Grand Cannon was a sham, and the UEDC were frightened men who had brought the world down around them rather than admit that they were wrong.

He shook it off, his oath to his duty coming to the fore again. But there was real pain in his voice as he told her, "I'm sorry, but—"

"But you won't."

"I can't allow you to throw your life away up there. Lisa, Lisa... you're my daughter."

"I'm an officer in the RDF!"

He said it very quietly, "I know that."

"Then reassign me!"

He looked at her angrily now. "Father or no, I promise you this: If you try to leave, I'll have you thrown in the brig."

She was only partly successful at keeping the tears out of her eyes, but her voice was steady.

"Yes, sir."

Admiral Hayes despaired of ever winning the battle; he saw that he had lost the last of his family.


Breetai looked up at the projecbeam image. "What now, Azonia?"

She didn't mince words; he had expected no less. "There are no options, great Breetai. Dolza will try to exterminate us now that we have been exposed to the Micronians. I will stay and face the Grand Fleet. It will be an honor to go into battle with you, my lord!"

Some part of him knew what she meant. Wasn't this the battle any Zentraedi dreamed of, a hopeless fight against overwhelming odds in the clash of dreadnoughts as numerous as the stars? Wasn't this the apocalypse to which the Zentraedi looked for their version of immortality?

"Commendable," he said. "May you win every fight."

She drew a breath at the high compliment he had paid her. "And you too, Breetai!"

Her face dissolved as the projecbeam image did, and he turned to another. "Khyron? Your intentions?"

Khyron, languid and condescending, smoothed his beautiful blue hair. "You know my answer. The odds are too great. Why fight if you can't win, Breetai?"

"Why be Zentraedi if you don't know the answer to that, Khyron? But this is as I expected; I wasn't depending on you, anyway."

And so it was all out in the light at this eleventh hour. Khyron had substituted the ruthlessness and savagery that were all he had for courage. The difference came forth only in moments like these, but it was plain.

Now Khyron's facade broke, and he screamed at Breetai, froth leaping from his lips. *"You will be destroyed!"* The projecbeam image vanished.

On his own flagship, Khyron sat slouched in his command chair like a wounded toad. "All right, let's go." He threw the command over his shoulder to his subordinate, Grel.

"What coordinates?" Grel asked carefully. In such a rage, Khyron was easily capable of lashing out and killing any around him.

"Anyplace else in the universe but here," Khyron brooded, staring off angrily at nothing. There was no response from Grel, and Khyron snarled, "Didn't you hear me?"

Grel calculated his next words carefully. "But sir, we can't run."

Khyron barked a galling laugh. "You think not? Watch, then!" He signaled, and the engines of his flagship came up to power, as did those of all the Botoru ships under his command.

Grel licked his lips, wondering how best to tell Khyron that he hadn't been speaking figuratively. Khyron cherished the practice of beheading the messenger who bore bad tidings.

Breetai paid little attention to the maneuvers of the Botorus. He considered the nearby fabric of space, where the first perturbations of the Cosmic String heralded the Grand Fleet.

Once he had been Dolza's most valued subordinate—had saved Dolza's life from the very lnvid attack that had killed Zor. Now he contemplated the stirrings of the universe in advance of the attack and reflected on the incredible way things had turned out there in the Micronian star system.

*Hear my thoughts, Lord Dolza! To go down in battle is all we seek, from the highest to the lowest. Mark me well, for this is the final battle of Breetai!*

In the hearing chamber, people were exhausted, but the marathon went on. Computers and analysts were hooked in; G-staff members and evaluation teams were ready.

"Dolza will assume you're too weak to fight," Exedore was saying, still animated and prim in the midst of the most tiring activity. "He will divide his fleet and attack from every side, sealing off any avenue of escape. But this maneuvering will give you your only chance."

"Enough background; kindly be specific," Gloval snapped. Exedore turned to a luminous tactical projection he had constructed with the help of the SDF-1 computers.

"Their flagships will be here, here, here, and here, and Dolza's mobile base will appear here; these are my best projections.

"If you can destroy these vessels, it will throw the entire Grand Fleet into chaos."

"Simple military strategy," someone muttered.

"No; *simple* military strategy—of all-out, straightforward attack and overwhelming numbers—is what has allowed our tactics to remain the same for so long," Exedore countered. "That and the fact that the Zentraedi have never lost a war."

Colonel Maistroff rubbed his face with his hand, as if he were washing. "So, in short, we crush the head of the snake!"

Exedore nodded. He stepped away from the tactical display, pacing toward the place where Gloval sat.

"With their attack forces in disarray, our only chance for survival is to utilize the combined forces of the SDF-1 and our battlefleet. We are already aware of the crude Robotech cannon in your planet's northern hemisphere but consider it a minor element at best."

Gloval came to his feet. "I'm glad that we're now fighting on the same side." He clasped hands with the gnomish little man.

"Yes, so am I." Exedore turned to Minmei, who was watching it all unbelievingly. "And without your singing, this alliance between our peoples would not have been possible."

Kyle had assumed a hard expression, eyes closed, chin sunk on chest, lip curled. But Minmei was in a sort of dream state. "Who, me? *Really?*"

Exedore nodded his head slowly. "While I don't profess to understand Micronians, I now realize the importance of your singing. It touches emotional resources to which we Zentraedi did not have access before—a courage that is beyond mere courage in battle."

He seemed to blush a little; nothing could have surprised them more. Even Kyle was shocked.

"Will… will you sing for us?" Exedore got out, face coloring furiously. "So that we may hope for victory? Please, Miss Minmei."

"Of course."

She stood up, in that room where the plans were coming together that would spell the death or life of worlds, the survival or slaughter of billions. She drew a breath and sang in a voice as clear as polished diamond.

She sang "To Be in Love," one of her first compositions, still one of her favorites. It was a simple song, and there was nothing in it of armies or battles. It was about a closeness between two lovers.

Exedore and the three former spies were mesmerized. Kyle, eyes closed, was cold and indifferent. Gloval, Max and Miriya, and the rest watched and listened, immersed. Her voice soared to rebound from the domed ceiling.

Rick was transfixed, too, at first. The fact that he'd lost her didn't make her any less desirable, especially now.

But then a new sound came to him, a sound he recognized even through the intervening decks and bulkheads.

On the hangar decks, the elevators were at work, lifting Veritechs for cat launch. For the final battle.

The finder beams had done their work. Now there was a brutal application of force, and the warp and woof of the universe were ripped apart.

The Zentraedi had refined their targeting. This time, there was no cosmic bow wave of incandescent fire. Instead, a green cloud of some kind seemed to appear—until it became clear that every last mote in the cloud was a warship.

Another cloud appeared nearby, and another. Then two at once, then three. And soon the stars were blotted out. It was as if handfuls of sand had suddenly become ugly battlecraft. More appeared, and more, in dense, well-ordered formations, thicker than any hive swarm.

"There are too many for sensors to count," Vanessa said, sweating, blinking behind her glasses. "Too many…"

...

"I have to go," Admiral Hayes told his daughter gruffly. "We'll talk about this later—"

The PA interrupted. "Sensors register immeasurable defold activity. Estimated enemy strength one million, three hundred—correction, *two* million, one hundred thousand—stand by! Stand by! More enemy units arriving!"

Some other, less hysterical voice cut in. "Battle stations. Repeat, battle stations." Alarms and sirens sounded, and nobody had to say that it wasn't a drill this time.

Admiral Hayes swallowed, going pale.

Earth was engulfed in a net of enemy warships. They blotted out the sun's light, appearing in their hundreds of thousands, taking up position for the ultimate confrontation.

Claudia's face appeared in the hearing chamber on a display the size of a movie screen. "Captain Gloval, monitor three shows enemy positions over the western hemisphere."

The view came up. Still the sinister warcraft poured into Earth orbit from nothingness. The drifting clouds of them stretched, established intervals, deployed for total coverage. Great blotches of green, whole clustered space navies, were painted into the picture.

"Well, I'm afraid this is it," Exedore said. It looked like the planet was falling, in time-lapse photography, under a leprous infection of Zentraedi combat green.

Minmei could only stare, her song forgotten. Max and Miriya took each other's hands, and he was grateful that he had been granted the time they had had together.

Even Kyle was aghast. If there was one there who was in the mood for the scene, it was Rick Hunter. He watched the Grand Fleet spread and grow. Nothing left to lose. Okay: A fight it would be.

Breetai, staring up at the displays that were still functioning on his bridge, watched in awe. It was the greatest single combat fold-jump operation in history, and it came off meticulously. Dolza was doing everything right so far.

Breetai's clifflike jaw set. Opening moves and endgame were two different things.

The night sky over the Alaska Base was lighter, with the reflections of sunlight from the light underbellies of the warships taking up orbit. The stars were obscured, hundreds at a time.

Watching the screens, Lisa heard her father moan. She turned and saw by his expression that he realized, far too late, that the reports of the aliens' strength were accurate and that five million ships were so many more than he had ever envisioned.

# 16

And so the Great Mandala spun,
Two halves had learned
They both were one

Mingtao, *Protoculture: Journey Beyond Mecha*

AMONG ALL THE ANNOUNCEMENTS OF THE LOADING OF Decamissiles, the manning of gun turrets, the frantic coordinating of target-acquisition and threat-priority computers, there came word that Skull Team was to report to its fighters.

"Well. That's us," Max said, looking at the deck and then up at his wife. He was really at a loss. Some traditionalism said that he should shield her from harm; but Miriya was a better flier than anyone else aboard except Max, and there was no safety, anywhere.

More to the point, she would never have allowed him to leave her behind.

"Yes, Maximillian," she said, watching him. Rick noticed that in an amazingly short time, they had both learned to smile *exactly* the same slow smile at each other at *exactly* the same moment. He did his best to suppress his envy.

Max put his arm around his wife's slim waist and gave Rick a wave. "See you out there, boss."

"Count on it." Rick waved at them with phony cheer, watching them go off to suit up.

Others were finding their way out of the hearing chamber; Gloval and Exedore and the other heavy-hitters were already gone. The recording techs were wrapping things up quickly, preparing to double in brass on combat assignments.

Only Kyle and Minmei were left, uncertain, with no place to go. Rick looked up at them and thought about what was happening out there where the void met Earth's atmosphere. Millions of ships were forming up for a greater battle than even the Zentraedi had ever seen before.

Which meant the future looked very dim for one little VT leader who had come late into the business of war. Rick decided in an instant and sprinted off to where Minmei stood.

She was at the top of the steps leading to the table podium; he stopped a few steps below. "Minmei!"

She looked at him oddly. "Yes, Rick?" He couldn't read her, couldn't understand what was going on behind the startling blue eyes. Kyle was at her shoulder, cold and angry, glaring down at him.

Not that Kyle mattered anymore; very little did.

Rick fumbled for words, not coming up with any that would express what he wanted to say, not even managing to get started. At last he got out, "You know I'm not good at this sort of thing."

She did; knew it from the long days and nights they had spent stranded together, knew it from more recent times, when he had been all but inarticulate.

"But I might not see you again," he went ahead. "I want to say that—that I love you."

Her hands flew to her mouth like frightened birds. She mouthed words that made no sound.

"Had to tell you." He smiled bittersweetly. "Take care."

Then he left to suit up, already late in the massive launch schedule of the apocalypse, heels clicking emptily on the deck. She was frozen by his words; she could move again only when he was out of the hatch, out of sight. Minmei hurried down the steps to catch up.

Kyle was next to her in an instant, catching her arm, bringing her up short. "*Don't try to stop him!*" The doings of the warmakers were their own concern; Kyle had loved Minmei too long to lose her to them now.

She struggled hopelessly to free her arm, the black hair whipping. "Let *go*! I have to *tell* him! Kyle, let me go or I'll hate you *forever!*"

Fingers that could have tightened like a vise released instead. He knew a hundred ways to force her to stay there but not a single one to take away her feelings for Hunter or to keep her from the pilot without making her hate him.

The grip, strong as steel, went limp, letting her go. Minmei wrenched her arm free and raced off after Rick. Kyle stood alone for a long time in the deserted hearing chamber, listening to the emergency directives, the RDF announcements, the preparations for battle.

Battle, death, oblivion—those were so *easy* to face, didn't the military war lovers understand? Living without the one who meant everything in life to you, *that* was the fear that couldn't be overcome, the abyss no courage could see you across.

In the hangars and bays and ready rooms of the combat mecha, thoughts of love and grief had been left behind. Now it was only kill or be killed. Men and women emptied their minds of everything else in a way no outsider would ever understand.

"Arm all reflex warheads," the command came over the PA from Kim Young. The missiles—Hammerheads, Decas, Piledrivers and Stilettos—became alive in their pods and racks. The attack mecha stood to readiness: lumbering giants heavy with laser-array and x-ray laser cannon, missiles, chain-guns, and rapid-fire tubes loaded with discarding-sabot armor-piercing rounds.

The Destroids stumped out first: waddling two-legged gun turrets the size of houses, running their clustered barrels back and forth in test traverses, ready to bunch up shoulder by shoulder and concentrate fire. Forming up behind them were the Gladiators, Excaliburs, the Spartans and Raidars, all making the reinforced decks resound to their tread, weighted with every weapon Robotechnology could give them.

The March of the Robotech Soldiers.

The SDF-1 gun turret and casemate barrels swung and readied, men and women sweating as they settled into the gunners' and gunners' mates' saddles. Targeting reticles were checked for accuracy; triggers were dry-fired.

The stupendous warrior that was the SDF-1 itself stood ready, covers lifted from its many weapon ports. The two supercarriers that were the ship's arms, *Daedalus* and *Prometheus*, set for battle and for the harrowing, fiercely dangerous business of combat launches and retrievals.

On the hangar deck, Skull Team warmed up. They would be one of the few teams flying the new armored Veritechs. Max, running things until Rick could get there, threw his wife a quick smile. Miriya blew him a kiss, as she often did when no one else was looking. Kissing was still an amazing thing to her; lovemaking left her at a complete loss for words. But then, it did the same to Max.

She turned back to a final check of her VT. Combat was something she knew intimately, too. Max got the rest of Skull saddled up, resisting the urge to be bitter and preoccupied with regret that he had had so little time with her.

Those were the distractions that got fighter pilots killed.

On the bridge, Gloval arrived with Exedore at his side, and no one thought to say it should be otherwise. The reports of the ship's fighting status came to him from the Terrible Trio and from Claudia.

Gloval led Exedore to the great bubble of the forward viewport, thinking, *Who would have dreamed we'd be fighting side by side?*

But there was an answer to that. It was Gloval, always Gloval— and sometimes *only* Gloval—who had anticipated this day from the moment he had heard of the enemy defections.

Over the UEDC Alaskan headquarters, fighters looking a lot like VTs but lacking their superlative Robotechnology screamed into the air on alert. It was a brave show that everyone knew to be hollow; Earth's only real hope lay with the dimensional fortress.

Admiral Hayes and several other senior officers stood on a balcony overlooking the vast situation room. They heard echoing updates on the Grand Cannon's firing status, the enemy fleet that was still pouring out of spacefold, the composite picture that made it unlikely that a single member of species *Homo sapiens* would live through the day.

"The projections turned out to be in error," an intel-analysis officer confessed, zombielike. "Against a force that big, we can't hope to win. We couldn't do it even if the Grand Cannon satellites were in place." He was shaking his head slowly. "No way, sir."

Hayes was used to hiding his dismay. He called down to a communication officer, "Lieutenant! Have we been able to establish contact with the aliens?"

Hayes burned at the thought of *why* his superiors were suddenly so eager to talk to the Zentraedi. He avoided any contemplation of how Earth's rulers sounded now that reality had at last been forced upon them. The brave words and the bold posturing had been blown away like smoke in the wind, and UEDC was eager, cringingly eager, to make any deal it could, starting with an offer to make itself an overseer government under alien rule.

Except the Zentraedi weren't making deals today, and Armageddon was apparently the only item on the agenda.

"We're trying, Admiral, but so far it's a no-go," a com officer called up to him.

Hayes himself felt betrayed and a fool. His daughter and Gloval had been correct all along, right down the line. The prestige and honor of his rank had fallen away to nothing, and he saw that he had, very simply, wound up an otherwise honorable career by being the instrument of craven and greedy men.

"Then there's nothing left to do but fight," Hayes said.

Under other circumstances it might have been one of those lines flag-rank officers could hope to have show up in history books. The fact was that Hayes knew he been duped again and again by the politicians. Besides, it was unlikely that there would ever *be* any more history books.

And the only reason to fight was that the enemy offered no alternative—it meant to wipe the human race out of existence.

The Grand Cannon prepared to fire, and the futile squadrons of Earth fighters went out to do their jobs as best they could. Lisa Hayes stared down at her screens and instruments and fought off the urge to weep for the men and women who were doing their jobs in all good faith and were kept, by the omnipresent UEDC propaganda and disinformation, from knowing that they were doomed.

During a few moments' lag time, she paused to regard a close pickup shot of the SDF-1 and to think of Claudia, of Gloval, and of Rick. She found, as her father had told her when she was a little girl, that there were only a few really important questions in life and that combat would make *anybody* ask them.

*Why are we here? Where do we come from? What happens to us when we die? And when I do, will I be with Rick, at last, or will I be alone forever?*

An update on the cannon's targeting status came in just then, and Lisa had to let those thoughts go.

Rick Hunter sealed up his flightsuit and made sure his gloves were firmly connected to his instrumented cuff rings. They fit smoothly, allowing him maximum dexterity.

The hatch to his quarters signaled, and he thought it was just another messenger with a mission update, all com channels being overloaded. Until the hatch slid back.

"Rick?"

He pivoted and saw her standing in the hatch, outlined against the harsh glare of the passageway lights. She came a step into his quarters demurely but looking him in the eye.

The hatch rolled shut behind Minmei.

They were there in every size and shape, those war-green vessels of the Zentraedi Grand Fleet. Never in their entire history had they been assembled for combat in such a formation.

From his command station, Dolza, supreme commander of the Zentraedi race, considered his target, Earth.

Space was filled with his ships; there had never been a marshaling like this in the infamous annals of the Zentraedi.

And yet he felt misgivings. Dolza knew the ancient lore of his race from Exedore's endless teachings. Against the forces that those records mentioned, the Grand Fleet itself might not be enough.

Perhaps nothing would.

Inside the boulderlike base that was Dolza's headquarters, a thousand miles through its long axis, the supreme commander received word that the fleet was at last all present.

He was enormous, the largest and, but for Exedore, the oldest of his race. Dolza's shaven skull and heavy brow made him look like a granite sculpture.

"My first attack shall be the Micronians' mother planet," he said. "Let all ships stand prepared."

All through the fleet, final preparations for battle were carried out. On the colossal bombardment vessels, the bows opened like giant crocodile jaws, exposing the heavy guns.

Targeting computers accepted their assignments from Dolza's base, ranging their sights across the surface of the world, fixing their aim. The Grand Fleet's engines howled like demons, supercharging the weapons pointed at the helpless Earth.

"I want to apologize to you, Rick," she said. "I mean, about Kyle."

"It's not really your fault," he told her. "I should have let you know what my feelings were. I should have tried harder, I guess."

"But, I—"

"Oh, Minmei, *it's all right!*" he yelled, frightening her a little. He got control of himself and went to get his flying helmet. *How do I tell her?*

He went to pick up the helmet but saw her reflection in the visor. She was standing silently, watching him.

"I'm a pilot, and you're a superstar now," he said tiredly. "You know it wouldn't have worked for us, anyway. Too much has changed, Minmei."

He went to the viewport, looking down at Earth. "It's strange to think how small our world is," he said, almost distractedly. "It's a pity how much time we wasted, isn't it?"

She flinched as if he had hit her. She could see that he was being cruel on purpose, hurting himself and her, to make the love stop. She opened her mouth to say something that would make him honest again, would clear the air between them.

But at that exact moment the universe lit up. The Zentraedi attack had begun.

# 17

Once I wrote here—a younger Minmei did—that I needed to be my
own person, that I had my own shadows to cast.

But, oh... I didn't realize how terrible that darkness would be.

From the diary of Lynn-Minmei

MILLIONS OF BURNINGLY BRIGHT BEAMS OF PURE ENERGY RAINED
down on the blue-white world.

First to go were the orbital defenses, the surveillance satellites and
the "armors"—the big conventional-technology space cruisers. They
were obliterated instantly, vanishing in clouds of expanding gas.

The incredible volley pierced the atmosphere, boiling away
clouds and moisture, striking through to the surface. Buildings and
trees and people were vaporized; everything flammable exploded.
The hellish rays set off tremendous detonations and superheated
the air like thermonuclear weapons.

Everywhere it was the same. Soldiers and civilians, adults and
children, and the unborn as well—the Grand Fleet favored none
and spared none. In the middle of a humdrum day marked only by
some sort of alert the UEDC wasn't explaining, nearly the entire
population of the planet was put to the sword.

For most, there wasn't even time to scream, only a hideous moment
when light and heat beyond any description engulfed them, making
their bodies as transparent as x-ray images, then consuming them.

Cities toppled, and blowtorch winds scoured the world. Seas
were given no mercy, either; Dolza had decreed a carpet-volley
pattern to get ships and aquafarming and aquamining installations
and the like. Untold cubic miles of water turned into steam.

The beams came like a fusion-hot monsoon all across the defenseless world.

In UEDC headquarters, the ground rumbled but miles of earth and rock saved the occupants from immediate death.

Lisa gaped at an illuminated situation map. The strikes were so numerous that the display computers couldn't discriminate anymore. The face of the world glowed.

"They can't be doing this!" she screamed. "They can't!

But she knew she was wrong. They were.

"Annihilation."

Gloval stood helplessly, shoulders bowed, looking out the forward viewport. Exedore stood mute at his shoulder. The alien decided that he must, in fact, have fallen victim to the contagious human emotions, because he felt them very strongly at that moment: rage that this should happen, a soul-wrenching sorrow, and an utter, utter shame.

Reading her instruments, a female enlisted-rating tech said in monotone, "They're gone. They're all gone."

In his headquarters base, the immense Dolza looked upon his handiwork and found it good. His guttural laugh echoed in the deep, eerily resonant tones of the Zentraedi.

The Micronian interlude would be expunged from history, he had decided. And any similar race encountered by the Zentraedi would be subject to instant and total termination.

Then, events could be put back on their proper track.

Dolza had to admit that even he, the supreme commander, hadn't had a *true* idea of Zentraedi power until the moment the Grand Fleet opened fire. The irresistible might of it! It filled him with new aspirations, new resolve.

When the humans were finished and the rebellious Breetai and his followers destroyed completely, it would be time to deal with the Robotech Masters.

For too long now, the Masters had treated their warrior servants, the Zentraedi, with the contempt one showed a slave. For too long, that had seared the Zentraedi pride. Moreover, it had come to light that the Masters had told the Zentraedi a colossal lie all along—they had deceived them about the giants' very origins.

The Protoculture secrets hidden in Zor's ship had been an important part of Dolza's master plan to overthrow the Robotech Masters and let the Zentraedi take their rightful place at the pinnacle of the universe.

The accursed Zor had been aware of that and had dispatched his ship to keep it from Masters and Zentraedi alike. The plan had ultimately worked, but in so doing it had brought this day. As Dolza looked out at nearly five million warships, all raining down destruction on Earth, he realized that he didn't need Zor's secrets, didn't need the SDF-1. All he needed was the might of the Zentraedi hordes.

He laughed again, a bass rumble that made the bulkheads ring. Today humanity died. Tomorrow the war against the Robotech Masters would begin.

Rick Hunter clutched the ledge of his viewport. As he watched, the night side of Earth, partly obscured by the enemy fleet, lit up with a myriad of red-hot specks, the work of that first terrible salvo.

"The whole planet," he said numbly.

Minmei came up behind him, walking like a robot, in deep shock. "Are they all… are they all dead, Rick?"

He watched the night turn red. "Yes, Minmei."

She tore her eyes away from the sight. "Mother. Father."

"Lisa," he said very softly. His cheeks were suddenly slick with tears.

She started to sing in a lullaby voice, crooning a little love song to life and to the planet that was dying. But it didn't last long, and soon her head was buried in her hands.

"So this is how we end," she sobbed. "First the Earth and then the rest of us."

He put a hand on her shoulder. "No, Minmei. This is *not* the end, do you hear me?"

He wished he could sound more convincing. But she wasn't blind; she could see the overwhelming might preparing to turn its guns on the SDF-1 and its Zentraedi allies.

"We still have our lives," he said, shaking her shoulder a bit roughly to make her listen to him.

It was all so unfair, so hopeless. He hadn't felt so angry and powerless since that day in Dolza's base when he and Lisa and Ben were helpless prisoners—

*THAT'S IT!!!*

He shook her shoulder again with a sudden new conviction. "It's not over yet! Listen, Minmei, I want you to go now and *sing for everyone!*"

She wiped tears from her lashes. "Sing?"

"Yes. I've got an idea."

The smoke clouds were already rising from the Earth, rolling to envelop it and bring on a winter that even the computers couldn't analyze reliably.

In the UEDC base's main control room, Admiral Hayes heard the report.

"There's been no word from any other Council member, sir. Marshal Zukav is still unconscious, and the doctors think they'll probably have to operate. What are your orders?"

In this election year, most of the UEDC members had been caught by surprise by the alien attack, out mending fences and fixing political support. Of them all, only Hayes and Zukav had been present at the base when the attack came, and Zukav had suffered a coronary on the spot.

Now the reins were in Hayes's hands, but they were the reins to a planet that was more cinder than soil.

"Damage estimate to all sectors exceeds any known scale," a voice was saying quietly to one side. "We have indications that a few scattered groups survived the first attack."

The first attack, yes. But now the enemy was no doubt preparing a second and a third—as many volleys as it took to turn Earth into a molten ball.

And so the world would end.

"Did the Grand Cannon survive the attack?" he asked.

An aide was quick to answer. "Yes, sir. It will still function."

Hayes turned to him. "Very good. Then we'll begin the countdown at once, Lieutenant."

The aide hurried off to relay the order. In moments, the vast base thrummed with power.

Gloval looked into the face of his onetime enemy. Breetai stared back, and it would have been an historic moment if everyone had not been in such a hurry.

Breetai gazed down at the mustached, almost disheveled—looking little creature who had outfought and outthought the best warriors in the galaxy; Gloval looked up at a frighteningly massive fellow with a chest as thick as an ancient oak and a metal and crystal cowl covering half his skull.

They spoke with virtually no preamble; they felt they knew each other well.

"Commander Breetai, I want you to please broadcast a simultaneous transmission of Minmei's song on all of your military frequencies."

Breetai's single eye fixed on Gloval intently. "I have no objection, but what is your plan?"

Exedore stepped into the picture to explain. "As yet, the soldiers in Dolza's fleet have had no contact with Micronian culture, m'lord! When exposed to the song, they will be thrown into confusion. And it will also boost the Micronians' morale."

Breetai rubbed his massive jaw. Gloval stared in fascination at the giant mauve hand, the dense black hairs on its back thick as wires. "That *could* provide us with the chance we need to catch them off guard."

Gloval was a bit breathless with this alien's audacity. He himself had been thinking more along the lines of a selective strike. "But—the Grand Fleet is not a force we can attack head-on, Commander!"

Breetai gave him a surprisingly winning smile, coming as it did from a cloned XT soldier whose head was half hidden by a metal and crystal sheath. Breetai plainly savored every word. "Precisely, Captain Gloval. They would never expect us to mount a surprise attack against them."

The main bridge hatchway slid open, and a slender figure stepped in. Minmei looked around nervously at the mysterious landscape of dials, lights, screens, and controls.

"Um, you wanted to see me, Captain?"

He went to her, Exedore trotting alongside. "Yes, Miss Minmei. Lieutenant Hunter has told me his plan. We're going to use it for our counterattack."

Minmei glanced nervously at the communications screen, then quickly averted her eyes from the metal-skulled alien who was staring at her with frank interest.

"You *will* be able to sing a song for us, won't you, Minmei?" Exedore said anxiously.

She forced a smile. How could you go on with life when the world had just died? Simple: You used your acting instincts, keeping introspection and sorrow damped well down.

"Yes, of course. Anything to help out."

Gloval nodded in approval. She had barely exchanged two words with him at the wedding, but there was something about his old-world formality, a kind of lovable stuffiness, that put her at ease somehow.

"I have one special request, Minmei," Exedore put in. "*Could* you do that, er, that is, that *thing* that you do in all your movies? I believe it is referred to as a kiss."

He couldn't have surprised her much more if he had done his Minmei imitation for her. "I—I suppose I could. But why do you need that?"

Exedore dropped into the pedantic, almost effete tones he used when trying to get his point across to stubborn Zentraedi. "I believe it would act as a kind of psychological shock to all the Grand Fleet attack forces, rendering them less able to fight."

She felt like laughing hysterically; there were some critics who would have agreed with Exedore's evaluation of her acting ability.

But outside the viewport, Earth smoldered. "Well, if it will help."

. . .

The clouds were already thick in the night sky over Alaska, lit from below by an infernal glow.

The base throbbed around her, preparing for the monumental cannon shot. Lisa stared at her screens and waited to die.

At the cannon's base, a small city of Robotechnology, subatomic fires whirled; energy crackled and struggled to get free.

Admiral Hayes heard the reports in stony silence. This would probably be the last, possibly the only human shot in the battle, on the last day of the human race; but *somebody* was going to be very sorry they had ever come seeking battle. To go down fighting was much better than simply dying.

The cannon's huge lens, lit with targeting beams, made the undersides of the black clouds closing in on the world red.

Dolza looked around suddenly at an emergency communication tone. "Your Excellency! We've detected a high-energy reaction coming from the third planet!"

But before Dolza could ask for more data or give a single order, hell spewed forth.

It had been apparent from the start that an energy gun buried vertically in a planetary surface would have a very limited field of fire. The planned system of satellite reflectors was supposed to have solved that, but interim measures had been put in place. They showed their worth now.

A beam as hot as the heart of a star sprang up from the devastated Earth. Widened by the lens, it lanced up into the Grand Fleet. A hundred thousand ships disappeared in an instant, burned out of existence like insects in a flamethrower's blast.

Brute servos tilted the lens, angling the beam. No one had been sure whether or not a shot like that would violate all the mathematics of the Grand Cannon and blow the installation to kingdom come, but it turned out that somehow everything held.

Like a flashlight of complete and all-encompassing destruction, the Grand Cannon's volley swiveled through the blockading fleet.

Ships were simply there and then not. Left behind were only component particles and the furious forces of destruction. In that single attack, the human race destroyed more warcraft than the Zentraedi had lost in any war in their entire history.

"The enemy ships are just disappearing, sir," Vanessa said. Gloval and Exedore stared at the screen, watching the angling and swinging of the Grand Cannon. "Alaska Base survived!" Gloval exulted. The Terrible Trio let out whoops and laughter.

"Lisa," Claudia whispered.

# 18

Well, that was when I decided that ol' Vance needed to ease out of being Minmei's manager and into a new setup. I mean, hey: what does twenty-five percent of Armageddon amount to in real money?

Vance Hasslewood, *Those Were the Days*

MINMEI'S BACKUP BAND AND ROADIES (IF THAT WAS THE PROPER name for them; they played only one town, but they clocked more miles than any other act in history) were used to taking their time setting up, running sound checks, getting mentally prepared for a concert or recording session. None of that today, though.

RDF techs and other personnel threw the setup together in a few minutes flat, a briefing officer making it clear to the musicians just how important this concert would be. The only one to object, a keyboard man who wasn't happy with the way his stacks had been arranged, was menaced into silence not by the military people but by the other band members. Everyone knew what would happen if the Grand Fleet carried the day.

In her dressing room, Minmei tried to keep her mind off the greater issues and simply concentrate on her performance. Humming, she leaned toward her brightly lit makeup mirror, examining one eyelash critically. It wasn't that she was unaware of the horrifying events taking place all around the SDF-1; it was just that she could do nothing about them except clear her mind and sing her very best.

There was a timid knock at her door, and three visitors entered. "Hi, Minmei," said a rough but friendly voice.

FORCE OF ARMS

Minmei smiled into her mirror at the reflection of Bron and the other two Zentraedi spies.

"We understand the pressure you're under, Minmei," Rico began.

"Going into battle can be very, um, *taxing*," Konda added helpfully.

"We just wanted you to know we're with you 100 percent and we know you can do it," Bron told her, blushing. The other two nodded energetically.

"Oh!" She turned to them and came to her feet. She had spoken to them only a few times, even including the official hearings and meetings.

But she felt a kinship to them, a bond of empathy. Song had made them leave behind everything they knew, made them risk the unknown and commit themselves to a new life, even though that life held dangers and frightening enigmas. In that, they were very much like Minmei herself.

She put her hands out to them, palm to palm. "Thank you, Konda—Bron, Rico. You're very kind."

Konda cupped his hands around hers, and the other two stacked theirs gently on top. "You three are such wonderful men."

"Minmei," came the stage manager's voice. "Two minutes."

She kissed each of them on the cheek, then she was gone in a swirl of long, raven hair.

Instead of the seats of the Star Bowl amphitheater or a glass wall that looked on a recording studio's engineering booth, Minmei and her band gazed at a great, concave sweep of viewport. The enemy warfleet was deployed before them. Below were the battle fortress's upper works, and beyond the bow, the curve of the blasted Earth.

Combat craft were swarming from the super dimensional fortress; the warships of Breetai's armada were forming up around and behind it, battlewagons and flagships at the lead for a do-or-die first impact.

The cameras and pickups focused on Minmei as she found her mark on the stage. She had decided to wear a simple full skirt and blouse, with a golden ribbon bowed at her throat.

"Wh… what's your opener gonna be?" laughed her manager, Vance Hasslewood, nervously, mopping his brow with his handkerchief.

"How 'bout 'My Boyfriend's a Pilot'?" the bass man joked weakly.

"No," she said firmly. "We'll do the new one."

They had barely rehearsed it; she had completed it only two days before. There was a chorus of objections from just about everyone, but she held up her mike and spoke into it firmly.

"This is the time for it."

*Now or never.*

Tactical corps and civil defense mecha had been brought out on the decks of the battle fortress and the supercarriers. With their massed weapons added to the turrets and tubes of the SDF-1, short-range defensive firepower was more than tripled.

Out where the VTs were forming, as the cats slung more and more of them into space, the RDF fliers listened over the command net as Gloval's voice came up.

"Attention, all fighter pilots. Once we enter the zone of engagement, there will be complete radio silence under all circumstances. Miss Minmei's song, and only that, will be broadcast on all frequencies. As you have been briefed, we hope that will distract the enemy and give us the advantage.

"We *must* make maximum use of this element of surprise. Good luck to you all."

Rick heard Gloval out, lowering his helmet visor. Skull Team was flying the few armored VTs the fabrication and tech people had managed to get operational. That meant that Rick, Max, Miriya, and the rest would be out at the very spearhead of the attack. Not something to dwell on.

In his heart, he wished Minmei well, and then he led Skull Team out.

She looked up to the camera and raised her mike on cue as the cone of spotlight shone down on her. In the control room, her image was on all the screens from many angles.

Life is only what we choose to make it,
Let us take it,
Let us be free

Rick hit his ship's boosters. The blue vortices of its drives burned and shrieked. The armored VTs left trails of light, leaping into the dark. Conventional VT teams came after.

Breetai's tri-thrusters, pods, and other mecha prepared to follow. Gloval and the Zentraedi had wisely agreed not to mingle their forces; in the heat of battle, human pilots would have a difficult time reading alien unit markings and telling friend from foe. Even the hastily added RDF insignia on the tri's and pods might not be spotted in time.

In the command station of his flagship, Breetai stood with arms folded across his broad chest, a characteristic pose, staring up at a projecbeam. As he had admitted so long ago, hers was a voice to wring emotion from any heart. Perhaps the course to this moment had been set when he first heard it.

A tech relayed word. "My lord, this transmission is being picked up by Dolza's ships."

He nodded, watching and listening to Minmei.

We can find the glory we all dream of,
and with our love,
We can win!

His flagship trembled as its engines came up to full power. The front ranks of the armada moved forward at half speed, picking up velocity slowly. The SDF-1, in Attack mode, was accelerating along in the thick of them, its back thrusters blazing, a fantastic armored marionette of war.

Still engulfing Earth, below them, the Grand Fleet lay in orbit, seemingly paralyzed.

The human-Zentraedi alliance swooped down at it.

. . .

"What's that on our monitors?" growled one of Dolza's communications officers, his voice harsh and guttural.

His subordinate could barely tear his attention away from the song to answer. Such distraction when a superior was asking questions would have drawn quick, terrible punishment at any other time, but they were both hypnotized by Minmei.

If we must fight or face defeat,
We must stand tall and not retreat.

The subordinate shook himself a little and answered. "I don't know, sir, but we're receiving it on all frequencies."

Then they both watched in fascination, ignoring the flashing of indicators and the beeps of comtones.

"We're within firing range," Vanessa said tightly. "No counterattack detected."

*"It's working!"* Exedore cried, watching the battle at Gloval's side.

"This is it," Gloval said calmly. "All ships, open fire."

In that first gargantuan volley, the attacking force's main problem was not to hit its own fightercraft or have its cannon salvos destroy its own missiles in flight. But the Zentraedi were used to that sort of problem, and fire control had been carefully integrated with the SDF-1's systems.

It was an impact almost as damaging as the Grand Cannon's; millions of Zentraedi, gaping at Minmei's performance, died in moments.

Alarms were going off. The few Grand Fleet officers who could force their attention away from the screens could get no response from their troops short of physically attacking them.

As many of the Grand Fleet crews were beginning to notice the alarms, though, Minmei paused in her song; the band vamped in the background. A tall, dark figure stepped out into the spotlight with her.

Lynn-Kyle wore a look of burning intensity, his long, straight black hair swirling around him, taking her hand. "Minmei—"

"Yes, Kyle; I know," she recited her line. "You've come to say good-bye."

"Yes."

Minmei wasn't exactly sure where the lines had come from; everything was so hurried, so improvised. Weren't they from one of the movies the two had done together? But Kyle was putting more into them than he had ever managed on screen. He had seen her run off after Rick. What was going through his mind?

No matter. He took her into his arms. She turned her face up to his. The camera cut from a two-shot of their bodies pressed against each other to a close-up of a long, passionate kiss, Kyle no longer acting.

In the Grand Fleet, alien warriors groaned and made nauseated sounds.

"How can they *do* that?" "Most disgusting thing I ever—"

And yet there was something about it that kept them from looking away, an appalled captivation. It should be added that among the female units like the Quadronos, there was more absorption and less repulsion than among the males.

But all through the orbiting fleet, moans and growls and other reactions to the kiss turned into shrieks of dismay and pain as the alliance's volley cut through the enemy ships, holing them, blowing them to nothingness.

Rick watched the kiss on a display screen and thought, not unkindly, *Farewell Minmei.*

Then, "Let's get 'em!" he snarled over the tac net.

Someone must have managed to cut off the Minmei transmission from at least *some* of the Grand Fleet's mecha. There were plenty of effective ships, more than plenty.

The Skull Team's armored VTs bore in at the enemy, releasing barrages of missiles, fighting their way through Grand Fleet pod and tri-thruster defensive screens. Quadrono powered armor came at the VTs, too, less effective now that Miriya no longer led them. Miriya avoided engaging those.

VTs shifted configuration according to the needs of the moment; Battloid and Guardian and Veritech modes were intermingled. Pods and tri-thrusters mixed it up with them and opened fire. Space was one big killing ground.

The armored VTs were faster and more maneuverable than anything else in the battle as well as being more heavily armed. They pierced the enemy formations, ripping a hole for the rest of the attack force to exploit.

Skull Team seemed to be everywhere, unhittable and unavoidable. Many, many Zentraedi saw their Jolly Roger insignia—the skull and crossbones—and died instants later. The heavy autocannon buzz-sawed; the missiles streamed, leaving boiling trails. But for every enemy downed, three more dove in to try to seal the gap.

It's love's battle we must win.
We will win.
We can win!

The range was close now. Around the bowl in which Minmei performed, the ship's mecha opened up. The Destroid cannon in particular put out staggering volumes of fire. Every battery the ship mounted—except for the monster main gun, whose energy demands might have damaged the SDF-1—was working overtime.

The Grand Fleet's losses in the first moments of the battle were awful, but its numbers still gave it a vast edge, and some of the enemy ships were returning fire. The SDF-1 and the armada dreadnoughts forged on, blazing away in all directions. Enemy mecha were starting to get through to the alliance capital vessels now, despite the best efforts of the VTs and the armada's pods, tri-thrusters, and powered armor.

But slowly, seemingly by inches, the allied force drew closer to Dolza's headquarters.

Max and Miriya were like avenging angels, beyond any mortal power to resist or stop. Faced with the red-trimmed armored VT or the blue, all any enemy pilot could do was resign himself to death.

Rick had part of his commo and guidance equipment tuned for signals of life on Earth, especially from Alaska Base. If there was *any* sign of life...

A light cruiser was trying to break past the VTs for a go at the SDF-1. He went in at it, letting go a torrent of mixed ordnance, aiming for the vital spots the defectors had told the RDF about.

The cruiser fired back, and Rick decided this was one head-on he wasn't going to survive. But all at once the cruiser expanded, armor flying off it like rind off a bursting melon, and then the vessel and its crew were scattered atoms and little more.

So violent was the explosion that Rick was distracted, avoiding being damaged by it. When he looked around again, he saw that a trio of Battlepods had loosed multiple spreads of missiles at him, and there was absolutely no hope of dodging them all.

He eluded some, jammed some of the others' guidance systems, shot a few right out of existence—and the special VT's armor protected him from several hits.

But that left still more to go for his vitals. In Battloid mode, he crouched, trying to shield himself. He nevertheless took several, right in the breadbasket. VT armor was good but not that good.

The damaged Battloid, leaving a wake of flame behind it, spun and tumbled for Earth, flopping lifelessly.

# 19

When you're in the upper-right-hand corner, pushing that envelope, and the "CANCEL" stamp comes your way, you do a lot of thinking.

The Collected Journals of Admiral Rick Hunter

THE CRESCENT MOON HUNG LOW ON THE HORIZON; THE landscape of Earth made the two bodies like twins now.

Compared to the barrage that had laid waste to the Earth, the stray beams and rounds from the colossal battle above were barely distant sniper shots. But they were enough to rattle an Alaska Base that was already mortally wounded.

The shattered mouth of what had once been the Grand Cannon was already ringed with bizarre energy phenomena. Crackling discharges, wandering spheres of ball lightning, and firefly-like radiation nexuses had sprung from the tremendous forces loosed by the Grand Cannon and their interaction with both local fields and the fury of the enemy's rain of death.

"Earth Defense Sector four-alpha, come in please," Lisa called into her headset mike as the room tossed. "This is Alaska Base!"

The base heaved again, shaking down dust and debris from the ceiling. The tremors were caused by stray shots from the battle and by the rebellion of the very planet against the obscene things that had been done to it. But they came as well from the interior of the base itself. The installation was dying; but from what Lisa could read from her instruments, it would not be a slow, quiet death.

She had found no one else alive in the base. She had been ordered to see about a glitch in a shielded commo relay substation, had been there just as the cosmic fireworks went off. Being the last survivor in an underground charnel house might be somebody else's idea of a stroke of fortune, but it wasn't Lisa's.

She fought to keep her voice and her nerve from breaking as she tried another call. She kept herself narrowly fixed on the job at hand to shut out the ghastly things she had seen and smelled and been forced to come in contact with in making her way back to her post.

The place was nearly dark, lit only by dim red emergency lights. The weak flow from the fallback power system was barely enough to keep her console functioning. There was plenty of power in the base, power gathering itself for a split-second rampage, but she couldn't tap any of it.

"It's no use. They're all gone," she said numbly. She wondered how long she would last, the only living thing in the city of the dead, perhaps the only human being alive.

Not long, she hoped.

Abruptly, multicolored lines of static zagged across her screen, and her father's face appeared, broken by interference, only to reappear.

"Is that you, Lisa? I'm reading you, but the transmission is very weak."

She let out a long breath. "Thank God you're alive!"

She could see that he was still in the command station. A few figures moved in the gloom behind him, lit by occasional flashes of static or electrical shorts. So others had been spared by the concussion, the explosions and air contamination, the fires and smoke and radiation.

"The Grand Cannon was severely damaged," he admitted. "I don't think it will fire again, but we have to try."

"Oh, Father."

He smiled weakly. "It seems you were right all the time. The Zentraedi forces are much too powerful for our weapons to handle. I should have listened to you."

Another shock wave shook the base. Admiral Hayes said, "Lisa, you have to get out of here now!"

Get out? What was he talking about? The surface was a radioactive execution chamber carpeted with molten glass for miles all around. She was about to tell him so, to make her way to him, to die with him because it was a better place than the one she was in now, and she knew she would die this day.

Before she could speak, there was some sort of eruption from the Grand Cannon base equipment behind him, and the screen broke up into rainbow distortion, then went dark.

"No!" She threw herself at the console, then sank to the floor, wracked by sobs, as the wailing of the base's power plant built and built for a final, terrible outpouring.

"Father… Father…"

As the battle draws on, we feel stronger,
How much longer must we go now?

Rick recognized the voice at once, even in the daze he was in from the missiles' pounding. He blinked and saw the Earth whirling before him. His flying sense told him his ship was spinning and sprawling toward the ground, its thrusters only marginally effective in slowing it. He was inside a big, loose-limbed fireball meteor.

*Where am I? What happened?* Then it came back to him in a rush. As he gained a little control over himself, his VT, taking its impulses from the receptors in his helmet, did the same.

*Gotta go to F mode!* The bucking and spinning of the dive made it difficult reaching for the one close control. He knew that if the ship hadn't made minimal attempts to control the crash, he would likely never have woken up.

It was the hardest thing he had ever done in his life, but he got his hand to the F lever and yanked it. Damage control systems in his Robotech ship made decisions and blew off the armor and pods with which it had been retrofitted. Somehow, the burning components were jettisoned too.

The Battloid folded, elongated here, shortened there— *mechamorphosed*. And in a moment, a sleek, conventional VT rode the thickening air down toward Earth.

*Seems to be handling all right,* he thought. *Maybe I wasn't hit as bad as I thought.*

The ship had automatically assumed a belly-flop attitude for atmospheric reentry. The speed of its descent reddened its ablative shielding a bit, torching the air around it.

*Oops! Better activate heat shields!* In another moment a protective blister of heat-reflective armor, bearing the Skulls' Jolly Roger insignia, slid into place over the canopy. Other vulnerable components were similarly protected.

The heat in the cockpit began dropping at once, and Rick tried to assess his situation. *I'm still alive.* That covered just about all the important stuff as far as most pilots were concerned.

Minmei was still singing. He recalled those last words he had exchanged with her in his quarters as the sirens shrilled for a VT hot scramble.

*You can do it, Minmei. Just remember: Today you sing for everyone.*

*But—I want you to understand, Rick. I'm really singing for you.*

And then she had given him a kiss that he had felt to his toes, a kiss that made him feel he didn't need a VT in order to fly.

*I love you,* he told her; *I love you,* she said.

But it was really good-bye, and they had both known it.

He shook off the recollection; that was the sort of stroll down memory lane that got pilots killed. He was deep in the atmosphere now, his VT trimmed, seeming to respond well. He slowed, bringing the wings out to minimal sweep, rolling back the heat shields, for a look around. Night lay over the wasteland, and clouds closed in above.

He tried to figure out why the VT was descending in the first place, why it seemed to be homing in on something. Then he noticed that the commo system had picked up a signal and remembered that he had given it a certain task.

He swept in lower over the ravaged surface, trying to get a stronger signal. The utter horror of what had been done to his planet made him lock his mind to the job at hand and that alone. His commo equipment had picked up emanations of some kind on the designated frequency.

He turned and banked, climbed through the smoky night. A minute of maneuvering went by, then two, and as if by magic he was rewarded with a signal that came in five by five—perfectly.

"I say again: This is Commander Hayes, Alaska Base. Anyone receiving this transmission, *please* respond."

There was a note of fear in her voice that he had never heard before. Something in it brought home to him forcefully how important she had become to him.

*Farewell, Minmei.*

He was so eager to reply, to tell her he was there, that he fumbled in opening his transmitter and ignored all proper procedure.

"Lisa! Lisa, it's me!"

"Rick?" She said it low, like a prayer. Then, wildly, "Rick, is it really you?"

"Yes! Are you all right?"

She suddenly sounded downcast. "Yes, but I think I'm the only one."

"Lisa, give me your coordinates. Send me a homing signal."

She waited a beat before answering. "No, Rick; it's far too dangerous here. But thanks."

"Damn your eyes! I've got a fix on your signal, and I'm coming! Now, will you help me or not?" She didn't say no, but she didn't say yes.

"Besides," he said jauntily, "what's a little danger to *us*? I'll get you out of there in no time." He wished he had his long white flying scarf so he could fling it back over his shoulder rakishly.

Suddenly, there was a homing signal. "Rick, I'm so glad it's you," she said in a voice as intimate as a quiet serenade. "Be careful, all right?"

Soon after, the VT dove straight down the shaft of the one-time Grand Cannon. It went from Fighter to Guardian mode, battered by rising heat waves and running a gauntlet of radiation that would have broiled an unprotected human being instantly.

We shall live the day we dream of winning
And beginning a new life
We will win!
We must win!

She had sung it through, taking longer because of the scene played with Lynn-Kyle, and yet it hadn't been very many minutes since Minmei had begun her song. Nevertheless, Khyron the Backstabber knew, the universe and war in particular turned upon such minutes.

He stood in his flagship, well out of the battle but within striking distance, watching the fight. Lack of sufficient Protoculture to make his escape from the solar system had forced him to come up with a new plan, and the plan seemed more promising every moment.

Grel, his second in command, watched Khyron worriedly. Khyron had shown no aversion to the singing, the kissing. His handsome face shone, his eyes alight with the gleam Grel had seen there when Khyron used the forbidden leaves of the Flower of Life.

"What is your plan now, my lord?" Grel ventured.

Khyron was still watching Minmei. "Mm. Pretty little thing."

Grel couldn't help bursting out, "What?"

Khyron looked at him coldly. "Get me the position of Breetai's flagship." Then he was smiling up dreamily at Minmei's projecbeam image once more.

Grel didn't know what to say and, moreover, knew that saying the wrong thing to the Backstabber had cut short quite a number of otherwise promising careers. He couldn't help blurting, though, "But my lord! Breetai is one of us! You cannot do th—"

Khyron whirled on him in a murderous rage. "How *dare* you? You will follow my orders or else!"

Grel turned very pale and hurried to obey. Khyron turned back to his enjoyment of the song.

But his enjoyment was sinister. He felt a physical, languorous pleasure as he concluded that he was at last coming to a clear understanding of a pure *true* definition of conquest; something more pleasure-giving, if he was right, than all the victories, booty, and worlds the Zentraedi had ever taken.

In seconds, Khyron's flagship was under way, followed by the tiny flotilla of those still loyal to him.

People in the control booth and even members of the band had sent the inquiry up the line: Shouldn't Minmei go to another song?

In the midst of the most important battle of his career, Gloval had taken time to give the order personally: no! This song, *this* song was the one!

Now, with Minmei's voice ringing through it everywhere that battle damage hadn't silenced the PA system, the SDF-1 waded deeper and deeper into the massed Grand Fleet. Out on the decks and outerworks, enemy fire was taking a vicious toll of the exposed attack mecha, but the crews of the war machines still kept up intense fire.

Breetai's armada had suffered badly, too, but hadn't slowed.

"Keep all power levels at maximum!" he bellowed as systemry and power conduits blew all about him.

His flagship and its escort, the SDF-1, side by side with them, pressed on, their volume of fire enormous, the rest of the armada striking after in a wedge, probing their way through the disorganized foe.

Many of the smaller fightercraft and mecha on both sides had been snuffed out of existence by the overwhelming volleys being traded; most of the rest had quit the battle's fairway.

"Hell or glory!" cried Azonia, holding her fist aloft, coming in to shore up the alliance's badly crumpling left flank. Her forces threw themselves into the engagement with fanatic zeal.

Dolza's faithful leapt at them with an equal thirst for death and triumph.

Inside the SDF-1, a direct hit pierced the hold in which Macross City lay. Atmosphere roared out at once like a great river, and more missiles penetrated the hold to score direct hits on the streets of the city. Armored curtains and sealing sections swung into place at once, but still there was grievous damage to the city. Rebuilt a half dozen times, it was fast becoming rubble again. Loss of life was relatively low because most of the inhabitants were on emergency duty elsewhere and practically all the rest were in shelters.

Just before the last curtain rolled into place to seal the compartment and allow it to be repressurized, a last heavy enemy missile somehow sizzled through the gap. By chance, it found a shelter in a direct hit, and the carnage was nothing that belonged in a sane universe.

Repair and rescue crews and medical teams wanted the ship to drop back to give them time to do their work. Gloval bit his lower lip but refused; perhaps all that was left of humanity was aboard the SDF-1, and if Dolza wasn't smashed now, in this moment, none of them would survive.

The request was denied. The battle raged on. It was not the first agonizing time Gloval had felt himself something of a villain.

# 20

Aside from Gloval, very few of our senior military people seem to be able to grasp the simple truth: The Zentraedi do not truly understand Robotechnology. They use it without comprehending how it works, as many humans use television, laser devices, or aircraft without the slightest idea what makes those technologies function. The Zentraedi were given their weapons and equipment by the enigmatic Robotech Masters. Their control over the Zentraedi is due, in part, to the giants' own ignorance.

This means that the Zentraedi are vulnerable in ways of which they are unaware.

Dr. Emil Lang, Technical Recordings and Notes

**M**ORE DISTURBANCES SHOOK THE UNDERGROUND CORRIDORS of Alaska Base as a terrier might shake a rat in its teeth. The titanic supports complained, and the ceilings showered rock dust.

Through it flew the Skull Guardian, maneuvering in very confining space to avoid exploding power ducts and ruptured energy mains. Rick brought the ship to an abrupt halt, hitting the foot thrusters hard so as not to collide with a thick shield door that dead-ended the cyclopean corridor.

But he was in no mood to be stopped. He lowered a phased-array laser turret and aimed with his gunsight reticle. The fearsome power of the quad-mount sent armor flowing in rivulets, but not as quickly as he hoped. He cut back his ambitions and tried for a man-size opening instead of a VT-size one.

In a few moments a circular plug of armor two feet thick

fell back from the shield door, leaving a makeshift hatch. Rick gave commands with his controls and with mental images; the Guardian bowed, its nose touching the corridor floor so that he could disembark.

He was barely at the smoking, red-hot opening when he heard her. "Rick!" Lisa was waiting for him patiently at the far end of the short, small connecting passageway.

He felt like sinking to his knees with relief and—something else. But there was no time for it, and so he tossed his thick, unruly black hair out of his eyes and flickered his eyebrows at her.

"You the lady who called for the cab? I'm your man."

She laughed fondly, nodding. "It's about time." She ran to him, laughing, and he caught her up in his arms, whirling her.

In another few seconds they were in the Guardian's cockpit, Lisa seated across his lap, Rick trying to concentrate on his flying. Strange energy phenomena coruscated and spat all around, a poltergeist zoo of deadly short-term exotica. Purple lightning grasped for them, and green rays ricocheted from surface to surface. Walls blew out into the corridor, sending pieces of shredded armor plate whirling like leaf fragments.

"The reactor's overloading!" she yelled over the din.

Rick somehow ran the dimly lit obstacle course, Lisa's head buried against his chest in case the canopy shattered. After several centuries' time juking and sideslipping through the maze of Alaska Base, the Guardian was back into the vertical shaft of what had been Earth's greatest weapon less than an hour before.

The last layer of defensive ships was riven apart by the irresistible wedge of the allied force. Before them hung Dolza's headquarters like some lumpy, dangling overripe fruit.

But Dolza didn't run; that wasn't the way of the true Zentraedi warrior, and Dolza embodied the Zentraedi warrior code. It was as Breetai had known it would be. Instead, the moonlet-size headquarters came straight at its enemies, surrounded by such escort vessels as it could gather around it.

"Objective now approaching," Vanessa reported.

"All units in position," Kim sang out.

"Target within range. Stand by, all batteries," Sammie said into her mike.

"All escort fighters, break contact and attack objective immediately," Claudia ordered. She paused for a quick glance at the headquarters. Its shape and lines and apparent texture reminded her so much of a mountain in space, falling straight at the SDF-1. Ready to crush them and the Zentraedi who had become humanity's friends; ready to crush everything in its path, as had always been the Zentraedi way.

Claudia's face hardened along grim, angry lines. *Not this time.* She thought of her slain lover, Roy Fokker, and of all the others who had died in the pointless war. *But not this time!*

Exedore, still at Gloval's shoulder, said softly, "Now, Captain."

It was as if someone had run a high current through Gloval. "Open fire!" he barked.

The SDF-1 fired again, in every direction, her carefully hoarded power being used at a fearsome rate now, at a moment that was late in the battle even though only minutes had elapsed.

The armada ships of Breetai fell away to all sides to engage the enemy or lend support as they could. The final mission was the dimensional fortress's alone, and no other vessel in existence could perform it or accompany the ship.

The giant warrior shape's thrusters blared, adjusting attitude, and now the SDF-1 came at Dolza's stronghold headfirst.

"Brace for ramming!" Gloval bellowed, and the orders went forth. The engines shook the great ship and drove it in a death dive.

The two great booms that reared above the ship's head like wings were now aligned directly at the space mountain that was Dolza's headquarters, the nerve center of the Grand Fleet. The booms were separate parts of the main gun, reinforced structures that were, with the exception of the mammoth engines, the strongest parts of the ship. And around their tips glowed the green-white fields of a limited barrier defense, making them all but indestructible.

The SDF-1 plunged at its objective; Dolza's technical operations people, prepared for an exchange of close broadsides, realized only in a last, horrified moment what the dimensional fortress's intention was. By then, it was too late.

The idea of being rammed hadn't occurred to them; no other vessel could have done it. Even Breetai's flagship could have caused Dolza's base little more damage that way than a child could inflict by crashing a kiddie car into Gibraltar.

But this was Zor's final creation, a machine that incorporated most of what he had learned about Protoculture and the secrets of Robotechnology. The booms went through the thick armor of the headquarters moonlet as if it were soft cheese. The SDF-1 was like some enormous stake being driven into the heart of the Grand Fleet.

Once the dimensional fortress was inside the outermost layers of the headquarters' armor plating, Dolza's stupendous ship was even more vulnerable. Bulkheads were smashed out of the way like aluminum foil; structural members snapped like toothpicks. The directed barrier shields glowed brighter but held.

An ocean of air began leaking from the headquarters, and the dying started at once. Power junctions and energy routing, severed or crushed, sent serpents of writhing electrical and Protoculture lightning into the thinning air and serpentining along the bulkheads and decks.

The SDF-1 brought its mighty forearms, the supercarriers *Daedalus* and *Prometheus,* into play. Their bows, too, had been reinforced and mantled with directed barrier shields. Like a giant punching his way through an enemy castle, the ship drove on, destroying all that was in its path, its thrusters making it an irresistible force.

Zentraedi were whirled through the air like dust motes in the tremendous atmospheric currents being sucked toward the opening the SDF-1 had made. They died in explosions and were torn apart, ground up, squashed to jelly, or impaled by the flying, whirling wreckage.

Through it all, Minmei sang. She knew the song was no longer a part of any surprise attack, but she felt now that if she stopped, it might bring about some disastrous halt in the desperate attack. It was as if her song was what was making it all happen; it was a form of magic that she couldn't stop in midspell.

Then the dimensional fortress was opening up with conventional weapons. X-ray lasers and missile tubes, cannon and pulsed beams hammered away at everything before and around them. The ship's path was often obscured by the demon's brew of flame and explosion all around.

Minmei watched, transfixed, at the huge sweep of viewport and sang, wondering if the universe was about to end. Because that was how it looked from where she stood.

But moments later, as suddenly as the drawing aside of a curtain, the SDF-1 broke out into a vast, open place. Behind it was a tunnel with its mouth edged by jagged, bent-out superalloy plate. The Zentraedi gaped as it drifted across the vast space within the headquarters mountain.

Gloval knew the timing had to be split second and perfect, and he had no leisure for preparation.

There were quite a few enemy vessels still inside the gargantuan base, something Gloval had been hoping against. But they were all at rest, unable to maneuver or open fire for seconds more at least, perhaps as much as a half minute. In a battle like this, that was an eternity.

"Prepare to execute final barrage!" he snapped as his bridge crew bent to their work. "Then full power to barrier shield!"

Missile ports opened to let loose the last volley the SDF-1 was capable of firing, the do-or-die knockout punch Gloval had saved for this moment. The fortress's heaviest projectiles—Deca missiles the size of old-fashioned ICBMs, Piledrivers as big as sub-launched nukes—were readied for firing.

The bows of the flatdecks opened like sharks' mouths, revealing racks of smaller Hammerhead and Bighorn missiles.

"Target acquisition on their main reflex furnace," Gloval ordered.

But Claudia was way ahead of him. "Target locked in, all missiles, sir," she said.

In his command post, the looming Dolza tried to believe what he saw before him. "What are they doing? They'll destroy us all!"

If the reflex furnace went, the resulting explosion would certainly destroy the base and everything in it, and quite possibly all ships in both fleets and even the planet nearby. But that didn't seem to be daunting the Micronians.

*This isn't war!* Dolza screamed within himself. *It's madness!*

So the tiny creatures were willing to die in order to avoid the disgrace of defeat.

*They are more like us than I thought!* Dolza realized. *They have some source of strength we must learn. What allies they would make in a war against the Robotech Masters!*

"Wait!" he bellowed.

"Fire!" Gloval roared on SDF-1's bridge.

The missiles gushed from the battle fortress, the smaller, faster ones getting a quick lead and leaving corkscrewing white trails. The heavier ones took a bit longer to get up to speed, but they quickly overtook and passed their little siblings. All angled in, on assorted vectors, for the base's reflex furnaces.

But Gloval had dismissed them from his mind as soon as he had given the order to let them fly. There was no time to spare.

"All power to barrier shields!" he snapped, but again his bridge crew had anticipated

The ship was standing stock still. Every erg of power in it was channeled to the shields, producing first a cloud of scintillating light around the ship, then a green-white sphere like some exotic Christmas ornament.

"Barrier shield coming to maximum," Kim said calmly. Then, a second later, just as the first missiles began to detonate on target, "Barrier at max, sir."

The enemy ships in the base were opening fire now, but their shots glanced harmlessly off the barrier system. Gloval barely paid attention to confirmation of that; he had little doubt the Robotech shield created by Dr. Lang could hold out against an enemy bombardment for a few seconds. The real test was coming up.

...

Dolza watched the awesome barrage hit home on the reflex furnace area of the ship's interior and knew he was going to die.

Even with the protection of its shielding, even with the defenses of desperate, brave Zentraedi captains who purposely threw their ships in the way of the all-out salvo, enough missiles got through to ensure that the base would be destroyed. Many *times* enough.

The reflex furnaces churned, then spewed forth utter destruction. Dolza, watching from his command post, had time only for one thought.

Years and years before, he had watched Zor die. Zor had spoken of some overriding Vision that made the megagenius send the SDF-1 here, to Earth.

Had Zor seen this moment, too? And things beyond it?

Then a terrible light seared him. Dolza howled a fierce Zentraedi war cry as he was rent to particles.

The interior bulkhead of the base began to bulge with secondary explosions, nodes of superhard armor being pushed out like putty by the force of the blasts running through the place. The rift in the reflex furnaces that had destroyed Dolza's command post was expanding, gushing forth blinding-white obliteration.

Ships only beginning to maneuver for the run to safety were caught in it, wiped out of existence like so many soap bubbles in a blast furnace.

The base swelled like an overfilled football, then split apart along irregular seams that hadn't been there moments before. Ruinous light spilled out of it, then it lit the sky over Earth like a star.

# 21

Francis Bacon said that "In peace the sons bury their fathers and in war the fathers bury their sons." My father warned me when I joined up that this didn't always apply to our family, because we were *all* military. He might have had some premonition that I would outlive him, but what he didn't foresee was that his daughter would hear taps played for an entire world.

Lisa Hayes, Recollections

THE THICK CLOUDS HAD DARKENED THE ALASKAN NIGHT TO pitch-blackness, but the fighter's night-sight capabilities gave Rick a clear view of what he was doing. The lurching Guardian barely cleared the rim of the Grand Cannon's shaft without snagging a wingtip.

It might be begging for a crash, but he kept going, nursing the fighter along until he was beyond the blighted, red-hot area around what had been Alaska Base.

He was barely clear of the blast radius when Alaska Base went up like a pyromaniac's fantasy of Judgment Day.

He flew in Fighter mode for a long while, casting back and forth across the charred Earth for safe landing, watching his radiation detectors and terrain sensors.

He swooped in over what had been a major UEDC base, according to the maps. But there was only a dry lake bed, its water vaporized by a direct hit, and the remains of what had been a major city. The plane started bucking hard, and he went back to Guardian. The place showed no signs of radioactivity or fallout; he decided to set down.

It was a little before sunrise on a smoky, darkened world that, it seemed, would never see the sun again.

Rick hit the foot thrusters and brought the VT to an erratic, slewing landing. The canopy servos had gotten fried in one of those last blowups, so he yanked the rescue handgrip and blew the canopy off.

Rick and Lisa stood up in the cockpit and looked out at the mutilated landscape of Earth. It was as pockmarked as the moon, with deep cracks and crevasses. Smoke was rolling into the sky from dozens of impact points and from fires that stretched along the horizon. The air was hot, thick with soot and dust. There seemed to be volcanic activity along a chain of mountains to the west. A scorching wind was rising.

The most frightening thing was that there was no water to be seen anywhere.

There was a patch of open sky, but as they watched, the clouds rolled in, blotting out the stars. He wondered how the battle had turned out. From the looks of Earth, it probably didn't matter very much.

Lisa looked at him, pulling the windblown strands of long brown hair away from her face. "Thank you for getting me out of there, Rick." She could bear dying on the surface, in whatever form that death might take. But to endure her last moments among the charred and smoking remains of the base's dead—that would have been more than she could have borne. She extended her hand.

Rick took it with a grin. "Oh, c'mon. It gave me a chance to disobey your orders again, after all." They shook hands, and she let herself laugh just a little.

Lisa sat on the edge of the cockpit. "I'll always be grateful. I admire you a great deal, Rick."

That wasn't what she really wanted to tell him, but it was a start. It was much further along than Rick had gotten in saying what *he* was feeling at the moment. It occurred to him that a world that was a mass grave, very likely smoldering ash from pole to pole, was a strange place to profess love for somebody.

Or maybe not, he saw suddenly. Maybe it was the best epitaph anybody could ever hope to leave behind. He had already yielded to the hard lesson that life wasn't worth much without it.

He almost said four or five different things, then shrugged, looking at his feet, and managed, "It was … it was a pleasure."

A ray of light made them turn. The rising sun had found a slit between clouds, to send long, slanting rays on the two people and their grounded machine. There was no sign of the stupendous battle.

"It looks like the fighting's stopped." She felt so peaceful, so tired of war, that she didn't even want to know the outcome.

"Um, yeah."

"I wonder if there's anyone else around?"

"Huh?"

She looked around to him. "What if we're the last? The only ones left?"

He looked at her for long seconds. "That wouldn't be that bad, would it?" he said softly. "At least neither of us will ever be alone."

"Rick…"

He had his mouth open to say something more, but there was a blast of static from the commo equipment as the automatic search gear brought up the sound on a signal it had located. There was a familiar voice singing a lilting, haunting hymn to Earth.

We shall have the day we dream of winning,
And beginning a new life!

"Minmei!" Lisa cried. She didn't know whether she could ever change her feelings toward the singer, but right now that voice was as welcome as—well, *almost* as welcome as the company Lisa was keeping.

"Up there!" Rick shouted, pointing. Something was descending on blue thruster flames hundreds of yards long, trailing sparkling particles behind it, weird energy anomalies from the interaction of barrier shield and reflex furnace obliteration.

Rick held Lisa to him. The dimensional fortress settled in toward the lake bed, the two flattops held level, elbows against its own midsection like Jimmy Cagney doing his patented move.

*All it needs to do is throw a hitch in its shoulders and sing "Yankee Doodle Dandy"!* Rick thought.

The enormous blasts of its engines kicked up dust, but the SDF-1 was landing with the rising sun directly at its back. They watched it sink down, silhouetted against the wavering fireball of the sun, until the land was waist high all around it.

Sunrise was throwing brighter light across the flattened terrain. "What a sight for sore eyes." Rick smiled, flicking switches on his instrument panel.

Lisa laughed outright, surprising herself. Was it right to be happy again so soon after so much carnage? But she couldn't help feeling joy, and she laughed again. "Oh, yes, *yes!*"

"This thing's still got a few miles left in it," Rick decided, studying the instruments. "Let's go."

*"Okay!"*

She settled back into his lap, and when he put his hand over the throttle, she covered it gently with her own, averting her eyes but leaving her hand there. He moved the throttle forward. Lisa's heart soared, feeling his hand beneath hers.

The Guardian jetted across the devastated landscape, into the sunrise, straight for the SDF-1 and the long shadow it threw. Lisa, her arms around Rick's neck, laid her head on his chest and watched a new future loom up before her.

Not far away, another survivor of the destruction saw his future go up in smoke.

# PART II:
# RECONSTRUCTION BLUES

# 22

Why were the higher-ups so surprised that we rebuilt right away, and so quickly? Human feel can wear down a stone, human hands can grind down iron, human perseverance can overcome any adversity.

Mayor Tommy Luan, *The High Office*

UPON ITS INITIAL ARRIVAL, GLOVAL HAD THOUGHT OF THE SDF-1 as a kind of malign miracle, since it had kept humanity from destroying itself utterly in the Global Civil War. There was another miraculous purpose it was to serve, to divert war away from Earth, fight off the Zentraedi, and ultimately break the invaders' power.

But there was a third role in this sequence of events that even Gloval hadn't guessed; indeed, he had unwittingly worked in opposition to it.

The SDF-1 was an ark, as well.

Even after the bombardments, the scorched-Earth attack that had very nearly come to a *no-Earth* situation, the boiling away of much of the planet's water—temporarily at least—into the atmosphere, pockets of humanity had survived. But what chance would they have to resume an advanced culture and technological base?

Very simply, none.

Take mining as an example. Most of the useful minerals that could be mined by primitive means were long since exhausted. The huddled groups of war-shocked people who survived the Zentraedi holocaust were unable to mount even steam-age mining efforts, much less the sophisticated operations it would take to get to the less accessible deposits still remaining in the planet.

An unbelievably complex and interdependent world had simply passed away, and there was no means to rebuild it.

Terran technology had used up its one bolt, and there was no such thing as starting over from scratch, because the resources that had let Homo sapiens start from scratch had been consumed long before.

The human race was on its way to becoming a permanent, dead-end race of hunter-gatherers with no hope of ever being more again. History was about to close the books on a vaguely interesting little upstart species; events and the simple facts of life had gone against it.

Except there was the SDF-1, with Macross City inside.

There had been few hard words or unyielding attitudes once the great starship set down in the dry lakebed. Who do you get mad at when the world lies dying?

In their years of wandering and persevering, the residents of Macross City had put most delusions and wishful thinking behind them. They saw what had happened, and it came to them quickly that against any expectation, *they* had been the lucky ones. The castoffs and pariahs were actually the cargo of a new ark.

So in the end that was the fate of Macross City. What was left of it was disembarked, person by person, piece by piece, around the lakebed, and the rebuilding began.

The intellectuals and experts argued about the best ways to reestablish ecological balances and manage moisture reclamation; the people of Macross rebuilt their homes and businesses and lives as best they could, trusting that such things were more important than all the computer projections.

The ship's engines provided power. Its mecha and military people enforced law and order in an ever-growing domain of security. The SDF-1's fabricators and other technical equipment quickly provided a new industrial base, and the population of Macross constituted an urban economic hub.

In the time after that last Armageddon, the SDF-1's name might better have been that of one of its constituent flattops, *Prometheus.* It was humanity's main source of medical care, technical resources, and most importantly, the accumulated knowledge and wisdom of the species *Homo sapiens*.

The nuclear winter scenario was much less severe than the computers had guessed. That was partly because the predictions had been based on faulty models. It was also because the RDF and civilian corps worked around the clock to make it so.

And they had allies. The explosion of Dolza's base had disabled or taken with it his entire Grand Fleet, but a considerable part of Breetai's armada had survived. Many Zentraedi had chosen to go to Earth and take up a life there either in Micronian size or in their own original bodies.

Both races hoped for a new golden age or at least a lasting silver one.

It was a world seared and barren, pockmarked with craters and split with fissures made by war. Everywhere were the rusting mecha of the last great battle. Most of the disabled Zentraedi ships had, for unknown reasons, oriented on the nearest center of gravity—Earth—and driven toward it.

The result was that the planet's surface was an eerie Robotech Boot Hill dotted with crumpled alien warships that had driven themselves partway into the ground like spikes. The reminders of that last day were everywhere, too many to ever dismantle or bury. Only time and the elements would remove the grave markers, and they would not do so in the life span of anyone then living.

But those who were left alive went on a new crusade, the one to heal the planet and put things right again.

Two years passed.

Rick Hunter's VT, in Guardian mode, complained at the strain he put on it in the tight bank. He gritted his teeth but held to it. The old ship, battered as it was, had never failed him yet. With replacement parts and maintenance time in such woefully short supply, the Skull Leader's craft wasn't in the shape it had been in during the war, but he trusted it.

The Guardian jetted in low over the rust-red, pitted countryside and foot-thrustered to a deft landing. It bowed, nose nearly touching the ground; he jumped from the cockpit eagerly, hardly able to credit what was happening to him.

"I don't believe it! It's impossible!"

He ran across the gritty, fallow soil, back toward what he had spotted. All around were gigantic, jagged shreds and peels of Zentraedi armorplate, twisted and mangled, slowly turning to rust and dust. Off to one side was an overturned Guardian wreck that looked like it had been put through a meat grinder. Its rusting legs stuck straight up into the air like a dead hawk's.

Rick skidded to a halt, the wind moaning around him. He looked down and was astounded.

At his feet, springing from a moist plot of earth somehow enriched enough to sustain it, was a field of dandelions. The irregularly shaped, few-square-yards patch of them was sheltered from the wind by the wreckage and yet, by chance, had good exposure to sunlight.

For a moment he couldn't find words. "Absolutely incredible," he murmured, but that was insufficient. Here, near yet another Zentraedi wreck, the soil had been fortified with something that would support life. He suspected that he knew what that something had been, and it suddenly made him feel very mortal and humble.

"Real flowers!" He knelt, handling them as gently as a lover, inhaling.

Certainly there were flowers in the greenhouses and protected fields of the reclamation projects, but this! It was a thing as wonderful as flight—no, *more* wonderful! Life itself!

He couldn't recall how many times, as a child, he'd raced across a field of those unglamorous flowers, eyes fixed on the blue sky, wishing only to fly. And now things had come full circle; he flew the most advanced aircraft ever known with his eyes trained on the ground, waiting and hoping for just such a sight as... dandelions.

*I hope this means the Earth is forgiving us,* he meditated.

It was a good and precious thing to know that at least one positive sign, however small, had shown itself. There were other omens that were not so good. Rick was privy to a lot of high-level information thanks to his experiences among the

Zentraedi and his value as an intelligence source.

There were things he tried not to think about, and three of them had disturbing names: Protoculture. Robotech Masters. Invid.

Three VTs swooped in low over the desolate land, forming up again after completing their aerial recons of assigned sectors. They were newer ships than Rick's, but they looked somehow less sleek and finished. There were those who said the true high-water mark of Robotech workmanship had passed.

"Commander Hunter, come in, please," said Rick's new second in command, Lieutenant Ransom. "This is Skull Four calling Skull Six."

No answer, after five minutes' trying. Ransom thought for a moment. "Bobby?"

Sergeant Bobby Bell, youngest of the remanned Skull Team, appeared on Ransom's display screen. "Yo?"

"I can't raise the boss, kid."

Bobby's round face looked pained. "What d'you think? Renegades?"

That was one of the big reasons for the patrols. Of the many Zentraedi who had gone forth among the humans to try a more peaceful way of life and a chance to open up the more feeling and compassionate side of their nature, some had found that it simply wouldn't work.

The renegades had begun slipping away into the wastelands more than a year before. There was an entire world of salvage for them out there: mecha, weapons, rations, and anything else they might need, provided they could find the right wreck. More importantly, there was the freedom to act as Zentraedi warriors once again, to follow their own brutal, merciless code.

"I think his last transmission came from his search quadrant," Bobby said worriedly.

"I know," Ransom said. "I got a DF fix on it. Let's go."

The VTs formed up, and their engines made the ground tremble. They shot away to the northwest.

The SDF-1 stood like a knight in a bath up to his waist. The two supercarriers floated at anchor, giving the corroding derelict added buoyancy.

Refilling the lake had been a major priority, since not even the fortress's colossal strength could support itself and the two giant warships for long. At the same time that RDF fliers were seeding clouds and Dr. Lang's mysterious machines were working day and night to head off the nuclear winter, combat engineers and anybody else who could be found to lend a hand worked feverishly to make sure the drainage would be ready.

And just over forty-eight hours after the ship's landing, the rains had begun. They gave back some of the moisture boiled away by the Zentraedi attack, but Lang's calculations, supported by subsequent data, showed that much of it was gone forever. Short of importing many cubic miles of water across space from some as yet unknown source, the Earth would never again be the three-quarters-ocean world she had been when she brought forth life.

In time, the rains stopped, and the generations-long job of replanting and refoliating the planet began.

Around the lake the new Macross rose, the stubborn refugees rebuilding their lives yet again. It was the only new population center on the planet so far, the only place where the concrete was uncracked and the buildings tall and straight. There was fresh paint, and there were trees transplanted from the starship. There were lawns and flower beds seeded from plants that had survived the billions of miles of the SDF-1's odyssey.

It was a city where energy and resources were used with utmost efficiency, a town of solar heaters and photovoltaic panels, with a recycling system tied to every phase of life. The Macross residents and SDF-1 personnel had learned the tough lessons of ecological necessity during years in space, and nothing at all was wasted. That was the sort of world it was going to have to be from now on.

In a neat, quiet suburb of the city served by an overhead rapid-transit system sat a modest little prefab cottage, its solar panels, guided by microprocessors, swinging slowly to follow the sun. As a senior flight officer, Rick Hunter rated off-base housing even though he was single, and liked the idea of getting away from the military when he could, even if his home looked like modular luggage. As Skull Leader, he seldom got a chance to be there.

So Lisa Hayes took it upon herself to tidy up the place when he was away. Her own rather more spacious quarters were nearby.

Neither of them was quite sure what the bond between them meant or where their companionship was going, but she had a key to his place, and he to hers.

Now she hummed happily to herself as she put away the last of the just-washed dishes. *Maybe I ought to bill him for maid services,* she thought wryly.

But she knew better; she enjoyed being in his place, touching the things he touched, seeing reminders of him all around. She hoped that the extended patrol up north didn't last too much longer—that he would be home soon so that they could be together again.

Lisa considered the sunlight streaming through the kitchen window. Polarizing glass was all well and good, but curtains were what that window needed.

*Will you listen to me? Curtains! Miss Suzy Homemaker!* She smirked at the apron she was wearing. It was doubly funny because she was due back at the base soon for more meetings and briefings on the final construction details of the SDF 2, the new successor to the battle fortress.

And she meant to have a berth on that ship, to be the First Officer if she could, and go to the stars. OI' Suzy Homemaker herself.

She snorted a laugh as she moved into the bedroom. Seeing it, she sighed. *Why does this place always look like a bears been wintering here?*

She raised all the blinds, opened all the windows, and moved around the room slowly, fondly. When she smoothed the sheets to make up the bed, her hands lingered upon them, and she touched the pillows tenderly, remembering his head on them, and her own.

Her wrist chrono toned, reminding her she had to go soon. When she straightened, her eye fell on something she hadn't seen before.

It lay on his desk, next to his spare flight helmet: a photo album bound in creamy imitation leather. Lisa moved toward it unwillingly, knowing she shouldn't do what she was about to do but unable to stop herself.

The album was well worn, had obviously been leafed through many times. The first page made her heart sink. There was a snapshot of Minmei seated on a park swing back in the Macross within the SDF-1, Rick standing behind her. The other picture was a close-up taken of Minmei back at the start of her career, a wide-eyed gamine with flowing black locks framing her face.

Lisa sighed again. *What does he see in her? What's she got except great looks, the singing voice that won the war, and superstardom?*

It was Minmei on every page, glamour poses and home snapshots, portfolio glossies and PR photos. Lisa got angrier and angrier as she thumbed through them.

*Why do I have the impulse to strangle this girl?*

Along with the anger came a pain so sharp and cold, it took her off guard. Lisa had assumed she and Rick were solidifying something, strengthening the ties between them. But the thought of his keeping this album, taking it out when Lisa wasn't there and fantasizing over it—that was too much to bear.

Having his companionship and friendship without his declared love was something she had accepted, albeit always with a secret hope. But the photo album made her feel she had been taken for granted, a kind of emotional consolation prize. Her self-respect simply wouldn't allow that.

Lisa slammed the album shut, tore off the apron, and strode for the front door. As the door rolled shut to lock, she tossed Rick's spare house key onto the living-room rug, leaving it behind.

# 23

We won? When you hear some military moron say that to you, spit on him! Point out the graveyard that is Earth! When he tells you how the military's going to make all that well again too, hold up the ash that used to be your home.

They won, all right, and they'd just love to win again. And every time, it's you and I who lose.

From Lynn-Kyle's tract, Mark of Cain

RICK HUNTER SAT IN THE COCKPIT OF THE GROUNDED GUARDIAN and watched white spores take to the wind like miniature parasols. Meanwhile, he wrestled with his thoughts.

The truth was that Earth was a dead end for a pilot. Oh, there was the problem of the rebellious Zentraedi, to be sure, and the various fractious human communities. But the war was over, and there were no flying circuses. Maybe it would be easier to put up with the growing boredom of peacetime life if bigger things weren't brewing out beyond Earth's atmosphere.

Breetai and Exedore seemed to be at the source of it, and Gloval, Dr. Lang, and Dr. Zand. Only everything was so secret that a mere squadron commander couldn't find out a thing. Even Lisa professed not to know anything. But scuttlebutt and the few hints Rick could get from his intel debriefings made him believe that the SDF-2 was slated for a big, big mission.

He was pretty sure that the SDF-2, and such Zentraedi warships as Breetai could get fully functional again, were going to carry the war to the Robotech Masters. Humans and Zentraedi would go out and end the threat forever or die trying.

How could he *not* go? Only... that was a voyage and a military operation that might make their previous campaign look like a weekend vacation by comparison. It would probably mean he would never see Earth and Minmei again.

Not that he'd seen much of Minmei in the last two years, but signing on for a trip to far-off star systems would strip away any hope.

But what else was there for him except flying? He wished and prayed that there could be Minmei, but Minmei was so bound up in her glittering career that he rarely saw or heard from her. On the SDF-2 mission, at least he would be with Lisa, and he was becoming more and more convinced that that was where he belonged.

Of course, the odds against surviving would be very high, but that was a combat pilot's lot. And what better cause was there to serve, and die for, if it came to that? He had a sudden vivid recollection of something Roy Fokker had told him.

*An American president once said that the price of liberty is eternal vigilance, Rick.*

It was on a "day" in SDF-1, out someplace by Pluto's orbit, when Rick joined the RDF. *There's no more flying for fun,* Roy told him, stem and grave. *From now on you fly for the sake of your home and loved ones, Rick.*

"My home and loved ones, huh?" Rick muttered to himself. He flicked a switch, and the canopy descended on whining servos.

"All right; time to go flying, then." He eased the throttle forward. The Guardian's foot thrusters blew soil away and lifted it. Rick was careful to skirt the patch of dandelions as he rose. But the backwash sent hundreds of thousands of spores wafting into the air in hopes of finding some other kind plot of ground.

Rick tucked a single dandelion blossom into a seam of his instrument panel, mechamorphosed his ship to Fighter mode, and went ballistic, climbing toward the sun. He set the commo rig to search for local traffic, part of the recon mission. The equipment scanned the band and stopped at a transmission that carried a female human voice.

—here by my side,
Here by my side.

He jolted against his safety harness, reaching to get a stronger signal. "Minmei!"

There was applause in the background. Another voice he knew well came up. "You're listening to the beautiful Lynn-Minmei, broadcasting live and direct from Granite City! This area is slowly rebuilding through the combined efforts of many wonderful people who are ceaselessly devoting their time and labor to a project that many considered hopeless."

Lynn-Kyle. He sounded more like a pitchman than a costar now, but he still had that same hostility in his tone.

*Granite!* Rick realized. *Not far away!* He was already checking his nav computers.

"People Helping People is the theme of our tour," Kyle went on. "And we don't consider the project hopeless at all! How do *you* feel about it?"

*Clapclapclapclap,* from the audience, and a few yays. Those shill questions always worked. Rick's expression hardened, and he brought his stick over for a bank.

Granite City lay in the shadow of a Zentraedi flagship rammed like a Jovian bolt into the red dirt. The outskirts of the place were still haphazard rubble from the war, but a few square blocks in the center had been made livable.

There were weakened foundations and angled slabs of paving and fractured concrete everywhere, but at least the streets were clear.

This most recent stop in what was to have been the triumphant Minmei People Helping People tour had attracted something under three hundred people in Granite, plus several Zentraedi who loomed over the crowd even when sitting and squatting.

The crowd was composed of sad-eyed people doing their best to believe they had a future. Most were ragged, all were thin, and there were signs of deficiency diseases and other medical problems among them.

But at the urging of Lynn-Kyle and others in the loose-knit network of antigovernmentalists, Granite persisted in refusing to drop its status as an independent city-state or allow military relief teams in.

The Zentraedi were in better shape than the humans; the rations in the spiked ship could sustain them, though for some reason those seemed to have no nutritive value for *Homo sapiens*. There had been a fine cordiality and hopefulness among the people of Granite at first, but now there was growing despair in this dissident model program. Thus, this morale appearance by Minmei.

"Yeah! Let's hear it!" Lynn-Kyle yelled, working the mike at center stage, making beckoning motions with his free hand. The crowd clapped again, a little tiredly.

"And Granite doesn't need any outside interference, either!" he yelled. He had spent fewer than four hours there in his entire life.

"The good people here will take care of themselves and make Granite the great metropolis she once was!"

The applause was even weaker this time around, and the more theatrically knowledgeable in the front rows could detect beads of flop-sweat on Kyle's brow.

"But let's forget, for now, what the military warmongers have brought us to," he said, almost scowling, then catching himself and flashing a bright smile. "As we listen to the song stylings of the marvelous, the incomparable Lynn-Minmei!"

Recorded music came up, and Minmei hit her mark right on cue, mike in hand. She sang her latest hit.

I've made the right move at the right time!
We're on our way to something new!
Just point the way and I will follow!
Love feels so beautiful with you!

Rick followed the song, entranced, until a transmission cut through Minmei's singing. "Commander Hunter, come in, please."

It was Ransom. Rick switched to the tac net. "What is it?"

"You all right, skipper? I've been trying to reach you for some time; thought you might've run into trouble."

Rick let a little impatience slip into his tone. "Is anything wrong?"

Ransom looked at him out of a display screen next to the yellow dandelion, speaking precisely. "Nothing specific, boss. Just wish you'd take your rover radio with you when you leave your ship to look around. I worry, y' know?"

Rick bit back the rebuke he had been putting together. Of course he knew; he would have chewed out a subordinate for doing the same.

He sounded contrite, and it was real. "Sorry, Lieutenant. But I came across something miraculous today."

Ransom stared. "Trouble with renegade Zentraedi? Boss, what is it?"

Rick took the dandelion from its place and held it close to the optical pickup. "Look what I found. An entire field of them."

Ransom considered the flower. "Wait a minute. Your zone wasn't inside the natural recovery planning zone."

Rick was ecstatic. "That's right! But lemme tell ya, there are flowers in the northwest quadrant!"

The usually morbid Ransom cracked a very slight smile. "I suppose we should have known the Earth would be starting her own recovery program. Great news, huh, skipper?"

"Roger that. Look, continue your patrol according to mission plan, Ted."

"I copy, but aren't you coming with us?"

"Not right now," Rick answered. "I'm dropping over to Granite City. If anything serious comes up, give me a yell."

Ransom nodded and hedged. "And, uh, boss…"

"Don't sweat it, Lieutenant! When I leave the ship, I'll take my rover! Out!"

Rick did a barrel roll for the hell of it and opened his throttle wide for Granite City.

If she wonders,
It's you who's on my mind.
It's you I cannot
Leave behind…

Rick followed Minmei's voice as someone else might have trod a yellow brick road. From overhead the Zentraedi battlewagon dominated the landscape, but a closer look at the ground showed that the rusting metal peak was a monument to defeat and that the teeming victors were still in turmoil.

Rick left his VT at the edge of town under the care of the local militia CO, who was well disposed toward RDF fliers even if the populace wasn't. Rick got to the concert and missed, by a fraction of a second, getting flattened by the hand of a Zentraedi leviathan who was sitting at the edge of the crowd, shifting his weight.

"I'm so sorry," the alien tried to whisper in his resounding bass. Everybody around them went *Shhhh!* Rick gave the big fellow a nod to let him know it was no offense taken.

It's me who's lost,
The me who lost your heart
The you who tore my heart
Apart…

*She's come a long way, but it's the same girl I spent those awful, wonderful two weeks with somewhere in the belly of the SDF-1. My Minmei.*
When the song was over, the crowd applauded. Rick applauded loudest of all.

Near a sidewalk café in Monument City, with the SDF-1's shadow coming her way like a sundial, Lisa stared dully at people passing by and ignored her cooling demitasse. The meetings had been delayed, giving her some unexpected free time. Idle hours were more a curse than a blessing.

As she watched, two down-at-the-heels *boulevardiers* ogled a very pert young blonde whose hemline came nearly to her waist. The two did not quite slobber.

"My man, the women were dealt all the aces in this life. They can have anything they want," opined one, a beefy kid who looked as if he stood a fair chance of growing up to be normal. "They can have anybody they wanna have."

Lisa considered that, her chin resting on her interlaced fingers. "That's all you know about it, my fat friend," she murmured, watching the two would-be rakes go on their way. "Here's *one* woman who'd trade every other ace, knave, and king in the deck for one Rick Hunter."

She drew a sudden breath as she looked across Monument City's main thoroughfare. Max Sterling strolled along there, looking as if he didn't have a care in the world, pushing a baby carriage. Miriya held his arm.

They stopped, and Max hurried around the carriage to scoop up his daughter and pat her back, burping her on his shoulder. Miriya looked on serenely with a smile Lisa almost begrudged her.

The very most secret eyes-only reports boiled down to the fact that nobody could quite figure out how Max and Miriya had had Dana, their baby girl. But as proved by exhaustive tests, the child was indisputably theirs.

No Zentraedi male-female reproduction had ever been recorded, making the whole thing that much more extraordinary. The likelier explanations had to do with Miriya's consumption of human-style food as opposed to the antiseptic rations of the Zentraedi and her exposure to emotions that had worked subtle biochemical changes on her. The word "Protoculture" cropped up again and again in the reports, only nobody seemed to understand quite what it was, at least nobody outside the charmed, secretive circle of Lang, Exedore, and a few others.

Like a lot of women and quite a few men, Lisa sometimes thought all that was a crock. Miriya and Max were in love, and so: little Dana.

She looked at the three of them, and for a moment Max wore Rick's face, and Miriya wore Lisa's. The SDF-2 would soon be ready for space trials, but that didn't mean the First Officer couldn't have a family. The starship had been built for a long voyage, for children as well as men and women.

Max and Miriya and their baby resumed their way, and Lisa watched them go. *They look so happy. If only I could make Rick understand!*

Just then, though, two RDF boot trainees wandered up to the café with a street-blaster stereo. The well-remembered voice boomed,

And the thrill that I feel
Is really unreal.

"Hew! That little mama sure can sing," the first one said, whistling. "I'd give a month's pay to meet her."

The other blew his breath out sarcastically as the pair sat down a few tables away. "Sure, buddy. Then she takes you away and signs over the deed to her diamond mine to you, right?"

The first one made a very sour face and signaled the waitress. On the eardrum agitator, Minmei sang,

I can't believe I've come this far.
This is my chance to be a star!

*There doesn't seem to be any way I can avoid you, Minmei!*
Lisa collected her purse and left her money on the salver, then rose and headed off down the boulevard.

She was so caught up in her own thoughts, regrets, and preoccupations that she didn't realize—had never realized—how many admiring glances she drew. She was a willowy, athletic young woman with brown hair billowing behind her, a delicate complexion, and a distant look in her eyes. Her insignia and decorations were enough to make any vet, male or female, take notice of her.

If there were an artistic competition for the concept WINNER, a simple photo of Lisa at that moment would have won it. Women in particular looked at her, her sure stride and air of confidence, and made various resolutions to be more like this self-confident superwoman, whoever she was.

But that wasn't the way it felt to Lisa. She allowed herself a rueful half smile. *I guess when the aces were dealt out, it just wasn't in the cards for me to get the one I want.*

It was near enough to a joke to make her smile cheerlessly. She quickened her pace, off to report to the SDF-2.

# 24

I've seen people like Lynn-Kyle before. I'm prepared to believe that he hates war; who among us does not?

But he has the attitude, set in concrete, that virtue is measured by one's disaffection from the power structure under which one lives. Such a person builds a fortress of self-serving piety, resisting authority of any kind at every turn whether for good or ill.

The RDF will continue to defend to the death the freedoms that make this possible.

From the log of Captain Henry Gloval

"WHAT A CRUMMY HOLE!"
Lynn-Kyle threw his arms wide to take in Granite City, off to one side, and the wastelands all around it.

Minmei sat despondently on a piece of rotting Zentraedi alloy, hugging her knees to her chest, a pink jacket draped over her shoulders against the evening chill, watching him take another slug from the bottle of brandy that seemed to be his constant companion these days.

Things had gone steadily downhill since Vance Hasslewood had moved up in the world to become a booking agent and aspiring theater maven, leaving Minmei's cousin, costar, and lover to take over the duties of manager. Lynn-Kyle's interests went far beyond show business, and he had come to realize that his own fame and popularity were only a pale reflection of hers.

Now he paused. "Lousiest booking so far!" Then he threw back another several ounces, making her wince.

Kyle wiped his mouth on the back of his hand, staining the purple cuff of his suit. "Let's get out of this burg! It's disgusting!"

He was red-eyed and close to the edge, but she said what was on her mind anyway; she had held it back long enough. "Do you have to drink so much?"

"Listen, don't change the subject!" he slurred. "We didn't even get any money! *This* is our whole paycheck!"

He toed over a wilted cardboard box; out spilled some canned goods, bath soap and so forth, a few vegetables—the same dole everyone else in Granite City was living on. Even though Granite refused to recognize the new Earth government's authority, the government gave what help it could; without it, the city couldn't have kept functioning.

"A stinkin' handout from our military overlords!"

"And what else do we need for survival?" she asked him, watching his eyes. Two years with Kyle had made her older, much older.

"Have you given any thought to taking in a little cash for a change?" he snarled.

She came to her feet, the jacket clutched to her. "No, I haven't!"

If it was going to be another argument, she decided, this time she was going to get a few things off her mind. "This was supposed to be a benefit concert for those poor people who're trying to make their lives work in Granite, not some big-deal career move for Lynn-Minmei!"

She had him, and they both knew it. All at once his ranting sounded like empty talk. He was suddenly contrite. "Aw, c'mon, Minmei. You know I didn't mean anything like that." It was not quite a whine, but somehow it only made her detest him more.

She knelt and began picking up the things he had spilled, brushing dirt from them. "We're getting paid like everyone else is, in the things that keep us alive. I think we should show a little appreciation."

That made him cough on the mouthful of brandy he was chugging. He almost finished the bottle, and his mood swung end for end, as quick as his martial-arts moves used to be.

"Appreciation? I should appreciate the great military mentality that brought us to *this*?" He opened his arms as if to embrace the blighted world.

She straightened and met his stare. "Earth was attacked, and it fought back. I don't want to hear anybody knocking the military. If it hadn't been for them, I wouldn't be alive right now. And for that matter, neither would you."

*So, we come to the core of the matter,* he thought blearily.

That moment on the SDF-1, with a planet dying at his feet and great fleets slaying one another while he kissed her, was two years behind him. And yet it played over and over in memory, as fresh as if it had happened that afternoon.

The secret that glowed in him like a reflex furnace, the one Kyle would never be able to bring himself to admit to her or even put into words to himself, was that he had exulted in that moment even as he had been repulsed by it.

*He had loved it!* He had been taken by the drama completely, swept up in the battle. He had cast aside every conviction he ever had and gloried in what was happening. He had hoped with all his soul for human victory.

His father had been a soldier; both family restaurants had catered to the military trade. Lynn-Kyle scorned all of that, scorned military and government and authority in every form. And yet when it had come down to a question of seeing his planet and people die, he had been out there rooting for the home team, as red of fang and claw, as contemptible, as any of them.

He had never lost a fight since his father had pummeled and shamed him into learning the martial arts. Indeed, he'd become a very genius of unarmed combat. But this contest with himself was one he felt fated to lose. As he hated himself, so he had come to make Minmei hate him.

He had seen that the military, with the SDF-1 and Macross as a power base and Breetai and his Zentraedi as allies, was destined to be the force that reunited the planet. Nevertheless, he resisted it every inch of the way, going deeper and deeper into despair as the vast egalitarian movement he had envisioned dwindled away to a few pitiful holdouts.

So if this was going to be the argument that had been building between Minmei and Kyle for so long, let it be so. He turned his face to an ugly mask with an elaborate sneer. "You're breaking my heart." He swallowed the last of the brandy.

*You're breaking my heart.*

Twenty yards away, behind a broken piece of cornice at the top of a rise, Rick Hunter squatted with his back against cold stone and listened to Minmei and Kyle.

He sat still as a rock or one of the pieces of dead mecha that now littered the world.

"*Must* you keep drinking?" Minmei said. "It's getting out of hand!"

Kyle upended the bottle and let the last few droplets fall on soil that hadn't tasted moisture in two years. Then he tossed it high, launched himself through the air in a reverse spin kick, a *ki-yi* yell coming from deep within him, turning twice, and popped the little brandy bottle out of existence like a trap shooter.

Pieces of dark glass landed at Minmei's feet. She watched Kyle steadily. "Did that make you feel any better about yourself?"

*How can she wound me so easily with just a word or two?* he wondered in confusion.

His mood swung again, and there was an endless affection in him for her. She was, after all, the sum of his life. All he had ever really accomplished, Lynn-Kyle saw now, was getting Minmei to love him.

But Minmei's mood was riding a different swing. "Whatever you think of the RDF, there are a lot of fine men and women in it," she said levelly. "Much better people than you are right now."

A moment that might have been a reconciliation and a new start was gone forever. Kyle ran the back of his hand across his mouth again. *All right; we might as well have it all out.*

"What's that crack supposed to mean?"

Minmei was actually shaking a *fist* at him. "It means they're trying to rebuild Earth, while all you can do is drink and feel sorry for yourself!"

"Is that so? Well, I've done a pretty good job of takin' care of your career, little Miss Superstar!"

She had been loud a moment before; her voice was quiet now. "Maybe we'd better split up then, Kyle. So you can look after your own career." She gathered her pink jacket around her.

She had been hurt until her endurance was all gone, and now she only wanted to hurt in retaliation. "I didn't realize I owed it all to *you*, Kyle."

He had his hands out in fending-off gestures. "Wait, wait. I didn't mean—didn't mean I wanted to split up our partnership." 'Partnership' was a weak word for what they'd had, but somehow the vocabulary of love was steamrollered by the vocabulary of argument. He felt something slipping away even as he made the choice of words.

She drew a long, deep breath, looking him m the eye. "Maybe not, but it's what *I* meant."

The compass of Lynn-Kyle's emotions swung a last time, and his mouth resolved into a straight, thin line. "Okay, go! Who needs you?" He kicked the empty carton high into the air.

Rick Hunter didn't know exactly what to feel. The fact that Kyle had alienated Minmei might have been enjoyable from a distance, but it was harrowing to see at close range.

And then there was the whole question of going out and intervening. Rick had no illusions about being able to take the tall, cobra-fast martial-arts expert hand to hand, and he had forgotten to bring along the survival pistol from his VT's ejection pack.

Suddenly the rover radio buzzed in its thigh pouch. "Commander Hunter, come in please!" It was Vanessa's voice, sending from the rusting, soggy-footed SDF-1.

He had turned the volume down low when he came out to the edge of the wastelands, following leads to find Minmei. Now he held the rover up to his ear. Minmei and Kyle didn't seem to have heard a thing.

He thumbed the transmit switch. "I'm here."

"Sir, you're directed to lead your flight to New Portland. A residential district is under attack by several Zentraedi malcontents."

"Malcontents." That was what the new world government was calling them so far. But those who had sworn the Zentraedi warrior oath and turned their back on human society were a lot more than malcontents. They had only to walk out into the wasteland and keep going, find the right wrecked ship. If they were lucky, they would find arms, mecha, rations, water, and shelter.

Rick poised for a moment in a pain so precise that it defied any random theory of the universe. Most of what he had come to believe in impelled him to get to New Portland with all possible speed.

Everything else told him to stay there, because this was the moment he could win Minmei back.

But he thumbed the rover's transmit button again. "What weapons?"

"Three battlesuits and four pods, a total of seven," Vanessa's voice came back. That wasn't exactly several, the way Rick saw it, but he had to admit that things probably looked a little different from a worldwide coordinating nerve center like the SDF-1.

These were Zentraedi who had defected to the human side in the Robotech War. They were onetime allies. He held the rover's voice pickup close and said softly, "It'll be taken care of. What's the status on Skull flight? Over."

"They are curtailing their current sweep and will rendezvous with you in New Portland. Out."

He shut off the rover before the sound of static could betray him. He raced off toward his ship. It was a kind of liberation to have some crisis so pressing that he could forget about Minmei for a while. He left the two Lynns to their own devices, and somehow he couldn't help wishing them the worst.

As his VT took off in Guardian mode, Rick saw the tiny, distant figure of Kyle go down on both knees before Minmei. She turned and opened her arms, cradling his head to her breast. Rick hit the throttle, and his VT left a trail of blue fire across the sky.

Lisa stared up through her window at the rotting hulk of the SDF-1. Beneath it was a thriving, growing city, but its presence put everyone in mind of the war.

"Hmmph! What a view!" As a morale builder, she was wearing a tight blouse with a high, upturned collar. Every once in a while she permitted herself to catch a glimpse of herself in a full-length mirror there in her quarters and admit, *not bad!*

The SDF-1 wasn't bad to look at either, really. The more so because the SDF-2 would be lowered into place, back to back with it, in another day or so. Lang and his disciples had worked out some way to move the sealed enigmatic engines from one to the other. Lisa had heard the briefings, could sort of understand the mathematics Lang scrawled all over every flat surface that came to hand, and had faith in him, but she still thought her new assignment was an unknown quantity.

The comset birred for her attention. She picked up the hand-set. In seconds she had word of the New Portland raid from Vanessa and was hurrying for the door.

Sunset had come, and a freezing rain, as the Zentraedi ransacked New Portland. They had cut a swath of destruction from the diminished Lake Oswego to the once-great Columbian River.

The pods fired and devastated without mercy. Local militia and police were victims just like the civilians; in the first hours of their rampage, the alien malcontents slew over four hundred men and women of assorted constabularies, police departments, and guard units.

They set buildings afire with a mere brush of their plastron cannon; they trod houses and people flat underneath their pods' huge, hooflike feet.

Now they loomed, three abreast, in the center of New Portland as black smoke roiled around them and the screams of the dying echoed through the rain-washed streets. Blood ran in the gutters.

Down from the night swooped the VTs of Skull Team under Ransom's command. Robotechnology made them all-weather fighters, as dangerous in blackness as they were in light.

"Nobody fires unless they have a confirmed target; they're civilians down there," Ransom said.

Just then New Portland came into view, burning like a skillet of molten metal, smoke funneling up from it to form thickening layers that threw back red light.

Bobby Bell began, "My God! This is horrible—"

"Shut up, Sergeant," Ransom cut him off. "All VTs form up on me. Let's get down there and stop this thing. *And watch your fire!*"

Jeanette LeClair and her best friend, Sonya Poulson, ran through the rain-slick streets of New Portland hand in hand, shivering in the frigid rain, crying for the loved ones who had died, pulses hammering because death was at their heels. Jeanette's birthday a month before had made her eight years old; Sonya's, four days later, had brought them even.

Behind them, a Zentraedi Battlepod stumped around the corner, kicking a traffic light through a brick wall and snapping power lines, then turned its guns on them.

Jeanette fell, and Sonya wanted to keep running but found that she couldn't. She dashed back to her friend, trying to help her up, but she fell instead, and the two of them sprawled on the rain-washed cobblestone street as a huge round metal hoof came down at them. They wept, held each other close, and waited to die.

The pod paused in the act of trampling yet more victims. The armored, lightbulb-shaped torso turned, as if listening to something. Jeanette and Sonya could hardly know that it was receiving an urgent message from one of its fellows.

"Warning! Warning! Enemy fightercraft approaching! Form up to take defensive action!"

The two little girls looked up at the ridges and features of the huge hoof and realized it was pulling away. In moments, the pod had turned and grasshoppered off for some destination they couldn't even guess at, riding its foot thrusters.

Moments later, thunder came down through the sky as Skull Team VTs arrived at full throttle. The two girls helped each other up. Buildings shook and windows broke to the sonic boom as the RDF fighters swept in vengefully.

The girls' voices were very small in the middle of all that, but they cheered nonetheless.

...

The pods chose straightforward battle, charging out in a group, firing the primary and secondary cannon mounted on their armored chest plastrons.

That suited Skull Team just fine; they flew down through the intense ground fire in Guardian mode, like eagles for the kill, gripping their chain-guns.

"Let's hit 'em," Ransom said.

"Sure, but we've gotta lead 'em away from the city!" Bobby Bell yelled.

He was right, and the formation split even while it exchanged fire with the rampaging pods. The Guardians turned back, and the pods, firing with every gun, rocketed and kangaroo-hopped after.

# 25

For the Zentraedi, peaceful life and a disengagement from their warlike culture was, after all, a profound struggle, a sort of sublimating battle into which they could hurl themselves. For a time they were content with it, as they were content with any other conflict.

Is it any wonder, though, that with the battle won, so many of them began to fall prey to a frustrated restlessness? The fight for peace can be a noble one, but as history and legend tell us, the warrior-born should beware the disaster of total victory.

And so should those about him.

Zeitgeist, *Alien Psychology*

IN THE FOOTHILLS AT THE OUTSKIRTS OF NEW PORTLAND, THE VTs stopped running and the mecha clashed in earnest.

Almost by instinct, the pods came abreast to set up a firing line. The Guardians dove at them, and the blue-white lances of energy beams jousted against streams of high-density slugs lit by tracers.

A concentrated salvo of alien cannon fire took off the left arm of Ransom's Guardian. "These dudes really wanna fight," he said grimly. He looped, trying to manage the damage, and unleashed a spread of Stilettos at them.

*No more tromping on little girls, bows! Let's see you pick on somebody your own size!*

"This could be defined as dereliction of duty, Commander," Lisa's voice said in Rick's ear.

"What're you talking about?"

"Where were you?" she said icily.

"Uh, on recon." Guilt made him snappish. "It's within mission guidelines. Why, any objections?"

Back in the command center, she looked down at the latest satnet locater profiles of military aircraft. He had been grounded at the edge of Granite City. No surprise.

"I object when you jeopardize the lives of the men under your command, Hunter."

He couldn't help it; the accumulated experiences of the day just made him lose control as no cool, competent combat flier is supposed to. "What's your goddamn problem, Lisa?"

"Your men are in combat, and you're supposed to be leading them, you unutterable moron!" she yelled into the mike, then snapped it off.

Well, there. They had had a grand argument over a command commo net about everything except what was really driving them apart. What satisfaction.

She stalked away from the commo console. "Oh, that man."

"Take cover, take cover," chanted Vanessa in a whisper to the rest of the Terrible Trio.

"I wonder what Commander Hunter did to cause the blowup this time." Sammie blinked.

"Whatever it was, it looks like he'll be on a steady diet of cold shoulder when he gets back," Vanessa replied.

Kim took off her headset and turned to them. "I dunno; d'you think she really loves him?"

"D'you mean to say you haven't heard the latest gossip?" Sammie almost squirmed in her eagerness to tell it. "They say she cleans his quarters. Yeah, yeah, *cleans!* While he's away on patrol. And he doesn't even take her out or anything."

The Terrible Trio thought poisonous thoughts about the male gender.

Kim fanned herself gently with her hand. "It's hard to believe Lisa would get herself roped into something like that. She's too smart!"

Sammie caught her arm. "But wait; that isn't all!"

"*Ixnay*," Kim murmured, turning a sidelong glance. "We're being watched."

"Uh-oh." Sammie hastened to put her earphones back on.

Lisa looked at them resignedly. *Go ahead, girls; I don't blame you. I guess it is funny.*

The pod's cannon hosed concentrated fire into the storm-wracked night sky. The Guardian sideslipped and counterfired with its autocannon.

"Won't these characters ever give up?" Bobby Bell gritted.

But there was a certain fear to it. Zentraedi who had returned to their warrior code, their death-before-defeat belief system, were enemies to be reckoned with.

And then there was a familiar face on an instrument panel display screen. "How you guys doin'?" Rick Hunter asked with elaborate casualness. It was the heritage; he was flying into the middle of a red-hot firefight, and he looked like it was all he could do to stay awake.

"Boss, look sharp," Bobby shot back. "These boys are murder."

Rick's VT dove down through the rain in Guardian configuration like a rocket-powered falcon. "It's okay. I'll take over now. Ransom, Bobby; all of you drop back and stay out of sight."

He went in at them as he had gone in at hundreds of pods—thousands—since the day he first stepped into a VT cockpit. He wove through their fire, rebounded from the ground, and sprang high overhead on Robotech legs.

The energy blasts skewed all around him. "Last chance," he transmitted over the Zentraedi tac frequency. "Cease fire and lay down your arms."

If they had, they would have been the first of the malcontents to do so. But instead, like all the rest, they fired that much more furiously.

He wondered what he would have felt like if their positions had been reversed. The human race was lost and struggling in its own ashes, but how much more so the Zentraedi defectors?

He wondered only for an instant, though; lives were at stake.

Skull Leader came in behind a sustained burst from its

autocannon, the tracers lighting the night, blowing one pod leg to metallic splinters. As the pod collapsed, Rick banked and came to ground behind an upcropping of rock, going to Battloid mode.

He reared up from behind the rock, an armored ultratech warrior sixty feet tall with a belt-fed autocannon gripped in his fist. "For the last time, I order you to drop your weapons!"

He saw the plastron cannon muzzles swinging at him, and hit the dirt behind the rock. Energy bolts blazed through the air where he had been standing.

When the volley was over, he came up again shooting. The high-density slugs blew another pod leg in half at its rear-articulated knee, toppling it. The third one ran, zig-zagging, evading his fire. Suddenly there was only the drumming of the rain on the field of battle.

The Zentraedi malcontents emerged from their disabled mecha slowly. He could see that they carried no personal weapons and knew that the New Portland police and militia would be able to deal with them. The rest of Skull Team went to mop up and make sure the armored Zentraedi on foot were taken prisoner. The malcontents would pay with their lives for the lives they'd taken.

*Tonight we won. What about tomorrow?*

He was the last one to deplane; Ransom, Bobby, and Greer were already far from the hangars and revetments when Rick dragged himself from his VT, feeling dog-tired. How could peace be so terrible? Peace was all he or Roy or any of the rest had ever wanted. He wondered if there would ever be an end to the fighting.

Then he saw Lisa standing by the fighter ops door. *No peace in my lifetime,* he decided. *Look at that warcloud.*

"Why do I feel like I should ask for a blindfold and a last cigarette, Commander?"

"Not very funny, Rick."

"No, I suppose not." He groped for a way to tell her all the things he had thought and been through in the last few days.

But she was saying, "You're ordered to report to Captain Gloval at once."

He considered that, brows knit, turning toward the SDF-1. "Wonder what he wants."

She couldn't hold back what she was thinking. "How was your visit with Minmei?" she called after him.

He stopped. "I enjoyed her broadcast from Granite City yesterday," she said softly.

He drew a breath, let it out, looked down at the hardtop beneath his feet. "Well, I didn't actually visit with Minmei."

He started off again. She caught up, walking right behind. She made it sound as spiteful as she could, hating herself for it the whole time. "Was that because she was so surrounded by adoring fans that you couldn't get close to her, Rick?"

"No."

"Anything happen?" *Why am I putting us both through this?* she wondered, and the answer came back at once: *Because I love him!*

"What *could* happen?" he growled.

"I don't know!" She raced to catch up with him, taking a pale blue envelope from her uniform pocket. She dashed around in front of him, bringing him up short, pressing it into the palm of one flightsuit glove. She turned and walked away from him.

"Lisa, what *is* this?"

"Just something to remember me by," she threw back over her shoulder, not trusting herself to look at his face once more. Her heels clicked away across the hardtop.

The envelope held photographs—Lisa with a niece, on a vacation; Lisa as an adorable teenager with a kitten perched on her head; Lisa on the day of her graduation from the Academy.

"What on Earth?" he mumbled, but he knew. The album, all the rest of it: What had happened came to him in a flash. He had left New Portland feeling like there was some good that he could do in the world, feeling that no matter how bad things looked, there was always hope, and feeling that he was on the side of the angels.

But now, holding the photographs at his side and watching her disappear among the parked combat mecha, he tried to ride out a tide of regret that threatened to wash him away, and he was suddenly sorry he had ever been born.

...

"Commander Hunter reporting as ordered, sir."

Gloval sat looking out the sweeping forward viewport of the SDF-1, at a blue sky flecked with white clouds. "Please come in, Rick," he said without turning.

"Thank you, sir." Rick came in warily; Gloval did not often use his subordinates' first names.

"I'll get right to the point." Gloval swung around to face him and came to his feet. "The aliens among us are reverting to their former ways."

Rick considered that. He had friends among the Zentraedi— Rico, Bron, and Konda; Karita and others. "The New Portland rebels won't give us any more trouble, sir."

"That incident was only a symptom, Lieutenant Commander." There was something about the way Gloval pronounced your rank that let you know you were a part of a thing greater than yourself.

"We cannot afford to have this occur again," Gloval went on, "or we'll be risking complete social breakdown. I've decided to have some of the aliens reassigned to new locations where we can keep an eye on them."

None of the importance of that was lost on Rick. *We promised them freedom!* It was all coming apart, everything that had seemed so bright two years before.

The rest didn't really have to be said. Gloval was counting on Rick to enforce his directives and letting him know what he would be in for.

Rick Hunter looked at the old man who'd been through so much for Earth, and for the Zentraedi, too, in truth. The younger man snapped off a brisk salute. "Whatever you decide, you have my support; you know that, sir. And you have the support of everyone on the SDF-1."

"Thank you, Lieutenant." Gloval acknowledged the salute precisely but rather tiredly. He didn't look like he had gotten any real sleep in a long time.

They met each other's gaze. "I understand," Rick said.

...

Minmei shivered under her jacket, leaning against a pylon of Zentraedi wreckage and staring into the sky as night came on Granite City.

*So much desolation. And so much bitterness, even between people who should have learned to love one another a long time ago!*

She looked to the few lights of the town. Kyle had gone off that way, and she had no idea whether he intended to stop or keep on going, had no idea whether she would ever see him again and no clear conviction as to whether she wanted to or not.

She looked up as the stars appeared. *Oh, Rick. Where are you?*

# VOLUME 03
# DOOMSDAY

FOR SHOJI KAWAMORI AND THE '80s GANG
AT STUDIO NUE; HARUHIKO MIKIMOTO; IPPEI KURI
AND KENJI YOSHIDA OF TATSUNOKO:
ROBOTECH MASTERS THE LOT OF THEM—ALTHOUGH
THEY DIDN'T REALIZE IT AT THE TIME.

# 01

Had the Robotech Masters the power to travel as freely through time as they did space, perhaps they would have understood the *inevitabilities* they were up against: Zor's tampering with the Invid Flower was a crime akin to Adam's acceptance of the apple. Once released, Protoculture had its own destiny to fulfill. Protoculture was a different—and in some ways *antithetical*—order of life.

Professor Lazlo Zand, as quoted in
*History of the Second Robotech War, Vol. CXXII*

*THE DIMENSION OF MIND… THE RAPTURE TO BE FOUND AT THAT singular interface between object and essence… the power to reshape and reconfigure: to transform…*

Six hands—the sensor extensions of slender atrophied arms—were pressed reverently to the surface of the mushroomlike Protoculture cap, the Masters' material interface. Long slender fingers with no nails to impede receptivity. Three minds… *joined as one.*

Until the terminator's entry disturbed their conversation.

Offering salute to the Masters, it announced:

—Our routine scan of the Fourth Quadrant indicates a large discharge of Protoculture mass in the region where Zor's dimensional fortress defolded.

The three Masters broke off their contact with the Elders and turned to the source of the intrusion, liquid eyes peering out from ancient, ax-keen faces. Continual contact with Protoculture had eliminated physical differences, so all three appeared to have the same features: the same hawkish nose, the flaring eyebrows, shoulder-length blue-gray hair, and muttonchop sideburns.

—So!—responded the red-cowled Master, though his lips did not move—Two possibilities present themselves: Either the Zentraedi have liberated the hidden Protoculture matrix from Zor's disciples and commenced a new offensive against the Invid, or these Earthlings have beaten us to the prize and now control the production of the Protoculture.

There was something monkish about them, an image enhanced by those long gray robes, the cowls of which resembled nothing so much as outsize petals of the Invid Flower of Life. Each monkish head seemed to have grown stamenlike from the Protoculture flower itself.

—I believe that is highly unlikely—the green-cowled Master countered telepathically—All logic circuits based on available recon reports suggest that the Invid have no knowledge of the whereabouts of Zor's dimensional fortress.

—So! Then we must assume that the Zentraedi have indeed found the Protoculture matrix, ensuring a future for our Robotechnology.

—But only if they were able to capture the ship intact... The organic systems of the Masters' deep-space fortress began to mirror their sudden concern; energy fluctuations commenced within the Protoculture cap, throwing patterned colors against all but breathing bulkheads and supports. What would have been the bridge of an ordinary ship was here given over to the unharnessed urgings of Protoculture, so that it approximated a living neural plexus of ganglia, axons, and dendrites.

Unlike the Zentraedi dreadnoughts, these spadelike Robotech fortresses the size of planetoids were designed for a different campaign: the conquest of inner space, which, it was revealed, had its own worlds and star systems, black holes and white light, beauty and terrors. Protoculture had secured an entry, but the Masters' map of that realm was far from complete.

—My only fear is that Zor's disciples may have mastered the inner secrets of Robotechnology and were then able to defeat Dolza's vast armada.

—One ship against four million? Most unlikely—nearly impossible!

—Unless they managed to invert the Robotech defensive barrier system and penetrate Dolza's command center…

—In order to accomplish that, Zor's disciples would have to know as much about that Robotech ship as he himself knew!

—In any event, a display of such magnitude would certainly have registered on our sensors. We must admit, the destruction of four million Robotech vessels doesn't happen every day.

—Not without our knowing it.

The terminator, which had waited patiently to deliver the rest of its message, now added:

—That is quite true, Master. Nevertheless, our sensors *do* indicate a disturbance of that magnitude.

The interior of the Protoculture cap, the size of a small bush on its three-legged pedestal base, took on an angry light, summoning back the hands of the Masters.

—System alert: prepare at once for a hyperspace-fold!

—We acknowledge the Elders' request, but our supply of Protoculture is extremely low. We may not be able to use the fold generators!

—The order has been given—obey without question. We will fold immediately.

High in those cathedrals of arcing axon and dendrite-like cables, free-floating amorphous globules of Protoculture mass began to realign themselves along the ship's neural highways, permitting synaptic action where none had existed moments before. Energy rippled through the fortress, focusing on the columnar drives of massive reflex engines.

The great Robotech vessel gave a shudder and jumped.

Their homeworld was called Tirol, the primary moon of the giant planet Fantoma, itself one of seven lifeless wanderers in an otherwise undistinguished yellow-star system of the Fourth Quadrant, some twenty light-years out from the galactic core. Prior to the First Robotech War, Terran astronomers would have located Tirol in that sector of space then referred to as the Southern Cross. But they had learned since that that was merely *their* way of looking at

things. By the end of the second millennium they had abandoned
the last vestiges of geocentric thinking, and by A.D. 2012 had come
to understand that their beloved planet was little more than a minor
player in constellations entirely unknown to them.

Little was known of the early history of Tirol, save that its
inhabitants were a humanoid species—bold, inquisitive, daring—
and, in the final analysis, aggressive, acquisitive, and self-destructive.
Coincidental with the abolition of warfare among their own kind and
the redirecting of their goals toward the exploration of local space,
there was born into their midst a being who would alter the destiny
of that planet and to some extent affect the fate of the galaxy itself.

His name was Zor.

And the planet that would become the coconspirator in that
fateful unfolding of events was known to the techno-voyagers
of Tirol as Optera. For it was there that Zor would witness the
evolutionary rites of the planet's indigenous life form, the Invid;
there that the visionary scientist would seduce the Invid Regis to
learn the secrets of the strange tripetaled flower that they ingested
for physical as well as spiritual nourishment; there that the galactic
feud between Optera and Tirol would have its roots.

There that Protoculture and Robotechnology were born.

Through experimentation, Zor discovered that a curious form of
organic energy could be derived from the flower when its gestating
seed was contained in a matrix that prevented maturation. The bio-
energy resulting from this organic fusion was powerful enough
to induce a semblance of bio-will, or *animation*, in essentially
inorganic systems. Machines could be made to alter their very
shape and structure in response to the prompting of an artificial
intelligence or a human operator—to transform and reconfigure
themselves. Applied to the areas of eugenics and cybernetics, the
effects were even more astounding: Zor found that the shape-
changing properties of Protoculture could act on organic life as
well-living tissue and physiological systems could be rendered
malleable. Robotechnology, as he came to call this science, could
be used to fashion a race of humanoid clones, massive enough to
withstand Fantoma's enormous gravitational forces and to mine

the ores there. When those ores were converted to fuel and used in conjunction with Protoculture drives (by then called reflex drives), Tirol's techno-voyagers would be able to undertake hyperspace jumps to remote areas of the galaxy. *Protoculture effectively reshaped the very fabric of the continuum!*

Zor had begun to envision a new order, not only for his own race but for all those sentient life forms centuries of voyaging had revealed. He envisioned a true mating of mind and matter, an era of *clean* energy and unprecedented peace, a reshaped universe of limitless possibilities.

But the instincts that govern aggression die a slow death, and those same leaders who had brought peace to Tirol soon embarked on a course that ultimately brought warfare to the stars. Co-opted, Robotechnology and Protoculture fueled the megalomaniacal militaristic dreams of its new masters, whose first act was to decree that *all* of Optera's fertile seedpods be gathered and transported to Tirol.

The order was then issued that Optera be defoliated.

The bio-genetically created giants who mined Fantoma's wastes were to become the most fearful race of warriors the quadrant had ever known—the *Zentraedi*.

Engrammed with a false past (replete with artificial racial memories and an equally counterfeit history), programmed to accept Tirol's word as law, and equipped with an armada of gargantuan warships the likes of which only Robotechnology could provide, they were set loose to conquer and destroy, *to fulfill their imperative*: to forge and secure an intergalactic empire ruled by a governing body of barbarians who were calling themselves the Robotech Masters.

Zor, however, had commenced a subtle rebellion; though forced to do the bidding of his misguided Masters, he had been careful to keep the secrets of the Protoculture process to himself. He acted the part of the servile deferential pawn the Masters perceived him to be, all the while manipulating them into allowing him to fashion a starship of his own design—for further galactic exploration, to be sure—a sleek transformable craft, a super dimensional fortress that would embody the science of Robotechnology much as the

Zentraedi's organic battlewagons embodied the lusts of war.

Unbeknown to the Masters, concealed among the reflex furnaces that powered its hyperspace drives, the fortress would also contain the very essence of Robotechnology—a veritable Protoculture factory, the only one of its kind in the known universe, capable of seducing from the Invid Flower of Life a harnessable bio-energy.

By galactic standards it wasn't long before some of the horrors the Masters' greed had spawned came home to roost. War with the divested Invid was soon a reality, and there were incidents of open rebellion among the ranks of the Zentraedi, that pathetic race of beings deprived by the Masters of the very essence of sentient life—the ability to feel, to grow, to experience beauty and love.

Nevertheless, Zor ventured forth in the hopes of redressing some of the injustices his own discoveries had fostered. Under the watchful gaze of Dolza, commander in chief of the Zentraedi, the dimensional fortress embarked on a mission to discover new worlds ripe for conquest.

So the Masters were led to believe.

What Zor actually had in mind was the seeding of planets with the Invid flower. Dolza and his lieutenants, Breetai and the rest, easily duped into believing that he was carrying out orders from the Masters themselves, were along as much to secure Zor's safety as to ensure the Master's investment. The inability to comprehend or effect repairs on any Robotech device and to stand in awe of those who could was programmed into the Zentraedi as a handicap to guard against a possible grand-scale warrior rebellion. The Zentraedi had about as much understanding of the workings of Robotechnology as they did of their humanoid hearts.

So, on Spheris, Garuda, Haydon IV, Peryton, and numerous other planets, Zor worked with unprecedented urgency to fulfill his imperative. The Invid were always one step behind him, their sensor nebulae alert to even minute traces of Protoculture, their Inorganics left behind on those very same worlds to conquer, occupy, and destroy. But no matter: In each instance the seedlings failed to take root.

It was at some point during his final voyage that Zor himself began to use the Flowers of Life in a new way, ingesting them as he had seen the Invid do so long ago on Optera. And it was during this time that he began to experience the vision that was to direct him along a new course of action. It seemed inevitable that the Invid would catch up with him long before suitable planets could be sought out and seeded, but his visions had revealed to him a world far removed from that warring sector of the universe where Robotech Masters, Zentraedi, and Invid vied for control. A world of beings intelligent enough to recognize the full potential of his discovery—a *blue-white world, infinitely beautiful, blessed with the treasure that was life… at the crux of transcendent events, the crossroads and deciding place of a conflict that would rage across the galaxies.*

A world he was destined to visit.

Well aware of the danger the Invid presented, Zor programmed the continuum coordinates of this planet into the astrogational computers of the dimensional fortress. He likewise programmed some of the ship's Robotech devices to play a part in leading the new trustees of his discovery to a special warning message his own likeness would deliver to them. Further, he enlisted the aid of several Zentraedi (whose heartless conditioning he managed to override by exposing them to music) to carry out the mission.

The Invid caught up with Zor.

But not before the dimensional fortress had been successfully launched and sent on its way.

To Earth.

Subsequent events—notably the Zentraedi pursuit of the fortress—were as much a part of Earth's history as they were of Tirol's, but there were chapters yet to unfold, transformations and reconfigurations, repercussions impossible to predict, events that would have surprised Zor himself… had he lived.

"*Farewell, Zor,*" Dolza had said when the lifeless body of the scientist was sent on its way to Tirol. "*May you serve the Masters better in death than you did in life.*"

And indeed, the Robotech Masters had labored to make that so, having their way with Zor's remains, extracting from his still-functional neural reservoir an image of the blue-white world he had selected to inherit Robotechnology. But beyond that Zor's mind had proved as impenetrable in death as it had been in life. So while Dolza's Zentraedi scoured the quadrant in search of this "Earth," the Masters had little to do but hold fast to the mushroom-shaped sensor units that had come to represent their link to the real world. Desperately, they tried to knit together the unraveling threads of their once-great empire.

For ten long years by Earth reckoning they waited for some encouraging news from Dolza. It was the blink of an eye to the massive Zentraedi, but for the Robotech Masters, who were essentially human in spite of their psychically evolved state, time moved with sometimes agonizing leadenness. Those ten years saw the further decline of their civilization, weakened as it was by internal decadence, the continual attacks by the Protoculture-hungry Invid, a growing rebellion at the fringes of their empire, and heightened disaffection among the ranks of the Zentraedi, who were beginning to recognize the Masters for the fallible beings they were.

Robotechnology's inheritors had been located—"Zor's descendants," as they were being called—but two more years would pass before Dolza's armada made a decisive move to recapture the dimensional fortress and its much-needed Protoculture matrix. There was growing concern, especially among the Elder Masters, that Dolza could no longer be trusted. From the start he seemed to harbor some plan of his own, reluctant to return Zor's body twelve years earlier and now incommunicado while he moved against the possessors of Zor's fortress. With his armada of more than four million Robotech ships, the Zentraedi commander in chief stood to gain the most by securing the Protoculture matrix for himself.

There was added reason for concern when it was learned that Zor's descendants were humanoid like the Masters themselves. The warrior race literally looked down on anything smaller than itself and had come to think of normally proportioned humanoids as "Micronians"—ironic, given the fact that the Masters could have sized the Zentraedi to any dimension they wished. Their present size was in fact an illusion of sorts: Beating inside those goliath frames were hearts made from the same genetic stuff as the so-called

Micronians they so despised. Because of that basic genetic similarity, the Robotech Masters had been careful to write warnings into the Zentraedi's pseudo-historical records to avoid prolonged contact with any Micronian societies. Rightly so: It was feared that such exposure to emotive life might very well rekindle real memories of the Zentraedi's bio-genetic past and the true stuff of their existence.

According to reports received from Commander Reno (who had overseen the return of Zor's body to Tirol and whose fleet still patrolled the central region of the empire), some of the elements under Breetai's command had mutinied. Dolza, if Reno's report was to be believed, had subsequently elected to fold the entire armada to Earthspace, with designs to annihilate the planet before emotive contagion was spread to the remainder of the fleet.

The Zentraedi might learn to emote, but were they capable of learning to utilize the full powers of Robotechnology?

This was the question the Robotech Masters had put to themselves.

It was soon, however, to become a moot point.

Hyperspace sensor probes attached to a Robotech fortress some seventy-five light-years away from Tirol had detected a massive release of Protoculture matrix in the Fourth Quadrant— an amount capable of empowering over four million ships.

# 02

Throughout the territories we traveled (the southwest portion of what was once the United States of America) one would encounter the holed hulks of Zentraedi warships, rising up like monolithic towers from the irradiated and ravaged wastelands... At the base of one such apocalyptic reminder sits the cross-legged skeleton of a Zentraedi shock trooper, almost in a pose of tranquil meditation, still clad in his armor and bandoliers, a Minmei doll insignificant in his huge metalshod hand.

Dr. Lazlo Zand, *On Earth As It Is In Hell:*
*Recollections of the Robotech War*

THEREFORE, IT IS OUR CONCLUSION, BASED UPON THE AVAILABLE information, that human and Zentraedi are descended from very nearly the same ancestors!"

Exedore leaned back in the chamber's straight-backed chair to cast a look around the circular table as the weight of his pronouncement sank in. Continued exposure to Earth's sun these past two years had brought out strong mauve tones in his skin and turned his hair an ochre red.

To his immediate right was the somewhat dour-looking Professor Zand, a shadowy figure who had emerged from Lang's Robotech elite; to Zand's right were two Zentraedi, micronized like Exedore and sporting the same blue and white Robotech Defense Forces uniforms. Clockwise around the table to Exedore's left were Claudia Grant, the SDF-2's First Officer—a handsome and intelligent representative of Earth's black race—Commanders

Lisa Hayes and Rick Hunter (*Made for each other*, Exedore often said to himself), and Admiral Gloval, serious as ever.

The rich golden warmth of Earth's sun poured into the fortress through two banks of skylights set opposite each other in the conference room's cathedral ceiling.

Exedore had been working side by side with Dr. Emil Lang and several other Earth scientists, deciphering some of the numerous documents Zor had thought to place aboard the SDF-1 over a decade ago. But his announcement of Terran and Zentraedi similarity came as the result of an extensive series of medical tests and evaluations. The distinction *human* or Zentraedi no longer applied; indeed, it was beginning to look as though there existed—lost somewhere in time—an ancestor race common to both.

Exedore had noticed that the Terrans accepted this with less enthusiasm than might otherwise be expected. Perhaps, he speculated, it was due to the fact that they continued to reproduce in the *natural* way, whereas the Zentraedi had long ago abandoned that unsure method for the certainty of genetic manipulation. In Earthspeak the word was "clone"; the Zentraedi equivalent approximated the English term "being."

New discoveries awaited them in the documents, especially in the latest batch of trans-vids uncovered. Exedore had yet to view these, but there were indications that they would provide answers to questions concerning the historical origins of the Zentraedi race, answers that might shed light on the origins of the Terrans as well. All evidence pointed to an extraterrestrial origin, an issue hotly debated by Earth scientists, most of whom believed that the human race *evolved* from a tree-dwelling primate species that had roamed the planet millions of years earlier.

But if all these protohistorical answers were coming fast, the whereabouts of the Protoculture matrix Zor had built into the ship remained a mystery. Hardly a place had been left uninvestigated by Exedore, Breetai, Lang, and the others; and Zand had even suggested that the Protoculture was *in hiding!*

Responses to Exedore's announcement proved varied: The misshapen, gnomish Zentraedi heard Claudia's sharp intake of breath and Lisa Hayes's "Ah-hah," voiced in a fashion that suggested she had expected no less. Commander Hunter, on the other hand, sat with eyes wide in a kind of fear—the personification of a certain xenophobic mentality that permeated Terran cultures.

Gloval was nodding his head, saying little. His white commander's cap was pulled low on his forehead, so Exedore couldn't read his eyes.

"So, Admiral," Exedore continued, leaning into the table. "There is little doubt—our genetic makeup points directly at a common point of origin."

"That's incredible!" Gloval now exclaimed.

"Isn't it? While examining the data, we noticed many common traits, including a penchant on the part of both races to indulge in warfare."

This brought startled reactions around the Terran side of the table.

"Yes," Exedore said flatly, as if to forestall any arguments. "Both races seem to *enjoy* making war."

Rick Hunter held his breath, counting to ten. How could the Zentraedi believe his own words, he asked himself, when it was *love* and not war that had doomed the Zentraedi to defeat? The Zentraedi race had started the entire conflict, and Rick nursed a suspicion that this pronouncement of Exedore's was his way of letting himself off the hook.

Exedore seemed to be enjoying his so-called micronized state, and Rick further suspected that this had more to do with a new sense of power the small man had gained than it did with exploring the ship for some alleged Protoculture factory. Exedore couldn't bear to admit to himself that his commanders had waged a war for something that didn't even exist; they had nearly brought destruction to both races, chasing after some goose that was supposed to lay golden eggs. Truly, this was the saga that would go down in their history as legend: the pursuit of a ship that supposedly held the secrets of eternal youth, the capture of one hollow to the core.

Rick looked hard into Exedore's lidless pinpoint-pupiled eyes. He didn't like the idea of Exedore poking into every nook and cranny in the fortress, acting as if it was more his property than Earth's. Only a moment earlier the Zentraedi had seemed to be sizing him up, well aware of the effect of his words. Rick wasn't about to disappoint him.

"Well, with all due respect," he began acidly, "I disagree. We don't fight because we *like* to—we fight to *defend* ourselves from our enemies. So, under the circumstances we have no choice in the matter. Do you understand?"

Rick's hand was balled up into a fist. Lisa and Claudia looked at him in surprise.

"That's nonsense, Commander," said Professor Zand, who was tall and unkempt looking. He stood up, palms flat on the table, to press his point. "There have always been wars in progress somewhere on Earth, even before the invasion from space. I think this clearly indicates the warlike nature of humans."

*Another Zentraedi sympathizer*, thought Rick. And talking like an alien to boot. He began to stammer a response, always feeling outgunned when up against academics, but Zand interrupted him.

"A perfect example: Look what happened on Earth when the *peacemakers* tried their best to prevail. They formed the League of Nations and the United Nations, *both* of which *failed!*"

Rick got to his feet confrontationally. What did all this have to do with humans *enjoying* war? The best he would allow was that *some* humans enjoyed war but most didn't. Most enjoyed... love.

"I can't believe you'd simplify the facts like that," Rick shouted. "You're practically rewriting history!"

"Facts, sir, do not lie," said Zand.

Rick was about to jump over the table and convince the man, but Exedore beat him to the punch, fixing Zand with that unearthly gaze of his and saying:

"We're merely telling you the results of our best data analysis. Please don't interject your opinions."

*So when we have something to say, it's an opinion, and when they have something to say, it's a fact*, Rick thought, restraining himself.

Gloval cleared his throat meaningfully.

"Fascinating... So we're all descended from the same race, are we? And who can say in what direction all of us are headed. We may never know..."

Rick dropped back into his seat, staring off into space. Whatever happens, he told himself, we mustn't ever allow ourselves to become like the Zentraedi, devoid of emotions—no better than robots. *Never!*

The conference room, scene of Exedore's briefing, was located on level 34 of the new fortress, the so-called SDF-2, which had been under construction for almost as long as the city of New Macross itself. The space fortress was a virtual copy of the SDF-1 and currently sat back to back with it, linked to its parent by hundreds of transfer and service corridors, in the center of the circular human-made lake known now as Gloval, in honor of the admiral. The arid, high plateaus of northwestern North America seemed ideally suited to the reconstruction of the city that had once grown up inside the original super dimensional fortress: The area was cool compared to the background radiation of the devastated coastal corridors, untainted water was plentiful enough, the climate was temperate, and there was no shortage of space. As a result the city had risen swiftly, prospered, and spread out from the lake, a burgeoning forest of skyscrapers, high rises, and prefab suburban dwellings. In the two years since its founding, the population of New Macross had increased tenfold, and it was considered (though not officially recognized as) the Earth's capital city.

New Macross had its share of Zentraedis, though not nearly as many as the cities that had grown up at alien crashpoints throughout the continent—New Detroit and nearby Monument City chief among them. The Zentraedi enjoyed less freedom than the Terrans, but this was conceived of as a temporary measure to allow for gradual readjustment and acculturation. Most Zentraedi had opted for micronization, but many retained their original size. However, control of the Protoculture sizing chambers fell under the jurisdiction of the military government, the Robotech Defense Force, alternatively known as the Earth Forces Government. Micronization was encouraged, but the return to full size of a previously micronized Zentraedi was rarely if ever permitted. This had given rise to a separatist movement, spearheaded by Monument City, which advocated the creation of autonomous Zentraedi free states. Critics of the proposals pointed to increasing incidents of Zentraedi uprising as justification for maintaining the status quo. The innate blood lust that had earned the Zentraedi their reputation as fearsome warriors was not always so easily overcome and controlled.

At factories in the industrial sector of New Macross City, humans and aliens worked together toward the forging of a united future. The Zentraedi were fond of work, having had no previous experience with it during their long history of enslavement to war. Manual labor or assembly line, it made no difference to them. Giants hauled enormous cargos of wood and raw materials in from the wastelands, while their micronized brethren worked at benches completing electronic components, adding Protoculture chips to Robotech circuit panels—chips that had been salvaged from the ruined ships that dotted the landscape.

But there was tension in the air on this particular day. Unused to a life without war, some of the aliens were beginning to question the new life they had chosen for themselves.

Utema was one of these. A massively built red-haired Goliath who had served under Breetai, he had worked in New Macross for eighteen months, first assembling steel towers in the Micronian population center, then scouring the countryside for usable materials. But on one of his forays, he had stumbled upon an encampment of former warriors who had abandoned the Micronian ways, and ever since he had harbored an anger he could not articulate. An urge to... *destroy* something—*anything*!

His eyes had seized on one of the factory trucks parked in the fenced-in yard, a harmless tanker truck used for the transport of fuels. He approached it now and booted it, experiencing a long-lost thrill as the toy vehicle exploded and burst into flames.

Laborers at their work stations inside the factory heard Utema bellow:

"I quit! I can't stand it! I quit! This is stupid!"

The explosion had rekindled his rage. He stood with his fists clenched, looking for something else to demolish, ignoring the protests of his giant coworker. The two faced off.

"It's worse than stupid—it's degrading!" Utema roared. "I've had enough!"

Violently, he side-kicked a stack of dressed logs, a guttural cry punctuating his swift move.

"Shut up and don't interfere," he warned his companion. "I'm leaving!"

The second giant made no move to stop Utema as he stepped over the chain-link fence and headed off into the wasteland. Two others had arrived on the scene, but they too let him walk.

"But where are you going?" one of them called out. "Utema— come back! You won't survive out there!"

"It's *you* that won't survive!" Utema shouted back, pointing his finger. "*War!* War is the only thing that will save us!"

At a supper club in Monument City, Minmei, wearing a gauzy blue dress that hung off one shoulder, stood in the spotlight, accepting the applause. It was nowhere near a full house, and, disappointed by the turnout, she hadn't put on her best show. Nevertheless, those few who had been able to afford tickets applauded her wildly, out of respect or politeness, she couldn't be sure. Perhaps because most of her fans rarely knew when her performance was off—she was her own most demanding critic.

The light was a warm, comfortable curtain she was reluctant to leave.

Kyle was waiting for her backstage in the large and virtually unfurnished dressing room, leaning against the wall, arms crossed, looking sullen and angry. He was dressed in jeans and a narrow-waisted jacket with tails. She could tell he'd been drinking and wondered when he would go into his Jekyll and Hyde number again. No doubt he'd caught all her off notes, tempo changes, and missed words.

"Hi," she greeted him apologetically.

"That was terrible," Kyle snapped at her, no beating around the bush tonight. It was going to be a bad evening, perhaps as bad as the night he had kicked a bottle at her.

"Sorry," she told him mechanically, heading straight for the dressing table, seating herself on one of the velour stools, and wiping off makeup.

Kyle remained at the wall.

"I'm worried about tomorrow's concert—if it goes like this."

"I'll be okay," she promised him, looking over her shoulder. "There were so few people tonight that I was really taken by surprise. Don't worry, I'll be all right tomorrow."

"This is a high-class club," Kyle persisted. "We let the patrons down."

She sighed. He wasn't going to let go of it. She couldn't do anything right anymore. He was constantly lecturing her and trying to change her behavior.

"I know," she said meekly, sincerely depressed—not for disappointing Kyle but for giving anything less than her all to the audience.

"Well, there's nothing we can do about it now—the damage is done."

She began applying crème to her face. "You could have reduced the admission price a bit, right?"

"Y' get what you can," Kyle said defensively, shaking his fist at her or the world, she didn't know which. He approached her. "And then, don't you forget, my pet—we'll be sharing the dough we earn with all the *poor* people, *right*?"

His scolding voice was full of sarcasm and anger, hinting that she was somehow to blame for his actions: He *had* to charge a lot for the tickets because *she* was the one who insisted on splitting all the profits with the needy. Little did Kyle know that she would gladly have worked for no profit. It just didn't seem right anymore to work for money with so much need, so much sadness and misery, in what was left of everyone's world.

"Then why don't we give *all* the money to charity?" she asked, meeting his glare. "We have enough."

Kyle was down on one knee beside her now, anger still in his eyes but a new tone of conciliation and patience in his voice. He put his hands on her shoulders and looked into her face.

"We have, but not enough to make our dreams come true. You

certainly ought to be able to understand *that!*"

"Yeah, but—"

"We promised ourselves we'd build a great concert hall some day and do all our work *there*—right?"

She wanted to remind him that they had made that promise years ago, when such things seemed possible. But a great concert hall now—in the middle of this wasteland, with things just beginning to rebuild and isolated groups of people working the land who never strayed five miles from home? Still, she just didn't have the energy to argue with him. She could imagine the accusatory tone in his voice: You're *the one who ought to understand about dreams—you had so many...*

"Now, get cleaned up," Kyle ordered, getting to his feet. "After you get dressed, I'll take you out for a good dinner, okay?"

"I'm not very hungry, Kyle," she told him.

He turned on her and exploded.

"We're going to eat anyway! I'll get the car."

The door slammed. She promised herself she wouldn't cry and went to work removing the rest of her makeup, hoping he would mellow somewhat by the time she met him at the stage door. But that didn't happen.

"Come on, get in," he demanded, throwing open the sports car's passenger door.

She frowned and slid into the leather seat. Kyle accelerated even before she had the door closed, squealing the tires as they left the club. He knew that she hated that almost as much as she hated the car itself—a sleek, dual front-axled all-terrain sports car, always hungry for fuel and symbolizing all that she detested in the old world as much as the new: the idea of privilege, status, the haves and have-nots.

"Where would you like to eat?" Kyle said unpleasantly, throwing the vehicle through the gears.

"Your dad's restaurant. We haven't been there in a long time."

"I don't want to go there."

"Then why do you bother asking me where I want to eat, Kyle? Just let me off and I'll go there myself!"

"Oh?" Kyle started to say, but swallowed the rest when he realized that Minmei had thrown open the door. An oncoming van veered off, narrowly missing them, as Kyle threw the steering wheel hard to the left to fling her back into the vehicle. But he overcorrected coming out of the resultant fishtail and ended up in a swerve that brought him into oncoming traffic. The car went through several more slides before he could safely brake and bring them to a stop on the shoulder. Afterward he leaned onto the steering wheel and exhaled loudly. When he spoke, all of the anger and sarcasm had left him.

"Minmei… we could have been killed…"

Minmei was not nearly as shaken by the incident, having achieved some purpose.

"I *am* sorry, Kyle. But I'm really going there, even if I have to walk." She opened the door again and started to exit. "Good-bye."

"No, wait." He stopped her. "Get back in the car."

"Why should I?"

"I'll… I'll drive you as far as the city line."

She reseated herself and said, "Thank you so much, Kyle."

The doors of the rebuilt White Dragon slid open as Minmei approached just short of closing time. Still the center of the city as it had been on Macross Island and later in the SDF-1, the restaurant was packed even at the late hour.

"Hi! I'm here," she called, cheerful again, the argument with Kyle behind her now.

Aunt Lena was cleaning up. Tommy Luan, the barrel-chested mayor of Macross, and his fusty wife, Loretta, were having tea.

"Oooh, you're back!" said Lena, a warm smile spreading across her face, the mother Minmei had lost.

"Heyyy!" called the mayor, equally happy to see his long-lost creation.

She greeted Lena with an embrace.

"Welcome back, darling! But shouldn't you be rehearsing for your concert?" Minmei was the daughter Lena had never had as well as a replacement for the son she seemed to have lost.

"Uh huh," Minmei told her and let it drop. "Mr. Mayor, how are you?"

"I'm just fine, Minmei."

"Good seeing you, dear," said his stiff wife. A head taller than her husband, she had a long, almost emaciated face underscored by a prominent chin. She wore her wavy auburn hair pulled back into an unattractive bun and kept the collar of her blouse tightly fastened at the neck by a large blue brooch.

Loretta and Tommy were almost as unlikely a couple as lithesome Lena and squat Max, who was just stepping from the kitchen now, his cooking whites and chef's hat still in place.

"Heyyy, Minmei," he drawled.

"Uncle!… Would it be okay with you if I stayed here tonight?"

"Of course it'd be okay! M' girl, you can even have your old room back again."

"Oh, thanks, Uncle Max," Minmei said, suddenly overcome with a feeling of love for all of them, happy to be back in the fold, away from the lights, crowds, attention… *Kyle.*

"Isn't that great?" the mayor crowed. "She hasn't changed a bit, even after becoming famous!"

Three male customers had left their table to surround her, wondering what she was doing there, taking advantage of the casual nature of her visit to ask for autographs.

"Success hasn't spoiled our Minmei."

"She's still our little girl," said Max.

Which is just what she wanted to feel like at the moment: to be the one taken care of instead of the one who always had to keep things going. But she said, laughing:

"Oh, no! That makes me sound like a little child who hasn't grown up at all!"

"Oh, I didn't mean it that way!" Max recanted, joining the laughter.

After signing autographs and having something to eat—Lena refused to take no for an answer—Minmei excused herself and went upstairs to her room. There were no questions about Kyle; it was as if he were no longer part of the family.

Lena and Max hadn't changed a thing even after the relocation of the restaurant from the hold of the dimensional fortress; they must have put everything back where it had been—even the whimsical pink rabbit's head bearing her name that she had tacked to the door.

Once inside, a flood of memories began to overwhelm her:

Her first night in this very room when she'd arrived on Macross Island from Yokohama—the balcony view from these very windows of the reconstructed SDF-1; the Launching Day celebration and the madness that had ensued; the years in space, and the strange twists of fate that had brought her fame... And through it all she saw Rick journeying along with her, accompanying her, though not always by her side.

She looked up at the corner of the room damaged by Rick's Battloid on the day fate had thrown him a curve. The cornice of the room had been repaired, but the place never seemed to hold paint for very long, as though the spot had decided to memorialize itself.

Minmei crossed over to her bureau, opened one of the drawers, and retrieved the gift Rick had given her more than three years ago on her sixteenth birthday. The titanium Medal of Honor he had received after the battle of Mars. She recalled how he had appeared beneath her balcony only minutes before midnight and tossed the gift to her. "It says what I can't say to you," Rick had told her then.

The memory warmed her heart, thawing some of the sadness lodged there. But suddenly she felt far away from the joy and love of those earlier times; something inside her was in danger of dying. She sobbed, holding the medal close to her breast:

"Oh, Rick, what have I done?"

# 03

What do I remember about those days in New Macross?
...Anger, strident conversations, despair—it almost seemed as if
Protoculture's shape-shifting capabilities had taken hold of fate
itself, changing and reworking individual destiny, transforming and
reconfiguring lives...

Lisa Hayes, *Recollections*

THE SUN ROSE INTO CIRRUS SKIES ABOVE NEW MACROSS CITY,
autumn's first crisp and clear day. The stratospheric dust and
debris that for two years now had led to blue moons, sullen sunsets,
and perpetual winters was at last dissipating, and there was every
indication that Earth was truly on the mend.

Minmei, dressed in a white summer-weight skirt and red
sweater, stepped out of the White Dragon and took a deep breath
of the cool morning air. She felt more rested than she had in
months; the comfort of her own room and the company of her
family were warm in her memory. A newsboy, brown baseball
cap askew on his head, rushed by and dropped off the morning
edition; she greeted him cheerfully and started off down the street,
unaware that he had turned startled in his tracks, recognizing
the singing star instantly and somewhat disappointed when she
hadn't stopped to talk with him for a moment.

She had a lot on her mind, but for a change she felt that there
was all the time in the world to see to everything. The band
would be expecting her for rehearsal, but that was still hours
off, and she wanted nothing more than to walk the streets and

say hello to the city in her own way. *That's no EVE projection up there*, she had to remind herself, unaccustomed to sunny skies. She had been a creature of the night for too long, victimized by her own needs as much as she was by Kyle's grandiose plans for the future.

Last night's argument seemed far removed from the optimism coursing through her. If Kyle could only be made to understand, if he would only stop drinking and return himself to the disciplines that made him unique in her eyes... Sometimes he appeared to be as displaced as the Zentraedi themselves, yearning for new battles to wage, new fronts to open. He detested the presence of the military and continued to blame them for the nearly total destruction of the planet. Minmei pitied him for that. The military had at least managed to salvage a place for new growth. And as for their presence, the threat of a follow-up attack was a real one —not manufactured, as Kyle claimed, to keep the civilians in line. The Earth had been ravaged once, and it could happen again.

But these were dark thoughts to have on such a glorious day, and she decided to put them from her mind. There was beauty and renewed life everywhere she looked. Skyscrapers rose like silver towers above the rooftops, and Lake Gloval looked as though it had been sprinkled with gems...

In the outskirts of New Macross Rick had already commenced his morning run, in full sweats today, a beige outfit Lisa had given him for his birthday. The city was still asleep, taking advantage of the chill to spend a few extra moments cuddled under blankets, and there was no traffic to fight; so he jogged without any set course in mind, along the lakefront, then into the grid of city streets. Flat-bottomed cargo crafts ferried supplies to and from the supercarriers still attached to the SDF-1, while launches carried night-shift work crews away from the SDF-2, back to back with its mother ship and rapidly nearing completion.

*Breathe in the good, breathe out the bad,* he chanted to himself as he ran—and there was a great deal of the latter he needed to get rid of. If asked what he was so angry about, he probably wouldn't have been able to offer a clear explanation. Only this: He was tense. Whether it had something to do with his situation with Lisa, or Minmei's situation with Kyle, or Earth's with the Zentraedi, he couldn't be sure. Probably it was a combination of everything, coupled with an underlying sense of purposelessness.

*"Both races seem to* enjoy *fighting,"* Exedore had said. Rick regretted now that he had turned the briefing into a debate—he would have felt differently had he been able to make his point—but was still certain of his feelings: that the Zentraedi, for all their genetic similarities to humans, were no better than programmed androids. All one needed to do was look around to see that he was right: The Zentraedi were hungry for war—*biologically* hungry. They were deserting their positions, sometimes violently—the recent incident in New Portland was a case in point—to take up with their fellow malcontents in makeshift compounds in the wasteland, off limits to humans, who would not be able to withstand the lingering radiation. Perhaps a mistake had been made in attempting to band together despite the gains to New Macross. But Rick was certain it was only a matter of time before all the Zentraedi followed suit and returned to war.

He exhaled harshly and increased his pace.

Just down the street from the White Dragon, only a few blocks from Rick's present course, a delivery van pulled to a stop in front of a two-storied building with a red and white striped awning and a rainbow-shaped sign that read CLEANING. At the wheel was Konda, one of the three former Zentraedi spies.

"Rico! Gimme a hand with this!" Bron called from the sidewalk, a full basket of laundry in his brawny arms.

The door to the shop opened, and the founder of the Minmei cult stepped out, affecting oversized and unnecessary eyeglasses, convinced that they enhanced his appearance. Rico had also let his hair grow and was dressed in a short-waisted blue and white uniform that fit him like a leisure suit.

The three former secret agents had secured jobs with the cleaning service several months before, their fascination for clothing as strong now as it had been when they first experienced Micronian life in the holds of the SDF-1.

"Hey, guess what happened?" Konda said, leaning out of the van.

Rico was quick to respond, leaving Bron (a good fifteen pounds lighter than he'd been two years ago) to fend for himself. "What happened?" he asked excitedly.

"Guess."

"What?" Rico repeated, enjoying the game but still vague about the rules.

"Minmei's back in town—she stayed at the restaurant last night!"

"No kidding!"

"I got it straight from his honor the mayor himself."

Rico made a puzzled gesture. "But I saw in the paper that Minmei's got a concert in Granite City today." He wanted to believe Konda, but still...

"Well, if she leaves early enough today, she can still make it," Konda offered as an explanation.

Rico snapped his fingers. "Rats! If I had known, I would have gone to the restaurant last night to eat." He dug into his pants pocket and produced a small notebook, which he immediately began to leaf through. It was possible he'd been mistaken about the Granite City concert. "Hmmm... let's see... It looks like I've forgotten her concert schedule in my other notebook." If Konda's information was correct, then perhaps Minmei would be spending another night at the White Dragon.

Rico reveled in the idea of "having a mission." He and his sidekicks had had their share of dull evenings lately. Things didn't seem to be working out too well for the three of them and Kim, Vanessa, and Sammie. He was at a loss to explain the reasons for this but reasoned that it had something to do with *procreation*, that mystery of mysteries so important to Micronian females. Not everyone could be as fortunate as Miriya Parino and her mate...

Just then Bron appeared behind him, a neatly folded stack of sheets in his arms.

"Hey! We're supposed to be dry cleaners, not gossipmongers." Bron took his job very seriously, judging it to be one of the most important things a Micronian could attend to—next to cooking, of course. The care and maintenance of uniforms especially. "Now, either you ship up or shape out or I'm gonna just have to—huh?"

Bron shouldered Rico aside and advanced a few steps along the sidewalk, staring at a woman pedestrian headed their way.

"Hey… Am I dreaming?" he said. Then: "It is!"

"Huh?" said Rico, tempted to remove his glasses.

Konda leaned from the van. "Is that…"

"*Minmei!*" the three of them said together, unable to believe their luck.

"Hi." She smiled, raising her hand. She hadn't seen any of them in months—since her last open-air concert in New Macross, where they had had front-row seats and carried artificial flowers.

Rico and Bron ran to her, Kanda quick to bring up the rear. "Minmei, would you… well, would you like to autograph this?" Bron said, offering her his pile of pressed linen.

"Hey, Bron, that belongs to a customer," Rico pointed out, confident that his knowledge of Micronian protocol would impress Minmei.

But Bron ignored him. "So what! I'll buy the customer a new one!"

This found favor with Rico and Kanda, both of whom reached for the sheets simultaneously, touching off an instant tug-of-war for what hadn't already fallen to the sidewalk.

Minmei backed up, worried that the battle might escalate; but finally she laughed and dug into her purse for a pen.

Elsewhere in the city a more violent battle was under way.

Mayor Tommy Luan had been attending to his morning ritual (putting on a tie, then taking it oft), when he saw something fly past his second-floor bedroom window—something large and red that had about as much business being in the air as a tie had around his neck. He moved to the window in time to see a compact car crash to the street and explode. Pedestrians were screaming and fleeing the scene. *Some idiot's driven off the roof of the parking garage,* Luan told himself as he made for the stairway.

By the time he reached street level, flames and thick smoke had engulfed what was left of the car. But he had scarcely stepped from the building when a second explosion filled the air, more ground-shaking than the first. Luan saw a second black cloud rise over the rooftops from somewhere nearby and ran toward the direction of the smoke, revising his earlier hypothesis. Was this a sneak attack or some new terrorist group at work?

As he approached the intersection, an airborne girder took out a streetlamp, sending up a fountain of sparks and stopping him in his tracks. From around the corner came two Zentraedi giants, one brandishing a long pipe and carrying a large sack stuffed with who knew what. Luan had begun a slow retreat down his street, but the two saw him and began to pursue him. Spent after a block, the mayor stopped, collapsing to his knees in front of his home.

The Zentraedi stood over him, threatening him with the pipe.

"I beg you—h-have pity."

"I'll spare you if you give me everything you've got!" growled the pipe wielder instinctively, with no real purpose other than intimidation in mind.

"T-That's easier said than done," Luan answered him, trying to figure out just what he might possess that would appeal to a sixty-foot warrior.

Inside the house, Luan's wife, Loretta, having glimpsed the terrifying street scene from the living room window, had already raised the base on the phone. The clenched fist of one of the aliens filled the picture window behind her.

"Right... right," she was saying, growing panic in her voice. "They've suddenly become very violent and extremely dangerous. They're trying to take our food and our possessions and everything we—"

Something took hold of her, cutting off her breath.

Now she was being lifted off the floor and carried through the front door, her narrow shoulders and fragile neck pinched in the grip of giant fingers. The warrior, who had gone down on both knees to fish her from her home, held her ten feet above the sidewalk, choking the life from her while he roared into her face.

"Whaddaya think you're up to? Sit down!" he said gruffly, slamming her to the concrete. This knocked the wind out of her and dislocated her back. Through the pain she recognized that she was sitting in a most unladylike position, her pleated blue skirt up around her thighs, but there was nothing she could do about it. Then suddenly Tommy was beside her, holding her and spitting at the aliens:

"You monster! You've hurt her." Luan wrapped his beefy arms around his wife. "Be strong, darling. We're going to get you to a hospital as soon as we—"

"You're not going anywhere!" the two Zentraedi bellowed, moving in to cast a grim shadow over both of them...

Rick was breathing hard, pushing himself into a sprint, when he heard his name called. He forced himself to stop, doubled over with hands on his knees, panting for a moment, before he turned around. *Lisa!* He had purposely avoided his usual route for fear of bumping into her. There had been some awkward moments between them these past few weeks. She had stopped coming by his quarters— even (in a roundabout fashion) returned the key he had given her. She thought he was seeing Minmei again, but he wasn't. Not *really*.

"What are you doing up so early?" he asked as she approached.

She stammered, "Um... well, I wasn't sleeping too well."

"Why not?" Rick said, feeling a sudden concern.

"Something's wrong."

"Wrong? Whaddaya mean?"

Lisa stared at him. Was he ever going to be able to *talk* to her? "I don't know," she told him. "I'm not really sure..."

"Well, working on patrol has made me pretty sensitive to what's going on—there's some tension, but we can handle it."

Was he talking about tension between the two of them, or did he mean tension among the Zentraedi? Lisa asked herself. Patrol was making him sensitive... to what? She wanted to believe that this was Rick's way of apologizing.

"I'd better be reporting in," he said, motioning toward the SDF-1. "It's breakfast time."

Lisa smiled to herself. It was like pulling teeth... but she wasn't going to give up on him. Not yet.

"Mind if I walk with you? I don't feel like going back to the barracks by myself, okay?"

"Come to think of it," Rick said as they started off, "you may be right about there being trouble."

It was as prescient a comment as Rick had uttered in quite some time—although subsequent events would erase it from his memory—because Minmei happened to be walking up the same street Rick and Lisa had entered when they rounded the corner scarcely ten paces ahead of her.

Minmei froze, sucking in her breath, as the haunting memories she had experienced in her room last evening returned. Seeing Rick now, practically arm in arm with another woman, only strengthened her earlier longings and, worse still, reinforced her worse fears. *What had she done?*

"Oh, listen," she heard Rick tell Lisa. "I forgot to tell you—I put your picture in my album."

"You did? That was sweet."

Rick turned to Lisa and started to say, "I hope you don't mind, but I—"

Then he saw her standing there.

The moment was full of real-life drama, but Minmei held the edge. She stood still long enough for him to hear her sob and see the tears; then she turned and ran.

Her performance wasn't lost on Lisa. But Rick was fully taken in, already chasing after her, calling for her to wait.

*Why?* Lisa yelled at herself. *Why does she have to manipulate him, and why does he fall right into it, and why am I chasing him now when he's chasing her?*

Rick and Lisa were right behind Minmei when she turned the corner, but all at once she was nowhere in sight.

"How could she have disappeared so quickly?" Rick said, looking around.

Lisa was out of breath. She had figured—correctly, in fact—that Minmei was hiding in one of the storefronts up ahead.

She was about to suggest they try a different direction, when a thunderous bass voice suddenly yelled: "I said shut up!"

Rick and Lisa turned. Towering above the building situated diagonally across the intersection from them, two Zentraedi workers were faced off in an argument. The red-haired one stepped forward and threw a sucker punch, catching the second across the jaw and dropping him to the street with a ground-shaking crash.

"Come on!" Rick said, hurrying toward the fracas.

By the time Rick and Lisa arrived on the scene, the red-haired Zentraedi was straddling his opponent, pummeling the other's face. A third Zentraedi, obviously allied with the winner, stood smiling off to one side. Tommy Luan was cowering on the sidewalk nearby.

Rick braced himself and stepped forward. "Stop that fighting right now!" he yelled. "Stop it, I said!"

The mayor, supporting his injured wife, ran to Rick's side from across the street.

"Commander! Thank goodness you're here!"

"What's this all about, sir?" Rick asked him.

"They were threatening to kill us! Then this one showed up, and they started arguing—"

"I can't live here anymore!" bellowed the red-haired Zentraedi, pinning his opponent to the street.

Luan, encouraged by Rick's presence, stepped forward to address the giant. "I told you—I understand your problem, but you have to be reasonable about—"

"Be quiet, fatso!" the former warrior said, getting to his feet. "I'll squash you, got it?!"

Luan and his wife hid behind Rick.

"Tell him not to get angry about it, Commander."

Just then the streets began shaking with a recognizable thunder. Civil defense sirens blared as four Excalibur MK VIs took up positions on either side of the Zentraedi, their twin-cannon arms raised. Bipedally designed relatives of the MAC II cannon, the mecha bristled with gatlings and were capable of delivering devastating volleys of firepower.

Rick wasn't sure what he was going to say next, but the sudden arrival of Robotech mecha on the scene was a booster shot to his confidence.

"The authorities are here. *Now* will you stop fighting?"

The upper gun turret of the lead Excalibur slid forward, and the mecha's commander elevated himself into view.

"Zentraedi!" his small but amplified voice rang out. "Stop! We've got you surrounded!"

The giant who moments before had been flat on his back got up and stepped out of harm's way, leaving the red-haired one and his cohort center stage. Rick, recognizing the voice of the mecha commander, cupped his hands to his mouth and shouted: "Dan! Hold it!"

Dan looked down from his cockpit seat, surprised to find Rick in the middle of this. "Commander! What happened here?"

"Let me handle this," Rick told him.

Dan gave a verbal aye-aye, and Rick moved in angrily to confront the giants.

"Now, you listen to me, and listen good! I know life with us is hard for you, but the authorities *want* to help you with your problems—if you'll give them the chance."

The red-haired Zentraedi, clutching his sackful of valuables once again, went down on one knee to answer Rick, equally confident and angered.

"Wait a minute!" he growled. "If your government is so worried about us and so concerned about our welfare, why don't they let us go out and be with our own people where we *belong*?"

"Uh, well, that's—"

"I am a warrior, *understand*?"

"Well, what about it?" asked the second Zentraedi threateningly. "Bagzent wants to fight—can you help him?"

"I'm good with my fists, and I can handle practically any weapon," continued the one called Bagzent. "So what do you say? Can you help? Speak up, I can't hear you… Well?… Are you gonna help me or *not*?"

The scene was turning ugly again. Mayor Luan, his wife, and Lisa sensed it and began to back away. The CD mecha shifted slightly, their guns traversing somewhat.

At the corner, unseen, Minmei gasped.

"Well," Rick began, "we have no firm guarantee you won't band together and attack us again. If you want to—"

"Huh!" Bagzent grunted, tiring of the game. "If you can't help me solve my problem, then what's the point in saying that you or your government will talk about it?" All at once his right hand had moved forward. "Micronian!" he uttered in disgust, flicking his forefinger.

Rick took the full force of the movement. The Zentraedi's log-sized forefinger caught him full body, from knees to chin, lifting him off his feet and tossing him a good ten feet through the air. Dazed and bloodied, he landed solidly on his rump at the clawlike foot of one of the Excaliburs.

Startled gasps went up from the humans pressed together on the street corner, but those were not as bothersome to the Zentraedi as the sounds of weapons being leveled against them.

"On my signal," said Dan. "Blast 'em!"

The two Zentraedi backed away, suddenly afraid. Gatlings were ranged in.

"Wait," one of them pleaded. "Don't shoot."

Rick shook the pain from his body, struggled to his feet, and raced back to the center of the arena. He raised up his arms and shouted to Dan again, "Hold your fire!" Then he held his face up to Bagzent, blood running from the corner of his mouth.

Bagzent snarled. "Listen to me, Micronian," he started to say.

"No! *You* listen to me," Rick interrupted him. "We've given you sanctuary and *this* is how you repay us?!"

The corners of Bagzent's mouth turned down. "I'm sorry," he grumbled—not apologetically, but as if to say: *I'm sorry it has to be this way.*

Bagzent and his companion turned and began to walk off, but the third Zentraedi stepped forward now, calling to them.

"Come back! You'll regret this! When we first came here, you thought their culture was a great thing—you were so impressed by Minmei's songs."

The Zentraedis stopped for a moment as if considering this, then continued their heavy-footed retreat.

"Stay and give it one more try!" the third was shouting. "It's worth the effort, isn't it? We've come so far, we can't give up now!"

When he realized his words were having no effect, he added: "Stupid cowards! Come back!"

Concealed from Lisa and the Luans, Minmei brought her hand to her mouth to stifle her sadness and terror. When she could no longer contain herself, she fled.

Lisa was at Rick's side now, watching the Zentraedis move stiffly away.

"They're getting more and more dissatisfied," said Rick, spitting blood. "We're gonna have to do something."

"I wonder... what'll they do after they leave here?"

"I know one thing," the mayor interjected. "Whether they survive out in that wasteland or not... *we're* responsible."

Rick spun around, angry and confused to find yet another sympathizer in his midst. But the mayor stared him down.

"That's right, Rick," Luan said knowingly. "We haven't heard the last of this."

# 04

The mythologies of numerous Earth cultures identified north and the arctic regions with evil and death. I don't believe it was convenience or coincidence that led the militaristic heads of the Earth council to construct their ill-fated Grand Cannon there; nor do I think that Khyron just happened to land his ship there. As water seeks its own level, so does evil seek its own place.

Rawlins, *Zentraedi Triumvirate: Dolza, Breetai, Khyron*

THE MILE-LONG ALIEN CRUISER LAY BURIED UNDER ICE AND SNOW, with only its igloolike gun turrets visible above the frozen, howling surface. No squad of Air Force personnel would come to investigate this one, nor would any human-chain prophylactic magic circle be formed to contain its evil intent. It was too late to watch the skies…

In the observation bubble inside the ship, Khyron, his burgundy uniform and forest-green campaign cloak looking none the worse for wear through two long years, sprang from the command chair as Gerao delivered his latest report.

"Are you absolutely sure of this, Gerao?"

"I'm certain of it, m'lord," said Gerao, thrice lucky for having lived through the explosion of the reflex furnaces on Mars, the holing of his ship during a *Daedalus* Maneuver, and now the holocaust itself. He brought his fist to his breast insignia in salute.

"Our spies have reported that thousands of dissatisfied Zentraedi are leaving town after town. They are estimated to be around ten thousand, sir."

"Ah, splendid," said Khyron, clenching his right hand, the

devilish eyes of his handsome face peering from beneath blue bangs. "A most interesting occurrence—well worth the two-year wait in this terrible place!"

Khyron, through either an act of prescient will or cowardice unheard of among the Zentraedi, had absented his ship and crew from the battle that had all but destroyed the last of his race. It certainly wasn't Khyron's plan to bring Breetai and Dolza into confrontation, so why allow the Botoru Battalion to get caught up in High Command's madness? All along Khyron had maintained that the best way to handle Zor's ship was to destroy it. Anyone should have been able to see that from the beginning. But instead the fools had attempted to capture the fortress, unaware of the Micronian malignancy spreading fast through the fleet. The existence of the Protoculture matrix Zor's fortress was thought to contain was not, however, so easily dismissed. Indeed, Khyron had saved himself for this greater purpose; but the fact remained that his warship's precious fuel and weapons supply were all but depleted.

He had hidden on the far side of the Earth during the catastrophic explosion that had wiped out Dolza's four-million-ship armada— the armada that had once made his race the most feared throughout the Fourth Quadrant. Surely the Micronians had the traitors Breetai and Exedore to thank for their success, although how those two had gained any knowledge of the barrier shield's inversion capacity was beyond him. In all likelihood it was a stroke of luck—and the judgment of fate for the Zentraedi.

Khyron had chosen to put down in the frozen wasteland of the half-dead planet in the hopes of salvaging something from the Micronian's reflex weapon, the so-called Grand Cannon. But nothing remained of it.

He was aware, however, that his elite group did not represent the last of the Zentraedi; somewhere in the quadrant between Earth and Tirol, there was Commander Reno's ship, along with the automated Robotech factory, still fabricating battle mecha for a handful of warriors. There were also the contaminated Zentraedi from Breetai's fleet who had elected to stand shoulder to shoulder with the Micronians. Khyron's own spies were at work infiltrating this latter group, in addition to the renegade bands of Zentraedi who had already abandoned the Earth population centers to inhabit the wastes; and Khyron knew that someday soon they would prove to be his allies. Then, Reno and Khyron would rebuild the Zentraedi war machine with the help of the Masters themselves. And once the Earth was incinerated, they would scour the quadrant for new worlds to conquer.

But first he needed to get his ship spaceworthy once again.

And now the word he'd been waiting for had finally come.

He turned to the one who had stood beside him through the long wait, in defiance of the old ways, a symbol of the new order of things.

"Our faith is vindicated, my dear Azonia."

"Indeed." The former commander of the Quadrono Battalion smiled. She was dressed like her lord, save that her cloak was blue. Her arms were folded, and she wore an arrogant grin. When her own ship had been holed by fire from Dolza's armada, it was Khyron who had come to her aid, convincing her to abandon Breetai's forces and join him. *"Let them battle it out together,"* he had said. *"We will live to see the rebirth of the Zentraedi!"*

"Their taste for the Micronian life-style was only temporary," Khyron was saying. "I knew that after a little while they'd grow tired of it. And you see I was right!"

Two years under the ice and snow had brought a strange new closeness between Azonia and her confederate—a closeness that had more to do with life than death: the stimulation of the senses, *pleasure*. Azonia believed it had something to do with the planet itself—this Earth. But she kept these thoughts to herself. If pleasure was the cause of the warriors' desertion, she couldn't blame them—Miriya included, although it remained a puzzle why she would bother to take a Micronian mate over a Zentraedi.

The fourth Zentraedi in the command center was Grel, who had been Khyron's trusted lieutenant through many long campaigns.

Azonia shook her fist, mimicking Khyroa's gesture of determination. "Now, look," she announced. "If things keep going as planned, we can put together a battalion that I guarantee will *take* them!"

Khyron smiled to himself. It was only right that his underlings echo his sentiments, but Azonia had a lot to learn. What could *she* guarantee, save that *Khyron* would be victorious in the end? That *Khyron* would take them!

Nevertheless, he humored her without seeming patronizing.

"Yes, of course we shall."

The Backstabber moved to the comlink of the cruiser's command bubble to address his troops, who had gathered in the astrogational hold below.

"Now, listen, everyone," he began. "You needn't hide yourselves any longer! You are Zentraedi warriors! I want you to see to it that our former comrades are led here. Those who have established camps for themselves in the wastelands and those who have yet to leave the Micronian population centers. And I want you to tell all the micronized Zentraedi that if they join us, I will return them to their original size so that they too may walk tall and proud once again!"

The soldiers began to cheer their lord and savior with cries of "Long live the Zentraedi, long live Khyron!"

Khyron's lips became a thin line as he took in the collective outpourings of his troops.

Yes, he promised himself, he would return the Zentraedi to their original size—their rightful place in the universe. And the destruction of planet Earth would be his first step in that direction, including the destruction of that secret weapon the Micronians had used so effectively against his race, that weapon the deserters had learned to embrace: that *Minmei!*

Kyle gave another look at his wristwatch: seven forty-eight and she still hadn't arrived.

He glanced out from the wings of the stage. It was a small crowd who had gathered in Granite City's open-air amphitheater (half a dozen giant Zentraedi in the far tiers, mesas and monoliths in the distance, a pink and blue sunset sky) but a vocal one nonetheless, clapping and shouting now, eager to bring Minmei on stage. The warm-up group was well into their second set, but the audience had already tired of them halfway through the first.

Kyle cursed himself for letting her out of his sight, especially after the previous night's fight and that crazy stunt she had pulled on the Macross Highway.

"Hey, Kyle!" said someone behind him. There was an unconcealed note of anger in the voice, and Kyle swung around ready for action, happy to vent his own frustration and rage if the opportunity presented itself. Vance Hasslewood, Minmei's booking agent, was striding down the corridor toward him.

"What's the idea? Where the devil is Minmei?" Hasslewood demanded.

Hasslewood was wearing his customary aviator specs, a sweater-vested white suit and tie, and a scowl on his clean-shaven face.

"Minmei'll be here," Kyle told him tiredly.

"But showtime's in just ten more minutes—you realize that?"

"She'll show," Kyle said more strongly. "Minmei is not the kind of singer who ignores her obligations. You oughta know that by now, Hasslewood."

"I *do* know that. But just the same, Kyle, I want her here at least half an hour before showtime."

"She'll be here!" Kyle repeated, his patience fading fast. He gestured to the audience. "You know, you put on a pretty good *act* as a promoter, Hasslewood-attracting an audience that size."

Hasslewood's nostrils flared. He was getting sick and tired of having to answer to Kyle's demands and criticisms and was of half a mind to turn his back on the whole deal. But he couldn't bear the thought of leaving Minmei in the care of a hothead like Kyle. A drunk and degenerate—

"Hey, she's here!" a stagehand called out.

As Hasslewood turned around, one of the band members ran up to him.

"Minmei's here. She's in her dressing room," he told them, feeling it necessary to point the way.

Kyle snorted and shouldered his way past Hasslewood. He didn't bother to knock at the dressing room door, merely threw it open and demanded:

"Where have you been?"

Minmei was putting on her face. She was wearing the same off-the-shoulder ruffled blue dress she had worn at the supper club the previous night.

"Sorry I'm late," she answered without turning around.

"I don't know why we're even bothering to do this gig—there's hardly anyone out there. This is the pits."

"I don't care that much about the size of the audience," she said into the mirror. "I'm through worrying about all this, Kyle. I'm just going to sing for my fans, just the way I always have."

"What's with you?" he said, standing over her now.

Minmei shot to her feet and faced him. "*You* worry about our *take*, Kyle! I'm just singing for myself, do you understand me? Just for myself!"

She pushed past him and left the room.

Her anger had taken him by surprise. *Minmei just singing for herself?* he asked himself, then turned to the door with a sullen look.

He'd see about that.


Back in New Macross, Rick, Lisa, and Max and Miriya Sterling were summoned to a briefing in Admiral Gloval's quarters aboard the SDF-1. Hunter and Hayes had spent most of the day filling out reports concerning that morning's incident with the Zentraedi malcontents. Rick was sore head to foot from Bagzent's finger flick. Max and Miriya were *sans* Dana, their child, for a change but joined at the hip nonetheless.

Gloval looked plain tired. Perhaps, as a former Earth hero had once remarked, "it wasn't the years, it was the miles." He'd been spending more and more of his time in the old ship, and on those rare occasions when he did put in an appearance elsewhere, he seemed impatient and troubled. Gone was the tolerant, accepting paternal figure who shared the sense of fear and purpose that united the rest of them. In his place was a man of secret purpose, bearing the weight of the world on his narrow shoulders. Exedore, who in a sense had become his right-hand man, was also in attendance.

"What I'm about to tell you is strictly confidential," Gloval told the four RDF commanders. "Not a word of this is to leave this room. If it were to get out, the damage would be catastrophic."

The old man was seated at his desk; behind him the clear starry night poured in through the fortress's massive permaglass window.

The commanders responded with a crisp, "Yes, sir."

Exedore stepped forward to address them now, the whites of his eyes practically glowing in the dim room.

"Yesterday, we finally spotted the Zentraedi automated Robotech factory satellite. Space cruisers large enough to destroy the Earth with a single blast are being constructed within the satellite." He caught their gasps of surprise and hastened to add, "Yes, it is a terrible thing."

"Listen carefully," said Gloval, more harshly than was necessary. He was standing now, palms flat against the desk. "I want you people to survey that system and bring me additional data on the satellite."

The four commanders exchanged puzzled looks. There was something the old man wasn't telling them—aside from answering how it was they were supposed to get offworld—unless of course he was planning to recommission the SDF-1 itself.

"Commander Breetai will fill you in on the details," Gloval explained after a moment. "We have no way of knowing if and when the remaining Zentraedi will attack us again, but for our own defense we have to have as many space cruisers as we can lay our hands on." He turned to them now to emphasize the point, "You understand that."

"Yes," Exedore said softly. His eyes were closed, his brow furrowed, and one could almost believe that he felt a twinge of pain at the thought of bringing warships to bear against his own kind once again.

Rick and the others voiced their assent: It not only meant that they would be leaving the planet again, it meant that they would be relying on the Zentraedi as well. And yet Gloval was right: *It was for their own defense.*

Minmei stepped onto the stage and grasped the microphone. Colored spots played across the plank floor, until at last a single rose-toned beam of light found and encompassed her in its warm glow. Her face was sad, blue eyes wide and full of loss. The crowd was chanting, "We love Minmei, we love Minmei," but all she could think about was Rick, Kyle, those giant Zentraedi who had fought in the streets of New Macross only hours ago.

She felt as though she had failed everyone.

She had decided to scrap the first upbeat tune of the set and go immediately into "Touch and Go," a laid-back number that started with a simple piano and string riff and bass slide but grew somber and melancholy at the F-sharp minor/C-sharp 7 bridge, with a sort of crying guitar distortion punctuation backed by a stiff snare beat.

I always think of you,
Dream of you late at night.
What do you do,
When I turn out the light?
No matter who I touch,
It is you I still see.
I can't believe
What has happened to me.

Tears began to form in her eyes as she sang. The audience was mesmerized by her performance. She sensed this and began to experience an extraordinary sense of nostalgia and yearning, entering the tune's bridge now:

It is you I miss.
It's you who's on my mind,
It's you I cannot leave
behind.

*If the connection could always be this strong,* she said to herself. *If only* she had the strength to *will* things right, and good, and peaceful. *If only* she had the power to become that symbol once again, that perfect chord everyone would vibrate to…

It's me who's lost—
The me who lost her heart—
To you who tore my heart
apart.

But *loss* was the world's new theme; loss and betrayal, anger and regret. And what could she hope to achieve against such malignant power? She had tried and failed, and the day would come soon when song itself was but a memory.

If you still think of me
How did we come to this?
Wish that I knew
It is me that you miss
Wish that I knew
It is me that you miss…

# 05

[The joint Terran/Zentraedi exploration of the SDF-1] was the only occasion when Breetai allowed himself to undergo the micronization process [prior to the SDF-3 Expeditionary Mission to Tirol]. As soon as it became obvious that Zor's prize [i.e., the Protoculture matrix] was likely to remain hidden for some time longer, Breetai immediately had himself returned to full stature. He had little of the curiosity for Micronian customs that Exedore had; nor did he share the same fascination for Minmei that was responsible for so many other deviations from the Zentraedi way. Breetai enjoyed being looked up to...

Rawlins, *Zentraedi Triumvirate: Dolza, Breetai, Khyron*

GROUND FOG LAY LIKE SPUN SUGAR ACROSS LAKE GLOVAL AND swirled through the early morning streets of New Macross like autumn ghosts. In the shadow of the gargantuan dimensional fortress—like some techno-Neptune protector—a three-stage rocket added its LOX exhaust to the mist. An RDF shuttle (the same that had carried Lisa Hayes from the SDF-1 to Alaska Base two years before) was affixed to the rocket's main booster pack.

In another part of the field, nine Veritechs were also holding in preflight status. Each ship was outfitted with deep-space augmentation pods and positioned atop individual blast shield transports.

The *Shiva* was fully primed for launch; gantries and attendance vehicles had already been pulled back, and the sound of the countdown Klaxons lent an eerie sound track to the scene.

In the control tower, techs ran last-minute crucial checks on the shuttle's propulsion and guidance systems. Readouts flashed across myriad monitor screens too quickly for the untrained eye to decipher, and two dozen voices talked at once but never at cross-purposes. Robotechnology had simplified things substantially since the pioneering days of space travel, but certain traditions and routines had been maintained.

"Calculations for orbital fluctuations have been received," one of the shuttle crew said through the comlink. "We have lock and signal, control."

"Shuttle escort," a male controller directed toward one of the Veritechs, "we are at T minus fifty and counting. Your lift-off is at T three."

A second Veritech pilot was being questioned by a female tech: "Escort V-oh-one-one-two, your gravitational tracking status is *what*? Please clarify."

"Tower control," the pilot responded. "Uh, sorry about that. Little snafu with the guidance switch, if you know what I mean…"

"Watch it next time, mister," the tech scolded him.

On the field Max and Miriya, strapped into their respective blue and red Veritechs, went through final systems checks. Max flashed his wife a thumbs-up from the cockpit as he lowered the tinted faceshield of his helmet.

Evacuation warnings were being broadcast through the field PA: "All ground support vehicles evacuate launch area immediately… All Veritechs complete final systems check… We are go for lift-off. Repeat-we are go for lift-off… Countdown commencing—T minus thirty seconds…"

In Skull One, Rick surveyed the field as the transport's massive hydraulic jacks lifted the Veritech to a seventy-two-degree launch angle. Simultaneously a thick blast shield was elevated into position behind the Veritech's aft rockets. Thinking about the importance of the mission, he was overcome by a wave of nostalgia, a curious sense of *homesickness* for space. He realized suddenly how disappointed he would have been had the admiral left him out of this one…

*"You are going to rendezvous with the Zentraedi flagship,"* Gloval had explained at the briefing. *"Only at that time will you receive your final*

*instructions. I have put Commander Breetai in charge of this mission for*
*reasons that will become clear to you later."*

Rick glanced over his shoulder at the *Shiva*, the shuttle
piggyback on its gleaming hull. It was amazing, he decided: going
off to rendezvous with Breetai, the Zentraedi who had once torn
his Vermillion Veritech limb from limb. He wondered if Lisa was
remembering that time, that kiss...

"Shuttle to tower control... all systems on-line and awaiting
green light."

"Roger, shuttle," the controller radioed to the crew. "Stand by..."

Inside the shuttle, Lisa leaned toward the permaglass porthole
closest to her seat. It was not an easy maneuver, but she hoped to
catch a glimpse of Rick's lift-off. One by one the Veritechs were
being nosed up now... Max's, Miriya's... Rick's... She pulled
herself away from the view and sighed, loud enough for Claudia and
Exedore to hear her and inquire if she was all right. It was a strange
mixture of emotions that tugged at her thoughts: memories of the
time she'd spent in Breetai's ship and recent events that continued
to confuse her feelings. In some ways this return to the stars was
less like a mission than a vacation.

"Shuttle escort launch at signal zero—*now!*"

The Veritechs lifted off, the sound of their blasts like a volley
of thunderclaps echoing around the lake. Then, with a more
continuous roar, the *Shiva* rose from its pad, a fiery morning star in
the scudded skies over New Macross.

Breetai's ship, one-time nemesis and subsequent ally of the SDF-
1, was holding at a Lagrange point inside the lunar orbit. More
than ten kilometers in length, armored and bristling with guns
like some nightmare leviathan, the vessel had never put down
on Earth. But teams of Lang's Robotechs, working side by side
with Zentraedi giants, had retrofitted the ship to accommodate
human crews. Elevators and air locks had been incorporated into
the hull; holds had been partitioned off into human-size work
spaces and quarters; automated walkways were installed; and the
astrogation hold now contained control consoles and the latest

innovations from Lang's projects-development labs. All this had been child's play for the Earth techs—many of the same men and women who had overseen the original conversion of the SDF-1, had later fabricated a city for 60,000 inside the fortress itself, and were currently involved in the construction of the SDF-2—but it had struck the Zentraedi (who had no understanding of the Robotechnology bequeathed to them by the Masters) as near miraculous.

Now, while the shuttle craft carrying Exedore, Lisa, and Claudia entered one of the flagship's docking bays, the nine Veritechs under Rick's command were reconfiguring to Guardian mode and putting down in formation on an external elevator. In the bay a human voice announced the shuttle's arrival in English.

"All personnel in docking zones D-twenty-four and D-twenty-five—attention: Micronian shuttlecraft now commencing final docking procedures in upper landing bay."

The use of the term "Micronian" was no longer considered to be pejorative, in spite of its derivation; it had simply come to mean "human-size" as opposed to "microbe-like." So Lisa and Claudia were not fazed; nor was Rick, topside, when a shock trooper welcomed the Veritechs aboard likewise.

The Zentraedi shock trooper stood a good sixty feet tall, but the fact that he was wearing armor and a helmet suggested that he might be one of the inferior class of warriors incapable of withstanding the vacuum perils of deep space unless properly outfitted.

"Uh, thanks," Rick told him through the com net. "It's good to be here." The trooper flashed him a grin and thumbs-up. "If you're ready, let's bring her down," Rick added.

The giant proudly displayed a device in his gloved hand. He tapped in a simple code, and the elevator began to drop into the ship.

Elsewhere, Lisa, Claudia, and Exedore exited the shuttle's circular hatch and descended the stairway to the hold floor. Breetai was waiting for them there, his blue uniform and brown tunic looking brand-new.

"My Micronian friends—welcome," his voice boomed.

Lisa looked up at him standing there with arms akimbo and found herself smiling. These past two years had worked a subtle magic on the commander. It was well known that he refused to micronize himself, but merely working with humans had been enough to change him somehow, soften him, Lisa thought. The gleaming plate that covered one side of his face seemed more an adornment now than anything else.

Meanwhile Exedore had stepped forward and offered a stiff human salute.

"Greetings and salutations, your Lordship. We are at your service."

Breetai bent down, a look of affection contorting his face. "It's good seeing you, Exedore... It's nice to have you back on the ship."

Exedore must have noticed the change as well, because he seemed genuinely *moved*. "Why, uh, *thank you*, sir," he stammered.

Breetai turned to Claudia and Lisa, their upturned faces betraying gentle amusement. "And I especially wish to extend a welcome to *you*," he told them, making a gallant gesture with his hand. "I am deeply honored to have you under my command."

Lisa, versed in Zentraedi protocol, returned: "It's a great honor, sir, to have this opportunity."

Breetai came down on one knee to thank her. "As you know, my people are unaccustomed to contact with beauty such as yours," he said flatteringly. "So don't be offended by any strange reactions you may encounter."

Lisa and Claudia turned to each other and laughed openly as Breetai drew himself up to full height again.

"Now then... if you'll permit, I'll show you to your quarters."

In the hangar space below the docking elevator, Max stood beneath Miriya's scarlet Guardian. He called up to the open-canopied cockpit, "Okay, that's it," signaling her with a wave of his hand. "Now bring the cradle pod down."

Miriya activated the device only recently installed in her Veritech. "Here it comes," she told him.

Servomotors whined, and a royal-blue cylindrical pod—which could have passed for a turn-of-the-century bomb—began to drop from the rear seat, riding a telescoping shaft down beneath the legs of the fighter.

A *Robotech delivery,* Max said to himself as he approached the pod. He went to work disengaging fasteners, and in a minute the pod's blunt nose swung open. Max peered inside the heavily padded interior, smiled, and said, "There…"

He reached in and pulled Dana into his arms, a tiny wiggling astronaut in a white helmet with tinted faceshield and a pink and white suit that fit her like Dr. Dentons. Dana cooed, and Max hugged her to himself.

Miriya saw him step from beneath the Veritech with Dana cradled in his arms. Max assisted Dana in a wave; Miriya smiled and felt her heart skip a beat.


Breetai paced the bridge anxiously. Terran techs had effected changes here as well. The observation bubble had been dismantled and an openwork semicircular flat-topped walkway installed in its place; human-size consoles occupied a flyout platform at the center of the arc. In addition, the circular monitor screen Max Sterling had once piloted a Veritech through was back in one piece.

"Any fluctuations from the satellite factory?" Breetai inquired into one of the binocularlike microphones.

"Negative," answered a synthesized voice. "Maintaining solar stasis."

"Notify me immediately of any change," he ordered.

"Yes, sir," the computer responded.

Breetai assumed the command chair and steepled his fingers. "Think, Breetai—think of a plan," he said aloud, as demanding of himself as he was of his troops. "If we are able to convince Reno that we have the Protoculture, we will have little difficulty in securing his complete cooperation… Otherwise, we will have quite a fight on our hands. Our forces will be vastly outnumbered."

Claudia turned from her console and monitor station on the walkway. "But we don't possess any Protoculture," she saw fit to remind him, her console mike carrying her words to the commander. "How do we convince him that we do… uuhh," clearing her throat here, her eyes going wide for an instant, "assuming we're given the chance?"

Breetai grinned. "We'll have our chance," he said certainly. "But for now, entering hyperspace is our immediate concern, wouldn't you say?"

Claudia traded looks with Lisa, seated at the adjacent station. It was obvious now that Breetai's musings were not really meant for their ears at all. Whatever the plan, it seemed likely they would be the last to know.

Max and Rick stood together on one of the moving walkways, marveling at the changes the ship had undergone and reveling in memories that time had rendered less severe.

"Hey, remember the last time we were on this ship?" asked Max.

"Heh! Being a prisoner wasn't much fun, was it?" said Rick, turning the tables on his friend's obviously rhetorical query. "I'm sure glad things have changed. I don't want to see Breetai on the other end of an autocannon ever again!"

"Yeah, after serving under Admiral Gloval, it'll be interesting to see what his ex-enemy's like."

"I just wish we knew more about this mission."

"Gloval asked me to bring my whole family along and left it at that."

Rick shook his head in puzzlement. "Why in space would the old man want you to bring Dana along?"

Max shrugged. "I don't know, Rick, but I want you to understand something: I won't put her in jeopardy, mission or no mission."

Rick looked at him squarely and said, "I won't let you."

"All polarities inside the reflex furnaces have become stabilized, Commander," Claudia told Breetai from her station.

A confusing array of data scrolled across the monitor screens, a mixture of English, Zentraedi glyphs, and the newly devised equivalency-transcription characters—phonetic Zentraedi.

A Zentraedi tech reported to Claudia that fold computations were complete, and she relayed to Breetai that all systems were go. "We can fold any time you like, sir."

He thanked her, then raised his voice to a roar.

"Begin fold operation immediately!"

As the fold generators were engaged, Protoculture commenced its magical workings on the fabric of the real world, calling forth from unknown dimensions a radiant energy that began to form itself around the ship like some shimmering amorphous aura, seemingly holing it through and through. The massive vessel lurched forward into a widening pool of white light; then it simply vanished from its Lagrange point, for one brief instant leaving behind globular eddies and masses of lambent animated light, lost moments in somewhere else's time.

# 06

Up until the end of the Second Robotech War (how Pyrrhic, how bittersweet that victory!), Protoculture was literally in the employ of the Robotech Masters; not only did it in effect keep tabs on itself for their benefit, but alerted them to changes in the fabric of the continuum. Not a single Zentraedi ship could fold without their being made aware of it.

Dr. Emil Lang, as quoted in *History of the Second Robotech War*, Vol. CCCLVII

**Y**ES... I FEEL IT...

The three Masters linked minds and once more laid their bony hands against the Protoculture cap. The mushroom-shaped device reacted to their touch, radiating that same pure light which spilled into the known universe when Breetai's ship had folded. The cap took them through the inverse world, through white holes and rifts in time, allowing them to see with an inner vision.

They were no longer in their space fortress now, but back on their homeworld, back on Tirol.

—Our former charges have allied themselves with Zor's descendants; our former charges would replace us as Masters.

—We must try again to resurrect a simulacrum of Zor.

Twenty clones had been created from Zor's body; they had been grown to maturity in biovats and held weightless in a stasis sphere. All matched his elfin likeness: handsome, dreamers all of them, youthful and graceful. But none of them had the spark of life that would replicate his thoughts and mind, that would allow the Masters to learn the whereabouts of the Protoculture matrix and the secrets of that rare process.

The Masters left the cap and stood gazing up at the stasis sphere that housed the remaining clones.

"I suggest we begin the prion synthesis immediately," said one of the Masters.

Away from the Protoculture cap they were forced to rely on ordinary, primitive speech to convey their thoughts.

"Yes, Master," a synthesized voice responded.

Three Masters positioned themselves around a saucerlike device fitted with numerous color-coded sensor pads grouped circumferentially around a central viewscreen, while a visible antigrav beam conveyed one of the lifeless clones from the stasis hemisphere of a circular biotable. The clone was placed flat on its back on it, as if it were resting on a sheet of pure light.

The three Masters placed their hands on the saucer's control pads. Roller-coaster-like readouts, hypermed schematics and X-ray displays began to flash across the circular viewscreen beneath them. Meanwhile the unmoving clone was bathed in a fountain of high-energy particles that rose from the biotable like an inverted spring rain.

"Altering positronic bombardment," said the gold-cowled Master, frowning as he watched the disappointing displays take shape.

"There's some bilateral cellular inversion," observed a second, the same one who had called for prison synthesis. "Commencing symphysis..." he announced, the sensor pads flashing like a light box.

The Masters concentrated, focusing the powers of their telepathic will, then broke off their attempts momentarily.

The clone showed no signs of cerebral activity.

"Cranial synapses are still not responding... There is the same disintegration of molecular substructures as in previous attempts."

"Yes, it has happened again... This time I think we've taken the clone from the suspension before complete maturation... We must stimulate its life function regardless," the red-cowled Master said, leaving the saucer pod.

"I suggest we alter the prionic bombardment of the upper strata," said the third Master.

Master two nodded his head and moved his left hand to a new location along the control rim. "We'll try... Augmenting prionic bombardment in increments of four..."

"Positronic emission is at maximum capability!" observed the third, his arms at his sides.

"Good—cellular agitation is critical..."

Still the clockwork schematics revealed no activity.

"It is useless... We are down to the minimum suspension material—we cannot waste it like this."

"Life is such an elementary process," said the first, standing over the now useless clone, its neural circuits fried. "Where have we gone wrong?"

Miriya relaxed back into the couch and sighed, her fingers playing absently with Dana's curls. Would she keep her dark hair? Miriya wondered; each day it seemed to be growing lighter and lighter...

The baby was peacefully asleep on her breast, and just looking at her, it was all Miriya could do to keep from weeping for joy. A miracle, she told herself ten times a day: that she and Max could produce some innocent loveliness; that she, a former warrior, could feel this way about anyone or anything. Such unknown contentment and pure rapture.

"Max." She smiled. "Look at our child. She's so peaceful."

Max glanced out from the kitchenette of their quarters aboard Breetai's ship. He was carrying a trayful of tall cocktail glasses to the sink—the aftermath of an afternoon's partying with Rick, Lisa, and Claudia—and wearing a knee-length apron that read: MAX AND MIRIYA: LIVE!

Peaceful and beautiful, both of them, he said to himself. But while Miriya seemed to be having all the fun, he was the one who was stuck with all the dishes and the cooking and more than half the time the midnight feedings.

So what he said to her in the end, without betraying any of these thoughts and just grateful for a few minutes of blessed peace, was: "Yeah... but we'd better keep our voices down or we'll wake her up."

. . .

Rick, Lisa, and Claudia were a somewhat unsteady trio returning to their quarters after the afternoon drinks they'd shared with the happy couple. Combined with the thrill of deep space (after so many planetbound months) and the effects of hyperspace travel, the drinks had left them with more than an ordinary buzz.

"… and I held little Dana the whole afternoon, and she didn't cry a bit the entire time!" Lisa was saying.

"Yes, but I don't think Miriya should have *thrown* Dana to you. She has to learn to be more careful!"

Lisa nodded, biting her lower lip. "Well, it's an adjustment for her. After all, her role model was probably the neighboring test tube."

Claudia cracked a smile in spite of herself and looked over Lisa's head at Rick, but he was too bleary-eyed to catch her gaze. "Sometimes I envy Max and Miriya for just having such a beautiful little girl," she said loudly.

"Mm-hmmm," Lisa agreed.

They had reached Lisa's quarters now, and Rick was standing off to one side vaguely thinking about how he was going to spend the rest of the day, while Lisa and Claudia exchanged good-byes. Suddenly Lisa turned to him and said: "Rick, I'm going to walk Claudia to her quarters, but if you have a minute, I'd like you to wait in my room for me—there's something I want to talk to you about."

Her request somehow managed to cut through all the cotton inside his head, and he found himself stammering, "Uhh… but…" all the while knowing that there was no way around it. It just didn't seem like she had *official* business on her mind, and he wasn't at all sure he was up to a heart-to-heart. Claudia cleared her throat. "May I remind you, Mr. Hunter, that Lisa *is* your superior."

"But I'm off duty," Rick protested, definitely not in top form today.

"So is she," Claudia laughed, throwing him an exaggerated wink.

The two of them left Rick standing there with some half-formed reply caught in his throat while they continued on down the corridor sharing a whispered exchange.

"Now then, Lisa, what can I do for you?" Claudia asked when they were some steps away.

"I just wanted to thank you for being understanding these past few weeks. It really helps to have someone to lean on."

"I know what you mean," Claudia said at the door to her quarters. "It can be rough sometimes—when you find you're in love."

Lisa still grew a little wide-eyed at hearing it stated so matter-of-factly. She blinked and swallowed hard, ready to defend herself, but Claudia cut her off.

"Go get him, okay?" A wink for Lisa also, and she was through the door.

Inside, she dropped herself on the bed and kicked off her heels, sighing: *I hope those two get it together soon.* Lisa had a habit of pushing "understanding" to the limit. And Hunter… Hunter was starting to remind her of Roy in his early days. And that wasn't necessarily a good sign.

Alone in Lisa's quarters Rick felt nervous and trapped. *His superior, huh?* Just how long was he going to have to put up with that remark? Almost three years ago—*on this very ship!*—Lisa had used that remark, and he had held it against her ever since.

Lisa had unpacked some of her things, and Rick was wandering around inspecting this and that when he saw a framed photograph on the room's desk. He picked it up and regarded it. By the look of it, it had to have been taken ten years ago. But here was Lisa looking cute in short hair and chubby face, standing alongside an older guy, taller than she was by a foot and wearing what looked to be an Afghani woven cap. Nice-looking couple, he decided. But there was something familiar about him… something that reminded him of… *Kyle!* Then this had to be Riber, Rick realized. Karl Riber, Lisa's onetime true love, who had bought it along with Mars Sara Base years ago.

His attention was so fixed on the photo that he didn't hear Lisa enter the room. She realized this and stood in the doorway a moment, not wanting to startle him or make him uncomfortable. Finally she called his name softly, and he reacted like a sneakthief caught in the act, dropping the photo sideways to the desk and apologizing.

"Oh, I'm sorry, Lisa. I didn't mean to snoop."

This angered her: after all they had been through together, after all the *time* they had spent together, sharing secret thoughts and feelings, after all the time *she* had spent at his place in New Macross familiarizing herself with *his* things...

"What do you mean 'snoop'? I have nothing to hide from you, Rick. Be my guest, look around—not that there's much here..."

"Uh, sure," he said, at a loss. "So, uh, what did you and Claudia have to say?"

Lisa dismissed her conversation with Claudia as nothing special and asked him if he wanted some tea. "You know, just a little chat," she told him from the kitchenette.

Rick righted the photo when she left the room. He joined Lisa on the couch afterward.

"Didn't sound like just a little chat to me," he braved to say, tea cup in hand.

"Well, as a matter of fact, we were talking about you." Rick squirmed in his seat. "If it concerns me and Minmei, I don't want to hear about it!"

"It wasn't at all about Minmei," she said cheerfully. "What would I possibly want to talk about her for?"

Unpracticed at this sort of thing, Lisa wished for a second that Claudia could stand over her shoulder during moments like these, feeding her the right lines or something. But oddly enough, Rick was apologizing for his tone.

"Minmei and I haven't seen much of each other in several months, and..."

"Oh, Rick," she said, perhaps too tenderly. "I know how you feel about her, so... well, there's nothing more to say about it."

*Acceptance* was the one tack she hadn't tried yet.

Rick breathed a sigh and was puzzling over how he could just politely excuse himself, when Lisa added:

"I don't know why, but I get the feeling sometimes that you... well, that's there's something you *want*..."

*Who doesn't?* Rick asked himself, wondering just what she was getting at now.

"What are you talking about?"

She made an exasperated sound. "Rick, you know what I—"

The PA chose just that moment to intervene: A female voice was calling Lisa to the bridge.

Frustrated, Lisa said, "The usual perfect timing," then laughed. "You've managed to escape unscathed once again." She stood up and bade him a resigned good-bye. "We'll try this again some other time."

Rick reacted as if a dentist had just told him to make another appointment.

Claudia had also been summoned to the bridge. She stood stiffly with Lisa now on the automated walkway that was actually the curved top rail of the observation bubble, her back to the astrogation hold. The ship had unexpectedly defolded from hyperspace, and they were once again feeling a bit shaky.

Exedore was manning one of the human-size duty stations. Breetai was seated in his command chair, a grim look on his face. When Lisa said, "Reporting as ordered," he uttered a throaty growl and inclined his head a fraction to the left, as if to indicate the object of his attention.

Claudia and Lisa about-faced and eyed an image now filling the rectangular field of the projecbeam. It was like nothing either of them had ever seen—a twisted convoluted dark mass of armor, tentacles, reflex thruster ports, and sensor devices, smoothed and eroded-looking along its dorsal side, like a monstrous hunk of extraterrestrial driftwood.

"What in space is *that*?" Claudia asked.

"That, my dear Commander Grant, is a ship from our reconnaissance force—a fairly late model if I'm not mistaken."

"B-But I've never seen anything like it!" Lisa exclaimed.

"That is not unlikely," Breetai told her.

Lisa turned to Exedore and ordered a status report.

"I have made a positive identification, and it is in fact a late-model reconnaissance vessel. It has been somewhat modified for hyperspace travel. Moreover, our scanners indicate no biological activity whatsoever."

Lisa noticed the concerned look on his face as he studied the image and attendant glyphic readouts. Sectional views and close-ups of salient features of the thing flashed across his monitor screen to illustrate his report.

Lisa sucked in her breath and turned to Breetai once more.

"Commander, we have to investigate!"

"That is completely out of the question," he snapped.

"Sir," she tried, "isn't it possible your scanning systems may have missed something? Perhaps there are Zentraedi aboard? Isn't there any margin for error?"

She didn't believe a word of it, and judging from the look on Exedore's face, neither did he. But it was possible there were weapons aboard—pods, tri-thrusters, something the Earth forces could use to beef up their arsenal.

"The information assimilated is in accordance with the galactic code," Exedore told her sternly. "'Errors' are not possible."

"We can't waste an opportunity like this—we must investigate!" she answered him, filing away "galactic code" for some future discussion. "The possibility of Zentraedi—"

"Your *compassion* is commendable," Exedore interrupted, still unconvinced. "However, it looks to me as though the vessel could be a trap."

"A trap?!"

"Yes," he continued. "We Zentraedi are known for such 'Trojan horses,' as you call them. It is not wise to take such a risk."

Claudia decided to step in. "He's right—we can't jeopardize the mission, Lisa."

"I suppose..." she said uncertainly.

"It is worse than you realize," Breetai intoned behind her. "This vessel belongs to the Robotech Masters. It is one of many which act as their eyes and ears."

*The Robotech Masters,* Lisa exclaimed to herself.

"You're saying that they could monitor our presence."

Breetai grunted. "I fear they already have."

# 07

Your Earth scientists are a fanciful lot: all this talk about time travel, relativity, looking through a telescope and being able to see the back of your own head... I suppose it all looked good on paper.

Exedore, as quoted in Lapstein's *Interviews*

DEFOLDING FROM HYPERSPACE ONCE AGAIN, BREETAI'S FLAGSHIP materialized in real time hundreds of parsecs from Earth.

If the image of the Robotech surveillance vessel had awed Lisa, the form and appearance of the automated factory satellite positively stunned her. It had the same vegetal look as the smaller vessel, the same external convolutions, cellular armor, and incomprehensible aspect, but all similarities ended there. The satellite was enormous, almost organically rose-colored in starlight, shaped in some ways like a primate brain, with at least half a dozen replicas of itself attached to the factory's median section by rigid stalklike transport tubes. In orbit around it were hundreds of Zentraedi craft: dreadnoughts, battle mecha, and Cyclops recons.

"My dear colleagues," Breetai announced as a close-up of the factory appeared in the projecbeam field, "we have arrived."

Lisa, Claudia, and Exedore looked up from their duty stations.

"It's incredible!" Claudia exclaimed breathlessly.

Lisa made a sound of amazement. "Whatever powers created that must be light-years beyond us," she said softly, recalling her first glimpse of Dolza's command center and the surveillance vessel they had left behind only hours ago. "It's still hard to believe that such things exist in our universe."

"Well, all I can say is you *better* believe it, Commander," Max Sterling chimed in from Lisa's monitor, his helmeted image filling the screen. Max and Miriya's Veritechs were in position on the docking bay elevator, preparing for launch.

Lisa went on the com net. "Max, remember: You must convince Reno that we possess the Protoculture."

"Right, Captain." He saluted and signed off.

"Exedore," Breetai said from behind Lisa. "Summon Commander Hunter to the bridge immediately."

Lisa swiveled in her seat to face the commander while Exedore carried out the order.

"What do you have in mind, Commander?" she asked rum. Breetai showed a roguish smile. "I must apologize for not having informed you sooner, but you are of course aware that diversionary tactics will be necessary if our plan is to be successful."

"I support the tactic," she said warily. "But I thought we had agreed to broadcast Minmei's voice."

"Correct," he responded, suddenly turning to Exedore. "However, we have devised a small modification."

Lisa didn't like the sound of it, especially when she saw Exedore return the commander's grin and add, "Your Lordship, that was your plan from the beginning, was it not?"

Breetai issued a short laugh. He was pleased to see that his adviser had not been completely changed by the Micronian ways; Exedore still refused to take credit for a plan, even when his inspirations had guided it.

"Your modesty equals your intelligence," Breetai told him. Then, turning again to Lisa: "Captain, *we* have decided that *the kiss* would be a more effective counterattack. Wouldn't you agree?"

Lisa's eyes went wide and unfocused; she began to slump down in her chair, her stomach in knots. "Umm… I suppose…" she managed.

"I'm sure you recall the extraordinary effect produced when you and Commander Hunter touched lips," Breetai was saying.

Claudia meanwhile had left her station and was coming Lisa's way, a sly smile already in place. "Liisaaa…" she said playfully, putting her hand on her friend's shoulder. "Come on, Captain, can't you see it's a *brilliant* plan! Nothing to get upset about."

Lisa was staring blankly at the monitor. *Plan?* she asked herself. Yeah, but what plan were they all talking about: the one to fool the Zentraedi Reno, or were these galactic events suddenly taking second place to a universal conspiracy meant to bring her and Rick together?

"Lord Breetai," a Zentraedi voice announced. "A transmission from Commander Reno. Shall I put it through, sir?"

Breetai raised himself out of the command chair.

"Yes. And use the translator so that our friends can understand him."

Reno's face and shoulders took shape in the projecbeam field. A swarthy male with large eyes, dark busy brows, and a square jaw, Reno wore a blue uniform with red piping and a green command tunic. He opened with formalities, although wariness was suggested by both his voice and his stance.

"Welcome," he told Breetai, the English translation out of synch with the movements of his full lips. "It has been a long time, Commander."

"Indeed," said Breetai flatly. They hadn't seen each other since that fateful day long ago when Zor had been killed; when Dolza had ordered Reno to return the scientist's body to the Masters; when Zentraedi and Invid had fought to the death... Breetai unconsciously stroked the faceplate that concealed scars from those less confused times...

"Do you come as friend or foe?"

"We have retrieved the Protoculture matrix from Zor's dimensional fortress, Reno. Our powers are limitless. I have come to demand that you surrender the satellite to me. Join me and my friendship is yours. Oppose me and perish."

Reno snorted. "So you've stolen Zor's science, have you?... And of course you and your new Micronian playmates plan to keep it from the Masters... Any other amusing anecdotes you wish to relate, Breetai?"

The commander smiled knowingly. "Actually, I do have something else you might enjoy—it should be arriving at any minute."

"I'll attempt to contain my boundless excitement," Reno responded sarcastically.

Rick was at just that moment arriving on the bridge. He saluted Breetai from the curved walkway.

"Right on time," said the pleased commander. He turned to Reno and issued his ultimatum: "This is your last opportunity to comply."

"Ridiculous!" Reno started to say. "The very fact that you have rejected the ways of the Robotech Masters indicates—" But his own projecbeam now closed on Lisa and Rick standing together on the walkway. Reno's bushy brows went up. "What?! A female talking to a male?!"

Breetai's one eye sparkled. "Yes, that's right, Commander. And now…"—like a master of ceremonies—"if you watch closely, you will witness the strange and glorious freedom that comes from Protoculture."

Rick meanwhile was baffled, casting confused looks to Breetai and the projecbeam image of Reno. He turned hopelessly to Lisa and whispered, "What the heck is going on?"

"It's all right," Lisa said soothingly.

Rick stiffened. If Lisa was telling him it was all right, he was *really* worried!


"Max," Miriya said over the tac net after hearing him laugh, "is there any chance Rick won't go along with the change in the diversionary tactics?"

Their Veritechs were wing to wing in deep space, closing fast on Reno's command ship, thrusters blue in the eternal night. The drama on the bridge was being carried over the com net.

"I don't think I'm going to like this one little bit," Rick was grumbling.

Max grinned. "Don't worry about him, Miriya. Remember: Rick Hunter is a *professional*." The humor was of course lost on her.

Miriya recognized Lisa's voice now: "Yes, mister, I'm making it an order!"

"It's his *job* to take orders," she heard Max comment. *He's so serious,* she thought. Perhaps there was another side to kissing that she wasn't aware of—some *strategic* method Max had yet to teach her. As a mother she was somewhat alarmed; but the warrior and fighter ace was downright angered. This was, after all, a dangerous mission they were flying. There might not be another opportunity...

"Do you think we'll ever have a chance to touch lips again, Max?"

Max regarded her red-suited image on his commo screen and smiled. "I *promise* we will," he assured her.

"The Veritechs are within range of the tracking systems now," Claudia reported from her duty station.

"Commence broadcast," Breetai told Exedore, ignoring for a moment the minor battle that was in progress on the walkway below him.

"No, Lisa!" Rick was shouting. "I'm not going to consent to the kiss, orders or no orders! I'm sorry, but my mind is made up!"

*Diversionary tactic,* Rick said to himself with distaste. Of all the cheap shots Lisa could have taken! Just something to divert him from thinking about—

*Minmei?!*

Rick blinked; Minmei's "Stagefright" was booming over the bridge PA system, and he seemed to be the only one surprised by it.

Although that wasn't quite true: Reno's crew wasn't prepared for this, either. Nor had they the chance to become gradually accustomed to singing, as Breetai's crew had. Consequently, they reacted as though a combination of nerve gas, high-frequency sound, and unbridled electricity had suddenly been leveled against the ship.

"Aaarh! Blast it!" screamed Reno, throwing his hands up to his ears.

"Can't stand it!" yelled his crew members, who were dropping like flies at their duty stations.

"No more!" Reno pleaded. "Please turn it off!"

It never failed to amaze Rick that Minmei's voice could elicit such contrary responses from beings who supposedly had common ancestors; but he had scarcely a moment to dwell on it. Lisa had grabbed him by the shoulders and was now putting all she had into *offensive osculation.* And *whew!*—this was a different Lisa from the one who'd kissed him closed-mouthed in front of Breetai three years ago!

"Well, Reno," Breetai was saying at the same time, a self-satisfied smile on his face, "perhaps *this* will please you."

Reno, who had averted his gaze from the projecbeam, turned back to it now that Breetai had lowered that "sound weapon." But the image that greeted his eyes was even more debilitating: Here were two Micronians...

"—*touching lips??!!*" Reno wailed. He stared at the field, nauseated by confusion and some *feeling* even more alien to his system. From the ship's astrogation hold came shrills of protest, pain, and caterwauling. Reno covered his eyes with his hand: He had barely enough strength to deactivate the projecbeam and felt close to fainting when he managed to do so. Below him, several of his troops had collapsed. But he would never admit to defeat.

"Breetai," he said into the mike, his voice a harsh croak. "That display gained you nothing."

Breetai looked exulted nonetheless, ready to lay down his trump card now.

"Reno has discontinued transmission," a tech informed him.

Then Claudia relayed that the Veritechs were approaching their mission objective.

"Contact in three seconds..."

Reno was just regaining his composure when a fiery explosion breached the starboard hull of the astrogation hold, the force of it throwing several of his goliath crewmen clear across the vast chamber. He cursed and at the same time complimented Breetai for the brilliant execution of his plan; his diversionary tactics— *those Micronian secret weapons*—having completely disarmed his crew. Regardless, he had the presence of mind to bellow:

"Attack alert!"

On Breetai's ship, Claudia updated that the Veritechs had made a successful entry.

"The baby is with Max and Miriya," Lisa said worriedly to a still dazed and confused Rick.

"Huh?!" he stammered in response, promising this was the last time he'd permit himself to be so far removed from mission planning.

When the smoke and fire had been sucked from the hold of Reno's ship, the hull self-repaired, and two Micronian battle mecha, one red, one blue, rested side by side on the deck, fully encircled by Zentraedi troops wielding pulsed-laser rifles.

"All units prepare to destroy Micronian fighters on my command!" Reno growled, his troops snapping to and arming their weapons. He asked himself just what Breetai was hoping to gain by the insertion of such a small strike force, then directed his orders to the pilots of the Veritechs, using what little he knew of their language. "Micronians! You are completely surrounded! Surrender immediately and you will be allowed to live!"

The augmentation packs of the fighters elevated.

"This is it, Max," Miriya said over the net. "Wish me luck."

"You've got it," Max returned. "Everything'll be fine—I'm right here."

From the observation bubble high above the deck, Reno watched as the canopy of the red fighter went up. The Micronian pilot stood up and removed its helmet, shaking its long green mane free. Reno's mouth fell open when the Micronian spoke.

"I am not a Micronian," Miriya announced in Reno's own tongue, "but a micronized Zentraedi warrior."

Reno didn't doubt it for a second; in fact, he recognized her.

"You are Miriya Parino!" he said in disbelief. "You were second in command under Azonia!"

Miriya pointed to Max's Veritech. "Allow me to present Lieutenant Maximillian Sterling, an officer with the Earth forces… and my *mate*."

Max removed his thinking cap and stood up in the cockpit.

"What is this thing, 'mate'?" Reno was asking. "He is merely a Micronian."

Max said loud enough for Miriya to hear: "Show him the baby."

And Miriya did just that, lifting Dana from the cockpit and raising her into view. The infant was cradled in her arms, wearing the same helmet and Dr. Dentons EVA suit.

For a moment Reno didn't know what he was looking at, but there was something about the thing that filled him with fear nonetheless. From his vantage it appeared to be some sort of… *micronized Micronian!*

"But this is impossible!"

His rough and ready troops were similarly nonplussed.

"What is that thing?" one asked.

"By the twelve moons— it's deformed."

"Look—it moves!"

"A mutant!" someone insisted.

In an effort to rub her eyes, Dana had brought her tiny gloved fists up to the helmet faceshield.

Miriya resumed, "In the Micronian language, this is what's called an 'infant'—actually created inside my own body. By both of us," she hastened to add, indicating Max.

Max nodded, humbly, and smiled.

"It is *love* that is the basis of Protoculture," Miriya continued. She lifted Dana over her head, the baby smiling and cooing in response. "You cannot conquer *love!*"

Reno's face began twitching uncontrollably at Miriya's mention of the shibboleth—*Protoculture!*

Still holding Dana aloft, Miriya pivoted through a 360-degree turn, preaching to the full circle. "Observe the power of Protoculture— the power of love!"

"It's a mutation," one of the troops shouted, letting his weapon fall and fleeing the hold.

"It's contagious!" said another, also fleeing.

More discarded weapons crashed to the deck.

Dana, innocent, continued to wave her arms and smile.

Overcome, the troops began to desert their posts.

Beads of sweat pouring from his face, Reno was ranting into the mike: "Stay where you are, you cowards! Come back! It must be a trick!" Ultimately he backed away, turned, and ran from the observation bubble.

# 08

Love, like *size*, had lost all meaning—love was a battle maneuver, kissing a diversionary tactic. The only one among us who seemed to know anything about that elusive emotion was Miriya, wedded to the infant she'd given birth to as much as she was Max.

The Collected Journals of Admiral Rick Hunter

Reports from Max and Miriya verified the success of the third stage of the ruse.

Breetai reasoned (correctly, as it would unfold) that Reno would retreat just far enough from the cruiser's command center to restabilize himself and sound general quarters. It was possible that the three-act tactic had convinced him to surrender—and indeed, Breetai was more than willing to give him the benefit of the doubt before mounting a full-scale assault on the heavily guarded satellite—but unlikely.

At her duty station well below Breetai's thoughtful look, Claudia Grant laughed. "I can't imagine why Reno's crew reacted like that," she was telling Lisa Hayes. "I think Max and Miriya's baby is pretty cute, don't you?"

"Oh, stop it, Claudia," said Lisa.

Breetai noticed that Commander Hunter appeared somewhat debilitated by the kiss he performed with Lisa before he had rushed from the bridge. It was no wonder that Hunter had expressed such initial reluctance, Breetai thought. *Obviously, kissing is something not to be taken lightly.*

"None of you should underestimate the opposition's capability,"

Breetai warned the humans now, putting a quick end to the jokes. "Inform your mecha pilots to stand by."

Claudia followed through immediately, ordering Blue, Green, and Brown teams to their launch platforms. And not a minute later Max reported that Reno had called for a counterstrike; he and Miriya were going to make a break for it.

*Dana!* Claudia recalled, suddenly full of concern.

"Launch all mecha!" Breetai bellowed.

Human and Zentraedi mecha launched themselves from the warship's bays while the vessels of Reno's fleet massed for attack.

Rick led his small squad of seven Veritechs against them, side by side with the Zentraedi's ostrich-like Battlepods, tri-thrusters, and pursuit ships. Two years had passed since he had engaged any enemy in deep space, but it suddenly felt like no time had elapsed. The silence, the zero-g spherical explosions that bloomed in the night like flowers of death, the eerie glow of thruster fire, the disinterested shimmer of starlight, the cacophony that poured into his helmet through the tactical net—a hallucinatory symphony of panicked commands, frenzied warnings, and final screams.

He knew that he would need to clear his mind of all thoughts, righteous and otherwise, to come through this unscathed. Out here thoughts were a pilot's number one enemy, because they invariably impeded productive interface with the Veritech. So he let it all go— the questions still there after four years of combat, the faces of those left behind—and the mecha picked up that vibe transmitted through the sensor-studded gloves and "thinking cap" to its Protoculture heart and led him once more through hell's gates.

"I don't want your excuses!" Reno screamed, slamming his fist down on the substation console—an elaborate control center even by Zentraedi standards, salmon-colored and organic in design with no less than a dozen circular monitor screens. "Now order your troops to battle stations! Do you understand?!"

The face of Reno's red-haired lieutenant seemed to blanch in the projecbeam. He raised his shaking hands into view.

"But sir, our troops are terrified of Micronian contamination!"

"Nonsense!" howled Reno. "You have your orders: Destroy the infected mecha at once! I have spoken!"

"We are within range, m'lord," Exedore reported calmly.

Breetai regarded the projecbeam. Reno's fleet had foolishly formed up on the commander's own cruiser, now itself bracketed in Breetai's deadly sights. *So much the easier, then,* he said to himself.

At one time the strength of Breetai's conditioning would have made such a thing impossible, but the Zentraedi imperative had been altered beyond recognition by the campaign directed against Zor's dimensional fortress. To remain on the side of the Robotech Masters was to be Breetai's enemy.

"On my command, Exedore..." said the commander.

Skull One's lateral thrusters edged the Veritech out of the arena—momentarily. There were still half a dozen Battlepods on his tail crosshatching space with angry bolts of cannon fire, *and these guys were on his side!* The non-allied pods were of course a concern, but the crazed random firing of Breetai's troops was life-threatening! From the sound of the shrieks and comments coming through the net, Rick knew that he wasn't alone in his fear.

Now, with no advance warning from the bridge, the warship's main cannon had been armed. Pinpoints of dazzling light had erupted across the blunt nose of the battlewagon; in a moment, Rick knew from previous battles, a lethal slice of orange death would streak from each of these, holing their targets with an immeasurable force.

Breetai's ship was within point-blank range of Reno's, taking aim at the bow of the smaller ship where the bridge and astrogational section were located. Rick went on the tac net, warning his fellow pilots to steer clear, and voiced a prayer that Max and Miriya had escaped safely.

The Robotech factory satellite, its secondary modules like small moons, spun slowly on its axis—a small world unto itself, barely visible now in the blinding light of a thousand small novas.

Miriya held Dana in her lap, her right hand gripping the Veritech's Hotas. Flashes of stroboscopic light threw flaming reds and blazing yellows into the cockpit. In no other battle (and there had been many) had she been possessed by such fury. Even that on-and-off dogfight she had waged against Max couldn't measure up to the intensity and *need* she now felt. It was as though her entire body was rallying to the cause; as though the small life she held in her arms was a treasure more precious than any the universe could offer, a life worth preserving at all costs...

She and Max had blasted free of Reno's ship, but they were far from safe.

"Enemy projectiles bearing 977L!" Claudia told her through the com net, the alarm in her voice unmasked. "Two triple-fins attempting interception!"

"Watch it, Max!" said Miriya, as concerned for his safety as she was for Dana's. "I've got them!"

She thumbed the trigger button on the Hotas, releasing four white-tipped heat-seekers, which tore from the Veritech's missile tubes. They found one of the tri-thrusters, blowing it to pieces, while the second craft disappeared beneath Miriya's own. She engaged the underside lasers as the enemy made its pass, the intensified light searing open the cockpit of the triple-fin, decommissioning it.

Miriya heard Max breathe a sigh of relief and thank her.

She returned the sign and clutched Dana more tightly to herself, the infant waving her arms joyously at the fiery spectacle.

"Fire!" said Breetai.

A rain of supercharged energy ripped from the nose of the warship, converging on Reno's ship, individual bolts tearing through it as if it wasn't there. And in scarcely a second, it wasn't— its superstructure flayed and bow blown open beyond self-repair.

Like a whale swallowing a stick of dynamite, Rick decided. He imagined Reno's swift death: energy brilliant as blizzard snow wiping him from life...

"Dead ahead!" one of his wingmen said through the net.

Rick looked forward into a swarm of Officer's Pods, triple-fins, and tactical Battlepods.

"Fire all proton missiles on my command," he told his squad. "Now!"

Hundreds of missiles dropped from their pylons and fuselage tubes, blowtorching into the midst of the enemy cloud, taking out fighter after fighter.

Meanwhile, Breetai's dreadnought had loosed follow-up fusillades against two more warships in what had once been Reno's fleet. Explosions lit local space like a brief birth of suns, Robotech husks drifting derelict in the perpetual darkness. On the observation balcony, Breetai stood rigid with his hands behind his back, impassively watching projecbeam views of the battle. Victory was assured: one more blow struck against the Masters. But he was aware that this was a minor triumph in the war that would someday rage at Earth's gateway; and as bright as this moment might seem, he would be powerless when that day arrived—

"Squadron leader requesting assistance in the Third Quadrant," one of his officers interrupted.

"Is the neutron cannon ready?" Breetai asked.

"Eighty percent," Claudia reported sharply.

"We have positive lock and focus on photon particle tracking beam," Lisa added, her monitor schematic resembling a star map overlaid with doodles. "All Veritechs and pods have cleared the field of fire."

"Neutron exchange complete," Claudia updated.

Breetai's lips became a thin line.

"Sanitize the area," he ordered.

Rick led his squad—Max and Miriya among them now—to the safe coordinates Lisa had supplied him. Hearing the go signal for the neutron cannon given, he glanced back at Breetai's ship, expecting to witness an outpouring of energy to make all previous discharges pale by comparison. But he saw no sign of fire, only the invisible particle beam's awesome and horrific effect: Nearly every mecha in the cannon's line of fire was disintegrated. Some exploded, others came apart, while still others simply vanished without a trace.

The number of dead was beyond his ability to calculate. And he found himself thinking about the Zentraedi on Earth—the micronized ones who were struggling to adapt to a new culture, the malcontents who wandered the wastes in search of new wars. With Reno's defeat (according to Exedore), the race would be close to extinction.

It was as if they knew somehow that their time had come. They had honored their imperative; they had chased Zor's fortress for their Masters and done their best to reclaim it. But in truth, they had traveled clear across the galaxy to fulfill a greater imperative: *They had come to Earth to die.*

"Lord Breetai," said Exedore. "The remaining troops have agreed to surrender." His voice gave no hint of sadness at the nearly total annihilation of Reno's forces; if anything, it carried a suggestion of relief. His commander's reign was now supreme—as it was always meant to be, with or without the Protoculture matrix.

Breetai was seated in the command chair. Regally, he stated, "Let the prisoners know that we will gladly accept all who wish to join us."

Exedore spoke into the mike at his duty station. "Lord Breetai extends his greetings to all Zentraedi prisoners. Furthermore, it is his pleasure to extend a full pardon to those who wish to join the United Forces under his command."

Standing now, Breetai announced: "Our victory may very well mark the dawn of a new era in galactic relations."

His ship was already closing on the Robotech factory satellite, a bioluminescent mollusk in the blackness of space, strings of lights girdling it like some Christmas ornament. The prize had been won. And if those defeated troops on bended knee weren't testament enough to the win, one had simply to look out on that seemingly limitless field of mecha and cruiser debris through which his ship moved, the remnants of the last remaining Zentraedi fleet.

# 09

The transport of the Robotech factory satellite to Earthspace was another one of the malign miracles visited upon us. Certainly Gloval and Breetai had only our best interests in mind, but shouldn't it have occurred to them that if the Robotech Masters had been able to track Zor's dimensional fortress here, they could surely do the same with the satellite? Like Zor before him, Breetai thought he was doing Earth a favor... This renders his comment (upon manifesting in Earthspace with the factory) doubly ironic: "We've made it," he is quoted as saying. "It is good to be back home."

Dr. Lazlo Zand, *On Earth As It Is In Hell:*
*Recollections of the Robotech War*

**A**RMAGEDDON PLAYED IN FULL COLOR ON OVAL-SHAPED VIEWING screen in Tirol's central ministry, an organic room like those in the Masters' space fortresses, cathedraled by columns that might have been living ligaments and sheathed neurons. Representatives from the Council of Elders, the Robotech Masters, the Young Lords, and the Scientists were in attendance—the Elders and the Masters in unvarying groups of three at their Protoculture caps. The Young Lords, a bearded trio, balding in spite of their relative youth, were intermediaries between the Masters themselves and the Empire clones. Three was sacred, three was eternal, the irreligious trinity ruling what remained of Tirol's social structure—what remained of a race long past decadence. Such had been the influence of the tripartite Invid flower, the Flower of Life...

One of the Masters had the floor now: With Reno's defeat at

the hands of the traitor, Breetai, their hopes for reclaiming Zor's fortress had been dashed.

—I think that the best plan is to completely educate another deprivation tank tissue, so that by the time we get to Earth, it will appear human.

One of the Scientists risked a question, approaching the Masters' station arrogantly, leaving his partners in the Triumvirate to labor at the spacetime calculations.

—What makes you think this clone will be different from the others that have been generated and failed?

—Mmmm?!

A second Master took up the challenge, regarding the Scientist with distaste. An exotic-looking, blue-lipped, and scarlet-haired androgynous clone. What had they accomplished, the Master asked himself before replying, in creating this young generation of long-haired, toga-clad beings who walked a thin line between life and death?

—Such insolence! Have you forgotten that these previous efforts have been undertaken without proper attention to the basic matrix generation process? This clone will have ample time to mature, but we must begin programming the tissue immediately. Of the fourteen remaining in the tank, one will surely take on the full psychic likeness of Zor.

—One more thing, Master: Why don't we check the matrix figures on the remaining Protoculture? Perhaps such a journey is unnecessary.

—The figures have been checked and rechecked. We don't even have enough to make the hyperspace-fold to the Earth system.

The female member of the Triumvirate turned from her calculations.

—I understand, Master.

—*So!* We will begin the trip under reflex power and rely on the remaining clone matrix cell tissue to complete our mission.

—Twenty long years by their reckoning…And how many of us will survive such a journey?

—If only three of us survive, it will be enough. This is our only chance to regain control of the Protoculture.

One of the Masters gestured to the oval screen—a view of deep space captured by their surveillance vessel: the mecha debris and litter that was once Reno's fleet.

—After all, look what is left of *their* culture; observe and survey the remnants of their once-great armada. We must have that Protoculture matrix! Even if it takes twenty years and the last developing clone from our tank! We have no choice but to proceed. I can see no other solution. *So!* If there is nothing further…

A member of the Elder Triumvirate spoke through lips as cracked as baked clay, a face as wrinkled as history itself.

"Elder Council is with you."

The central speaker of the Masters inclined his head in a bow.

"We acknowledge your wisdom and appreciate the generosity of your support, Elder. It is out of loyalty to you and our forefathers that we have decided thus."

"We understand the importance of this mission, not only for our race but for all intelligent life in the quadrant."

A second Elder bestowed his blessings on the voyage.

"Proceed with your plan, then; but know that there can be no margin for error without grave consequences."

"The future of all cultures is in your hands."

A *twenty-year journey through the universe,* the Masters thought in unison. Twenty years to regain a prize stolen from them by a renegade scientist. Would they prevail? Was there not one loyal Zentraedi left?… Yes, there was. But could even he succeed where so many had failed?

*Khyron!*

Khyron was their last hope!

Human and Zentraedi teams labored long and hard to ready the factory for a hyperspace jump. In less than a week's time it defolded in lunar orbit, winking into real time without incident Breetai's dreadnought, his human and Zentraedi crew, and thousands of converted warriors inside the satellite's womb. The commander's prime concern had been the removal of the factory from the Robotech Masters' realm; their reach, however, was to prove greater than even he had anticipated.

The Veritech Team, as well as Lisa and Claudia, returned to New Macross, and in their place arrived scores of Lang's Robotechnicians, who dispersed themselves through the factory like kids on a scavenger hunt. Finally, Admiral Gloval himself was shuttled up to Earth's new satellite; well aware that the factory was now Earth's only hope against a potential follow-up attack by the Robotech Masters, he traveled with his fingers crossed. Claudia Grant was his escort.

Dr. Lang and several of his techs were on hand to greet them. Pleasantries were dispensed with, and Gloval was led immediately to one of the factory's automated assembly lines, where alien devices, still only half-understood by Lang, turned out Battlepod carapaces and ordnance muzzles.

Gloval marveled at the sight of these machines at work: Pods were being fabricated as though they were chocolate candy shells. From a basic sludge vat of raw metals to finished product in minutes; servos, arc welders, presses, and shapers doing the work of thousands of men. Unpiloted pods, controlled by computers even Lang refused to tamper with, marched in rows, one above the other, along powered transport belts, pausing at each work station for yet another automated miracle. All the while a synthesized Zentraedi voice actually *spoke* to the devices, directing them in their tasks. Exedore had substituted a translation, which was playing as Gloval stood transfixed.

"Make ready units one fifty-two and one fifty-eight for protobolt adjustments and laser-bond processes. Units one fifty-nine to one sixty-five are on-line for radio-krypto equipment encoding…"

"But what does it mean?" Gloval asked Lang.

The scientist shook his head, marblelike eyes penetrating Gloval's own. "We don't know, Admiral. But do not be deceived by what you see. This entire complex is but a ghost of its former self—nothing is running to completion." Lang made a sweeping gesture. "Whatever fuels this place—and I see no reason to suppose that it is any different than that which runs the SDF-1—has lost its original potency."

"Protoculture," Gloval said flatly.

Lang gave a tight-lipped nod and pointed to the line of half-finished pods along the conveyor belt. "Observe…"

Gloval narrowed his eyes, not sure what he was supposed to be looking at. But shortly the Doctor's meaning became obvious.

"Warning! Shut down! Warning! Damage!..." the synthesized voice began to repeat. Suddenly one of the pods on the belt was encased in a spider web of angry electrical energy. Servowelders and grappling arms flailed about in the fire, falling limp as the pod split apart and the great machines ground to a halt.

"Status report on the way," one of Lang's techs said to Gloval.

The admiral rubbed his chin and hid a look of disappointment.

No one spoke for a moment, save for a human voice from the PA calling maintenance personnel to the process center. Then Exedore arrived on the scene. Gloval had not seen him since the evening the satellite mission was first discussed.

"How are you, sir?" Exedore asked, concerned but having already guessed Gloval's response.

"Not as well as I was hoping," Gloval confessed. "When can you start operating again?"

"I'm afraid the situation is worse than first thought." Never one to mince words, Exedore added: "We may be down permanently."

"Are you certain?"

The Zentraedi adviser nodded, grimly.

Claudia gasped. "But our defense depends on continued operation!"

Gloval clasped his hands behind his back, refusing to accept the prognosis. "Carry on," he told Exedore. "Do what you can to get things running again. Do something—*anything!*"

"Veritech team leader," said the female voice over Rick's com net. "We have a disturbance in New Detroit City. Can you respond?"

Rick accessed the relevant chart as he went on the net. "Roger, control." He glanced at the monitor: His team was over the southern tip of Lake Michigan, close to what was once the city of Chicago. "We are approximately three minutes ETA of New Detroit City. What's up?"

"Zentraedi workers have broken into Fort Breetai. They've taken over the sizing chamber and are attempting to transport it from the city."

Rick gritted his teeth and exhaled sharply. "Listen up," he told his wingmen. "We're on alert. Hit your afterburners and follow my lead."

New Detroit had risen up around a Zentraedi warship that had crashed there during Dolza's apocalyptic attack; its mile-high hulk still dominated the city and the surrounding cratered wastes like some leaning tower of malice. The population of the city was predominantly Zentraedi, many micronized by order of the New Council and hundreds more who were full-size workers in the nearby steel factories. In addition, though, there was a sizable contingent of civil defense forces stationed there to guard a sizing chamber that had been removed from the derelict ship but had yet to be transported to New Macross, where similar ones were being stored.

Rick caught sight of the chamber on his first pass over the high-tech fort. A convoy of vehicles was tearing along the rampart that led to the underground storage facilities. Updated reports from control indicated that at least twelve Humans and three Zentraedi giants lay dead inside.

The clear-blue nose-cone-like device had been placed on an enormous flatbed, hauled by a powerful tug with tires like massive rollers; two micronized aliens were in the drivers' seats, three more up top, along with three blue-uniformed giants, two of whom were attempting to stabilize the hastily guy-wired and turnbuckled chamber. Behind the flatbed were two more enormous eight-wheeled transports, each bearing malcontents armed with autocannons. Rick saw them open fire on the laser-sentry posts. At street level, they turned their cannons on everything that moved, scattering workers and pedestrians alike.

"We're over the disturbance now," Rick reported in. "Left wing, wait until they've reached the outskirts, then go in low and give them a warning."

The renegade Zentraedis spotted the Veritechs and opened up with indiscriminate volleys as the fighters fell from the sky. Rick and his team rolled out, dodging autocannon slugs and gatling spray as they broke formation.

*So much for scare tactics,* Rick said to himself, Skull One flying inverted and low over the tortuous landscape outside the city limits.

"Left wing, knock one of the giants off the lead unit immediately!"

Rick completed his roll as his wingman went out, reconfiguring the Veritech to Guardian mode and swooping down on the convoy. The Zentraedis were loosing continuous fire, but Rick could discern the early stages of panic in their flight. The highway was full of twists and turns here, and the converter had made the flatbed dangerously top-heavy.

The armed alien on the flatbed got off one last shot before Rick's wingman, now in Battloid mode, blasted him from the vehicle. The road was also proving too much for the drivers to handle; Rick watched the vehicle screech through a tight S-turn, leave the road, clinging to a raised course of shoulder, then bounce back to the tarmac, where the giant's micronized accomplices decided to call it quits.

Meanwhile, the rest of the Veritech group had reconfigured to Battloid mode and put down ahead of the halted convoy.

Rick completed his descent and advanced his mecha in a run, chain-gun gripped in the metalshod right hand and leveled against the giants on the flatbed. One Zentraedi was dead on the road. The others began to throw down their weapons as Rick spoke.

"Don't move or you'll be destroyed!" he called out over the external speakers. The Battloids came to a stop and spread out. "It's useless to resist," Rick continued. "You are completely surrounded. You must understand that what you have done is unacceptable behavior by Human standards and that you will be punished." Rick stepped his mecha forward. "Now, the Protoculture chamber will be returned to the fort."

Three hundred miles to the northeast of New Detroit a thick blanket of newly fallen snow covered the war-ravaged terrain. Khyron's ship had landed here, having used up almost all of the Protoculture reserves that drove its reflex engines to free itself from Alaska's glacial hold.

Zentraedi Battlepods sat in the snowfields like unhatched eggs abandoned by an uncaring mother. Deserters from the Micronian population centers and factories continued to arrive in stolen transports and tugs. The hulk of a Zentraedi warship overlooked the scene, its pointed bow thrust deep into the frigid earth like a spear, alien tripetaled flowers surrounding it, hearty enough to pierce the permafrost.

Khyron had followed a trail of such ships clear across the northern wastes, salvaging what he could in the way of weapons and foodstuffs, marveling at the resilience of the Invid Flower of Life, gone to seed and flower as the Protoculture in the ship's drives had disintegrated.

Now in the command center of his ship, he received word that his plan to steal the sizing converter had failed.

"Idiot!" Khyron said to his second, Grel, standing in stiff posture before the Backstabber. Azonia was seated in the command chair, her legs crossed, a mischievous look on her face. "Your feeble plan has failed us again!"

Grel frowned. "I'm sorry, sir, but our agents failed to eliminate the communications center and the Veritechs—"

"Enough!" Khyron interrupted him, raising his fist. "Our soldiers couldn't even defend themselves!"

"But sir, if you had only listened to…" Grel started to say, and regretted it at once. The plan had been Azonia's, not his; but there was little chance that Khyron would blame her—not now that a *special* relationship had been forged… And especially since his commander had begun to use the dried Invid leaves once again. As if that wasn't enough, the troops had all seen the Robotech satellite appear in Earth's skies, and that meant only one thing: The Micronians had somehow defeated Reno!

"Shut up, Grel!" Azonia barked at him. "Under your leadership they couldn't possibly have succeeded!"

"Well, I wouldn't exactly say—"

"Do not interrupt," she continued, folding her arms and turning her back to him.

Khyron too mocked him with a short laugh, and Grel felt the anger rising within him despite his best efforts to keep his emotions in check. It was bad enough that he and the troops had been forced to live these past two years with a female in their midst, but now to be humiliated like this...

"You should have had no trouble capturing the sizing chamber," Azonia was saying when he at last exploded, murder in his eyes as he leaned toward her.

"It might appear that all of this is my fault, but the truth is that you—"

"Enough!" Azonia screamed, standing, nearly hysterical. "I don't want to hear any excuses from you!"

Khyron stepped between them, angrier and louder than the two of them combined. "Stop arguing, Azonia! And Grel, I want you to listen, understand me?! I don't have to tell you what the appearance of that satellite signals—the last hope for the Masters lies with *us*!"

"Sir, I'm listening," Grel said, spent and surrendering.

Khyron, spittle forming at the edges of his maniacal snarl, waved a fist in Grel's face. "Excellent... because my reputation is on the line, and I need that sizing chamber to save *face*, and if I don't get it... *I shan't spare yours!* Now, get out of here!"

Grel stiffened, then began to slink away like a beaten dog.

When he had left the room, Azonia moved to Khyron's side, pressing herself against him suggestively, her voice coy and teasing.

"Tell me confidentially, Khyron, do you really think he can handle it?"

"For his sake, I hope so," Khyron said through gritted teeth, seemingly unaware of Azonia's closeness until she risked putting a hand on his shoulder.

"You know how to handle your troops, Khyron," she purred in his ear.

He pushed her away with just enough force to convey his seriousness, not wanting to confront the hurt look he was sure to find on her face. There was no use denying the bewildering attraction he had come to feel for her in their joint exile—these novel pleasures of the flesh they had discovered; but she had to be made to understand that there was a time and place for such things and that war and victory still came first—*would always come first!* No other Zentraedi had more right to these sensual gifts than he, but his troops deserved more than a commander who was less committed to them than they were to him. He had promised to return the deserters to full size, and he meant to do it—with or without Grel. And, should it come down to it, with or without Azonia.

"Now, listen," he confided. "There is something I couldn't tell Grel but I'm going to tell you... I'm going after that sizing chamber myself—I can't count on him to do it. I want you to stay here and take command while I'm gone."

He turned and walked away from her without another word, unaware of the smile that had appeared on her face.

Azonia savored the thought of commanding Khyron's troops in his absence. "This is starting to get good," she said aloud after a moment.

# 10

If we accept for a moment the view expressed by some of our twentieth-century colleagues—*that children live out the unconscious lives of their parents*—and apply that to the Robotech Masters and their "children," the Zentraedi, we will arrive at a most revealing scenario. It is clear at this point that the Masters were the ones devoid of emotions. War though the Zentraedi did, their true imperative was centered on individuation and the search for self... One has to wonder about Zor, however: He served the Masters yet did not count himself among them. Who can say to what extent he himself was affected by Protoculture?

Zeitgeist, *Alien Psychology*

RETURNED TO NEW DETROIT, THE SIZING CHAMBER WAS BEING hoisted back into its cradle, a four-poled hangar similar to those used to support freestanding tents. A large crowd had gathered, Humans and coveralled Zentraedi giants as well as their micronized brethren. Rick was supervising the crane operation, while the rest of his team, still in their Battloids, patrolled a cordoned-off area in front of Fort Breetai. There was palpable tension in the air.

"That's it... just a little more and we're there," Rick instructed the operating engineer. "Fine, fine... just keep it coming..."

As the chamber's round base was sliding down into the cradle's cup, a black sports car screeched to a halt nearby. Rick glanced over his shoulder and spied Minmei in the passenger seat.

New Detroit's Mayor, Owen Harding, a well-built man with a full head of thick white hair and a walrus mustache, was in the back seat. He recognized Rick from the days he himself had served with the RDF aboard the SDF-1. Harding stepped out and asked if everything was well in hand, whether there was anything he could do. Minmei had been recognized by the crowd, and two policemen moved in to keep them from gathering around the car.

Rick saluted and gestured to the sizing chamber. "I need your people to provide security for this device."

"I can't do that, Commander," the mayor said firmly. "Most of the population here is Zentraedi—as you can see. Securing this 'device,' as you call it, is a military matter. We've already had enough trouble, and I'm not about to add to it by throwing my police force into the middle of it. Let's not beat around the bush, Commander, we all know what this machine is for."

Rick shook his long hair back from his face and squared his shoulders, trying not to think about the fact that Minmei was only fifteen feet away. "That's exactly why I need your support, sir— just until my superiors dispatch a proper unit to guard it. We can't afford to allow this chamber to fall into the wrong hands."

The crowd didn't like what they heard. Even before Rick finished, they were letting the mayor know where they stood. "What're you saying, *Commander*—that we're all thieves?!" someone shouted.

"Just who is the 'wrong hands,' flyboy?!" from another.

The mayor made a hopeless gesture. "You see what I'm up against."

"Look," Rick emphasized, "I know you don't want any more trouble here, but I'm only asking for your cooperation for a matter of days—"

"I can't become involved in this."

"It's for *their* protection, too," Rick said, pointing to the crowd. "We all agreed to honor the Council's—"

"Then tell all the facts," a familiar voice interrupted.

Rick turned and saw Kyle walking toward him from the car.

"Military business, Kyle—stay out of it!" Rick warned him sternly. Kyle was the last thing this situation needed: Mr. Agitation.

"This isn't just military business," Kyle started in, addressing Rick and the crowd. "It's everyone's, *Commander*, because you're talking about the Zentraedi's right to return to their normal size whenever they want."

Rick was incredulous. *Sure, why not let them all change back—especially now that they are hungry for warfare again and the closest targets are one-tenth their size.*

"You're nuts, Kyle."

"If you think I'm kidding, you're even a bigger fool than I thought. And I'm sure that most of the people in this city would agree with me… isn't that right?"

Rick didn't bother to look around. Shouts of agreement rang out; micronized Zentraedi raised their fists, and the giants growled. Kyle's violent scene with Minmei in Granite City replayed itself in Rick's mind, along with Max's remarks about Kyle's false pacifism. *Minmei,* he said to himself, giving her a sidelong glance and reading some sort of warning in those blue eyes. *How could you be blood with this—*

"Well, do you…" Kyle was demanding. Picking up on Rick's inattention, he followed his gaze, reading his thoughts now… *So he's still in love with her.*

Rick heard Kyle snort, then say to the crowd:

"When they take away your right to use the Protoculture chamber, it's the first step toward martial law! You lived under that for long enough before you came to Earth! This chamber should be controlled by the people of this city!"

One of the giants stomped his feet, rocking the area.

"You better listen to us right now!" he bellowed.

"This is our city," said a human female, much to Rick's amazement, "not the military's!"

*Was there some sort of reverse contagion at work here?*

"Why don't you just climb into your little plane and get out of here while you still can!" yelled a second giant.

"Listen to me!" Rick pleaded, actually managing to quiet them for a moment. "Isn't it better to have this machine secure from people who would use it against you than to endanger the whole city with it!"

"I'm getting sick of your lies, Hunter!" Kyle ranted at him, furious.

"Beat it!" the crowd shouted.

"We're not going to take this anymore!"

The mayor edged over to Rick, eyes on the alert for airborne bottles or rocks. "They mean business," he said warily.

"I've heard enough!" Rick began to shout back at them. "This is military property! I've been ordered to secure it, and I intend to carry out those orders!"

"We'll see about that!" one of the giants threatened.

Rick signaled his squad lieutenant. Two of the Battloids raised their gatlings and stepped forward.

The crowd took a collective intake of breath, but the comments persisted, helped along by Kyle, who was now attempting to lead them in a chant: "Leave here now! Leave here now!" punctuating his call with raised arm gestures.

The crowd joined him, holding their ground.

"Please, *Commander*," said the mayor, "You have to go."

Rick narrowed his eyes and shot Kyle a deadly look. He scanned the crowd-angry faces and towering Zentraedi. If the Battloids opened fire, there would be all hell to pay; and if they didn't... if they just let the chamber sit...

*No win!* Rick screamed at himself, sending a tormented look Minmei's way before he turned his back on all of them and walked off.

In the snowfields at civilization's edge, Khyron received word of the turnabout in New Detroit. He couldn't have been more pleased.

He stood now at the head of a double-rowed column made up of twelve of his finest troops, each, like himself, suited up in Zentraedi power armor.

"Listen to me," he instructed them. "We are the *last true Zentraedi!* We must take that sizing chamber! *No* sacrifice is too great!"

With that, he fired the body suit's self-contained thrusters and lifted off, his elite squad following him into the skies.

Having left two of his Veritech corporals to stand guard over the chamber, Rick and his remaining team were on their way back to New Macross. Bill "Willy" Mammoth, one of Skull One's wingmen, had raised Rick on the tac net.

"Go ahead, Willy, I'm readying you," Rick told him.

"It's just that it's bothering, sir. All that power. Leaving it there'n... well, forget it..."

"Say it, Willy. I told you, I'm reading you."

"Well… I just hate to see a bunch of innocent people get hurt because of some hare-brained troublemaker."

An image of Kyle's angry eyes flashed in Rick's memory. That fight long ago in the *White Dragon*, Kyle's *pacifist* speeches, his violent temper…

"Yeah, so do I," Rick said grimly.

Mayor Harding was having misgivings. Two of Hunter's Battloids along with one of New Detroit's own civil defense Gladiators were supervising the transfer of the sizing chamber from Fort Breetai to its new resting place inside the city's exposition center, a sprawling complex of pavilions and theaters constructed in the "Hollywood" style—a pagodalike multistoried building here, a Mesoamerican temple there.

"But will it be safe?" the mayor wondered aloud.

Lynn-Kyle and Minmei were with him in the center's vast rotunda, observing the transfer procedure.

"Something's bothering you, Mr. Mayor?" Minmei asked leadingly, hoping Harding had had a change of mind and would recall Rick and his squad.

The mayor bit at the ends of his mustache. "To be honest, I was just thinking about the consequences of having the sizing chamber here should we be attacked… I only hope I made the right decision."

"Attacked by whom?" Kyle said harshly. "The war's *over*."

"Not to hear Commander Hunter tell it." Harding shrugged. "All these disaffected Zentraedi who have been leaving the cities and setting up camps *out there*…"

Kyle made a dismissive gesture. "Forget about it—all that's just disinformation. They'll say anything to convince us that we still need their protection. Besides, there are a lot of peaceful Zentraedi citizens here. They'd help us if things got bad."

"I hope you're right."

"Don't worry. We did the right thing, and the people appreciate it. This chamber rightfully belongs to the Zentraedi people, and that's all that really matters."

The mayor cleared his throat.

Kyle said, "Trust me."

Harding, however, remained unconvinced. Kyle noticed that Minmei seemed preoccupied and uneasy, her face inordinately pale. The mayor had insisted on taking them on a tour of the center's new theater, and it was here that Kyle decided to change strategies.

"I've got an idea," Kyle told both of them, a lighter tone in his voice now. "How about a goodwill concert to promote brotherhood between the Human and Zentraedi citizens of New Detroit?"

All at once Harding grew excited. "Why, that would be great! I mean, if Minmei would consent… on such short notice and all…"

"Of course she'll do it," Kyle continued, although Minmei hadn't so much as acknowledged the idea by word or movement.

"The whole city'll turn out," said Harding, the wheels turning. He began to lead them down one of the theater aisles toward the large stage. "We can seat almost three thousand in here, and wait till you see our lighting system." Cupping his hands to his mouth, he called to the balcony: "Pops! Open up the main curtain and hit the spots!"

An unseen old-timer answered, "Sure thing, Mr. Mayor," and the curtain began to rise. Kyle took advantage of the moment to turn to Minmei and whisper, "What's your problem today, Minmei? You're going to upset the mayor."

"I just don't feel like singing," she said firmly.

Kyle raised his voice. "And just why not?"

"Because I don't think this place is safe with that Protoculture chamber here and because of what you did to Commander Hunter," she answered, not looking at him. "He is my close friend, you know. *He saved my life.*"

Kyle smirked. "You make it sound like it's a lot more than friendship, Minmei."

"You asked me, so I told you."

"Take it easy," he said. "First of all, we're not in any danger. And second, it didn't hurt your flyboy any to have his feathers ruffled. It keeps him sharp."

Minmei gritted her teeth.

"Here they come, Mr. Mayor!" the veteran stagehand yelled.

Two intense spots converged center stage, and Mayor Harding turned to Minmei proudly.

"How 'bout that?"

Kyle put on his best smile and stepped forward. "I think the whole *place* looks great, sir."

The mayor beamed and started to say, "Thank you—" when a loud concussion rocked the theater. A second and third explosion followed in quick succession, violent enough to send them all reeling in the aisle.

"What the—"

"Quick! Outside!" Kyle ordered.

No doubt a Minmei concert would have worked wonders in New Detroit, but how could Kyle have known that Khyron had made a previous booking?

Immediately upon his return to New Macross, Rick was ordered to report to Admiral Gloval in the briefing room of the SDF-1. There he found the admiral, Exedore, Lisa, Claudia, Max, Miriya, and the infamous Terrible Trio—Sammie, Vanessa, and Kim—seated at the room's circular table. Rick made his report directly to Gloval, summarizing the events that had transpired in New Detroit.

Gloval wore a look of despair. "I want to commend you for exercising good judgment, Captain," he told Rick after a moment. Then he gestured to the table. "I wanted you to be included in this. Exedore…" he said, sitting back to listen.

The enigmatic Zentraedi inclined his head. "I have finished my research on the relationship between Protoculture and the Zentraedi," he began rather soberly. "My race…" Exedore's face appeared to blanch. "My race was bio-genetically engineered by the Robotech Masters for the sole purpose of fighting. Protoculture, the discovery of the Tirolian scientist Zor was utilized in both the initial cloning process and the enlargement of our physical being."

Miriya gasped. "You're saying that the Masters *created* us? It can't be true, Exedore. I have memories of my youth, my upbringing, my training…"

Exedore shut his eyes and shook his head sadly. "Implants, engrams… The Masters were clever to equip us with both racial and individual memories. But they neglected what is more important…"

Gloval cleared his throat. "Exedore, if I may?…"

Exedore gestures his assent, and Gloval addressed the table.

"These people you call the Robotech Masters were extremely proud of their advanced and powerful civilization. Hyperspace drives and advanced weaponry were already a part of their culture. But soon after the discovery of Protoculture and the science of Robotechnology, they dreamed of ruling a galactic empire. And they decided to develop a police force to protect their acquisitions—the Zentraedi."

The table went silent.

"For hundreds of years," the admiral continued, his eyes finding Miriya and Exedore, "you secured worlds for them—these *Masters* you were programmed to obey. But this scientist, Zor, the very genius who designed and built this ship, was silently working at tearing down what his co-opted discoveries had unleashed. It was believed that he hid his secrets somewhere in this ship and tried to send it from the Masters' grasp.

"And you, Exedore, and Miriya, Breetai, the old one you called Dolza, even Khyron, you were ordered to reclaim this ship at all costs—because without Zor's secrets the Robotech Masters won't be able to fulfill their dreams of empire. Without *Protoculture*, they will fall, as surely as their race of giant warriors fell. Confronted with emotions and feelings for the first time, the Zentraedi were powerless. For surely that race of perverted geniuses had no love left in their hearts. And they will be defeated for the very same reasons."

Exedore looked up now. "Do not underestimate them, Admiral," he cautioned. He was impressed by Gloval's summary and evaluation, but the admiral spoke as if all of this was behind them, when in fact *it was just beginning*. "We Zentraedi no longer pose a threat to you, it is true. But believe me when I say this: The Masters are out there waiting, and they will not rest until the Protoculture matrix is theirs. Earth has been brought once to the brink of extinction by their power. Do not mislead yourselves by thinking that it can never happen again."

Gloval absorbed this silently. "Are there any questions?"

"Are the people of Earth… are they Protoculture?" Miriya asked, full of concern as she looked at Max. There was Dana—how could they explain *Dana*!

Gloval said, "I know what you're thinking, Miriya. But no. You see, we go back millions of years. And the Zentraedi…"

"But how can you explain that our genetic structures are nearly identical?" Max wanted to know.

Exedore spoke to that. "Nearly identical. *Nearly* identical. What is most plausible is that our genetic… stuff was cloned from the Masters themselves. They are, after all, er… Micronians like yourselves. Look for a similarity there, Lieutenant Sterling, not among the Zentraedi."

Max shook his head in a confused manner. "But I don't see that it matters any!"

"It doesn't," Miriya said, putting her hand over his.

"Then it must figure," Lisa pointed out, "that the people of Earth and the people of Tirol *did* have a common ancestry."

"I no longer believe that to be so," said Exedore. "A coincidence, I'm afraid."

Rick's eyebrows went up. "A *coincidence*?! But Exedore, the odds on that have to be nothing less than… ah—"

"Astronomical," Lisa finished.

Gloval snorted. "And the odds against our coexisting together?… They might be even greater."

"So the truth is," Exedore concluded, "that although our races are similar, they are not identical. My race, the Zentraedi, are devoid of everything save the bio-genetically engineered desire to fight. We were nothing but *toys* to our creators—*toys of destruction*."

# 11

I had wandered into an inviting, friendly-looking house that sat flush
with the street, thinking it would be a shortcut to Rick (who was
speeding away in his Veritech). The house was filled with antiques
from the last century, and I was running around touching everything.
But then when I remembered Rick and began to search for an exit,
I couldn't find a way out! I started opening doors only to find more
doors behind them, and more doors behind those, and more doors!
...I woke up more frightened than I've ever been in a long time. It was
more frightening than real life.

From the diary of Lynn-Minmei

YLE, MINMEI, AND MAYOR HARDING REACHED THE THEATER'S
main entrance in time to see the descent of Kyron's airborne
assault team.

They fell upon the city like a storm loosed from hell itself,
resembling deep-sea divers and Roman gladiators in their powered
armor. Civil defense Destroids were already in the streets, pouring
missiles and transuranic slugs into the skies. An Excalibur MK VI,
its slung cannons blazing, caught two enemy projectiles, which
blew it off its feet, continuous fire from one of the cannons holing
storefronts all along the avenue. Nearby, a Spartan was faring better,
having taken out two of the enemy raiders with Stilettos launched
from the mecha's drumlike missile tubes. But it too fell when one
of the Zentraedi, easily as tall as the Spartan and better equipped to
maneuver, barreled into it, sending the thing reeling back against the
facade of the exposition theater, sparking out as it collapsed to the

street, missiles dropping from one of its shattered drums.

Kyle and the others pressed themselves deeper into the theater's doorway, shivering with fear, as cries for help rang out from the demolished Spartan.

"Our worst fears are realized!" yelled Harding.

Minmei clutched Kyle's arm, eyes shut tight, mouth wide in a silent scream.

Khyron's troops were bent on nothing less than extermination; they had had two years to work up to this, two unrelieved years, just waiting for an opportunity to make the Micronians pay for all the hardships they had been forced to endure. Now all the tension and hatred left them in a frenzied rush, with New Detroit left to reap that violent harvest.

Everything was a target, and no one was spared—human or citified Zentraedi.

"Fight to the end!" the Backstabber yelled into his comlink. "Find that chamber! No sacrifice is too great for a cause dearer than life itself!"

Still, the Earth forces would not surrender; courage and valor were the words of the day, although few remained by battle's end to sing the praises of those who died.

A Gladiator went hand to hand with one of the alien berserkers, dropping the Zentraedi with a left uppercut when its own cannons were depleted of charge, only to have the downed enemy blow it to smithereens with a blast from its top-mounted gun.

Another of Khyron's elite paused before a parking lot simply to incinerate the vehicles and huddled groups of humans inside.

"I'm getting high reflex-activity readings," Khyron announced, his suit displays flashing. Locators were helping him zero-in on the exposition hall. "All troops converge on my signal immediately!"

Minmei and Kyle, wrapped around each other in the theater's entrance alcove, watched as enemy troops made for the hall, the streets vibrating to the crash of their metalshod boots.

*What have I done?!* Kyle asked himself, close to panic.

Inside the hall, the RDF sentries received word that the first defenses had been overrun; the enemy was headed their way. A

446                                           JACK McKINNEY

Battloid raised its chain gun at the sound of pounding on the hall's foot-thick steel door. The three-member crews of the Gladiators readied themselves.

Mayor Harding had left Kyle and Minmei and rushed to the basement of the building. He and an unfortunate office worker were looking in on the hall and sizing chamber now, a Permaglass shield the only thing separating them from fire, as the door was suddenly blown open and Khyron's troops poured in.

One of the Gladiators stepped forward to engage a Zentraedi, spitting harmless machine gun fire into the face of its enemy as the two of them grappled. Khyron's soldier got hold of the mecha's face plates, swung it clean off its feet, and sent the hapless thing crashing through the building's reinforced concrete wall.

The second Gladiator was similarly engaged, one-on-one and winning his close-in fight... until a Zentraedi appeared without warning overhead, blasting his way through the ceiling and descending on the mecha forcefully enough to split it wide-open, crown to crotch.

All this time, the Battloid was emptying its gatling against a Zentraedi wall of armor. When the pilot saw the Gladiator take that terrible overhead blow, he ran his mecha forward, autocannon raised high like a sledgehammer, only to receive a paralyzing spin kick to the abdomen by an enemy with eyes behind its head.

"That finishes it!" exclaimed the mayor, turning away from the carnage. "We've lost the sizing chamber!"

"Chances are, no matter how much they are exposed to humans, the Zentraedi are still a war-loving race," Exedore told the admiral after the session. He, Gloval, and Claudia had walked together from the briefing room to one of the fortress's enormous supply holds.

"But many of your people have discovered an entirely different kind of life here on Earth, Exedore," Gloval argued. "You shouldn't be so... *hard* on yourself."

"Admiral Gloval's right," Claudia added. "Many of your people supported peace as soon as they were exposed to the possibility, and most still do."

"I agree that many want it," Exedore countered, unmoved by their obvious attempts to put him at ease. After all, it wasn't a question of *feeling* this way or that way about it; it was simply a fact: The Zentraedi were warriors. Exedore wondered sometimes if humans didn't carry the emotional mode too far. "It's just that I now worry about those who still want to fight. Surely you understand that, Admiral."

"Yes," Gloval admitted, lifting his pipe to his lips, uncertain where this discussion was headed.

"Doesn't it seem strange, then, that no matter how far even *superior* civilizations have progressed, there never seems to be a solution to the problem of aggression and warfare?"

"How true, my friend."

"That applies to humans, too," Exedore continued. "In fact, there is no known species in the whole of the Fourth Quadrant that has ever turned its back on war."

"Regrettably so," Gloval said.

A comtone sounded, and the admiral reached for a handset, grunting yeses and nos into it, his nostrils flaring. He re-cradled it with a slam and barked at Claudia:

"Find Hunter immediately!"

Claudia stepped back somewhat. "Sir?"

"Zentraedi have attacked New Detroit!"

"A toy of destruction," Rick was repeating to Lisa. "That's what he called himself, right?"

The two of them were standing in one of the SDF-1's open bays, twenty feet above the shimmering lake, staring into orange and pink sunset clouds.

"Genetically programmed for fighting… it's pretty sad."

"If you ask me, it sounds a lot like us," said Lisa.

Rick frowned at her.

"Aren't *we* always fighting?" she asked him.

"That's not fair, Lisa."

"I wasn't trying to be… Just making a point."

"Oh, yeah?"

"Rick! Lisa!"

They turned together to find Claudia striding toward them.

"I'm glad I found you two," she said, out of breath. "Zentraedi forces have attacked New Detroit!"

Rick's eyes went wide. "Forces?! What d' ya mean? Who—malcontents?"

Claudia shook her head. "Not from the sound of it. Their communication signal was lost about ten minutes ago, but one of our recon ships spotted the fighting. It looks like a coordinated attack. At least a dozen Zentraedi in power armor."

Lisa watched Rick go livid. He clenched his fists and cursed.

"Rick, it's not your fault!" she said quickly, reaching for him. But he was already through the doorway in a run.

"Who?!" Lisa demanded of Claudia. "Who?!"

The reinforcements from New Macross arrived on the scene too late. Rick, in Skull One, had a bird's-eye view of the battle's aftermath: fire, smoke, and several square blocks of total devastation. New Detroit's central avenues were torn up and cratered; civil defense mecha lay smoldering in the streets, while rescue crews worked frantically to free trapped crew members. The area around the exposition hall was unrecognizable. The main buildings had been reduced to rubble.

Rick blamed himself.

It had been his assignment to secure the Protoculture chamber, he told himself, but he had let Kyle and those easily influenced Zentraedi take charge.

Below him now, cranes and bulldozers worked to haul a damaged Excalibur MK VI to its feet; the mecha's twin cannons had been blown from the body. Elsewhere, the hulk of a Gladiator was being towed from an intersection; it looked as though it had been split down the middle by an ax.

Though Rick was shouldering the blame, he couldn't very well charge himself with the attack, and this was what began to concern him. The only incident that approached the level of destruction here was the raid on New Portland some weeks earlier. There, renegade Zentraedi had broken into one of the armories, commandeered three Battlepods, and indulged themselves in a brief orgy of terror. But that was the isolated case; most often, the trouble was confined to fighting—the recent fistfight in the streets of Macross was a perfect example. But now, within twenty-four hours, there had been two major raids.

The recon pilots who had witnessed the attack saw no battlepods; Zentraedi power armor, they said. Rick thought about it: Many of the warships that had crashed on Earth had been stripped of weapons during Reconstruction two years ago. But of course it was possible that a band of outlaw giants had chanced upon a ship and found the power suits... but what would they want with the sizing chamber? A blow for independence? Furthermore, the attack on New Detroit had been too well coordinated: It was purposeful, nothing like the sprees of random violence Exedore was worried about—the resurgence of the Zentraedi programming.

Rick found himself thinking about the Zentraedi's raid on Macross City, when it was still located in the belly of the SDF-1. As he looked over New Detroit, he began to feel that there was something familiar about this patterned ruination, almost as if it bore the earmarks of someone thought to be dead—someone whom the Zentraedi themselves had feared..

While Rick was dropping the Veritech in for a closer look, searching for an uncluttered stretch of street to put down on, Kyle and Minmei were preparing to flee the city. The black sports car, which had been parked near the theater entrance, had miraculously survived the destruction, and Kyle was behind the wheel now, twisting the ignition key and cursing the thing for not turning over. Above the sleek vehicle towered the lifeless body of an Excalibur, spread-eagle in a death pose against the theater facade.

"You crummy no-good pile of junk!" Kyle shouted at the car, pumping the accelerator pedal for all it was worth.

"Hurry, Kyle!" Minmei yelled from the street. "They might be coming back!"

"I'm doing the best I can!" he told her angrily.

Minmei was wringing her hands and pacing, a victim of fear and self-torment. Like Rick, she was blaming herself for the tragedy.

*I could have stopped Kyle, and none of this would have happened! How could I let him do that to Rick?! If I had just stepped in when Rick looked at me like that...*

The sports car's engine fired, and Kyle hurrahed.

"Minmei, get in! Let's go!" She was either in shock or lost in thought, he decided, because he wasn't getting through to her. *"Minmei!"* he tried again.

She turned to him as if they had all the time in the world, pure loathing in her eyes. She reached for the handle of the back door and threw it open.

Rick spotted her.

He had the Veritech reconfigured to Guardian mode and was setting down on the theater street several blocks behind Kyle's sports car. Kyle was revving the engine, too preoccupied to take notice of the mecha's descent, but Minmei caught sight of it in the rearview mirror and spun around in her seat.

She sucked in her breath. "Kyle, please don't leave yet—it's Rick!"

Skull One had landed. The radome of the Veritech was on the ground, tail up in the air like some mechanical bird searching the earth for worms. Rick had sprung the canopy and was climbing out of the cockpit.

Kyle said, "We're late already!" and gunned it, patching out on the pavement.

Rick was chasing them on foot, and Minmei could read his lips: He was calling her name, asking them to stop.

"Turn around, Minmei!" Kyle yelled at her from the front seat. "It's too late!"

Her eyes filled with tears.

"Good-bye," she said softly to the small figure in the distance. *It's too late!*

# 12

The Zentraedi are not inferior beings, nor should they be treated like second-class citizens. They should enjoy the same freedoms the rest of us do—life, liberty, and the pursuit of happiness! No one can say for sure that some of them won't turn to crime or evil purpose, but at least we won't have repressed their right to express themselves—we won't have acted like fascists!

From Lynn-Kyle's *Pamphlets on Pacificism*

"THE LINE FORMS TO THE RIGHT!" ONE OF KHYRON'S SHOCK troopers bellowed, gesturing with his massive hand.

Forty feet below the giant's angry face, a micronized Zentraedi, recently returned to the fold, wondered whether he had made the right decision in joining the Backstabber's battalion. It had been an arduous journey from New Detroit to reach these snowbound wastes. And now there was a certain *hostility* in the cold air...

But all at once the shock trooper was grinning, then laughing and slapping his knee. Other soldiers were, too, and all along the line of micronized Zentraedi the laughing was spreading.

"Well, that's what the *Micronians* are always saying, isn't it?" the shock trooper asked his diminutive counterpart. "'Line forms on the right,' 'no parking,' 'no smoking'... I mean, we Zentraedi warriors have *learned* something from the Micronians, haven't we? We want to do things orderly from now on—*peacefully!*"

"Yeah, we're *all* for *peace!*" said a second trooper, brandishing his laser rifle.

A third added: "We love their homeworld *so much* that we're just gonna *take* it from them!"

And everyone laughed and threw in comments of their own, giants and micronized Zentraedi alike.

The line led to the sizing chamber, back where it belonged in Khyron's command ship now, where one by one, Zentraedi were doffing their Micronian outfits and being returned to full size in the conversion tank. It was a slow and tedious process, but no one seemed to mind the wait.

Khyron least of all.

He and Azonia were sitting some distance from the tank, sipping at tall glasses of an intoxicating drink one of the former micronized Zentraedi had introduced to the growing outlaw battalion. Khyron had taken a fancy to sipping straws, and his consort humored him by having one in her glass also. Close by, Grel watched them nervously.

Word had spread quickly through the wastelands that Khyron had captured the sizing chamber and was ready to make good his promise to return to full size any who would join his army. Each day the lines of micronized Zentraedi males and females grew longer, and Khyron was reveling in his victory. He had instructed his spies in the population centers to make it known just who had taken the chamber.

*Let them know that* Khyron *had returned!*

Laughing hysterically, the warlord lifted the glass in a toast to a soldier who stepped from the chamber, naked and powerful once again.

"Now that Khyron is in possession of the chamber, he will rebuild his army and crush the Micronians! This wretched world will have known better days!"

With that, he heaved his glass at the line, shattering it against the interior hull of the ship and showering those waiting with glass and liquid.

Azonia looked at her lord and grinned proudly. She was half in love with his insanity, though "love" was hardly the word she would have used.

But suddenly Khyron wasn't smiling.

He made a guttural sound, stood up, and began to pace back

and forth in front of her, his clenched fists at his hips holding the campaign cloak away from his scarlet uniform.

"Not enough," he said at last. "Not enough!" He whirled on her without warning, devilish fire in his eyes. "We must have the Protoculture matrix itself—Zor's factory. It's somewhere still in that rotting fortress, and we will have it!"

"But m'lord, surely the Micronians—" Azonia started to say.

"Bah!" he interrupted her. "Do you think they would even bother to guard this chamber if they had the factory in their possession?! No, I don't think they've found it yet."

"Yes, but—"

Khyron smashed a fist into his open palm. "We will do what we should have done all along. We will *take* something from them— something they deem *precious*. And we will hold it in exchange for the dimensional fortress. There is a Micronian word for it…" He turned to Grel and said, "The *word*, Grel—what is it?"

"'Ransom,' m'lord," came the speedy reply.

"Ransom, yes…" Khyron repeated softly. He gestured to the sizing chamber and instructed Grel to speed things along. "We're going to be leaving here shortly," he told him. "But we must not forget to leave a little surprise for our Micronian friends…"

New Detroit had been placed under martial law. There was little reason to expect a follow-up attack, but the theft of the chamber had the resident Zentraedi up in arms. Some of them believed that the Earth Forces had *staged* a Zentraedi raid in order to gain possession of the chamber. Reconstruction crews and civil defense reinforcements had been flown in from New Macross, and a field headquarters (with Lisa Hayes in command) had been set up outside the city limits.

Whether a band of malcontents from the wastes were responsible for the assault had yet to be confirmed, but reconnaissance flights north of the city had revealed the existence of a base of some sort, hastily constructed around the remains of a crashed warship whose towering presence dominated that snowy region. A squadron of Veritechs under Rick Hunter's command was on its way to the site now, Lisa Hayes monitoring their progress from field HQ.

Her screen had indicated no activity at the base, but when the Cat's-Eye recon dropped in for a closer pass, the displays had lit up: Enemy missiles had been launched at the approaching fighter group. Lisa went on the com net to warn them.

"Uh, we roger that, control," said one of Rick's wingmen.

"Enemy projectiles maintaining tracking status. Onboard computers calculate impact in twenty-three seconds."

"Evasive!" Lisa heard Rick say over the net.

Lisa watched her screen: The missiles were altering course along with the fighters.

"They're still on your tail, Captain Hunter."

An elisted rating at the adjacent duty station turned to her suddenly. "Picking up a sudden heat emission."

Lisa was already back on the net. "The projectiles have activated protoboosters."

"All units," said Rick. "Send out ghosts."

Lisa studied the screen once more. The missiles had gained on the group, but the false radar images had confused them. Only momentarily, however. "They're swung around, Commander."

"Roger, control," Rick answered her. "We've got them in our tracking monitors. We're planning a surprise of our own."

Skull One led the group in a formation climb and rollout that brought them nose to nose with the incoming projectiles. Though eyes saw nothing but blue skies ahead, the Veritech screens read death.

"Impact in seven seconds," said Rick's wingman.

"Hammerheads on my mark—now!"

Missiles tore from launch tubes as the group loosed a bit of their own death; projectiles met their match head-on, annihilating one another in a series of explosions that fused into an expanding sphere of fire. The Veritechs boostered through this, scorching themselves but holding their own, the route to the enemy base clear as day.

They came in hugging the barren terrain, the tail section of the leaning hulk looming into view over the horizon. Rick ordered reconfiguration to Guardian mode when they hit the edge of the target zone and released a score of heat-seekers to announce his arrival.

The ground at the base of the Zentraedi warship was instantly torn up. Snow and dirt were blown from the area, and when the smoke cleared, there was a newly formed crater fully encircling the ruined warship. But no return fire or signs of activity. Rick guessed what the Cat's-Eye indicators would reveal.

"Scanners indicate no sign of life," the recon plane's pilot said after a moment.

Rick ordered half the team to put down and reconfigure to Battloid mode for entry into the warship itself.

The fact that the hulk might contain unknown traps was on everyone's mind, so they were to proceed slowly and methodically, compartment by compartment, checking for timing devices or infrared trips.

Three hours in, they reached a central cargo hold filled with Zentraedi ordnance and supplies. Still there was no sign of occupation.

"Looks like the place was deserted when we hit it," Rick proposed. "The missiles must've been controlled from a remote outpost."

Rick's wingman gestured the arm of his Battloid to the weapons cache.

"Take a look at all this stuff."

Rick did just that: If whoever had been here could afford to leave all this behind, he didn't want to think about what they were packing when they left.

He moved his mecha toward one of the supply crates, absently brushing dirt from the lid. As he did so, the insignia of the Botoru Battalion began to take shape.

*Khyron's battalion!*

One thousand miles west of New Detroit, through land that had once been home to dinosaurs and buffalo, ran the strangest group of creatures to appear in many a day: a small band of giant humanoids and ostrichlike machines—in some cases a commingling of the two, with giants riding piggyback on the pods, hands clamped tightly on plastron guns, legs wrapped around the pods' spherical bodies. Inside an Officer's Pod at the head of the pack sat the Backstabber, a crazed smile on his face while he addressed the images of Azonia and Grel on the mecha's circular screens.

"Everything is going just as I planned," he congratulated himself. "These Micronians are so easily fooled."

"Battlepods are now approaching objective," his consort reported.

"No sign of any resistance," said Grel. "They fell for it!" Khyron cackled.

As a cowboy would the rump of a horse, he slapped the console of the pod to hurry it along. He could hear the mechaless giants give out a war cry as they crowned a small rise in the terrain and moved on the city.

Denver, Colorado, as it was once known, had been rebuilt so often since the Global Civil War and had undergone so many name changes that people now referred to it simply as "the City." An enormous hangar used decades before by America's NORAD had been converted to a concert hall large enough to accommodate several thousand Humans and close to a hundred giants. There was a small crowd tonight, but Minmei was singing her heart out nonetheless, memories of the raid on New Detroit fresh in her mind and the *need* to cement relations between Human and Zentraedi foremost in her thoughts.

She had the crowd, small as it was; the band was tight, and there were moments of perfection in her performance. For a while she could put Kyle from her list of concerns; he hadn't said ten words to her on their cross-country trip from New Detroit, and even now she was certain that he was glaring at her from the stage wings.

Minmei, in that same ruffled dress she had sported in New Macross, was two verses into "Touch and Go" when the real trouble began. The giant Zentraedi seated in the upper tiers were the first to notice it: a rhythmical undercurrent of mechanical articulation, the beat of metalshod hooves in the streets, a sound like distant thunder.

The singer herself became aware of the noise a moment later and stopped midsong. Most of the audience was on its feet, staring up at the curved roof of the hangar: Something was *moving* up there...

When the building began to quake, everyone made a run for the exits, but they were a bit late: The roof seemed to tear open, and all at once it was raining Battlepods. Several more broke through the hangar walls, followed by Zentraedi shock troopers armed with laser rifles and autocannons. The hall was pandemonium, even though not a single shot had been fired.

Minmei stood paralyzed center stage, Battlepods close enough to be reflected in her azure eyes. She was aware of Kyle's presence at her side but incapable of moving of her own free will.

"Minmei," he was screaming, "they're heading right for us! You've got to snap out of it!"

An unusual-looking pod had positioned itself in front of the stage; it had a red snout, a top-mounted cannon, and two derringer-like hand-guns—one of which it slammed against the stage as Kyle was leading her away.

She felt herself thrown off her feet by the violence of the force, but even that wasn't enough to restore her will.

So she surrendered herself to Kyle, allowing him to pull her up and lead her to the stage steps, down into the orchestra pit, down into that grouping of pods closing in on them…

"Well, look what we have here…" an affected voice boomed out far above her.

Minmei looked up into a handsome, clean-shaven face framed by attractive blue hair. The giant Zentraedi who had climbed from the unusual-looking pod was wearing a scarlet-colored uniform trimmed in yellow and an olive-drab campaign cloak that fastened on itself over one shoulder. He reached his hand out and grabbed hold of her and Kyle, crushing them together in his grip as he lifted them high above the stage.

"Let us go!" Kyle managed to yell. "You're going to kill us!"

The warrior titan held them up in front of his face; Minmei saw the devil in his steel-gray eyes.

"I wouldn't dream of it," he said, some unspoken purpose in mind.

"No harm must come to Minmei, Commander!" she heard one of the other giants insist. She craned her neck to see past the warrior's thumb, fighting for breath to get a look at the one who had spoken in her defense.

Khyron gestured to one of his Battlepods, and without warning the mecha kicked the friendly Zentraedi, catching him in the groin and sending him sprawling back against the wall of the hangar, where he rolled over in agony.

"I will not tolerate disobedience!" Khyron bellowed, raising his other fist.

He shot Minmei a look that chilled her heart; then he threw his head back and roared with laughter.

Khyron's name was being shouted in the streets of New Portland, New Detroit, and several other cities that had seen incidents of Zentraedi uprising. Lisa Hayes had heard as much at field headquarters, and she was the one who first reported the rumors to Admiral Gloval. But Gloval remained skeptical: If history had taught him anything, it was that heroes, regardless of their orientation toward good or evil, were often resurrected in times of cultural stress. The Zentraedi were no exception, so it was natural for them to suddenly *believe* that Khyron, their evil lord, had not perished along with Dolza and the commanders of the armada but had somehow escaped and had merely been lying in wait these two years, ready to strike back at the Earth with an equally ghostlike battalion of warriors when the time was right.

Of course, there was no actual *proof* that Khyron had met his end in battle, and the most recent attack on New Detroit and the theft of the sizing chamber were suggestive of his style. There was also Commander Hunter's discovery of an arms cache bearing the Botoru Battalion insignia...

The admiral ran through all of it once more as he paced in front of the large wall screen in the SDF-2 situation room. He was about to put a match to his favorite briar when Claudia called to him from her duty station.

"We're receiving a transmission from someone claiming to be *Khyron*," she told him. "Shall I put it on the screen?"

"Yes, by all means," he replied, stoking the pipe. "And be sure to get a fix on the source of the transmission."

Gloval fully expected to encounter the likeness of an imposter. After all, no one in the Earth Forces had met the so-called Backstabber face to face (although God knew how many had met him mecha to mecha and regretted it). The admiral had, however, seen trans-vids of Khyron supplied by Breetai and Exedore during the long debriefing sessions following the defeat of the Zentraedi armada.

…Which explains Gloval's sudden start when Khyron's devilishly handsome face appeared on the wall screen. A collective gasp went up from the command center personnel; even those who hadn't been privy to the trans-vids recognized the real item when they saw it.

Khyron sneered: "What a pleasure it is to interrupt you, Admiral Gloval."

"He sounds like that sixties actor," someone in the control room commented. "James Mason."

Gloval made up his mind that he was not going to allow himself to be rattled. He cleared his throat and chomped down on the mouthpiece of the pipe. "On the contrary," he said with appropriate sarcasm, "the disgust is all mine, I assure you."

Khyron seemed to like that and said as much. He made a gesture with his hand to indicate something off to his left, and the camera swung slightly to find a second Zentraedi officer—a female, at that. She was not unattractive, with close-cropped blue-gray hair, fine features, and a pointed chin, but she wore the same malicious look on her pale face as that worn by her commander. Gloval didn't have to guess: This had to be Azonia, also believed to have been killed, the dreaded Quadrono leader who was Miriya Parino's superior.

"I have some friends of yours here," Khyron was saying quite matter-of-factly.

Gloval didn't have time to wonder to whom or to what Khyron was referring. Azonia had raised Lynn-Kyle into view, pinched by the scruff of the neck between her thumb and first finger. Khyron, too, raised his fist, shoving Minmei toward the remote camera. The singer looked pale and frightened.

"Minmei!" Claudia said in surprise.

"This can't be happening!" seethed one of the techs.

Dropping his act of feigned indifference, Gloval pulled the pipe from his mouth. "You filthy swine!" he said to the screen image.

"You're mad!" someone added.

Khyron reacted by tightening his fist around his helpless captive, his face suddenly contorted in anger. "Don't try my patience, Micronian—I am known to have a violent temper!"

The implication was obvious, and Gloval signaled everyone to remain calm. "We're sorry," he told Khyron.

The Zentraedi laughed shortly. "Well, then, your apologies are *humbly* accepted. But listen to me carefully: I want you to know I mean business, Admiral."

"We understand. What do you want?"

"Don't hurt her—I beg you!" a tech shouted.

Khyron smirked. "Then deliver the dimensional fortress to me tomorrow by twelve hundred hours."

No one had expected this, least of all the admiral.

"That's impossible! The fortress is no longer spaceworthy."

"Don't lie to me, Admiral. I'm warning you…"

"I'm not lying," Gloval told him firmly. "Listen to me for a moment… The war is *over*, Khyron. Dolza and his armada—"

"The war is not over, Admiral!" Khyron threw at the screen. "Not until I have that fortress in my possession!"

Gloval knew what was on his opponent's mind. "The Protoculture matrix doesn't exist," he tried calmly. "Ask Exedore and Breetai if—"

Khyron was livid. "Those traitors are alive?!" Suddenly he laughed maniacally. "Just deliver the fortress to me, Admiral—if you value your little… songbird."

"You *are* mad!" said Gloval.

"Ah, but there's method to my madness," Khyron returned with a grin. "First, the fortress for Minmei. Then, the Robotech factory satellite for this second hostage." He gestured to Kyle, who was dangling by his coattails from Azonia's pinch.

"Don't do it!" Kyle exploded. "Don't listen to them, Admiral!"

"You mind your manners," Azonia said playfully, wiggling him about roughly.

"It's too dangerous," Kyle managed, in obvious pain. "You can't… you can't just give in to this guy…"

"You're hurting him!" Minmei screamed.

Khyron gestured to his consort to take it easy. "I'd of course prefer to avoid *violence*, Admiral. But believe me, I'm more than willing to carry out my threats."

"I'm sure we can arrange something," Gloval answered him. In fact, he wasn't at all sure *what* could be arranged, but it was essential to start by buying time.

"That's better." Khyron sneered.

Just then a third officer entered the screen's field of view, a large, square-jawed man who deferentially tapped his commander on the shoulder.

"Uh... excuse me..." said Grel.

Khyron turned to him briefly, then back to Gloval. "I must take my leave now, Admiral. But remember: tomorrow by twelve hundred hours."

He flashed a smile, V-ed his fingers, and cut off transmission.

Gloval bowed his head and chided himself silently for believing that evil could so easily be laid to rest.

# 13

When I first heard Khyron announce his demands for the SDF-1 in exchange for the hostages he'd taken, my fear was that his agents had actually penetrated our most top-secret operations. Then, when I realized that his request was more in the nature of a formality, I began to relax some. But the knowledge that he did in fact present a continued threat to our security made me reevaluate the plans I had so carefully formulated for the coming months.

From the log of Admiral Henry Gloval

SOMEONE HAD THOUGHT TO CALL THE DENVER HANGAR/THEATER "Zarkopolis"—as close a translation from the Zentraedi as the Micronian language allowed. The structure bore no resemblance to the original Zarkopolis—the Zentraedi mining base on Fantoma—but it was in keeping with the rekindled spirit of conquest to rename it thus.

Cross-legged on a raised portion of the stage that had become their command post sat Khyron, Azonia, Grel, and Gerao. In attendance were several aides and shock troopers in full battle armor. Stationed in the vast hall below were troops of Khyron's elite strike force and half a dozen battlepods. Minmei stood bravely in the Backstabber's open palm; Khyron regarded her as though she were some zoological specimen.

"It's hard to believe that this helpless little creature in my hand is the key to our freedom," he mused aloud. "To think they'd give up the fortress for you…" His closed his hand on Minmei. "This Micronian sentimentality—it makes me quite ill just to think about it!"

Khyron got to his feet, striking an orator's pose.

"Oh, to be free of this miserable planet!... I can hardly wait, I assure you..." He had turned his back on his audience and was once again eyeing Minmei, now on her knees in his open hand. "Well... why doesn't Minmei perform for us, eh?"

He swung around again and extended his hand, a small stage for her act, almost forty feet off the ground.

Minmei was quick to comply; in fact, she'd been waiting for just such an opportunity. Hers was the voice that had toppled a mighty empire, so surely a handful of disaffected warriors would present little problem. She feared and hated Khyron, but somewhere in the back of her mind endured the idea that she possessed the power to open his heart to love and peace.

"To be in love..." she began, standing up and looking him in the eye. "...must be the sweetest feeling that a *man* can feel... To be in love, to live a dream..."

Khyron's expression was softening. The giant hand that was sweeping her in front of a shocked and dumbfounded audience of hardened soldiers was shaking and sweating.

" ...with somebody you care about like no one else." Minmei was practically shouting out the lyrics now as choruses of groans and words of disbelief rose from Azonia and the others.

Khyron's body was trembling; his eyes were rolled back in his head.

"A special woman, a dearest woman..."

And suddenly, his knees were buckling and he was down on the floor, seemingly ready to release her from his hold. Minmei started to step from his palm, singing: "...Who needs to share her life with you alone..." Without warning, he grabbed her again, a sly grin splitting his face as he squeezed the song and breath from her.

"Well, it was a brave attempt, Minmei. But unfortunately for you, as you can see, I am immune to your witchcraft."

"You had me fooled!" Azonia laughed, her hand to her mouth.

But Khyron silenced her. "I am speaking to my little songbird." He looked hard at Minmei. "And she's going to help us get what we want, isn't that so, my little pet?"

Minmei flailed about in his hand, struggling to free herself. "I won't help you—you big overgrown... *clown!*"

Khyron faked a look of hurt. "That was not very nice, Minmei... In fact, I'm rather surprised at you—losing your temper like that. Very unladylike."

Minmei folded her arms in defiance, fighting back tears.

"I may have to teach you some manners," her captor was threatening, his anger building, his grip on her tightening. "You think that just because you're the *magnificent* Minmei, you're better than we are... Well, I despise your *music!* Despise it! Do you hear me?!"

She could no longer breathe. Khyron was ranting and raving, and she was rapidly losing touch with the world. Blackness circled in on her from the edges of her vision, silencing thoughts and fears alike.

Khyron felt her go limp in his hand and realized he had gone too far. Azonia was shouting at him to be careful, but he was certain he'd already overstepped himself.

"Cosmos! What have I done?!"

Minmei was unmoving in his hand, deathly still. "She enraged me so, I forgot how important she was to our plan..." Gently, he poked at her with his finger, hoping she'd revive; and in a moment she did, dazed and possibly hurt but certainly nowhere near dead. Khyron acknowledged his relief with a smile.

"She's all right," he told Azonia. "They're well-built little things."

Azonia had picked up Kyle and was now holding him by one foot and one arm, twisting him about as though he were made of pipe cleaners. Kyle was far less important to the plan, so she wasn't concerned about breaking him up a bit.

Kyle, on the other hand, felt differently about it, and it was only his many years of martial-arts training that kept him from suffering major dislocations. The blue-haired Amazon seemed hell-bent on *reconfiguring* him like some sort of mannikin mecha.

She joked: "Surely this is as much fun for you as it is for me!"

And Kyle could only hope he would see the day when she micronized herself; because if he lived through this, there was going to be a score to settle.

· · ·

Admiral Gloval called an emergency session with his chiefs of staff following Khyron's transmission, which had been traced to New Denver. They had less than twelve hours to decide on a course of action. Claudia Grant, General Motokoff from G3, and several officers from various departments of the RDF were gathered around a long table in the SDF-2 briefing room. Exedore, still aboard the factory satellite, was in communication with them via comlink; his image appeared on one of the monitors.

"The situation is without precedent," Motokoff was saying. He was a young man in spite of his rank, former head of the CD forces aboard the SDF-1 during its two-year ordeal in space. "Since the Zentraedi have never taken hostages before, we have no way of knowing if they'll make good their promises."

Gloval drew at his pipe, nodding. "Or their threats," he told the table.

"May I respond to that, Admiral?" Exedore said from the screen.

"Go ahead, Exedore," said Gloval.

The Zentraedi looked squarely into the remote camera. "Khyron will make good his threats, of this I can assure you. Lord Breetai concurs with me that this hostage taking suggests he has gone beyond the bounds of his Zentraedi conditioning, which would have rendered such an act unthinkable. There is no telling how far he is willing to go now. But I must caution you *not* to accede to his demands under any circumstances. Lord Breetai wishes me to inform you that he is at your service should you require him in settling this most unfortunate matter."

Gloval took the pipe from his mouth and inclined his head. "That will not be necessary, Exedore, although you may convey my appreciation to the commander. Your people have already spent far too many years acting as a police force. We won't ask you to fight our battles for us."

"I understand, Admiral," Exedore said evenly.

One of the officers stood up to address Gloval. "I agree with Breetai, Admiral. Putting the SDF-1 into Khyron's hands would be an act of suicide!" The officer had gotten himself so worked up that the pencil he was holding snapped in his hands.

"Calm down," Gloval told him gruffly. "I have no intention of giving in to his demands."

"I hope you're not suggesting that we ignore Khyron's threats to Kyle and Minmei," said Claudia.

"No," everyone was quick to say.

"We're all in agreement on that, sir," said another officer. "But this is a blatant act of terrorism, and we must refuse to bargain with him."

Claudia nodded in agreement.

Gloval cleared his throat. "For two years now the Zentraedi have lived with us as equals. And in that time we have all come to know many of them as friends and allies. Khyron took advantage of this by infiltrating his spies into our cities. We have no way of knowing who they are or where they might be."

"I don't see what bearing this has on the problem, Admiral," Motokoff interjected.

Gloval made a dismissive gesture. "I'm coming to that. We don't know who our enemies are, but we *do* know our friends…" The chiefs of staff waited for him to finish. "So, I suggest we use the Zentraedis to trick him, as he used them to trick us."

"Commander Hunter, engage your scrambler," Lisa said over the net from field headquarters.

The Skull had been ordered out of the deserted Zentraedi base where the arms cache had been discovered. In minutes the place was going to be a memory, thanks to the explosive charges they had set to self-destruct.

"Engaging voice scrambler for encoded transmission, control," Rick radioed back after tapping in a series of commands on the Veritech's console.

He had been expecting new orders since word had been received that Khyron was responsible for the attack on New Detroit. Unlike Gloval, Rick saw no reason to doubt that Khyron had survived the Zentraedi holocaust. Khyron had always been the most self-serving of the lot; he was a born survivor, and it was not unlike him to go in hiding for two years—to *stage* his own resurrection. Rick recalled the many times he had faced Khyron in battle; without adequate proof, he blamed Khyron for Roy Fokker's death. And as anxious as he felt about a renewed contest, one part of him was actually looking forward to it.

Lisa wasn't sure she wanted to break the news to him about Minmei, but orders were orders. "Operation Star-Saver," the High Command was calling it.

*"It looks like it's going to be a tough one, this time,"* Claudia had told her. *"But you, you lucky devil, you'll be coordinating for Commander Hunter once again."*

Somehow Claudia had missed the point: *Rick was being ordered to save Minmei—again!* How much longer was fate going to build these rescues into their relationship? Lisa wondered. Just when the singer was no longer a threat to what little happiness Lisa and Rick shared, another crisis would present itself.

*"And why was it that Rick is called to respond to every crisis?"* she had asked Claudia, not really expecting a response and certainly not having to be reminded that *Rick was the best there was.*

That was why she wanted him.

"Good to hear your voice again, Lisa," Rick was saying.

Lisa sucked in her breath and decided to take the plunge.

"Rick," she began. "Your team is to report back to New Macross for special orders. Khyron has kidnapped, ah, two… people. He's holding them hostage in New Denver for the return of the SDF-1."

"That's insane! The fortress isn't even airworthy, is it?"

"Of course not. But—"

"Man, somebody really must have slipped some elephant juice into the punch bowl when that guy was cloned… And since when do the Zentraedi take hostages?"

"Since Khyron got back to town."

"So who'd he grab? Lynn-Kyle, if it's my lucky day."

Lisa raised her eyes to the domed ceiling. "It's your lucky day," she told him.

She heard his gasp, then: "Who's the second person, Lisa? Give it to me straight."

*Make it short and sweet,* she told herself, and said: "Minmei. Khyron attacked a club in—"

"Where are they?!"

Lisa stiffened at her station. *He'd fly to the sun and back,* she said to herself. But to Rick, she cautioned: "There is no place for amateur heroics on this mission, Commander."

Rick went silent, and it was too late for her to take it back. "Uhh, really?" he said after a moment, cold as ice. "I wasn't aware that amateur heroics were my stock in trade."

Lisa fumed, her face coloring. The woman tech at the adjacent station was staring at her as if assessing her professionalism. "That is all! Out!" she hollered, and slammed her palm down on the comlink button.

Four hours later, Skull Team was assembled on the flight deck of the *Prometheus;* they had been briefed and were ready for action.

Lisa, also recalled to New Macross, was braving the cold evening winds to wish Rick well. She couldn't bear the thought of his going off into combat while that foolish argument remained unresolved. But he wasn't helping her out at all, clinging to his anger.

"Please be careful, Rick," she called up to Skull One's cockpit. "Khyron will stop at nothing, you know that."

Rick stopped on the top step of the Veritech's ladder and turned to her, "thinking cap" in place. "Look, I appreciate your concern, but we've been over the operation, and I know what I have to do."

"That's not what I'm talking about," she said as he climbed in. "I'm just afraid you'll lose your objectivity and do something rash..."

Again her words brought him to a halt, but this time he leaped from the Veritech and strode toward her.

"Rick—"

"Yes. I love her very much—I won't lie to you, Lisa. I've never tried to conceal that from you. But I settled my feelings about her a long time ago. Minmei and I can *never* be together... I'm flying this mission as a pilot."

"And you're a fine pilot, Rick. Just don't lose your perspective, that's all. If anything happened—"

"I'm commanding an entire squadron, Lisa! Do you think I'd jeopardize their safety just because of my feelings for Minmei?!"

"Emotions are so compelling…" she said, averting her eyes. "I just can't be sure…"

Rick struck a challenge pose, gloved fists on his hips. "What? You can't be sure of *what*?!"

She lowered her head. "It's nothing… Forget I said anything."

Rick put his hands on her shoulders. "Look, I'll be back," he said, hoping to put her at ease. He didn't even know why they were going at each other like this. Two hostages: It didn't matter who they were…

"Good luck," Lisa said as he walked away.

In celebration of his imminent victory, Khyron had emptied the coffers of the last remaining Zentraedi foodstuffs and provisions—bottles of Garudan ale and sides of yptrax from Garuda, too long in the freeze-dry bins. Most of the Zentraedi subsisted on chemical nutrients, but Khyron had always strived to individualize himself. *To be unique in all things.* He respected the Micronians' taste for organic food; it was only fitting that life feed on death, as death fed on life. .

Khyron toasted their success, took a long pull from the bottle of ale, and refilled Azonia's glass. She was on the floor to the left of Khyron's improvised throne—an enormous storage crate turned on its side—Grel, a drumstick of meat in hand, to the right.

"There you are, my dear."

Khyron and Grel watched her empty the glass and laughed drunkenly.

"She's amazing, my lord," Grel commented. His feelings toward Azonia had changed somewhat, especially now that there were other Zentraedi females in camp. And of course the ale helped considerably.

"I believe I'll have another," said Azonia. "Fill it up."

Khyron smiled and poured. "My dear Azonia, I believe you could outdrink all of us."

"And I'm just starting." She beamed.

Khyron leered at her. "Excellent, Commander … excellent."

Minmei and Kyle were imprisoned in an ingeniously designed cage fashioned from a circular arrangement of giant-size forks— the downward-pointing tines anchored by the inner lip of a shallow bowl—and a similarly sized pan lid that enclosed and held fast the backward-bending upper ends of the fork sterns. To offset the fear, and really for lack of anything better to do, the two captives pulled at their makeshift bars to no avail.

Exhausted, Minmei fell to the bowl floor, Kyle beside her, breathless, his body racked with pain from Azonia's manhandling.

"We'll have to try another way," she managed, gasping for air.

"There is no other way—we'll never get out of here!"

"No, Kyle, don't say that…"

"Whatever happens to us—no matter what he does to us— Gloval must never give in to that barbarian's demands." Kyle wiped sweat from his brow. "Imagine the SDF-1 in Khyron's hands!"

"Won't they try to rescue us?" she asked, suddenly even more frightened.

"I wouldn't hold my breath, Minmei."

It was difficult to know just what Kyle wanted. He didn't want the admiral to give in to Khyron's demands, but at the same time he was already condemning him for not mounting a rescue. This was all too typical of his recent behavior, and Minmei was further saddened.

"Then there isn't much to hope for," she sobbed. It didn't seem possible: Hopes and dreams were so very *real*…

Kyle was getting to his feet. "There's *nothing* to hope for."

"But we *can't* lose hope—that's all we've got," she told him, unsure whom she was trying to convince.

But Kyle came back at her with his usual: "All the hope in the world is useless in a situation like this."

Minmei felt sad for him. She didn't want to hurt him but nevertheless found herself saying, "If only Rick was here—*he'd* save us."

Kyle didn't hear it or perhaps didn't want to hear it; in either case, he had turned his attention to their captors and was now leaning between the forks and shouting at them.

"Hey, you Zentraedi! Hey, you overgrown gorillas! What a bunch of brainless baboons! All you can think about is your own bellies, huh?!"

Khyron and the others fell silent, listening to him.

"What about your own comrades? What do you think about that? Does it make you happy knowing that you've slaughtered your own people?!"

Minmei noticed Khyron's eyes narrowing. She wanted to tell Kyle to stop. What was he trying to gain by this, anyway? but he went right on provoking them.

"Why can't you goons learn to live in peace for a change? I'll tell you why—because that would take courage, and you're all a bunch of cowards, that's why!"

Khyron had been getting a kick out of it—the spunk displayed by this tiny creature—but accusations about *cowardice* were never amusing, especially since the defeat of the armada and Khyron's decision then to absent himself from the battle...

The Backstabber got to his feet in a rush, smashing a bottle of ale down on the table that held the cage.

"Careful, Khyron," Azonia said as her commander stomped toward Kyle and Minmei. "Remember the fortress..."

"You puny little things," Khyron sneered, towering over them. "If it weren't for the fact that I need you, I'd... I'd *crush* you—just for pleasure!"

Minmei was shaking uncontrollably, ready to feel that hand come down on their cage. She stammered, "Be careful, Kyle, he's been drinking!"

The female, Azonia, was by his side now, and Khyron suddenly reached out for her and pulled her to him, passionately.

"You see," he whispered to his captives, "I've learned something about *pleasure*..."

And with that he embraced Azonia and kissed her full on the mouth, savagely; she responded, groaning and holding him fast. Kyle and Minmei were aghast—every bit as shocked as Dolza had been by Rick and Lisa's kiss years before, the one that had started it all.

Kyle dropped to his knees as though defeated while the two Zentraedi drank in each other's lust. And there was no telling just how far Khyron and Azonia might have been prepared to go. But fate, as is its wont, chose that particular moment to intervene: Grel, nervous at the prospect of disturbing his lord, stepped forward with news to drain the life from the best of parties.

"I'm, er, sorry to have to interrupt your... *demonstration*, Lord Khyron," Grel faltered, "but I, uh, thought you might want to know that we seem to be, uh, under attack."

# 14

Hierarchy, hegemony... these words have no meaning to a Zentraedi. They were a... *compartmentalized* military body. Dolza was created to oversee them, Exedore to advise them; Breetai, Reno, Khyron, and innumerable others to command; and the rest, to serve. But there was never any male/female fraternization. And that very repression of natural drives and instincts was in part responsible for the tremendous energy they consequently gave over to warfare— *displacement drive* as it was once called... How like the matrixed seeds of the Invid Flower itself, the basis of Protoculture.

Dr. Emil Lang, *Ghost Machines:*
*An Overview of Protoculture*

PART OF AZONIA'S INITIATION INTO SENSUAL PLEASURE WAS TO be pushed aside and told that the time wasn't right.

Khyron had rushed to the nearest viewscreen, leaving Azonia where he had pushed her to the floor, hungry for more of his attention. A red-haired Zentraedi soldier stationed at a forward outpost saluted the Backstabber from the screen.

"Greetings and salutations, Lord Khyron, master of the peoples of—"

Reflexively, Khyron leaned back from the monitor as a fiery blast erased the soldier's words and carried him clear out of the remote camera's field of view.

"What's happening there?!" Khyron shouted into the comlink, fooling with the console control knobs. In a minute, the soldier rose into view once again, hand to his head where he'd been wounded.

"Fighters are everywhere, sir! They've taken us completely by surprise! We'll try to hold them off for as long as we can!" Earth mecha streaked across the screen's starry background, leaving contrails in the night sky. "Please, sir, you must send reinforcements—" And the monitor blanked out.

Khyron frowned. Behind him, one of his shock troopers suggested that the Micronians might be mounting a diversionary raid, but Khyron didn't think them foolish enough to risk such a thing.

"So this is how they answer my demands!" he said, suddenly getting to his feet. "Well, it seems as though our little songbird has outlived her usefulness—to them *and* to us!"

Khyron ordered his troops to their pods and began to suit himself up in Zentraedi armor, bandoliers, and hip belt. Azonia approached him cautiously.

"Khyron, may we please continue the… demonstration?"

"Just as soon as I return," he told her firmly. "But why don't you come with us? The Micronians won't stand a chance with you by my side! We'll enjoy a moment's pleasure with them."

Azonia hesitated; it was certainly an inviting notion, but she had been trained to lead, not to follow. Besides, it would mean that one of the troops would have to give up his mecha, and they were looking forward to battle to the last man.

"And what about Minmei?"

Khyron glanced over at the cage he had fashioned and spat.

"We'll deal with her later." He put his arm around Azonia and offered to find her a Battlepod, as if offering to take her on a vacation.

"That would be wonderful!" Azonia gushed.

"We'll share the experience our people love most!"

"Yes, we'll go into battle together!"

"Good." Khyron smiled. "I sense a great victory!"

Outside the hangar theater, the Zentraedi commander lowered himself into a harness seat astride an Officer's Pod, which had been modified to support four top-mounted cannons. The mecha was piloted by a three-man crew of micronized warriors. Somewhat below him, Azonia clambered into one of the standard versions. "Show no mercy!" she shouted to the troops lined up behind them.

Khyron kicked the side of the Officer's Pod to signal the pilots to move out. Inside, one of the crewmen asked whether one kick meant "forward" or "reverse."

"Neither, you fool!" said a second. "It means advance to the left."

"What does it matter?" asked the third. "We better do *something* or he'll start screaming at us again."

Sure enough, Khyron opened the hatch to the control room and snarled: "Get moving, you idiots!"

Zentraedi war cries filled the air as Khryon's alliance of troops and mecha charged into the night.

Undiscovered by Khyron's sentries, two members of an RDF long-range reconnaissance team witnessed the charge from their position atop a granite outcropping not far from the hangar theater. They were outfitted in sensor-reflective antirad suits, complete with jetpacks, full helmets, and survival gear. The radio man had raised SDF-2 control.

"Pelican Mother," he whispered. "This is Eyes-Front. The Dark Star has fallen; repeat: The Dark Star has fallen…"

"Roger, Eyes-Front, we copy you loud and clear," returned Lisa Hayes. She then switched over to the corn net.

"Skull Team, you now have green light, over."

Winging his way toward New Denver in Skull One, Rick copied the message.

"Roger," he told Lisa flatly. "We're going in."

*There was so much more she wanted to say, so much more.*

Khyron's forces crested a small rise and dropped into a barren hollow in time to see three of their comrades locked in hand-to-hand combat with three RDF Battloids.

"Micronians!" Khyron snarled from his seat. "Prepare to meet your doom!"

Vastly outnumbered, the Battloids turned and fled as expected, but the sight of the three Zentraedi giants fleeing along with them came as a complete surprise. Khyron began to shout: "Where are you going?! We have come to save you!" He didn't bother to repeat himself, though. His warrior sense told him that he'd been led into a trap. Ordering his team to a halt, Khyron spent a moment puzzling out Gloval's move.

*Of course!* he said to himself. *Gloval had managed to infiltrate his unit with Zentraedi traitors!* Khyron turned in his seat and regarded his forces warily. But there was no time to pick out the good from the bad: On the high ground all around them, Micronian mecha were popping into view.

"Fire!" ordered Khyron, barely getting the command out before the enemy guns opened up. Six of his Battlepods were taken out in an instant, and an explosive close call almost toppled him from his seat.

"*Fire!*" he yelled again, hearing the immediate report of friendly cannons. "*Charge!*"


"Skull Team, this is Pelican Mother: The trap is sprung! Over!"

"Roger, Pelican Mother," Rick's wingman radioed Lisa. "Approaching assault objective."

"Commander Hunter," said Lisa. "That's your signal to begin."

"Roger."

*The heck with rules,* she told herself. "Be careful, Rick. Khyron left several Battlepods behind to guard the hostages."

"Going in low," he replied, Lisa's last words to him echoing in his mind. *Don't lose your perspective.* But Minmei's voice was running at the same time in wishful daydream thoughts.

*It can't end this way, Rick,* she was telling him lovingly. *Soon we'll be together.*

Rick's face had a determined look as he nosed the Veritech still lower, the target looming into sight.

Inside the hangar, three Zentraedi giants were playing cards, trying to shake off the buzz from that premature celebration bash. The fork cage was beside them on the table. Before they had time to know what hit them, a Veritech had blown its way into the building, swept-back wings bringing down two soldiers in its flight path.

Three Battlepods guarding the entrance had already been blown to smithereens.

The hangar was pure chaos; every soldier with an autocannon or assault rifle was loosing fire and bolts of deadly energy against the fighter, a bird of prey streaking overhead.

Rick circled the stage, looking for Minmei and Kyle while he dodged steady bursts of ground fire, blinding searchlights in the dark building. In Guardian mode now, he nosedived his mecha to within twenty feet of the floor and made a pass between two Zentraedi, bowling them over with the Veritech's wings. When he put down, a third giant wielding a depleted autocannon rushed at him, connecting once with a blow that narrowly missed the cockpit canopy before Rick dispatched him with a savage thrust of the mecha's metalshod left fist. The warrior was propelled a good three hundred feet to his final resting place.

Rick walked the mecha forward to the cage, pulling off the lid as he dropped the Veritech's radome to the tabletop.

"Minmei, are you all right?!" he called anxiously through the external speakers.

She was standing inside the fork enclosure, somehow tidy-looking and effervescent despite the ordeal she'd suffered through.

"Yes, Rick! I knew you'd come for me!"

"Of course I would."

Looking up at him in the cockpit, she felt her heart suddenly swell with love and longing. Rick was like some guardian angel in her life, always there when she needed him—for support, protection, *affection*. And in that moment, she vowed to act on the strength of these renewed feelings, to demonstrate to him how much he meant to her.

"It's been a... long time," she said softly.

But it was doubtful that Rick heard her over Kyle's shouts. "Will you get us outta here!" he was demanding.

Rick thought the mecha through a series of motions that allowed him to rip open the remainder of the cage, flattening the forks like a hurricane wind. As Minmei and Kyle clambered up the mecha's left hand and arm, Rick raised the base:

"This is Skull Leader, Operation Star-Saver... Mission accomplished!"

. . .

Lisa Hayes was already on her way to New Denver's theater when word arrived that the two hostages were safe and sound. But no sooner had her plane put down than she began to get an earful of complaints from an infuriated Lynn-Kyle.

"I'm telling you," he was hollering in her ear, "he came blasting in without any regard for our safety!"

Lisa could never figure Kyle out, but she had no patience with anyone who criticized a successful mission—especially when that mission had saved two lives.

Kyle thrust his forefinger at her like a weapon. "That maniac almost got us killed!"

"We executed the mission to the best of our abilities," she countered, angered beyond control. "If Commander Hunter's conduct was unacceptable, then file a report."

"A report?!" Kyle screamed, flexing his hands. "Just lemme get my hands on him!"

Suddenly Minmei was between them, holding her arms out like a crossing guard—a living cross to Kyle's vampire. "Stop it!" she shrieked. "Can't you see that all of these people risked their lives for us, you ungrateful oaf!"

Lisa waited for Kyle to deck his cousin, but Rick's equally sudden appearance caught Kyle off guard. The Skull Leader came walking out of the night shadows cast by his crouched Veritech, helmet cradled in his right arm.

"I did it for *you*, Minmei," he said, approaching the three of them. "I sure didn't do it for *Kyle*."

Kyle took a step forward, threateningly. "I'd expect that from you, Hunter." *Now*, Lisa said to herself. *Now all hell is going to break loose*. Things had been building to this showdown for three years...

But thankfully, the argument didn't escalate to violence. Quite the opposite: Minmei stepped out from between Kyle and Lisa with a warm "Thank you" for Rick, and he smiled. "I was happy to do it."

She seemed to stand there staring at him for a moment, then broke out into a run that led her straight into his arms.

Lisa heard Rick tell her: "You must know that I'd be willing to risk my life for you again and again." And as Lisa's mouth dropped open, the two of them began twirling around together, sobbing with joy like long-lost lovers.

Just that, in fact.

Elsewhere, Khyron's troops and the Earth Forces were annihilating each other. The last thing the RDF commander had expected was a charge; but then, he had never faced the Backstabber in battle.

Battlepods and Gladiators met head-on, going at it with a ferocity neither side had experienced before. Here, a pod rammed itself into a MAC II cannon, self-destructing on impact, while close by two pods down on their backs and cracked open like eggs fought their assailants with blasts of heat and fire sent blowtorching from their foot thrusters. Azonia, the Protoculture charges of the Officer's Pod weapons system depleted, windmilled the mecha's hand-guns against its Battloid opponent. Zentraedi infantry troops armed with control rods torn from ruined Battlepods dueled Excaliburs, swinging autocannons like baseball bats.

Khyron was still astride his undamaged cannon pod, directing rotating fusillades of fire against ridge guns and attacking mecha. Battloids challenged his position, charging in from all sides and scaling the four-cannon machine to engage him one on one.

He wrestled a gatling away from one of these would-be heroes and turned the gun on it, blowing off the top of the pod. As the Battloid hit the ground and exploded, Khyron emptied the gun on a new wave of Micronian mecha, laughing maniacally, as was the Zentraedi way to welcome death.

Khyron was cursing the depleted galling when one of his micronized crewmen appeared briefly in the cockpit hatchway to inform him that the cannon's Protoculture charge was likewise used up. Distracted, the commander didn't see a second Battloid that had reached the top of the cannon until it was almost too late. He sidestepped the mecha's lunge and knocked it off balance with a gatling blow to the abdomen. But now a third had suddenly appeared behind him, and again he twisted and swung the gun, nailing the mecha with a shot to its chest.

Grel had also survived the initial surprise attack and was contributing his blood lust to the kill zone. Out of weapons charge, he ran his Battlepod at full throttle into the swarm of Battloids attacking his commander's position. But a miscalculation inadvertently brought him crashing against one of the mecha's hand-guns, setting loose the cannon's final charge. The force of the blast threw Grel's Battlepod into a back flip, while the slug itself ripped from the muzzle and blew away the arm of Azonia's Officer's Pod.

Khyron saw her go down in a fiery fall and leaped from the cannon seat to run to her aid. Bolts of energy criss-crossed overhead and explosions erupted around him as he ran, a broken-field runner in hell. A Battloid thought to stop him, but he felled it with a gatling blow to the thing's head.

He lifted the plastron hatch of Azonia's smoldering pod and called out to her, the first time he had ever demonstrated such feeling for one of his own kind. She was lying injured inside, on the brink of unconsciousness, until she saw him and felt the light return to her.

Was she all right? he wanted to know.

She smiled slightly, even though there was nothing good to report; oh, she was unhurt, but the pod's weapons were empty. And it didn't matter, she wanted to tell him, because she had at least lived to experience the joy of battle and the knowledge that he had cared enough to come to her side.

But Khyron surprised her by ordering a retreat.

She got the pod to its feet and scooped Khyron up in its one good arm, running away with him into the dawn light, a badly beaten band of Battlepods trailing behind.

Lisa and Kyle stood silently side by side, identical scowls on their faces, while the happy reunion continued. Lisa was thinking: *We must look like twins.*

She wasn't aware of the female flight officer who approached her from the shuttle plane until she felt the light tap on her shoulder.

"Khyron is in full retreat," the woman reported.

Lisa glanced back at the lovers. The sun was up, and it would have made a pretty picture—the two of them embracing, the Guardian behind them against a powder-blue sky—if only Rick hadn't been a featured subject. But this sudden news had presented her with a way to break it up. After all, it was Rick's *duty* to go after Khyron, wasn't it. *He was the best there was…*

If Lisa wrestled with the idea of using her rank to come between them, she didn't show it. She turned to the woman officer and told her to notify Admiral Gloval that she was sending Commander Hunter in to mop up.

With that, she walked over to them, tapping Rick roughly on the shoulder to put a swift end to their lingering kiss. She demonstrated none of the nervous reserve Grel had shown earlier with Khyron and Azonia.

"I hope I'm not interrupting anything *important*, Commander, but Khyron is on the run, and Skull has been ordered to give pursuit."

"Huh?" Minmei said, as if waking from a dream.

Rick shot Lisa an angry look. "I almost didn't make it back the *first* time—isn't that enough for you?!"

"Are you refusing orders, mister?!" she said, raising her voice.

Rick threw his helmet to the ground. "You're darn right I'm refusing! You want Khyron so bad, you go out and get him!"

"Fine!" Lisa shot back, squatting down to retrieve the helmet. "I'll go bring him in, and you can just go put yourself on report!"

Minmei made a startled sound, looking back and forth between them. Rick snatched the helmet away from Lisa's grasp.

"Forget it! I've come this far—I might as well finish the job, Captain!"

Lisa berated herself silently. *How could I allow myself to do this to him?* She started to apologize, but he cut her off.

"It's my *duty*, right?!" He turned affectionately to Minmei and told her that he'd be back soon.

"I know you will," she sighed.

Lisa stood with her arms folded, her foot tapping the tarmac fitfully. She wanted to throw up, apologize again, scream, do *something!*

Rick donned the "thinking cap" and made an athletic jump to the lowered nose of the Veritech. As he was snuggling down inside the cockpit, Minmei saluted and said, "I'll be waiting for you."

He returned both her smile and her salute before bringing the canopy down.

The Guardian righted itself as Rick fired up the rear thrusters, and some sort of silent communication passed between Minmei and himself: words and thoughts from the past, suddenly intertwined and confused with these renewed trusts.

Minmei stood unmoving while the Veritech initiated its launch, riding over the barren land on its own blasting carpet. But when it had reached the end of the field, she began to chase after it, shouting out Rick's name, afraid all at once that she would lose him forever.

Lisa took off after her, concerned for her safety. She saw Minmei collapse a short distance off, burying her face in her hands.

# 15

I don't know who I want to strangle more—Lisa or her idiot flyboy. I only know that if something doesn't put a quick end to this little duet they're dancing, I'm going to get myself transferred to the factory satellite, and I'm going to see to it that Lisa Hayes comes with me.

The Collected Letters of Claudia Grant

THE ISSUE, LISA DECIDED AFTERWARD, WAS CONTROL. IT HAD nothing to do with Minmei, Kyle, or even Rick. She couldn't bring herself to blame him no matter how much effort she put into it; she couldn't accuse him of deceit—he had been honest about his feelings for Minmei all along—lack of consideration, or outright selfishness. Nor was his behavior manipulative or *controlling* in any way. Damn him. That left only herself to blame, unless she could somehow pin the whole thing on *Khyron*!

This made her laugh: Here she was, sitting in the officer's mess feeling like the world was about to end because she and Rick had had another tiff, when *Khyron* was on the loose, kidnapping people, demanding the return of the SDF-1, and threatening to wipe out what little remained of the human race. But her preoccupation with the *little* things didn't surprise her. For what could one person do up against the *big* ones? She played her part, Rick played his; all of them, Minmei included, had roles to enact. Sometimes, though, it felt as if someone else had written the lines they all delivered with such force and passion. But in the end it all came back to control: how she was going to regain control of herself.

Lisa sat there sipping at lukewarm coffee, so wrapped up in

replaying dawn's events that she took no notice of Claudia's arrival.

"I thought I might find you in here," her friend said, slipping into the seat opposite her "Why so glum, chum?"

Lisa looked up, startled and in no mood for good cheer.

"Come on," Claudia pressed. "Tell me what Rick has done now, Lisa."

"Please, Claudia…"

"Not in the mood for talk, huh? Well, honey, sometimes it clears the air… just helps to get it in the open."

Lisa loved Claudia dearly, but ever since Roy's death she seemed to have become the absolute font of optimism. Whether this was simply *her* way of running from reality—her path of control—Lisa had no idea. Just now she didn't feel like "clearing the air"; instead, she tossed her head back as if to shrug off her dark mood and asked Claudia what made her think she was upset.

Claudia almost smiled. "Uh, woman's intuition. And even if I'm wrong, I want you to try my prescription for pain." She produced a box of blended teas from her jacket pocket and slid it across the table. "Hot tea can do wonders for open wounds."

Indefatigable optimism and a reliance on health potions and panaceas, thought Lisa. But after a moment she surrendered.

"Is it really all that noticeable?"

"Only if someone happens to be glancing in your general direction," Claudia told her. "Or maybe to someone who's been there…"

Lisa could only shake her head.

Claudia reached out for Lisa's hand. "I know how it is… but you've got to loosen up. Stop trying to control how you feel—just *tell* him."

Claudia stood up.

"What am I supposed to tell him?"

Now Claudia shook her head. "How you *feel* about him, silly."

Lisa thought about it as Claudia walked off. She picked up the package of tea and began to fool with it absently. *Rick Hunter,* she said to herself. *This is the way I feel about you: I-I love you.* Suddenly she gave the box a sort of hopeless toss. Even her inner voice was stammering! This was not going to be easy.

. . .

Mirroring the emotional state of its pilot, Skull One came in fast and furious, rocking side to side as it screeched along the *Prometheus*'s flight deck.

Rick was like a raw nerve just waiting to be touched. Effectively he'd been in high gear since leaving the abandoned Zentraedi base over forty-eight hours earlier. For the past eight, the squadron had been scouring the countryside for signs of Khyron's forces. Beginning with the site of the surprise attack (now a place of unspeakable carnage, littered with the remains of scores of Battlepods and RDF mecha), Skull Team had traced Khyron's retreat north to yet another hastily abandoned base. Sensor readings indicated that a Zentraedi warship had been launched from the base shortly before Skull's arrival, but there was no trace of its heading or any way to determine the strength of Khyron's remaining army. Given the number of Zentraedi who had deserted the cities, the size of the ship (Zentraedi cruiser class), and the fact that Khyron was in possession of a workable sizing chamber, troop estimates ranged anywhere from one to three thousand.

Then there was Lisa to think about—the other front in this war without end. Bad enough that most of his waking life was spent following orders, but to have to take them from someone who expected to regiment his personal life as well was more than he could stand. Even the memory of Minmei's sweet embrace wasn't enough to wash away dawn's sour start.

"We'll put her away for you, Commander!" one of the ground crew said as Rick was raising the canopy.

It took Rick a second to realize that the man was talking about Skull One. He took a deep breath of fresh air and climbed from the cockpit, dead on his feet.

The ground crew chief called out to him as he was leaving. "Excuse me, sir, but Captain Hayes wants you to report to her as soon as possible."

"Did she say why?" Rick asked him.

"No, sir."

Rick turned and stormed off. It was time to have a showdown with *Captain* Hayes.

Lisa, meanwhile, was at her station in the SDF-2 control room. She had made up her mind to apologize to Rick, perhaps go a step further if her courage held up. Humming to herself now while she toyed with the tea package, she didn't notice Rick's vexed entry. Vanessa, at the adjacent duty station, tried to whisper a warning, but Lisa had turned and caught sight of him, somehow misreading his mood.

"Oh, hello, Rick," she said cheerfully.

He answered her by practically throwing his written report at her. "With my compliments, *Captain*."

Lisa's eyes went wide; she hadn't anticipated this.

"Will that be all?" he continued in the same sarcastic tone. "I don't want to take up too much of your time."

"Rick, I—"

"I said, will that be all, Captain?"

"What's the matter with you?" She raised her voice, but it came out confused-sounding.

"What's the matter with me?! I come in after chasing Khyron halfway across the continent and the first thing I hear is that I'm supposed to report to you—you think I don't understand military procedure by now, or what?!"

He was standing over her, red-faced and shaking.

"If you'll just give me a chance to explain…"

"And another thing." He made a fist. "My personal life is just that—*personal*! D' ya understand, Captain?! I'll speak to whoever I want, whenever and wherever I want!"

So that was it, Lisa thought. He believed that she had manipulated this morning's situation for her own purposes. In other words, her motives had been transparent.

"I understand," she told him meekly.

"Like Vanessa here, for example," Rick added suddenly, walking over to her station. "Am I right or not?"

Vanessa adjusted her glasses, glanced briefly at Lisa, and slid down in her seat, wanting no part of this. "Uh, I don't really think I'm…"

But Rick was bending over her, his hand on the back of her chair, full of false charm. "Hey, why don't we grab a bite to eat?"

Vanessa blanched. "Please," she told him, not wanting to have to state the obvious. "As you can see, I'm still on duty…"

"So what? You can still play hooky, can't you?" Rick stole a look at Lisa; she was getting to her feet, her back to both of them.

"If you'll excuse me," Lisa said, "I think I've had enough of this." She was hurt, but at the same time she felt sorry for Rick. That he would stoop to such transparent gestures to get even with her; that he would drag her friend into it; that he was a *man*…

When Lisa was out of earshot, Vanessa turned sharply to Rick and told him off. "That was the worst, Hunter. I mean it."

He had an arrogant look on his face. "Oh yeah, why's that?"

Vanessa shook her head in disbelief. "You've been relying on instruments too long, hot shot. Open your eyes: Did you stop to think about how Lisa feels about you?" This was none of her business, and she knew she had no right to be speaking for Lisa, but *somebody* had to get this guy to wise up.

"Feels about me?" Rick was saying as if he couldn't believe what he was hearing. "You gotta be kidding—the only thing Lisa cares about is her job."

Vanessa frowned, and Rick walked off. She gave herself a moment to calm down, then went over to Kim's station to fill her in on this latest chapter in the Hayes-Hunter miniseries.

"What's Lisa's problem?" said Kim after she'd been briefed.

"She doesn't have any problem," Sammie defended her commander. "It was just a lovers' quarrel. It's none of our business."

Vanessa disagreed. "You weren't there. She loves him, but she doesn't have the courage to tell him."

"That's absolutely ridiculous!" said Kim, suddenly angry. "Why doesn't he just be a man about it and tell her how he feels?"

Vanessa gave her a quizzical look. "Has it ever occurred to you that he doesn't share the same feelings? He asked me out, you know."

"Oh, come on," Kim said, dismissing it. "He knows how she feels about him, and he *does* feel the same. He's just being a stubborn idiot."

Vanessa restated her doubt. Sammie, though, had a dreamy look on her face. "Well, if I felt that way about a man, I'd come right out and tell him."

Kim turned to her and laughed. "Yeah, but you do that with almost every man you meet!" This cracked Vanessa up as well. But it didn't last long.

Kim sighed. "The only reason we're laughing is because it isn't happening to us."

Vanessa nodded. "The only other man Lisa ever loved was killed in action."

"This makes me so sad…" Sammie said tearfully.

*Yeah,* Vanessa thought, putting her hand on Sammie's shoulder. *But what would we do for entertainment around here without Lisa and Rick?* What was there in her own life—or in Kim's or Sammie's—that even approximated passion and the dream of a new start? Rico, Konda, and Bron? That was a dead end on several counts. She grew tearful herself, for all of them. For the emptiness at the center of this brave new world they had all been thrown into.

In spite of the threatening skies, Lisa had decided to walk home from the base. The clouds opened up before she had made it halfway to the New Macross burbs, drenching her instantly and chilling her to the bone. A long winter was on its way.

*When the world is out of sync with your inner life, you come to think of it as a heartless, godless realm; and yet when it mirrors those thoughts and feelings, you dismiss it as pathetic fallacy.*

She stood thinking this to herself in front of Rick's quarters. There were lights on inside, and once she saw his silhouette pass briefly behind the picture window perma-glass. It wasn't aimless wandering that had brought her here, but she couldn't summon up the nerve to go up to the door. Rather, she had a peace offering in mind: She'd leave Claudia's tea in Rick's mailbox, go home and phone him, and—

"Planning to drink that tea in the rain?"

All at once there was an umbrella overhead and Claudia was beside her, smiling. "Why don't you go up and knock?"

"He doesn't want to see me," Lisa told her, raising her voice above the sound of the rain.

"You've made up his mind for him, huh? Well, listen, if you're not ready to talk to him right now, why don't you come on over to my place? We'll dry off and talk some—what do you say?"

Lisa hesitated, and Claudia put the umbrella in her hand.

"Well, while you're thinking about it…"

"Claudia, I…" Lisa began, but her friend was already trotting off. Lisa gave another hopeless glance toward Rick's window and followed after her.

"I've made some nice hot tea," Claudia called out from the kitchen.

Lisa was on the living room sofa towel-drying her hair. Tea sounded all right, but the chill she was feeling ran clear through to her heart. "At the risk of sounding like a pushy guest," she said when Claudia entered with the tea serving, "you wouldn't happen to have anything stronger lying around, would you?"

Claudia's eyebrows went up. "Like what?"

"You hiding any wine around the house?"

A big grin appeared on her friend's handsome face.

"You got it."

"Well, go get it!" Lisa said playfully. She had a low tolerance for alcohol and drugs of any sort, which was both a good and a bad thing: On the one hand, her body simply rebelled at overindulgence, a fact that kept her from turning to drugs for escape in times of stress; while on the other hand, she could count on a little going a long way—one or two drinks and inhibition was a thing of the past. A classic "cheap date," she reminded herself.

"Burgundy all right?"

"Right now I'd settle for Zentraedi zinfandel."

Claudia returned with two wine goblets and sat down facing Lisa on the matching recliner. A framed photo of Roy held center stage on the low table between them. She pulled the cork from the bottle and poured two full glasses. Lisa offered a silent toast and drained the entire glass, sensing an almost instantaneous warmth suffuse her body. She settled back against the couch and smiled at Claudia.

"So how long does it take for the hurting to stop?" she asked her.

"You sound like you're giving up."

"When he came in with his report this morning, I really wanted to apologize, but then, before I could, he started chewing me out."

Claudia refilled Lisa's glass. "What did he say?"

"Only that his personal life was his own business and that I should stay out of it." Again Lisa drained the glass.

"What did you expect?" Claudia was saying. "He doesn't know how you feel about him. You've both shared some ordeals and some close conversation, but as far as he knows, you're just his fellow officer and sometime friend."

"I know… I've *tried* to be honest about it… but I don't think it would matter anyway."

Claudia had never seen her friend quite so loosened up. Lisa was holding her glass out for yet another refill, but she already looked pretty low-lidded. Claudia didn't want her to get sick or pass out, but she poured a little more burgundy, anyway.

"You don't *know* that it wouldn't matter to him. Stop trying to outguess him all the time. Just do it, Lisa."

Lisa blinked and shook her head. "Okay, toss it up to the wine."

"Fine. But you weren't drinking out there in the rain twenty minutes ago when you decided he wouldn't want to see you… The situation's *not* as hopeless as you think—at least the man you love is still alive… Of course, I know that you've had that experience also," Claudia was quick to add.

Both women turned to the photo of Roy.

Claudia continued. "When Roy passed away, *this*," she said, holding up her wine, "became a very necessary crutch for me… Now, nothing seems to be important anymore."

Lisa was stunned, almost brought back to the edge of sobriety. *But what about all that optimism?* she wanted to ask—all those *teas*? Instead, she said: "There's a difference, anyway… You and Roy hit it off from the very start… Rick and I were… enemies, I mean, enemies." Lisa stopped and took a breath: *"Enemies."*

Claudia chuckled, then grew somber. "It wasn't like that at all—Roy and I were at each other's throats all the time. It nearly drove me crazy."

*A second revelation!* thought Lisa.

Claudia reached for Roy's photo. "Do you want to laugh? I'll tell ya 'bout him!"

Lisa laughed up front. "Lemme tell ya something—right now I'll take all the laughs I can get!"

Rick was too exhausted to sleep; it was as if he had somehow passed beyond the need for rest. And that cold prewinter rain beating down on the flat roof of his small modular barracks home seemed to be keeping time with his racing heart.

He had tried to focus his thoughts on Khyron's whereabouts; the latest intel reports pointed to a southern route of retreat. But where, Rick had asked himself while pouring over the reports and reworked maps—somewhere in what used to be Mexico, or the decimated Panamanian land bridge, the Amazon jungles, such as they were? Where was he hiding, and what was his next move likely to be? Even Breetai hadn't a clue.

He gave up on this after a while and collapsed on his back to the bed, still in his uniform, hands locked underneath his head.

*Why did I have to go and shoot off my big mouth like that?* he asked himself, getting at last to the center of his confusion. *The least I could have done was to listen to what she had to say!*

That tall, blond, smooth-talking, and guitar-strumming Roy Fokker had been a ladies' man came as no surprise to Lisa; but to hear Claudia tell it, he had also been something of a scoundrel and *womanizer*. Lisa had always known Claudia and Roy as the happy couple—this went back to the early days on Macross Island when the SDF-1 was first being rebuilt. But the stories Claudia had regaled her with for the past two hours painted a much different portrait than the one Lisa had imagined.

Claudia met Roy in 1996, during the initial stage of what would come to be called the Global Civil War, when the two of them were stationed together at a top-secret base in Wyoming: Roy the eager young fighter jock, half in love with death and destruction, and Claudia the naive recruit, easily impressed and often taken advantage of. Claudia described an arrogant Roy to Lisa: a whacko flyboy who would be plying her with gifts one week, then showing up for a date with three adoring women in tow the next. A Roy who would down enemy fighters in her honor but who would rarely call in advance to cancel an appointment.

"Talk about a complex personality," Claudia said. "At first I didn't want anything to do with him, and I avoided him as much as possible. I even told him so, point-blank. But… it didn't work— Roy Fokker was nothing if not persistent.

"But what I'm trying to tell you is that our first impressions can be all wrong. Roy and I never really *talked* to each other, or said how we actually felt, until it was too late… And then he was gone."

Lisa was momentarily confused; then she realized that Claudia was referring not to Roy's death but to his overseas transfer during the Global Civil War.

For over a year Claudia didn't hear from Roy; but ultimately they both wound up on Macross Island soon after the "Visitor" crash landed. Still, it was rough going. Roy now had a new love: Robotechnology—specifically, the Veritech fighters that Dr. Lang's teams of scientists were developing.

"He used to look at those experimental aircraft the way I wished he would look at me," Claudia explained.

She had actually left unopened all the gifts Roy had given her in the old days and returned them to him years later, hoping he would come clean with her about how he felt. But Roy had simply chalked it up to fate, telling her with a shrug, that you couldn't win them all! And it was Claudia who had ended up hurt. On another occasion she saw him dancing and carrying on with three women in a way that suggested that they knew him much more intimately than she did.

But finally—on a rainy night much like tonight, Claudia went on—Roy confessed his love for her. As obsessed as he was with flying and combat, he was equally obsessed with death; he was certain that he would die in a fighter, and it was only Claudia he could talk to about his hidden fears.

"It was quite a revelation for me to realize that underneath all that mechamorph bravado, there was a sensitive human being, full of real dreams and real fears," said Claudia. "Deep down I knew it all along. But look at all the happiness I lost with him just because I wasn't able to say what was in my heart. I just hope that you won't let the same thing happen to you, Lisa."

Lisa polished off the last sip of wine and set her glass on the table, staring at it absently. Rick had never pulled half the stunts Roy had; she at least had that to be thankful for. But in some ways her problems with Rick ran even deeper than Claudia and Roy's: Their arguments centered on issues like… competition and control… and *Minmei*! Roy had stepped out from behind his mask, but Rick Hunter didn't wear a mask.

The ball remained in Lisa's court, and even now, after all these hours of wine and honest conversation, she still didn't know how to play it.

While Lisa was visiting Claudia's past, Rick was running through his own. He recalled his first exchange with Lisa, when he had called her "an old sourpuss," and their first meeting after he had embarrassed himself in a lingerie shop. Then there were the countless arguments, most of them over the com net, related to procedure and such. Their capture and interrogation on Breetai's flagship. *That first kiss…* The decoration that followed their escape, the complex crosscurrents that developed after Lynn-Kyle entered the scene. The time Lisa had visited him in the hospital—after inadvertently shooting him down. Roy's death, and how she had tried to comfort him … Ben's death on that horrible afternoon over Ontario… The final battle that brought them all together, the way they ran into each other's arms after he had touched down near Alaska Base, thinking themselves the last survivors of their race. And the two long years of Reconstruction following that fateful day. He and Lisa as a team: planning, supervising, rebuilding. She would come over to his quarters for a late-night snack or just hang out and read while he was off somewhere on patrol—often clean up the mess he invariably left behind. And that day not long ago when she had presented him with a picture of her to add to his album…

For the first time he felt as though he were seeing the whole progression of their friendship clearly. And isolated from its various backdrops—Minmei, Kyle, the war without end, Reconstruction blues—their relationship suddenly leapt out as the most significant one in his life. What leapt out with equal clarity was that he had been an absolute *fool!*

How, he asked himself now, could he have run that lame number on Vanessa—just to hurt Lisa?! He realized that his stubborn refusal to believe that Lisa was in love with him was all wrapped up in the Minmei dreams he himself perpetuated. Lisa represented a *threat* to those dreams, much as Minmei was a threat to Lisa's dreams. Dawn's harsh words were crystal clear, and so were Rick's thoughts: He jumped out of bed feeling as though he had slept for a month, refreshed and revitalized, with one purpose in mind—to find Lisa.

He grabbed an umbrella and ran through the rain to her place, but she wasn't there. He tried a spot in town she frequented; no one had seen her. He phoned headquarters, and the SDF-2 duty chief told him that Lisa had signed out hours ago… That left only one more possibility.

He deposited another token in the pay phone and tapped in the numbers as rapidly as he could.

"You're kidding," Lisa slurred when Claudia informed her that Rick was on the phone.

"He called from across the street." Claudia smiled, re-cradling the handset.

"You're serious."

"You bet I am." Claudia picked up Fokker's picture and regarded it. "Now I wanna have a drink with this fella," she said. "So don't plan on hanging around here with your friend."

Lisa was suddenly flustered. "What'll I say?"

"What'll you say? If you don't know by now, then we've wasted the whole evening."

In a moment Rick was pounding on the door, and Claudia was handing Lisa yet another box of tea. "Your Prince Charming is here. Now, go on, and take this with you—it's a great little icebreaker."

...

They walked silently, shoulder to shoulder beneath Rick's umbrella. Lisa was carrying on a running dialogue with herself, and by the looks of it, Rick was too. After all they had been through together, tonight had all the uneasiness of a first date. Something as yet unspoken had altered the way they reacted to each other.

"Uh, you aren't going to be too cold, are you?" Rick asked her.

"Oh, no… Are you?"

Rick suggested they call a cab, even though it was only a few blocks to either of their quarters—and that was the general idea, *wasn't it?* She smiled and said that she enjoyed walking.

Rick agreed: *Yeah, it felt good to walk.*

"I walk a lot at night," said Lisa.

"That's great—it's terrific exercise."

Finally, when she couldn't stand the small talk anymore, she said: "Rick. We've got to talk."

They were at the corner nearest his place. Rick gestured. "We could go to my quarters, but I don't have anything to offer you—er, wine or…"

She produced the package of tea. "I've got just the thing."

Rick smiled. "You're a lifesaver," he told her.

# 16

First and foremost we must accept who we are; only then can we gain a clear view of our motives. How well I recall being one of the *important* people, and how well I recall the effect that illusory self-image had on my decisions and motivations. Fallen from grace, I was rescued from what might otherwise have been a transparent existence. *Unimportant*, I learned to know myself. This forms the basis for the following lesson.

Jan Morris, *Solar Seeds, Galactic Guardians*

NOVEMBER 2014 CAME AND WENT, THANKSGIVING FOR THOSE who remembered it—not in remembrance of the pilgrims, though, but in memory of the feast held two years before, when the SDF-1 returned to its devastated homeworld and founded New Macross. Wild flowers covered the western slopes of the Rockies, and blue skies had become an everyday event. The cities had been peaceful, and there was no further sign of Khyron. Minmei was back on tour.

Rick and Lisa had been seeing a lot of each other. This morning she was in the small kitchen of her quarters, humming to herself while preparing sandwiches and snacks for the picnic she and Rick had planned. On routine patrol only days ago, he had discovered an ideal spot in the nearby forest. Lisa was in high spirits. She had a map of the area spread out on the table. It seemed like months since she had taken personal leave and years since she had done anything like this. And she owed at least some of her happiness to Claudia for getting her to be more honest with Rick; she had told him how special he was, and surprise of surprises, he had said he felt the same way toward her.

In his own quarters a few blocks away, Rick was getting himself ready. Lisa had said she wanted to take care of the food; all he had to do was show up on time. He was certain he could handle that much. It was strange to be out of uniform, almost frightening to contemplate a return to normalcy, days and days of uninterrupted peace. And that very sense of discomfort made him ask himself how similar the human and Zentraedi races had become: in their own way grown dependent on war.

The phone rang while he was shaving. He turned off the razor and went to answer it, figuring it was Lisa trying to hurry him along.

"I'm almost ready," he said into the handset, not bothering to ask who was on the line. "I'll be there—"

"Hi there, it's me!"

Suddenly uncertain, Rick looked at the phone.

"It's Minmei!"

"Oh, Minmei!" he answered, perking up. "Where've you been?"

"All *over* the place," she said dismissively. "Where are you now?"

Rick looked at the phone again. "*Home.*"

Minmei laughed. "Oops, I completely forgot! I called to thank you... for saving me and... Kyle. I mean it."

"You don't have to thank me, Minmei," Rick said plainly.

After a moment she asked him if he was free for the day. Rick hemmed and hawed but didn't mention the picnic. She was hoping that he could make it over to Monument City—she had a few hours free before tonight's concert. "I kinda made plans already."

"Oh, please, Rick," she purred. "I'm only here for today, and I'm sure whoever you're going to meet won't mind."

Rick thought back to his conversation with Lisa, how he'd asked her to cancel whatever plans she had made so they could get together for the picnic. He looked at his watch and wondered what sort of last-minute excuse he could come up with. Sickness? A new war?

"Pleease..." she repeated.

"Uh, I guess it's okay," he said, relenting. "It's not every day that I get to spend time with you."

"It'll be fun," Minmei said excitedly. "You can see your friend any time, right?"

"Yeah…"

"Great! I'll be waiting for you at the airport. And dress up," she told him.

*An old school chum showed up,* Rick thought, replacing the handset. *Somebody who just wandered in from the wastelands.* Quickly he punched up Lisa's number, but of course she had already left; more than likely she was already at the Seciele coffee shop waiting for him. Better to say nothing, he decided at last. Just not show up at all.

*There are a hundred reasons why this* is *a good idea,* Rick said to himself as he dropped his fanjet in for a landing on Monument's new strip, not the least of which was the chance to put his little craft through some paces—it had been months since he'd taken it out. And of course it was good for his relationship with Lisa: putting his feelings for Minmei to rest and such. But "sudden business in Monument City" was what he planned to tell Lisa; he promised himself that he would take her on *two* picnics to make up for this.

He cut quite the dashing figure in his new gray jumpsuit as he jumped from the cockpit. He had changed from denim and flannel to his one and only suit and was wearing it underneath, a black scarf tied around his neck.

"I'm over here, Rick!" Minmei waved from behind the chain-link fence. "How've you been, flyboy?"

He approached her, smiling. She was wearing a tight-fitting sweater and skirt, heels, a large red hat that matched her belt, and big round tinted glasses.

"I don't think I would have recognized you," he confessed.

She laughed. "That's the point, silly."

Rick got out of the jumpsuit and stowed it in his carry case, while she ran to the gate, coming around to his side of the fence.

In a moment they were walking arm in arm, not saying much to each other. Rick felt uncomfortable in his button-down shirt and tie but tried not to convey it.

"Listen, Rick," Minmei said at last, biting her lower lip. "I'm sorry to drag you away from your appointment. I hope he wasn't mad at you, whoever he was."

Rick cleared his throat. "Uh no, *he* wasn't mad… I rescheduled my appointment with him…" Minmei pressed herself against him, her hand caressing his arm. People were checking them out as they strolled by. "Aren't you worried that someone might recognize you… and me, and, er…"

"I'm never worried with you," Minmei sighed. She turned him around and reached for the knot in his tie, adjusting it. "I've never seen you in a suit before. You're very handsome—you look important."

*Important?* he asked himself. He remembered how good it felt to be in denim and flannel—strange but good. And here he was in a suit, wandering around Monument City with a *star* on his arm, looking *important,* and receiving compliments left and right. What did Minmei have in mind? he wondered. Lisa had wanted to picnic and hike.

Minmei had rented a vehicle for them to use. Rick climbed behind the wheel and followed her directions into the city. Monument was about the closest thing Macross had to a sister city. It had been founded by Zentraedi once under Breetai's command, who had rallied around the crashed warship towering out of its lake the way humans had around Lake Gloval's similarly situated SDF-1. Monument had spearheaded the separatist movement and had recently been the first to be granted autonomy from the Macross Council.

She sensed that she might have done something wrong, but she had only been trying to show him how she felt about him. If flattery wasn't going to work, she had hopes that the restaurant she was leading them to would do it: beautiful view, great food, soft music… It was probably more suited to quiet dinners than early lunches, but it had been difficult enough to block out even a few midmorning hours from her busy schedule. And there were only so many excuses she could come up with to convince Kyle that she needed private time.

Chez Mann was an anachronism, a sumptuously decorated theater restaurant with window walls, crystal chandeliers, and tuxedoed waiters, which, for all its pretensions, ended up looking like an airport cafeteria. An arrogant maître d' showed them not to the secluded table Minmei requested but to a deserted-looking one along the window wall, while a lifeless pianist noodled his way soullessly through an old standard.

"Do you like it?" Minmei said when they were seated. "My producer has a friend who's part owner. Movie stars come in here all the time," she continued, pressing her point.

Rick regarded her quizzically. Minmei seemed incapable of accepting the present state of the world. *Movie stars:* There weren't more than a handful of entertainers left on the entire planet, let alone in Monument City! In fact, if anything, the notion of entertainment was reverting back to much earlier forms of storytelling and what amounted to religious drama and reenactments.

"Who cares about movie stars?" Rick said harshly.

Minmei smiled at him. "Well, *I'm* a movie star, and you like *me.*"

"I liked you *before* you were a star, Minmei."

Her first reaction was to tell him: *I've always been a star.* Miffed, she said: "You mean you don't like me just because I happen to be famous?"

"I like you," he reassured her, but she had already turned her attention to something else. Rick glanced down at his watch and thought again about Lisa. When he looked up, Minmei was sliding a present toward him.

"Just my way of saying thank you, Rick."

He didn't want to accept it. It wasn't, after all, like he'd done her some sort of *favor.* But she insisted, claiming that she had looked all over for something special. Finally, he shrugged and opened the wrapping; inside was a winter scarf of handwoven alpaca wool, as rare as hen's teeth these days.

He put it around his neck and thanked her. "I'll think of you whenever I wear it."

"It looks good with that suit," she commented, hoping the nervousness she felt wasn't visible. It was so important to her that he understand how she felt.

"Makes me feel like Errol Flynn," Rick joked, striking a pose.

She laughed. "All you need is a sword."

Minmei wanted to reach out and take his hand, but just then the waiter appeared with cocktails and set them on the table. The moment spoiled, she looked across to Rick and said: "Why do waiters always seem to serve people at precisely the wrong time?"

The waiter, a long-haired would-be actor with a pencil-thin mustache who had had a bad morning, returned: "And why is it that movie stars always seem to find something to complain about?"

Rick stifled a laugh, happy to see Minmei taken to task. But it hardly fazed her. He joined her in a toast to "better times" and began to feel suddenly at ease. They began to talk about the old times—for the two of them, a period of scarcely four years. To Rick it felt like yesterday, but Minmei seemed to think those times a million years ago.

"Some things time can't change," Rick said cryptically.

She nodded. "I know. Sometimes I think my feelings haven't changed at all."

It was an equally vague sort of response, and Rick, recalling Minmei's feelings, wasn't sure he wanted things to return to yesteryear. He decided to be straightforward—the way Lisa had been with him recently—just to see where it would lead.

"I still think about you, Minmei," he began. "Sometimes at night, I—"

There was some sort of commotion at the door; the maître d' was shouting, insisting that the man who had shoved his way past him was required to wear a tie before entering. The long-haired man turned out to be Lynn-Kyle.

Both Rick and Minmei had turned their attention to the scene; now they were staring at each other blankly. Minmei took Rick's hand, squeezing it, her eyes brimming with tears.

"*Please* Rick, you've got to promise me: Whatever he does, whatever he says, you won't interfere."

"But—" he started to protest.

"Promise me!"

Rick's lips became a thin line, and he nodded silently.

In a moment Kyle was standing over Minmei.

"I've been looking all over for you," he said, controlled but obviously angered. "You knew I scheduled a press conference. Come on, we're leaving."

He made a move toward her, but she refused to budge. "Don't be obstinate, Minmei! Do you realize the strings I had to pull to get those reporters out here today?!"

Rick held himself in check, the scarf still around his neck; Kyle hadn't bothered to acknowledge him. Rick guessed he was still sore about having had to be rescued. *The dirt bag.* Still, this was business, and maybe Kyle had a right to be angry. He decided to help Minmei out by offering to leave. But instead, she put him right in the middle of things.

"We don't have to leave—I'm not going!"

Now Kyle grabbed her by the wrist. "Oh yes you are!"

"Get your hands off!" she retaliated. "You're hurting me, you bully! Who do you think you are, anyway?!"

Surprisingly enough, Kyle backed off, and Rick offered silent thanks to the heavens, because if it had gone on another second, he would have been all over Kyle, promise or no promise, martial arts or no. The piano player had stopped his noodling, the restaurant patrons having found more accessible entertainment.

Kyle grinned knowingly and turned to Rick. "This is how a professional acts... Attractive, isn't it?" He swung back to Minmei, raising his voice parentally. "That's enough of your whining! Why don't you try acting your age for once? People are waiting for you!"

Minmei was standing at her place, her fists clenched. She grabbed her cocktail and downed the thing defiantly, shivering and trying to brave it out. Rick looked out the window.

"I'm tipsy..." he heard her say. "I couldn't *possibly* talk to any reporters now."

Kyle issued a low guttural growl, a dangerous signal that Minmei might have overplayed her part. With lightning speed he scooped up the water glass and threw it in her face.

"That oughta sober you up."

Rick was halfway out of his chair, his teeth bared, waiting for the next move. Minmei had begun to sob, and once again Kyle had her by the wrist.

"Now, stop acting foolish and let's go."

Kyle tugged, she followed; then she suddenly turned and shouted for Rick.

"Kyle!" he screamed, expecting him to let go of her and come after him. Kyle, however, chose a subtler way to disarm him.

"Don't you understand, Hunter?" he said, reasonably and in full possession of himself. "She's got too many things that have to be taken care of. It comes with the territory." When he saw Rick relax, he added: "Oh, and don't worry about lunch: We'll cover it—that's what expense accounts are for. Maybe you should just report back to your base, huh? Get back into your uniform or something."

Rick saw Minmei nod to him, sobbing but gesturing that he should do as Kyle said. Kyle tugged at her again, lecturing her about how he had given up everything, how she didn't care about her career anymore. Most of the patrons were bored by now; many had simply gotten up and left the restaurant.

Rick avoided their stares and reached for his drink, fingering the new scarf. *Some swashbuckler,* he said to himself.

It was almost noon, and the Seciele coffee shop was beginning to gear up for lunch, although the majority of its outdoor tables remained empty. The weather had taken a sudden turn, and most people were electing to take indoor seats. Lisa, however, was still at the table she had occupied since nine o'clock. She had already downed four cups of coffee and was sweating despite the sudden chill in the air. There had been no word from Rick, but she had decided to remain in case he tried to get a message through. Obviously he had been called in, but no one at the base knew anything about it or knew where he might be. If there had been an alert, she would also have been notified, but no such orders had been given. Still, Rick's being called in was the only possible explanation.

The good mood she had enjoyed only hours before had long since abandoned her along with the morning's unnatural warmth.

Were these quick turnabouts a sign of the times? she questioned—the mood swings, the reversals, the confusion? Only moments ago she had witnessed a small misunderstanding between a pedestrian and a motorist escalate into a violent argument. It made her wonder if Rick had been involved in an accident, perhaps run over!

Anxiously, she checked the time and hurried to the vidphone. There was no answer at Rick's quarters, so she toned in the base again, contemplating a fall leaf that had blown her away—the closest she might come to nature all day.

"Communications. This is Lieutenant Mitchell."

Lisa identified herself, but before she had an opportunity to inquire about a possible alert, Nikki Mitchell said: "Captain Hayes, I thought you were with Commander Hunter."

Lisa instantly regretted phoning them. Her life had practically become an open book to the SDF-2 control room crew, Vanessa, Sammie, and the rest. It was one of those damned-if-you-do, damned-if-you-don't situations: When she was cool, calm, and collected, Lisa Hayes "the old sourpuss," no one bothered to interfere with her private life; but now that she had taken some of Claudia's advice and was speaking her mind, everyone was tracking her moves as if she was a regular entry in some sort of gossip column contest.

"Aren't you supposed to be on a picnic?" Mitchell asked. In the background, Lisa could hear Kim say: "I bet that creep stood her up." Vanessa reinforced it: "See, I told you he wasn't interested in her."

"Shut up!" Nikki yelled, and Lisa held the phone away from her ear. "You two sound like a couple of old hens!"

"And what does that make you—the rooster?" Sammie countered.

Lisa was furious. Not only was her private life being discussed behind her back, but it was being wagered upon and argued about!

"Oh, never mind!" Lisa yelled, and hung up. "Busy bodies," she muttered under her breath.

Cut off by the Chez Mann bartender after countless drinks, Rick had drifted back to the right-hand-drive rented vehicle and started out for the airport. The scene that had taken place between Minmei and Kyle now seemed just that: an orchestrated act put on for the public, with a cameo by Rick Hunter, occasional hero. In the end Minmei had chosen to run along with Kyle, and that was all that really mattered: She hadn't changed, and Rick had been a fool to think she could. Presents, wistful walks down memory lane, post-rescue embraces: it was all part of her repertoire. And now he had lost her for the umpteenth time and stood up Lisa to boot.

Up ahead of him on the two-lane airport highway was a roadblock manned by a CD corporal wearing a white beret. The road was closed, Rick was informed.

"Is there an alternate route to the airport?" he asked, leaning out the driver's window.

"Airport's closed," said the corporal. "We've got Zentraedi trouble."

"My plane's out there!" Rick shouted, not clear-headed enough to show his ID.

The corporal's hand edged toward his sidearm. "I told you, buddy, the road's closed."

Rick cursed him and stomped on the accelerator. The minivan shot forward, swerving around the barricade, while the sentry drew his weapon. In thinking about it later, Rick would ask himself why he had done this, wondering whether to blame Minmei or the alcohol. In the final analysis, however, he realized that he had done it for Lisa: He was going to have to tell her *something*!

"Damn fool!" the sentry yelled, thinking twice about firing a warning shot and hurrying to his radio phone.

A Battlepod ambled along the runway, destroying grounded Veritechs with blasts from its plastron cannon, while nearby a giant Zentraedi armed with an autocannon picked off fire and rescue vehicles that were tearing across the tarmac en route to crisis points.

"These Micronians are no challenge at all!" he yelled in his own tongue, the lust for battle erasing all memories of his two peaceful years on Earth.

A second giant in Botoru powered armor lifted a fighter from the field, pressed it over his head, and heaved it at a speeding transport truck several hundred feet away. The Veritech fell squarely on the vehicle and exploded, obliterating both.

Veritechs appeared in the skies now, just as Rick was arriving in the minivan. Dodging gatling slugs, he made his way to the CD hangar, showed his ID, suited up, and commandeered an Excalibur. He had counted five giants—all armed with autocannons—a sixth in powered armor, and at least two Battlepods. Whether these were malcontents or members of Khyron's beaten band was immaterial: The CD unit was outpowered. And yet the base commander was giving him a lot of flack about clearance and warning him *not to damage the mecha!* Rick realized that Monument's recently gained autonomy accounted for this, but without a little help, there wasn't going to be much of a Monument left; so he humored the commander, shaking off the last of his alcoholic stupor.

Meanwhile, a Battlepod was holing the passenger terminal with volleys of fire. His ally with the cannon had tired of firing on the private craft and now turned his attention to the terminal. Peering through a horizontal row of permaglass windows, he spied several Micronians huddled together behind the desks of a spacious office—the most laughable sight he had seen all day. It was too easy to blow them away as a group, so he first drove the muzzle of the autocannon through the plate glass to scatter everyone. Only then did he train the weapon on them, bolts of white energy flinging bodies to gruesome deaths.

One of his less exacting comrades emptied his cannon against the building in an effort to collapse the entire wall.

Rick stepped his mecha from the hangar in time to see a pod with its left foot posed above his small fanjet, preparing to stomp it out of existence. He got off a shot without thinking and managed to take the pod's leg off at the knee, sending the mecha backward and down on its back to the field. This captured the attention of the remaining Zentraedis, who swung around to find themselves face to face with two Excaliburs and a Battloid.

"Zentraedi rebels!" Rick yelled through the external net. "Throw down your weapons at once or we will be forced to take immediate action!" He repeated it even as the soldiers and mecha were leveling their weapons against him.

"Prove it!" said one of the giants, a purple faced, blue-haired clone with gorilla features. He gestured to his fellow warrior and opened fire, autocannon slugs raining ineffectively against the armored legs of Rick's Excalibur.

"They're bluffing!" he shouted when his weapon had expended its charge.

Rick smiled madly inside the cockpit. "Give them a demonstration," he ordered.

Suddenly a drum-armed Spartan was looming into view on the other side of the airport terminal. Rick gave the word, and scores of missiles streaked heavenward from the mecha's launch tubes. The three Zentraedi giants tracked their course with frightened eyes and screamed as the missiles plunged homeward, exploding like strings of fireworks at the giants' feet. The three were blown from the strike zone, one flung to his death against a massive conduit, the others gasping for air as paralyzing nerve gas released from the missiles began to sweep over them.

"Move in!" Rick said over the tac net.

Reconfiguring to Guardian mode, the Battloid went after the remaining Battlepod; but the Zentraedi mecha juked and sidestepped, facing off with Rick's Excalibur instead. Rick dropped his mecha to a crouch and tackled the pod, shearing off one of its legs as it passed overhead. Out of commission, the mecha hit the field with a ground-shaking crash, its severed leg bouncing along with it.

The one giant who had survived the gas was easily dispatched by the second Excalibur, while the Veritech just as easily dropped the alien in powered armor.

Rick ordered the civil defense units to collect the bodies, separate the living from the dead, and lock the former away for interrogation.

"And radio the SDF-2 for me," Rick added as an afterthought. "Make sure you mention that I was here."

With a little luck, Lisa would receive word of the uprising even before he made it back to New Macross.

. . .

Lisa had switched over to cocktails, and by the time the robo-waiter cruised over to inform her that outdoor service was being discontinued, she had had so many Bloody Marys that she was seeing red. The waiting game had become some sort of crazed exercise in self-control. She had visions of Rick finding her skeletal remains here, her withered hand permanently affixed to the thermos or the picnic basket. The temperature had fallen a further fifteen degrees since noon, and the wind had picked up, gusting in autumn leaves that swirled around her feet. Once, a puppy had wandered by and she had fed him snacks from the wicker basket. She had been eyed by more than one Veritech jock and coffee shop poet. But now she was ready to throw in the towel. That Rick Hunter had *died* was the only excuse she was ready to accept.

But no sooner did she hear Rick's voice than she went back on her word. He was running up the street toward her, dressed, oddly enough, in his one and only suit and wearing a long scarf around his neck. Hardly the picnic and hiking outfit she had expected, but she decided to at least give him a chance to explain.

"Let's hear it, Rick," she said coolly from her chair.

Rick was panting. "I didn't think you'd still be here… I checked your quarters first… You see, there was a Zentraedi uprising in Monument and—"

"An uprising?!" Lisa said, surprised. "Is everything all right?"

"Yeah, now it is. But there were a number of deaths and—"

"Wait a minute," she interrupted him. "We have no jurisdiction in Monument. What were you doing there?"

"Well, I… had some official business—"

"Which is why you're wearing your suit, of course."

Rick looked himself over as if noticing the suit for the first time. "This was for our date."

Lisa laughed. "It was supposed to be a picnic, remember—not a cocktail party."

"Look…"

She made a dismissive gesture and stood up, taking hold of the basket and thermos. "It's too late for a picnic now. And it's a shame, really, because I spent all morning cooking. It's the first time I've had a chance to do that in years."

Rick stammered an apology.

"You should have called me," she told him. "I've been waiting here all day, worried that something had happened to you and figuring you would try to get a message to me somehow. Now you give me this story about an uprising and some mysterious business—"

"There *was* an uprising! Check with the base if you don't believe me. Besides, I did try to call you…"

She threw him a suspicious look. "You're here now. We can at least take a walk."

Lisa didn't hear Rick's sigh of relief. She was too busy concentrating on the fact that he was cozying up to her, draping one end of that scarf around her shoulders. The temperature was continuing to plunge, and there was a winter dampness in the air. She reached up to feel the weave; it was so soft, she touched the cloth to her cheek. And suddenly stopped dead in her tracks.

She might have had a poor memory for faces and two left feet when it came to dancing and a habit of picking derelicts for boyfriends, but one thing she prided herself on was her talent for remembering aromas and tastes. And she sure as heck recognized the perfume on that scarf: *Innocent*—Lynn-Minmei's favorite!

"Take that thing off me, Hunter!" she exclaimed. "You seem to have wrapped it around the wrong person!"

"Lisa, I can explain everything! It's not what you think!" Rick said, as she threw one end of the scarf over his shoulder.

"I recognize the scent, you idiot! So *that* was your official business, huh?" she began to walk away. "And don't bother calling me!"

She shouted it without turning around because she didn't want him to see the tears in her eyes.

Snowflakes had begun to fall.

"Good evening, ladies and gentlemen of Monument City," Lynn-Kyle announced from that city's bandshell by the lake. "Congratulations on your autonomy from the central government. Tonight, in celebration of that event, we have a special treat in store. Minmei has graciously agreed to come and sing for you. Let's all hang *our* hopes for a bright future on her songs… And so, let's have a warm welcome… for a great talent—*Lynn-Minmei!*"

The audience of mostly Zentraedi giants applauded and cheered as the orchestra commenced the opening bars of "Stagefright." The bandshell blacked out, and Kyle moved off to the wings. On the stage's upper tiers, a wide spot found Minmei; she stood unmoving, arms at her sides, the mike dangling from one hand.

Even *after* the song's intro.

Kyle looked up, full of concern. The band had broken into a low-volume vamp, awaiting her entrance. "Minmei, that was your cue!" Kyle whispered. When she didn't respond, he tried another tack. "Quit fooling around! Are you all right?!"

"Yes," she said with a sad smile. The band had broken off altogether now, and murmurs were running through the audience. Some thought it part of the act—a new form of dramatic effect or something—and a rhythmical clapping began, punctuated with shouts of "Minmei! Minmei! Minmei!"

"What's the problem?!" hissed Kyle. "Sing!"

She had one arm across her chest self-protectively and her eyes averted from the audience. Kyle heard her sigh; then she suddenly turned to them. "I'm sorry—I can't perform!"

The clapping died down.

"I won't sing," she continued, on the verge of tears. "I can't perform when my heart is breaking!"

And with that she dropped the mike, turned, and fled. The audience surged forward, refusing to believe this, and Kyle was all at once stunned and worried about a riot. Quickly, he signaled the stage manager to lower the bandshell's eyelid-like curtain.

The audience fell back to watch its descent. And the moment carried with it a discomforting note of finality; the Zentraedi ship in the lake loomed behind the closed bandshell like a spike driven into the all-seeing eye.

Kyle found her on the littered beach behind the bandshell. She was alone, hugging her knees, staring at the ruined Zentraedi ship. He wasn't sure that anything he said would turn the trick. And for the first time he didn't care. She had moved away from him, withdrawn from the high goals they had both set themselves. Unreachable, she had ceased to interest him any longer; she was beyond his control.

"This is all your fault," Minmei said, sensing somehow that he was standing over her. "Since I've been with you, I've lost touch with the things that are really important to me."

Kyle laughed shortly. "You haven't changed a bit, have you? Still the selfish brat! You know, you only think about what *you* want, just like you've done since you were a kid. Well, it's about time you grew up. Don't you have any idea how those people felt when you refused to sing for them tonight? You should've seen their faces… They're your fans, and they love you. And what do you do? You go and let them down. That's just like you!"

Minmei struggled with his words, determined not to let Kyle get to her. She knew what he was up to: pulling out all the stops now to convince her to come around. And she knew it would get worse—*uglier*.

"I just can't do it anymore," she said firmly.

Kyle reconfigured his tone. "If you just opened your heart and let the love flow through you, you could be the greatest talent ever. Through your music, we could transcend all the evil in the universe and bring people together… That's a precious gift, Minmei, but it has to be properly presented. That's why I've worked so hard for three years… But now, this is the end. I'm going to take a long trip, and I probably won't see you again—at least not for some time…"

A ferry was crossing the lake, its mournful horn sounding. Minmei clenched her teeth, hating Kyle for his hypocrisy, his years of abuse. He had almost succeeded in dragging her down to that plane of misery and cynicism he lived on—despite the *noble* sound of his words, the *peaceful* thrust of his speeches. And now he was simply going to walk out on her—his standard approach to interpersonal challenge when martial arts wouldn't do it. So of course it was important for him to make her realize that she'd been rotten all along, that he could do nothing with such flimsy stuff, that she was no longer worth the effort. He had done the same thing to his parents.

He had draped his jacket over her shoulders in preparation for a theatrical exit.

"I hope that someday," he was saying, "you can find happiness for yourself. I'll always love you…"

*Creep!* She was shouting to herself. *Rat! Fool!* But at the same time she seemed to have a vision of him, off somewhere in the wastelands, probably living among the Zentraedi renegades organizing a new movement… perhaps seeing if he could get himself enlarged to their size—a dream at last fulfilled.

A sudden breeze came up, sending watery crests of moonlit brilliance across the waves. She felt a chill run through her, and when she turned, he had disappeared into the night.

# 17

The symbolism of the SDF-1 as New Age Ark wasn't lost on the residents and crew of that fortress—Macross, *thrice-born* city of the stars. But unlike the Old Testament Ark, which was really Noah's Ark, the dimensional fortress was thought of by some as the savior itself; the reappearance of the culture hero, the second coming, clothed in the guise of technology—Robotechnology—befitting the times, much as the Nazarene was his own world. This, however, remained the stuff of esoteric cults; underneath it all, the old religions continued to thrive. A return to the basics was universally stressed; the original untampered-with versions of creation and regeneration. And even the Zentraedi found their way over to these.

*History of the First Robotech War*, Vol. CCXIII

ALTHOUGH DOLZA HAD RAINED DEATH ON THE EAST AND WEST coasts of the South American continent, the Amazon basin, with its complex river systems and millions upon millions of acres of virgin forest, was left relatively untouched by his deadly storm. Ironically, many of the indigenous people who had once abandoned their dwellings on the jungled shores of those many slow-moving tributaries for the coastal cities had found their way back into that verdant wilderness after the devastating Zentraedi attack. Green hell or green mansion, its untamed prehistoric disorder was currently home to more survivors than ever before.

And among the most recent arrivals was Khyron.

So different from those bleak icebound reaches he had come to hate, this landscape of perpetual murder—where one waged a daily

battle for survival, and where pain, misery, and death ruled supreme—
it was hardly his world, but it was most certainly his element.

Chased by unrelenting squadrons of Earth Forces mecha, Khyron
had been forced to put down here, his own troops reduced to a
mere handful, and his cruiser all but depleted of its Protoculture fuel
supplies. The small amounts of precious fuel that had spilled from
ruptured Protoculture lines had found sympathetic roots in the
forest, working vegetal miracles in the thin surface soil—Khyron's
ship, wrapped in creepers, tendrils, orchids, and vines, looked as if it
had landed there eons ago. But there were things to be thankful for:
Some of his troops had served for many months in the Micronian
population center factories, learning about that strange custom
called "work" and that more important process known as "repair";
moreover, his agents were still at work in the so-called cities of
the north, reporting to him on matters of mecha deployment,
Protoculture storage, and the growing separatist movement in the
Zentraedi cities such as New Detroit and Monument. Soon the time
for his reappearance would be at hand...

In addition, Khyron learned that scores of Zentraedi ships had
crashed in the jungle, and already the survivors of those wrecked
ships were finding their way to his new stronghold.

For several weeks the tech crews had worked feverishly to effect
repairs on the cruiser's weapons and navigational systems, while
squads of giants had scoured the thick forests for food and supplies,
often raiding the simple Micronian settlements they stumbled
upon. The hot, steamy jungle succeeded in dragging them down
to its own primitive levels, *humanizing* them in ways even Khyron
didn't notice. Discipline had loosened somewhat, especially with
regard to fraternization between males and females and the wearing
of uniforms. The men, sometimes stripped to the waist or in tank-
top undershirts, grew accustomed to sweating—something new
to their bodies, despite their having labored on infernal worlds like
Fantoma. And Khyron got used to his troops calling him by name.

"Commander," called one of the techs now. "I can give you
auxiliary power."

"Then do it," Khyron told him.

There were four of them in the control center of the cruiser, all in sleeveless T's, enervated by the afternoon heat. The man who had addressed Khyron was seated at one of the many duty station consoles; he engaged a series of switches, and illumination was returned to the bridge.

"Good," Khyron complimented him. He reached for his communicator and inquired after the reflex furnaces.

A tech wearing an earphone, a flex-mike communicator, and a monocular enhancer responded from elsewhere in the ship. He was one of those who had spent more than a year in the New Detroit mecha factories.

"Not yet, Khyron. And probably not at all unless we acquire some Protoculture soon."

"What is the status of the main reactors?" Khyron asked.

"Barely functional. Takeoff is still impossible."

"Not good enough! Is there some way to shunt primary power to one of the smaller ships?"

"Yes…" the engine room tech said hesitantly. "But its range would be very limited."

"Enough to get us to New Macross and back?"

"Yes, but—"

"That's all," Khyron said, breaking transmission. He adopted a thoughtful pose for a moment; then, wiping sweat from his brow, he turned to Grel, who was tinkering with a monitor at the opposite end of the control room.

"Grel, are your spies in the Micronian cities to be trusted?"

"I believe so, m'lord," Grel said over his shoulder.

Khyron walked over to him, bending down to repeat his question. Again Grel stated that the agents could be trusted.

"I have a plan…" Khyron began. "This 'hollow day' that approaches—"

"'Holiday,' m'lord. A feast day of sorts."

"Holiday," Khyron repeated, trying the word out. "Yes 'Christmas,' you called it. The Micronians will have their minds on celebration."

Grel smiled. "I understand, Commander. It would be an ideal occasion to strike."

"And you're certain about the whereabouts of the Protoculture matrix, Grel? Because I warn you—if you're not..."

Grel swallowed hard. "Certain, m'lord."

Khyron ordered him to open all communications channels within the cruiser. When Grel nodded, Khyron picked up the comlink mike.

"Now hear this," he announced. "We are mounting a raid on a Micronian population center. Our objective: the Protoculture-matrix drive housed in the storage facility at New Macross. I want all of you to go on standby alert."

Khyron signed off.

"What is this 'Christmas,' Grel?"

Grel raised his eyebrows. "A feast celebrating the creation of one of the Micronian culture heroes, I believe."

"Culture hero?!" Khyron spat. "It is the name 'Khyron' they will speak of after our raid! Khyron the destroyer of worlds!" He threw his head back, laughing maniacally and crushing the communicator in his hand. "Khyron, the *Protoculture* hero!"

"Sometimes I think life was easier when we were Zentraedi," Konda said sadly.

Bron and Rico responded at the same time: "You don't meant it!"

"We're still Zentraedi, Konda!"

Konda pushed his long lavender hair out of his face and looked at his comrades. "I know that. But I mean when we were soldiers." He turned and motioned to the shelves of Christmas toys that lined the back of their small Park Street stall. "We wouldn't have to worry about selling all this stuff!"

Snow had begun falling on New Macross two hours earlier, lending further enchantment to an already cheery and magical Christmas Eve. It was the first snowfall in several weeks, the first Christmas snow many of Macross City's residents had seen in a decade. Shoppers and pedestrians moved along the sidewalks in a kind of wonder, as if questioning their surroundings: Was it possible after four long years of war and suffering that joy was finally returning to their hearts? One could almost feel the radiant warmth of their collective glow.

All except Rico, Konda, and Bron, that is.

Their jobs at the laundry had come to a sudden end months ago, when they had returned from a routine-pickup with a stack of expensive linen sheets, each bearing Lynn-Minmei's indelible ink autograph. There had followed a succession of menial jobs since, culminating with this Park Street stall full of toys—transformable robots, lifelike dolls, and huggable stuffed puppies, all of which had peaked three seasons before and were little more than memorabilia now. They had managed to sell two items during the past week— and that was only by reducing the prices to less than they had paid.

"We just have to learn to be more *aggressive*," Rico said knowingly.

"What d' ya mean?" said Konda.

Rico thought for a moment. "Uh, you know: *forceful.*"

Bron looked confused. "Are you *allowed* to do that?"

"That's what someone told me." Rico shrugged.

"Well, okay," Bron echoed, beginning to roll up his sleeves to expose his brawny arms. "But I don't see how we can do that from inside this stall."

"He's right," Konda suddenly agreed. "We should put all these toys in sacks—"

"Like Santa Claus," Bron interjected proudly.

"Right. And take them over to the mall. We'll have more knee room there."

Rico stared at the two of them. "Elbow room, you idiot."

Konda grinned sheepishly. "Whatever."

"I say we do it!" Bron said decisively, slapping his friends on the back. "We'll be the most *aggressive* salesmen in town!"

In the deserted children's playground across from the mall where Park Street emptied into Macross Boulevard, Minmei rocked herself side to side on one of the swings. The newspaper gossip columns were filled with rumors linked to her sudden disappearance from Monument City almost three weeks ago, and this was the first time she had ventured out of the White Dragon since returning to Macross. Even so, she wasn't disguised, dressed in a plain burgundy-colored dress and black sweater barely heavy enough to keep her warm. She reasoned—rightly so—that people wouldn't recognize this *new* Lynn-Minmei, who was as far removed from that eternally optimistic star of stage and screen as one could get.

Singing was a part of her past. So was Kyle and everyone else connected with her career. She had spent a few days with her agent, Vance Hasslewood, after the scene with Kyle, but he wanted to be more to her than a sounding board. So she returned to Uncle Max and Aunt Lena; they took her in with open arms and helped her secure a few moments of peace. But she realized she wouldn't be able to remain with them: One day Kyle would wander in, and she didn't want to be around when he did.

If only it weren't Christmas, she kept telling herself. If only it were summer, if only everyone else didn't seem so *happy* and complacent, if only...

She stretched her hand out to collect some snow, and as the flakes melted against her warm skin, she thought about Rick. Where was he now? Would he even be willing to talk to her after what had happened in the restaurant? He was probably off having a wonderful Christmas Eve dinner with someone that girl Lisa, perhaps. *Everyone had somebody they could turn to.*

Suddenly someone was calling her name. She looked up and saw three men running toward her from the boulevard entrance to the park. One of them, the shortest of the three, was pushing some sort of cart in front of him; the other two were carrying enormous backpacks and bedrolls. All three had on baseball caps and orange jackets, and there was something familiar about them...

"Minmei!" one of them shouted again.

And then she knew. Disguise or no disguise, new Minmei or old, these three would *always* recognize her!

She jumped up from the swing seat and began to run for the street.

Rico, Konda, and Bron gave chase, but encumbered by the toy sacks, backpacks, and such, they couldn't keep up with her.

"Minmei!" Rico called again, out of breath.

Aggressive sales tactics had gotten them thrown out of the mall—they'd actually been grabbing kids and forcing toys upon them—and so they had wandered over to the park in search of fresh quarry.

"Maybe she didn't hear us," Konda suggested mildly.

"Maybe it wasn't her," said Bron.

Rico nodded. "Couldn't've been. We're her best fans."

Rick was in the kitchen of his quarters, waiting for water to boil, when he heard the television announcement.

"Last night we reported that famed singer and movie star Lynn-Minmei had been taken ill. But we have since learned that she is listed as officially missing, following her hasty departure from Monument City three weeks ago. Official sources believe that this has something to do with the disappearance of Miss Minmei's longtime friend and manager, Lynn-Kyle. There has, however, been no mention of foul play…"

Rick listened for a moment more. He was certain that the two of them had wandered off somewhere together. After what he had witnessed in Chez Mann, it was obvious that Minmei was completely under Kyle's spell. Rick didn't dwell on it, though; people made their own choices in life. Besides, he had problems of his own to dwell on: Lisa would talk to him only over the com net, and even then her tone left no doubt about how she felt toward him. She refused to talk about it, wouldn't so much as have a cup of coffee with him.

The newscaster was saying something about a discovery in the Amazon region when Rick heard the doorbell ring. He threw off his work apron and went to answer it.

It was Minmei, although he almost didn't recognize her. She had a forlorn and downcast look about her, snowflakes like a network of disappearing stars in her dark hair. She asked to come in, not wanting to impose, apologizing for not having called first.

"My friends don't have to call," Rick said, offsetting his initial stammering.

She began to cry, and he held her.

Inside, he put his wool officer's jacket over her shoulders and made some coffee. She sat on the edge of his bed and sipped at her cup, happier by the moment.

"I feel so tired of everything," she told him after explaining her fight with Kyle and her flight from Monument. "I'm sick of being fussed over all the time... Now, when I think about my life, I remember the things that I've lost instead of being grateful for what I have. I just don't have anyone to turn to for support anymore."

She was standing by the window now, her back to him, staring out at the snowfall. Rick, on the other hand, was staring at her long bare legs; even while he tried to listen to her complaints, he wondered if she was going to spend the night.

"You've still got your music," he said after a moment, not sure what he meant.

"If that's all I've got, then I don't want to sing anymore."

"Your songs are your life, Minmei."

"My *life* is a song," she demanded, lower lip trembling.

Rick made a face. "You can't be serious."

"I can't perform anymore, Rick."

"It's Kyle, isn't it?"

She frowned at him. "That's not it! I don't care if I ever see him again! We spent all our time together, whether we were working or not. He smothered me with his stupid attempts at affection, then yelled at me when he couldn't control me." Minmei looked hard at Rick. "I have nobody who understands, nobody who'll take the time to listen to me."

Rick resisted a sudden impulse to run. He was aware of what she was leading him into, and even though he'd played this scene through a hundred times before, he didn't want to win her from weakness. As much as he desired her, he didn't want to get her on the rebound from Kyle.

At about the same time Minmei showed up at Rick's door, Lisa was enjoying a holiday eggnog with Claudia, Max, and Miriya at the Setup, a health spa-pub on the boulevard. Later, she cabbed over to Rick's place, told the driver not to wait, and headed for his quarters, leaving footprints in the thin layer of snow.

She had a present for him—a shirt she had shopped long and hard for, yet another peace offering in the seemingly constant war they waged with each other. She had considered drenching it in her own favorite scent ("SDF No. 5," Claudia called it) but thought Rick wouldn't appreciate the joke. He had been calling her every other day with one suggestion or another—coffee, a movie, a *picnic!*— and she had turned him down each time. But with some distance from the battleground (her hours at the outdoor table forgotten), and this being holiday time, she decided that the time was right for forgiveness. Rick had been inconsiderate and all, but it probably wouldn't be the last time; and if she was going to make this thing work, she would have to learn not to hold on to her anger.

As she approached the house, she noticed that the front door was ajar. She neared it just as Minmei was saying: "I have nobody who understands, nobody who'll take the time to listen to me." The voice was as recognizable as the perfume.

"None of my friends in the business really know who I *am*," Minmei continued. "You see, Rick, you're the only one who cares. That's why I came: I was wondering if I could stay here for a while."

Lisa sucked in her breath and almost shoved her fist into her mouth. She *knew* she had no right to eavesdrop, but her legs refused to put her in motion.

Minmei was pleading with Rick: "I don't have anyone else to turn to!"

Lisa's life seemed to be hanging in the balance. Then she heard Rick give his okay and felt herself going over the edge. Silently she pulled the door closed and began to run, crying harder with each step. A short distance down the block a man stopped to inquire if she was all right. She turned on him like a harridan, telling him to mind his own business.

Claudia, meanwhile, had been hopping from bar to bar, party to party. Her brother, Vince, and his wife, Dr. Jean Grant, had invited her over for Christmas drinks, but she had declined. Likewise, she had no desire to return to her quarters and confront the intense loneliness that plagued her on each holiday. For all his bravado Roy had had a traditional side that revealed itself on holidays, and they had passed many wonderful moments together: quiet dinners, walks through the snow on moonlit evenings, midnight exchanges of gifts and affection. She saw this same shared magic in the eyes of each couple that passed her on the street, and it wasn't long before she found herself back at the Setup, hoping she would run into a friendly face or two.

The last person she expected to find there was Lisa, but there she was, draped over the bar, an almost empty wine bottle in front of her. She was singing—trying at any rate—one of Minmei's songs, "Stagefright," by the sound of it. Claudia's face dropped, then she gave a small shrug and took the adjacent stool.

"Misery loves company," Lisa slurred, and smiled.

Several hours and countless drinks later, after toasting everyone they knew or had known and solving all the world's problems, they kissed each other good-bye just as the sun was coming up over Lake Gloval. Claudia had the day off, but Lisa had put in for the morning shift. A young staff officer who had been a frequent visitor to their private party ran Lisa over to the SDF-2 in his open-air jeep.

Surprised at how sober she was—figuring she had somehow pierced the hangover envelope—she tried to let herself enjoy the ride, the cold air rushing at her face. But all that seemed to do was sober her to the point where last night's problems had little trouble creeping into her consciousness once again. It was time to give up, she told herself, give up and let Minmei have Rick once and for all.

As Lisa was approaching the command center, she heard Kim and Sammie discussing her—a common enough occurrence these days—so she waited outside the door until they were finished, wondering how much more of this she could stand.

Apparently, word of her all-nighter in the Setup had spread fast. Sammie was saying: "Well, you shouldn't believe everything you hear."

"You'd do the same thing if you wanted to forget him," said Kim, making Lisa think back on the evening to ascertain if she had really done something to be ashamed of. If only she had come into this a little sooner...

"Lisa's too nice a person to do something like that!"

"Of course—she's not as perfect as you," Kim teased.

That seemed to take the conversation in a different direction entirely, and a minute or so later Lisa felt safe to enter. Kim, Sammie, and Vanessa were, of course, all smiles by now, but

Lisa didn't hold anything against them. Vanessa mentioned a Christmas party, the first Lisa had heard about it.

"You mean no one told you? It's for the bridge. Why don't you invite Rick—I'm sure he'd love to come."

Was Vanessa goading her? Lisa asked herself. "Ah, I don't think he'd be able to make it."

"But he's off today."

"Yeah, but he's at home with a miserable little…"

"Oh," said Vanessa. "Sick, huh? Too bad."

Just then the bridge PA came alive. A female voice said:

"This is ground base security! Zentraedi forces are attacking the industrial section! Emergency communique to all sectors!"

Khyron's Officer's Pod ran through the streets of New Macross, five tactical pods alongside it. They had entered the city before dawn, submerging themselves in the cold waters of the lake before the early-morning surprise attack. Grel's Battlepod had taken the point, but something was wrong: He had led them past the same storage tanks three times now.

"What are you doing?!" Khyron screamed into his communicator. "You're leading us around in circles!"

"The Protoculture has got to be here somewhere," Grel returned. "My agents—"

"Your agents are idiots! Now listen to me: Your incompetence may end up costing you your life! Now, find it!"

Jeeps and CD vehicles sped through the city announcing the attack and instructing the early-morning crowds to seek shelter immediately. Thus far the Zentraedi were restricting themselves to the storage facilities and factories across the lake, but there was no telling where their blood lust and thirst for destruction would lead.

Max and Miriya were opening presents for Dana when the alert sounded. They left the baby with their neighbors, the Emersons, and headed for the base, awaiting further instructions from Admiral Gloval's headquarters. It was like old times, after all.

Gloval had been roused from sleep and was now putting in a rare appearance on the SDF-2 bridge. Exedore, recently returned from the Robotech satellite to continue his study of Micronian customs, was by the admiral's side. Surveillance cameras located throughout the industrial sector had captured the Zentraedis' curious movements. Both Gloval and Exedore were in agreement that the Officer's Pod was manned by Khyron.

"They seem to be looking for something," Gloval commented. "There has been very little destruction. Several sentries were killed when the pods made their first appearance, but nothing since."

The micronized Zentraedi adviser nodded his head solemnly. "Correct, Admiral. If this were an attack, he would be concentrating on military targets. Or whatever suits his fancy, as you say. It would be my guess that he is here to obtain the Protoculture he needs for his battlecruiser."

"We'll concentrate our defense in the industrial sector, then."

Exedore concurred. He then glanced about and added in a conspiratorial tone: "May I be permitted to make a suggestion, Admiral?"

Gloval's brow furrowed. "Of course, Exedore."

The Zentraedi said: "Let him find what he's looking for."

Frustrated by Grel's failure to zero in on the storage facility, Khyron left his mecha behind and went into the streets on foot to reconnoiter. He was armed with a single autocannon and his own brand of reckless abandon. He held his ground calmly as Veritechs dove in for strafing runs, picking them from the skies with hardly a lost step.

Across the lake Azonia headed up a diversionary force consisting of powered armor units and Quadrono Battalion Invid scout ships. Someday Earth would see many more of these in the skies...

She directed her squadrons against the city proper, successfully drawing off the Veritech teams that were going in after Khyron. The opposing forces met above the lake, filling the chilled air with furious exchanges of heat, harnessed lightning, and swift death. Max was at the center of the sudden hell storm, his blue Veritech reconfigured to Battloid mode, juking and dodging volleys of enemy missiles while his gatling cannon retaliated, spewing transuranic slugs against the invaders. Miriya went wing to wing with him, dropping one, two, then three scout ships and wondering which of the remaining mecha might hold her former commander, Azonia, now Khyron's consort!

Rick, ever the gentleman, had taken the couch. He was aware that Minmei had stood over him in the middle of the night while he pretended to sleep; she had fixed his blankets and smiled at him in the dark. But he hadn't slept well at all; his neck was cramped, his left arm was tingling, and some sort of fireworks had roused him much earlier than he wanted to rise—always the case on a day off.

He went to the window and saw thick columns of smoke in the clear skies above the lake. Quickly he switched on the television, conscious of Minmei's rustling around in the kitchen. Rick was already pulling on his clothes when he heard the announcement from the MBS newscaster, Van Fortespiel, "the Boogieman":

"This special bulletin just in: The Zentraedi attack force is believed to be concentrated in the industrial section of the city. Casualty reports are expected in at any minute now…"

Rick was stunned. "Why wasn't I notified?!" he shouted to the screen, pulling off his V-neck sweater and reaching for his uniform. "Lisa's on command watch—she knew where to find me!"

Minmei waited nervously by the front door. Rick saw her troubled look and tried to reassure her.

"Don't worry—this is routine."

Her eyes were wide with a sudden fear. "If something happened to you, I don't know what I'd do!" She held him. "Please don't let me lose you now that I've finally found you!"

Rick took her face between his hands and kissed her lightly.

"I'll be back soon," was all that he said.

Khyron's years—long familiarity with the Invid Flower of Life had imbued him with senses above and beyond the ordinary, especially when it came to homing in on the flower itself, or in this case its repressed matrix—Protoculture.

He ripped away the metal chamber's tarpaulin cover and smiled to himself, his heart pounding and blood rushing through his system. "The storage matrix," he murmured aloud.

The cylinder was easily half his height and perhaps twice his weight, but he lifted it easily onto his back nevertheless.

Returning to his mecha, he attached servoclamps to the chamber and winched it tight against the underside of the pod.

A savage battle was raging throughout the sector between Battloids and giants, but he put an end to it now by issuing a recall order to his troops. They regrouped and headed out in formation to the southwest.

Airborne in Skull One, Rick received an update from Max and signaled his team of Veritechs to follow his lead.

"Prepare to block their escape route in sector November! We can't let them get away with that Protoculture!"

Max broke off to join Skull, leaving the rest of the scout ships to Miriya and her fighter team.

"It's getting bad back there," he was telling her. But just then his eyes fixed on the Veritech's topographic display. Something massive was putting down in sector N... "A Zentraedi escort ship," he yelled.

Rick saw it land, the escort's four polelike legs spearing through the roofs of buildings and settling deep into tarmac roads. A bizarre-looking ship, shaped like the body of a bloated walrus, with legs that could have been an architect's compass and an enormous rear thruster like some outsize megaphone. Kyron's battlepods and attack mecha were ascending into its open steel-trap belly, while Battloids and Excaliburs poured ineffectual fire against its armored hull.

"Attention, Micronians!" Khyron's voice suddenly blurted out as the ship began to lift off. "Khyron the Destroyer wants to wish you a merry Christmas, and I send you a special greeting from Santa Claus. May all our foolish hollow-days be as bright as this one!..."

New Macross didn't know what had hit it, only that the entire city seemed to go up in flames. Later, piecing together what passed for facts—Khyron's cryptic remarks and the observations of people in the street—evidence would point to a certain sidewalk Santa, an uncommon Santa with empty eyes and skin like polluted clay, a Zentraedi who might have been in radio contact with "the Destroyer" and set off the myriad bombs his agents had planted throughout the city...

The Veritechs abandoned their pursuit of the escort ship and returned to Macross to battle the blaze, diving into the citywide inferno again and again with fire-retardant bombs.

By the end of the day, the fires were brought under control and the city began to count its dead. The hospitals were filled to overcrowding, and whatever Christmas spirit remained was more funereal than festive. Still, by nightfall, most families had been reunited and a strange post-holocaust calm prevailed. So often destroyed, so often reborn, the people of Macross were hardened survivors, nothing if not adaptable, and well accustomed to death. Church bells sang to one another from distant sectors, carolers took to the streets, and the SDF-2 crew went ahead with its preplanned surprise, lighting the ship with garlands of light, a sacred tree grown from the navel of the world...

Rick met briefly with Lisa afterward. He was angry in spite of the exhaustion he felt.

"I talked to Vanessa," he said sharply. "She told me you said I was sick in bed! And you know that's a lie! I should have been notified at the very first scramble alert!"

"I didn't say you were sick," she answered, averting her gaze for a moment. "Anyway, I didn't think you'd want to be disturbed..." She waited for his puzzled look, then added: "You should be more discreet when you have people coming over—or at least learn to close your front door... I came by last night to say merry Christmas. I know all about Minmei staying with you."

He let it go at that and returned home, entering the house like he was returning from a day at the office, with a cheery "Hi there!" for Minmei, who was visibly overjoyed to see him.

"Thank goodness!" she gushed, wiping tears away.

"I told you I'd come back." He smiled.

She ran off to fix her face. Rick noticed that she had prepared an entire dinner for the two of them—even a white-frosted cake with a candle and a small Santa.

"I made it for you," she said softly, hugging him from behind. "My sweet Rick... I was so worried."

Rick was speechless, feeling her pressed up against him like that, too good to be true.

"Do you think you could ever give up your commission with the Defense Force?" she asked him. "Please think about it because I never want to lose you, Rick—never again..."

She lit the candle after dinner and wished him a merry Christmas.

"May we have a million more like it," said Rick, the dog fights and fireworks suddenly forgotten.

Minmei sighed and leaned forward, closing her eyes. Rick followed her lead until their lips met...

# 18

I believe Khyron suspected that Gloval's allowing him to leave Macross with the Protoculture matrix was a form of peace offering. It was Gloval's judgment for deportation as opposed to incarceration; Gloval's way of saying: *You have what you need to get home—now leave!* But it remains unfathomable to me that Gloval and Exedore could so misread Khyron at this late stage. *Home—with the imperative unfilled?* Unthinkable. And yet, could the war have ended in any other fashion?... I have asked myself over and over again how events might have reshaped themselves had Khyron simply left.

Rawlins, *Zentraedi Triumvirate: Dolza, Breetai, Khyron*

VENGEANCE, SNARLED KHYRON.

If there had been doubts regarding Khyron's leadership, the raid on New Macross not only erased them but instilled within his rank and file a sense of loyalty hitherto unknown, even among the Zentraedi. He was "the Destroyer" now, no longer the Backstabber who had sacrificed thousands along his own vainglorious campaign trail. By capturing the Protoculture matrix, he had effected a rescue; he had provided them with the means to take leave of the miserable world that had held them captive these two long years—a way to return home. His troops would have followed him into hell itself... And that was precisely where he meant to lead them...

"All energy inputs building to operative levels, sir," an engine room tech reported to the observation bubble command center.

"Check the reflex furnaces," Grel shouted into the communicator. He sat rigidly at his duty station, grateful to be alive after the way things had turned out in Macross. Had Khyron failed to find the matrix, Grel wouldn't have survived the day.

The Destroyer himself was pacing the deck, his hands clasped behind his back, the olive-drab campaign cloak swirling as he turned.

"Stable," relayed the engine room tech.

"We have full power," Azonia updated. Seated at the duty station adjacent to Grel's, she too was in full-dress uniform.

Khyron clenched his fists and approached the curved console of the command center. His eyes held a look that went beyond anger. "Excellent!" he hissed. "We will leave immediately to rejoin the Robotech Masters!"

Grel and Azonia were raising their hands in salute when he suddenly added: "But before I leave Earth, *I want to destroy the SDF-1!*"

His subordinates stared at him in disbelief, their protests ignored. The Earth Forces weren't foolish enough to permit a second sneak attack; they would be lying in wait, the guns of their newly constructed fortress primed and aimed! Surely Khyron recognized this, surely he wouldn't allow freedom to slip from their grasp now!

"I will have my final revenge on these Micronians," Grel and Azonia heard him mutter under his breath. Then he turned on them and ordered lift-off. They glanced at each other wordlessly and initiated the launch sequence.

The cruiser shuddered, vibrating to a bone-shaking bass rumble that was more feeling than sound. Protoculture surged through the ship's atrophied systems, empowering the massive reflex furnaces in its holds. Thrusters erupted with nearly volcanic force, inverted against the tangled tenacious growth that was partly of the ship's own creating. The Earth itself sensed the force of the cruiser's withdrawal, replying in kind with tectonic movements created and relayed from deep within its core, the last gasp of some opposing telluric intelligence bent on holding fast its dangerous captive.

But ultimately the powers of evil proved superior and the Destroyer's dreadnought tore loose, taking great hunks of earth and forest with it as it climbed toward freedom and headed north for its rendezvous with vengeance and death.

*The end of the world,* Lisa cried to herself.

Two weeks had passed since Khyron's Christmas morning attack, and Macross had yet to recover. Initially the residents of that often devastated place had rallied, once again prepared to pick up the pieces of their lives and rebuild the symbol of their dreams. But then a sort of delayed shock set in, sapping even the strongest of the will to prevail. People remained in their homes, leaving the streets deserted, the recent damage untouched; some had even taken up what amounted to residency in the shelters themselves. And yet others fled to other cities or wandered off into the wastes, a new breed of pioneer, abandoning the one thing that had brought salvation and devastation alike—the SDF-1.

Lisa Hayes was on the lookout bridge of the fortress now, her inner world as overturned as that one she glimpsed along the curve of the lake. Rick was lost to her, and his leave-taking had emptied her, much as the city itself. She contemplated the single decision that would free her, sobbing for all that might have been.

"Lisa!" Claudia yelled from behind her.

She wiped her eyes and turned around.

"Admiral Gloval sent me to look for you," her friend told her. "Why aren't you on the bridge?"

"I needed to be alone," she answered, the cold wind mussing her hair. "I'm thinking about resigning."

Claudia had sensed this coming for weeks now but found herself surprised nonetheless. "You've got to be joking," she said plainly.

"No, I'm serious, Claudia." Lisa's voice cracked. "I just can't take it anymore. The army… Rick… I'm giving up—I'm just not as tough as everybody seems to think I am."

Claudia sized her up for a moment, deciding to get tough herself. "Come off it, Lisa—you're not fooling anybody but yourself!"

So much for the sympathy, Lisa thought, startled by Claudia's reaction. Maybe she just wasn't explaining all this properly— Claudia wasn't *seeing* it through her eyes.

"You're talking like some silly, simpering, weak sister schoolgirl!" Claudia stepped in to confront her further. "You're a military woman, born, bred, and trained, and you're too much of a scrapper to give in like this without a fight!"

But Lisa held her ground. "There's no use fighting—it all comes down to a battle with myself, Claudia. And I'm losing. If Rick prefers Minmei, that's just the way it is, and there's nothing I can do about it.

"Except *get over it and move on!*" Claudia emphasized. "The military is your *life*, girl. You give up and resign your commission, you might as well throw everything else away."

Lisa's lips narrowed to a thin line. "I have to get away."

"You mean *run* away."

Lisa turned her back to Claudia. "Call it what you want. I can't work with Rick and then watch him go home to *her* every day. If you can't understand that..."

*He shouldn't have the power over you,* Claudia wanted to tell her. *You shouldn't* permit *him that power!* But her heart understood only too clearly. "I do understand," she said quietly.

*The loneliness of command,* Gloval said to himself for the third time that morning. He wished Exedore hadn't chosen to return to the Robotech factory satellite so soon; he missed him, finding in the gnomish Zentraedi a keen mind unencumbered by emotional restraints. And yet far from being pure intellect, cool and remote like Lang, the man—and Gloval would always refer to him thus— the man had a loyal and unbiased nature, along with a compassion rarely encountered among Humans or aliens alike. The two had forged a unique friendship, built on shared interest, mutual trust, and nothing less than awe for the events that had shaped their histories, both racial and individual.

Gloval was in his favorite chair, the command seat on the SDF-1 bridge, staring out at Macross through the wraparound permaglass bays. Everyone knew to look for him here, more than anything his place of retirement. And indeed, the issue of retirement weighed heavily on his mind; he wanted the untaxed freedom to think back through the past two decades and make personal order out of the chaos he had so often seen there in moments of reflection. He needed to take a hard look at his successes and failures and evaluate his performance record, if for no other reason than to *justify* the decisions that had affected so many lives... countless lives.

He recalled saying once that he was allowed to make more mistakes than the rest of the crew, and indeed he had. He only prayed that his latest decisions wouldn't fall into the same category.

When Lisa finally reported to him, he stood and walked to the forward portion of the bridge, his hands behind his back.

"I have called you here to brief you on your new assignment, Captain."

"I'm... sorry, sir, but I can't take a new assignment," Lisa told him directly.

Gloval pivoted through his rehearsed turn, raising his voice a notch. "And why not?!"

Lisa's head was bowed. "Sir, I've decided to resign. In my state of mind I'm no good to myself or the service."

"And what state of mind would that be?" Gloval wanted to know.

"I... I need to get away for a while, Admiral—for personal reasons."

Gloval beamed. "Well, that's perfect, then, because this assignment calls for a certain amount of travel."

"No, sir." Lisa shook her head. "I'm sorry, sir."

Another tack, Gloval said to himself. "Nonsense. You can't disregard your duty just because of some unrequited romance—you're just going to have to get over it because I need you now more than ever before."

Lisa was staring at him wide-eyed. "You mean, y-you *know*?!"

The admiral made a dismissive gesture. "Good grief, I have eyes, don't I?! I've probably known about you and Commander Hunter longer than *you* have known!"

Lisa brightened somewhat and smiled. "I'll bet you have, sir... This new assignment, then—is it in the way of a favor?"

"Nonsense," Gloval snorted. "You're the most capable and experienced officer in the entire command. The choice was an obvious one."

"Sir…"

Gloval cleared his throat. "As you know, construction of the new fortress has just been completed. I want you to command it."

Lisa put her hands to her breast. That she was to command the SDF-2 had been hinted at but never actually stated.

"What?! My own command?"

"It's a long-term commitment," he cautioned her.

"I accept—whatever it is."

"Good," he said, asking her to step over to the forward bay. She did so and began to follow his gaze.

Stratified layers of blue sky and crystalline white arced across the eastern horizon. Above this was a darker, more menacing ceiling of swiftly moving storm clouds pierced by brilliant rays of winter sunlight. It was a majestic morning sight, breathtaking.

"Yes," Gloval was saying, "our Earth is a beautiful planet. And we must preserve its glories. That's why I must ask you to leave our world behind for a time."

Lisa experienced a fleeting moment of fear.

"The time has come for humankind to grow up and leave its cradle behind," the admiral explained. "To go forth and claim its place in the universe… Your assignment is to lead a diplomatic mission to the homeworld of the Robotech Masters."

"To Tirol, sir?!" Lisa said in disbelief. "But how?"

"That is the new purpose of the SDF-2. Commander Breetai and Exedore will accompany you, although it might be easier to follow Khyron's lead."

Lisa's brow furrowed.

"We let him have that Protoculture matrix for a reason, Captain. I'm only sorry we hadn't anticipated the explosions."

"Khyron's ticket home," Lisa mused. "But why Tirol, Admiral?"

"Because the Human race couldn't possibly survive another holocaust like the last one. Our defense system has been vastly improved, but even that would prove useless against the

sophisticated technology of the Masters—or worse yet, to hear
Exedore tell it, the Invid. It's essential that we make peace with the
Masters, perhaps for the sake of both our races."

"Peace," Lisa said, as though hearing the word for the first time.
"And we have to travel clear across the galaxy to secure it."

*The downside of getting your wish,* thought Rick.

From the picture window of his suburban quarters, he
watched a formation of Veritechs streak overhead. He hadn't
been airborne in more than a week, having taken the leave to
spend time with his new roommate/partner/significant other…
and that didn't begin to tell the tale of his confusion. As pleasant
as it was with Minmei, Rick felt unfulfilled; without flying,
without a mission, without something to strive for, it was just
the two of them playing house. They would sleep late, cook
together, watch the screen, and suddenly there would be nothing
to talk about. She had stopped writing love songs, and he had
stopped telling tales.

Minmei entered the room just then and seemed to pick up on
his distance. Was he tired of her already?

"Rick, why not just quit the service? We could move somewhere
else if you want. I mean, could you be happy if we settled down to
a normal life?"

"Normal?!" he said, more harshly than he had to. "Take a look
outside, Minmei. There isn't any more *normal!*" He shook his head.
"I don't think we could even if there was."

"But why not? There's so much more to life than this, and we're
missing it."

Rick held his breath, then exhaled slowly through clenched
jaws. "People are depending on us. They look to people Like me
for protection, and to you for inspiration. How can we just walk
away from that?"

She put her hand on his shoulder. "Life is funny, isn't it? Nothing
turns out the way you think it will… When we first met, I was
totally caught up in romantic dreams, and some of those actually
came true. But not the dream I had for you and me, Rick."

"What *dream?*"

She tried to hold his eyes with hers. "Let's get married."

Rick reacted as if he'd been punched. *Wasn't she listening to anything he said?* ...But even as he thought this, he knew that it was more black and white than he was making it out to be: Somehow the war and their separate careers weren't the real issues at all. It was something else...

When the doorbell rang, both of them jumped up to answer it, thankful for the intrusion. Lisa was standing there demurely, her uniform as bright as the patches of snow on the front lawn. "I came to say... good-bye, Rick. I've received new orders, and I'll be going back into space soon." She pushed on through Rick's surprised reaction, fighting to maintain her even tone. "It's true. I can't believe it, but Admiral Gloval has given me command of the SDF-2." She grew almost cheerful now. "It's like a dream come true. Aren't you happy for me, Rick?"

"When are you leaving?" he asked her anxiously.

"Transfer of the reflex engines from SDF-1 will begin tomorrow. But we're bound for deep space soon afterward. To Tirol, the homeworld of the Robotech Masters. It's going to be a diplomatic mission—a mission of peace."

*That could take years!* Rick thought.

"So I just wanted to say good-bye and... see you in a few years." Lisa smiled at Minmei. "It's been a pleasure, Minmei. Your music has been a great inspiration to all of us."

Minmei thanked her, warily at first but more sincerely when Lisa wished Rick and her happiness in the future.

"I just have one more thing to say," Lisa stammered, her voice failing her all of a sudden. "I love you, Rick! I always have! And I always will!"

Rick was speechless. Minmei had latched on to his arm with a tourniquet-like grip. Lisa was apologizing, holding back tears.

"I may never see him again," she was explaining herself to Minmei. "And I had to tell him... Take care of him for me."

She saluted Rick, turned, and began to run.

Rick stood in the doorway a moment, then shook himself out of his stupor and called for her to wait. He took off down the walk, but Minmei was there in front of him, her arms stretched out to stop him.

"You can't go!" she said in a frightened rush. "What about me?! You've already done *more* than your share! How could you even *think* of going back into space again?!"

"Because… they *need* me," Rick lied.

And all at once the sky fell…

# 19

Entropy—your belief that systems, biophysical and otherwise, are predestined to move from a state of order to disorder—is the one concept that continues to fascinate me; and I do believe that it has indeed shaped your thinking as a race as powerfully as Protoculture has shaped mine, This dissolution, this winding down... how typical of your thinkers to conjure up such a *poetic* ending.

Exedore, as quoted in Dr. Lazlo Zand,
*On Earth As It Is In Hell: Recollections of the Robotech War*

A HAIL OF MISSILES FELL ON UNPREPARED MACROSS TURNING THE sky a radiant yellow and leveling the heart of the city. Rick and Minmei were thrown to the ground by the concussion of a thousand blasts that filled the air with suffocating heat and fiery debris.

When Rick saw that Minmei was unhurt, he began a frantic search along what was left of the street in the direction Lisa had run. The sky was an orange fireball now, much of the city a memory. High-rise towers had crumbled like sand castles; houses imploded. Park Street and Macross Boulevard were buckled and heaved like roller-coaster courses.

Rick heard the high-pitched whine of secondary assaults above the howling of an alien wind; then that deadly thunder returned as explosions continued to punish the city and the surrounding hills.

He found Lisa lying in the street, miraculously alive though the buildings on the block had been utterly destroyed.

"What happened?" she yelled above the firestorm.

"We're under attack!" he returned, helping her to her feet. "The Zentraedi! One ship!"

*Khyron!* she said to herself. "We've got to get back to the SDF-2!"

Lisa took a step forward and would have collapsed, but Rick held her, his hands under her arms. "You're too weak," he spoke into her ear. "Let me take care of you… *I love you!*"

She turned in his arms and took his face between her scorched hands. "Am I dreaming this?" she said weakly.

Minmei was suddenly alongside them, urging them to get to the shelters and pleading with Rick to stay with her.

Projectiles shrieked like banshees in that chrome sky.

"Get yourself to safety!" Lisa told her. "Rick and I have our duty to perform!"

Minmei took a faltering step forward, confused.

"If you really love him," Lisa continued, "let go of him! He's a *pilot*—that's his *life!*"

"Life?" Minmei screamed, hysterical, her arms flailing about. "You call this a *life*?! War! Devastation! Battle after battle until everything is destroyed!"

Rick took her by the arms and tried to calm her, urging her to leave. "We're trying to put an end to all this. We hate it as much as you do, but the future of our race has to be preserved!"

Missiles exploded nearby, raining vengeful lightning on them and erasing words and thoughts. The three of them huddled together, showered by cinders and unheavenly tongues of airborne fire.

Minmei looked at Lisa and Rick, angry now. "There *is* no future!"

Rick turned to leave, and she grabbed hold of him, begging him to remain by her side. *If he loved her, he would stay with her.*

But he shook himself free.

"Someday you'll understand!" he shouted.

"I'll *never* understand!" she screamed to his back.

Lisa entered the bridge of the SDF-2 at a run, making straight for her station. Vanessa was already at her console, the threat screen in front of her flashing with display information.

"Give me a status report!" Lisa ordered.

"A single battlecruiser—ten degrees southwest. Present position twenty-seven miles but closing very fast."

"Right," said Lisa, and reached for the air com net switch...

The projecbeam field on the bridge of Khyron's cruiser showed the Micronians' new battle fortress, sitting in its circular puddle back to back with its crippled cousin, the SDF-1—Zor's ship, cause of so much *undoing*.

The Destroyer stood proudly in the observation bubble command center, his facial features distorted by intense hatred. "The dimensional fortress now coming into range, sir," Grel reported from his station.

"Main gun at full power and standing by," said Azonia.

"My revenge was well worth waiting for! Admiral Gloval is going to wish he'd never heard of me!"

Azonia straightened in her seat. "Awaiting your orders, m'lord."

"Take out the new ship first," he commanded. "Then we'll finish them off. Zor's ship will soon be little more than a footnote in Zentraedi history!"

"Enemy ship still closing!" Sammie told Lisa from her station below the balcony area of the SDF-2 bridge.

Kim suddenly swung from her console screen. "I'm getting high-level radiation readings!"

"Vanessa?" Lisa said, asking for confirmation.

"They're firing on us, Captain!"

Glyphs of unharnessed lightning began to take shape along the blunt bow of Khyron's leviathan-like cruiser, leaping pole to pole across what could almost have been a full-lipped mouth, crowded and underscored with twin-muzzled spiked cannons like tusks on its armored hull. The energy danced and stretched, animated by the Protoculture charges enlivening the dreadnought's weapons systems.

Localized storms were unleashed as the ship tore through the winter clouds above Macross, orange thrusters aft propelling it swiftly toward the lake and the immobile fortresses.

The bolts crackled and hissed in the thin air as the bow began to open, revealing a network of blazing vertical shafts of power, fangs and incisors filed to gleaming points in the mouth of the beast. Ultimately, from somewhere deep within its black heart a cone of blinding light burst forth, spewing from the cruiser and fanning out to encompass the Earth itself, then narrowing and collapsing upon itself as it found its focus. It surged forward across the rooftops of the city, buildings collapsing in its wake, and struck the heart of the fortress, rending the fabric of spacetime on impact and opening gaps into antiworlds.

Colors reversed themselves; what had been light was now darkness, and what had been blackness glowed with an infernal radiance. The heavens rolled and gyrated as though the very stars had been thrown into chaos by the force of the explosion.

"SDF-2 has taken a direct hit!" a hurried and frightened male voice informed Rick over the tac net. "We've lost communications!"

Rick looked over his shoulder, dropping the Veritech's left wing as he turned. Below him Lake Gloval was a cauldron of fire and smoke, less a reservoir of water than a volcanic cone. The new fortress was in ruins, holed through and through by the annihilation ray.

"They're listing!" the voice updated. "They're sinking, Captain!"

"Come in, SDF-2," Rick shouted into his helmet mike. "Lisa, do you read me?! Captain Hayes?!" His commo screen was a grid of black and white static, then a vertical column of blue and white bands. "Answer me!" he shouted once again.

Approaching Skull Team from twelve o'clock came an angry flock of Zentraedi mecha, pursuit ships, tri-thrusters, and Battlepods.

Rick locked onto his targets and pulled home the Hotas.

"You'll pay for this!" he snarled through bared teeth.

*The rain was harsh but blessedly cool against her raw skin. Why hadn't she thought to include sunscreen in the beach basket? And was Rick as burned as she?... The wailing of tortured seabirds was taking her rapidly to the surface of the world, the roughhouse voices of beachgoers at play...*

Lisa opened her eyes to a close-up view of her console keyboard and touch pads, water cascading between the tabs and puddling on the floor. Her hands were under her face, and the screen in front of her was blank and silent. She raised her head, pushed wet hair from her face, then struggled to her feet to ascertain the extent of the damage to the bridge.

On the floor below the flyout balcony, Sammie and Kim lay sprawled near their duty stations, seemingly dazed but uninjured. Klaxons were sounding throughout the ship, and the overhead fire control system had drenched everyone and everything in the hold. Lisa turned to check on Vanessa before opening the comlink to request assistance.

"Fire control teams needed on levels four through twenty," she managed.

Back at her station, Kim put in a call for medics.

"All section commanders file status reports as soon as possible," Lisa heard Vanessa say.

"Tell 'em we need more help on the flight deck!" a paramedic shouted from the floor.

Kim was working frantically at her controls. "Computer's dead!" she told Lisa. "No manual override. We have no control whatsoever!"

"Losing power, Captain," Vanessa said behind her. "Recommend we abandon ship!"

Lisa's mouth dropped open as she felt the impact of those words and understood what it meant to lose a ship. She swept her eyes across the bridge: The fortress had taken a direct hit some floors below the control center, but secondary missiles had razed the bridge as well. There were huge holes in the bulkheads behind her, acrid smoke was coiling from the ventilation systems, and for the first time Lisa was aware that the ship was listing hard to starboard.

*Think!* she screamed to herself, as if to chase the demons of defeat from her mind. *What would Admiral Gloval do in a situation like this?*

She pictured him sitting in the command chair on the SDF-1 bridge, his white cap pulled low on his brow, the tobacco-stained fingers of his right hand gently tugging at the ends of his thick mustache... She could almost hear him:

*"Lisa, you know that you'll always be able to find me right here."*

And suddenly she understood why he had told her this; she understood why he had been absent so often these past months while the SDF-2 was nearing completion, why he had given her command of the fortress...

"Of course!" she yelled. She beckoned her bridge crew to follow her and hurried from the control room.

A winding service corridor still connected the two fortresses, a dark and spooky place now, but the four of them barely took notice of its sinister elements as they ran toward the mother ship, Lisa in the lead. Barely breaking stride, she hit the control switch for the bridge hatch, and they rushed in, surprised to find the overhead lights on and the display boards lit. They were equally surprised to find Claudia standing at her forward station, already initiating the lift-off sequence.

"Welcome aboard, ladies," she said calmly and with a hint of humor. "What took you so long?"

"Don't just stand there," Gloval barked from the command chair. "We have a job to do. Battle stations—everyone!"

Lisa smiled to herself while she and the others hastened to their consoles and screens. So it was true: Gloval had half expected an attack of some sort. He had sworn to Kyron (and the entire crew, for that matter) that the SDF-1 was nonoperational, when in fact it was not only spaceworthy but armed to the teeth. Robotech crews had to have carried out the top-secret reconstruction months ago, purposely leaving the battered exterior of the fortress untouched.

"What about the main gun, sir?" she asked Gloval.

"Enough power for one firing. We'll have to make sure it's effective."

"Computer countdown is already programmed, sir," Claudia reported.

Gloval called for maximum power on all thrusters.

"Antigrav power levels at optimum capacity," Sammie updated.

"All systems go," said Kim. "Ready for immediate lift-off on commander's mark!"

Claudia tapped commands into her overhead control board.

"Drive system is operational, and the chronometer is running. Four seconds to ignition. Three! Two! One!..."

"Take her up!" shouted Gloval, almost rising from his chair...

Minmei, her aunt and uncle, Mayor Tommy Luan, and thousands of others were pressed together in Macross's main shelter, an enormous aboveground structure of steel and reinforced concrete that also housed the city's communications system and data storage networks. Minmei had been entertaining everyone with songs and stories. They were all maintaining, despite the despair they felt when word of the destruction of the SDF-2 had reached them. Recent arrivals to the shelter described how that Zentraedi dragon had belched a flow of irresistible force and how the new fortress had slipped like a corpse beneath the frothing surface of Lake Gloval. The crowds in the shelter had keened and offered up their prayers.

But now incredible news had arrived: The SDF-1 was lifting out of the lake! And people all over the city were beginning to leave their shelters, heedless of the burning buildings and ravaged land, the death wind that blew like a gust from hell through the deserted streets. Their guardian was resurrected, and this was all that mattered. Even annihilation itself held no sway.

Minmei, too, left the shelter in time to see the fortress liftoff, parting the water as it rose from the lake, still a gleaming techno-knight despite its sorry appearance. The supercarriers that were its arms were held out in that characteristic gesture of supplication, and already the main guns were elevating into position above the knight's visored helmet...

Khyron's cruiser was continuing its deadly descent, disgorging blast after blast of white light from its unholy gullet. Streaks of blue lightning shot from pinpoint gun turrets, while power-armored Zentraedi troops steadfast along the warship's rusted hull loosed cannon fire against the Earth Forces mecha.

Rick skimmed Skull One along the cruiser's organic-looking surface, offing missiles as he broke and climbed across its bow.

When the recipients of those Stilletos and Hammerheads exploded beneath him, he threw the fighter into another dive, reconfiguring to Guardian mode as he dropped. The skies were alive with tracer rounds, hell flowers, and annihilation disks. Veritechs and Zentraedi pursuit ships were locked in crazed dogfights amid it all, adding their own slugs and rounds to the chaos, their own deaths to the escalating body count.

In Battloid mode now, legs splayed on the sickly-colored hull and the autocannon at the ready, Rick's mecha emptied his rage at barbed turrets and solitary troops alike. Explosions encircled him, filling the air with white-hot shrapnel. But the great ship held to its course, hurtling toward the lake undeterred.

All at once there was a voice on the com net.

"Rick! Rick Hunter—is that you?!"

"Lisa!" Rick cried. "I must be hearing things!"

"You're not," she told him. "I'm aboard the SDF-1, and we're preparing to fire the main guns. So I strongly suggest you get yourself out of there!"

He was already reaching for his mode selector stick. "You don't have to tell me twice!" he exclaimed, running his mecha along the deck and lifting off.

Rick raised Max and Miriya on the tac net. Wing to wing the three fighters peeled away from the targeted cruiser...

"Main gun is in ready position," Claudia announced. "Energy reading at present... niner-five-zero."

Lisa ran calculations at the adjacent station, reporting the results. "The admiral was right—that's only enough energy for one shot, so make it a good one!"

Vanessa gave the word: The cruiser was centered in the computer reticle.

"Now, fire!" yelled Gloval...

The two columnar towers of the main gun were set in position side by side, a continuous cat's cradle of scintillescent energy uniting them running fore to aft. As Gloval issued the command to fire, the power web seemed to solidify itself for an instant; then the twin-boomed gun blowtorched.

A near hemisphere of incandescence erupted from the fortress, dematerializing the winter clouds and igniting the sky like a second sun. The collective force of an infinity of hyperexcited subatomic particles tore through Khyron's approaching cruiser like a radiant stake driven into its icy heart.

But the cruiser's forward motion was not yet arrested. Flayed of armor and superstructure and trailing a dense pillar of swirling black smoke, it continued to fall...

Khyron tasted blood in his mouth. In the dim illumination in the observation bubble provided by the cruiser's auxiliary power system, he traced the blood's course to a deep gash over his left eye. The eye itself was closed, swollen and hemorrhaging in its fractured socket. Azonia was in the command chair beside him, unscathed though the rest of the bridge was in ruin.

"All right," he said, as though taken in by a minor trick, "they've had their fun, and now it's our turn! I'll show them!"

Behind him, both Grel and Gerao had met their deaths. Weapons systems and communications were out; likewise the computers and projecbeam screens. But the ship's navigationals were alive—the ship itself could be used as a final weapon.

"Now what?" Azonia asked eagerly.

Khyron took the second chair. "They can't erect a defense barrier without any power, correct?!"

"Right! They're helpless! Get them!"

He turned to her and smiled. "We both will," he rasped. "But it requires a sacrifice... are you willing to face it with me, Azonia?"

She reached out for his hand. "It will be glorious."

"Yes... glorious. Locking on guidance systems, now."

Its power systems depleted, the SDF-1 had dropped back in the lake, helpless.

Vanessa glanced up at the schematics on the threat board. The enemy hadn't altered its course. "It looks like he plans to ram us, sir!"

Gloval turned to Sammie: "Do we have *any* power left?!"

"Not enough to activate the main gun again, sir."

"Kim? said Gloval.

"Same story here... I have no helm control!"

Claudia turned from her station : "Reserves and backups are out."

Gloval stood up. "Ready the ejection modules," he started to say. But Sammie was shaking her head, tears rolling down her freckled face.

"Only module C is operational. The rest are..."

Lisa felt her heart begin to race. Everyone looked at each other, saying more with their eyes than would have been possible through words alone. Sammie and Kim were crying, holding each other. Vanessa was tight-lipped, stoic, almost angry.

Lisa saw Claudia and the admiral exchange glances, then suddenly felt her friend's graceful hand on her shoulder.

"Lisa..."

Lisa stepped aside and clutched at herself, feeling a wave of hysteria mount inside her. "No!" she screamed.

"Lisa, *yes!*" someone said—it could have been Sammie, or Kim, or Vanessa.

Claudia and Gloval took a step toward her.

She began to shake her head wildly...

Max and Miriya, Rick and what remained of the Skull Team, had put several miles between themselves and Khyron's warship. Circling out over the lake, they regrouped and headed home, the SDF-1 at twelve o'clock, now resettled in the choppy waters.

Rick had witnessed the counterstrike leveled against Khyron's vessel and had naturally anticipated its complete destruction. But the cruiser had survived and was locked on a collision course with the dimensional fortress.

The Veritechs began to pour everything they had toward it: missiles, armor-piercing depleted transuranic rounds, heat-seekers, and the rest. Phalanx guns of the SDF-1's close-in weapons system were similarly engaged, challenging the gods with their volleys of thunder and blinding light.

All at once Rick knew in his gut that all the firepower in the world wasn't going to slow that skeletal ship's suicide descent...

The cruiser was a fiery javelin in a ballistic fall, called by the Earth's own inherent powers to deadly rendezvous with its techno-savior.

On the bridge of the Zentraedi ship, Khyron and Azonia stood hand in hand facing that *divine wind* in a way only warriors could, victorious in their final moments as much for destroying the object of their years-long pursuit as for the strength of their extraordinary bond, their marriage in death.

Gloval, in his place, hugged his crew to him, stretching his long arms around them all, courageous and loving father, while the Destroyer's warship eclipsed the sky.

The mile-long cruiser rammed into the main guns of the fortress, splintering the twin booms as it continued its dive. Metal shrieked against metal, shafts, connectors, and joints snapping and roaring in protest.

The bow of the leviathan ship forced the booms apart and impacted against the main body of the SDF-1, shearing off the head and going on to crash and explode once, twice, and again. The fortress took the full power of these against its back and itself exploded, blowing the supercarriers from their mountings and ripping away the battle-scarred armor that had seen so much violence.

The lake boiled, releasing massive clouds of steam into the cold air, and lightning storms appeared spontaneously in the skies overhead.

A fireball rose and mushroomed there, announcing the event to the rest of the world...

When the smoke cleared, three ruins stood in the much shallower lake: the burned-out hull of Khyron's cruiser, the remains of the ill-fated SDF-2, and the blackened, headless torso of the original dimensional fortress—monuments to madness.

Most of the city along the lakeshore had been obliterated.

Veritech teams swept the littered waters and frontage lands for survivors but found none.

Rick made a pass over the leveled suburbs where his quarters had once stood—where Lisa and Claudia, Sammie, Vanessa, and Kim had lived; then he flew over the heart of downtown, where survivors were already leaving the shelters.

But there would be no rebuilding this time—not here at any rate. Rick guessed that the area would remain hot for decades to come. Evacuation and relocation of the thousands who had lived through the day would have to commence immediately. No simple task given the extent of the destruction, but there were nearby cities that would lend a hand, and the Earth would prevail, rid of its enemies at last.

He tried not to think about Gloval and the others; this was what waited for all of them at the end of the rainbow.

He piloted his fighter past the lake hulks, circled, and put down in Guardian mode at an intact landing zone not far from the shore. People were beginning to gather, many in shock, others staring at the fortress in stunned silence. He raised the cockpit canopy and climbed out, only to hear a ghost call him by name.

Lisa was walking toward his ship.

Rick approached her cautiously, more than willing to settle for hallucination but worried that real emotion might frighten it off. But the quaking shoulders he touched with his equally anxious hands were flesh and blood, and the feel of her brought him close to fainting.

"At the last moment," Lisa was saying, "Admiral Gloval and... Claudia forced me into the ejection module." She regarded the fortress for a moment, silent while tears flowed freely down her cheeks. "They wanted *me* to live..." She turned Rick and studied him intensely. "They said that *I* was the only one who still had something to live for!"

Rick held her while she cried, her body convulsing in his arms.

"I thought I'd lost you," he whispered. "Just when I realized how much you mean to me." He tightened his embrace. "You *do* have something to live for—we both do now."

Neither of them heard Minmei approach. Reflexively, they separated when she spoke; but Rick, in a rush, began to stammer an explanation.

Minmei spared him that.

"You're in love with Lisa," she said quietly. "I knew that."

"I would have told you sooner, but… I don't think I knew until today." Rick reached for Lisa's hand. "Forgive me, Minmei."

Now Minmei faltered. "Well, uh, only if you can forgive me, Rick. For trying to make you into something you're not. And, uh, for pretending to be something I'm not." Rick and Lisa looked confused, so she continued. "You see, I wasn't really that eager to get married. I realized that my music means as much to me as the service does to you."

Lisa seemed to stiffen, somehow able to locate just a hint of anger through her heavy sadness. "Oh, really?" she said flatly.

"My life is music," Minmei said innocently.

Lisa smiled to herself and gave Rick's hand a squeeze. Minmei couldn't bear to admit that she had lost Rick; and why bother to think that when it was so much easier to rearrange the facts? Looking around, Lisa wondered if she could do the same: just pretend all this hadn't happened, see blue skies instead of storms ahead.

"Good luck on your mission, Lisa," Minmei said straight-faced.

*As though all this hadn't happened!*

"I knew you'll be a bigger star than ever by the time we return," Lisa told her, willing to give Minmei's blinder game a try.

Rick, too, wore a slightly puzzled look. But this began to fade when Minmei turned to him, wishing him well and kissing him lightly on the cheek.

"Don't forget me, Rick—you have to promise me you won't!"

"I'll never forget you," he said, meaning it.

She spun on her heel in an almost weightless turn and walked away, stopping once to wave to him before rejoining the crowds of survivors, already welcoming her with open anus.

Snow was beginning to fall. Lisa put her arm through Rick's elbow and snuggled up against him.

"What about our mission, Rick? Is there a chance—even without the SDF-1?"

Rick nodded slowly. He had already given it some thought.

"There's still the factory satellite and Breetai's ship. With his help, and Lang's and Exedore's, we'll make good Admiral Gloval's assignment. We'll reach the Robotech Masters' homeworld before it's too late. This time *peace* comes first."

Mesmerized, Lisa watched the snow begin to blanket the devastated city, the ruined warships that were to be its massive grave markers.

Perhaps Max and Miriya would sign on, she said to herself. Even *Minmei!* What did she care now? It was going to be a diplomatic mission, a proper meeting of two cultures bound to each other by a mysterious past and separated by nearly the breadth of a galaxy.

She looked over at Rick and managed a smile, which he returned though tears filled his eyes.

And if their plan failed for some reason, if it wasn't possible for Breetai's ship to undertake the journey... then other solutions would present themselves. Earth *would* rebuild itself and prevail. Perhaps, she speculated, the Robotech Masters would come here instead...

And it turned out, new solutions would present themselves. Earth would rebuild and prevail. And as for the Robotech Masters... *come they would.*

For more fantastic fiction, author events, exclusive
excerpts, competitions, limited editions and more

VISIT OUR WEBSITE
**titanbooks.com**

LIKE US ON FACEBOOK
**facebook.com/titanbooks**

FOLLOW US ON TWITTER
**@TitanBooks**

EMAIL US
**readerfeedback@titanemail.com**